Dear Target Reader,

I am so honored that Target has selected *The Matchmaker's List* for its Diverse Book Club! I grew up in a community where everything from modern-day arranged marriages to Tinder dating was the norm, and I was inspired to write about the experiences, hiccups, and cultural pressure women like me sometimes face on our own romantic journeys.

Enter Raina. She's twenty-nine years old and her loving—if overbearing—grandmother Nani is hell-bent on getting her married before she hits the big 3-0. Although Raina is still hopelessly in love with her ex-boyfriend, she agrees to the plan and starts dating men from Nani's preapproved list of bachelors. Some of the dates go well, while others are downright awful, but the plot thickens when her ex, Dev, reappears in her life.

Dev is "the one that got away," but he's also the man who broke her heart two years earlier, and so she chooses to hide his reemergence in her life from her nani and best friend, Shay, who aren't his biggest fans. At the same time, Raina struggles with the pressure from her nani and their community to settle down and find an eligible bachelor from the list. Raina wants to make her grandmother happy. Unfortunately, when it comes to love, the solution that would make Nani happy would make her miserable. Or so Raina thinks . . .

The Matchmaker's List is a novel about love, friendship, acceptance, family, and self-discovery. It explores themes that I hope will resonate with everyone. Like all of us, Raina must figure out who and what she wants in life on her own terms—and following her own timeline!

I hope you'll enjoy reading this book as much as I enjoyed writing it. Raina, Nani, Shay, and the entire cast of characters live very close to my heart, and I'm delighted that you'll get to know them, too.

You can find out more about what I'm up to at sonyalalli.com, or come find me on Instagram or Twitter @saskinthecity. I'd love to say hello!

Thank you so much for reading,
Sonya

"Bright and vivid, and fresh and funny—I was utterly charmed by this insight into Raina's struggle to be the perfect Indian daughter. A delightful debut."

—Veronica Henry, bestselling author of
How to Find Love in a Bookshop

"A riotous odyssey into the pressures of cross-cultural modern dating that will chime with every twentysomething singleton."

—*ELLE* (UK)

"A funny and moving exploration of modern love. Sonya Lalli's observations on being single while Indian and female certainly resonated with me, and reminded me of the challenges of balancing family pressures with my desire for independence in my twenties. I enjoyed meeting all the men on Nani's list, even the disastrous dates, because they reflected the hit-or-miss reality of the modern arranged-marriage experience."

—Balli Kaur Jaswal, bestselling author of *Erotic Stories for Punjabi Widows* (Reese's Book Club Pick)

"An absolute treat—I loved it. My senses were buzzing with delight as I read it."

—Milly Johnson, bestselling author of *The Queen of Wishful Thinking*

"A delightfully different story of friendship, family, and getting over heartbreak. It's fresh, funny, and fabulously written—it had me hooked from the get-go."

—Anna Bell,
bestselling author of *The Bucket List to Mend a Broken Heart*

"Heartwarming and funny."   —*Woman's Own*

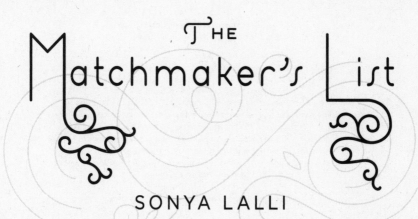

The Matchmaker's List

SONYA LALLI

BERKLEY
NEW YORK

BERKLEY
An imprint of Penguin Random House LLC
1745 Broadway, New York, NY 10019

Previously published in the UK as *The Arrangement*

BERKLEY and the BERKLEY & B colophon are registered trademarks of
Penguin Random House LLC.

ISBN: 9780593098172

Orion Books trade paperback edition / August 2017
Berkley trade paperback edition / February 2019
Berkley trade paperback Target Book Club edition / February 2019

Printed in the United States of America
1   3   5   7   9   10   8   6   4   2

Cover art and design by Vikki Chu
Book design by Kristin del Rosario

For my grandparents

ACKNOWLEDGMENTS

First and foremost, I want to thank my parents, Anita Chakravarti and Parm Lalli. You have been my rocks from day one, and I couldn't have asked for more loving and supportive people to call Mom and Dad. Thank you for showing me what it means to live with an open heart and open mind, and for encouraging me to chase after my dreams. Any achievement to my name is not mine, but ours. None of this would have been possible without you.

I am overwhelmed with gratitude for my grandparents, Maya and Aninda Chakravarti and Surjit and Bikkar Lalli, whose sacrifice and bravery brought our families to Canada. Thank you for instilling in us the values of our culture, while supporting us when we chose our own path. Thank you Nani, for your grace, love, and selflessness; Dadima, for your generosity and laughter; Papaji, for teaching us strength and kindness; and my gentle and loving Dadu, who is with me in spirit every single day.

Thank you to my brother Jay Lalli, for challenging me to be my best self; my sister Anju Sohal, for teaching me about the real world; our baby sister Georgia Lalli, for your unconditional love; my new sister Heather Lalli, for bringing so much joy into our family; my lovely Buaji, Meena Lalli, for your patience and everything you do for our family; and my uncle Baljit Lalli, for your kindhearted and free spirit.

A huge thanks to my brilliant agents Federica Leonardis and Martha Webb for your insight, perseverance, and for believing in this book as much as I did. Thank you to my fantastic editor, Kerry

Donovan, and her colleagues at Berkley for your enthusiasm and support, and also to Katie Seaman and Orion Books for publishing the UK edition of this book.

Many thanks to Kathleen Grissom for a telephone conversation that changed my life and taught me that a woman from Saskatchewan can be a writer; to my City, University of London creative writing tutors, gurus, and friends Clare Allan, Julie Wheelwright, Lesley Downer, Bea Pantoja, Stephanie Reddaway, and Lin Soekoe; and to my mentors in both life and the law, Terry Zakreski, Ken Norman, and Dwight Newman.

I am very grateful to Saskatoon's wonderful Indian community, who have been my second family, and to my earliest readers and dear friends, Annie MacDonald, Beshmi Kularatne, Sasha Kisin, Sofie Riise, Crystal Robertson, Qi Jiang, Anusha Jegadeesh, Kanika Sharma, Nick Vassos, Liz Miazga, Fafa Ahiahonu, Stephanie Hernandez, Mike Fowler—and of course Raina Upadhyay, my heroine's namesake.

Finally, I want to thank my husband, Simon Collinson, for putting up with me through all the highs and lows of this process. You have brought balance into my life and have believed in me through every twist and turn. Thank you for sharing this experience with me.

The Matchmaker's List

BOYS FOR MY RAINA

Sachin—Reetu's son in Scarborough, some kind of doctor—birthday lunch??

Jagmohan—Pinky's nephew in Jodhpur (visiting Canada this summer?)—but may be looking for immigration

Jayesh—Sharon's cousin, science professor at university . . . ~~divorced~~!!!

Rohit—Sarla's nephew, lawyer in Boston

~~Arjun~~—Sonia's son, pediatrician, probably will want to have babies soon!

Vishal—Bengali boy, also likes business things—but may be ~~too short~~

Rahul—Sarla's physiotherapist, says he very good-looking boy ☺

ONE

Nani opened the front door as I was still crossing the lawn. Her nose twitching, she looked me up and down as I forced myself up the steps.

"Is *that* what you're wearing?"

I shrugged and glanced down at my weekend jeans, my favorite checked shirt. It's what I always wore home during one of my weekly visits, but I supposed today wasn't an ordinary day.

I was twenty-nine today, and walking into an ambush.

"I was hoping you would dress up, *nah*? We have guest."

A *guest*. A guest implied a cup of chai and a tray of sweets quickly defrosted from the Deepfreeze. A guest was small talk, compliments, gossip.

A *guest* was not an unannounced blind date chaperoned by your grandmother.

"What kind of guest?" I asked evenly, deciding not to tell her that my best friend, Shay, had already warned me about the blind date. Nani didn't answer the question, clucking her tongue as I bent over and brushed a kiss on the top of her head. She smelled the way she always smelled, like cocoa butter and roasted cumin. A touch of garlic. She stepped back and continued her evaluation, her tiny fingers pinching at the fleshy part of her chin as I kicked off my shoes.

"Find something more suitable." She flicked her hand up the staircase, and I bounded up the stairs to the second floor, knowing full well there was nothing nicer in my old room. Too-large T-shirts from summer camps and music festivals where my favorite band that year had headlined. Jogging pants, the type with black or white snaps running up the leg. My old trumpet.

It was odd how little of me I kept here. But of all the places I'd lived since moving out—a dumpy apartment with Shay; a shared flat in London; and now, a new condo with my name on the mortgage—it was this house that I'd always considered home. I heard Nani calling, her voice staccato and sweet, and I ran a brush through my hair and then made my way back downstairs.

She looked up at me expectantly. "Nothing?"

"All my clothes are downtown."

She arched her brows. "Anything in guest room?"

Again, I shook my head. Mom's old room. Starch white walls and a beige linen duvet, not a trace of her left in the closet. Nani sighed as I reached the bottom step, evaluating my outfit one last time. And then she shrugged, squeezed my hand, and said, "Still my pretty girl. Even in *that*."

Anywhere Nani lived would always be home.

I tucked in my shirt and followed her through the kitchen, ducking my head beneath the crossbeam as we took the eight steps down to the lower level. To the "entertaining room," as Nani called it: orange corduroy couches wrapped stiffly in plastic; the walls packed with street art bought for a few hundred lire on my grandparents' one trip abroad; Lord Ganesh presiding on the mantel, a choir of porcelain Siamese cats chiming in unison. And our *guest* stood at the room's rapturous center, awkwardly in place, his dark brown skin the same shade as the varnish on the wood paneling.

"Raina," said Nani, clutching my wrist. "Meet Sachin." She dragged me closer until the top of his forehead was square to my mouth, and I tried to ignore the dull sensation in my belly. He looked vaguely familiar. Perhaps someone I'd known as a child, or seen in the stack of pictures Nani had started leaving on the kitchen table. He was quite short, albeit symmetrical—handsome even. He smiled and brought his palms together at his chest, bowing slightly to both of us.

"Hello, Raina," he said, like my name was a word he'd invented.

"Hi."

"Sachin drove far to come for your birthday lunch."

"It's your birthday?" His face stiffened. "I didn't mean to intrude."

"No intrusion, dear." She pinched his cheek. "My Raina and I are *so* happy you joined. *Nah*, Raina?"

I nodded.

"Raina is *such* a good girl. Always coming home from her busy job to take care of her nani." She gasped and turned to me. "Sachin is a busy man, too. Raina, did you know he is doctor?"

"No, I didn't." I turned to him. "My best friend is a doc—"

"I'm a cardiologist, actually." He glanced away. "To be more precise."

I clamped down on my lower lip. *Precise, or just plain arrogant?*

"Subspecialized at Columbia," he said.

"Mhm." I tried not to roll my eyes. "Is that right?"

He nodded, fingering his wristwatch. "Diverse city. Beautiful campus. One of the top programs in the country—world, even. Some might say."

"I think I've heard of *Columbia*." I folded my arms across my chest. "Is that in Cleveland?"

"Actually, New York—"

"And you're the kind of doctor that cleans teeth, right?"

Nani jabbed me on the arm, and I tried not to laugh.

"No, no. It's—"

"*Cardio*-logist. Oh! You're a sports doctor."

He shifted from side to side. "Actually, cardiac electrophysiology is a—"

Nani clucked her tongue, waving him off. "Don't listen to her. She's a silly one, my Raina." She wrapped her arms around my waist as if she were a coconspirator in the charade.

"Oh," said Sachin.

Evidently, they didn't teach sarcasm at Columbia.

"Dear," Nani said, turning to Sachin. "Would you like chai before lunch?"

"Chai sounds lovely, Auntie."

She waddled up the stairs, leaving me alone with him, and I sat down on one of the couches, the plastic screeching beneath me as I settled onto the cushion. Sachin joined me a moment later, his legs spread so wide he was nearly touching me. To my dismay, he actually smelled pretty good: the way rich men tended to smell, like Dev used to smell. An understated potency that still dominated the entire room.

"Your nani is very sweet," he said after a moment.

"She's the best."

"What's her name again?"

"Belinda."

"Oh."

I looked straight ahead, deadpan, trying not to look at him out of the corner of my eye.

"Is that . . . Bengali?"

"No," I sighed. "Her name is Suvali."

"But, you just said—"

"It was a joke."

"A joke, right"—he let out a stiff laugh—"good one."

Growing up, everyone just referred to family friends as "auntie" or "uncle," but I still felt mildly offended on Nani's behalf that he didn't even know her name. I reclined slightly on the couch, and stared straight ahead. Lord Ganesh—eyes, trunk, and all—stared right back.

Upstairs, I could hear Nani bustling around in the kitchen. She would be setting out her favorite teacups on the silver tray Nana had bought her as a wedding present, placing teaspoons equally spaced along the paper napkins—garish, a bold red and gold—that she'd once bought in bulk at a discount store going out of business. Fifty packages for a five-dollar bill.

"Raina, hey, listen," Sachin said after a while.

"Yes?"

He played with his rounded fingernails, picking beneath them. "I really hate to ruin your birthday, but—"

"You have to go?" I asked, a little too eagerly.

"No." He flashed me a smile, two rows of square white teeth. "Don't worry. I'll stay for lunch. But I would hate to mislead you on my intentions." He looked up at me quickly, and then back at the floor. "I'm not interested."

"That's fi—"

"You seem like a really nice girl, Raina. Really nice. And I don't mean to hurt you." He sighed again. "I'm just not in that place, you know? I'm not ready for the kind of commitment that our families— that *you*—seem to be after."

I bit my tongue. The only thing I was after was for him to *leave*.

"I know, I know." He stood up and paced in front me, his hands partially shoved into his pockets. "I'm a doctor, I get it. The biology of it all just isn't fair. It's harder for women. More pressure after they—uh—reach a certain age?"

I let out a deep, writhing sigh. "It's *so* hard."

"And your nani finding you a single doctor is—" He paused and looked me dead in the eye. "Well, it's the dream, isn't it?"

A dream? More like a nightmare.

"But really, Raina, you seem like a nice girl." He knelt down in front of me and petted my knee. "*Really* nice. And I'm sure you will find someone—soon."

I resisted the urge to tell him what I really thought of him, and studied him as he crouched at my feet. Sachin was the definition of the man Shay and I had spent so many years avoiding: the *Westernized* Indian. The one who used to be captain of the chess club or math team, and although brutalized for it in high school, now threw out the stereotypes about his culture as an anecdote to make the C-cups and hair extensions laugh as he chivalrously paid for their drinks. He was the archetype who watched sports and drank beer, had the uncanny ability to mock his father's accent, yet would still want his wife to learn how to make curry the way his mother did. He was the hybrid of east and west; the immigrant mentality distilled and harnessed, his arrogance the forgivable by-product of ambition.

Sachin looked up at me and heaved out a patronizing sigh. "Are you going to be okay?"

He was also the type of man that any nani would want her granddaughter to marry, and as I patted his shoulder reassuringly, I tried to convince myself that Sachin—that *his* type—wasn't what I was interested in, either.

There seems to be a great deal of misinformation around the modern-day arranged marriage. I am often bombarded with questions by coworkers or middle-aged women sitting next to me on long-haul flights after they've picked up on the fact that I'm half Indian. After explaining to them that I was raised by the Indian side of my family, and that whichever white guy fathered me was never in the picture, they smile and tell me that being Indian is all the rage these days. And in an exertion of worldliness, I am cited anecdotes they've picked up in the frozen food section at Costco while buying paneer, or watching twenty minutes of *Dil Chata Hai* on the Bollywood channel that comes with their deluxe cable packages. They love the bright colors and gold chains. The eccentric music. The food—oh, how they love the food. And of course, they are curious about my love life. They want to know more about this whole "arranged marriage" thing, whether soon I, too, might be enlisted.

But the protocol of today's arranged marriage in my community is less glamorous than they might anticipate. It is choosing from a roster of carefully vetted men, men whose family, religion, background, values, and sometimes even astrology match your own. It is having parents who want their children to marry into the "culture," and so they hurl them against a brick wall of blind dates until one finally sticks. It is arranged dating, really; an agreement to decide quickly whether you are in love.

I grew up with dozens of girls who went this route; women fast-tracked down the aisle, business class on a nonstop flight toward happily ever after.

And they *seemed* happy.

After all, they tell me—their mouths full of champagne and vanilla cream cake, cocooned in flowing bridal *lenghas* worth as much as a new car—what was the big deal about being set up by your family? Isn't "today's arranged marriage" equivalent to being set up by a friend, or an algorithm in your go-to dating app? Aren't their chances of having a successful marriage as high as the girl who ends up marrying her one-night stand? Or the one who met

her leading man in college? I am one of the very few in my generation still unmarried in my hometown, and I never know what to
say. How much to smile. And so I help myself to another drink—
sometimes, another piece of cake—and reverently congratulate
them on their Bollywood ending.

But I always wonder what happens after the ceremonial fire
goes out and the guests go home, stuffed and slightly drunk on
Johnnie Walker. Nani's marriage was arranged, and unlike today's
blessed nuptials, she didn't have much of a say in the matter. Her
father showed her a black-and-white photo of a lanky boy with
round wire spectacles, and later, someone smeared red powder on
her forehead, and just like that—well, *nearly*—she was married. It
was simple. Clear-cut. A transaction performed not out of love for
a would-be spouse, but for one's own family.

But wasn't an arranged marriage beneath me? I wasn't *really*
Indian, after all. I was Canadian. A girl who refused to feel out of
place in her mostly white, middle-class suburb in west Toronto. I
had Rollerbladed and held lemonade stands, rolled my eyes on
"Culture Day" at school when Shay and I were forced to wear *lenghas*, the other kids crowding around us for a chance to paw at the
fake crystals sewn onto the sleeves. I only saw other Indians when
I was dragged to dinner parties, and at temple every Sunday. When
we went bulk grocery shopping in Scarborough because the corner Safeway didn't have the right brand of lentils or coconut milk.
And even though Ravi Shankar always seemed to be playing on
the radio at home, and my clothes perpetually reeked of masala, I
grew up fully committed to my role in what otherwise seemed to
be a white narrative. I played a girl who couldn't believe in arranged marriage—not only because of the cliché of her own family shambles, but because the cynicism of her Western world, the
literary fiction on her bookshelf, barely allowed her to believe in
marriage at all.

So I resisted. I resisted the idea of a planned union that might make me happy. That might make Nani happy.

"Did you like Sachin?" she asked after he had left. She stood beside me as I washed the dishes, the side of her head lightly resting on my shoulder.

Did I like him? I didn't *dislike* him. After he told me he just wasn't interested, and Nani came back with the tea, the pressure had evaporated. It wasn't a chaperoned date, a three-hour festival I'd have to immortalize in the diary I'd outgrown so I could one day tell my daughters about all the silly things their father said the first time our eyes locked.

It was just lunch.

"Will you see him again?" Nani asked.

"No." I shook my head. "I don't think so."

"Don't *think* so?"

I didn't answer, and she leaned forward on her tiptoes and turned off the tap.

"You got along with him, *nah*?"

"I don't know." I turned to face her, not quite sure how to tell her I'd already been rejected. "What did you think of him?"

"Only you know what you need in husband, Raina. What you need to be happy."

"I am happy."

She wiped a fleck of foam off my neck and stared at me, attempting to read my expression the way she attempted to read English.

"I am!"

She grimaced and glanced away, as if she'd heard it, too. The urgency. The insistence. I attacked the rice cooker, knuckles and steel wool, my palms burning red in the hot water. The suds washed off, and I held it up, set it sideways on the dish rack. Why did I sound like I was trying to convince myself? I was happy, wasn't I? I had everything, less the one thing that, to Nani, defined the rest. The boxes for college and career had been ticked; only marriage remained.

She rolled up her sleeves and handed me a frying pan. Staring at it, she said, "You agreed to this."

"I know. But I said thirty."

"You're twenty-nine now, Raina. What difference is one year?"

"Yeah, what *is* the difference?" I squirted dish soap onto the pan, and set the bottle down firmly. "What's the difference if I get married now, or in five years, or *never*—"

"Don't talk nonsense."

"Really, Nani. What's the rush? Kris isn't married."

"When he's ready, he will."

"It's because he's a man."

She didn't answer. She walked around me and inspected the rice cooker propped up on the drying rack. Tapping on a spec of white caked onto the side, she handed it back to me.

"Just because he's been married before, or just because he can have children whenever he feels like it, and his *sperm*—"

"*Beta*. Enough."

She finally met my eye. The slight scowl that had formed on her face vanished, and she reached for my cheek. "A husband, a family—it will bring you so much joy. You remember how happy your nana made me?"

I wasn't so sure I agreed, but I was too tired to argue. Her hand was soft, slightly wet from the dishes, and I let my head rest against it.

"You remember, I told you, when I was young, my father was in army and we had to move. Moving, moving constantly—and I never had anything of my own." She nodded, pressing her lips together. "And then I had your nana. I had *family* of my own."

I turned back to the sink.

"And don't you want children?"

I sighed. "I do, but—"

"*Beta*, you are getting older. Your auntie Sarla, everyone at temple—they always ask me: Why is Raina not married? Why always at that office? You cannot marry your Blueberry!"

"It's called a BlackBerry, Nani. And I'm not picky. I'm just not ready."

"You work, and work, and life is passing by. Men are passing by. Tell me, when is the right time? When will you be ready?"

I watched the pan fill with water, bits of brown bubbling in the froth. To Nani, a man unmarried in his thirties was fine—but for me, it wouldn't be. I took a deep breath, and willed myself not to fight back.

She reached for my hand, and as her slight brown fingers interlocked with my own, that's when I realized that in my silence, I was being complicit. I realized how much I truly loved this vivacious, slightly insane little woman, and what I would do to be the only person in her life never to break her heart. I would go along with it. I would live up to her expectations, and that promise I made to her two years ago—brokenhearted and desperate for my life to make sense once again—that if I wasn't married at thirty, I'd let her make the arrangements for me.

"So we will try again?" she asked. "We will find you someone else?"

"Sure, Nani." I forced out a smile. "We'll try again."

She dried her hands on her slacks and headed into the den. "Good, stay there," she called. "I am bringing the list." A few moments later, she reappeared in the kitchen, light steps on the hardwood, a piece of loose-leaf paper fluttering like she was bidding at an auction.

Was my future husband's name somewhere on that list?

She sat down at the kitchen table and pulled out the chair next to her. Dragging her thumb along the edge of the page, she muttered names under her breath.

Did I want it to be?

I abandoned the sink and sat down next to her. Looking through the list, I feigned interest as she enthusiastically explained who each of the candidates were. Going on these dates would make Nani happy, and I supposed it didn't really matter who I wanted—or who I still wanted. *This* was happening, and with only three hundred and sixty-four days to go, the arrangements had already begun.

Sachin — Rittu's son in Scarborough, some kind of doctor — birthday lunch??

TWO

It was light out now when I left; summer, it seemed, was on its way. I ran most mornings before 6 A.M., before the commuters clogged the streets and the city became a mess of traffic, delivery trucks, and the hammering from a nearby construction site. I loved the feel of bare concrete and unbreathed air, of the urban sprawl temporarily abandoned. My legs twitched, and I picked up speed, nothing but the sound of my feet beating against the pavement. I headed north past the still-closed shops, St. Michael's Cathedral, then cut through Queen's Park. The paths were damp and crusted in last season's leaves, and as the sun peeked through the branches and the sweet scent of dew filled my lungs, I exhaled and smiled into the light. Running was how I survived sitting upright in an office chair, sometimes eighteen hours a day; how, as a child, I had learned to survive.

I ran home through the university, the boundaries of four years of my life walled in brick and mortar, paper and pencil, the glare and hum of a screen. I brushed by the buildings dotting St. George Street, each of which harbored memories that became vaguer with each run: the eastern brownstone where I had a class on political economy and advanced econometrics; the building perpetually under construction where I took a seminar on microfinance in the developing world.

Had it really been over ten years since I started university? I thought back to myself in those days: slightly skinnier, commuting back and forth from Nani's house on overcrowded buses, highlighting textbooks and writing in the margins as I awkwardly stood in the aisles. There hadn't been wild frat parties with beer pong and hours of missing memories, or shots of tequila after a Monday evening lecture.

I'd studied. I'd graduated. And, exactly according to plan, I'd gotten a well-paying job.

I was soaked by the time I completed my loop. I sprinted up the stairs of my building, and each floor greeted me with a new smell. Week-old garbage and wet dog. Compost and fresh bread. I heaved my body up the last few stairs and smelled curry—like Nani's, but tangier—from the Sri Lankan family who lived across the hall. I opened my front door, and for a moment just stood in the entrance, panting as I tried to catch my breath. It never failed to strike me how, two years after moving in, my condo still smelled of absolutely nothing.

Between scenes at the office, only a shadow of me even lived here in this catalog-clean condo with two bedrooms and a view, a gallery of wicker and eggshell and midnight blue accents. Here, there were only egg whites and salsa in the fridge, vodka in the freezer, and thanks to the previous owner, everything seemed to match but me.

I'd bought it as is a month after flying home from London and hadn't changed a thing except for the handful of framed photos I'd nailed indiscriminately to the walls. Shay and our group of high school friends at graduation next to the fridge. A rare, complete family photo hanging in the front hall: Nani and Nana, me in a frilly dress sitting on their knees, Kris and Mom standing just behind. If anyone asked, I wouldn't know how to explain each of these characters in a way that made sense, or my relationships to them all. Kris is your uncle—but grew up with you like a brother? And your mom is alive, but didn't raise you?

I poured myself a glass of orange juice and, leaving the empty carton on the counter, finished it in one long swig. But no one ever asked those questions. In the two years that I'd lived here, I hadn't had anyone over who didn't already know the answers.

I showered and changed into a linen suit, and by the time I left again, the city was awake. I turned south on Yonge Street toward downtown, maneuvering through pedestrians and lampposts as I answered e-mails on my BlackBerry. Shay was already at the diner, slumped over in our usual booth, and I slid in across from her.

"Already ordered." She leaned back, her eyes half closed, and I grabbed a sticky newspaper off the seat. There were mornings when neither of us spoke—when I read, and Shay, straight from a night shift at the hospital, napped at the table. We'd been coming to the same diner since we moved out together into a shared apartment in the building above it. At the time, she was still in medical school, but tired of living with her parents, and I'd received my first big-city paycheck. I'd get home after work and find her studying her medical textbooks at a booth, and we'd nurse our free refills of coffee beneath the neon light of a decorative Hollywood sign, Shay learning how to make a differential diagnosis, while I kept her company, and stuck straws in my nose and tried to make her laugh.

Our usuals arrived: black coffee, three fried eggs and ketchup, crunchy breakfast potatoes, and four thick slices of rye; and for a while, we ate in silence. She looked exhausted, and I waited until after she'd had her first cup of coffee, and was well onto her second, to bring it up.

"Aren't you going to ask me how it went?"

"Sorry." She smiled groggily, and then nodded her head. "What was he like?"

I shrugged. "He was okay, I guess."

"Are you glad I warned you?" Shay asked, setting down her fork. She was nearly finished with her meal, and she rested her elbows on the table. "I was worried you wouldn't turn up."

Somehow, Shay's mother, Auntie Sarla, had found out Nani was inviting Sachin over—and, of course, Auntie Sarla had told Shay. Seemingly, there were no secrets in our community, and nothing Auntie Sarla wouldn't involve herself in. She was my best friend's mother, and one of Nani's closest friends, but it was hard to be in the same room with her. She judged and criticized and berated, and treated Nani and me like inferiors. She was particularly critical of her own children, even though Shay and her brother, Nikesh, had lived up to every expectation.

Sarla was a matriarch of our community, and in a way, she represented everything that was wrong with our traditions. At the same time, Nani owed so much to her—making it difficult to despise her.

After they moved to Toronto, Nani and Nana made their living as restaurant owners, running an Indian café that is now called Saffron. But the trendy, upscale establishment was nothing like it used to be: strip mall locations and empty plastic seats, Nani and Nana packing up yearly, rifling through the classified pages of the *Toronto Sun* after getting evicted. They were a homely couple, food (not business) savvy, and intent on viewing the world the way they were themselves: honest. Business parks were rezoned, neighborhoods gentrified, but more often than not, landlords took advantage. And back then, the idea of taking a slum landlord to court, asking an authority in broken English for help, was simply too foreign a concept.

It was Auntie Sarla who had turned things around for them. One of the useful features of a woman who never shut up was, well, she never shut up about their food. She and Nani became friends, and Saffron grew to be the unofficial caterer to the Indian doctors, professors, and obnoxiously rich that populated Auntie Sarla's inner and outer circles. Gradually, as Nani and Nana could afford to move the business to Roncesvalles, and brand their humble business as more grandiose, they graduated from being one of Auntie's philanthropic pursuits into full members of their community.

"Would you see him again?" Shay asked after a moment.

"Maybe. I'm not sure. But it doesn't matter, because he's not interested in *me*." I reached for my coffee. "When Nani was in the other room, he said he wasn't interested."

"In you?"

I nodded. "In me."

"Sachin, in the middle of your date, *actually* told you he—"

"Can we drop this?"

Shay bit her lip, and then nodded slowly. "Sure. Sachin doesn't matter—"

"Thank you—"

"Because I have someone else for you."

"Tell me he's not a cardiologist."

"He's one of Julien's groomsmen," she said, her mouth full again. "He spent the last ten years abroad teaching, traveling—something like that."

"You want to set me up with a drifter?"

"Asher's not a drifter. He's amazing. He's—"

"Homeless?

"Don't be bitchy."

"I'm not."

"You're being skeptical, Raina. You're *single*, it's okay, but you need to start giving guys a chance. Asher, or"—she gestured to a balding man eating alone at the counter—"that guy over there. Can't you just try and date, or do something—for once?"

I groaned at Shay's authoritative voice. Just because she had her own love life sorted, my best friend was allowed to control mine, too?

When Shay and I had lived together, I'd never taken the men that stumbled out of her room too seriously. They were disheveled, red-eyed boys who groggily waved to me as they slipped past the kitchen, Shay still sound asleep. At first, Julien seemed no different. But unlike the rest of them, he kept coming back and, recently, proposed. And so Shay got to skip the queue of suitable Indian men Auntie Sarla had been lining up for her since birth, opting for the debonair French Canadian boy in her class, the fellow pediatrician.

She didn't need an arrangement. And I couldn't help but think, then why did I?

Shay's eyes flicked back from the balding man and onto my plate, and I pushed my last piece of toast toward her. She lunged for it, watching my face as she stripped the edge off with her teeth.

"So Sachin's a no." She looked up at me hopefully. "Asher is . . ."

"A no."

She took another bite of toast. "Last week I met a few residents from South Africa. There's one who might—"

"Actually," I said, looking at my hands, "I've already decided to start dating."

"Really?" Shay nearly screamed.

"Nani gave me this . . . list. I told her I'd look it over, maybe start making a few calls."

"Can I see it?" She grabbed my purse. "Is it in here?"

I watched her rifle through my bag and dump its contents onto the table—Kleenex, pens, tampons, passport, and all. She eventually found it, and started scanning the list.

"Nani knows them through the temple, or they're friends of friends, or—"

"My cousin Rohit is on here!"

"Have I met him before?"

She shook her head. "No. He is *such* a jerk. Even Ma knows that. I don't even want him at my wedding."

"Why would Nani put him on the list then?"

"I guess because he's"—Shay shrugged—"well, *single.*"

"So she'd rather have me be with some Indian guy nobody likes than be alone."

"She just wants you to be happy—and *open.* You don't only have to date Indian men"—she shook the paper—"from *this* little list."

"My birthday was *three* days ago, and do you know she's called me every day just to ask if I've met anyone from the list yet? If I've e-mailed or called any of these guys?" I shook my head. "A date I find online, or one with *Asher* or that bald guy, isn't going to be enough."

"So you're really going to do this then. Date, and"—she hesitated—"marry one of them?"

I didn't answer, and watched Shay as she deliberately crossed out Rohit's name with my pen.

"So this is . . . it," she said after a moment.

"I guess so."

"But I've never pictured you with an Indian, Raina."

I shrugged, and reached for my coffee. An Indian—one, in particular—was the only man I'd ever pictured myself with.

Rohit—Sarla's nephew, lawyer in Boston

Absolutely NOT

Date #1

"So here we are," Vishal said, tugging at the sleeves of his white collared shirt, which were sticking out from his navy blue suit. I looked down, wondering what kind of omen it was that I was wearing virtually the same outfit.

"Have you been here before?"

I shook my head. "It just opened, didn't it?"

"It's been two years, actually."

"Two years?" I glanced around the coffee shop, one that I could have sworn until recently used to be a take-out sushi joint. "Are you sure?"

"Positive."

A waiter brought us each a latte, and I tried to brainstorm conversation topics as I laconically stirred a packet of sugar into my cup. Had it only been one week since I turned twenty-nine? For a woman who once spent three months deciding on what handle she wanted as an e-mail address, Nani sure didn't waste any time.

Within days of receiving *the list*, I'd received a text message from Vishal—the fellow Bengali boy who also liked "business things." Unfortunately, he happened to work in the building next door to my office, and I wasn't able to find an excuse not to see him.

I thought I'd be nervous, but I wasn't. It was like having an awkward meet and greet with a client, or a job interview for a position you really didn't want. He wasn't *that* short, and sure, he was handsome—but within thirty seconds of shaking hands, I could tell we lacked chemistry. Or for that matter, failed to have anything in common. Funny how Nani thought that we could be a match made in heaven just because we both worked on Bay Street and understood how the stock market worked. The conversation was stilted, awkward, but eventually we found some things to talk about. Afterward, I insisted on paying for my own coffee, and then he walked me back to my office. Shaking my hand, he held eye contact just a bit too long. Was he also thinking about how he would spin this date to his family? I was about to joke that we should make up an excuse together for why there wouldn't be a second date, when he sighed loudly.

"Look, I'm dating someone. I have a girlfriend."

I guffawed. "Are you kidding me?"

"I'm sorry—"

"Don't say sorry to *me*," I said, crossing arms. "You should be saying that to your girlfriend!"

"I know, I know . . ."

"What on earth are you doing?"

"My mom doesn't like the fact that she's not Indian. And she's been on my case to meet you for months." He shrugged. "I just thought this would make everything easier."

"On you, maybe."

"I know." He shrugged. "This was a stupid idea."

"Stupid is an understatement, Vishal."

He smiled at me for the first the time. He didn't seem so dull when he smiled, and I half wondered whether we would have been friends had we met under different circumstances. Vishal ran his hands through his hair, and I wasn't sure what to say to him. Shay was right; Nani wouldn't care one way or the other if the guy I ended up with wasn't Indian—but that was Nani. Not everyone was lucky enough to have that.

"It sounds like you need to call your girlfriend," I said after a moment. When he smiled, I added, "And maybe stand up to your mom?"

"Perhaps." He cocked his head to the side. "But it's not like you wanted to meet *me*, either. I mean, how many times did you check your BlackBerry in the last forty-five minutes?" I hesitated, and he continued. "Sounds like *you* need to stand up to someone, too."

I nodded, even though I knew I wouldn't. What was the point of standing up to Nani? So I could let her down like the rest of her family had?

I didn't have a boyfriend, or even a prospect. The only men I met were through work—and they were all married, or single for a reason. And Dev . . . Well, Dev was nothing but a memory.

~~Vishal—Bengali boy, also likes business things—but maybe too short~~

Not single!

THREE

The humidity of early summer was starting to set in, and the air conditioners were ill prepared as the sun arched over Bay Street and streamed in through the windows. I heard the usual chatter of the break room across the hall; the slow drip of the percolator, the opening and shutting of the fridge as Emma from reception gossiped to someone in a low whisper. I sat back down at my desk, and as my wrists hovered above the keyboard, I realized I'd completely forgotten what it was I'd been working on before I'd left for coffee.

To me, *work* meant doing a lot of sinfully boring things that, regrettably, I'd once found interesting enough to get me through a minimum eighty-hour workweek without dabbling in self-mutilation. These days, I wasn't sure what kept me going. Everything had become routine. Work meant graphing variables and predicting outcomes for clients. Analyzing NASDAQ figures, Excel spreadsheets, and financial statements, and researching and sourcing investment products. It meant keeping my passport on hand and an extra pantsuit at the office just in case I needed to fly somewhere last minute to talk to or learn from people who did largely the same thing.

I'd once tried to explain to Nani the macroeconomic world and how exactly I fit into it, but she'd smiled sweetly, blankly, and then turned back to the television. She enjoyed strangers' reactions when she told them her granddaughter worked at a multinational investment bank, but that was as far as her pride went. She didn't want to understand what my job really was, or why choosing this career meant I had so little time for her, let alone anyone else.

It had been a few weeks since my date with Vishal, and I'd started texting with two other men on Nani's preapproved list. It felt wrong to have more than one guy "on the go," but Nani insisted. "Sprinkle your seeds, and see which flowers grow," as she liked to say. Arjun seemed normal, as did Jayesh—although with conflicting work schedules, I had yet to find a good time to meet either of them.

I'd overworked myself on my morning run, and my thighs and lower back throbbed. I reached up my arms and stretched, then closed my eyes. When I opened them again, Zoey's face had appeared in the doorway.

"Have a sec?" Without waiting for me to respond, she pushed through and closed the door behind her. She sat down in the chair opposite my desk, stretched out both legs, and drummed her stomach with her palms.

"You all right?"

She shrugged, and then glanced up at me slyly. "I accidentally saw Alice last night."

"Accidentally?" I laughed.

"How many weeks did I last this time?" She started counting on her fingers, and then gave up.

"Six," I said. "It's been *six* weeks since you last broke up."

"And I did really well. I didn't see her once—"

"Until last night!"

"Raina, she just showed up out of the blue. Handed me a bottle of wine, and waltzed in like nothing had happened. Like we had never broken up. And then . . ."

"And *then*?" Zoey didn't reply, and I grabbed a pen and gently lobbed it at her to get her attention.

She caught it and, blushing, set the pen down beside her. "It's fine. *I'm* fine. Really. It'll be—it'll be different this time. Won't it?"

"I may not be the best person to give you relationship advice."

"No one's perfect. You can't be worse than anyone else."

I laughed, trying to figure out what to say. Zoey was several years younger, the most junior—and intelligent—analyst on my team. I'd been assigned to train her on her first day, and by the time I'd showed her around the office and she'd laughed at one of my jokes, we were friends. Over a year later, she'd become more than that. We'd confided in each other quickly, and she'd told me about her life growing up in Canada's prairies, the difficulties she had experienced coming out as gay to her family, her on-again, off-again relationship with Alice—a law student she'd met her first week in Toronto.

I'd always considered Shay to be my best friend, but these days it was Zoey who seemed to know me best. She was the person beside whom I battled each day. These days, when Shay and I saw each other, we talked about her wedding plans, or she analyzed my text messages with Arjun and Jayesh—and then she'd lecture me about how I needed to be more "open." But Zoey and I actually *talked*.

My cell phone vibrated. It was an unknown number, and tentatively, I answered it.

"Hi, is this Raina?" The voice paused. "It's Sachin."

I covered the receiver with my palm and looked up at Zoey.

She'd heard all about the birthday ambush, and when I mouthed to her who it was, she swiped the phone from my hand and set it on the desk with a thud. She pressed the speakerphone button, and his voice, the tone now less formal, blared out.

"Hello? Hi? Is anyone there?"

"Hi," I said, slowly. "It's Raina."

"Yeah, hi! It's Sachin, the, uh—"

"Cardiologist. I remember."

He cleared his throat, his voice scratching through the room, and I tried not to laugh as Zoey gestured vulgarities at the phone.

"And how are you today, Raina?"

"I'm fine. And you?"

"Great—great, thank you. Well, no." He cleared his throat again. "Actually, I lost a patient this morning."

"I'm so sorry . . ."

"It happens." His voice trailed off, and as I caught Zoey's eye, her hands dropped slowly back to her lap.

"I had a great time with you and your nani a few weeks back," he said after a moment. "I'm sorry it's taken me so long to call."

"I didn't know you were planning to."

"Yeah . . . About that. I'm sorry I was so rude to you. My mother only told me that morning about the lunch, and I was annoyed with her. I shouldn't have taken it out on you. I'm sure you understand."

I did understand, but I didn't say anything.

"I really shouldn't have said that I wasn't interested. I hadn't even met you yet, and—well, you really are a nice girl, Raina. I am interested in getting to know you." I opened my mouth to speak, but nothing came out, and after a few seconds of static, he spoke again. "Would you like to have dinner with me?"

"Did your mother tell you to call me?" I blurted.

"No, I wanted to."

"Really."

"You're intelligent and forthright and *attractive* and—well, frankly, there's no reason why I shouldn't want to get to know you. So will you have dinner with me?" He spoke quicker, as if he had somewhere to rush off to. "Just dinner. With no pressure or anything. Just a normal date."

I listened to Sachin as he breathed heavily over the speaker, to Zoey's fingernails against her BlackBerry as she seemingly grew bored waiting for my answer.

Except for my coffee with Vishal—with whom I'd had less chemistry than my toaster—I hadn't been on a date in years, and I wasn't sure I'd ever even been on a *normal* date. My brief relationships in college had started in the library—and then there was Dev, although nothing about that date had been normal.

I could barely even remember the last time I was alone with a man. Last winter, was it? The securities seminar Zoey and I had flown to New York for last minute. Zoey had been on a break with Alice then, and she'd briefly disappeared with a woman she'd met at the hotel lobby a few hours before the flight home. Sitting there alone, I'd somehow become tipsy chatting to a broker from Atlanta. I could vaguely recall his hand grazing my waist next to the empty coat check, ignoring the longing in his glances when I refused to take a later flight home. But that was as far as it went: turning away from the kiss, forgetting the business card in an airplane seat pocket. I never let it lead to normal. I leaned forward against the desk and stared at the phone. Getting to know each other over dinner. This was what normal meant. Later, we'd go for more dinners, movies, and lunch dates—and then what? Months of sex and the superficial? A natural segue into the serious?

"Dinner," I repeated slowly, conjuring up Sachin in my mind. Indian. Intelligent. Handsome.

Nani-approved.

If I was going to do this, *really* going to do this, then it might as well be Sachin. And squinting into the glare from the window, I said, "I could do dinner."

Sachin ~~Reetu's son in Scarborough, some kind of doctor~~birthday lunch??

*Dinner 9:30 P.M., Tuesday @ Eldorado

FOUR

My boss, Bill, was pissed that I left work early, but Nani had insisted I come see her before my date with Sachin. After nearly an hour battling through rush-hour traffic, I arrived home to find that she wasn't even there yet.

She'd left all the lights on, and I walked around the house turning them off and then put the kettle on to boil. My head throbbed, and I flopped down on Nana's side of the couch and closed my eyes. I knew I was imagining it, but the sofa still smelled of him. I could picture him there reading me *Little House on the Prairie*, my head resting against his knees, impatiently tugging on the cuff of his trousers whenever he stopped mid-sentence to sip his tea.

No one was home with Nana the morning he died, and I don't think Nani ever forgave herself for believing him when he claimed his chest pain was merely indigestion. Watching her lose him was harder than dealing with my own grief. The horror of finding her collapsed sideways on the stairs clutching his parka, her wet eyes and nose buried in the garlicky tobacco scent of the goose down, would never leave me. She became a widow at the age of sixty. An arranged life drastically rearranged, Nani had to start over; create a life from scratch that didn't revolve around the man to whom she'd been assigned.

It took her years, but her vivacity returned, as did the color in her cheeks. She was always practical and compassionate—most of all toward Nana and I—but these days it wasn't strange to find Nani teasing the busboys and running Saffron better than Nana ever did; driving her Mini Cooper from an afternoon tea to temple, from one charity project to another. I suppose she had to find a new balance in the equilibrium that life had imposed on her.

In a way, Nani and I grew up together. Discovered each other all over again as adults. I'd learned the way she watched the *Ellen* show, her toes wiggling in her pressure socks whenever Ellen DeGeneres and the audience danced. The way Nani showed she loved you through food—and then, through more food. The way she only called me *beta* when she was upset or irritated. How she pronounced "vegetable"—*veg-ee-table*—or invented idioms like to "take a sleep" or "open the light." English was her fourth language, she liked to remind me, after Bengali, her mother tongue, Hindi, and Punjabi. English for her came last, not until 1969 when Nana moved his new bride across the world to Canada. To the land of opportunity.

To the land of, well, *land*.

I also learned that Nani could be vain, ignorant of what didn't concern her or her own family. I'd switch on the news, or buy her a book I thought she should read, and she'd sigh like the idea of something new tired her right out. For a while, I'd tried to get her interested in politics, coming home on election night—provincial, federal, American—and she'd cluck her tongue and leave the room, annoyed that I'd disrupted her favorite Hindi soap. She thought the oil sands were polluted beaches and didn't understand why Palestine and Afghanistan, and not India, was on the news so often.

Nani had never been like the other "aunties" in the community. She wore Western clothes most of the time—Sears pantsuits and polyester sweaters—and had refused to stay home and play house. She'd worked side by side at the restaurant with Nana and kept her chin high when her teenage daughter brought home a baby. She was *modern*, generations in front of so many of her friends—small-minded women who gossiped and pettily talked about one another's children. But still, for Nani, getting married and having children was a woman's one true path.

Her daughter had become a mother too young, and now she feared I'd become one too old or not at all. But couldn't she try and understand how it worked now? Women didn't have to get married and have children anymore—and even if they did, it didn't always mean they were happy.

I was tired of arguing with her, but at the same time, maybe Nani and Shay were right: Work consumed my life, and I *was* lonely. So what reason did I have to resist?

I heard the back door open, and I leaped up. I beat Nani to the kitchen and had the tea poured into two china mugs by the time she sat down at the table. She sighed as she brought the cup to her lips, and I watched her face, the fine lines dancing and stretching as she blew on the tea.

"How was work?"

She smiled, and sank back in her chair. "I am very tired."

"I can make dinner?"

"But you will eat with Sachin, *nah*?"

"Sure, but that's hours from now."

"*Aacha*. Make some rice, and we will heat up dal I have in freezer." She took a sip of tea, and then shook her head. "But first we must discuss Sachin. I called his mother today."

"You did *what*?"

"She is in my sewing group with temple, *nah*? I had to call anyway. And then I mentioned your dinner tonight, and she grew very happy."

I groaned. "Nani, I asked you not to tell anyone."

"Reetu is his mother. She has every right to know where her son is."

"But Sachin and I said we wouldn't involve the families yet, that it wasn't any of their business until—"

"None of our business?" Nani snapped. She stared at me, and I shrunk back into my chair.

"I'm sorry, I didn't mean—"

"None of *my* business." Nani's glare tore through me, and then landed on her hands. "Your mother used to say this to me."

"I'm not like her, Nani," I said, and for several long minutes, she didn't answer.

I drove back downtown and found the door to my condo unlocked, and Shay going through my wardrobe. Nani had put me in a bad mood. Her trump card for any argument: comparing me to Mom. Telling me that I, too, wasn't good enough.

I mindlessly changed in and out of outfits Shay selected for me. Leather pants I'd bought on a lark and never wore; skinny jeans from college that, when I sucked in, still sort of fit. Work blouses paired with too-short skirts I hadn't worn since London; dresses Shay brought over, silky and static, tight or loose in all the wrong places.

"You look great," Shay said as I stood in front of my mirror, only a wisp of pale peach chiffon differentiating me from a nudist. "I'm jelly of your legs."

I whipped around. "My legs look like jelly?"

"No, it means *jealous*." She bit into an apple, crunching loudly. "It's what the kids in my ward say."

I turned away slowly, pulling down the hem of the dress. The evening before, I'd waxed and filed and moisturized and polished. Groomed and straightened. Shay, lying sideways on my bed, still in hospital scrubs, nodded or shook her head vigorously at each outfit I tried on—but still, everything felt so wrong. My clothes felt like costumes, designed to impress the guy that may or may not become my husband. I just wanted to wear one of my work suits, what I felt most comfortable in and most like myself, but I had the feeling Shay wouldn't agree.

Through the mirror, I saw Shay lean down from the bed and smirk as she felt my smooth leg.

"You're going to sleep with him."

"No, Shay." I pulled at the hem of a skirt, forcing it down past my thighs. "I'm not going to *sleep* with him."

"It's an urban myth that men won't call you after."

"And they always called you?" I saw her stick out her tongue in the mirror, and I turned around. "Sorry. I meant . . . I meant I don't even know if I like him."

"Then why do you care so much?"

"Nani's the one who cares," I grumbled.

"You did this with Dev, too." Shay got off the bed and started walking toward the bathroom. "You built everything up in your head before you even knew him."

"If you came over just to lecture me, you didn't need to bother." I turned back to the mirror, and a moment later, I heard the bathroom door shut.

I sat down on my bed. I felt the skirt digging into my stomach and the sides of my thighs. I groaned, and rolled over and grabbed my BlackBerry from where it was charging on the nightstand. I had one new text message from Zoey wishing me luck on my date, and a handful of grumpy e-mails from Bill.

I could hear Shay still in the bathroom, and so I scrolled down to Dev's last message. For more than a year after we broke up, we'd stayed in touch, e-mailing every few days or at least once a week from our work accounts. But then weeks turned into months, and that last message I'd sent him more than four months earlier had gone unanswered.

It was only a few sentences: I'd told him about Shay and Julien's engagement, a new coworker in the New York office, and then asked after his family. It was small talk; really, it was nothing. Then why was I still unable to bring myself to delete it?

I heard the toilet flush, and I stuffed my phone into my bag. A moment later, Shay appeared in the doorway. The irritation had disappeared from her face, and now she just looked tired; the dopey blue of her hospital scrubs poking out from the top of her hoodie. I wasn't sure if she'd come over straight from work, or was on her way to a night shift; I'd forgotten to ask.

"How's work?"

She flopped onto the bed beside me, and put her arm around my neck. "Okay. It's going by quickly."

"When are you done with your residency again—less than a year, isn't it?"

She nodded. "I'll be done just a few weeks before the wedding. It's perfect timing."

Her arm felt heavy, and I shifted away from her on the bed.

"Raina, my ma set the date. It's—"

"I know," I said, holding a top against me in the mirror. "Nani already told me. Don't worry about it."

Auntie Sarla had confirmed Shay's wedding date. The day Shay got married to the love of her life and fulfilled her mother's wishes would be the day I turned thirty.

Thirty.

I grabbed a cardigan from the closet, nearly tearing the sleeve as I ripped it from the hanger, and walked back to the mirror.

Perfect timing.

DATE #2

I arrived early and waited outside the entrance, and at exactly 9:30
P.M., I entered the restaurant. Sachin had suggested it. It was modern looking, all burgundy and glass, and as soon as I noticed the
soft smell of roasting chicken, I realized how little I'd eaten that
day. I walked up to the hostess, and right behind her, to my surprise, I saw that Sachin was already there. He was seated at the end
of the bar, a scotch glass nestled between his palms, watching the
news on a small flat screen on the wall.

I walked slowly toward him. His suit jacket was open, a lavender tie loosened around his neck, and when I was a few feet away,
he looked over and smiled.

Before I could even say "Hi," he loosely hooked his finger
through my belt loop and tugged me in closer.

"Hi, beautiful."

He pulled me in for a hug. He smelled good, like whiskey and
paprika, and a part of me swooned. The other part of me kicked her.

"Hi, yourself."

"What's your poison?"

"Gin and tonic?"

"Josh? Double gin and tonic." Sachin picked up his glass, drained it, and then set it back on the bar. "And another Dalmore while you're at it."

A muscular blond behind the bar threw a dishrag over his shoulder, and rolled up the sleeves of his black collared shirt. "Sure thing, Sach."

"You have a preference?" Josh asked me.

"Hmm?"

He smirked. "Of gin."

"Oh." I blushed, forcing myself to look back at Sachin. "Barman's choice."

Sachin's eyes were glossy, his smile a bit crooked, and I wondered how long he'd been sitting there; how many Dalmores he'd already drunk.

"You look amazing," he said after a moment, as if he, too, had to think about what to say. His gaze flicked between my mouth and my eyes, and I tried to think of something to say in response. *Thank you? You, too?*

A heavy silence hung in the air, and when I looked up, Josh was making our drinks less than a foot away. He smiled at me— laughed, almost—like he could feel how awkward I suddenly felt.

"Don't do that," I heard Sachin say.

"Pardon?" I looked back at him. I was playing with my bracelets, winding them rapidly around my wrist with my fingers.

"Don't be nervous." Sachin steadied my hand with his, traced his pinky finger in a circle around my palm. "Do I make you nervous?"

"Why would *you* make me nervous?"

He grinned. "Then quit acting like it."

"I'm not acting like anything."

After a few minutes of stilted conversation, Josh led us to a table at the back of the restaurant, and as we walked, I tried to ignore the weight of Sachin's hand on my lower back. It felt good, but heavy, and I wondered whether I wanted him to move it.

We were through the first bottle of wine by the time our entrées arrived. I could feel it pooling in my stomach, trickling down, and my body relaxed. The waiter brought another bottle, and as time slicked by, I tried to make a list of what I liked about Sachin; reasons that this date—that we—maybe could be something more.

Sachin was nothing like dull, distracted Vishal. Sachin was intelligent and liberal, his views extending well past the dimension of the operating room, which I hadn't expected. We had mutual friends in banking, in medicine, had spent one of our rare vacations at the same Cancún resort; even our nanis had been born in the same village. And with each course, the list of similarities and commonalities between Sachin and me grew, and I found myself again warming to the idea of being with another Indian. He, too, had been raised with a mixed bag of expectations, straddling the cusp of Western culture and Eastern values. Like most people I knew, Sachin, too, never felt good *enough*; always being compared to others.

Didn't I need an Indian man to understand that about me?

I looked down at my glass. It was full, but I didn't remember Sachin pouring more. I reached for it, and a wave of nausea shot through me. A dessert was sitting between us, thick chocolate and cream, and as I watched Sachin bring a spoonful to his lips, Dev's face flashed in front of me. And just as quickly, I made it disappear.

"I'm having a great time with you, Raina."

I had to think about the words as they came out of my mouth, and I smiled. "You—too."

"You asked me if I *cleaned teeth*. Funny stuff." Sachin pinched at a piece of stray bread on the white tablecloth until it crumbled. He looked up at me—almost past me.

Was he going to reach for my hand? I pulled my hands down to my lap and, a moment later, made myself put them back on the table. I leaned into the table, thinking maybe he might kiss me. But we were talking again—about partition? His ex? I couldn't tell. His mouth was a blur of words, and I couldn't focus on what he was saying. Just his lips. His hands. He lifted his wineglass as if to toast me, and then set it down abruptly and reached into his pocket. "Sorry." He glanced down at his phone and then set it on the table.

"You can answer it."

Dev hated it when I asked him to keep his phone off during dinner.

Sachin waved me off. "No, it's not important. Really."

"Maybe it's a patient? You should answer."

His head swayed lazily. "Raina, it's nothing." And as he leaned in toward me, the phone buzzed again. I felt the vibrations pulsate across the table and through my hands, and I didn't mean to look at the screen, but I did. *Anika.*

Sachin flipped over the phone.

"Who is that?" I whispered.

"Nobody."

"Do you have a girlfriend?"

I'd once accused Dev of having another girlfriend.

Sachin reached for my hand. I pulled it away.

"Do you?"

He pressed his hands into his thighs, looking tense, suddenly alert. "I thought we talked about this—that we're in the same boat?"

"What boat is that?"

"That we're both at that age where our parents really want us to get married, and—"

"And?"

"And Anika and I have . . . gone on a few dates. You know I'm getting set up a lot, Raina. Just like you." He shrugged. "What's the big deal?"

But Dev had never cheated. He didn't have the time. Work—always work—was his priority; above his own family; above starting his future with me.

"Do you realize Anika has probably picked out a wedding sari? And here you are playing the field?"

"Slow down—"

"A rich and handsome guy though, right, *Sach*? You can get away with it. You can get away with leading girls on—"

"Are you kidding me? This is our first date."

Our first date. He was right. I didn't know him. This—he and I—meant nothing. It would never mean anything. I could feel the tears brimming at the corners of my eyes and the sudden sensation that everything was caving in around me.

"I should have gone with my instinct on this one," I heard Sachin say. "I *knew* you'd be like this."

Vishal. Sachin. Arjun. Jayesh. They were names on a list. Names to appease Nani, to fill the page, to fill time, the gaping hole in my chest. They were nothing to me, and they would never be Dev.

I looked up, surprised suddenly to see Sachin sitting across from me. He was leaning away from me in his chair, his eyes fixated on the pepper shaker. I grabbed my purse, unsteady on my feet as I stood up. I turned around looking for the door, and flung myself forward until I felt the cool night air on my face.

Outside, Yonge Street was exactly as it was before; exactly as it was every night. Dark storefronts and eateries, dive bars giving off a sickening red glow. Clusters of kids on skateboards, bored stiff, slouching in their skinny jeans. I walked past them and took a deep breath, gulping for air.

Is this what Nani wanted?

For me to be the fool. To reduce myself to just another Indian girl desperate to get married.

I could hear myself panting, my legs like jelly as I turned onto College Street, and I waited until I was around the corner—away from the kids, their faultless youth—before I let myself cry.

~~Sachin — Rittu's son in Scarborough, some kind of doctor — birthday lunch??~~

~~·Dinner 9:30 P.M., Tuesday @ Eldorado~~

What was I THINKING!!!!

MAY 20, 2014

Raina turns twenty-five at 5:52 P.M. local London time. Her co-workers toast her, pints of cider and lager clinking together above the wooden pub table, the stale chips no one has yet to touch. She finishes her drink in one long swig, slapping the empty glass down in celebration. Colin's ginger hair brushes hers as he leans in and asks if she'd like another. She shakes her head and glances around the room. It's unoriginal, dank, and cold. Dark wood paneling, a brick wall boasting an oil painting of the Queen. Raina reaches for her extra cardigan, and Colin laughs at her—*with* her. She is always cold, it seems, and being from Canada, he teases her about this endlessly.

She has been living in London for several months on a shared third-floor flat just off Upper Street. It has an unfocused smell of damp laundry, burned hair extensions, Heinz beans eaten cold from the can. Raina is rarely home, but when she is, they keep the flat lively with hip-hop, Sunday roasts, and girls-nights-in. Two of her flatmates are still students at uni—bottles and books perpetually in hand—and the third is a graphic designer with the face of a model, and "Chatterbox Pink" lips. They are British girls, lovely and loud, and with them, Raina feels safe.

They are a break from her sometimes sixteen-hour workdays, a splash of color onto what would otherwise be a life walled in by the dreary, pale demands of working in the City of London. The girls introduce her to the real city—gigs outside Zone 1, wine bars in repurposed churches—and also to the boys they know. Immature, ashy brown–haired boys who find her witty when drunk, intimidating when sober. To them, Raina downplays her job at the investment bank, her life among the three-thousand-pound suits marching up and down Cheapside and Cannon Street. She was chosen from among fifty applicants in the Toronto, New York, and Chicago offices for a temporary transfer to the overseas office, but these aren't the things that interest them.

Nor do *they* interest her.

His name is Dev Singh, and at present, he is a mere silhouette.

They have never spoken directly, yet two months earlier, at her very first meeting, it was his voice she noticed first. The way he gently commands a boardroom, she can tell he's humble. Dedicated. He's a man unaware of his impact on others, and this only affects her more.

They still haven't spoken directly, yet she's conscious of him always. How she is slightly taller than him in heels, or the way he crosses and uncrosses his legs when he has something to say. How he stays at the office later than most people—even Fridays, never joining the rest of them at the pub. Already, he is unlike any man she has ever met. He is more than the men she talks to at clubs through gritted teeth, her flatmates giggling nearby. The ones in the cash-only line at Tesco. Already, he's more than either of her college boyfriends, flings so brief, inconsequential, she often forgets she had them. She is startled by the way Dev affects her. She has never been attracted to an Indian man before, and this is how she knows it must be real. She knows that Dev is different.

She has already given up hope that he might turn up to the pub that evening, when she sees him. Her heart pounds. She stiffens as he walks past her, and slyly, she leans back in her chair and looks after him.

He is greeted with enthusiasm by a cluster of bankers—those more senior, sitting separate from her crowd. He leans forward against the backs of two chairs, and she struggles to hear what they are saying over the chatter, over Colin, who again asks if she'd like another pint. Dev says something she misses, and it makes the group laugh, especially the woman—Becky—who heads the fixed-income division. She throws her head back as she laughs, and the blond hairs of her ponytail catch on his suit.

Raina has never liked Becky.

After a moment, Dev turns and walks toward the bar. Raina exhales. This is it, she tells herself. Today is her birthday, and unlike any other day, she is sure that this time she will think of something to say. Witty. Original—though not overly curated. She has been waiting for a chance to approach him. To impress him. And somehow, she knows that now is the time. She counts to five before following, and as she slinks toward him, navigates through the after-work crowd, her mind once again draws a blank. Her stomach churns. She is only a few feet away, and she is considering turning back, when he looks over his shoulder and smiles.

"Ah." He leans back on the counter. "Raina Anand. Our newest import from *Ca-nada*."

She is giddy about the fact he knows her name and bites her lip to keep from smiling. She loves how he says "Canada," and her country suddenly appears elegant in her mind. She struggles not to picture him there with her, already; running to catch the streetcar on

King Street, handing Nani a bouquet of wildflowers the first time he comes for dinner.

"That's me."

"I've been meaning to swing by and chat, but—"

"But you're a busy man," she says, surprised by the evenness of her voice.

"Too busy, it would seem." He is looking at her neck. Her lips. Her hair in wisps around her shoulders. "So," he says, sliding a beer toward her. "What can you tell me then, Raina?"

She smiles coyly and reaches for the beer. As she had hoped, she knows exactly what to say.

They stand there for hours. She is dizzy from the smell of his cologne, the glasses of *hefeweizen* that keep appearing in front her. They are speaking, and at times, she has no idea what about— redemption funds and Chelsea football. The pub's fresco-style ceiling. She has never laughed so hard, been so inebriated by another human being. He is teasing her. Enveloping her. He pinches her nose, and his thumb falls slowly, parting her lips. And suddenly, they are no longer laughing.

He grabs her hand and leads her outside. Beneath the moony streets of St. Paul's, she reminds herself that she's not supposed to believe in casual sex. But the way Dev is kissing her, his fingers lightly wound through her hair, already this doesn't feel casual. Minutes pass, and then he pulls away and tilts her chin to the side. She looks up at him and cannot meet his eye, and she prepares herself to say no when he inevitably asks her to go home with him. But he doesn't ask. Instead, he thumbs the leather of her purse, wonders out loud whether she happens to have her passport.

His hand stays on her knee in the taxi as they head north on Farringdon Road toward St. Pancras station. Their wide smiles fill the back seat, and he apologizes three, four, five times, telling her that Paris would have been more romantic, more fitting for birthday spontaneity—if only the Eurostar to Paris wasn't already booked up. Brussels is perfect, she says into his shoulder. Raina has never been to Brussels, and she senses now that she'd always wanted to go.

He buys them orange juice and chicken avocado sandwiches in the cafeteria car, and as they dip beneath the English Channel, her ears pop and he tells her about growing up in West Harrow. She senses his shame as he talks about his family. She doesn't understand his resentment, but she intertwines her fingers with his and tells him that she does.

It is nearly midnight by the time they reach Gare de Bruxelles-Midi, and after hailing a taxi, Dev looks surprised when Raina begins to converse with the driver, asks him in stilted French to take them anywhere he likes. He drops them off on a lively street across from La Grand-Place. Brass lampposts and cobblestone streets, twinkle lights and fogged-in windows. Hundreds of men stripped down to their boxers parading through the square, whipping their red, sweat-drenched football shirts around like batons, chanting, "*Allez la Belgique!*"

Dev squeezes her hand as they maneuver through the crowd and onto quieter lanes. They are soon lost, and everything smells of white wine and rain. They wander past marble fountains, through alleys and impossibly green parks, and every so often, he pulls her aside—against a railing or black brick wall—and kisses her. Every time, she falls further. Becomes more convinced about the connection between them. That rushing sensation. The inability to catch her breath. And right there, on the darkened streets of Brussels, for the first time, Raina falls in love.

It's nearly dawn when they find a hotel. Dev leads her to the room, and her mind races. Her body trembles. She's twenty-five now, and a virgin. Isn't she ready?

Wasn't she waiting for *this*?

She sits on the foot of the bed, and Dev kneels down in front of her. Kisses both of her knees. And then he reaches up and kisses her, pulls down her face to his, and she's on the floor, too, pressed hard against him.

Nani's face flashes before her eyes, and then her mother's. Every time this is what has happened, and every time it's the reason she stopped.

She thinks about pushing Dev away, ending it before she becomes weak—before she becomes her mother. But he's kissing her neck, her collarbone. His tongue darts in and out of her ear, and then her mouth—and then it is consuming her. His hands around her waist, Dev lifts her to the bed, pushes her down. Raina's blouse, Dev's trousers are flung to the side, and with them her doubts. With Dev, she's alive, finally, and nothing can stop her.

Date #3

I followed Arjun's eyes, which were glued to a chubby-cheeked Asian toddler with a Spider-Man hoodie and chocolate on his face. He was perched on the shoulders of his dad, yawning and at the same time attempting to have another lick of his ice cream cone.

"Adorable." Arjun squeezed my forearm. I tried not to flinch. "Isn't he *just* the cutest?"

"Very cute," I admitted, subtly drawing my arm back. What had Nani written on that list, which was now buried somewhere at the bottom of my handbag? Arjun was a pediatrician, so he probably wanted to have kids soon? She wasn't kidding. Arjun and I had been at Canada's Wonderland for several hours, and he'd already pointed out a dozen children to me. All of them Asian. All of them spitting images of him. Gulp, or *me*.

"Do you have any nieces or nephews?" He hesitated, probably realizing I'd already told him I was an only child. "Or small cousins?"

I shook my head, as we shuffled forward in line for the park's largest roller coaster. "My experience with children is limited."

"Ah."

"But I like kids of course." I attempted a smile. "You know, my friend Shay and her fiancé are both pediatricians, too."

"Oh, Shaylee Patel? Yes, I'm *sure* I've met her." The roller coaster sped over us, and Arjun rubbed his hands together in delight. "I'm so excited! This one's my favorite."

"I've never been to Wonderland."

"No?" Arjun smiled at me, and then rested his hand gently on my shoulder. "Clearly, no one's ever spoiled you before."

The line trudged forward, and the optimism I'd embraced at the beginning of the date waned. After Shay had scolded me for overreacting with Sachin, never mind getting plain drunk on a first date, I decided I needed to try anew. Try to make an effort with the men Nani had selected. And so when both Arjun and Jayesh asked me if I had plans the following Saturday, I cleared my calendar and tossed a coin.

Heads for Arjun.

He was lovelier in person than he was via text message. Respectful. Sweet. Fun. Attractive. He'd mentioned in passing that he'd broken up with a long-term girlfriend just months before, and I knew this sort of guy wouldn't be single for long. Everything about Arjun seemed suitable, and appropriate, but as the attendants buckled us into the ride, it struck me that I was entirely bored. Not bored with him, but with myself. Who exactly was I pretending to be meeting him? A nice Indian girl devoted to her nani? A hardworking investment analyst with high-flying ambitions—that is, until she became the mother of our adorably South Asian babies?

Arjun wanted to marry a woman like the character I was playing. He wouldn't want the real me, and by the end of the dizzying ride, I was confident that I didn't want to play that role for him, either.

When we parted ways in the parking garage, I let him down gently. Afterward, I fished the list out of my purse, found a pen in the glove box, and crossed out his name. Sure, maybe there wouldn't be anybody on this list that was *more* right for me than Arjun, but I knew I was doing him a favor. There was bound to be an amazing woman on Arjun's own list who'd feel lucky to have him.

~~Arjun—Sonia's son, pediatrician, probably will want to have babies soon!~~

Has B-A-B-Y fever!

FIVE

The clear blue skies of summer continued. The bodies of Bay Street moved at a slower pace, stilled by the humidity, the souring heat coming off the Great Lakes. Summer had always meant studying and taking temp jobs at the library or as a research assistant. Coaching community basketball. Now, summer blended into the rest of the year.

My job felt stagnant, even mindless, and at least twice a day I'd find myself lying on my keyboard staring sideways at a pile of papers, eyes blurred, until one of the senior bankers' voices in the hallway startled me upright. When I was dating Dev, I'd loved my job. Or had I? He'd traveled abroad for work every few days or weeks, and when he was in London, we both spent most of our waking hours in the office. But we'd been happy. We'd made it work, although I had no idea how. London felt so long ago, and a heavy fog seemed to block me from remembering the details.

I broke up the summer monotony as best I could. There were

rooftop bars or music festivals with colleagues after work; midnight movies alone at the cheap theater near my condo; short weekends away at a cottage with Zoey and Alice—now back together "for good"—and other friends, complete with chopped logs and icy beer, sunbaked split ends and aloe vera for the drive home. And, of course, there were my morning breakfasts with Shay— although because of the wedding plans and conflicting work schedules, I saw her less and less. When we did see each other, she was distracted by the latest wedding crisis, and I'd get snappy at the mention of Auntie Sarla or Nani, and one of us would end up making an excuse to leave early. Because Nani had been a young grandmother, and Sarla had had Shay in her early thirties, the two women were close in age—and "close competitors." Seemingly, all they wanted to talk about these days was Shay's impending nuptials, and the fact that mine were still TBD.

I *thought* I was making progress on the list—although, according to Nani, two first dates that didn't turn into first husbands didn't count as progress. Sachin was a tool. Vishal wasn't single. Arjun was—well, not the one. I went to Nani's house after leaving Wonderland, and after I had made up excuses about how Arjun and I weren't a good match, she squished up her face as if she'd stuck a lemon beneath her tongue, and said, "Not him, *too*?" Nani was young enough to be my mother, but the generation between us could feel endless. Raising my mother, raising *me*, had made Nani modern quickly. Unwillingly. But she still couldn't understand that women no longer needed to get married.

Was that unfair of me? Hadn't I wanted to get married? Fulfill every fantasy and stereotype? How many hours had I wasted wondering when Dev would propose, envisioning garlands of marigolds and traditional saris, silk drapery and bhangra music. Dev in a kurta pajama, and everyone in my family—for the first time— sitting peacefully in the same room.

One Sunday in late August, the first day in over a month where I had the option to sleep in, Nani insisted I come home and spend the day with her. I relinquished my plans of sleeping off my hangover, of spending the day on the balcony with a tub of ice cream and the book I'd been meaning to read for over a year, and instead, Nani and I made paratha.

It had been years since I'd helped her in the kitchen, and I was proud of the result. Parathas, gold and flaky, smothered in butter, stuffed with spicy *aloo*. After, we ate them beneath the backyard awning, cooling ourselves down in the lazy summer breeze. Nani had slipped a disk in her back the summer before, and I'd hired a neighbor's son to mow the lawn, to trim the hedges and plant, while Nani pointed and prodded, sat on a stool as she instructed him on how she wanted the beds arranged.

"Andy's doing a good job with the yard," I said, yawning, admiring the lawn, almost a forest green.

"What is *that*?" She reached forward and pulled at my ear, and then squinted at the blue paint that rubbed off onto her fingers. "Paint?"

"Um, yes?"

"*Vhy*? Are you renovating your apartment? This is not a good color."

"No. I went to a—uh—pride party last night." I thought back to the evening before—Zoey, Alice, me, and some of our other friends bodysurfing, drunk off electronica music at a warehouse in the Gay Village—and decided to leave out the details.

"Pride?" she asked after a moment.

"Like, you know"—I hesitated—"a celebration for LGBTQ—"

"Huh?"

"For gay people, Nani. It was a party celebrating gay people," I said, trying to rack my brain for the most straightforward way of explaining the term. "I went with my friends. With Zoey—you remember her, right?"

"Oh. Was Ellen there?"

"Ellen DeGeneres lives in Los Angeles."

"But I thought you said you were too busy this weekend to see Jayesh. His mother is calling me *many* times."

"I was busy," I grumbled, refusing to feel guilty about the fact I kept postponing my date with Jayesh. "I was at the party."

"Raina . . ." She clucked her tongue. "You are pushing luck— just like your mother used to. Please *try*. Jayesh comes from very good Hindu family."

"So he's automatically perfect for me?"

"I am not a silly woman." Nani sighed, and turned to face the lawn. "His family is very educated, very stable. These things become important in raising children. *Values* are important."

"Being Hindu. Being . . . Indian." I buried my toes into the dirt in front of me, twisted them in the damp earth. "Is that what's important to you?"

"*Nah*, Raina. Julien is Catholic, he is white—and look, your Auntie Sarla is fine with it. Please just stop looking for things that are wrong. They are men. White, brown, yellow, blue; they all have *something* wrong with them." Nani guffawed. "Just pick one!"

I knew she was trying to be funny, and so I laughed. But I had picked one—and in the end, Dev wasn't ready to get married. Did that mean I should just pick another now? One that I liked well enough, and one day could maybe fall in love with?

I watched the geraniums shudder as the sun grew fierce. I checked my watch. It was nearly noon, and our temple's Sunday service usually went until 1 P.M.

"Nani, you want to go to the *mandir*?"

"*Aacha?*" Nani smiled, and sitting forward on the lawn chair, she squeezed my chin. "Okay, let us go."

Our temple, all limestone and Mughal-influenced architecture, was only a ten-minute drive away. It sat at the edge of a public park, its grounds clean lines of lawn and concrete. The puja was already under way as Nani and I walked in. The front altar was decorated with tin bells and displays of fruit and sweets, rose petals, shiny jewelry, and garlands strung of marigolds. Nani maneuvered her way through the crowd toward the front where she always sat with Auntie Sarla, and I lingered near the back searching for space on the crowded floor.

I was surprised to find Shay sitting against the back wall. Both of us went to temple so rarely these days that I figured she would have texted me about it beforehand to see if I wanted to go, too. She made room for me, and I sat down and closed my eyes. The priest continued chanting, the room echoing in unison. I had never had the patience to meditate, to practice yoga like Nani—but this time I didn't mind. His deep voice soothed something in me. The long, reverberating vowels. I breathed in and out, and a few minutes later when I came to, the sharp lights lifting me back to the present, Shay was looking at me.

"Ma is making us go to India," she said, a little too loud. An auntie in front of us coughed loudly, her doughy back rippling out of her blouse as she whipped her neck around to glare at us.

I leaned closer to Shay after the woman turned back around. "When?"

"In January," Shay whispered. "To shop for outfits and gifts. Stuff for the wedding. Julien's actually excited about the whole thing. He cannot *wait* to see the Taj Mahal."

"That's exciting."

"Is it?" Shay argued. "No sleeping in the same room. No meat or alcohol. Having to dress like a monk. It sounds *terribly* exciting."

I'd only been to India once—a two-week trip with Nani and Nana as a child: a quick collage of coddling distant relatives and rich goat curry; the smell of putrefied garbage and endless compliments about my fair skin, my light hair; pails of sliced mangoes and having to rinse my toothbrush with boiled water. And the memory, as vague as it was, polluted by the smog that seemed to settle into eyes and chests, still felt like home. The sprawling courtyard and the mango tree in my grandmother's village an hour outside of New Delhi. Her talcum powder scent as I fell asleep on a bed beneath the stars. It was Nani's history. Nani's home. In its grounds, built of baked bricks and timber, it was my home, too.

But Shay hated India. It repulsed her. The people, the country, the heritage, the politics. The dichotomies of injustice: excess and poverty; humility and greed; men and, much further down— women. Growing up, Shay and her brother, Nikesh, had been dragged "home" yearly to their family's estate in Rajasthan, a fortress of over thirty relatives. An extended family, an entire culture, which Shay grew to despise. She'd come over after every trip, throw both herself and a bag of gaudy souvenirs down onto my bed, and moan. Moan about her three weeks locked in a metaphorical interrogation room. The way they soaked her twine-like hair in coconut milk, stuffed her with sweet *rasmalai* and then faulted her for gaining weight. How she was rarely let outside for fear of a suntan or, slightly worse, being accosted by the local men.

Shay said the men there leered at her, smacked their lips, and tried to pull down her skirt. They would drive back and forth on scooters calling her names until she'd yell at the top of her lungs for them to screw off. They didn't treat their own Indian women like that, Shay said to me, her smile limp; even though she spoke both Hindi and Rajasthani fluently, to them, she wasn't really Indian.

I suppose neither was I.

The priest resumed chanting, and I spun Nani's heavy gold bracelets around my wrists. I looked toward the front. Auntie Sarla was hovering beside the priest, assisting him as he poured holy water out of a silver tin. Shay's engagement party was less than a week away, an elaborate affair in its own right, and over the past few weeks, I'd spent hours on the phone with Auntie Sarla helping her organize the party—answering her calls and running errands whenever she couldn't get a hold of Shay.

"How did the fitting go?" I asked her.

"The *lengha* fit, but Ma said 'not well enough.'" Shay shook her head. "I have to go back again tomorrow."

"Do you want me to come with you?"

She looked over, as if surprised. "Yes, oh my God—*yeah*. I need a buffer between me and Ma." She smiled, and then leaned over and kissed me on the arm. "I wish I was getting married next week. Get it over and done with, you know?"

I nodded.

"Who needs an engagement party anyway?" Shay glanced at me. "But at least the 'drifter' will be there."

"Who?"

"Asher. The guy I told you about, remember?" She sounded irritated. "Julien is picking him up from the airport right now. He just flew back from Bangkok . . ."

The auntie sitting in front of us turned around again, her glare forcing Shay's voice down to a whisper as she nattered on about Asher. The photos he posted online of the lychee orchards on a trek near Chiang Mai. How she and Julien might now honeymoon there on his recommendation. I refrained from rolling my eyes as Shay spoke. Mom had gone to Thailand when I was in high school, and none of us had known she'd been gone until she was home again, arriving at the house in the middle of the night needing a place to sleep. Tanned skin and bleached hair, a backpack the size of a small child clamped onto her shoulders. A tattoo on her calf—a Hindi phrase inked in pitch black—one that was supposed to mean *peace*, but, Nani had claimed, meant nothing at all.

"—so is that okay?" Shay nudged me again. "I'll introduce you guys."

"No," I whispered, turning to Shay. "I've been meeting enough men."

"How was your date with Jayesh?"

"I didn't go in the end." I shrugged. "Maybe next week . . ."

"Oh." Her voice conveyed her annoyance, like I should have already told her that detail. "Well, have you met anyone else—anyone I should know about?"

I hadn't told Shay about Arjun. I knew she would harass me for a play-by-play if I did, and force me to explain in detail how I could be so sure after one date that Arjun and I wouldn't work out. That I wasn't ready—or maybe didn't want—what he had to offer. She'd accuse me of comparing him to my ex, or self-sabotage, or say a dozen other go-to phrases she'd probably picked up from a handbook on "how to manage lonely best friends"—and I didn't feel like another sermon when I'd had plenty from Nani.

So I shook my head, pressed my lips together for a moment, and turned back to face the priest. "Nope. There's no one else."

SIX

Nani and Shay left right after the puja, but I stayed behind to help the volunteer caretakers water the flower beds and trees lining the temple grounds. When I arrived home, I found the driveway full of cars I didn't recognize, and when I opened the front door, I could hear Nani and her friends downstairs in the entertaining room.

I lingered in the foyer, evesdropping on Nani, Auntie Sarla, and the others speaking together in Hindi; Auntie Sarla's shrill exclamations steadied by Nani's voice, low murmurs of what I sensed to be assent. I'd never learned to speak Hindi properly, and only knew the most basic nouns, verbs, and phrases, but it was everything else that made the language so identifiable to me; it was a language of pitch and tone, emotive cadence and expression. As their voices ricocheted up the stairs from the entertaining room, even though they weren't saying my name, I could tell they were talking about me.

I leaned against the wall and slid down onto the floor. I flattened my legs and felt the cold linoleum on my bare calves. I leaned back, and my hair caught onto the fibers of the wallboard, the way it always had when I'd sat in this spot as a girl.

What exactly was Auntie Sarla saying about me?

That every day I was letting another potential husband slip through my fingers, and not getting married like her Shaylee? That I was twenty-nine, and with each breath, each step, inching closer to thirty?

Without saying hello, I went upstairs and stretched out on my bed. Soon after, I heard that someone had started playing on the harmonium, and the disharmony of singsong voices blared upstairs through the vents. I focused on the glow-in-the-dark stickers I'd stamped onto the ceiling as a child, now just flecks of mild green.

Except for the dirty laundry on the floor, Nani had left everything exactly as it had looked the day I moved out. The vintage tea-stained map I had framed. My bookshelf, an antique maple hutch well stocked with Puffin Classics and novels from garage sales and the clearance shelves of supermarkets. The mash-up of throw pillows and raw silk curtains that we'd sewn together. I had been a hopeless student of basic domestics and slammed my foot on the treadle like I was race car driver, and she'd had to undo every stitch I made with her Hobbycraft sewing machine.

I thought about going back downtown. I had client meetings to prep for, recycling to take out, groceries to buy. But I knew I wouldn't do any of that. I knew that if I went back downtown, I would just sit on the chaise lounge by the window and close my eyes in the sun. Listen to the faint noises of families walking their dogs and buying gelato. The teenagers shuffling aboard the streetcar with H&M bags and neon headphones. I yawned, and before I could decide one way or another, the doorbell woke me up.

"Nani?"

I could still hear the harmonium's music, Auntie Sarla's voice shrieking over the rest of the voices. The doorbell rang again, and I pulled myself off the bed and down the stairs. I opened the front door, and squinting into the afternoon light, it took me a moment to realize who it was.

"Depesh?"

"Raina, hey." Depesh was at least six inches taller than the last time I'd seen him, and not nearly as scrawny. His muscles were more defined now and filled out his shirt, his dark wash jeans. The black, wayward curls I remembered on him as a kid were flattened and slicked behind his ears.

"Wow." I crossed my arms. "I haven't seen you in forever! You grew up nice."

He rolled his eyes.

"How old are you now—sixteen, seventeen?"

"Eighteen."

"Eighteen. God, you make me feel old."

"Well, you look exactly the same, Raina."

I led him into the family room, and sank into the couch. He looked around the room, his hands on his hips, and then tentatively took a seat in Nana's armchair.

Depesh had once been like a brother to me. His mother had been diagnosed with MS when he was ten, and I'd spent the summer after my junior year of college babysitting him. His parents—a rotund lady I called Sharon Auntie, and her husband, whose name I still hadn't figured out—had spent long days at the hospitals, at clinics for drug trials, three-day trips to Boston or San Jose for experimental procedures. So Depesh and I baked cookies and played Monopoly, went to the park and watched television until our eyes hurt. At the end of the summer, his parents moved him to New Jersey to be closer to a specialized facility, and I hadn't seen him since.

Depesh's hands were perfectly still and straight on his lap, and he stared at them.

"Do you want some tea?"

He shook his head, and looked up. "Just picking up Ma."

"Oh, I didn't know she was over."

He nodded. "Your nani is like the only one who's been able to get her to leave the house."

"Wait." I sat up. "You moved back?"

He nodded. "We've been back a month already."

"Nani didn't tell me"—I racked my brain, trying to remember—"or maybe she did, shit. I can't remember."

"It's okay."

"She calls me a lot. Sometimes at work I put her on speaker and drift off . . . God, am I a terrible person?"

"No, you're not." He laughed nervously. "But what do I know? I haven't heard from you in, like, a decade."

I knew he didn't mean to make me feel guilty, but I did. Depesh had been a kind, genuine kid—and I could still see that about him; in his eyes, his smile—it was impossible to miss. But he was different, too. He had been playful and silly when I'd known him. Exuberant. Brave enough to climb to the tops of the jungle gyms, face the tallest slides while I trailed behind.

Now he seemed awkward in his own skin. Nervous, unsure of himself. I realized that I didn't know him anymore, either. For the past eight years, I'd basically forgotten all about him.

"Do you want to go get some ice cream?"

He rolled his eyes. "Raina, I'm not a kid anymore."

"Maybe *I* want ice cream."

He glanced over at me nervously. "Well, you could buy me beer."

Nani rarely kept alcohol in the house, and the bottle of whiskey Kris stored beneath the sink was missing. So we slipped out the front door and walked a few blocks north on the wide suburban streets toward the strip mall nearby. He waited outside while

I went in and bought two large bottles of beer, and on the walk home, we stopped at the park beside my old high school. A few other people were around—kids about Depesh's age smoking weed by the basketball courts—and we picked a spot to sit a fair distance away in the grassy field.

I opened my bag, and then reluctantly handed him the beer. "I'm a bad influence on you. Don't tell your mother."

He laughed. "I'll be legal in a few months."

He twisted off the cap of the beer, and brought the bottle to his lips. He stared at it for a second before taking a sip, and I saw him wince.

"Do you like beer?"

He wiped his mouth with his hand, smiling. "Not really. I never really drank in high school. I wasn't invited to the parties."

"Me neither. But my best friend was, so sometimes I tagged along."

"I didn't really have a best friend . . ." Depesh looked down at his beer, and with one hand started to peel back the label. "Actually, down there I had trouble making friends."

I put my hand on his shoulder.

He continued. "Jersey was . . . hard. And now I don't know anybody here anymore, you know?" His fingers shook, and the label—partway off—split in two. "I'm starting university in a few days. That will be good."

"It will be, Depo." I smiled at him, and then took a quick sip from my own beer. It was already warm, tasted stale, and I set it down beside me. "And until then, you know you have me, right?"

"I don't need your pity or anything."

"It's not pity." I stared at him until he looked me in the eye. "I promise. I'm really glad you're back."

He nodded, and looked back at his beer.

"So, what classes are you taking?"

"Bio, chemistry, math"—he sighed—"you know, the usual pre-med stuff."

"You want to be a doctor?"

"Doesn't everybody?"

"So what if everybody else does? You should be what you want to be."

He grew quiet, and stretched back on his elbows. It was hot, and the sun was in my eyes, scorching my face.

"I heard you're getting married."

My stomach dropped, and I turned to face him. "Who told you that?"

"My mom did." He paused. "Is it that British guy? I heard something a while back about a British guy."

So that's what Nani and her friends were talking about in the entertaining room: that I was about to get married? How many in our community were preparing to shove me down the aisle, had picked out a punch bowl for a wedding gift, when I—when *Nani*—had yet to find me a husband?

I grabbed the beer and swigged it, drank until it was nearly half gone.

"So you're not getting married?"

Slowly, I set the beer back down. The aftertaste was disgusting. "No. I'm not."

"But there was a British guy? I'm not making that up?'

I pressed my lips together. "There was. We broke up when I left London."

"I'm sorry. That sucks. But London—that must have been *amazing*, hey?" Depesh's smiled brightened. "I would love to live in Europe—or *go* to Europe even."

"Yeah, it was wonderful . . ." I trailed off. A moment later, I realized Depesh was still looking at me.

"What's London like?"

"Busy. Diverse. In some ways, entirely overwhelming." I shrugged. "Lonely, in other ways. Like any big city."

"Lonely? But you had a boyfriend."

I cleared my throat. "So you've never been?"

"No"—he shook his head—"I really want to, but we could never travel because Ma's treatments cost too much." He paused. "That's actually why we moved back. Tuition to a good school down there was *expensive*."

"Oh . . ."

"It's a lot here, too, though," he said. "I took out a loan, and I'm working part-time at Star Labs to save up."

"Star Labs is across the road from my company. You can drop by sometime." I picked up my bottle. "Like if you need beer, or something."

He laughed.

"Or you can borrow my car if you want to take a girl out, or whatnot."

He smiled at me vaguely, and put his hand out in front of his face. The sun cast a shadow across his eyes, his nose, and I couldn't tell what he was looking at. After a while, he fished his phone out of his pocket and looked at the screen.

"Ma is wondering where I am." He pushed himself up onto his knees, and wiped his hands together, grass and dirt falling from his palms. "We should probably go back."

I nodded, and we walked back together in silence, my mind racing. In Nani's eyes, my marriage was a done deal. But what if it wasn't?

I stopped short at the foot of the driveway, breathing through the tightness in my chest.

What if I already knew that what Nani wanted for me wouldn't be enough?

DATE #4

"So you're Auntie Suvali's granddaughter," he said, without standing up to greet me.

"And you must be Rahul." I shuffled into the seat across from him. He was reading the *Paris Review*, and bookmarked his page with a peacock feather. Then, as if on purpose, he set the magazine down on the table between us facing toward me.

I was exhausted, and as I made introductory chitchat with Rahul, I realized I was not prepared for yet another blind date. I'd worked crazy hours all week, all the while fielding panicked calls from Shay and Auntie Sarla about the engagement party—which was tonight.

I'd stayed up late the evening before with Shay's younger brother, Nikesh, designing, printing, and manually cutting out place cards for the table settings. Afterward, I'd thought seriously about canceling on Rahul, but Nani had called me excitedly at the crack of dawn asking me what I was wearing and where Rahul was taking me—and I didn't want to let her down again.

To Nani's dismay, Jayesh had given up on me. I guess postponing a first date for an entire summer does that to a guy. To make matters worse, earlier in the week I'd bailed on a Skype date with Jagmohan in India, something Nani had organized so I could check whether he was still coming to visit.

"Absolutely not. Nani, he just wants a marriage visa," I'd said, pointing at the list. "You wrote it down yourself."

"Even nice boys can have ulterior motives, *nah*?"

Rahul was the very last name on her list. So when she asked me to call him, I didn't know how to say no.

A server with gray-blue hair dropped off two jam jars full of water and a wicker basket full of what appeared to be—and nearly smelled like—dog shit.

Rahul lunged for the dung, and popped one in his mouth.

"What is it?"

"Gluten-free vegan raw bread," he said, his mouth full.

"Can bread *be* raw?"

He scowled at me as he swallowed. "Don't you have a dehydrator?"

I shook my head.

"Wow, okay." He looked alarmed. "Well, it's a must-have when you're on a gluten-free vegan raw diet. It's as indispensable to me as my NutriBullet."

I snuck a look at my watch. I'd been at the restaurant for *four* minutes, and already I wanted to leave. Rahul seemed insufferable, but maybe we had gotten off on the wrong foot? Maybe I was judging him too quickly.

I forced out a smile, trying to make an effort. I picked up a piece of the "bread" and nibbled on the corner. It tasted like mildew.

"Mmm," I purred, nodding heavily. "What's in it?"

"Vegetables, mostly. Onions, tomatoes, peppers, broccoli. Sunflower seeds, too, I think." He chewed loudly. "Whatever it is, it's ethically sourced. Everything here is farm-to-table fresh."

"My nani owns a restaurant."

"Oh yeah? Which one?"

"Saffron. It's in Roncesvalles—"

He waved me off. "Oh, I know it. It's quite . . . popular, isn't it? I imagine a lot of tourists go there. Must be in the guidebooks or something."

"What's wrong with tourists?"

"Where you should really go is to this place I know on Keele Street." He grabbed another turd, and I thought about telling him that he still had pieces of the last one all over his teeth. "It's less overplayed. You walk in, and you think it's a run-of-the-mill ciggys and gum convenience store, right?"

"Right," I deadpanned.

"And then the guy takes you through the back door and . . . BANG!"

"He shoots you?"

"Best Vietnamese food in the city. And *decent* virgin cocktails."

"Naturally."

"All in all, the evening will cost you around fifty bucks." He eyed my handbag, which I'd hung off of my chair's armrest. "I'm guessing that's less than that purse you have there. That isn't real leather, is it?"

I glanced at it, suddenly recalling that the ebony black tote was Shay's. I'd borrowed it the year before, swearing to give it back, but never had.

"I'm not sure . . ."

"Consumer culture. Am I right?"

I laughed, and it sounded about as awkward as I felt. "I sure could consume a *drink* right about now—"

"Raina, this place is alcohol free."

"Oh, I was kidding . . ."

He rolled his eyes, and after handing me a menu, I resisted the temptation to hit him with it.

Rahul suggested we try the five-course lunch tasting menu, and I obliged. He ordered an aloe vera smoothie, and despite his rave reviews of the birch juice, I wasn't quite in the mood for tree. I settled on an organic root beer, and while it tasted nothing like root beer, it was actually pretty good.

We discussed the weather—hot, but not sticky hot—and then took turns commenting on the restaurant's decor. The twinkly lights and green-brown ferns. Persian rugs and throws in piles, as if to enforce a sense of coziness.

Rahul had strong opinions, even on things that you wouldn't think warranted such fervor—such as the choice between wood flooring and carpet. Everything was right or wrong, authentic or "trying too hard." I glanced at the hemp necklace dipping between the V of his distressed T-shirt, the twisted tuft on the top of his head that very nearly fell into man-bun territory, and wondered which category Rahul fell into.

My favorite Drake song came on, and Rahul groaned. "Really? *Drake?*" He glanced around accusingly, as if prepared to prosecute whomever it was who had dared to play popular music.

"What's wrong with Drake?"

"Nothing, I suppose." Rahul rolled his eyes. "He's just so passé."

I suppressed a smile. Authentic. Rahul certainly was authentic.

"We should have met up tonight," he said after a moment. "I

know this hole-in-the-wall club around the corner. Great vibes, low-key—and like, you know—*fresh* beats."

"I thought I mentioned already; it's my best friend's engagement party tonight."

"Oh. Right."

"And it's been a bit stressful I suppose, with the planning and—"

"Ah," he said, blinking at me. "*Stress.*"

"What about it?"

"I feel sorry for you."

Mister pays-fifty-dollars-for-noodles-in-a-broom-cupboard felt sorry for *me*?

"I just don't get worked up about that kind of stuff."

I sat up in my chair. "What kind of stuff?"

"You know. Logistics. Details. Everyday . . . *stressors* that wig everybody out—and to be honest—make life unpleasant for those around them."

I nodded earnestly, thinking that maybe if I was unpleasant enough, he'd leave, and take all the organic shit-bread with him.

"Stress. The mental, physical, sometimes even spiritual reaction to the world outside of us. Aren't they all just feelings we can control?"

"You're kind of a superhero then, if you have the power not to feel. How do you do it?"

He smiled at me coolly. "Meditation. Yoga. Eating clean. It's all about bringing balance to the everyday."

"Like a Jedi."

"Huh?"

"They bring balance to the force? *Star Wars*?" The muscles around his lips twitched, and I sat back in my chair. "Oh, let me guess. *Star Wars* is also *passé*."

"I really don't get what all the fuss is about."

Our food arrived, if you could call it that. A vegan cheese board. A course of dandelion salad and eggplant bacon. A bowl of bloodlike broth that claimed to be pureed avocado, beets, and tigernut milk. (Note to self: It's not from a tiger, or a nut.)

No matter how hard I tried, Rahul shot down every topic of conversation I attempted. The Toronto Blue Jays? *Too pedestrian.* His favorite band? *You wouldn't have heard of them.*

What school did he go to? *What does it matter? We live in the present.*

I let the conversation dry up, much like the prunes, figs, and apricots that had gone into making our next course: a granola bar. At least I had chia and oat pudding to look forward to, and then, a cross-examination by Nani about how the date went.

I knew she would laugh when I told her about Rahul's raw, meat-, bread-, and milk-free diet, and how definitively incompatible we were. But then again, Rahul was the last name on her list . . .

"You're not enjoying the food," Rahul said, as I poked at a loose fig with my fork.

"Sure, I am," I lied.

"Raina, one must always be true to oneself."

Was he being serious? Did he think of himself as some kind of wise, Gandhi-like pundit? "I'm just not used to it," I said finally, wracking my brain for something nice to say. "But I admire your discipline."

Smugly, he laughed, shaking out the elastic in his hair. His man bun parted into an inverted pyramid at the top of his head.

"It's not discipline, Raina. It's being informed." He held out his hand, as if signaling an oncoming vehicle to stop. "Do you know how many pesticides you have in your body? How many you've accumulated"—he pointed at my stomach, which was still growling for food—"that are compounding in you right *now*?"

I was about to ask him to enlighten me, but then he did anyway.

"Let me guess, for breakfast you drank coffee, which is an addictive stimulant, and had some sugar-and-gluten-based cereal?"

"Are you sure you're not a Jedi? Because you just read my mind!"

He smiled. Had I been too rude? I was about to apologize, but then realized he'd taken it as a compliment.

"I had Special K for breakfast today, yes."

"See? What did I say? And I bet that when you're home with your nani, she makes you paratha in the morning, which is made from white flour, white potatoes, and butter—which, by the way, was *stolen* from a helpless cow imprisoned in some industrial farm outside the city. A cow that, as a Hindu, you should be honoring."

"Hindus honor cows because they help sustain life, and provide sustenance like *milk*."

"Whatever, Raina. My *point* is that all you need is three dates with me. Eat three of *these* meals, and you'll see how much better you feel, and realize how much crap you've been putting in your body. You'll be happier, sleep better, might even be able to lose some weight—"

I guffawed. Audibly. Did he just tell a girl to lose weight?

His cheeks reddened. "No, I didn't mean it like that. You look great—"

"How can I look great?" I grabbed my handbag, wondering what the hell I was still doing there. "I had coffee for breakfast!"

"I've really put my foot in my mouth, haven't I?"

"Rahul, it was really . . . *interesting* to meet you, but I have an engagement party to get to, where I'll be poisoning myself with tandoori chicken and cowy paneer." I stood up. "Lots of alcohol, too."

"No, don't go." He stood up after me, and reached for my arm. "I'm sorry. I'm just being defensive. My whole family thinks my lifestyle is ridiculous. Most Indian people do, and—"

"Your lifestyle isn't ridiculous," I snapped, turning to leave. "Your manners are."

~~Rahul—Sarla's physiotherapist, says he very good-looking boy~~ ☺

OMG UGHHHHH!!!

SEVEN

"Holy. Shit. I am *so* underdressed." Zoey hesitated at the entrance and glanced down at her beige suit. I'd offered to let her borrow a sari, but she'd claimed to be allergic to sparkles.

"Don't worry. It's just an engagement party."

Zoey turned to face me, eyes wide. "*Just?*"

The mezzanine level of the hotel had been transformed. I had tagged along for an inspection the week before, nodding mechanically as Auntie Sarla waddled about with a measuring tape, the back of her chubby arms swaying as she visualized her masterpiece. And it was. It practically wilted in decadence; an eruption of crystal and light turquoise. At its center was Shay, gilded like a Christmas tree, eight hundred people—mostly Auntie Sarla's own friends—milling by the open bar.

I led Zoey through the foyer, past the twenty-foot fountain of peach punch, through the clusters of families, mothers and daughters in matching *lenghas*; men in stiff suits, their white girlfriends gowned in spandex dresses, blissfully unaware that in *this* crowd, showing that much leg was the equivalent to being stark naked.

In the main hall, the tables were clothed in satin, a monstrous cake and head table at the front. At Indian celebrations, the families sat at the front, I explained.

"I guess that makes sense," said Zoey, darting into the queue for the bar. "They're the ones paying for it."

"*Wooow.*"

I turned around and looked down toward the voice. Nani and a few of the aunties had found us. Nani was dressed up—pink lips and shawl, a gin and tonic in hand—and when I leaned down for a hug, I could smell the perfume she rarely had the courage to wear. Chanel No. 5. The last gift Nana had ever bought her.

"You look wonderful, Nani."

"Me?" she exclaimed, her accent thickened with gin. "No one is looking at me next to *this* beauty model." She squeezed my chin and tugged until my face was level to hers, plopped kisses over my cheeks. After a moment, she leaned back, and then started picking imaginary lint off of me like a chimp.

"Nani, stop."

"The boys here will be lining up for you." She winked. "And about time, too."

"Nani, you remember Zoey?"

As if she hadn't noticed her before, Nani turned slowly to look at Zoey. She studied her oddly, and looked her up and down.

"How have you been, Mrs. Anand?"

"Oh, fine"—she looked between Zoey and me, and then down at the floor—"and yourself?"

"I'm well, thank you." Zoey touched my arm. "Work has been surprisingly busy this summer, plus we had those weekends away—"

"We rented a cottage with friends, remember?" I looked at Nani. "I told you, didn't I?"

She nodded slowly.

"I love your sari." Zoey smiled eagerly. "I'm regretting my outfit choice, now that I see how beautiful they look on you and Raina."

"Thank you, dear." Nani smiled at us faintly, and then snapped her head toward me. In a loud whisper, she said, "You met Rahul today, *nah*?"

"Yes . . ."

"Tell us"—Nani winked—"was he a *dish*?"

I laughed. "Yes, Nani. He was handsome, but it's *not* going to happen. First off, Rahul took me to a *vegan*—"

"Enough," she snapped, cutting me off. "I cannot hear another of your stories. It is too much now."

I could feel myself shrinking. I looked down at the ground. "But Nani . . ."

"And here I thought . . . soon, I would also have engagement to celebrate."

I heard her sigh, and then felt her beside me as she brushed a kiss on my cheek.

"Zoey, maybe you have boy for her? She is so hard to please, *nah*? No one I suggest is good enough for her."

By the time I looked up again, Nani had disappeared, and I felt Zoey squeeze my hand. "Are you okay?"

I nodded, without meeting her eye. "Yeah. Come on. Let's go find our seats."

Our table was disguised in a garden of gerbera daisies, cream wax candles, and chiffon seat covers. Zoey and I were seated across from Shay's older cousins and their husbands—women who as girls used to bully Shay and me. They arrived with smiles and hellos, and then seemed content to ignore us. Soon Kris arrived with

Serena—Shay's good friend and bridesmaid. I hadn't seen Kris in months, and wondered whose idea it was to seat us together.

Kris was thirty-eight, halfway in age between Mom and me, and I'd never really known what to make of him. He'd moved out for university when I was still a kid, and it wasn't that we weren't close; I'd just never really gotten to know him.

It was strange seeing him a suit, and not in gym clothes, or his uniform of khakis and ill-fitted T-shirts that he wore as an engineering consultant. He pulled out Serena's chair, and she folded into it suppressing a smile, tucked her hair and sari perfectly into place.

Ever since his divorce, Kris avoided going to temple, Indian weddings, or parties—anywhere he said the aunties and uncles would stare at him judgingly. But as I watched Kris and Serena effortlessly interact, pour each other water, eat each other's appetizers, I realized that already they seemed to be the community's next "it" couple.

Serena was the golden girl of my generation, so as her date, the community must have pardoned him.

I helped myself to another glass of wine as the main course was brought out, and then another. Serena and Zoey became engrossed in a discussion about politics, and Kris and I sat together in silence. I had nothing to say. I glanced behind me, and saw Nani in fervent conversation at her table with Auntie Sarla and a few other aunties.

Had news gone around already that I'd walked out on Rahul in the middle of our date? Was this evening's gossip that Raina, yet again, was being too picky—and not that Rahul was just a complete dick? My wineglass emptied again, and I reached over and poured more in.

"Quite the fish tonight, aren't you?" I heard Kris say, and I didn't answer. "I saw you talking to Ma earlier. She must be thrilled to see you all dressed up. You actually look nice, Raindrop."

"Please don't call me that."

He leaned in. "Are any of them here?"

"Any of who—" I stopped, seeing his smirk.

"She's even asking me if I have single friends for you." He laughed. "That would be strange, hey? My little *niece* marrying—"

"Kris, can we please not talk about this tonight?"

He brought his wineglass to his lips, and winked. "Come on. Lighten up."

I gestured toward Serena. "Why don't we talk about you two, then?"

"What do you want to know?"

"You two seem pretty cozy."

"So?"

"So when are you getting married?"

"Funny, Raina." His eyes glinted. "That's what everyone here wants to know about you."

At the front of the hall, Shay and Julien stood up in front of their audience, waving and holding hands—the most public display of affection they were allowed in front of this sort of crowd. It was the first time I'd seen them that evening. She was wearing a harvest gold sari. Her eyes were painted, her black hair winding into a bow at the back of her neck, and Julien, dressed up in an embroidered kurta pajama, smiled down at her.

"She looks wonderful, doesn't she, Raina?" Serena asked me.

"Yes," I said, wineglass in hand. I surveyed the room: everyone paired off and smiling. "Absolutely wonderful."

An hour later, the speeches continued as the backlog of Shay's extended family were still toasting her and Julien at the podium. I was restless, my feet vibrating, and finally, I couldn't take it. With a quick excuse to Zoey, I found my heels beneath the table and then snuck outside of the main hall.

My throat was parched, and outside in the foyer I grabbed another drink and wandered around. Others had gathered outside, too, perhaps sick of the frills and gimmicks, the insincere congratulations and tears from everyone fighting over a chance at the microphone. The wedding was still eight months away, yet everyone inside was acting like they were already married, as if something was about to change. Everyone thought that Shay and I still lived together—that she rented my spare room, but the only thing in there was a rack of my winter coats, a few boxes of junk, and a treadmill. Shay and Julien already lived together. They had a mortgage together. They had stupid things like a butter dish and a garlic press. Matching bureaus they'd picked out together and bought on their joint credit card.

And what did I have? Dates with men who told me to *lose weight*. A Nani who acted like she was disappointed in me because I refused to settle for a partner she'd arranged for me.

I wanted to fall in love; who didn't? But I wanted it on my terms. With a guy *I* got to choose. A man who accepted me for me, and wouldn't expect me to raise our children on my own, or have a three-course Indian dinner prepared for him when he waltzed through the door.

I wanted something real. A *real* partner. Not some random Indian guy who would look handsome standing next to me in a wedding photo. Was that too much to ask?

From inside the main hall, I could hear Auntie Sarla speaking into the microphone, making a rambling speech about family and community and marriage. What gave her the right to stand up and tell people what was right and what was wrong?

I moved farther away from earshot and examined the desserts. Carts of fruit, meringue and lemon pie; custards and salted caramel cheesecakes. Another cart full of Indian sweets. Lassi and *gulab jamun* and *rasmalaii*. My stomach felt unsettled just looking at all of it, and I grabbed a fistful of green grapes and walked onward. Just behind the dessert spread, I saw three long tables full of small sandalwood boxes, each hand carved with the name of a guest. Auntie Sarla had spent months organizing the shipment from India—delaying the engagement party for their arrival, even though surely everyone would be too drunk to remember to take one home, or would throw it in the trash as soon as it started to collect dust.

I weaved through the tables, looking for my box, and just as I found it, something fierce blew in like a foghorn. She was singing. Auntie Sarla's voice crescendoed, a throaty hum traversing the scales of a traditional Indian *bhajan*, and I couldn't help myself. I snorted, needing to reach up to wipe my nose, as I tried to stifle my laughter.

"I saw that."

I covered my face and whipped around. He was tall, much taller than me, his honey brown hair clumped behind his ears, a thick beard dripping down like moss. He smirked at me and rocked back and forth on his heels.

"What? I sneezed."

"You *sneezed*."

"Yes, I sneezed."

"Well," he said, rubbing his large hands together. "Then bless you."

Auntie Sarla was still singing, her voice blaring through the speakers. I pressed my lips together and started to turn away.

"Wait," he said. "You're Raina. Shaylee's best friend."

"I might be. And who are you?"

He chuckled.

"What?"

"Nothing?"

"*What?*"

"Nothing." His eyebrows arched high. "Although I wouldn't have thought you were that kind of bridesmaid."

"What is that supposed to mean?"

"It just makes sense. Laughing at Sarla's singing"—he motioned around the room with his hand—"pretending that this entire thing is funny."

I crossed my arms, my cheeks flushing. "What are you trying to say?"

"I'm *saying* that while that sari looks beautiful on you, Raina, envy does not."

"I am incredibly happy for Shay, okay?"

"Jealousy and being happy for a friend aren't mutually exclusive."

"What are you, a bumper sticker?" I moved to brush past him, and as I did, I caught hold of his scent. Like pepper and musk. Blackened greens and burned aluminum. Like Mom's winter coat, or the sixth-floor fire escape in my and Shay's old apartment.

I stopped. "What's that smell?"

"What smell?"

"Are you *high*?"

His idiot grin gave him away.

"You can't just come to an engagement party high, okay? Have you no respect?"

"I wasn't the one 'sneezing' at my best friend's mom."

"Who the hell do you think you are?"

He turned away from me, eyes laughing, and picked a box up off the table. *Klein*. Asher Klein.

"Oh. Well *that* makes sense."

"Seems like you've heard of me."

I uncrossed my arms.

"Come on now. What have you heard?"

That he was Julien's oldest friend from Montreal and, after

years abroad, had just moved to Toronto. That he'd dropped out of teachers' college a semester away from graduation. That he'd just gotten back from Southeast Asia after ten years of traveling and doing whatever it was that his type—the *drifter*—seemed to do.

"That you existed," I said flatly.

"And does my existence"—he paused—"interest you?"

"I'll buy your story when it comes out in paperback."

"And in this story—am I the hero?" He smiled. "Do I get the girl in the end?"

"You wrote it. You tell me."

"I think I do." He nodded to himself. "Adventure. Thriller. Romance. It'll be a bestseller."

"A regular Jack Kerouac."

"I'm handsome like Jack, aren't I?"

"You know he died from alcoholism?"

He knocked his glass against mine. "He died a happy man."

I crossed my arms again. "So—Jack—what did you do while *on the road*? Bit of a drifter, were you? Bounced from hostel to hooker?" I touched his elbow. "Tell me. Have you gotten yourself checked lately?"

"Gossip is a powerful thing, Raina."

I leaned up on my tiptoes, and whispered close to his ear, "So is herpes."

Asher laughed, and the creases around his eyes deepened. I could feel him looking at me, and my cheeks burned. Seconds passed, and he was still laughing, like I was the funniest thing in the world.

"Done?" I asked after a moment.

He nodded. "You're—"

"Hilarious, I know. But it's so easy to be funny around you," I said, gritting my teeth. "A thirtysomething with nothing to show for himself—"

"Better than being a thirtysomething drunk bridesmaid, don't you think?"

"I'm twenty-*nine*—"

"Always the bridesmaid, never the—"

But then I shoved him. Hard. He wobbled, nearly regaining his balance before toppling behind him and straight into a dessert cart. The metal trays clanged together as they spilled onto the ground and all over Asher. A few people standing nearby turned to look, and he picked himself up off the floor, his shirt a soppy swell of mango lassi and graham cracker crust.

"Shit." I covered my hands with my mouth. Had I just pushed him? I wasn't sure I'd ever pushed anyone in my life. Asher slowly pulled himself onto his knees, and I stretched out my hand toward him. He took it, pulling on me lightly as he stood back up. I had to concentrate not to fall over, too, and I realized that Asher was right. I *was* drunk.

I ran toward the restroom. It was all too much. Everything—Nani and Auntie Sarla, Shay's preoccupation with the wedding, work—it was boiling up and out, and I didn't want any of it. I locked myself in a stall, the seafoam green walls spinning, and I flicked down the toilet seat lid. Sitting down, I took three deep breaths, and then opened my eyes.

What was happening to me? What was I *letting* happen?

I thought I might cry, but the tears refused to form. I wanted, I needed *something*—but I didn't know what. I reached into my purse and found my BlackBerry. It was dead, and I resigned myself to the fact that I'd have to leave without telling Zoey. I couldn't face going back inside that hall again. I would make it up to her.

Outside, I slipped away from the main area and found a service staircase. I took off my heels, and toed my way down step-by-step, trying not to trip on my sari, my hand dragging behind me on the banister. I got to the last step and was about to push my way through the fire exit door when I heard a rustling behind me. I whipped around, thinking Asher had followed me. But instead, I saw a young, muscular blond, who I found vaguely familiar, rolling a cigarette on the landing behind me.

He held my eyes as he licked the rolling paper. Then he slid the cigarette through his fingers, and stashed it behind his left ear.

"It's Raina, right?" he said, still holding my gaze. "I remember you."

I pressed my lips together, and shook my head.

"I used to bartend at Eldorado. You came in a few months back with that jerk. *Sachin.*"

Slowly, it came to me. The bartender who had given me the eyes and made me a stiff gin and tonic. I nodded in recognition. "What's your name again?"

"Josh."

I nodded. "Sorry."

"You should be. You ran away before I could steal you away." He took a few more steps toward me, and suddenly, I felt self-conscious. Woozy. I put my arm back on the rail.

"I just got off my shift. You leaving already?" Josh opened his jacket, and motioned to a bottle of gin wedged into his inside pocket. "I nicked this from the bar upstairs."

"Don't worry. I won't rat you out."

He smirked. "Looked like a great party."

I shrugged. "It wasn't so great."

"Oh?" He took another step down. He was inches away, and I could smell the cigarettes, the stench of beer and wine and detergent, his breath from whatever he'd had for dinner. "Then maybe we should start another one."

He seemed like such a cliché, but then again, wasn't I? I held his gaze as he moved toward me, as he touched my neck with the very tips of his fingers. "Come home with me."

Josh up close was surreal. He was beyond attractive: blond, with a cheeky boyish grin and sculpted arms. He could have been a model. I would never be able to trust a man that handsome, but what he was suggesting wouldn't require that kind of trust.

My head pounded at the thought that, after only a few months of dating, I'd just crossed off the last name on Nani's stupid list. Now what would happen? Now what would she make me do? I didn't want to date. I didn't want to get married. And right then, exhausted and overwhelmed, I wanted something else. I hadn't ever been with anyone except Dev, and just looking at Josh, I thought about letting that change.

Josh leaned forward and brushed his lips against mine. For a moment, I just watched him kiss me. Hungrily, the muscles expanding and contracting on his cheeks and forehead as he moved his mouth—and I, in turn, moved mine. He put his hands on my waist, and a second later, I felt them slide down to my ass as he pinned me against the rail. His stubble ground coarsely against me, his tongue prodded and his hands pulled, and eventually, I closed my eyes and surrendered.

Josh—hotter than Nani's chicken vindaloo (BUT ONLY 23!)

I was already standing by the door when he woke up. He lifted his face an inch off the pillow and squinted at me.

"You're leaving?"

I nodded, and his head fell back on the pillow. I was sober now, filled with heavy guilt at having left Zoey at the party, and I noticed how his bedroom smelled like the inside of a hockey bag—how the walls were covered in creased *Lord of the Rings* posters. I vaguely remembered seeing them from just hours before—dim lighting, the bottle of expensive gin—teasing him for being a dork, while admitting that I, too, used to have those same posters. Later, falling back onto the bed, laughing so hard that one of his roommates banged on the wall and told us to shut up. Josh had smothered our faces beneath a thin pillow, and in a muffled voice, told me I was the most entertaining girl he'd ever had over.

Most entertaining *woman*, I'd reminded him.

He made a sleepy noise—a yawn, whimpering like a hungry puppy—and I sat back down on the bed. The flannel sheet crunched beneath my weight, and I wondered how long it'd been since its last wash. He rubbed his eyes, and then looked up at me smiling.

"My phone's dead. Could you call me a cab?"

He propped himself up on one elbow, and I resisted the urge to rub the sleep out of his eyes. "I can drive you," he said, kissing me on the lips. His mouth had crusted white overnight, and when I pulled away, I could still taste his morning breath.

He drove me home, the late summer wind blowing in through the windows, a strange voice singing at me through the dashboard, a random wool sock hanging from the rearview mirror. The passenger seat belt was missing, and I tried not to grip the seat as we sped east on Queen Street. Outside my building, he asked me for my phone number, and I gave it to him, knowing he'd never use it—and surely, Josh knew I didn't want him to. After one more dry kiss, he left.

I took the elevator up, and sighed as I unlocked the door. My sari stuck to me, and I felt the grime on my teeth, my hair in greased pieces behind my ears. I found an extra charger in the kitchen and plugged in my BlackBerry, left a trail of clothing down the hall, and stepped into the shower. Standing beneath the pressure, I opened my mouth and drank until my stomach hurt.

I closed my eyes, and tried to decide how I felt about what just had, and hadn't, happened. Damp sheets. Josh's eyelashes. Falling asleep with my head on his shoulder, both of his hands secured around my waist. The heat of a body at rest next to mine.

I lathered, and then rinsed it all away. I stepped out of the shower and wrapped a fresh towel around my body, walked around the apartment and opened all of the curtains. The light flooded in. My phone had powered on, and it lit up in beeps and flashes. I grabbed it and scrolled through the alerts. I had missed calls from Zoey, Shay, and Nani—surely, each of them wondering where I'd disappeared to the evening before. I made a mental note to call them all back and then kept scrolling. Surprisingly, Depesh had texted, wondering if I was also at the engagement party. Feeling bad that I'd missed seeing him, I texted him back asking if he enjoyed his first week at university, and then opened my work e-mails.

I'd received seventeen since my phone had died the evening before. Not bad for a Saturday night. Two were from Bill, another six from other analysts on my team. Five were from clients. Another three were spam. And then, I saw it.

My Raina,

It's been too long. There's so much to say, but I suppose now isn't the right time to say it. I'm not sure London is right for me anymore . . . if it ever was. There's been some rearranging, and the transfer paperwork was filed today . . . Will start shortly at the Toronto office. I'll see you then, darling.

Dev xo

EIGHT

Autumn set in, but Nani's hot stove kept out the cold. The countertops overflowed with baking sheets of raw chicken cut into cubes marinating in the masala she had taught me how to make. Onions, ginger, cumin, turmeric. Just the right amount of fresh coriander. Standing beside me, she guided me as I stirred the biryani and marinated the chicken, fried two vegetable *subjis* side by side on the back burners. It had been over a month since Dev told me he was moving to Toronto, and every weekend since, I'd come home to watch movies with Nani, or get cooking lessons to keep myself preoccupied.

I still hadn't figured out what it might mean. In the e-mail, he'd called me *darling*, and he hadn't called me that since the weekend before I left London—while we made spinach and goat cheese omelets, and he'd said, sipping his espresso, "Darling, you take the one that hasn't flopped over."

That morning had only just reappeared in my mind. Others,

too—the ones I had been pushing away for two years. Mere flashes of our life in London. Kissing after hours at the office with the curtains drawn. Brunch with his friends in Covent Garden, his hand sliding up my thigh beneath the table. After months of begging, going on an afternoon date to the Victoria and Albert Museum because I'd never been; licking scoops of gelato and rolling our eyes at wedding dresses from the Renaissance. Standing next to him in a crowded elevator; Dev leaning into my neck, and whispering, "You know that I love you, right?"

October crawled by. I jumped whenever I heard a British accent in the corridor at work, and checked my e-mail fifty thousand times a day. I trolled through the bulletins posted by HR checking to see if his start date had been announced, needing to confirm that he really was transferring. In his e-mail, Dev hadn't mentioned what day he was coming, or how long he might be staying—and I didn't know how to ask.

Was it his choice to move to Toronto?

Then there was that other question that I always typed out, and always deleted.

Are you moving here for me?

I hadn't seen him in two years, but the more I thought about it, the more it made sense. Of course he was supposed to move here. I hadn't spent the happiest years of my life with a man just so we could break up. And relationships like that—like the one Dev and I had—were never just a relationship. It was a love affair with a screen of its own on the Central Park lawn. The heartbreak had to be worth it, and suddenly, I knew that Dev was going to be my happy ending.

A sputter of oil escaped the pan, and I noticed that Nani was watching my face.

"Do you want to watch a movie after this?" I asked her. "Shah Rukh Khan has a new one out, doesn't he?"

"Do you not have other plans tonight?"

Other plans. Nani's code words that suggested I should be out on another date, trolling the streets, bars, and temple for another suitable Indian.

I thought maybe she'd lay off after I'd exhausted the list. Stupidly, I'd assumed that it would be over—and that I could wait for Dev in peace—once I'd met up with (or ruled out) everyone on her list, and she'd realized her arrangement just didn't work. But she continued to push, pulling eligible Indian bachelors out of some sort of magical hat. A new list she hadn't given me access to. I wasn't even sure where she was finding them—and whose sons, nephews, or cousins they were—but they wouldn't leave me alone. She'd started to give out my phone number, and now I couldn't go more than twelve hours without receiving weird texts from guys named Billy or Harpreet, voice mails from mouth breathers who'd forget to leave their name.

Each time my BlackBerry lit up, I'd hope it was Dev, and get that sinking feeling in my stomach when it wasn't. He'd be here soon, wouldn't he? Surely, all of this would be over *soon*.

"No, I don't have plans," I said to Nani after a moment, trying to sound firm.

"Did Neil not call? He sounds very promising—"

"Please. Not today?" I gave her a pleading look. "Work has been really busy, and right now I just want to cook and hang out with you."

Nani nodded slowly, and then kissed me on the cheek. "Well, you are natural cook. I am very proud. Your mother was never good like this."

"She liked to cook?"

Nani sneered. "Manu liked to do a lot of things."

"It's so relaxing," I said after a moment. "I never realized that before."

"*Aacha.* When you have time, yes. But when cooking for hungry customers, hungry children—it is not so relaxing."

Nani rarely spoke about the past, and I thought about pressing her. How had she felt about leaving her parents, one day suddenly packing her things and moving in with a husband she barely knew? What was it like getting on a plane for the first time in her life, crossing into a new country—cold, barren, and raising children in a land you knew nothing about?

I reached up to the spice rack and grabbed a small glass jar full of *methi*. I pinched some between my fingers, and then carefully sprinkled it over the pan. With a wooden spoon, I folded it in, another rich wave of aromas escaping.

"Was it hard?" I finally asked.

"Do you know I still am not sure the English word for *methi*?" I felt her beside me, watching me as I cooked. "Yes, Raina. It was very hard."

"Zoey said her grandparents were immigrants, too," I said. "From the Ukraine, but still."

"You spend a lot of time with Zoey, *nah*?" She paused. "Is she—"

I heard the front door open and, a moment later, slam shut. My eyes locked with Nani's as we heard a jingling of keys, the rustling of the hall closet. Nani's lips were pursed as she watched the kitchen door.

"Mom?" I called out.

Footsteps dragged across the hardwood in the other room, and a moment later, a deep voice. "It's me."

Nani's shoulders relaxed as Kris opened the kitchen door. His hair was wet, and he had at least a week's worth of stubble on his face. He sat down heavily at the kitchen table, tossing his gym bag in the corner.

"I didn't know you were coming," she said without turning around. "Not with Serena today?"

"No." He sat down at the table. "We broke up."

Nani leaned forward against the counter, and massaged her temples. Eyes closed, she inhaled deeply, and then exhaled like she did while meditating. It was only the week before that I'd overheard Nani and Auntie Sarla gossiping in the living room—calloused feet on the coffee table, plates of sweets on their stomachs—speculating on who, after Shay, would be the next in the community to get married. *Kris.* They'd been confident. Kris and Serena were the right age, and had established careers. *What was he waiting for?* Auntie Sarla had wondered aloud.

"Sorry to hear that," I said finally. Beside me, Nani was still crouched over, slowly shaking her head. "Nani, do you want to sit down?"

She whimpered.

"Ma, stop being so dramatic. We weren't even together that long."

"But *why*, Krishna?"

He winced. He hated it when Nani called him by his full name.

"Serena was *nice* girl—"

"All my girlfriends were nice. Maybe it's not—"

"Your auntie Sarla has practically planned your wedding. And now?"

"And now you tell your beloved Sarla to cancel it."

"What will I say? That you—again—have broken up with a girl for no reason? This time with that lovely Serena? That my Krishna is refusing to settle down? Just like Manu, never considering others—"

"That right there," yelled Kris, staring at me. He stood up from the table and reached for his gym bag. "That's why I never fucking come home."

Nani didn't say another word after Kris walked out. She went up-stairs, and after a few minutes, I realized she wasn't coming back down. I tried to finish cooking alone, but I was frazzled, uneven, and ended up burning half the dishes.

I scraped the tray of blackened chicken into the garbage, trying not to focus on the way Kris had just left like that. I managed to salvage the biryani and one of the *subjis*, but I didn't feel like eating any of it. I put the food away in Tupperware containers, washed and dried the dishes, and scrubbed down the stove top and kitchen surfaces I'd splattered.

When I was done, I found my way into the living room and slumped into the couch. I glanced up at the cuckoo clock. It was early evening, and it was already getting dark. I had a lot of catch-up work to do before the end of the weekend, but I didn't want to leave Nani alone. Not yet.

Her tablet was on the coffee table, and I grabbed it. I'd discov-ered the year earlier that she didn't like using the desktop com-puter I'd bought her because the den was too cold, so I'd given her my tablet. She'd been an infuriating student, wanting to play with it like she had with my old Nintendo before I'd even taught her what meant what, but eventually, she'd learned. Now she used it to Skype her sister in India, and send e-mails to her friends about temple gatherings and her charity projects. I'd even seen her play-ing games on it, which she'd taught herself to do.

I keyed in her password—1 2 3 4—and spotted in the bottom right-hand corner that the e-mail icon displayed thirty-eight unread messages. I clicked on it, determined to set up a spam filter for her.

But when the e-mails appeared, all of them—every single one—was from IndianSingles.com.

My mouth dropped.

I stared at the screen; was I imagining this? I blinked hard, but the words didn't change. Hesitantly, I clicked on one of the e-mails, and I could feel the blood pumping through my stomach, my throat, my ears.

A welcome message appeared that was addressed to me, and it said I had another "suitor" interested. I scrolled down, and a profile appeared.

> **Pradeep. 35. Accountant. Toronto. Hindu, olive skin, 5'9.5". 80k salary per year, looking for educated, fair-skinned <30.**

I exited the e-mail, and without thinking, clicked on another.

> **Neil. 32. Dentist living in Oakville. Jet-setter and avid reader. Open to meeting the love of my life.**

And then another.

> **Nish. 27. Computer science geek, Taurus, 5'8", searching for grl w/ good values + vegetarian chef.**

I clicked through each of the e-mails. One after another. *Jeetu. Vinod. Baljit. Ajay. Gopal. Amar.*

Nani had made a new list, given out my number to men on the Internet, and hadn't even told me. Had I exhausted all the single men she knew? Now she had to go online to pawn me off? All this effort to make sure I found a husband before I turned thirty?

I clicked through the link in the final e-mail, and the web browser flashed to life. IndianSingles.com, it read: "An online destination for Indian singles living abroad searching for that special someone."

I scrolled down, and there I was. My very own profile. My entire life summarized. Everything a man would ever need to know.

Raina. 29. Works at investment bank in Toronto. Nice Hindu girl in search of husband.

I felt the bile rising in my throat. *In search of husband.* Is that all that mattered about me?

And what about after I'd found a husband? Who was I then: A wife? A mother? Eventually a grandmother? Is that all an Indian woman would ever be? *Could* ever be? Someone defined by her relationship to others?

I stared at the photo Nani had used in my profile. She had taken the picture when I wasn't looking, at a café in Southwark during her one visit to London. I was wearing a leather jacket, a cream and poppy red scarf we'd bought that morning on Portobello Road. My hair was combed back into a ponytail, and I'd worn makeup that day. Mascara, black-blue liner. Even lipstick. The canvas tote bag on my shoulder was full of honey-cinnamon cashews and a piece of German chocolate cake that we'd bought at Borough Market for Dev, before we realized that he wasn't coming to meet us.

He'd been called away to Zurich. A merger on the brink of collapsing. I didn't see him for three weeks, and Nani never saw him at all.

I found Nani upstairs meditating by the foot of her bed. She sat cross-legged, her eyes closed on the grape-jam purple yoga mat I'd bought her for her last birthday. Her glasses were off, and there were clumps of balled-up tissues on the floor beside her.

After a moment, she opened her eyes. They were red. "There's my sweet." With her left hand, she tapped on the floor next to her, and I obliged.

I lay down on the mat and rested my head in her lap. She stroked my forehead, brushing the hair out of my face, as I looked up at her. From that angle, I could make out the faint lines in her neck and at the corner of her lips. Her broad cheekbones, the roundness of her small, delicate nose.

"How is chicken? I smell burning."

"That's because it's burned," I said curtly. Her face fell, and I was immediately filled with regret.

Nani playfully pinched my nose, looking down at me. "Well, I would have eaten anyway. I will eat anything my Raina makes for me."

I could feel the tears forming. The lump in my throat. A heaviness in my chest. I wanted to reply, but what was there to say?

Your son is angry with you, just like Mom is, but maybe you deserve it? Maybe it was you who pushed them away?

I thought about the list of men in her inbox waiting for a response. My marriage ad she'd posted online without telling me.

Nani loved me. I was her whole life. But why couldn't she see that she was pushing me away, too?

I rolled toward her, closing my eyes, breathing in her scent. Baby powder. Ginger. Paprika. I started shaking, the tears forming, and I felt her arms wrap around me.

"Don't cry, my Raina," she whispered. "We have each other."

Nani and I would always have each other. But as I buried myself against her, I'd never felt so alone.

~Pradeep. Neil. Nish. Jeetu. Vinod. Baljit. Ajay. Gopal. Amar.~

Not in a million years.

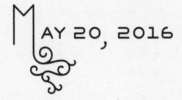

MAY 20, 2016

Twenty-seven and alone. Twenty-seven, and starting over. She watches marathons of *Degrassi* and *James Bond*. *Golden Girls* and *Star Trek*. She cries most of the day, and then again as she lies in bed trying to fall asleep. She stares at the fading star stickers taped to the ceiling of her old bedroom, thinking how, at twenty-seven, her nani ran both a business and a household in a country that wasn't hers.

How at twenty-seven her mother had had an eleven-year-old daughter and the vivid life of a flight attendant. How even Shay, not quite twenty-seven, is a doctor—and has just moved in with her boyfriend.

And what do I have? Raina thinks to herself.

She has a new condo that she'll get the keys to the following week. She has her old job at the Toronto office, one that they are anxious for her to resume. She has Nani. Shay and her other friends. But the thing she wants most of all—what she must relearn to live without—she has lost. And she has no idea what to do. Raina has no memory of the woman she was before she met Dev, or how that woman managed to function. She barely eats, and moves listlessly from bed to couch. Couch to bed. She is heartbroken and unkempt. She is carelessly adrift.

Nani bakes a cake for her birthday, and in the evening Shay arrives, still gowned in her mint green scrubs. Raina can hear them talking about her in the kitchen.

"This is not depression," she hears her nani say. "This is a breakup. She will be fine."

"She's stopped running." Shay's voice lowers. "I've never seen her like this before."

"Time will heal her. It heals all of us . . ."

Raina rolls her eyes and turns up the sound on the television. She is tired of them. Tired of hearing how that much passion was unhealthy, about their rage for the "asshole" who hurt her. But Dev was not an asshole; it was Raina who walked away, and as she stares blankly at the television, she thinks maybe she shouldn't have.

Was she asking for too much?

Marriage. Kids. Love. A *life* with Dev. She had grown tired of the bits and scraps he left for her to gather up, scavenge for between work hours and out-of-town meetings, between 12 and 6 A.M. when they lay in his bed, half undressed, beaten down from exhaustion. But did she need him to propose? They weren't that old, and it's Nani that wanted to see her married, was it not? It was Nani who *really* wanted the lavish Indian wedding; the weeklong celebrations and the showing off. The expense and traditions. Raina didn't need it, and as she feels acid spark in her stomach, she regrets having asked Dev for it.

Had it only been three weeks since she left? One day they had been lying next to each other, their ankles intercrossed, deciding whether to make Earl Grey or honey lemon tea. And the next?

She plays their breakup scene over and over again in her mind, rewinding and fast-forwarding. Agonizing over every word, every look, every pause.

She had surprised him with plane tickets and a hotel reservation: a two-night stay at a resort in Tuscany for their anniversary.

"You didn't even ask," he had said, not looking at her.

"That was the point." She sat down next to him at the kitchen table. His head was on his hands, and she watched him stare at the surface—shiny, varnished—that neither of them ever ate on.

"I told your assistant not to book any meetings, and even Raymond was—"

"You asked my boss?" He scoffed. "Jesus, Raina, don't you know how unprofessional that is? This is my career—sometimes I don't get a choice about when I have to work."

"It's always a choice—"

"It makes me look bad enough I'm dating a coworker."

She stood up, tears threatening to spill, and slammed the bedroom door behind her. He came into the room seconds later and cradled her, held her until he made her believe he didn't mean it.

Then she had asked him, for the first and last time, the questions that were—and still are—constantly on her mind. Was she ever going to come first? Would he ever meet her nani?

Would he ever ask her to marry him?

When she thinks of what came next, she feels the entire world buckle around her. She was the one to make unreasonable demands, force him to talk about the future, their plans. She had triggered everything, pushed and pulled, molded their relationship, their unhappiness, until there was nothing left to do but leave.

And even though he didn't stop her, she knows it was all her fault.

She reaches for her laptop. With trepidation, she begins typing on the keyboard, drafting an e-mail without knowing what she wants to say, or what purpose it would serve. She is clicking at the keyboard, more furiously now. The pads of her fingers type and clack, and then she hears a floorboard creak.

"What the hell are you doing?"

Raina snaps the computer shut. She turns around, and Nani and Shay are standing behind her, trays of tea and cake in hand. They are glaring at her.

"Were you e-mailing him?" Shay shoves a cup into Raina's hand, and hot tea spills onto their fingers.

Raina sets down the cup, wipes her hands on her shirt. "No."

"Don't lie to me." Shay turns to Nani. "They've been talking still. They text all the time, and *e-mail*, and—"

"Shay!"

Nani gasps. "Why, *beta*?"

"We love each other," says Raina, looking down at her hands. "I don't know if it's really . . . over."

"Oh, it's *over*, all right." Shay shakes her head. "After how he's treated you? You can't stay in contact with him. I refuse. It's masochism."

"*You* refuse?"

"Yes, I refuse. This isn't your call anymore. You have no judgment right now."

Raina turns to Nani. "She's being ridiculous. Are you listening to her?"

"Yes," says Nani. "I am listening, and Shaylee is right. It is time to move on."

Shay has crouched down in front of Raina. She opens the laptop, and skims the screen. Dramatically, slowly, she presses the delete key. "Absolutely not."

"Shay!"

"Don't *Shay* me." She tugs on Raina's ankle. "What's it going to take to get through to you?"

With birthday cake and tea comes another sermon. How Dev is now a lesson learned. How the years she gave him are not a waste; they will make her stronger. She tunes them out, still thinking of Dev. Minutes pass, and when her mind reenters the room, she realizes that Nani and Shay are discussing arranged marriages—*her* arranged marriage. They are discussing how Raina is not ready to start dating again, but how—in a few months, maybe a year—she would be.

Raina starts to resist, but Nani is adamant. She says she does not want to see Raina hurt any longer. She wants to find her a match. See her happy and settled. She wants to make an arrangement and help Raina find the right partner.

As much as Raina wants to please her nani, as much as she's always wanted to, she doesn't want *this*. She wants Dev. She will always want Dev.

"A couple years from now, Raina," says Shay. "If you're single at—thirty, let's say. Why not consider it?"

Nani smiles, rubs Raina's forearm until the fine brown hairs stick upright. *Thirty* feels infinitely far away, the destination elusive. She cannot imagine not yet being married by then, not having Dev in her life.

Nani and Shay are talking on either side of her about what type of man Raina might like—or rather, *should* like. Someone who is tall and handsome, says her nani, but will provide a stable home. Shay disagrees, and says that above all else, he must be humorous and kind; that Raina doesn't need a good match—but someone who can match *her*.

Raina tunes in and out of the chatter. She doesn't bother telling them to settle down, stop planning something that, surely, will never come to fruition. Instead, she nods her head and agrees to the plan. She is suddenly famished, and cutting herself another piece of cake, she glances at the computer. Already, she is crafting another e-mail; just the thought of Dev—the mere suggestion that it's not yet over—has revived her.

NINE

It was well into November already, and I woke up one morning unable to get warm. It hurt to move, to swallow, to think. Still, I was restless, and I almost wished Dev would e-mail me and tell me that he wasn't coming, and my life—however small it was—could get back to normal. But what did normal even mean these days? Tackling Nani's new *online* list, the one with seemingly an infinite number of men? It had been weeks since I discovered her online escapades, and still she hadn't confessed to taking out an ad on IndianSingles.com. She pretended that the men who were calling me—men who I told her I was simply too busy to see—were potential suitors she'd somehow found through her friends.

I abandoned my suit jacket for a thick wool sweater, and swaddled myself in my heaviest parka for the walk to work; still, the late autumn wind tore right through me. Chilled me to the bone. Most of my colleagues' offices were empty when I arrived. My brain felt like a block of ice, and I shut my door, rolled my coat into a thick pillow, and put my head down on the desk. Still, with my eyes closed, I felt queasy, and a sickening dread washed over me.

Did I have the flu? I wanted to call Nani, but I felt too weak to reach for the phone. I kept my eyes closed, thinking I would try in a moment, but the next thing I knew, Zoey's face had appeared in front of me.

She was squatted down next to my desk. A dull sunlight filled the room, and instinctively, I glanced over at the clock.

"Shit!" I tried to lift up my body, but I couldn't.

Zoey touched my forehead, and I wasn't sure if it was my skin that was wet—or hers. "Raina, you're super hot."

I closed my eyes. "A babe, I know."

"I'm being serious . . ."

I noted the tone of concern in Zoey's voice. I felt her tuck my hair behind my ears, and I opened my eyes again. "How was the meeting?"

"Fine . . ." Her eyes hit the floor. "Don't worry. I don't think Bill noticed you weren't there."

"Liar."

"Raina, you're sick." She cushioned me as I tried to sit up again. "You should go home."

Once I sat up, the room spun, and I blinked until it stopped. "I'm fine."

"You look like shit."

"Really, I'm fine." I fumbled for the keyboard, for the button to switch on my PC. "So how was the meeting?"

She stood up and sat on the edge of my desk, her legs waving in and out, knocking against each other. She wouldn't look up from the floor.

"What is it?"

She looked away.

"Zoey, what? Am I fired or something?"

Her eyes darted up and around, out the window, and by the time they finally landed on me, I already knew.

"Boardroom D," she whispered.

I tried not to sprint, to walk at a normal pace, but I kept stumbling. My shoes refused to keep up with my feet, catching on the carpet. I let my hand drag against the wall for balance. A right. Another sharp right. The hallway seemed longer, endless, a mirage of doors and suits, impractical art and sharp edges.

Then finally, I was there. And so was he.

Dev. Exactly as I'd left him. The way he still looked in my mind. The same Dev I knew—and now here—not thousands of miles away, but sitting right in front of me. Handsome and angular, a few sprigs of gray feathered into his sideburns. He was so close, only a glass wall between us; thin, angular lines of fog. He was facing away from me, toward Bill and a few other senior bankers lined up on the opposite side of the table. Dev reclined into his chair. Crossed his right ankle over his left knee, and from where I stood, I could only just see him thumbing the silk of his tie. I knew he would turn around before he did, and sure enough, a moment later, my palm resting on the glass between us, his neck craned slowly around. He looked right at me.

It was only a moment—but that one moment dragged on and on, frozen between heartbeats. Then he waved. A small wave. His hand traveling no more than a couple of degrees. A second later, he turned back around.

Was that it?

I turned and ran. My senses boiled up to the point I couldn't breathe. I felt the weight of it all rising. Tipping. I barely made it to the restroom before it all came retching out.

Dev . . . ?

TEN

Later that week, I saw him through the glass door before he opened it. He hesitated, surveying everyone in the fifty-fourth-floor conference room before slowly pushing through the door. A waiter standing just inside the entrance offered him a mimosa, and Dev, startled, almost dropped it as he picked it up off the tray.

I maneuvered myself farther behind the bar, so he couldn't see me. Watching him, I felt numb, and I didn't know what to say. Or how to feel. I'd been waiting to see him—waiting for *this* moment for so long, and now it felt too sudden. Sprung on me before I was ready. I'd been off sick for two days and had kept my BlackBerry off the whole time, unable to face whether a message from Dev awaited me—or didn't.

"Are you hiding?" I heard Zoey say.

I didn't answer, my eyes glued to Dev. Was I ready to face him? Ready to just walk up like our reunion was the most normal thing in the world? The truth is, I wasn't. I hadn't even fully recovered from the flu, but it was Bill's sixtieth birthday, and his assistant had organized a reception for his division. I had to come in.

A woman I didn't recognize clustered with some of the junior analysts waved Dev over. He smiled, and then walked in their direction.

"Who's that?"

Zoey looked up from her phone, and followed my eyes across the room. "Bridget," she said after a moment, and then looked back down. Zoey had been cool with me ever since I'd left her alone at Shay's engagement party. I'd apologized profusely, and she said she'd forgiven me, but I wasn't so sure she had.

"Are we okay?" I said after a moment.

"Yes, we're fine."

"You're still mad—"

"I'm *not*." Zoey looked up, and sighed. "I'm not mad. It's just hard to see you pine after him like that."

I looked back in his direction. He was talking to the group, and I watched Bridget flick her long, shiny black hair. She was very pretty, and young, with a healthy glow like she was vegetarian and never ate junk food.

"Raina, stop staring. She's just sucking up to him—she's like that." Zoey touched my elbow, holding it until I turned to face her. "Let's go eat."

"Do you like him?"

"Who—Dev?" Zoey scrunched up her mouth, then took a sip of her drink. "Yeah, I do. We had a training seminar with him yesterday. All the juniors like him." She nodded again. "Very experienced—"

I nodded, and looked back toward Dev. He was still talking to Bridget, and I wondered if Zoey was right. Was she really just trying to make a good impression? Or was she flirting—trying something with him? I shuddered. I'd looked at him like that once, too.

"What does Shay think?"

"About Dev being back?"

"Yeah."

"I don't know. Haven't told her." I turned back to Zoey. "Don't look so surprised. She hates him."

"Raina, she's your best friend. I understand your nani not knowing . . . but Shay?"

A waiter passed by with a tray of mimosas, and I wished I could reach for one. But Nani had called, again, saying that I needed to drive home after the party and help her move old boxes out of the garage.

"She doesn't need to know." I glared back at her. "She's busy with work. With Julien, and planning her wedding. Plus, she'd probably kill him before I . . ."

Before I what?

I started to walk over to the buffet, ignoring Zoey's glances as she trailed behind me, knowing she wanted to ask me the same question. What was I doing?

I reached for two plates and handed one to Zoey. We waited in line behind a few bankers I recognized from Chicago. They hovered over the olives, debating the greens and blacks, chili and salty, oiled and preserved.

I felt Zoey's hand on my wrist. "I think you should tell Shay," I heard her say. "I can't help you the way she can, Raina. You're going crazy in there, I can tell. This isn't you. You need some perspective."

"I have perspective," I said coolly. "It's been two years, and I"—I lowered my voice—"truthfully, I am still in love with him, Zoey. What am I supposed to do?"

"You're supposed to tell your best friend—"

"I can't." I grabbed the spoon, dished olives onto her plate, and then another spoonful onto mine. "I won't. I *can*—but I won't."

We inched forward in line, stopping again in front of the salads.

"Your nani. She seems modern—"

"Zoey, please try and understand." I turned to face her. "I'm not telling anyone he's back. I need time to figure this out on my own. So either you help me *deal* with that, or leave me to deal with it my own way."

"Fine," she said, evenly. "I'll help."

"Thank you."

"What do you need help with?" She reached over me for the bread. "Besides all your work Bill keeps sending *me*."

"I need Nani to stop pressuring me to find a husband. That's what I need." We reached the end of the line, and I glanced around, looking for a free spot at the tables. "I need her to stop forcing me on so many dates until I figure out everything with Dev."

"You mean the guy who didn't bother to tell you when he *moved* here?"

"Let's change the subject," I said, looking at her. "How are you? How's Alice?"

"She dyed her hair blond. Raina, it's terrible."

I laughed, which surprised me, because I wasn't sure I'd laughed in weeks.

"Do you think I should tell her?" She followed me to a nearby table and, sitting down next to me, said, "I don't know the protocol."

"Well, does *she* like it?"

"She thinks she looks like Beyoncé. I mean, I think my girlfriend is *hot*, but brown skin and blond hair only works on the queen."

"Do you have a pic—? What is it?" I followed Zoey's eyes to the opposite corner of the room, to Dev and Bridget. They were standing near the entrance, away from everyone else. He was leaning against the wall, her hand on his shoulder, and he was laughing.

He was fucking laughing.

And I was the butt of the joke.

I could feel myself shaking, and I pushed my plate toward Zoey.

"Raina, where are you going?"

"Home," I said, without turning around. I pushed my way through the crowd, trying to keep cool, trying to keep from crying. I had to pass them to leave. I kept my face down as I walked by, but he saw me.

"Raina, hi. How are you? It's been . . . It's been so long."

I had to stop. I forced my feet to slow down, come to a deliberate halt. I looked up, tensed the muscles in my cheeks. "Hello, Dev." I nodded, and then glanced briefly at Bridget. "Hi, there."

"Hello." She had a slight Chinese accent, and perfect teeth.

"I tried ringing you a few times . . . after . . ."

After you turned up to my office without any warning?

"Did you get my messages? How are you feeling? Unwell, still?"

"Oh? I'm just fine." I tried to sound nonchalant, and I avoided his gaze. "Actually, I'm just heading out."

"You're leaving already?" he asked softly.

Why was Bridget staring at me? Why did I feel like I had interrupted something? As if it were Bridget who knew Dev, the one who had the right to stand there speaking with him, and not me? My heart was beating fast, too fast, and I took a deep breath. And then another. "Yes. I have to go. I . . . have a date."

I pushed through the glass door without replying. My feet sped up, and I maneuvered down the hall, trying not to run. I pressed the elevator button, two, three, four times—praying it would hurry. I pushed again, and finally, it arrived. I could sense him running behind me, and I flung myself into the elevator, and a second later, as the doors were closing, he wedged his leg in and the doors stopped short.

"What was *that*?"

He was angry, his jaw tense, and I pushed the close button again, and again, but it wouldn't shut with him there.

"Dev, I'm late. I have to go."

"Raina, stop it." He fought his way into the elevator as a bell started to ring. He put his hands on my arms as the doors closed, and we started drifting downward. "What was that all about?"

"What was *what*, Dev?"

"Please—" He pulled me closer as I tried to move back, as I tried to distance myself for my own good.

"I—"

But then his mouth was on mine; his body, his heat, pressed up against me. My back to the wall, he kissed me—his hands through my hair, on my neck, my waist. I was burning, my senses on overload; and I wanted to push him away, and bring him closer at the same time.

Another bell chimed, and he pulled himself off me just as the door opened. I was out of breath, and I pushed myself off the wall and forward through the door. I walked slowly through the lobby. I could feel him a few steps behind me, and right before I reached the door, I turned around to face him.

"I don't know . . ." I breathed out. "I can't—"

"I didn't mean to make you jealous," he said. He inched closer toward me. "She's on my team. She's just young and ambitious. That's it."

I nodded, looking at my hands, wondering how he managed to make me feel so small and like I was his entire world in the exact same breath. "Why did you move here, Dev?"

"It's not exactly clear. It's been decided I'll go back and forth between here and the New York office for a while—others, too, perhaps."

"So it's temporary that you're here."

"Maybe. Well, I'm not sure." He drew closer to me. "But, now that I'm here, Raina. Now that I see you . . ."

"What?"

"I don't know. But I know I need you in my life. You've always been so good for me."

I *was* good for him. Before me, he'd go weeks without eating green food. Forget to eat, to sleep, obsessed by a file, a problem he couldn't figure out. I'd bought him vitamins and baby aspirin, towels that didn't reek of mildew. Outside, he was tailored suits and the brick walls of a flat he could afford to buy outright, but inside, he was cavernous. Undiscoverable. A boy who played with his power like a small child played house.

"Do you really have a date?"

His voice weak, I knew he still cared. After what we'd shared together, how could he not?

"It's okay if you do." Dev crossed his arms, and I could see on his face he was struggling, putting up a fight.

But for what? When, still, after all this time, he couldn't give in—give in to *us*?

I thought about how Nani had instructed me to come home to move boxes that evening at precisely 7 P.M., but how we didn't have anything in the garage she'd want to throw away or donate. I did have a date. By now, she was fed up with me refusing to meet the new men she'd been suggesting, so tonight, there'd be another ambush. There would be an Ajit or Sheev or Raj waiting for me at home, and there was nothing I could do about it.

"I wouldn't like it." He put his hand gently on my face, on my neck. "But you need to do what makes you happy, love."

Dev made me happy. He *would* make me happy.

"You're off on a date, then?"

And even though I hated myself for it, I knew that I would keep waiting. All I wanted was this second chance.

"No, Dev." I shook my head. "I don't have a date. I'm . . . still under the weather. And I need to go."

I walked home in a trance. Two years later, Dev was back in my life, exactly how I had left him. Still threaded in ambition. Still a man who wanted me. Still a man who needed time.

Date #5

"Raina, did you hear that?"

I looked up from my food. "Sorry?" I looked between Nani and . . . I'd already forgotten his name. I shook my head.

Nani touched her napkin to her lips, as if embarrassed on my behalf. "Neil was telling us about—"

"Auntie, it's nothing—"

"What is this *nothing* business?" She sat up proudly in her chair. "You protected this country—like in the movies, like that man with brown hair—"

"You were in the army?" I asked him, trying to make an effort.

"Just so they would pay for dental school."

"Clever."

Nani pressed another naan into his hand. "More?"

"I'm good, Auntie."

"Please. Eat *more*." She lunged for the raita, ladled it onto his plate. "You're too skinny."

"Let me finish this, and then I'll have more." Neil wiped his hands on a napkin and touched her hand. "Auntie, please sit down and join us. I can't eat until you eat."

"Nonsense—"

"I insist." He stood up and guided her to her own chair. "Don't tell my ma," he said, leaning in close to her as he helped her sit, "but this—*Auntie*—it's incredible. Much better than her cooking."

Nani arched her eyebrows at me. "So cute, Raina. And *so* sweet."

I zoned out again. I'd been remembering that time that Dev almost proposed. Or could have. Two months before I'd left London, when we took a Sunday morning off from work, caught the 55 to Chinatown for dim sum. The sun was out, and in the February chill, we walked back, wound our way through Soho, Holborn, and then right through Hatton Garden. The Jewelery Quarter. Where men like Dev came to buy a ring.

We walked by one shop, and then another—endless windows of round cuts and princess cuts, gold and platinum. In the reflection of one of the windows, I caught him staring, and I looked down at my shoes.

"What if—"

"Do you reckon—"

"You first." He pulled me out of the sidewalk traffic and against a shop wall. The wind had blown a strand of hair into my mouth, and he gently brushed it aside.

"No. You go."

Was this it? I remembered thinking—hoping—as he looked at the sky, the brick walls, anywhere but me. He leaned in. He opened his mouth. And then, just when it could have happened—when, in a million times replayed over in my head, it *should* have happened— I felt a vibration through his touch, and he reached into his pocket.

It wasn't it.

"I should take this," he'd said, darting briskly across the street, his BlackBerry wedged against his shoulder, me half a stride behind him the whole walk home. And by the time we got back to his flat, and he set down his keys on the coffee table with a tired clang, the moment had passed. Our laptops were back open. And our lives resumed their usual course.

Nani's voice roused me. "The one with Tom Hanks?" she asked. She reached over the table and spooned more dal onto my plate. Eyeing me, she knocked the spoon hard on the ceramic. "Raina, what do you think?"

"Huh?"

"*Saving Private Ryan*," said Neil. "Great movie."

"I haven't seen it," I said.

He clutched his chest. "You haven't seen it?"

"No."

"It is on the movie channel all the time," said Nani.

"I'll have to check it out."

"You should." Neil pinched off a piece of naan and dunked it in the *saag*. "Maybe we should watch it sometime . . ."

"Raina loves reading, too," I heard Nani say. "Not just movies."

I winced, and I felt Nani and Neil looking at me.

"Don't you, Raina?"

I nodded, avoiding their glances. Did Nani see Neil as the picture-perfect son-in-law and father of my children? A man who would rouse me from my own limp life and, magically, make everything okay? Nani wanted me to fall in love with him, leap after him. Skip over Mom's generation and turn right into her. She wanted this kitchen table full, full of hungry, smiling people—a fantasy no one in her family had ever been able to fulfill. Neil was exactly what she wanted. But wasn't I finally ready to admit to myself I didn't want her to choose for me?

"What do you like to read?" Neil asked.

I moved my food around with my fork. "You know. Whatever's around."

"And who's that written by?"

I looked up. He was smiling at me. His perfect, genuine smile. Straight teeth—unlike Dev's, pale white and splintered—hidden beneath a smirk. Was Dev still at the party? I wondered. Why wasn't *he* at our kitchen table?

"Well," I said finally, looking at Neil. "I have a lot of favorite books."

"Pick one." Neil leaned toward me.

"My friend Zoey just lent me *The Catcher in the Rye*." I shrugged. "I never read it when I was young. I liked it."

"That's one of my favorites."

"Yeah, well, a lot of people like it."

Neil grinned, and I caught him looking at my neck. I saw that familiar flaring of heat, and I winced.

"Neil," said Nani. "I can make you chai?"

Was it only that afternoon that Dev had finally pressed his lips against mine the way he used to? A moment of blinding exhilaration, and then the metal doors parting, the fluorescent light pouring in. I squeezed my eyes shut. But what about Nani? I loved them both so much. *Too much*, as Shay liked to say. Loved them more than I knew how to understand. Why couldn't they fit together somehow?

"Sure, Auntie. Would you like some help?"

"You sit. I will make."

Nani stood up from the table, and the moment she turned around, I grabbed my phone from my back pocket. I checked the screen, and there it was. A message from Dev—from thirty-eight minutes ago.

Raina—I need to know you're all right. Are you feeling better? The party is shit without you here.

Just then, another e-mail popped up.

I can't stop thinking about that kiss.

Dev wanted me. I knew he still wanted me.

Why had I run—*again*? Why hadn't I stood there, face-to-face, and told him that he had to choose? That it was time for him to pick me—this time *really* love me—or let me go?

"Are you okay?" I heard Neil's voice. "Raina?"

What was I doing here? With Neil? I needed more time. My breath came uneven. Jagged. I felt my body flashing hot and cold.

Nani's voice, drawing closer. "Ill again?"

"I'm sorry." I stood up so hard my chair flung backward. "I can't do this now."

I could hear her saying good-bye to what's-his-name at the door. Making excuses for me—that I was still ill, overburdened at work. After a moment, the front door thudded shut, and when I heard her start to climb the stairs, I shoved her list back into my purse where I'd kept it all these months. I heard the door creak open, the hum of the light as she switched it on.

"I made ginger tea."

I felt her sit down on the edge of my bed; the shifting of her body weight as she released a sigh. "You should have told me you were still feeling ill. I would have postponed."

Postponed something I hadn't even agreed to? That she and

Auntie Sarla, and probably even Shay, had concocted together? So there was no more single Raina to worry over?

"Tell me, where are you feeling ill?"

"I'm not *ill*." I tugged at the covers and wrapped myself tighter. "I'm a lot better today."

"You didn't eat much." I felt Nani's hand on my back, and I resisted the urge to pull away. "I wrapped your plate and put it in fridge."

I didn't answer.

"Okay, so you didn't like Neil. Maybe he is a bit boring, *nah*?" She laughed. "I have found another. His name is Chirag. He—"

"Will you just cut it out?" I barked into the pillow, because I couldn't look at her. "I saw my profile on IndianSingles.com. I know where you're finding them now. Did you really have to put up a marriage ad for me?"

I heard Nani sigh again. "I am sorry, my sweet."

"Well, you should be."

"I should have asked first. I can take it down, *nah*? It was silly idea your Auntie Sarla gave me. We can look elsewhere. Not online, then. I'll find others."

It suddenly occurred to me that she wasn't going to stop. This was it. Until I got married, this would be my life.

If only I could marry *Dev*. He was Indian. He would understand that I was almost thirty, and that there'd be pressure on us to get married quickly. We were two years older, and we were still in love after living an ocean apart. Now, wouldn't he be willing to meet Nani? I had to trust that he would be ready for our future.

"Sarla says she knows a nice boy in—"

"Nani. *Please*." I was choking. I couldn't breathe. "Please, *please*, stop." I was crying now. "Just stop. I know I agreed, but I can't—can't take this anymore."

She didn't reply, and my face burning with shame, I buried my face deeper in the pillow. How could I tell her? Would she understand why I was waiting for Dev?

"Raina," I heard Nani say after a moment, her voice wavering. "I must ask you something."

"What's that?" I grumbled.

"Again, at dinner you mentioned this Zoey girl. You mention her often." Nani paused. "Is she more than friend to you?"

I opened my mouth to answer, and then realized what she meant. Was she asking me if I was in a relationship with Zoey?

"I have seen things in movies, you know. And on *Ellen*." Her hand, momentarily frozen, had resumed its comforting massage on my back. "And I was thinking it is so common now, *nah*? It is very *normal*. And I thought that maybe, maybe this is why you are resisting marriage. Maybe I am not finding you the right match because . . ."

She trailed off, and the silence hung thick in the air. I could hear her breathing, the hum of the lights. The sound of a car driving by. The distant tick of the cuckoo clock echoing in the kitchen. Seconds passed, and it occurred to me that Nani didn't just think I was gay: She was okay with it.

"Is this why you've been unhappy with me, my sweet?" Her voice came out tentatively, and I felt her lean down and kiss me on the back of the head, her other hand brushing stray hairs away from my cheek.

What had just happened? Was it really possible that the idea of me being gay didn't upset her? When she was so traditional about other things in her life? My breath was trapped in my lungs, and my heart pounded. I knew I should say something. Letting her believe I was gay couldn't be right. But for some reason, already it made more sense than the truth. If I were gay—just for a while— there'd be no more dates. No more pressure or ambushes. There'd be time. There'd be Dev.

I should have told Nani the truth. I wanted to—everything, all of it—but I couldn't.

I didn't know how. So I didn't say anything.

~~IndianSingles.com guy w/ Tom Hanks obsession~~

(Ned? Neil? Nigel?)

ELEVEN

Within days of Nani offering me an excuse for my behavior, strangely, I was beginning to feel like my old self. I'd started sleeping through the night. Running. Eating normal meals, and not bags of chips for dinner. It was as if all the pressure was off my chest and I could finally breathe. No forced dates and looming marriage deadline. No worrying about Nani, or whether Dev would be ready before Nani shoved me down the aisle toward some guy whose name I could barely pronounce. Finally, I had time.

"I don't see how this is a good idea," Zoey had said, when I finally worked up the courage to tell her.

"You think this is a bad idea?"

"No. Not necessarily." She scratched her head. "But it's not a good one. Letting your nani believe you're gay to get out of a few bad dates? It's actually the stupidest thing I have *ever* heard."

"A few? I was practically getting an e-mail every morning with her top ten matches. Organized by height, weight, income tax bracket—"

"All right. I get it. There was a lot of pressure." She bit her lower lip. "Does anyone else know?"

"About Dev?" I shook my head. "No—"

"Raina, no." Zoey rolled her eyes and, her voice lowered, said, "Does anyone else know that you're a 'lesbian'?"

"Kris does. He came over that evening, and I kind of had to tell him."

"And what did he say?"

"Called me a brat and then poured us both a whiskey." I shrugged. "He's never been that interested in my life."

Zoey nodded slowly. "So the damage is minimal. Good. It's not too late to undo it."

I looked at the floor.

"But you don't want to undo it, do you." She paused. "Raina, why are you doing this? I want you to admit it to me."

"I . . ."

"If you have to lie about him to the people you love—can he really be worth it?"

Was she right? Zoey knew me well, and I usually trusted her judgment.

Dev had taken me for lunch only the hour before—a full forty-five minutes between meetings with our BlackBerrys on silent. Reminiscing at the corner table over pesto and chardonnay, it was as if nothing had changed. He was the man that I had fallen for—and I was still the woman in love with him. Every time he e-mailed, whenever I heard his voice passing by in the hall, my mouth curled into a smile. Dev was back in my life—and I was happy again. Couldn't it be as simple as that?

Now that Nani's matchmaking arrangement was off the table, every morning there was that same flutter in my stomach. A feeling of delight, rather than the weight of constantly disappointing the person who meant the most to me.

Sure, Dev traveled constantly, and was just as likely to be in New York, Chicago, or Los Angeles, but he was part of my life again—and I was in his. In every passing moment, I grew more and more sure that this was it. I knew that the last two years would only be one chapter of our story. Dev needed time to fully commit—and finally, we had it. The Bollywood struggle behind us, it was time for the third act.

"He's worth it," I said. He had to be.

The moment I hadn't denied to Nani that I was gay, everything changed. Harder than her questions I didn't know the answers to, more disconcerting than a fresh list of potential husbands, was her concern. Her empathy. Accepting who she thought I was seemingly defied everything she had grown up to stand for. It was as if ten years of the *Ellen* show had changed her into a woman I hadn't realized she'd become. And while it impressed me, it was downright baffling.

Shouldn't she have been angry? No one in our community was gay, or at least publicly out of the closet. It just wasn't something Indian people did. No matter how progressive she'd become in recent years, how was this acceptable to her?

The idea of me with another woman did not upset her; rather, she couldn't wrap her head around why Zoey and I were just friends. Didn't I care about her? Wouldn't Zoey make a great partner for me? Nani wouldn't let up, and I started to avoid her, and visited her less and less often.

It was harder to put on the act face-to-face, and until Dev was ready for a real commitment—until I could face her with the truth—I didn't want to see her. I didn't know how I would "come out" again, or how she would respond. But as I wrestled with my relationship status with Dev, the few hours we spent together every time he was in town never culminating in more than a hug, sometimes a kiss, I couldn't bring myself to think about what would happen next. I couldn't even imagine what I would say, or how long—another week, or month—I would have to keep up the charade.

But surely, after he'd settled into his new job, he and I would meet Nani as a united front.

"Just a few months now! Can you believe?" Auntie Sarla's voice boomed from the back seat of my Jeep.

"Coming quickly, Shaylee!" said Nani, reaching forward and patting Shay on the shoulder. Shay glanced over at me, grinning, shaking her head from side to side in mock excitement.

I turned up the heat, and wrapped my scarf tighter around my neck as we waited at a red light. The four of us had spent the day running wedding errands together. Shay, who it felt like I hadn't seen in months, and I barely had time to catch up as Nani and Auntie Sarla remained fixated from the back seat on discussions of tiered cakes and Hindu priests, chiffon lining and perfectly timed flower deliveries. The whole time, Shay listened to Auntie Sarla plan her wedding with glazed disinterest, piping in only to change the radio station during the drive from one vendor to another, or to mock Auntie Sarla's accent.

After our last appointment with a ribbon vendor, we drove back toward home. It was only late afternoon, and already it looked like dusk, night slowly falling over the icy roads. While Nani and Auntie Sarla were speaking in Hindi about the guest list, Shay leaned in toward me.

"Are we okay?" she whispered.

I concentrated on the road, carefully steered around a patch of ice. "Not really. I still haven't put on my winter tires."

"You know what I mean, Raina."

From the side, I could see Shay still looking at me, and then she looked back at the road.

"Yeah, Shay. We're fine."

"How's the dating—have you met anyone you liked?"

Mid-sentence, Auntie Sarla stopped talking, and her face appeared between us. "You live together—and you don't *know*, Shaylee?"

Shay looked at me, and then back at Auntie Sarla. "Raina and I work different hours. Remember, Ma? I don't see her a lot."

She nodded, and then slid a stubby finger across the armrest. "Raina, do you ever clean your car?"

"Sarla," I heard Nani say. "Don't interfere. We're going to have accident."

Auntie Sarla's face disappeared. "Well. *Someone* should interfere with that girl."

"Ma," said Shay. "Don't start."

"Speak to this child, Suvali. She will never get married this way."

I pressed my foot hard against the brake pedal, wishing I could kick it.

"There is nothing to speak of, Sarla," I heard Nani say after a moment. "Who Raina marries is *Raina's* decision."

"What marriage? There won't be a marriage if she keeps on like this. Not like my Shaylee—"

"Ma, don't bring me into this."

"Raina is being selfish—"

"Sarla, enough!" Nani's voice prickled my skin, and the car fell silent. "Do not lecture us like this. I will handle my own girl." I turned back to face the front, slowly lifted my foot off the brake as the light turned green.

"I have confidence in whatever she decides," said Nani.

I saw Nani glancing at me in the rearview mirror, and as I accelerated through the intersection, a wave of guilt tore through me.

I'd decided to create a mess, one that Nani and I might not be able to get out of easily.

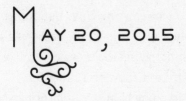

MAY 20, 2015

"You're getting old, love."

Raina giggles, and rolls over to face him. "How sweet of you to remind me."

It is still dark outside on the Clerkenwell Green, and the only light comes from the touch lamp on Dev's nightstand. In its warm, buttery glow, Raina can vaguely see the outline of his body nestled next to hers, the profile of his nose and eyelashes as he moves his head on the pillow.

"You're properly over the hill now."

"Oh, *shush*."

"Let me think," he says, moving his face closer to hers. "When I turned twenty-six, I—"

"Bawled like a baby?"

"Got promoted."

"Well then," whispers Raina, as he kisses her nose. "Why don't you promote me."

They hit the snooze button three, four times—and on the fifth push, Dev declares he will forgo his morning routine at the gym. Raina kisses him, sleepily, and smiles. They both work long hours, but despite the demands on their time, their health—even, at times, their relationship—Raina has never been this happy. It is her birthday, the one-year anniversary with the man she loves— and she lives in *London*, a thriving, humming city that fiercely loves her back. She works in the very heart, the very center of the world, and sometimes, lying there in a dreamlike state, Dev curled around her, it's hard to believe this is her life.

It is nothing like her nani's; a limb of her husband's journey into a new world, working hard with little respect for a community to which Raina never even felt she belonged. It is nothing like her mother's, either: a life disjointed and misunderstood, carelessly formed at the fringe of others'.

For the first time, Raina is finding her own way. She is doing things on her own terms, without anyone telling her who and why, how and where; she is living a life that is completely her own.

With him, Raina feels like a different kind of Indian.

Together, they are modern Indians. Ones who don't go to temple just to prove to others they believe in God, who can try a non-Indian cuisine—blander, with less spice—and enjoy it. Together, they command power and respect; dine, drink, and travel without worrying about money the way their families did. And, Raina often muses, they will raise their children differently, too. They will teach them that they don't need to be a doctor to succeed in life; they will teach them to believe that they are good enough exactly as they are.

Raina and Dev are kissing and his hand is up her shirt when a phone buzzes on the bedside table. Dev removes his hand and reaches for it.

"Oh, it's yours."

Raina grabs it, and a moment later, frowns. "It's Nani."

"Go on, then."

Raina takes a deep breath, and accepts the call. "Hi, Nani."

"Haaaaappy bird-*day*," she sings, almost screams, into the phone. She is loud, so loud that Raina uses her hand to cover Dev's mouth, muffle the laughter. Raina has tried many times to teach her nani that cell phones these days are better than landlines; that she needn't yell into the phone just because Raina is overseas.

"Are you having a happy bird-day?" Nani asks. "Did I wake?"

"No, no. I'm up. Just getting ready for work."

"*Aacha*."

Raina glances at the clock. It is past midnight in Toronto. "Why are you up so late?"

"Oh, just missing my Raina," says Nani. "You are twenty-*six*, now, *nah*?"

Dev mouths "so old," and Raina lightly pushes him away. He smiles and closes his eyes, rests on his back beside her.

"How is Dev?" Nani asks.

"Good."

"He will have a nice birthday for you? If you were home, I'd make you your favorite—"

"Yes, Nani. I'll see him at work, and then we're having dinner with friends."

"What are you eating?"

"Turkish, I think."

"It is not Thanksgiving—"

Raina laughs. "No, Nani. Turkish—from Turkey, the country. Middle Eastern food. Like couscous?"

"Huh?"

"It's kind of like rice."

"Are you eating enough? Are you being healthy?"

"Yes, Nani."

There is a pause—long, palpable—and Raina wonders if her nani is still there.

"I'd like to meet Dev," she says finally.

Raina turns to look at him. His eyes are discernably closed, and Raina pokes him until he opens them.

"He wants to meet you, too."

"When?"

"I don't know." Raina leans back in bed, stares at her toes poking out from the covers. "You know you can come visit anytime."

"He can come here?"

Raina nods into the phone, and a moment later says, "Yeah. Maybe."

She had asked Dev to come with her on her last trip home, but he said he was too busy with work. Lately, she has been thinking about asking again for him to come home and meet Nani and Shay, to see a glimpse of her old life, but she is afraid to bring it up; afraid he'll say no again.

"*Beta*, it has been long time now. It is time for Dev to visit—"

"Nani, please, not today."

"You are planning to marry him, and I don't know if he's nice boy. I don't know his family—"

Nani continues, her voice growing louder, and Dev rolls over on his side.

"He cannot come and meet us? He is Indian, *nah*? He does not understand how things should be—"

"*Please*, not now," Raina says firmly. She looks over at Dev, and sees that he's crawling out of bed. Without looking at her, in only his pajama shorts, he walks out of the bedroom.

". . . Dev cannot at least *call* and tell me his intentions? His parents cannot call me—"

A panic boils up inside of Raina, the warmth beside her suddenly gone.

"—and you will stay in that country for *him*? You—"

This is what she fears: Dev walking away. Dev leaving her, taking everything—her whole life—away with him.

"Nani," she says sweetly, placating. Her hand on her chest, she forces herself to calm down; forces out the words that her nani needs to hear—that, right now, Raina herself needs to say.

Dev and Raina will get married.

Dev and Raina are in love, and there is absolutely nothing to worry about.

After a few moments, she hangs up and sets her phone back on the nightstand. The bedroom door has closed behind him, and she can't hear anything—just a garbage truck outside the window, beeping, rumbling back and forth along the Clerkenwell Green.

"Dev?"

She is cold, and pulls the blanket around her. Has he already hopped into the shower, started his day without her?

Is she—is her nani—scaring him away?

They are together, committed, in love—but marriage, a life in permanency, is still far away. Together, Raina and Dev decided they wouldn't be *Indian* about their relationship: Their families wouldn't be involved, and they would date and take their time. They would enjoy life, and only talk about the future in an abstract way that didn't tie them down, didn't tie them together.

They decided it *together*, didn't they?

Raina sits up. She is about to get out of bed, when Dev pushes the door open. He stands in the doorway with a sleepy smile, and holds out two cups of tea.

Raina's mind releases, her muscles thaw. He walks to the edge of the bed, and sets the tea on the nightstand.

She smiles at him. "Come back to bed."

He drops to his knees on the mattress, and crawls over to her. "Anything you say, love."

"Sorry about that," Raina says after a moment.

He laughs. "I have a nani, too."

His family lives only a forty-five-minute tube journey from the city. She thinks about asking when she'll meet them, but decides against it.

Raina hears the metal gates opening from the shop across the road, and she glances at the clock. "Wait, what time is it?"

He groans, rolls more fully on top of her.

"What time is your meeting?"

He opens one eye, and then shuts it again.

"Honey, you really need to get up." With half strength, she tries to shift him, but he is deadweight on top of her.

"Dev?"

Sleepily, he kisses her chest. "Five more minutes?" He rolls onto his other cheek. "I can't make it through the day without this, Raina."

TWELVE

No one said much on the drive back to the suburbs. We dropped off Shay and Auntie Sarla, and then I drove Nani home. She insisted I come inside for dinner and wouldn't accept my excuse about work deadlines, my wet laundry still in the machine. After almost five minutes of bickering in the driveway, her voice crawling an octave higher with each breath, I turned off the ignition and agreed to come in.

Dread washed over me as I walked into the house. I knew what was coming, and I wasn't ready to deal with it. I'd skirted around the truth before—small lies about my blind dates, and in high school, about missed curfews or why my hair smelled like cigarette smoke—but never like this. I followed her into the kitchen, and I sat down at the table as she washed her hands and started to dice an onion. Halfway through, she set down the knife and looked at me.

"Why have you not told Shaylee?"

"Nani . . ."

"I am *proud* of you, Raina. She will be too, *nah*?"

"Not now, okay?"

"And you won't bring Zoey here for dinner? So I can get to know her properly?"

"I've told you a hundred times we're not together. Zoey is just a friend."

She wiped her hands on a dishrag. "You know, I read a blogger today. Do you know an Edith Windsor? She married a woman, and changed the American constitution."

"That's not exactly how it happened."

"This *Edith*—very strange name for a woman, but—"

"I really appreciate you trying to support me, but I just don't want"—I struggled for words—"I don't need—"

"Yes." Nani's voice cracked. "You do *need*. I refuse to be one of those mothers who say it's okay for everyone else to be gay, but not their own child." She bit down on her lips, and looked away. She always looked away when she cried, even when I was young. Even when the worst had just happened.

I walked toward her, wrapped my arms around her, and gave her a hug, and she turned around and pressed against me. She was so tiny in my arms, frail yet plump, her head resting beneath my shoulders. After a few moments, she pulled away, and wiping her face with the backs of her hands, she looked up at me.

Why was I putting up this wall between us? She loved me. She *supported* me—even with something like this that was foreign to her. Why wouldn't she approve of me getting back together with my ex-boyfriend?

Except I wasn't with Dev. Not yet. And if I told her that two years later I was still waiting for him, what would she say? Would she look at me the way she looked at Mom?

The daughter who had a child at sixteen. The daughter who

wanted nothing to do with her family, culture, or traditions. The daughter who seemingly lived with a new man every time she called home.

"What do you need, Raina, *nah*?" Nani brushed my face with her hand. "Tell me."

"I . . ."

It was the first time we'd spoken alone and in person since that evening, and I couldn't look at her. What the hell was I doing lying to her about something like this? I opened my mouth, keeping my eyes on the floor.

"I . . ."

Where did I even begin?

"You are seeming very tense." Nani touched my chin, tilting it upward until we were face-to-face. "I have idea. I know what always makes you feel better . . ."

"Vodka?"

She tutted at me.

"*Fine*. Gin then."

"Oh, *beta*." She pointed up the stairs. "Do you still have running shoes here?"

I nodded, suddenly grateful for the escape.

"Then *jao*. I will have hot dal *makhani* waiting for you!"

I dug through my closet and found my old pair of bright pink sneakers and ratty sweatpants. Nani had chopped off the frays around the ankles, and my winter-themed socks peeked out. She stopped me at the door, and tucked one of Nana's old newsboy caps on my head, a vomit brown fleece around my arms.

I stepped outside the door, immediately thankful for Nana's coat, which, surprisingly, fit me perfectly. I slammed the door behind me and picked up speed as I hopped down the front steps.

The air had chilled, and I took a sharp breath—concentrating on breathing in and out—while closing my eyes briefly as I hopped off the sidewalk, over a partially frozen puddle, and ran toward the park. I focused on my breath, on the feel of the road. Anything but Nani, but Dev, trying to will myself to once again feel light.

As I ran faster, my nose and mouth grew numb. I darted off the road and onto the dirt path toward the school, and the faster I ran, the lighter I felt. I ignored the sharp feeling in my lungs and pushed on. I started to sprint, the wind shrieking into my ears as I crossed onto the football field. It was close to dark, the streetlights faint behind the old brick of the school. My legs were tired, but I pressed on, forcing myself to go faster, and faster, my fingers clenched as I swung my arms back and forth.

I ran the long way around the field, and on the final side of the square block, it struck me that it had been fifteen years since the first day I had walked through the doors of a school where so much of consequence seemed to have happened. It was where Shay and I had gone from being the offspring of two friends to being best friends ourselves. Where I'd thrown the winning basket in the city basketball championship. It was where Mom, crying and bloated in the nurse's office, had found out she was pregnant.

I was less than fifty meters from the school, and again, I picked up speed. In the distance, I could see a lone silhouette shooting a basketball in the courts beside the parking lot. I drew closer. He looked too old to be a student, too tall, and I watched him arc the ball effortlessly through the hoop again and again. Even in the dark, I could almost see the creases on his face, the square of his jaw. I rubbed the sweat from my eyelids with the back of my hand, and just as he went up to take another shot, right when I passed him, our eyes met. He missed the shot, and the ball ricocheted loudly off the rim.

"Well," he called out to me, his arms still poised in the air. "Look who it is."

"Asher?" I panted, walking up to the fence. I barely recognized him without his beard. "What are you doing here?"

"Me?" The ball bounced back to him and he grabbed it. "What are you doing here?"

"This is"—I breathed—"my school."

"This is *my* school."

"What, you never graduated?"

He ducked the ball between his legs and caught it on the other side. "I teach here—thank you very much. The university let me re-enroll, so this year I'm going to finish up my teacher training."

"I see. Well, I used to go here. My grandmother's house is right over there," I said, gesturing across the field.

"You lived with her growing up?"

I nodded. "Mom's in Philadelphia. But Nani is here."

"A family saga?"

"It's not important."

"I imagine it's quite important."

I'd caught my breath, and I ducked through a tear in the metal fence and walked onto the court. Up close, in the shadows of the streetlights nearby, I noticed again how different Asher looked. His wide nose and lips. The slate gray of his eyes. And even though his beard was gone, there was still something wild about him.

He caught my eye, and I looked away. I bent down and tucked my laces into my red and white socks. "What happened to your face?" I mumbled, standing back up. "It was quite the ecosystem."

He smirked. "I decided to shave it. Thought the kids would take me more seriously."

"They certainly won't take your ball skills seriously. That last shot there." I shook my head. "Just brutal."

"I was frightened. Thought I had a stalker."

I lunged forward and tipped the ball out of his arm, catching it with one hand. "I used to play, you know. Varsity."

"Really? I coach the girls' team here."

"Oh yeah?" I dribbled the ball between my knees in wide figure eights. "And how are they?"

"They play like a bunch of girls."

"So they're *much* better than you." I shot the ball. It arced too high and bounced off the backboard.

"Someone's out of practice."

I ran for the loose ball, turned back to him, and then sliced it into his chest. "At least I'm not out of shape."

"Is that smack talk?" He dribbled the ball toward me, and I crouched down, preparing to swat it from his hands. At the last moment, he jutted out to the left, and then right again, dribbling the ball around me and up to the hoop for a layup. He caught the ball after it swished through the net, planted it slowly on his hip, and winked.

"Game on."

Asher won—by a long shot. For every point I managed—a fluke toss from the top of the key, a blind hook shot from beneath the basket—Asher scored five. He had at least fifty pounds on me, and a good six inches. I had forgotten how much I loved the game when challenged.

After I'd graduated high school, Nana hadn't wanted me to try out for the university team; he wanted me to focus on studying. So instead, I joined rec leagues when it fit into my class schedule. Played pickup games on the weekend when the girls from the team—who'd gone off to play college ball all over Canada—were home for Thanksgiving or summer vacation. My skills stalled while theirs got better. And even though those games reminded me of what I could have been, or not been, I loved that feeling of having to work for something. Work *at* something, and having the motivation, the passion, to be better.

After over half an hour of mocking each other, Asher overpowering me, effortlessly swatting the ball down whenever I tried to shoot, I was laughing too hard to keep playing. Panting, I lay down in the middle of the court and sprawled into a starfish.

"That's it?" In the shadows, I saw his smirk hovering above me. "Did I *beat* the infamous Raina?"

After I nodded, he disappeared from my view, and a few seconds later reappeared. He sat down next to me and handed me a water bottle. I took a long sip, some of it spilling down my chin, and handed it back.

"Good game."

I smiled. "Shut up."

"What?"

"You're being smug."

"I'm not being smug. I'm being *civil*." He knocked his knee lightly against mine. "I think someone just isn't used to losing."

"I let you win."

"Really? And here I thought I was teaching you a lesson."

"And what lesson is that, Mr. Klein?"

"It's not over yet—I don't want to spoil it."

"Is there going to be an exam?"

He grinned at me. Crooked, almost naughty, and I blushed. I could feel Asher's eyes still on me as I sat up. I reached over him and grabbed his water bottle, and before taking a sip, aimed it at him like a sword. "Don't think this means we're friends."

"Of course not," he said. "You and I are enemies."

"Sworn enemies."

"And besides." He leaned in close, and I could smell him—like pepper and laundry detergent, and the sticky way boys smell after being outside. "I don't think I can be friends with you. I don't have any sparring equipment."

I rolled my eyes. "I see you're still whining about that."

"I was attacked! Pushed into some desserts—*delicious* desserts, mind you."

"You were bruised for weeks, I'm sure."

"Me?" Asher smiled. "Or your ego?"

I shoved him.

"Ow!"

"As if."

"You're so *physical*." He massaged his shoulder. "What did I ever do to you?"

"Besides embarrass me at my best friend's engagement party?" He didn't answer, and I glanced toward him. He was looking at me, a plain expression on his face. The muscles in his cheeks and around his eyes were relaxed. Genuine.

"I shouldn't have pushed you," I said after a moment, looking back at the pavement between my feet. "I'm sorry."

"Me, too."

"I'm under a lot of pressure from my nani right now." I shrugged. "I'm not—I *wasn't* in the greatest place."

"It's okay. I could tell." He smiled. "I can read you like a book."

"I didn't know you could read."

He grinned, and then a second later, added, "Could that bartender read?"

"Who?"

"He looked a bit young." Asher pressed his lips together, as if thinking hard. "Pass along my number if he needs a tutor, would you?"

"Wait, what?"

Asher's mouth scrunched tight as if he was trying not to laugh, and when I caught his eye, something flickered. Then it hit me.

Josh. The bartender I'd gone home with. Asher had seen us.

"Oh. My. God."

"Please tell me you didn't wear *that*," he said, glancing down at my socks. "Kids these days don't understand fashion."

I hid my face in my knees, and I felt Asher's hand brushing the back of my head. "I like your hat. My dad had one just like it."

"Please. Stop talking."

"Oh, quit worrying so much. It's really not a big deal."

My face was red-hot, and I was sure my entire body flushed. "I'm so embarrassed. I'm never talking to you again."

"What?" He laughed, moving his hand to my back.

"Asher, I can't believe you saw that. I never—"

"Raina," he said loudly. "Look at me." Slowly, I peeled my face up from my knees. He straightened out my shoulders with his hands, waited until I was looking him in the eye. "I was just teasing you," he said gently. "Seriously. Who cares?"

"I care."

"Why?"

I turned away from him, not able to say it out loud: *Because Nani would care. She expects more from me.*

Asher dropped his hands to the pavement and leaned back, his legs outstretched in front of him. The sweat was starting to cool on my skin, and I shivered.

"You know, I dated an Indian girl once. We were like—twenty-one, twenty-two, maybe?" He dug the heel of his sneaker into the pavement. "Her family was very traditional. And they put a lot of pressure on her . . ."

"Is this an analogy?" I asked drily.

"Anyways"—he patted his finger against his lip, shushing

me—"even though she wasn't 'allowed' to date, I convinced her to go out with me. As you can imagine, she was conflicted about—you know—*sex*. Hugely conflicted. But then one afternoon after class she came over, and I thought maybe she finally liked me enough to—"

"Get it on?"

Asher laughed. "Yeah."

"And did she?"

"Not even close. The moment I came near her she started crying—*bawling*, actually—and then left. She refused to speak to me for the rest of the term. And as I'm sure you know, I left university early and—uh, well, I never saw her again."

"You think my problems are about *sex*?"

"No, Raina, my point is that she hated herself. I see so many kids raised to feel shame about who they are, what they want, who they love. And whether it's about sex or identity—or even just making mistakes—when people grow up, sometimes, they screw up. Isn't that the point?"

I looked back at the ground.

"This girl I dated—she was under so much pressure to do the right thing, she didn't even know what it felt like to make a mistake. She didn't have the courage to go out and try something new, something different, and know that she'd still be okay."

I could feel him looking at me, waiting for me to say something. His eyes bore into the side of my neck, and after a minute, I couldn't handle his scrutiny. I jumped up and grabbed the ball.

"Another game?" I turned to face him and dribbled the ball, hard, down and through my legs.

He was biting his lower lip, and I turned back around. I lined up the shot and took it, and it swished through the net.

"You see that?" I ran a lap around the court, pumping my fists in the air, and then ran back toward Asher. "Did you see that?"

"Yeah. I saw it."

I extended my hand. He grabbed it, and I leaned back from his weight as he used my support to pull himself off the ground.

"You know what we should do?" I asked.

"What's that?"

I glanced around the empty field. "Smoke," I whispered.

"You're a smoker?" He winced. "That would explain how easily I beat—"

"No. I mean a *joint*," I mouthed. "Let's smoke up."

"You want to smoke up."

"Yeah, I haven't in years." I grinned.

"You're kidding, right? Shaylee mentioned you liked to joke around."

"No, I'm not joking." I shook my head. "I'm kind of in the mood."

"Being here with *me* . . . puts you in the mood."

"Yeah." I laughed, touched his arm. "So do you have any?"

"You know what, Raina . . . No. I don't have any on me right now." He grabbed the ball from my hand. "Not today."

"Oh. Okay—"

"Must have used it all up at work this week," he said frowning. "Teaching *children*."

"Asher—"

"Look. I've got to run. Dealers to meet. Things to blow up. Irresponsible stuff—you wouldn't understand." He grabbed a tuque from his pocket and shoved it on his head, and without looking at me, turned away. "I'll see you around."

"Asher, wait, I didn't mean—"

But he was gone, already jogging toward the parking lot, his basketball tucked beneath his arm.

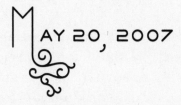

MAY 20, 2007

Raina turns eighteen and smokes her first joint. Before this day, she has never thought seriously about smoking marijuana. Even as it billows at the edges of the school parking lot, on back decks, and in the basements of parties, she has never considered it. Her coaches tell her to stay away, threats of slowness and sluggishness, and Raina listens. But on her eighteenth birthday, the season is already over. Basketball, volleyball, track and field—all the games are over. The scores tallied. In the muddy spring schoolyard, the one around which she has jogged thousands of times, there is no one left to race. In a way she is relieved, allows her body to slacken, but knowing graduation is less than a month away, she is also ter-rified.

The final bell rings, and Raina rushes out of sixth period ahead of her friends. Shay told everyone it was her birthday, and they dec-orated her locker with dollar-store stickers and ribbons, tacked-on messages penned on hot pink construction paper. Raina tears it all down as she throws her textbooks into her locker, and then races outside the front door. She is greeted by the heat of a May afternoon, the air still fresh with spring. She can smell nothing but the green of the lawn, the clipped hedges running along the sidewalk, and she smiles as she takes a deep breath. She is about to walk home, and she is still smiling when, right in front of the school, she sees Manavi.

Raina hasn't seen her mother in over a year. Her hair is different than the last time she visited. It is now cropped short, light blond and browns like a patchwork quilt. She sits cross-legged on the hood of a cherry red convertible parked in front of the school, and as Raina approaches, she looks up from the magazine open on her lap.

"Happy birthday, Raindrop."

Raina smiles. Now that she is older, she doesn't know what to call her. Manavi. Manu. Ma. Raina has always just avoided addressing her directly, but this time, when she says hello, calls her "Mom," she notes how natural it feels.

Manavi slides off the hood and wraps her arms around Raina. She is a few inches shorter, slightly wider, and she beams as she pulls back. "Shit, when did you grow up?"

"What are you doing here?"

"It's your birthday. Where else would I be?"

She has missed Raina's last three—maybe four—birthdays, but Raina doesn't remind her of this. Raina throws her backpack into the trunk next to her mother's worn-out duffel bag, and they get into the car. Manavi slides on a pair of cat-eye sunglasses and smiles at herself in the rearview mirror, pursing her lips together. Then, she opens her purse and hands Raina an identical pair.

"Really?" Raina can tell they are expensive. She recognizes the brand from airport billboards. Department stores that don't accept cash. She slides them onto her face. "Thanks, Mom. I love them." Their eyes hidden, their noses partially obscured, Raina notes how similar their mouths are. Rosebud lips that bloom into wide, slightly crooked smiles, just a hair too close to their equally soft chins. Manavi starts the car, and Raina turns to face her. "Where are we going?"

"*C'est une surprise.*"

They snack on Dr Pepper and cheese fries Manavi buys at a truck stop outside Belleville, racing down the highway with the windows down, Top 40 music blasting through the speakers. It is dusk by the time they reach Montreal, and they drive to an apartment in Laval that belongs to a friend of Manavi's. He isn't home, and she lets them in with a key. The rooms are tattered—peeling wallpaper, blue carpets with zebra patches of brown. Slits for windows that peer into a back alley. Manavi drops her bag in the middle of the hallway, steps over it as she searches for a radio. They listen to French Canadian pop and get ready for the evening squeezed side by side in the tiny bathroom. Raina is wearing Manavi's dress, sleek red and short, while Manavi has put on emerald green pleather pants, a black top that drips beneath her rib cage. Raina realizes with some surprise that her mother is thirty-four. *Only* thirty-four. Yet, as they stand next to each other, the same light brown foundation highlighting their faces, Raina can barely see the age difference; she can barely see a difference at all.

"You always look tired, kiddo," Manavi says, sorting through her makeup kit. Raina glances sideways in the mirror as Manavi applies black paint to her lids and lashes, erases the faint circles beneath Raina's eyes with a beige pencil.

"I stayed up late last night." Raina notes Manavi's bemused expression, and then shakes her head. "No, not that. I had a math test today."

Manavi rolls her eyes, and Raina, momentarily, feels embarrassed. She tries to think of something to say, wonders why it's so hard, and then it occurs to her that she can't remember the last time she was alone with Manavi. No Nani hovering in the background, disapproving of whatever it was they decided to watch on television, or ordered for dinner. No Nana and Kris making sarcastic comments, sucking the air out of the room. No Shay, filling the void, whenever the silence became too much.

While waiting for a taxi, Manavi sends Raina across the street to a liquor store. She is nervous when she slides her driver's license across the counter, prepared to confirm out loud that she is eighteen and, in Quebec, finally legal. The man slides it back without looking, and Raina smiles to herself. She stuffs the bottle of vodka into her purse, the expensive brand with gold glitter floating in it like a snow globe, and with her chin up, she walks back across the road to Manavi.

Raina is drunk by the time they stumble out of the cab in Montreal. Over half of the glitter floats in her empty stomach, and Manavi buys them both a hot dog from a street vendor on St. Catherine's. Now, Raina feels like talking, and she natters pointlessly to Manavi as they eat—about the lights, the churches, the strip clubs they pass—and when a group of boys stop to talk to them, Manavi slyly wipes the crumbs off Raina's lips, and winks.

The boys take them to club, and once they are standing in line, Raina begins to waver, a flood of nausea passing through her every time she blinks, and she grabs on to the black metal bars stretched across the window for support. Manavi pulls her hands away, and a moment later, the boys are leading them to the front of the line, and Raina sees one of them shove a fistful of bills into the bouncer's hand.

Raina can barely walk. Electronica pounds through her ears. With her eyes closed, she stumbles around aimlessly, guided by hands, people's breath like wet fog on her face. She can smell mold, the sweat on everyone around her, and soon she finds herself leaning on Manavi. She hands her a shot. Mindlessly, Raina drinks it, and then another—shiny blue liquid burning the back of her mouth, trickling down. Every time she opens her eyes, Raina thinks she might be sick, epileptic flashes of light, emerald green pleather, and clusters of faces she keeps pushing away. Raina is disoriented, and every time she hears her mother's laugh, the blinking lights that blister her eyes, she thinks of her nani.

She wants to go home.

The taste of blue rises in her throat, and then she smells Manavi's perfume, and feels her tuck a stray hair behind her ear. She catches Manavi's eye and points to the door. Manavi glances at her watch, rolls her eyes, and without saying good-bye to the others, they leave.

They don't speak as they turn off of St. Catherine's, as Manavi leads her to the Latin Quarter. They wind loosely through cobblestoned streets—some pitch black between the crossroads. The sound of traffic grows more distant, and in the hollow silence, Raina can hear nothing but the even click of Manavi's heels. It strikes her that her mother knows exactly where she's going, her footsteps assured and direct, as if, without Raina ever having known, Manavi has lived in Montreal before.

Ahead, Raina sees a group of men standing on the stoop of an old apartment building, and the men stop talking as they approach. Raina glances behind her. No one else is around, and she slows her feet. She feels hesitant, but Manavi's heels keep pace.

"*Mademoiselle,*" says the one with a goatee. His mouth is open, and Raina can make out his tongue as it slices across his front teeth. He is looking at Manavi. "*Vous êtes belle ce soir.*"

"*Merci. Toi aussi.*" Manavi smiles. Flashes him her white teeth. He beckons her, and to Raina's surprise, she walks up the stairs. They speak French to each other, quickly, effortlessly. She tries to catch what they are saying, but Raina has never been good at

French, and until tonight, she has always assumed Manavi wasn't, either. Every so often, one of the other men, his eyes black, glances down at Raina and gestures for her to join him. Raina shakes her head. She still feels nauseous, light-headed, and she wants to go home.

"*La soeur?*"

Manavi laughs, and then glances down the stairs. "He thinks we're sisters."

Raina inches up the steps. She stands at the edge, watching them converse. After a few minutes, the man with the goatee—the one whose hand is now tucked around Manavi's waist—pulls out a joint. He sets it on Manavi's bottom lip, lights it, and she inhales until the end glows amber. She breathes out, smoke billowing, and then offers it to Raina.

"No, thanks," Raina mumbles.

Manavi turns to her. "Just take it." She looks irritated, and when Raina hesitates again, she pushes it into her hand. "Be chill, Raina. Stop worrying about everything." She glances back at the men, mumbles something in French, and everyone laughs. And they keep laughing until Raina takes a long, thick puff, and her lungs start to burn.

Raina doesn't remember the rest of the night. Bits and pieces. Faint smells and feelings. Coughing so hard she thinks she just might die; her cheek, cold against a toilet seat reeking of shit. The night—and well into the morning—is a trance. An unfamiliar room spinning above, her eyelashes batting to a beat she makes up in her head. Vaguer memories, still, of how she falls asleep on a couch next to the man with the black eyes, the one who, as she dips in and out of sleep, smells like pot roast and keeps trying to touch her.

Manavi shakes Raina awake, smiles down at her weakly. It is

light outside, and Raina notices that Manavi's top is inside out. Without saying a word to each other, they slip out and take a taxi back to the apartment—and ten minutes later, they climb back into Manavi's rental convertible. Raina's head pounds the whole way home, made worse by the music—brash and loud—that Manavi insists on listening to. Finally, hours later, they are home. Raina swings open the door, and she is surprised that no sounds or smells are there to greet her. Nothing is cooking, and Nani's voice does not bubble out beneath the crack of the kitchen door, ushering her into the kitchen for a cup of chai or a taste of whatever is simmering on the back burner.

Manavi throws down her bag. "Anyone home?"

Nana appears at the top of the stairs, the cordless phone pressed into his chest with both hands. His hands slowly drop to his sides.

"Is Ma home?"

He glances between Raina and Manavi, and without saying anything, he turns around. Raina hears his door upstairs click, the lock slide into place, and she is overwhelmed with a sense of dread. She glances at Manavi, who is seemingly unchanged, and follows her into the kitchen. Nani is sitting at the kitchen table. She is motionless, her hands clenched white into two fists resting in front of her. She doesn't look up to greet them, and when Raina leans in to hug her, she shudders.

"Nani, what's wrong?" Raina steps back. She remembers that she hasn't washed off the makeup or brushed her teeth, and she wonders if her hair smells of smoke. "Nani?"

Still, Nani won't speak. Her hands unclench, slowly, and she sets her palms lightly on the table. They are shaking.

"Yeah. About that." Manavi has propped herself on top of the counter. She opens a bag of chips, and stuffs a handful into her mouth. Crunching loudly, she says, "I took Raina to Montreal last night. For her birthday."

Raina stiffens. She feels as if she's been punched, and she squats down beside her nani. She searches her eyes, only to find they have chilled. "Nani, I'm so sorry. I didn't realize you didn't know—"

"You are *both* adults." Nani looks different. Her voice is changed, and Raina feels as if she is speaking to someone who has emerged from the past—a woman of whom she heard rumors and, until now, never had the misfortune of meeting. Nani stands up suddenly, walks out of the kitchen, and Raina resists the urge to follow. She can hear Manavi crunching chips behind her, the plastic crackling, and she turns around. Manavi swings her legs in small circles, and when Raina finally meets her eye, Manavi is grinning.

"Raindrop, pass me a bowl—would you?"

THIRTEEN

"So he's gone."

"Until the spring."

"That's that, then." Zoey stood up from the chair facing my desk. I thought she was going to leave, but instead she shut the door and sat back down. "Are you okay?"

"What do you think?" She handed me the box of tissues next to her, and I pulled out three. My nose was running, but surprisingly, I had no tears left. Was I surprised that Dev, after being based in Toronto for merely five weeks, was being carted off to Singapore to temporarily oversee an emerging markets division—and that he wouldn't be back in town for months?

Did it surprise me that he'd dropped the news on me during dinner the day before he left, so casually that I felt tempted to laugh?

I always tried not to care about his lack of work/life balance, or his constant need to travel or push harder than any other banker we knew. Hadn't I been inspired? There was a certain nobility about a self-made man—the work ethic, the passion, the devotion it took to become one of the few people in the world who—rightly or wrongly so—had influence on the economy; on how the world worked. He was bright and powerful, and this man, the one who left and returned on a moment's notice, the one who had so few moments to spare—but wanted to spend them with me—was the *real* Dev.

I'd learned quickly that the man I fell for in Brussels had been on holiday. A chance glimpse, really, because he rarely took vacations. The Dev who had the inclination to read in bed with me, whisper secrets between the hotel sheets, was as rare as the London sun. And I was fine with it. It had always been clear what life would be like holding Dev's hand. Sleeping beside his furrowed brow. Cajoling him to cheer up during dinner, his mood soured by a deal gone bad.

Our life would be Dev hunting for a Wi-Fi connection, leaving me to sun myself on the beaches of Corfu alone while our complimentary bottle of champagne chilled in the honeymoon suite. Dev e-mailing a client during our child's Christmas concert, leaving during his solo to take a call. Dev having to keep a flat near the office for all the late nights and last-minute meetings; the rest of us in our town house in Totteridge or Haywards Heath—a light therapy lamp beside the davenport desk where I'd watch the clock and try and figure out my life's passion.

Life would be Dev growing older and even more powerful. Meeting him for a quick bite near his office in Westminster. His hand on my waist as he avoided eye contact with the waitress our daughter's age and I massaged my wrinkles, convinced he didn't have time for an affair. Life with Dev would be fast and slow at the same time; a waiting game between moments of bliss—between trips to Brussels. It hadn't bothered me. It had all been fine back then, but now I didn't feel so certain.

Why was I misleading my nani—and for what? What if I was waiting for nothing?

"How did you guys leave it?"

I leaned back on my chair. Zoey's patience with me was waning, but I appreciated so much that at least she was trying. "He said he would call me as often as he could—"

"Uh-huh. *Sure*—"

"And that we would figure 'us' out when he got back."

"Is that what you want?"

I nodded, but I wasn't sure which one of us I was trying to convince anymore. I was so busy with work, and went home so rarely these days, that surely I could maintain the lie to Nani for a short while longer? Surely, when Dev got back, we *would* figure it out.

"Just do me a favor, would you?" Zoey leaned forward and gave my forearm a squeeze. "It's almost Christmas. Try and enjoy the holidays, and do your best to forget about him. For now, at least?"

I promised her I would try, and surprisingly, it kind of worked. I took off the week before Christmas, and from the moment I arrived home, I felt better. Just being home and away from downtown, I felt ready for the holidays without Dev.

I established a new routine—a suburban, more relaxed life away from the city. In the morning, I'd wake up early and bring Nani her tea, two digestive biscuits resting on the saucer. I'd help her with housework, and at Saffron if she needed it. In the evenings, we cooked dinner, and Nani and I watched TV huddled together on the couch, and after she fell asleep, I'd go on a run, sometimes past the school's basketball courts. Once, I saw the girls' team practicing—running drills, shuttles, and layups. Asher was standing in the corner with a clipboard, and I'd slowed down and waved as I jogged past. But he didn't see me—that, or he purposely turned and looked in another direction.

The only downside of staying home with Nani was having to deal with her questions—questions it was becoming harder and harder to avoid.

Why were Zoey and I not together?

Did I have a different girlfriend?

Would I have natural children or adopt?

How did I define my sexual orientation, and was that different from my gender identity?

It wasn't until Christmas Eve, while surfing on Nani's tablet after she'd gone to bed, that I found out where those questions were coming from.

Her browser history was littered with LGBTQ websites. Organizations, support groups, blogs, and chat forums. Terminologies, ideologies—tips on *how to set aside your feelings on homosexuality* and *how to redefine your relationship with your gay child*. There was even a link to some gay porn (which, I gathered, she'd stumbled across by mistake). I laughed out loud at first, as I made my way through the websites—the new *list*—feeling rather proud of my progressive nani.

But then I imagined her on the couch, her wrinkled brow mouthing along with the words, and I realized that maybe it wasn't so funny. I kept scrolling, and more websites appeared. Ones outlining in layman's terms same-sex civil marriages, how Canada had been the fourth country in the world to legalize gay marriage. Sites with advice on raising kids of gay parents—for *grandparents* of kids raised by gay parents. Sites on adoption. Donor insemination. IVF treatment. Another on adoption. Then it hit me like a frying pan to the skull. Nani didn't just support me being interested in women.

She wanted me to marry one.

Nani and I both pretended not to notice that Kris didn't come home on Christmas morning, or that Mom hadn't even called. We spent the day cooking together and watching old movies, and then got ready for Auntie Sarla's party. She had first invited us over for Christmas dinner after Nana had died. It had started out of sympathy and included just our family and Shay's, but over the years the numbers had grown, and these days, Christmas dinner felt like just another one of Auntie Sarla's famous parties. Her two dining tables became a hodgepodge of salads, curries and dals, shrimp fried rice and oversalted stuffing. And in true potluck style, sometimes there were six turkeys—and other years there were none.

Their marble foyer was already littered with winter boots by the time we arrived for dinner. The house was all extravagance and no taste, a house of oversaturated colors. Rosewater pink carpets and blindingly gold walls; an indoor swimming pool only the dog used; a six-foot statue in the middle of the living room—just because.

Since their engagement, Shay and Julien had decided to alternate holidays with their families, and this year was Shay's first Christmas away from home. It felt odd being in her house without her; usually, we'd sneak upstairs away from the party, hide in her old bedroom with a plate of stolen desserts, ignoring everyone until Auntie Sarla found us and insisted we come back down and socialize. I thought about going up to her room alone, but it felt too strange. I wasn't sure how it happened—or when—but these days, Shay and I barely spoke.

Sure, I'd become more distant since Dev moved to Toronto, and avoided seeing her for fear of letting the lie slip, but I wondered whether it had started before then. Things hadn't been right since she got engaged, and started pressuring me to settle down, too. Maybe there'd be time over the New Year to talk things out, at her bachelorette party in New York City. Julien and his grooms-men would be there, too. Ironically, they'd both be spending their last "singles' trip" together—a group holiday I'd had planned for months. But ever since my misunderstanding with Asher, I wasn't sure I looked forward to it.

Shay's house was packed with some familiar faces and a lot of new ones. Most of the girls Shay and I had grown up with had moved away—Los Angeles, Vancouver, Calgary—or were away on vacation with families of their own. The few I did know sat in clumps in one of the living rooms, holding hands with their hus-bands or boyfriends, chasing after toddlers dressed up like rein-deer, in tiny novelty onesies bought specifically for the occasion. I quickly said my hellos, my congratulations, and then moved to-ward the kitchen.

I peered around the corner and saw Nani and Auntie Sarla arguing in front of the stainless steel oven, their faces flushed. Quietly, I drew closer, coming within earshot.

"This is not right, *ji*."

"Suvali. I am helping her. I am helping *you*. Raina needs a husband."

"Raina doesn't need—"

"You know what everyone is saying? They are saying none of the men she meets like her, that she is too difficult to please—"

"Why are you making up lies?"

"Suvali, why would I lie?"

"Raina doesn't need a husband, and—and—"

Nani's voice dropped off, and they both turned to look at me.

"What's going on?" I asked slowly.

"Nothing." Auntie Sarla turned back to the stove. "Have you eaten?"

"Not yet."

"*Jao.* Go make a plate." She nodded at me, and then threw Nani a glare. "Take your nani with you. She is looking pale."

I led Nani into an empty hallway. She was perspiring, fanning her face with a folded piece of paper towel. I found a table nearby with fresh glasses of champagne, and I thrust one into her hand.

"What's going on?" I asked.

"That woman is going on and on—always talking, talking." Nani tapped her fingers together. "She knows nothing—and still? Always talking. Who is that woman to talk like that about my Raina? We need to tell them. Band-Aid"—she flicked her hand like a musical conductor—"off."

I set my hands on Nani's shoulders and took a deep breath, trying not to imagine what would happen if everyone found out about the lie I'd told. Another scandal in the Anand family. Another daughter who didn't live up to expectations. What would Nani have to endure if everyone thought I was a lesbian? Most of Nani's friends couldn't even pronounce "homosexuality"—let alone support it.

"Should we tell them?" Nani reached up and stroked the side of my cheek. "I am *okay.*"

I shook my head.

"Raina, please—"

"No, Nani." I looked her straight in the eye. "Promise me you won't tell anyone yet—not until . . ."

Until when? Until Dev was back from London or Singapore— or wherever the hell he was going? Until I could admit that it was *him* that I wanted to marry, and not another woman? The man who humiliated me? Who humiliated Nani?

"Just promise me you won't say anything yet. Please?" I took a deep breath. I would come clean and tell Nani everything. Dev would return, and we would get back together—and I would make Nani realize he was right for me.

I would make them both realize.

"Okay." Nani sighed, and her hand slid to my chin. "But Raina. Eventually, you will have to face them."

No, Nani, I thought, my stomach wrenching. *Eventually, I will have to face you.*

FOURTEEN

I worked the next five days straight to make up for my "ill-timed Christmas holiday," as Bill had called it, and then just before 5 A.M. on New Year's Eve Day I took a taxi to the airport for the first flight out to LaGuardia. Serena was already there, a coffee in her hand and a crime thriller tucked between the thighs of her skinny jeans.

I sat down beside her hesitantly. I hadn't seen her since she and Kris had broken up, but she seemed happy to see me. Slowly, the rest of the group started to trickle in—Shay's twin cousins, Nikki and Niti, who'd been a few years behind us in school, and now had jobs in brand management and social media. Then came Julien's friend from the hospital, another resident named Matt, and Julien's younger brother, Victor, who'd sworn up and down that his fake ID would work.

Finally, Shay and Julien arrived, hugging us all through fatigued smiles. I hadn't made time to see her since they got back from Quebec—and I couldn't even remember the last time we saw each other, or spoke on the phone. Lately, our only contact had been brief texts hours apart, which were always about plans for the wedding or for the trip to New York.

Shay eyed me oddly as she drew closer. I thought she was going to lean in and hug me, but then she stopped, and patted me on the arm. "You look good."

"You, too."

Did she know I was avoiding her? That I was hiding something?

"Good Christmas?" she asked.

I nodded. "You?"

She didn't reply as she looked around the terminal and, after surveying the crowd, looked back at me. "Where's Asher?"

I shrugged, and a moment later, I saw him.

"There he is," said Julien.

Asher jogged down the moving sidewalk toward us, a duffel bag swinging in his hand. He'd let some of his beard grow back, a soft scruff on his chin and cheeks, and instead of a suit or sweatpants, he was wearing loose jeans and a faded leather jacket. Along with a white T-shirt and sneakers. He slowed down as he approached us, and without looking at me, smiling broadly, he wrapped an arm around both Julien and Shay and steered them toward security.

He avoided me as we waited, and then at the front of the line, when Shay bent over and took her time unclasping the buckles on her boots, I veered in front of her, angling myself behind him.

"Hi, Asher."

Whether he heard me or not, he didn't answer.

"How was your Christmas?" I said a little louder.

He retrieved his passport from his back pocket. "Festive."

"Were you with family?"

"Sure was."

"Did you guys have fun?" I paused. "Play any basketball?"

"Guess that depends on your definition of fun." He leaned on the metal rail and slid off his shoes. "My nephews prefer *SpongeBob* over—you know, *weed*—"

"I am really sorry about that."

He tossed his wallet and keys into the plastic bin.

"Asher, come on. I said I was sorry."

But he walked away through the metal detector, and didn't turn around.

There were only a handful of others on board, and after takeoff, we spread out sideways on the seats. I blinked in and out of sleep, and it felt like only minutes passed before we started our descent into New York City. I sat up and peered outside my window, watching the clouds feathered above the Rockaways. The snow sprinkled over the city like icing sugar.

I had booked ahead for transportation, and a square black van was waiting for us outside the airport. I sat in the front seat chatting with our driver, Ramón, about the state's public school system, the newest speakeasy that just opened beneath a pho takeout in the Lower East Side, camouflaged in red and yellow string lights, and we drove down the expressway toward Manhattan. I'd been to New York often—with Shay or other friends for weekend shopping trips or music festivals. A dozen conferences with colleagues, with days at the office on East 55th, nights in the hotel bar on Lexington in a black pencil skirt, charging Gray Goose martinis to the expense account. It was one way to live. It was Dev's way. But as the chalky gray peaks of Midtown rose onto the horizon, I tried to push thoughts of Dev out of my mind. Whether he, on those countless fall trips to New York, winding around that last bend on the Long Island Expressway, had thought of me, too.

On the other side of the Queens-Midtown Tunnel, we hit traffic, and after thirty minutes of crawling, block by block, Ramón muttering about tourists and the traffic reroutes around Times Square, we reached our hotel. I'd booked us two suites at a hotel in Hell's Kitchen the week after Shay got engaged. She'd showed up to my apartment, drunk, with two butter chicken burritos, and told me I was her maid of honor, and instead of Vegas, or some cheesy night doing the limbo with a tanned stripper, she wanted her bachelorette party to be during the New Year. And she wanted to share it with Julien.

We said good-bye to the guys, dumped our things in the room, and set out for Fifth Avenue. It was still early, foot traffic in the shops and on the sidewalks sparse, and Shay was acting unlike herself. Bubbly, almost, and she couldn't stop smiling, picking up clothes and modeling them, her eyes glossed as she walked by a storefront, exclaiming at something showcased in the window, and then hustling in to buy it. She chatted ruthlessly with the girls working at Chanel and BCBG, trying everything on as she stood in front of the mirror and surveyed the room for an opinion.

"So, what do you think?" she asked us, her fingers playing with the sequins of a stiff black dress. "Is it too much?"

Everyone chimed their approval as Shay twisted and turned in front of the mirror, sucked in her stomach and elongated her arms behind her. Surprisingly, she had the perfect figure. Petite and curvy from a diet of hospital cafeteria food, from the exercise of running from patient to patient.

"You look like that new movie star," I said to the mirror. "Priyanka Chopra."

"Priyanka Chopra's not new," said Nikki. "She's been around for more than a decade."

"Who's that new one then?

"Parineeti Chopra?"

"Yeah." I nodded. "You look like *her*."

"You have to buy it, Shaylee," said Serena.

"Can't. What if Ma sees the pictures?" Shay shrugged and turned away from the mirror. "She'd hate it."

"Shay—"

"And I'm ten pounds heavier and a thousand shades darker than any girl who makes it in Bollywood." Shay unzipped the dress, and stalked back into the dressing room. "Parineeti Chopra, my ass!"

"What a nut bar," Niti whispered to the rest of us. "We're going to buy it for her anyway, right?"

We bought the dress when she wasn't looking, and when we stopped for glühwein at the German Christmas Market, Serena handed her the bag. Shay eyed us suspiciously.

"I told you guys not to get me anything."

"Just open it," I said, and when she did, she started to cry.

"You guys"—she spluttered—"I can't believe it."

"Calm down." I rolled my eyes. "It's just a dress."

"It's not just a dress," said Shay, wiping her nose with her wrist. "It might be the only thing in this whole wedding I actually pick out for myself."

"You're our Parineeti Chopra," said Serena, hugging her, and the rest of us joined, and soon all of us were clumped madly together in the middle of Union Square, shopping bags and scarves flung to the side with pigeons knocking at our feet, the tourists walking by, nodding and smiling at us like we were some interesting occurrence that made up the landscape of the city.

"Should we take a picture here?" I asked Shay.

Shay nodded, and her eyes landed on a miniature wooden lodge selling wicker crafts and discount Christmas wreaths. "Yeah. Over there in the light. Raina, do you have him?"

I nodded, tapping the side of my purse. "I have him."

Him was Draco, and as maid of honor, or, perhaps, because he didn't fit in Shay's clutch, I was in charge of lugging around the stuffed teddy bear Julien had bought for her on their first real date. Ever since, Julien and Shay had carried him around like a child, ready for every photo op: Draco perched on one of their shoulders at the CN Tower or Niagara Falls; in the operating room with a clinical white mask over his face; in sunglasses on the beach; or riding the neck of an alpaca at Machu Picchu. The last time I'd seen him was the weekend before my twenty-ninth birthday when Shay, Draco, and I went camping, and we took pictures of the three of us canoeing Lake Nipissing, then chugging beer by the campfire. By now, Shay had accumulated enough Draco photos to warrant his own slide show at the wedding, and although Auntie Sarla had originally vetoed the idea, it was the one thing Shay insisted on.

After, we caught the 4 train uptown and took more pictures with Draco at Wollman Rink in Central Park, in Christopher's shadow on the steps of Columbus Circle, and later, propped on a velvet chair at the Ritz. High tea was a surprise for the bride-to-be. We walked into the hotel on the pretense of looking around, and when I took them up to the hostess and told her we had a reservation for a "Shaylee Patel," Shay looked at me, and again started to cry.

"You remembered."

We went to New York City on an overly chaperoned class trip in high school. We snuck off to the Ritz just for a moment to take a look: the dining room was full of old men and money; the decor of another century, wine red–colored carpet, and classical music. We fantasized about the lives of the people who were allowed inside—what they ate, what they did. We promised each other that one day we would get there—wherever *there* was.

I handed Shay a Kleenex. "Of course I remembered."

After tea, we went back to the hotel to change—Shay, into her new dress—and we were still full of foie gras and lavender macarons by the time we arrived at our reservation in Chelsea: a jazz-themed seafood grill where all the waiters—like in any fine city establishment—appeared to moonlight as models. An Italian with sideswept hair flirted with Shay as he took our order, and she giggled in response, played with her hair, and ordered everyone the chef's tasting menu, and several bottles of wine.

The table was large, and we were spread out. I was at the end, Shay sitting closest to me, and as the other girls chatted, Shay and I looked at each other. I realized that neither of us knew what to say.

"Did your Ma tell you?" I finally asked. "She booked that band from Vancouver for the wedding. They'll fly in before the *sangeet*—"

"Are you seeing anybody?" she asked suddenly. "Is there anyone you haven't told me about?"

"No. Why?"

"Where have you been then?"

"I'm right here."

"No," she said. "Where have you *been*?"

I shrugged. "Busy working."

"And before?"

"And before"—I trailed off—"before, well, I've just been busy. I've been working, Shay. Same as ever."

"Is this about Asher?"

"What?"

"This morning"—she paused, and looked away from me—"it looked like something was going on with you two."

"At airport security?" I shrugged. "He walked through with change in his pockets, was subject to a frisk and search, if you know what I mean . . ."

I trailed off when she didn't crack a smile.

"It was nothing, Shay."

"Nothing."

By the way she bit her lip and dropped the subject, then promptly engaged herself in conversation with the other girls, I knew she was hurt. Whether it was the offhand comment some guy in history class had made, or how a few unwanted edamame beans got on our order from the bitch at our favorite salad bar—with us, it was never *nothing*.

I didn't know what I was supposed to say to her. Nani thinks I'm a lesbian, and—*oh yeah*—Dev sort of moved to Toronto and we might get back together, but he's still not quite sure he wants an actual relationship? Just like you would have predicted? I knew what she would say, and I didn't want a lecture. Not from a girl who could memorize an algorithm or an amino acid structure in the blink of an eye. Not from a girl who it seemed never had to work hard for anything. Shay was my best friend. She always had been. But some things she just didn't—she *couldn't*—understand.

My stomach felt queasy throughout dinner. Unsettled. And I had to keep reminding myself that I was lying to Shay for a reason. She wouldn't understand why I was waiting for Dev, and letting Nani believe I was a lesbian—so what was the point of telling her? When I poured my wine into Nikki's glass, everyone had drunk too much of their own to notice—most of all Shay. The waiter had flirted with her throughout dinner, sneaking her shots of ouzo from the back room, and I had to peel his hands off her waist as he helped her into her coat. She was practically catatonic. Outside, I ducked into a mini-mart and bought her water, and then we walked toward Hudson Street, most of her weight collapsed onto me.

The guys were waiting for us outside the club. I saw Asher first, several inches taller than everyone else, leaning against a handrail with his coat open, a charcoal gray suit beneath. Shay unfastened herself from me and stumbled straight into Julien, but somehow we managed to get her into the bar without drawing too much attention.

The hostess led us toward our reserved area at the back. We were seated in a corner section with two long plush couches facing each other, a table full of glass bottles of vodka and gin, cranberry and Coke, lined up in between. We were at the edge of the dance floor, just in front of a terrace. The doors were wide open, and each gust of wind brought in the citrusy smell of perfume, the diesel of the heat lamps. I sat at the end of the group, disengaged, at the fringe of the conversation.

Asher was sitting across from me, and I kept catching his eye. But every time I turned to face him, he looked away. Annoyed, I finally waved at him, and to my surprise, he waved back.

"How was your day?" I yelled over the music.

"What?"

"How was your day?"

"Great." He smiled. "Smoked *loads* of weed—"

"Okay. Cut it out."

He grinned. "Cut *what* out, princess?"

I leaned forward. "You know what? I said I was sorry—three times, now. And I'm done. So if you don't want to—"

"See the thing is"—he walked around the table, perched himself on the armrest beside me—"you don't even know what you're apologizing for."

"Yes, I do."

"Do you? Because you're *hilarious*, Raina. Always making jokes. And you can't offend anyone if you're kidding."

"I really didn't mean to offend you. I just thought—"

"You just *thought* I smoked weed because you smelled it on me at the engagement party—which, by the way, you were wrong about. I was outside on the phone with my sister, and some kids were smoking right next to me, so that's why I smelled like it. I haven't even touched weed since college."

"Oh."

"And you also assumed that I had drugs on me at my workplace." He grabbed his drink from the table. "I mean, I'm just some shaggy guy who hangs around on a high school basketball court, must be—"

"Look." I took a deep breath. "I knew you'd been traveling and that you'd barely been back since you left—and everyone I know like that also—"

"Well, obviously, I'm just like them."

"Yes, okay? I made an assumption. I know your type. My own mother is *your* type. I mean, who leaves their family for *ten* years?" The lights around the dance floor kept slicing me in the eyes, and I blinked hard. "But it's all fine, right? You've been 'finding' yourself. Learning about the world. Not really having to deal with how selfish you are."

"Sounds like you have me all figured out."

"Don't I?" I snapped. "And don't *you* have me all figured out?"

"All I did was try to get to know you."

"But you *did* know me, didn't you? You knew that I was twenty-nine and my best friend was getting married before me"—I coughed, my voice catching—"so obviously, I'm desperate to get married, right? I take home bartenders to feel some validation?" He had looked away, and I glared at him, shaking, until he looked back. "So go ahead. Validate me. I *really* need it."

He rubbed his lips together, and then his hands, and when he looked at me as if he might say something back, I heard Shay calling my name. I looked over. She had hoisted herself off Julien's lap and was inching toward us.

"What's going on here?" she asked, leaning down between us. She dipped down and planted a wet kiss on my cheek. She moved for the other cheek and missed, hitting my chin.

"Do you want some more water?" I asked.

She shook her head, hair falling onto her chest as she wavered in front of us. "No. It's picture time."

"Now?"

She nodded. "Group shot."

"Sure. I'll bring Draco over right away."

"Okay," she said, slurring. "Let me know when you're ready."

She stumbled toward Julien, and I grabbed my coat from the back of the couch—kicking myself because I'd forgotten Draco at the hotel.

"Are you leaving?" asked Asher.

I nodded.

"Why?"

"It's nothing."

"Who's Draco?" He followed me as I cut through the dance floor, trying to lose him, and then up the stairs toward the club entrance. Outside on the sidewalk, I stopped, trying to catch my breath. I felt him behind me, his hand on my shoulder.

"Raina, who's Draco?"

I rolled my eyes. "Oh, you know. Just another guy who won't marry me."

FIFTEEN

"Shit." I stepped back on the curb as another cab drove past me. I let my arm fall down by my side and turned around. Asher was still leaning against a lamppost, his left foot propped up, his arms folded across his chest.

"What time is it?"

He glanced at his watch. "Eleven twenty. Do you want a hand?"

"No, thanks." I raised both my arms and waved frantically at another cab as it whizzed past.

"You know," I heard Asher say, "if the light's off, it means it's taken."

"You're being a nuisance."

"That's because you're not letting me be helpful." He uncrossed his arms, and then crossed them the other way.

"Fine." I gestured to the street. "Be my guest."

Asher pushed himself off the lamppost, and as he walked toward the edge of the sidewalk, a cab pulled up. The door opened, and three girls in stilettos and long parkas filed out. Asher placed his hand on the roof of the car as he helped them out, and then looked at me smugly.

"Lucky bastard." I got into the cab, and before I realized what was happening, Asher slid in next to me and pulled the door shut.

"Thirty-eighth and Tenth, please—we're going to the hotel, right?"

"Wait, *we?*"

"No problem," said the driver, steering sharply into the traffic.

Asher reclined in his seat and drummed his fingers on his lap and, a moment later, looked over at me. He smiled. "What?"

"What are you—why are you—"

"It's eleven"—he glanced back at his watch—"twenty-two. In New York City. On New Year's Eve. I'm not letting you go alone."

"So you're being chivalrous, are you?"

"Something like that."

We made it to the hotel in good time, and Asher waited in the lobby while I ran upstairs and grabbed Draco, who was still sitting on the windowsill where I'd left him. I stuffed him into my purse and then ran back downstairs. Asher was talking to someone at the concierge desk, and as I walked up, he shook the man's hand and walked briskly toward me.

"They can call us a black car, but it will take a while to get here. Or we can walk over to Eighth Ave. and try and catch a cab there. Apparently, we won't find one around here."

I reached for his hand, and rotated his wide wrist until I could see the face of his watch. Eleven thirty-five.

"Subway?"

He shook his head, looking at his wrist where I'd touched him. "It's out of the way—walking there and then back again—we might as well just walk down."

"Well, why don't we?"

"Walk?"

"Yeah. We'll go fast." I lifted up my right boot, the flat edges covered in salt. "We might even make midnight."

We cut toward Ninth Avenue and then turned south. Our strides long and brisk, we walked silently in step, the faint smell of salt and gasoline hanging in the air. We passed delis and tapas restaurants, low-income housing and upscale condos alike; the windows light and dark like a checkerboard. The crowd thickened outside of Penn Station, and we darted through the throngs of pedestrians, delivery boys on bikes, pizza boxes and steaming white paper bags strapped over the back wheels. And after a few blocks, the sidewalks thinned out, and the silence between us once again became palpable.

I looked at him out of the corner of my eye. "Are you still—uh—mad at me?"

"Not really." He dodged to the right of a couple walking their dog, while I curved around to the left, and when we'd passed them, he said, "Are you still mad at *me*?"

I shook my head. "No."

"Good." He smiled. "Your apology is officially accepted."

"I haven't apologized . . ."

"But you're about to."

"Yes, I guess I was." I laughed, hopping over a crushed beer bottle. "I'm sorry."

"I'm sorry, too."

I sighed. "I'm sorry I misjudged you, Asher. I'm sorry I assumed you were a stoner and an irresponsible drifter. And a nuisance. And—um—implied you were a slut."

"Ouch." He raised his eyebrows. "When you say it like that, I'm not sure I have forgiven you yet."

"Oh, calm down," I teased. "You're fine."

"Raina," he said after a moment, in a tone I couldn't quite read.

"Did you really think that badly of me? I know I've led an unconventional life, but I'm just not as scandalous as some may think."

"No Thai ladyboys during your travels?"

He laughed.

"Because I hear you can never be quite sure."

"Nope," he said grinning. "And no bastard children, either."

We dashed through another intersection, the streets dirty with melted snow. I looked down at my boots. Mud had caked onto the edges, and with each step, I tried to rub some of it off.

"Did I say something wrong?"

I shook my head.

"Tell me, Raina," he said softly.

"Really, it's nothing." I shrugged, and as his pace slowed even more, so did mine. "But I guess, technically, *I* am a bastard child."

"Oh."

"It happens all the time, doesn't it? Same story. Different characters. I never knew my dad, and Mom's kind of all over the place. He had blue eyes and blond hair—and was *tall*. That's all she ever told me." I smiled. "She was too young."

I felt Asher's hand on my shoulder.

"My grandmother—my nani—was different back then. Different with my mom. She wasn't allowed to do anything, not even take swimming lessons, because a swimsuit was too revealing. She rebelled, she had me—and then when I was young, I guess she'd had enough. Mom left, and has barely been back since."

"I'm sorry."

I shrugged. "It's not your fault. It's not really hers, either, though."

"Your nani was tough, sure. But that doesn't mean your mom is allowed to blame everything on her childhood, forever, don't you think?"

"To be honest, I'm not sure *what* I think." I glanced at him. "Anyway, Mom is still finding herself. She travels, she switches

jobs when she feels like it—kind of like you did. We all find ourselves in different ways . . . although I suppose your way is far more
interesting than mine."

"Interesting—sure." Asher kicked at a loose rock. "But being
away from everything and everyone you've ever known—it's so
easy to get lost. You can lose your perspective on life, rather than
find it."

"Is that what happened to you?"

"Who knows. I've been everywhere, tried everything"—he
winked at me—"almost. And I don't regret much. Except that I
wasn't home when I was needed."

"What did you miss?"

"My sister's wedding, for one. It's taken her a long time to forgive me."

"But she forgave you."

"Of course, she's my sister. But she has kids now. I'm an *uncle*,
and a pretty great one, too. And I know that when I have kids, I
would need Anna to be around for them. So now, I want to be
around for her. It's a small family." His voice quieted. "Our parents are dead."

"Asher. I'm so sorry."

He smiled. "I was at university—my last semester, actually.
Their car slid right off the road."

"Was that why you quit school?"

"It's life, you know?"

I felt his hand brush against mine, and I squeezed. "*Life* doesn't
make living through that any easier."

His fingers stayed intertwined through mine until the light
changed. On the other side, people had started to gather on the
sidewalk in front of a yellowing sign with "Punjabi Hut" painted
on in dark blue lettering. I'd seen shops like this in New York before: twenty-four-hour Indian eateries with platters of authentic

dishes served up on plates for a five-dollar bill. Never more than three rickety tables inside, yet always full, always ready for the next wave dashing in and out for a quick taste of home.

"What's going on?" asked Asher as we walked toward them. More people were arriving, from the handful of cabs parked halfway up the curb, pouring out from the restaurant, the scent of spices and oil trickling outside as they propped open the door. Someone was setting up a speaker outside the shop, and we gathered at the edge of the growing crowd, watching everyone speaking excitedly in Hindi or Punjabi, buttoning up their coats over saris and kurta pajamas.

The speaker pulsed to a start. Bhangra. Asher smiled at me in recognition, like he'd heard the lively, low-swinging beat before. Soon, everyone around us—old and young—was dancing with their hands clapping or twisting, their hips moving as fluid as a belly dancer's. A woman who reminded me of Nani, petite and with a kind face, walked by with a Tupperware full of *laddoo*, popping the sweets into people's mouths at random. She walked up to Asher and tapped his stomach. He opened his mouth, and she plopped the whole thing in, and part of it crumbled off his lips. He caught it with a smile. "What is this?"

I wiped the crumbs off his chin. "It's a blessing."

"It's good!"

The crowd formed a circle on the sidewalk, and everyone took turns dipping in and out of the middle, bobbing their shoulders with the beat, dancing with such vigor Asher and I couldn't stop watching. On an impulse, I dragged Asher inside, and laughing, I taught him the *lehria* step, and he jerked his arms from side to side, a silly, childish grin painted onto his face. We danced and spun, and the saris swished, the smell of masala overflowed, and being there—right *there*—with Asher, I felt something I hadn't in such a long time.

Happiness.

The music swelled, and in a chaos of shouts and laughs, the countdown began. I could feel Asher looking at me. Our bodies pressed together. I was sober, but suddenly woozy, drunk on the scent of pepper and his aftershave.

"We're missing midnight."

He was inches away, and it was like the crowd was pushing us closer. My ears rang, my neck prickled, and I could feel the heat of his body as he stepped closer.

"No, we're not."

As the numbers fell away, reverberated through the street, the mass of people, I couldn't breathe. I couldn't move. My hands were so close to Asher's, and his fingers brushed against me.

"Five . . . Four . . ."

I could smell him. Pepper, earth, aftershave. Our fingers locked together, and I looked up.

"Three . . . Two . . ."

And I couldn't look away.

"One."

Then, in the middle of New York City—as I thought of nothing and no one else—he kissed me.

Asher . . . What just happened!?

SIXTEEN

I woke up alert, ready to hop out of bed and grab my sneakers. I peeled back the covers, then noticed the floor-to-ceiling window with a view of the West Side Highway, the bleach white linen, and remembered where I was. I stretched my arms far above my head, and then let them tumble back onto the pillow. I looked over. Shay's side of the bed was empty, the evidence of the rest of last night scattered around the room: our boots and coats and dresses in piles on the chairs and dresser; wine and water glasses still half full of champagne. An empty carton of Chinese takeout, its grease dripping onto the bedside table. I sat up and wiped it with a napkin, and then scrambled for my phone. I had a handful of work e-mails—from Bill, mostly, sent just after midnight about a file I hadn't finished on time. One new voice mail from Nani, and a text from Asher.

Good morning :-)

I smiled until my cheeks hurt, and rolled sideways onto the duvet. *Asher*. Who would have thought—and what was I thinking?

I wasn't thinking. I still wasn't. But, for whatever reason, I couldn't stop smiling. The rest of the night had passed by in a blur, even though I'd barely had a sip to drink. No one had even noticed Asher and I had disappeared, and after taking the photo with Draco, we spent the rest of the night partying with the group, dancing to old-school R&B. Then, after a quick hug at the end of the evening, the bride's and groom's parties had gone their separate ways.

I lay there, staring at the ceiling, wondering what to text back. A simple good morning? A mentioning of last night? But what *was* last night?

Would there be time to talk about it in New York? We were flying home that afternoon and likely wouldn't have a moment alone together until we were back in Toronto. I wondered where Asher lived, whether he'd want to see me again.

I swung my feet over the bed and pulled on a bathrobe hanging in the closet. Shay was sprawled across the futon in the main room, her morning-after hair tied in a bun at the top of her head. She had an ice pack on her forehead, her cell phone on her stomach, and Nikki and Niti were limp on the other couch, half dressed, their eyes half closed. Serena was in the kitchen pouring coffee, and she pushed a full cup toward me as I sat down at the counter.

"Coffee?"

"Sure, thanks." I took a sip, and then glanced back at Shay. She was glaring at me now, and I wondered if she'd figured out what had happened with Asher.

"How was everyone's night?" I asked to no one in particular. I took another sip, and then glanced over at the twins. "Nikki, you seemed to be having fun."

She groaned, lifting her head slightly before letting it flop back down on the pillow. "I made out with Justin Bieber."

"You made out with a guy who told you he was Justin Bieber," Niti said, "and you believed him."

"But his name *was* Justin, right?" Nikki sighed. "I hope I didn't post any pictures."

I heard Serena laugh behind me, and when I turned to look at Shay, I saw that she was still staring at me.

"Shay, you feeling okay?"

She didn't blink. "I talked to Ma this morning."

I crossed my arms. "How was her New Year's party?"

"It seems she had a nice little chat with your nani." Shay sat up slowly, curled her fingers around the edge of the futon. "Want to guess what it was about?"

I laughed. "Did your dad get drunk and sing again . . ." I caught her eye, her icy glare, and when seconds passed and still she didn't say anything, I knew. And my stomach dropped. "I—"

"Is this all some kind of elaborate *joke* from you?"

"Shay—" I stopped. I glanced at Serena, coffee cup frozen halfway to her mouth, a blank expression on her face.

"Look," I said, turning to face Shay. "I can explain. Can we go talk in private for a second?"

"In private?"

"Shay, come on—"

"What the fuck is going on, Raina?"

I hopped off the stool, walked past the twins, and started to pull her up by her wrist. "Please, let's just talk—"

"No—"

"—in private. Shay, please—"

"Get off me!"

"Shaylee? What's—"

"Stay out of this, Serena," Shay growled. The air in the room had gone flat. Nobody spoke, and I could hear my heart beating furiously.

"So," she continued after a moment. "You have an audience now. Always begging to be the center of attention—well, here you are, Raina. We all want to hear your joke now. Since when does your nani think you're a lesbian?"

I heard a shuffle behind me, and turned around. Nikki and Niti were off the couch, one behind the other, walking toward the door. Serena was already gone. A moment later, the door clicked shut, and all I could hear was the hum of the fridge, its door still slightly ajar.

"Well?"

I looked back at Shay. She was standing there, staring at me with an anger I'd never seen from her before.

"What's going on with you?"

I sat down on the couch. I couldn't breathe, and I wished that I could open the window. Everything felt trapped inside me, and I didn't know how to—I couldn't—let it out.

"Unbelievable." She threw her hands in the air. "You're going to sit there, and not even look at me? After everything we've been through—you're going to *keep* lying to me?"

I concentrated on my toes as I tried to steady my breath. But what was the truth? That I wasn't as strong as her? That I hated myself; that I hated the way Dev treated me, yet I couldn't stop it? That I was ashamed, and alone?

"Fine," I heard her say. "Lie. Let's go with that. Let's go with you being a fucking *lesbian*."

My mouth dry, I swallowed, tried to find words—*any* words.

"You—coming out to your nani." Shay's voice cracked. "*You*— a lesbian—the same girl who became a doormat for the first guy to really look at you, some guy who didn't give two shits—"

"Shut. Up."

"And now—you're telling people you've given up on men? Want to try the *ladies* for a while?" She laughed cruelly. "Good fucking luck."

I looked up at her. "I said. Shut. Up."

"You know what." She shook out her hair. "I'm not going to 'shut up,' not like I did when Dev turned you into a puddle and *I* had to deal with that mess—"

"Shay—"

"It was pathetic—and *this*"—she threw out her hand—"whatever you're doing now, is really pathetic."

"You know, I always thought that I was the judgmental one. Not you." I scratched my chin, and I heard my voice grow cold. "I wonder if Julien would still marry you if he knew what a slut you used to be."

Her mouth dropped.

"Who knows, maybe you still are."

"You know I would never cheat on Julien," whispered Shay.

I stood up. "How would I know that, *Shaylee?* Maybe I don't know you at all. After all, you didn't know I was *gay*."

"Raina, you're not gay."

"How the hell would you know?" I screamed. "You haven't been around. You've been off with the man of *your* dreams, lecturing me about my problems whenever—"

"*I'm* not around? You're the one that keeps disappearing, keeps shutting me out—"

"If one day, you and Julien were just over—*over*—would you want me to tell you to 'get over it'? Tell you to grow a pair, and be strong?"

"I never said that. I was always there—"

"You didn't even try to understand what I was going through. You lectured. You sat up on your high horse telling me what to do, telling me to *move* on, telling me I could fix it all by screwing other guys—"

"How long was I supposed to let you sulk? Look at you—how long has it been—and you're still not over that jerk—"

"He's not a jerk—"

"Your nani flew all the way to London, and he wouldn't even meet her."

"It wasn't like that. He was called to Zurich, and then he—"

"You're still defending him. Why? You need to delete that picture in your head. That guy who rolls in cash and runs the world, because guess what"—she poked me—"you already dated him. And he never had time for you. He didn't even—"

"You don't even know what you're talking about. You with your perfect family and job, perfect fiancé—you growing up with Auntie Sarla's silver spoon stuffed down your throat."

"Right, because only *your* mother was the fuckup. No one else gets to screw up their child." Shay had tears in her eyes, and she took a step backward.

"So I'm screwed up," I said softly. I was crying, too. "I'm pathetic, and screwed up, and *gay*—"

"You're not gay!"

"Maybe I *am*, maybe I—"

"You won't even tell me what's going on."

"And why do you think that is, huh?" I walked toward the bedroom door and slammed it behind me, screamed, "Because you're so *fucking* understanding."

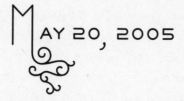

MAY 20, 2005

The girls are spread out around the room; groups of three and four on each couch, some flopped down or cross-legged on the shag carpet, others with their knees up, their backs against the sprightly papered wall. They take turns switching their favorite CDs into Raina's portable player—Macy Gray and Destiny's Child, Missy Elliott and Creed. The coffee table is full of kettle corn and fuzzy peach candies, ketchup and salt and vinegar chips. Birthday cake. Sprite—although some of the girls have brought cans of beer, water bottles full of vodka and lemonade mix, and they drink this instead.

It's Raina's birthday and, decidedly, a girls' night. Who decided it, Raina cannot remember, but nonetheless, Nani's entertaining room is now full of them. Girls from the team. Girls with bad haircuts who play the clarinet or the trumpet. Ones who run track, or met Shay in Chemistry Club. They are all shuffled in together at random, high on sugar, on one another, and they are giggling about boys.

Boys—thinks Raina, listening to them—the only thing of any concern on a girls' night.

Shay stands on the couch cushion, and everyone watches her body wriggle as she talks about Theo. He is a senior, and after class, Shay recounts, he drove her home in his dad's Mercedes, first parking the car behind the hockey rink. Raina is anxious to hear more when she hears the door open. Shay slinks down, slides her can of beer beneath the seat, and a moment later, Nani shuffles into the room. She sets down a tray of *pakoras* and samosas, tamarind and mint chutney in adjacent clay bowls, and smiles to the girls. Everyone murmurs their thanks, and Nani hovers expectantly as they examine the food.

All the girls in the room except for Shay are white, and they follow her lead, carefully selecting one of the flaky fried chunks like a chimp with a new toy, biting off tiny pieces. Selecting the smallest of morsels to place on their tongues. It is a success. Their eyes pop, and their expressions brighten in thanks. Raina suspects most have never tried Indian food before, and they lick their fingers clean.

"Thanks, Mrs. Anand!" they cry, as Nani turns to leave.

"Please," she replies, heading back up the stairs, "call me *Nani*."

Shay waits until the door clicks shut, and then turns back to the group. She is smiling from ear to ear and, Raina knows, waiting for someone to prompt her.

"So," says the girl beside her. "What happened with Theo? Did you . . ."

Shay smiles coyly. "Did I *what*?"

"Just tell us!"

"Come on, Shaylee," says another.

"What happened?"

Shay squeals and topples off the couch, rolls back and forth on the floor. After a moment, she sits up, arcing one arm high in the air. "Okay, okay. I'll tell you." She is breathless. "We didn't do *it* . . . but he—" She smiles and, after a moment, points between her legs, and there is a chorus of gasps around the room.

"Down *there*?"

Shay nods, and another girl chants, "Shaylee, no way!"

"Did it feel good?"

She squishes her nose like she's about to sneeze. "I think so."

"You think so?"

She nods again. "He says he knew what he was doing."

"Of course Theo knew what he was doing," says one of the girls from track. "He always knows what he's doing." Two other girls laugh.

"Shay," says Raina. "You never told me that." And after Shay turns to her and shrugs, Raina asks, "Is he your boyfriend?"

Shay glares at her, as if she is irritated. "I don't care about things like that."

"Do you think you'll have *sex* with him?"

But Shay has already turned away, turned her attention to another girl, another question, and they launch into a discussion about things Raina has never done—things she can barely fathom. Shay reaches into her backpack and pulls out a *Cosmopolitan* magazine—bright yellow and pink, Sarah Michelle Gellar posed on the front cover. Everyone leans in, and as they paw over the glossy pages, shrieking, Raina slips out of the room unnoticed.

Upstairs, Nani is splayed out on the couch, her calloused feet resting on Nana's lap. And although he appears to be asleep sitting up, eyes closed, his fleshy chin pillowed onto his neck, his hands are in motion. Softly stroking Nani's feet.

"What are you doing?" asks Raina, watching them from the hallway.

Nani looks over, and Nana snorts himself awake. "Raina." His yawn lands in a wide smile. "How is the party?"

"Good." Raina walks over to them as Nani slides her feet off the couch, and Raina wedges herself between them. She sinks into the cushion. "What are you watching?"

"*Mohabbatein*," says Nana, wrapping his arm around her shoulder.

"Again?"

He nods toward the TV. "Your nani loves this one."

"Should we start it again?" asks Nani. "Your friends want to watch?"

Raina shakes her head and stares at the screen. The actors are in a market throwing colored powder into the air, dancing beneath the festive debris. It seems like the DVD has been on a loop ever since Nana brought home a pirated copy from the restaurant, and from time to time, Raina has watched it with them. The characters have just started college and are falling in love for the first time, and as Raina watches them, her stomach drops. Their lives, their experiences—it all seems like an eternity away. But Raina is now sixteen, and college is not so far off in the future.

Raina cannot imagine having to decide what to do with her life. What—or whose—path she should follow. Shay already knows she will be a doctor, but Raina is not strong like her, and she cannot see herself in a hospital, in the witness-box of death and decay. Kris studies engineering—but Raina does not know what that means. She likes math, physics—even wants to understand his job, but these days Kris rarely sleeps at home. Nani despised his Sri Lankan girlfriend, a nutritionist with buckteeth and giant breasts, but she convinced him to propose, and now talks excitedly about the wedding even though a date has yet to be set.

Her nana tells her that she would make a good lawyer, but Raina has never met one before, and other than episodes of *Law &*

Order, she has no idea what lawyers actually do. Often, she wonders if she should go to university at all. Nani didn't, and neither did Manavi. The last time her mother lived at home, instead of a degree postered above her desk, she had a map. Tea-stained and pricked with a slew of red and blue pins. All the places that Manavi had been—or wanted to go. Places that Raina knows nothing about.

"Are you okay, my sweet?" Nani brushes Raina's cheeks with both hands. "Are you having fun?"

Raina nods. "Yes, thank you. Everyone loves the food."

Nani wiggles her eyebrows. "Don't worry. I saved spicy ones for you." She grabs a plate of *pakoras* from the end table and hands them to Raina, and Raina pops two in her mouth at once. She smiles, crunches the spicy warmth between her molars.

"Now," says Nani, setting the plate back down. "Go have fun."

Raina stands to leave, but lingers by the doorway. "Hey, guys?"

They both look at her.

"Manavi had just turned sixteen." Raina looks at her socks, toes the lines in the hardwood. "She was sixteen when I was born." Her lips quiver, and inexplicably, she wants to cry.

"Raina." Nana's voice is strong and sweet. Raina feels him, both of them, as they draw near her and stand on either side of her. Nani takes Raina's hand into hers.

"Listen to me." Nani squeezes her hand. "You are such a capable girl."

"A *good* girl," adds Nana. "With such bright future ahead."

A tear drops, and Nani wipes it away. "You are *nothing* like your mother."

"Do you understand?"

Raina nods. Forces out a smile, and a moment later, she says, "I understand."

Raina rejoins the party. Her seat has been taken, and so she curls up on the floor by the coffee table. The girls have moved on from the magazine. They are sillier now, passing cans and bottles around to one another, giggling, already thinking they are drunk. A bottle of beer reaches Raina. It has gone warm, and her hand sticks to the green glass. She takes a deep breath, wraps her mouth around the lip of the bottle, and throws back her head. As she drinks, Raina cannot stop thinking about what if Nani is wrong. What if she actually is like her mother? What if Raina, too, is a disappointment?

SEVENTEEN

For the first time ever, I was grateful for the long hours and sleepless nights at the office, the distraction of the cutting-edge, thankless world of banking. Winter churned on outside my window, and I sat in my twelve-foot-square cell poring over financial statements and market data, working and reworking a balance sheet. Dissecting a cash flow problem, an economic implication. I worked without really working; I spat out what I was supposed to, and as I sat there on the phone with a client discussing pharmaceutical investments and market shares, made notes on a risk analysis, I was thankful. For the diversion. The disturbance. Thankful that I didn't really have to think. I tore through reports faster than they were assigned, and Bill warmed up to me again, happy to see that I was "back to my old self." Ironically—although, predictably so—I felt further away from myself than I'd ever been.

January and then February dragged on, and still the winds sliced brisk and sharp, the sleet and snow creeping in through the revolving doors, at the edges of frosted windowpanes. It seemed like spring would never rear its willowy horns, fill the city with light and sun. It seemed that Dev would never show up, either. He'd been temporarily assigned to a project in Jakarta now—something about an emerging market, heading up a risk analysis. These days he called often, and his texts and e-mails were flowered with *darling* and *missing you*, constant reassurances that he'd *be back in a jiff*. But even when—even *if*—he came back, I wasn't sure what I'd do or say, or how he'd fit in to the spectacular mess I'd created and, with each passing day, obstinately ignored.

I mean, it wasn't every day that someone managed to single-handedly divide a community.

After New York, I'd gone straight home and asked Nani what had happened, and she'd simply apologized and collapsed sound-lessly onto the couch. I prodded, but she couldn't remember all that much about Auntie Sarla's New Year's Eve party, except that she'd reacted when Auntie Sarla made a derogatory remark about two men kissing on television. And then, partway through the argument, Nani had told Auntie Sarla—told *everyone*—what she thought to be the truth.

Nani outed me to a room full of people born in a country where homosexuality was still a crime, to a room full of people who quickly took sides. Overnight, everyone knew, half of them disgusted with Auntie Sarla, the other half disgusted by me. And in the months that followed, Nani had cut ties with at least half of her friends, despite my urgings that it wasn't necessary. She'd dis-invited herself to dinner parties and to the movie club, to any so-cial gathering organized by someone on "Team Sarla." Anyone who believed homosexuality was wrong.

"You should have *seen* her reaction, Raina. Terrible!" Nani had sobbed, clutching me in her arms. "But if you saw—you would have done the same. In front of everyone, she *screamed* at me, asking me how I could allow this"—Nani panted, exhausted from the dramatization, and then continued—"and I reply, 'What is there to allow?' Then, that *voman*, she told me to leave the party. Told me of course I would make all my girls turn strange."

My stupidity and weakness had ignited a war between Auntie Sarla, a social pillar of west Toronto's Indian community, wife of a neurosurgeon and mother to two successful children, and Suvali Anand: a blue-collar, social-climbing widow. Mother of rebels. Grandmother of, apparently, a lesbian.

Right then, I'd opened my mouth to tell her the truth: that I was straight. And this spectacular mess was actually about a *man*, a man I'd barely heard from over the holidays—a man who probably didn't even deserve me. But I'd pressed my lips together, and turned away. Because I wasn't strong like Nani, or Shay, or Zoey. Or even Mom.

I was much, much worse. I was a coward.

Now I sat in my office, my belly full of a Vietnamese noodle bowl Zoey had brought me for lunch, and I let my face fall onto my desk. My forehead stuck to the varnish as I breathed against the hard surface. I was bored and restless; it was becoming harder and harder not to think about Shay. She'd gone to India with Auntie Sarla and Julien, and had already been back for a week, Nani had told me. At yoga classes, she'd seen Auntie Sarla, who'd refused to turn around and look at her as she attempted chair pose at the front of the temple rec room.

"That woman is so inflexible—it is not *stool* pose," Nani had said cattily, waiting for me to laugh.

For the millionth time, I flicked through my phone, scrolled back to my last message from Shay. It was dated from over a month before: New Year's Eve. 11:51 P.M.

Where are you Raaaaaina?

I peeled my head off the desk and stared out the window. It was the middle of the afternoon, dark and miserable outside my office, and I missed Shay.

I missed my best friend.

I looked back at my computer screen, inundated with numbers, formulas, and I tried not to think about her. Concentrating, narrowing in on my work, there was something else I tried not to think about; *someone* else I hadn't seen since New Year's.

I'd left New York in a rush, and I was sure the rumor that I was gay had spread to Asher. No wonder he hadn't texted or called me.

Had he chalked up our kiss to a New Year's frivolity with a lesbian? Or did he think about it, too? A part of me wondered if I did call him, if he did know the truth, if anything would happen between us. The other part of me was sitting on my hands like an idiot. Screwing up my life—and worse, Nani's—while I supposedly waited for a guy I wasn't sure was coming back.

My intercom buzzed, and I hit the button. "Yes?"

"Raina, you have a—uh, visitor here."

My stomach fluttered. "Who is it?"

"A Dep-oosh Sax-ee-na?"

"Oh." I caught my breath. "All right, thanks, Emma. Send him up."

I opened my office door and waited out in the hall. A minute later, the elevator opened and Depesh appeared; fresh-faced, even taller it seemed than when I saw him the previous summer.

"How's university?" I asked. "Haven't heard from you in a while."

"Haven't heard from you, either."

As he followed me into my office, and sat down in Zoey's usual chair, I guiltily remembered that I'd never made an effort to see him.

"You're right." I sat down beside him. "I'm really sorry."

He shrugged.

"You want some coffee?"

"Hmm?"

"Coffee."

"Oh." He shrugged, and then looked down at his feet. "Nah, it's all right. I'm fine."

"Okay."

He went silent, and I watched him as he shook his foot wildly, refusing to meet my eye.

"Is everything okay?" I paused. "Is it Sharon Auntie?"

He shook his head. "Ma is fine."

"And you don't want coffee?"

He shook his head.

"Uh, tea?"

"No"—he stood up, started pacing the office—"I *don't* want tea, all right?"

"Depo?"

He stood by the door, and when he put his hand on the knob, I thought he might leave. But then he closed the door and sat back down. He paused, and then said, "I heard you're gay."

"Oh." I sank back onto the chair. "*That.*"

He glared at me. "Thanks for telling me, by the way. And what are you, like, thirty?"

I blew out air through my teeth. "Nearly."

"*Everybody* knows now, do you even know that? Like, everybody is talking about it."

"Yeah. Thanks." I scratched my head. "I am acutely aware."

"Why couldn't you just keep it a secret?" He looked at me like I'd done something wrong, like I was being ridiculous.

"Excuse me?"

"What made you come out?" He shook his head. "You hid it this long—and now—explain it to me."

"Explain what exactly?"

"You knew it would cause a scene with everyone, our whole community, and still—"

"Listen, I really don't have time for a lecture."

"Raina, please just explain it to me, okay?" His voice came out softer. Pleading. "I need you to explain because"—he paused—"I *am*, too."

"Come again?"

"I'm gay, Raina. Just like you." He slumped forward in his chest, and his head fell into his hands. "And I have no idea what to do."

We waited in the cocktail bar on the ground floor of my office building, and I sat there playing with my hands, watching Depesh drink his second whiskey and Coke in ten minutes. He'd slurped down the first in three clean sips and noisily chewed on the ice cubes until a waiter came back and asked if he wanted another. At first, I was surprised they hadn't asked for his ID—Depo, a kid in Converse sneakers and a T-shirt on Bay Street; a kid who, to me, still looked like the ten-year-old I used to babysit; who I'd seen cry after I let him watch a horror movie. Whose eyes lit up whenever I'd suggested ice cream.

But then I looked again. He had stubble on his chin and above the lip, and the baby fat had been sucked from his cheeks, exposing a chiseled jaw and brow bone, a beaky nose. He wasn't the kid I knew anymore. He was eighteen—nineteen, now—and I struggled with what to say. I could feel my heart pounding in my stomach, and I checked my watch. Zoey was on her way. Thank *goodness* Zoey was on her way.

It was the middle of the afternoon, and the bar was empty except for us; all the waitstaff were cluttered behind the bar unloading glasses and chatting about whether this year—finally—the Leafs would make it into the playoffs.

"They're not going to make it," I murmured.

"Pardon?"

"The Leafs," I said, gesturing at the waitstaff. "They're not going to make the playoffs."

"Of course not. But neither are the Devils."

"I have a New Jersey fan sitting next to me?" I scoffed. "And here I thought we could be friends."

"As long as you're not a Canucks fan . . ."

"I don't think the Canucks have fans. Just suckers."

He laughed, and just then, I saw Zoey waft through the entrance.

"There she is."

We were at a booth by the window, and she pulled up a chair to the end. She looked at Depo curiously, and then extended her hand toward him.

"I'm Zoey."

"Depesh," he said. He shook her hand, and then set his own back on his lap.

"Hi, Depesh." She glanced between us, and her eyes landed on me. "You texted this was some sort of emergency?"

"Not quite . . ." I looked at Depesh. "You're sure?"

He nodded, and I looked back at Zoey.

"Zoey, my friend Depesh wants to talk to us about something." I swallowed. "He is . . . gay."

"Also," he said, his eyes flicking between us, "Raina says you guys are, too."

"*Also* gay," repeated Zoey, her eyes still on me. I saw her press her lips together, and I could feel my cheeks flush.

What was I doing? This boy who'd been like a little brother to me was gay, and I was going to lie to him?

For a few seconds—what seemed like an eternity—nobody spoke. Depesh stared at his hands, Zoey stared at me, and all I could hear was the bartender's ignorant position on which Leafs players deserved to be in the Hall of Fame, the elevator jazz drifting from a distant speaker.

"Sorry," I heard Depesh mumble, and I looked up at him.

"What on earth are you sorry about?" I asked.

Looking as if he might cry, he shrugged his shoulders.

"No, we're sorry"—Zoey flicked her eyes at me, and then back him—"just a little stunned, is all." Smiling, she pulled her chair closer to him. "Is there anything in particular you'd like to talk about?"

He shrugged.

"Raina, do you want a drink or something?"

"I'm good."

She flagged down the waiter and ordered a small glass of chardonnay. While he walked away, lingered chattily behind the bar, and then sauntered back with the wine, none of us said a word. Zoey then lifted the glass to her lips and took a slow sip.

"Perfect." She set it back down, wiped off her lip print with her thumb. "What are you studying, Depesh?"

"Biochemistry." He shrugged. "I'm going to apply to medicine."

"That's pretty cool."

"Not really. Like, everyone wants to be a doctor."

"Well, why do you?"

He looked at me like he was expecting me to answer for him, and when I didn't, he glanced back at the table. "My mom is sick."

"I'm sorry to hear that."

"Don't be." He chewed another ice cube. "You didn't give her MS."

Zoey nodded her head slowly.

"We're close, you know? I'm the only son. The only *child*, and I gotta help out a lot. My dad has to work a lot more now, too—" He glanced at me again, like he was surprised I wasn't interrupting, offering my own version of events. "We used to live in Jersey, but her treatment got too expensive. Gotta love American health care."

"No kidding." Zoey chuckled. "How long have you been back?"

"Six months or so."

She nodded again.

"And there's treatments here, too, but"—he shrugged—"there's just not a lot *anyone* can do. It's secondary progressive, and sometimes between attacks, she's back to normal—almost—but it's a waiting game. Like, you never know who or what the trigger is going to be." His voiced quieted. "Whether *I* would be the trigger."

Zoey nodded, and as I sensed what was happening, what she was doing, I fought the urge to leap over the table and hug her. She was patient. Empathetic. She knew people, how to read them, and what they needed, and I felt an overwhelming sense of gratitude for her being there for me; being there for Depesh.

"Did Raina tell you my coming-out story, Depesh?" she said after a moment.

He shook his head.

"Well. It's a pretty standard story. I was about your age, and I'd known for a while." Zoey stared intently at her wineglass. "And because I'd figured myself out so easily, I just assumed everyone else would, too, and"—she paused—"that my parents would someday just figure it out."

He nodded.

"So I just didn't think about it. I didn't think about the fact I was always hiding, or lying, or making excuses for why I never had a boyfriend. Of course my best friends knew, and I dated—well, I *slept* with women. And then one day I met a girl, a girl who turned out to be pretty special to me. This girl was *gorgeous*, intelligent, sassy as hell. And of course she went on to break my heart, but in retrospect I swear to you, Depesh, it was still worth it."

He nodded, his eyes still down on the table.

"I told my parents about her. And they screamed and they cried—and they threw shit—"

"Did they forgive you?"

"Depesh, there was nothing to forgive. I am who I am—and they simply can't or won't accept that. Don't get me wrong, I sacrificed my relationship with them for a new relationship, but those feelings are part of who I am. They're a part of all of us. Love and heartbreak—it's everywhere, it's universal, and there's no shame in any of it."

I thought of Dev, and how my whole mess had started because I was ashamed.

As if she knew what I was thinking, Zoey reached for my hand beneath the table. I grabbed it, and it gave me strength.

"And"—I said, looking Depo in the eye—"if there's anything Zoey and I can impress upon you . . . it's that *you* have absolutely nothing to feel ashamed about."

EIGHTEEN

A young Rani Mukerji danced in a train station wearing a blue tube top, shaking her hips, lip-synching to a voice likely a full octave higher than her own. An actor I didn't recognize—wearing aviators, dressed like a sailor—appeared behind her, sang to her as he did push-ups and made the street children laugh.

I looked over at Nani. She had her feet on the coffee table, one toe bouncing along with the beat, but her eyes were glued to her tablet, her finger winding in long, slim lines across the surface.

"If you're not watching, can I put something else on?" I grabbed a pillow from the floor, and wedged it behind my back. "*Anything else?*"

Nani didn't reply. She pushed her glasses up her nose with the back of her hand, and then resumed her finger positioning at the tablet.

"What are you doing?"

"Candy Crash."

"Candy *Crush*?"

She smiled at the screen, and a moment later, let out a mild shriek. "I *von*! I beat the level." Turning to me, she winked. "Pretty good for old woman, *nah*?"

I laughed. "Good job."

"While you are here," she said shuffling over to me, "can you teach me how to download new game?"

I grabbed her tablet and clicked on the app store. "Sure, what's your password?" She didn't answer, and I looked over. "You wrote it down, right?"

"Raina, there are so many, *nah*? I don't know." She clucked her tongue. "Banking. Restaurant banking. U-*teel*-ity bill. Security code—"

"Don't you have a password manager?"

"Don't I have a granddaughter?" She winked at me, and I burst out laughing. It took about twenty minutes to find all her passwords and organize them in a way she'd remember, and by that time, the Rani Mukerji movie had ended, and a Madhuri Dixit one had begun. As Nani settled in to watch, I looked over at her face. She was smiling, her neck bobbing slightly to the melody.

Was she really watching? What was she thinking? Why was her granddaughter—supposedly successful, in the prime of her life—home with her watching Hindi movies on a Friday night?

And then I shuddered. Because as long as I could remember, Nani had never been home on a Friday night, either. She had dinner parties, temple gatherings, and pujas; was helping with festivals and volunteering.

"Why are you staring, *beta*?"

I sat up, and leaned in closer to her. "Have you spoken to Auntie Sarla recently?"

She pressed her lips together, and then after a moment, looked back at the screen.

I wanted to say something, to come clean. It felt like a wall had been built between us, and I'd never been so far away. And I knew that no matter how many evenings per week I came home to visit, no matter how many new *subjis* I learned to cook, I couldn't fix the fact that I'd ousted her from the community she'd helped build without telling her the truth.

And now Depesh thought I was gay, too. What the hell had I done? Why hadn't I realized such a lie would never be harmless?

This had all started because of Dev: I didn't want to take Nani's matchmaking seriously, because I thought he was the man of my dreams. The man I had to lie for. The man who was working half a world away, but still called once in a while, still e-mailed. Still wouldn't leave me alone.

I loved him, didn't I? And I *knew* he loved me, even if he didn't say it. But Dev coming back wouldn't fix anything anymore. I had to fix it on my own. I'd been selfish—thought only of myself—and now it was my turn to face the consequences.

I looked back at Nani, and watched the TV glow flicker across her face. "Hey, Nani?"

"Hah?" She didn't look up, and I took a deep breath. How was I even supposed to start this conversation? There'd be no good time to tell her the truth—not now. This was as good a time as any, wasn't it?

"I . . . uh—"

The phone rang, and my stomach dropped with relief, even though I knew I needed to fix things between us. Nani reached for the cordless phone and then pressed the answer button as she held the receiver to her face.

"This is Mrs. Ah-Nund. Hello, who is speaking?" She made a face into the phone, and then looked at me. "Raina, for you."

I reached for it. "Hello?"

"Raina, it's Julien."

"How did you get this number?"

"From Shaylee's phone—when she wasn't looking."

I looked over at Nani, staring at me curiously. "Work," I mouthed to her, hopping off the couch.

"You didn't try my cell phone?"

"If you saw my number, I wasn't sure you'd pick up." He paused. "And I saw your car there when I was driving home from Sarla's tonight."

"Ah." I walked into the kitchen, and the door swung closed behind me. "How was *that*?"

"All right." I heard the faint whir of a coffee machine, a few echoing voices, and I could tell he was in the doctors' lounge Shay used to call me from. "I was over there for dinner."

"I see."

"You know we went to India?"

"I heard."

"We've been home for weeks already," he said. "I was hoping you guys would have made up by now."

"Yeah, well . . . I wouldn't hold my breath." I sat down at the table, slumped my body onto its hard, cold surface. I could hear him breathing into the phone, and as I waited for him to say something, anger surged through me. She was getting her fiancé to call for her?

"Raina, listen . . ."

A moment passed. "I'm listening."

"Okay, here it goes." He sighed hard. "I wasn't going to say anything about this—but—to hell with it. Listen, Raina. I'm Catholic, so I guess I understand why some people reacted the way they did—"

"Are you really calling me to defend your mother-in-law?"

"No, of course not—that isn't even why I called."

"Why did you call?"

"Let me start over." He sighed again. "Something has happened with you and Shaylee—and I'm not even going to pretend to know what that is—or what's even going on with *you*, for that matter. You haven't exactly been there for her."

"Helping plan the wedding, organizing the trip to New York—that wasn't being there for her?"

"You know what I mean, Raina. Things have been off with you and Shaylee for a while. Well before New York . . ."

I could almost picture Julien, brow furrowed, chewing his lip, sitting there on those hideous orange couches Shay had described to me a thousand times, her hand buried beneath the cushion while she guessed how much change she would find, what gadgets she might excavate.

"Whatever happened between you two, she won't talk to me about it. She won't say a word. But I know her—and she feels terrible."

"Good. She should."

"Whosever fault it is, whatever it was that caused this—don't you think it's time to make up?" He laughed. "For Christ's sake. She still brought you home a bridesmaid outfit."

I didn't respond. In the other room, I heard the cuckoo clock start to chime, and a shiver crept down my spine.

"I don't know if I can forgive her, Julien."

"Don't you want to try? Don't tell me that you of all people haven't said anything in the heat of the moment. There's nothing you wish you could take back—something you took too far?"

I bit my lip.

"You have been best friends—you've been *sisters*—for over twenty years. You know her better than anyone in the entire world. Whatever you fought about, ask yourself, is it really worth it?"

"I'll talk to her," I said slowly. "But she has to apologize first."

"Funny. That's exactly what she said."

"Well"—I rolled my eyes—"we were best friends."

"You *are* best friends. And Shaylee needs you right now—what with the wedding coming up. And I know that Sarla is driving her crazier than usual because of—"

"All the drama I've caused?"

"You said it, not me."

I smiled, and I realized that even though they'd been together for nearly five years, this was the first time Julien and I had ever spoken on the phone. Indeed, it was the longest conversation we'd ever had.

"Will you think about talking to her?"

I nodded. "I'll think about it."

"Good. And just so you know, Raina, you may be Shaylee's best friend—but she's *my* best friend. And I know everything about her. Everything." He paused. "And I love her just the same."

I thought about it. And the more I thought about it, the more I realized how much I missed Shay, and how the last few months had felt empty without her. I wanted to know if she'd liked India this time around, and what it was like visiting her family now that she was *finally* getting married. I wanted to be filled in on the wedding plans, on her favorite patients at the hospital; find out if she ever bought that phallic-shaped figurine—of what, exactly, we never figured out—that we once saw at Urban Barn.

I wanted to know if she missed me, too.

And so the next weekend when Julien asked me to meet him, Shay, and Asher at the diner, I reluctantly agreed.

I only had an hour's notice. I showered and changed, and tried to style my hair—curled, jutting out at the back—the way Shay had once said suited me. I found my makeup bag beneath the sink, and outlined my eyes. Curled my lashes.

It was only a quick walk to the diner. On the way, I tried not to think about the fact that Asher would be there, and remained focused on Shay. What I would say. What *she* might say. And with each step, I grew more nervous, and less confident about what the hell I was doing, or what the right thing to do was. Why should I be nervous? It was Shay who owed me the apology, wasn't it?

I pushed through the front door of the diner, and saw Shay, Julien, and Asher sitting in our usual booth at the far corner, right beneath the neon Hollywood sign. Shay and Julien were both in powder blue scrubs, hoodies open over them. Asher was wearing his leather jacket again, a gray T-shirt underneath, the same color as his eyes.

I could feel my heart beating in my stomach.

Did he still think about New Year's Eve, too? Did he think about me at all? So much had happened since. In a way that night— that *kiss*—felt so far away, so surreal, I often wondered if it'd even happened.

I started to panic, and just as I was about to turn around, Asher saw me. I took a deep breath and kept walking.

Julien looked up first and, a moment later, Shay. She followed his gaze to the side, and looked up at me like she was waking up from a dream. I blinked, and a moment later, she snapped her head back toward Julien.

"I *knew* you didn't want to eat here."

"Wait," I said, dumbfounded. "She didn't know I was coming?"

Julien smiled at us sheepishly, and then he and Asher scooted out of the booth.

"I'm not staying."

"Me neither," said Shay.

"Babe. Yes, you are."

"*Her* babe—or me babe," said Shay, cuffing Julien on the arm. "Traitor."

"You're the traitor," I mumbled, just as I felt Asher's hands on my shoulder blades. His peppery soap smell clung to me as he gently guided me into the booth.

"Hey, Raina," he said without looking at me.

"Hey . . ."

"Julien, can you please tell *her* I'm not speaking to her?" I heard Shay say.

"Shay, she's right there. You need to talk to *her*."

"And since when do you tell me what to do?"

"Since now." Julien drummed the table with both of his palms. "You both are talking. Right now. This is enough."

Julien brushed a flyaway hair from Shay's forehead, and when she slapped his hand away, he laughed. "We're going to be outside guarding the door, so don't even think about leaving." He took a step backward, Asher in stride, and said, "That means you, too, Raina."

After they'd gone, Shay wouldn't look at me. Instead, she rolled her eyes, and then rolled her head back against the seat. She stuffed a french fry into her mouth, chewed it purposefully, and still, she wouldn't look at me.

"Child," I muttered.

She looked up, stuck her tongue out, and took out her phone.

"Typical *Shay*."

Another moment passed by, and then she set down her phone, dug into her purse, and retrieved a copy of *White Teeth*. My copy of *White Teeth*. She roughly flipped through the pages and lifted up the book so it blocked her face.

I slid her plate toward me—three-quarters of a chicken sandwich, a fistful of fries—and then reached to the side for a bottle of mustard and noisily opened the lid. She moved the book down an inch. I smiled as I slowly flipped over the bottle and then squeezed it as hard as I could, yellow mustard in thick swirls pooling over the entire plate.

Shay hated mustard.

"What the hell?" She tossed the book to the side. "I was eating that."

"I'm sorry." I stuffed three fries into my mouth. "Did you just speak to me?"

"You're such a child."

"Yes." I nodded. "*I* am the child."

"A child. And a liar." She reached for the plate, and I swatted her hand away. "And a brat—"

"Shay." I pulled the plate back, so hard that her butt rose off the seat. "Let go!"

"You let go!" She tugged on it, and then I tugged back, and just then, the plate flipped over and everything toppled onto the table in a big angry flop. "Look what you did!" cried Shay.

"Me?"

"Yes—*you*." Her voice was hoarse, and as we used paper-thin napkins to scoop the mashed fries back onto the plate, I looked up at her and saw that she was crying. Thick tears rolling down her cheeks. I handed her a napkin, and she roughly wiped her face.

After a moment, she stopped crying. She balled the napkin up in her palms, and then tossed it at me. It ricocheted off my shoulder and dropped into my lap. I picked it up, and then threw it back at her, hitting her square in the nose.

She smiled, and then a moment later, the happy expression on her face disappeared.

What had happened to us?

A waitress came by and glared at both of us as she grabbed the dirty plate, and then again we were left in silence. The diner was mostly empty, a few quiet tables closer to the front with children and grandparents, teenagers on day-dates. A speaker above us was playing the easy listening radio station, the tune and lyrics barely audible, but entirely familiar.

Shay stared at her hands, and I knew she was working up the courage to apologize. That face—sheepish, red, and sullen—I'd seen it a hundred times; Shay facing up to her mistakes, Shay acknowledging when she was wrong and trying to make amends.

But this time, if I were honest with myself, was it really *her* fault?

Why did it feel so awful that my best friend fell in love before me? Even after she started dating Julien, hadn't Shay always been there for me? Hadn't she always supported me whenever Mom came home, and when Nana died? And when Dev and I ended, how many times had she shown up in the middle of the night with half a caramel cheesecake and a bag of popcorn, determined to cheer me up? Belted out Coldplay until my sobs turned to laughter and the neighbors complained?

And what had I done for her?

I'd been too busy making sure my calendar matched Dev's to invite her to visit me in London. I'd pushed her away whenever she tried to help. I'd distanced myself as her wedding approached, as her residency drew to a close: whenever her life went right and, seemingly, mine went wrong. I'd lied to her, abandoned her when she needed me.

It was my fault: The fight. The lie that ballooned with each day that passed. It was all my fault.

"I'm sorry," I said finally.

Shay looked at me, a surprised look on her face. Her smile reappeared, and then she shrugged. "I'm sorry, too."

"No, *really*, I'm sorry—"

"I was such a bitch to you."

"What I said was horrible, too, Shay."

"I was just so angry, you know? I was angry, and I just didn't—

I *don't*—understand what's going on, why you're lying to everyone—"

"It's okay, Shay." I paused, and took a deep breath. "And I guess . . . I just couldn't believe you're getting married."

I looked away, embarrassed by the blunt and bitter truth: I couldn't believe Shay was getting married, and I couldn't believe it wasn't me.

Shay reached across the table and found my hand. "It's okay."

I blinked, trying to force away the tears, and she squeezed my hand until I looked her in the eye.

"Are you ready to tell me the truth now?"

Wasn't this why I came? Wasn't I ready?

"What can be so bad, Raina, that you're lying to everyone about *this*?"

I told her. Over two pieces of fresh pecan pie and cups of coffee, the whole story came out. I told her how Dev was back in my life—sort of—and I still didn't know what to do or what it meant. I told her about Nani—the dates, the pressure, the slip-of-the-tongue lie—and how annoyingly supportive she was being. I told her about Depesh, that I'd been talking to or texting him almost every day. How we'd talk about his feelings of isolation and disappointment, of having to lie about who he was to everyone he knew.

I told her about the situation snowballing, how I had no idea how to fix this without hurting him, without hurting Nani, and that I needed her help; I needed my best friend's help.

When I finally stopped talking, I was close to tears. Shay hadn't said a word the whole time, her face expressionless.

"Well?" I asked.

"Well"—she paused, pressed her lips together—"truth is, Raina, I don't know what the hell we are going to do."

Despite everything, I smiled. *We.* Shay and I were back.

"Jesus, don't *cry*," she said. She stood up from the booth, walked around the table, and sat down next to me. She wrapped an arm tightly around my shoulder, and I let my head fall onto hers. I could smell her shampoo, her soothing tang of sweat and hospital scrubs.

"You okay?"

I shook my head. "Seriously, what am I going to do?"

Abruptly, she pushed me off her, and then angled her body to face me on the seat.

"You can't go on pretending forever, but we're not going to tell anyone until we've figured out how to handle it," Shay said a moment later. "At some point, this is all going to come out. You're going to have to tell Depesh and your nani. We're just delaying the inevitable."

I looked up at her and nodded. I knew that, too.

"And your nani . . ." Shay sipped her coffee, and then set it back down. "She'll be okay, I think. She's resilient. Maybe we *should* tell your nani now. It would be hard, but she'll understand, won't she? She'd keep the secret until the time is right?"

I'd been asking myself those questions for weeks, and I still didn't have a clear answer.

"When is the right time though, Shay?"

"Down the road, after Depesh comes out? After he's more—I don't know—comfortable with himself?" Shay sighed, and wrapped her hand around her coffee cup. "At some point—whenever that is, whenever you tell him the truth—you're going to hurt him, and he may never trust you again. There's no way around that."

I'd racked my brain so many times, conjured up a million scenarios where he, my nani, didn't get hurt; but there weren't any.

"Everyone thinks I'm gay," I blurted. "How is it going to be okay? Now, how is anyone ever going to look at Nani the same after the truth comes out?" I laughed, despite myself. "How is *she* going to look at me after this? I've seen her browser history. You know, she's been *so* supportive, I think she might actually want me to marry a woman? Have children with a woman? I don't know how I let it get this far."

"You'd do anything for her, Raina. Everyone knows that." Shay shrugged. "And she'd do anything for you, even accept—"

"That her granddaughter isn't actually a lesbian?"

"Just a bit of a liar," said Shay, rolling her head backward onto the booth. "Shit, I should really go."

"Already?"

Shay nodded. "I have to train the new residents, and then go help Ma with—I don't know—*something*."

"How are the wedding plans?"

Shay groaned. "She has been such a pain. The three of us brought home *eleven* suitcases from India. Eleven. Can you believe it?" She reached for her coffee cup. It was empty, and she slammed it back down on the table. "I don't even know what's in the stupid things. It's turning into such a spectacle—ugh—and to think, Julien and his family wanted a tiny church wedding."

"And what did you want?"

She shrugged, and then in the clearest of voices, said, "I just wanted him."

I turned around in the booth and glanced out the front window. Julien and Asher were still standing on the sidewalk just outside, arms crossed, talking to each other. I looked back at Shay.

"Do they know I'm . . ."

Shay smiled. "Julien thinks whatever Ma has been telling him. I haven't said anything about this; that bozo can't keep his mouth shut. Did you know they have dinner together when I'm working late?"

"I did know, actually."

"And Asher—well, he thinks it was a *damn* good kiss for a lesbian—"

"You know about that?"

"Of course I know." She glanced at her watch, and then reached across the table for her purse. "But I have to go back to work. And you're going to call me tonight and tell me what the hell has happened between you two, okay?"

"Promise."

She stood up, fumbling with her coat and scarf. When she was all wrapped up, I got out of the booth and stood beside her. She came up to my nose.

"Shay"—I paused, struggling to find the words—"all this time, you never told anyone I was lying? Not Auntie Sarla, not Julien or Asher? . . . Why?"

"I was *mad*," she said, rolling her eyes. "But I'm still your best friend. I was never *not* going to cover your ass."

NINETEEN

After she disappeared from the diner, I took my time finishing my pie. When I finally left, I saw Asher standing across the road propped against a lamppost, waiting for me. For some reason, I wasn't surprised he was still there. I put on my sunglasses and, through their shelter, took in his broad, shadowy physique. The strong line of his jaw, upturned corners of his mouth. He smiled as I crossed the road toward him, and I found myself smiling back.

We wandered aimlessly, wrestling our way through the downtown sidewalks. It was one of those rare winter days that almost felt like spring, and the whole city felt alive; everyone seemed to be outdoors, their winter parkas tied hastily around their waists, shopping or sporting bags flung over one shoulder.

It wasn't until we'd walked past my office building that I realized that some twenty floors above, Bill and Zoey were probably waiting for me; that I'd told him I'd come in and help with the next report. I looked behind me as the skyscrapers fell away and followed Asher toward the lake, resolving not to think about it. Resolving, for now, not to care.

Cherry Beach was spotted with snow, and as we walked westward along the lake, a breeze picked up and I shivered.

"Are you cold?" he asked. "Do you want my coat?"

I shook my head. He took off his sunglasses and squinted at me for a moment, and then, smiling, he put them back on.

"Have you and Shaylee made up?"

I nodded.

"In New York, she didn't take your news well, I'm guessing."

I didn't say anything, timed my footsteps with his.

"People don't always understand what's not right in front of them." Asher's feet kicked sand up onto mine. "Not right away, at least. And how much can we really blame people for not knowing better? But then—when they do know better—I think we can blame them for not trying."

I swallowed loudly. Asher thought I was gay; he thought the fight was about me being gay.

"I think she's trying." I felt him looking at me, and after a moment, he continued. "I haven't told you about my sister, Anna, have I?"

I kicked a loose rock. "Have you?"

"About the time she swallowed everything in the bathroom cabinet and had to have her stomach pumped?"

"Asher, that's horrible."

"It was. She's okay now—thank God—but at the time, Anna was just a kid who needed help." He shrugged. "She's gay, and she didn't know how to deal with it—not even in a progressive family like ours. I can't imagine what it would have been like for someone growing up someplace less . . . tolerant."

He looked over at me expectantly, and my stomach felt as if it might tear in two.

Asher's sister was gay?

"Anyway, Anna's happily married now," he said after a moment. "Jess is great. They have two kids in the suburbs. Piano lessons, bake sales, the whole deal. But it just terrifies me to think how easily none of that could have happened. Actually"—he glanced at me—"it's one of the reasons I wanted to be a teacher. Kids should be happy, you know? I never want to see what happened to Anna happen to anyone else."

I nodded, stared furiously at my shoes as we toed our way across the sand. Asher's sister was gay, and like Depesh, it had been a struggle for her to accept it. I was making light of that. I was making a mockery of everything.

Would Asher understand? I wanted to tell him the truth, too. I barely knew him, but I already sensed that I could trust him, that despite everything he *would* understand. We stopped at a part of the sandbar that jutted out into the lake; a small peninsula of granulated rock and glass, and I stared across the water.

"I heard you're done with teacher training?"

"Yep. I've got a full-time position at your old high school. I'm teaching history, English, politics—"

"Basketball?"

He grinned. "Of course."

My stomach tightened. "Asher, look"—I breathed out—"I need to talk to you about something."

"If it's all the same to you"—he glanced away—"I'd rather not."

"But—"

"In New York, I"—he hesitated—"I got carried away. That's all."

Was that all?

"It's all behind us, for better or for worse. I've thought about you a lot since New York. And in hindsight it really does make sense."

"What does?" I whispered.

"Maybe it's growing up with Anna, or traveling and meeting so many other—I guess you could say—*lost souls*. You have that same look. Like you feel completely inadequate despite your accomplishments. Like you're struggling to fit in, searching for something else, and—"

He paused, looked me straight in the eye, and I knew this was my chance to tell him the truth. Tell him that I had lied, and dug myself into a hole so deep that I needed help getting out. That I *was* searching for something else—and even though I wasn't quite sure what it was, or how my life might ever make sense—that maybe, around him, it didn't need to make sense.

He was looking at me, his breathing deep, but I didn't know what to say—or how to say it. His gaze was too heavy. His longing— I felt it—was too much. The moment passed, and I didn't say anything.

"—and, I suppose," continued Asher, glancing back at the water, "what you were looking for . . . I just never guessed it was this."

Asher . . . What just happened!?

WAY TOO GOOD FOR ME

TWENTY

Asher invited me to go watch the Toronto Raptors game with him and a few of his friends, but I declined with an excuse about work, even though I'd already e-mailed Bill to tell him I couldn't come in. I walked Asher to a sports bar just off Queen West and continued north, but I didn't go straight home, either. And it was somewhere between Dundas Square and College that it hit me.

I had feelings for Asher. Real feelings. And the more I thought about it, the more palpable and real they felt. How was it even possible? Sure, he wasn't Indian. We'd led polar opposite lives, and I wasn't sure we had that much—if anything—in common. Then what was it about him that made me feel so stable? With Dev I'd been out of breath constantly, chasing him, always pushing for a different kind of life, but when I was with Asher, it felt like everything was exactly how and where it was supposed to be.

When I got home, I flopped down on my bed and texted Depesh, asking him if he wanted to catch up for dinner that evening, and then opened my laptop. I was staring at the home screen, trying to figure out what it was I needed to do to prepare for the week ahead, when I received a notification from Dev requesting a video chat.

I don't know why I answered. He was in Hong Kong now, and I lay faceup on my bed as Dev nattered away to me about the politics of our foreign office, even though all I wanted to do was tell him to shut up so I could be alone to eat a bag of salt and vinegar chips, and watch bad TV.

He steered his webcam around the patio of his suite, out toward the view of the harbor.

"Look what's just cropped up there—the Central Plaza, you see it?"

I nodded, and then realized he wasn't looking at me. "Yes, I can see it."

"Huge, innit?"

He turned the camera back to face him. He was wearing sunglasses and a tangerine polo with the top two buttons undone, and as his pixelated smile filled up my screen, I felt that familiar surge. The shortness of breath. That smile—the way he could wield it as both shield and sword.

"It's great, Dev. Looks like you're having a nice time."

I didn't recognize the shirt. Had a woman bought it for him? I wondered whether he even had time for women with the hours he worked—and it was me he had been calling whenever he had a spare moment, wasn't it? A part of me wanted to scream, ask who had bought him that shirt, and what we were, and why he couldn't have made up his mind to commit already.

The other part of me was just too exhausted to care anymore.

"Your work all right, darling?"

"It's okay. Busy. But okay."

"That's the beauty of it though. The business, the rush, don't you reckon?"

"Yeah, sure."

"Complacency, Raina. It doesn't suit you."

"Yeah, well . . ." I thought about what to say next: that neither does this job—after Dev and I split, had it lost its last redeemable feature? Dev glanced behind him and out onto the harbor. The image wasn't clear, but clear enough, and I could tell from his tensed chin, the square of his jaw, that his mind had already wandered off. He wasn't looking at the blues, yellows, and grays of the morning skyline, enjoying the few minutes he would spend outdoors. He was already thinking about that day's agenda; the intense session at the gym he'd fit in between client meetings, the conference call in the back seat of the 5 Series on the drive back to the office.

Dev had traveled constantly while we were together. Direct flights from Heathrow, gone for two days, or two weeks—then the fast train to Paddington, and back to the office. After each business trip abroad, I'd swing by his office with two coffees and pastries from Pret, and he'd have nothing to say about the observation deck on the Burj Khalifa or the white sands of Copacabana. Wiping the crumbs from his chin, he'd tell me about the swanky boardrooms in our Dubai office, the portfolio he'd sorted out in Rio—complaining about what went wrong, or what they had but we didn't. Dev wanted it all, to be a part of the whole world. But going that fast, I always wondered if he'd end up missing out on everything.

I heard my cell phone buzz on the end table.

"Where'd you go, love?"

"Hmm?" I said to the screen. Dev's picture had frozen—his mouth open, tongue slightly curled—and I waved my hand.

A second later, his screen unfroze. I picked up my phone. It was

Depesh, suggesting a ramen place nearby my condo, and I replied with a thumbs-up emoji.

"I have only twenty minutes, and you're going to chat with someone else?" I heard Dev say.

"Excuse me? You can run off for however many months, but I can't look at a *text*?"

"Raina, please don't."

"You call me when it's a good time for you, but did you even ask whether now is a good time for me? Did you ask me how my day was, except for *work*? Do you even know what else is happening in my life? Have you once asked me how Nani is doing? Or Shay?"

He held up a hand to the screen, and I heard him sigh. "Sorry, you're right. I don't want to fight, darling. I'm knackered. I slept like shit last night, and—"

"And it's always about you, isn't it?" I pressed my lips together. He repositioned his screen, and his face was closer now.

Was this the man I was waiting for? Was I—months later—still waiting for *him*?

"I need to know," I said, looking at my hands. "Are you coming back to Toronto?"

"Soon, Raina."

"What does *soon* mean? In a week, a few months? Maybe never—"

"Where is this coming from?"

"You're a smart guy, Dev. It's not that difficult."

"Raina, we've never played games with each other. Yes, I'll be the first admit I wasn't—I *haven't*—been great to you." He ran his hands through his hair. "But being away, bouncing around between offices . . . It's been hard for me, too."

"I'm so sorry this has been hard on *you*. Truly sorry."

"I've never led you on, darling. I've always been honest—*we've* been clear about the situation between us. You knew when I came to Toronto we weren't quite sure whether I could . . . that I was still . . ." He trailed off, and I could feel my ears burn.

He was right. I'd gone along with what he said, what *he* wanted, desperate to make him happy; convinced that it would make me so, too. But what for? When had I become this woman—weak, desperate—my everything dependent on him? I'd lied—I'd created this whole mess—because I loved him, but I was so tired of it.

All of a sudden, I was so fucking tired of him.

". . . you know how I feel about you. I just don't know what else to—"

"Dev," I said, interrupting him. "Let *me* be clear then. Crystal clear." I took a deep breath, and stared straight into his pixelated eyes. "Come back. Don't come back. It doesn't even matter anymore."

"Darling, you *can't* mean that."

Didn't I mean it, though?

"I mean it," I said, slowly. Firmly.

"Raina—"

"Because I'm done waiting for you."

I slammed the laptop shut. My bedroom was silent. Murky dark, except for the sliver of light coming in from beneath the door. I got off the bed and opened the curtains, stared out into the dark night.

And then I closed my eyes, let the tears drop; finally ready to let Dev fall away.

~~Dev . . . ?~~ Never. Again.

TWENTY-ONE

"You are inviting that woman *here*?" Nani had asked me, when I announced I'd invited Auntie Sarla and Shay over for tea.

I nodded, pulling a box of *laddoo* out of the Deepfreeze.

"And she agreed?"

"Yep."

She stared at me as I set the sweets out on a china platter, and then disappeared upstairs. Shay and I had been planning the reconciliation for weeks—an afternoon tea where we'd force Nani and Auntie Sarla to set their differences aside, and be friends again.

They'd always had an unusual relationship, one based on both rivalry and genuine affection. Auntie Sarla had been Nani's saving grace when our family had moved to Toronto. She'd helped Nani grow the restaurant, and had supported her after Mom got pregnant. Even though Auntie Sarla was everything negative about our Indian traditions incarnate, Nani had lost her friendship because of me. And while I would never truly forgive Auntie Sarla for her judgment, I wanted Nani to.

"Raina?" I heard Nani call, as she walked down the steps.

"Yes?"

"Can you give me hand?"

I went into the living room and stopped short in my tracks. She was holding up a giant rainbow flag, and it was nearly as tall as she.

She had bought a pride flag? What the hell had I done? My stomach lurched as I wrestled with whether to just spit it out: tell Nani I wasn't actually gay. Zoey and now Shay were on my case to tell her the truth, but I kept finding excuses. One week Nani had the flu, and the next I had to be in Montreal for a few days for a seminar.

"I was thinking we should put above the mantelpiece."

And in moments like these, when I did find myself face-to-face with Nani, I knew deep down that I should tell her. That I *wanted* to tell her.

But I never managed to do it.

"Amazon sent it to me." Nani moved her hands, and it sent a wave down the fabric. "Don't you think it's nice to have it out for"—she smiled sweetly—"our *guest?*"

I opened my mouth. I was ready, wasn't I?

"Nani . . ."

"Hah, my sweet?"

I hesitated, and then I shrunk back. "Do you think the flag matches the room?"

"It matches perfectly," she snapped. "It is absolutely *perfect.*"

They were an hour late. Auntie Sarla opened the front door and marched in like she lived there, Shay following, rolling her eyes in my direction as she sat down on the couch opposite us. Nani turned off the television, and as Auntie Sarla stood in front of the three of us, her hand planted firmly on her hips, no one said a word. Shay and I looked at each other, trying not to laugh as Nani and Auntie Sarla stared at each other in silence. Finally, Auntie Sarla sighed, and dramatically folded herself onto the couch next to Shay.

"Sarla." Nani smiled at the ground. "Do you like our new decorations?"

Without looking up, Auntie Sarla growled. "Suvali, I am saying this once. I am here against my will. Shaylee is the one who insisted—"

"Ma, please—"

"No, no," Auntie Sarla cut her off waving a hand. "*She* should know. I am not okay with this—I am not okay with either of you, but"—Auntie Sarla cleared her throat, and glared around the room accusingly—"Shaylee *insisted* that we all get along."

"I threatened to cancel the wedding." Shay smiled at me as she reached for the bowl of cashews. "And I was serious, too."

Through gritted teeth, Nani and Auntie Sarla spent the next hour discussing preparations for the *sangeet*. The billeting of various relatives and friends flying in from Jaipur, Singapore, and Dubai; where they would stay and what they would eat. It was almost back to normal, and Nani and Auntie Sarla were bickering about something inconsequential when Shay sidled over to my couch.

"I need to tell you something," whispered Shay.

I glanced over at Nani and Auntie Sarla. They were still discussing Shay's great-uncle's dietary restrictions and weren't listening to us. I looked back at Shay. "What is it?"

"Asher is seeing someone."

I felt my heart drop.

"Thought you might want to know."

I nodded, and wondered what gave me the right to care so much. He and I were friends. I let him believe I wasn't interested in his entire sex. What else could I expect?

"She's another teacher at his school. I'm sorry . . ." Shay kissed me on the forehead. "But she's a bit of an idiot. I wouldn't worry"— her head turned—"*what*, Ma?"

I looked up, and Auntie Sarla was staring at us, her mouth frozen mid-sentence.

"What, am I not allowed to *kiss* my best friend?" Shay snapped.

Auntie Sarla growled, and then she tore her eyes away from us. "*Disgusting.*"

"Stop it." Shay's voice shook. "Raina's no different than before."

"This is true. Raina was *never* a good girl."

"Sarla," said Nani. "Do not speak about Raina like that. Not in my house."

Auntie Sarla laughed, and gestured to Nani. "But what could we expect? Another one raised by *her*."

"Ma," said Shay unsteadily. "I'm warning you. You think I'm kidding, but so help me—if you don't stop—"

"Fine, fine." Auntie Sarla smiled and reached for her tea. "It's all fine." She glanced pointedly at Nani, and then toward me. "I am sorry." She smiled, and spoke slowly. "I am very, *very* sorry."

Nani's face was bright red, and I could tell she was breathing hard. I tried to catch her eye, but she just kept staring at Auntie Sarla.

"Would you like some water?" I asked Nani. She didn't answer. "Nani?"

She was shaking, and I felt myself shaking, too. She was fighting for me, but why was I putting her through this? Whatever her reaction to my deception, it couldn't be worse than this. I needed to tell her the truth, *now*, but first I needed to get Auntie Sarla out of the house.

"Auntie, maybe we should continue the plans later—"

"Yes. Very good idea. She needs to *leave*. I am not taking this—I am not taking *her*—any longer," said Nani. She stood up and pointed at the door. "Leave, Sarla. Right now. This is not acceptable treatment. You have been an interference *too* long—"

"I am being honest. Are friends not honest?" Auntie Sarla stood up also, face-to-face with Nani. "We have been friends for more than *thirty* years, Suvali—"

"You insult us. You insult Raina. She is a wonderful girl, and I am proud of her." Nani reached for the phone. "Let's call her girlfriend. I'll *show* you, you ignorant woman—this Zoey girl is more decent than—"

"Nani, Zoey and I are just friends—"

"—some of these boys she could have married. She is more decent than your husband, than *my* husband—"

"Can Zoey give her children? No. It is *wrong*, Suvali. I am trying to help. Have I not always helped you?"

"No, you—"

But then the phone rang, a shrill, reminding pierce that silenced us all. It was Depesh.

Sharon Auntie was in hospital.

TWENTY-TWO

The waiting room was full, and I crouched down on top of a vent in the hallway opposite. It was chock-full of Indians—some I recognized, some I didn't—and I kept my eyes low. Beneath the white fluorescent lights, my hands looked ghostly pale. I picked at a piece of dirt beneath my fingernails.

Shay had used her ID badge to sneak Nani and Auntie Sarla into the ICU, past the barricade of nurses and attendants who refused to let Sharon Auntie's other friends through. I checked my phone again. Shay hadn't responded to my last text, but as I scrolled through my alerts, I saw another e-mail from Dev.

These days, his messages came often; they were verbose, but said absolutely nothing. And every time I read one, and then forced myself not to reply, I tried not to wonder what my life would have been like if I'd listened to Nani and Shay when they first told me I should cut off all contact. What my life would have been like if I'd given myself the chance to move on.

"Raina? Is that *you*?"

I looked up. An auntie was standing just in front of me, and I stood up to hug her. She smelled like old clothes and soured perfume, and I racked my brain for her name.

Poonam? Vish-*mi*? She was in one of Nani's temple community groups, but I couldn't remember which one. I smiled at her, and we made stilted brief small talk—in English, with whatever Hindi words I knew thrown in—and then she continued on her way.

I watched her as she found a free seat at the far end of the waiting room. She sat down between some other aunties I recognized, and a moment later, I saw them all turn and look in my direction.

I looked back at my hands. It was the first time I'd seen any of them since Christmas. What were they saying? Which ones cared that I was supposedly gay, and which ones didn't?

Did it matter?

I looked up and saw Shay walking toward me, and I stood up.

"How is she?"

"She's good." Shay smiled. "Completely fine. It's not a relapse. She fainted, and Depesh brought her in to be safe. They're going to keep her overnight."

"Is Depesh in there?"

"He said he was going down to the cafeteria. Ma and your nani took over the room the instant they got in there. I'm surprised the doctors are letting them stay."

"What are they doing?"

"They're coordinating a phone tree to raise money for home care, figuring out who gets to cook Depesh dinner"—Shay rolled her eyes—"arguing over whose Tupperware they should use."

"Wow."

"Yeah," said Shay. "Looks like the gruesome twosome are back together."

I nodded, and looked back down the hall.

Within the hour, the news had traveled and dozens in the community had shown up in support of Sharon Auntie. It was strange—how connected we really were. An invisible safety net that I'd never really stopped to think about. As frustrating as they could be . . . I knew that they'd be there for Nani and me, too. They always had.

"Who are you looking at?"

I shrugged.

"It's embarrassing, isn't it?" Shay said after a moment. "The way some of them are acting."

"And what are we supposed to do? Do we accept them for how they are, and blame it on their upbringing? Appreciate everything that's good"—I turned back to Shay—"and try and not focus on the bad?"

"I guess so, *yeah*"—she pushed her hair out of her eyes—"but I don't know, Raina. I don't know if I have an answer for that."

There was good and bad, light and dark—yin and yang—to everything, wasn't there? Their homophobia, their reluctance to accept what they didn't understand—wasn't that just a relic of tradition? Something bound to be trampled on over time?

I heard Shay sigh, and I glanced back at her.

"I don't know if I've ever explicitly said it to you—if I've ever said—but I'm sorry for the way my mother has treated you and your nani."

"I brought it on myself, didn't I?"

Shay crossed her arms, and I knew exactly what she was about to say. "Depesh didn't."

I found him at the farthest table in the cafeteria. His hair was greasy, and he had dark rings under his eyes. He was staring out the window—a dark sliver peeking out into the parking lot—and he didn't see me until I was right next to him.

"Mind if I join?"

He shook his head and dropped his legs off the chair. I sat down, and he leaned in, hunched over the table. His eyes and the tip of his nose were red.

"How are you doing?"

He didn't answer, smiled halfheartedly at the table.

"Your mom can go home tomorrow," I said. "Have you heard? She's completely fine."

He wouldn't meet my eye.

"Depesh, what are you thinking?" I whispered. "You can tell me."

"I don't know, Raina." He sighed—an exasperated, frustrated sigh. "My mom is in hospital, she has a disease that one day might actually kill her, I'm in the middle of writing final exams—and all I can think about right now is a guy." He shrugged. "A *guy*."

"You met someone?"

He nodded.

I smiled and poked him in the arm. He didn't look up, and I kept poking him until he smiled, too.

"Tell me about him." I leaned back in my chair. "But only if you want."

"His name is Caleb, and we met in Human Biology a while ago . . . He's one of the friends I told you about."

"So he's a friend?"

Depesh smiled, shaking his head. "Not anymore. Yesterday, we"—Depesh paused—"Raina, I'm falling for him. I want to be with him."

"Depo, you *can* be with him."

"No." He shook his head. "I can't. Not the same way everyone else is."

"What do you mean?"

"I want to hold his hand. Like, I want to show him the house I grew up in—and bring him as my date to—I don't know, Thanksgiving dinner with my family. I'll never be able to do any of that stuff."

"You don't know that . . . Remember what Zoey said?" I sat up straighter in my chair. "You have to work up to telling your parents, work *yourself* up to it. Besides Caleb, you've talked to people, right? You told me some of your new friends know now?"

Depesh nodded.

"And how was that?"

He shrugged. "It was fine. They were great about it. But my parents, Ma is sick, and—and—"

"Your mom is getting the treatment she needs. She's getting stronger overall." I leaned in closer. "There's never going to be a right time, Depesh. If you want to come out to them, then—"

"They think I'm some kind of *dream* child, Raina. They respect me and love me, and *rely* on me—how am I supposed to take that away?" Depesh shook his head. "Raina, you think Auntie Sarla is bad. You should have heard what they said about you."

I pressed my lips together.

"They are who they are, and if they can't—or *won't*—change, how are they ever going to look at me the same again?"

A strange silence passed between us, and I became conscious of the wind-like rustling in the vent along the wall; a vacuum roaring faintly in another wing of the hospital.

"When I was younger—maybe you were too young to remember—but you should have seen the way people used to look at me when I was little, before my mother moved out. You should have seen how they looked at my whole family." My breath caught. "Do you know she was sixteen when I was born?"

He shook his head.

"And do you remember Vikram Prasad's wedding, about ten years ago?"

Again, he shook his head.

"Half his family didn't show up for the wedding because he didn't marry a Hindu."

"Really?"

I nodded. "And now? I'm all grown up, and does anyone care about how I was born? Does Auntie Sarla—does anyone in our community—care that Shay is marrying a white Catholic guy?"

He shook his head. "No. They don't."

"A lot of them are behind the times. It's going to be hard for the first person to do anything different." I smiled. "But as much as Auntie Sarla—as much as everyone—talks shit, and bickers, they stick together. Yes, they're judgmental—and *yes*, it's fucking frustrating when they don't see things the way we do, but this community is a family, and it's always stuck together."

I heard him swallow.

"And whether your parents kick you out, cut you off, cry, scream, disown you—they're still your family. And they're still going to love you."

He nodded.

"If you tell them, it's going to be hard, Depesh. I'm sorry that I can't change that for you. But—but you're brave enough to be that person, okay? I know you. I know that you're the one who's supposed to do this."

"You did it, Raina—you're *doing* it now."

I swallowed hard, and the guilt tore through me.

"But, maybe you're right." He took a deep breath, and looked me right in the eye. "Maybe I can be brave, too."

TWENTY-THREE

A few days later, I found myself parked outside of Depesh's house. He was sitting on the front step, elbows on knees. The summer I babysat for him, we used to sit on the porch step of his old house and wait for his parents to come home from the hospital; we'd eat ice cream or grape Popsicles, wash our sticky hands and faces with the garden hose before going back inside. He was a kid then, and now? I got out of the car and walked toward him, hopped over the cracked cement, and realized that he wasn't a kid anymore. He was going to face the truth about himself to the people he loved; he was going to do what most adults never have the courage to do. What I didn't have the courage to do.

I sat down beside him. The block was more run-down than it had been the decade before; trees and shrubs overgrown, taking over the sidewalks and fences; graffiti trimming the lampposts and the fire hydrants.

"How did your Chemistry final go?"

"It was good." He shrugged. "Physics is tomorrow . . . Human Biology the day after that."

"That sounds heavy . . . Are you sure you're—"

"I'm ready, Raina. I'm as ready as I'll ever be."

Was this the definition of bravery? Someone who didn't make up excuses, or find reasons to put off the inevitable? A boy—no, a man—who was about to come out to his parents, and stand up for who he was—in the middle of his exams?

"It might even be better this way, right?" He laughed. "They can't come down on me too hard if I have to study tonight."

"You know, Depo . . . I'm really proud of you."

He didn't reply, and then after a moment, he whispered, "They won't be."

"No," I said. "Probably not." I turned to face him, waited until his eyes met mine. "But you'll be proud of you."

"You don't know that."

"If you respect yourself, your own choices"—I looked back out toward the road—"isn't that what matters?"

A group of kids were walking by, drowned in skipping ropes and plastic traffic cones, soccer balls and netting, giggling, stamping across the pavement in a tight pack. They were oblivious in their own happiness. In silence, we watched them pass, and I wondered how many of them would one day have to go through what Depesh was experiencing right now.

As they grew up, as they discovered life in its imperfection, weren't there greater problems to dwell on, to agonize over? Far greater than fearing the implications of one's own sexuality. The world was disturbing enough as it was; not just across the world—deserts and oceans away—but right here at home. And before anyone could grow up, grow the courage to change any of it, surely, *home* was where it had to start.

The kids disappeared around the corner, and after their high-pitched voices faded behind them, I could hear Depesh breathing hard beside me.

"I've never disappointed them before, Raina. I've never not been what they wanted me to be."

I turned to him, and steadied his hand in my own. "Who do you want to be, Depesh?"

It went exactly how one might have expected it to go. Yelling and crying. Complete and unabashed outrage. Depesh defended himself. And when Sharon Auntie didn't drop dead in front of us, and his father's yells became hoarser, Depesh suggested that I leave; told me he wanted to handle the rest of it on his own.

It was dark by the time I pulled into the driveway, next to Kris's car. I turned off the ignition, but my legs and spine were frozen to the seat as I prepared myself to go inside and face Nani. I had made light of something I had no right to joke about. Depesh had come out, and I would tell him the truth next, but first, it was finally time to face Nani honestly.

What would she say? I shook my head. It didn't matter. I had to face it—I *wanted* to face it.

It was late, but for some reason, the front door was unlocked. I stepped into the house. The hallway lights were off, the house coated in silence; no television or kettle whistling, or Nani humming or singing or snoring in the background like white noise. All I could hear was the discerning tick of the cuckoo clock as the handle tapped its way around.

I stepped out of my shoes and crept into the living room. It was empty, and as the pale light of the muted television ghosted through the room, I noticed a full mug of tea abandoned on the coffee table.

"Hello?"

I turned, drawn by a noise in the kitchen, a sliver of light beneath the doorway. And when I pushed through, the door swinging wildly open, there they all were sitting at the kitchen table. Space and time, backward and forward; my childhood playing tricks, playing out right in front of me. Nani and Kris in their usual spots, jaws tensed, shoulders slouched. And across from them, seated cross-legged on my chair, there she was.

"Hi, Raindrop." Chin resting on her palm, Mom grinned at me. "So I hear you're a lesbian."

MAY 20, 1996

Nani surprises Raina with all of her favorites: thick yogurt, mango chutney, an *aloo paratha* with extra butter. Raina sits at the kitchen table eating her breakfast, sipping her glass of apple juice from the table without touching it; her top lip curled over the glass, her greasy hands held up as if in surrender. She eats carefully, tearing a piece of the paratha off with one hand the way Nani taught her, dipping it, and then bringing it slowly to her mouth. She has covered herself with three paper napkins. It is hours until her party, but she is already wearing her new dress. Manavi reappeared with it—a belated Christmas present after a trip to Las Vegas last year—and only now has Raina grown into it. It is lavender, the same shade as the pillows on Raina's bed, and she admires herself as she chews; the white and violet frills on the cuffs, the hem that skirts around her knees.

Her feet do not touch the ground, and she swings them as she eats, kicking a ball across an imaginary field. Raina is only partway through her breakfast when the murmurs from downstairs become louder. Staccato and sharp. She slips quietly off her chair and tiptoes toward the door that leads down to the entertaining room. She slides down onto her knees and presses her ear against the door, trying to make out the sounds.

Before, Kris used to take Raina to her room, turn on the radio. If that wasn't enough, he'd press her hands over her ears and tell her to keep them like that until they stopped. But these days, Kris is rarely home, so when they yell, Raina tries to listen; she is curious to understand why everyone seems to be so angry all the time. They yell about the mess of long hair Manavi left in the bathtub drain, or the door she slammed too hard, or the boy who dropped her off. About the right way to teach Raina to tie her shoes. Raina listens hard, but this time their voices are too muffled, as if they know she might be listening.

Raina hears a thumping up the stairs, and she bolts back to her seat, reaches for her glass of juice. Manavi swings open the door, followed seconds later by Nani. Manavi crouches down beside Raina and tugs on one of her braids.

"Do you want to go to Wonderland, Raindrop?"

Raina's eyes widen. "Wonderland?" Her face breaks out into a smile. "Really?"

"Manu . . ."

But Nani stops short when Manavi snaps her head in Nani's direction.

"Yes, Raindrop." Manavi turns her head slowly back to Raina, and blows her bangs from her face. "Let's go. Get your coat."

"Now?" Raina slumps forward. She wants to go, but not today. Today is her seventh birthday, and there will be a party at the new restaurant. "But there's going to be a magic show!"

"Raina, come *on*." Manavi leans back, balancing on her heels. "I got us tickets for today—"

"Please, Manu." Nani is now standing at the kitchen sink, her hands leaning against it like she's trying to catch her breath. She turns to them, and says, "Please, not—"

"I *told* you they're only valid for today!"

"Did you even remember it was her party?" Nani's voice is strained, and Raina looks down. Her eyes start to water when she notices that, despite how careful she's been, a fat droplet of juice has found its way onto her dress.

"So, are we going?" Manavi snaps. "I don't have all day."

Raina's eyes are locked on the stain, and after a moment, she says, "Can we go tomorrow?"

"Tomorrow?"

"But today is—"

"No, we can't go tomorrow," Manavi growls. She stands up in one fluid motion. "I'll go with my friends." And with that, she grabs her leather jacket off the hook, and marches out, mumbling inaudibly until the kitchen door bangs heavily behind her.

The new restaurant is bigger than the last one, Nani says, although to Raina it looks very much the same. Raina and her friends sit around two of the long restaurant tables pushed together. Nani and Nana have decorated them with white plastic tablecloths and gold confetti, pink and purple helium balloons. They have set out supplies like it's art class—with every color of cardboard construction paper, pipe cleaners and Popsicle sticks, cotton balls and glue. The expensive Magic Markers.

Raina makes her crafts sitting next to a boy from her soccer team, and an Indian girl named Shaylee that Nani keeps inviting to the house. When the magician arrives, they are all herded toward a makeshift stage in the corner. Raina sits at the end of the row, and when the magician makes a rubber duck disappear into a hat, her friends gasp. Raina thinks she knows how he did it: the hat is wide and long, and surely, the duck is being hidden inside; in a secret pocket, perhaps. She thinks about raising her hand, or leaning over and telling Shaylee how it happened, but she doesn't want to ruin the trick. So she doesn't say anything.

Next, the magician pulls out a deck of cards, and Raina blinks hard, trying to memorize the sequence, trying to unlock the secret of this trick, too, when she thinks she hears Manavi's voice behind her. She turns around, and is excited to see that Manavi has decided to come to her birthday party. Nani is whispering to Manavi, and although Nani is smiling, flicking her eyes toward Auntie Sarla and the other adults at the back, Raina can tell that her nani is angry. After a moment, they go into the kitchen, and silently, swiftly, Raina follows.

Inside, she can hear their voices, and she ducks behind a garbage bin, carefully peers around the side.

"I don't care—"

"Shh!"

"—what the fuck—they think about me."

"Manu!"

"And don't *shhh* me." Manavi stamps her foot like a child. She is crying, and her words are slurred. Raina has never seen her like this before; at least, not in the middle of the day.

"There is party happening, *nah*? Sarla is here. You must settle down."

"Who cares about *Sarla*?" She grabs a frying pan from the stove and tosses it between her hands. For a moment, Raina thinks she might hit Nani, swing at her with it like a baseball bat, but after a few catches, Nani lunges for it. She knocks it out of her grasp, and it clambers to the floor. Nani reaches down to get it, one hand on her lower back, and then sets the pan back on the stove.

"Never could let me have a little fun, could you?"

"You've been having your fun for a while."

"It didn't start out that way. Did it, Ma?" Silence, and then a moment later, Manavi says, "I'm moving out."

"You've been saying for years. Go ahead. Move out."

"And Raina?"

"She will stay with us."

"You don't have the right—you think *you* have the fucking right to decide that about her?" Manavi laughs. "I dare you. I dare you to stop me."

"You are not taking that girl with you."

"I'll take you to court."

"Take me wherever you like"—Nani takes a deep breath—"but you will not take my Raina."

"She's *my*—"

"Boozing, men—doing God knows what. You coming, going— we never know. Raina never knows. You think you can be her mother?"

"I *am* her mother," cries Manavi, tears rolling down her face and leaving black mascara tracks. "I am her fucking mother!"

"You are not a mother. Grow up. Stop being child. Start acting like you care about Raina, like you want to *be* mother to her—"

Manavi cries harder, slams her fists against the counter.

"—always blaming others. Never your fault, *nah*? Never taking responsibility—"

"I hate—you—you self-righteous *bitch*." Her words pour out in chokes and gasps, and Nani turns her head.

Manavi inches closer to her, and by the way Manavi is leaning against the counter, sobbing, their shoulders nearly touching, Raina has the feeling that if only her nani would turn around, there wouldn't be so much yelling.

But she doesn't turn around, and after a moment, Manavi stops crying. She grabs a roll of paper towels, uses the whole of it to dry her face. Nani is motionless, still facing away. Manavi inches toward her—and then, she retreats.

"You want her?" Manavi stares at Nani's back and, a moment later, whips the roll at her head. "You can *fucking* have her."

TWENTY-FOUR

How long did it take a freaking kettle to boil? I tapped my socks against the linoleum floor as I waited for the water to heat up, crushing cloves, cardamom, and fennel into Nani's favorite teapot. I couldn't find the cinnamon sticks.

"Sugar?" I asked the wall.

No one answered. In fact, no one had said another word since I walked in, and it made me wonder what I'd interrupted. I snuck a look behind me. Kris was pouring himself a glass of whiskey, Mom was looking at something on her phone, and Nani—well, something was wrong. Nani always froze up whenever Mom turned up unannounced, but this time it was different. Worse. Nani's chest was moving up and down too rapidly. And she was sitting down; how could she be out of breath?

When the kettle finally boiled, I poured the water over the tea bags and spices, and then set the teapot on the table next to a carton of milk, Nani's polka-dot sugar bowl, and a few teaspoons.

"Are you not forgetting milk jug?" Mom asked, mocking Nani's accent. "One must never pour guests chai from milk carton, *nah*?"

Nani didn't even flinch. Rolling my eyes, I went into the dining room to fetch the milk jug, and set it down on the table. Mom just laughed, and turned back to her phone.

I sat down fuming. What the hell was she doing here? Had she dumped her latest boyfriend and needed a place to crash? Run out of money again? Around nineteen, I'd stopped wondering when she'd call or visit, and stopped caring when she did.

It was the days after she left that were the hardest. Days when I'd come home and find Nani sitting alone somewhere, her eyes puffy and red, just staring at her hands. Days when I could do absolutely nothing to help.

"No one's talking?" Manavi asked, reaching for the teapot. "What, am I boring y'all?"

Y'all? Was she trying to be funny, or had she really been living in America *that* long?

Nani stood up abruptly from the table, and when Mom looked at her accusingly, Nani just shrugged her shoulders. "I am cold. I am getting something warmer to wear. Do I need your permission?"

The moment Nani stepped out of the kitchen, Mom let out a huge yawn. "Well, this is boring. You, me, and Kris—we should go out after she goes to bed."

I glanced at my watch. It was nearly 8 P.M. I hadn't eaten, and I could feel the beginnings of a headache.

"Why don't we go to a gay bar . . ."

"Hilarious."

"Google tells me there are *six* in a three-kilometer radius. Since when did this neighborhood become cool?"

"Since Drake," Kris said. "I heard somebody in his entourage lives nearby."

"Drake. *Really?*"

"Guys, I'm not going out."

"Don't be such a party pooper, Raindrop."

"Can you *not* call me that?"

Mom's eyes widened as she reached for the teapot. She poured out the cups and then pushed one toward me.

"Thanks."

"Look, Raina . . . I'm sorry I didn't know." I heard her sigh, and I looked back toward her. "You know I'm not in touch with anyone here. If I knew you were going through something like that, I would have called more. I would have come home sooner."

I snorted.

"I'm serious." She nodded earnestly. "Kris called me the other day. He's been having a tough time since Serena broke up with him"—she shrugged—"anyways, he told me you're gay. And I thought . . . I thought that maybe I should come home."

Her voice trailed off, and I didn't respond. She'd come home to make sure I was okay? This time, had she shown up out of the blue for *me*? And not because she needed something? I glanced at Kris. He was staring at his phone, but eventually I caught his eye.

How was it that I had no idea Kris was having a difficult year, or that he had emotions at all? Sometimes I forgot she was his sister, and that they'd grown up side by side. The same parents and upbringing, and the same lethal mix of genes: Nana's nose and Nani's mouth. Big, wide eyes that, when shone right at you, almost hurt.

"I want you to know I'm proud of you," I heard Mom say. "This is really cool."

My cheeks burned. "It's not *cool*."

"Of course it is."

"No, it isn't, I'm . . ." I shut my mouth as Nani walked back into the kitchen, wrapped in the woolly shawl I'd bought her for her sixtieth birthday.

"Hi, Nani."

"Hi, my sweet."

"Should I cook us some dinner?"

"Finally, yes," Mom said, slapping her hands on her thighs. "I'm starving. Anyone else starving?"

"You must be," Nani said, sliding into her chair. "In your condition."

I turned to face Mom, and her pale brown skin looked to have reddened. "What condition?"

The air in the room seemed to have lost its oxygen. Everyone was just staring at me.

"What's going on?"

"Thanks, Ma. I was going to tell her on my own time."

"Wait, what?" I searched Nani's face, then Kris's, but they weren't giving anything away. Mom had leaned forward on the table onto her elbows, and she was rocking side to side. Then, as she stood up, it hit me. Her fuller cheeks, arms, and thighs. The dark circles beneath the eyes. The slight curve of her belly.

"You're . . ."

"Having a baby, yes."

I was frozen to the seat, and only my hands were moving. Shaking.

"You're going to have a baby sister, Raina."

She smiled. Was it a smile?

"Are you going to say anything?"

"I . . ." What was there even to say? "You're forty-*six*."

"So—"

"Are you out of your fucking mind?"

"Hey, now. I have a good doctor—"

"Was it an accident? You just forgot to use a condom, *again*?"

She didn't reply. She leaned toward the counter and grabbed a bag of popcorn, ripping it open.

"You planned it."

"IVF." She nodded, shoveling the popcorn into her mouth. "First try, too. You see, Roger doesn't have kids. We're planning to stay put in Philadelphia. Roger's got a sister there, and his dad's in a nursing home. It'll be good." She paused, sitting down again. "And you know it's only a quick flight from here, an hour and a half. You could do it in a weekend—"

"Why the hell would I visit you?" I was livid, seething, and I didn't recognize my own voice. "I haven't even *met* Roger. And how many times have you come home to see me? How many—"

"Raina, seriously. *Calm* down—"

"I'm *your* daughter!"

"What am I supposed to say, huh? That this is how I thought *my* life would turn out? That I got what I wanted out of life? No. Not even close. But, like I said, Roger never had any kids, and . . ."

And *what*, Mom?

You didn't really come home to make sure I was okay, but to tell your old family you'd started another one?

You actually weren't that different from us "good Indian girls," and you wanted a marriage and children all along?

You just didn't want me?

"Get out."

"Excuse me?"

"This is not your house." I grabbed the milk jug and slid it hard toward her. "Drink from the jug, Manavi. You're only a fucking guest here."

"Can you calm down—"

"A guest no one wants!"

"*She* didn't want me."

"Quit blaming Nani. All the time—"

"Hah," Nani said, standing up. "Manu, you have no responsibility, no shame, no—"

"And *you* were so perfect, Ma?" Mom folded her arms across her chest, and she stood up to meet her. "It's not like this house was a fucking prison!"

Suddenly, it was like I was six years old, powerless, as Mom and Nani stood over me screaming at each other. Kris looked at me blankly, and all I could do was stare back. I half expected him to grab my hand and lead me to the other room, distract me by letting me play with his Lego sets or Game Boy. And between the shouts, couldn't I make out the sounds of Nana shuffling back and forth in his bedroom upstairs? Ignoring everyone? Waiting for it to end.

But would it ever end?

Tears running down my face, I stood up and held my arms out.

How many times had we been here? How many times had I done nothing—just waited, watched, avoided.

But I wasn't a child anymore. I wasn't just helpless Raina.

"Both of you need to stop." I wiped my face, steadied my voice. "It's enough."

Surprisingly, they stopped. Or maybe they were tired of it, too.

I leaned my weight forward onto the table, and stared hard at the surface. "Mom, you're selfish and careless, and even though I know you love us, it wouldn't hurt for you to fucking show it sometimes."

She didn't respond, and I couldn't look up. I couldn't face them.

"Nani, you wanted Mom and me to be perfect daughters . . . find the *perfect* husband." I laughed through my tears. "You think we don't remember how it used to be? How you took care of us, and Saffron, and Nana—and he didn't even lift a finger for you? After watching that, why the hell would we *want* a husband?"

"Do not speak ill of your nana—"

"Did you even love him?" I reached down into my handbag, and pulled out the list. It was crumpled into a ball, and I flattened it before I set it firmly on the table. "Did you even care if I was happy?"

"Raina, my sweet." Was she crying, too? "All I wanted was your happine—"

"No, Nani. You cared about what people at temple thought about *her*, about *me*. And what good is there *possibly* to say about an unmarried Indian girl?"

"My sweet—"

"Why am I not good enough on my own? First I needed a husband, then Zoey, or *someone* else to complete me as a woman?"

I was gasping for air. Was this it? The moment of truth.

"What's the *point* of having a brain, or dreams, or even a heart, if this is all we'll ever be good for, huh?"

She was sobbing into the table now, but I couldn't look at her. I couldn't look at any of them.

"I'm not gay, Nani." I sat back down in the chair. "I was just *sick* of buying into this bullshit."

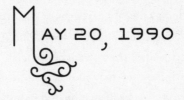

MAY 20, 1990

"Make a wish, my sweet."

Raina sits on her nani's lap, her chubby legs dangling. One of her socks falls off, and Nani reaches down to retrieve it.

"I can do it, Ma." Manavi lunges for the sock, and her head bangs against Nani's with a loud thud.

"*Oy!*" Nani turns to Manavi as she sits back up, plucks the sock from her hand. "Clumsy girl." Nani massages her head with the back of her palm, shifts Raina on her lap.

Raina giggles as her nana brings out a pan of brownies. He slowly cuts them into squares, and the chocolate drizzle drips onto the kitchen table as he sets a thick slice on a small white plate.

"Mine!" Kris licks his lips as he eyes the brownie. He reaches out and digs his finger into the icing, and Nani swats it away.

"First the birthday girl," Nana says, gently scolding. He cuts more slices and passes them around. A cassette of Ravi Shankar plays in the background as they sit and chew the warm cake, as Raina squirms in delight, her pudgy cheeks dropping like jowls. She is still teething and smacks her lips together often, dark brown crumbs falling out of her mouth, and after each bite, her nani licks a napkin, dabs the stains from her chin.

"Just leave it until she's done," says Manavi. "Babies get dirty." But it's as if no one has heard her, because nobody answers.

Raina no longer likes eating baby food. She likes unspiced *aloo gobi*, rice and dal mashed together, spoon-fed by Nani's fingers. She drinks apple juice and mango juice, bottles of fresh whole milk. She knows only the scent of a heated home and a warm bath, the beige and wood paneled walls insulating her existence. She knows only love and security. Abundance and affection.

Raina's skin is lighter than the rest of her family's; and this seems to be something that excites her nani. Her hair sticks out in two short pigtails above her ears, and saliva bubbles out of her lips as she tries to blow out a candle.

Nana focuses the lens of the Pentax. "Say cheese!"

Everyone else is smiling, and so Raina smiles, too.

"Good girl!" Nana sticks out his tongue, and Raina giggles. She claps her hands together as if the performance is just for her.

"Can I hold her now, Ma?"

"Manu, clear the dishes."

"Ma, I want to—"

"Dishes." Nani shifts Raina to her other knee. "*Now.*"

Manavi gets up from the table, a load of dishes piled on her forearm. She turns back to Nani, and whispers, "May I at least put her to sleep tonight?"

"Did you finish schoolwork?"

Manavi breathes hard, sharp, and then she turns back to the sink.

Raina has chocolate frosting all over her face, in her hair, and on her clothes. Nana and Nani carry her upstairs to the bathroom, where they fill a warm bath with strawberry bubbles. Later, they carry her to bed, envelop her in a baby blue sleep suit, and tuck her into her crib.

"How fair she is, *nah*?"

"A beautiful girl," the deeper voice says. "She will have no trouble finding husband."

"It is Manu that will cause trouble. What boy from good family will take her knowing she has mother like this?"

Raina is drifting, her eyelashes batting.

"There are options, Su. We will explain . . ."

Raina's in a dreamlike state, full of chocolate and love and laughter. Nearly asleep, she hears the door shut, then open again. Light cuts into the room. She opens her eyes and, startled, sits up in the crib. Manavi is in the room, and Raina squints as she watches her tiptoe across the carpet, sit down on the floor beside her. Manavi reaches her hand through the rails and strokes her hair, brushes her fingers along her face.

"Say MA-MA."

Raina whimpers.

"MA-MA?" And when Raina says nothing, no noises come to her lips, Manavi stands up, lifts Raina out of the crib. She squeezes her tight, presses their cheeks together. Raina struggles to pull free. She squirms, tries to unfasten her body from Manavi's grip, and when she is unable to, Raina starts to cry.

"Oh, baby. Please don't cry," begs Manavi. She rocks Raina back and forth, pats her on the back lightly the way Nani does. But Raina keeps crying, marble-size tears rolling down her cheeks, and she presses her tiny fists against Manavi. Pounds them—trying to push her away.

"My Raindrop, please—"

"Manu!" The light flicks on, and Nani sweeps into the room. She pulls Raina into her arms and cradles her. "Manu, look what *you* did."

Raina is quickly soothed. She is basked in a warm light and the soft touch of her nani. Comforted, firm in her nani's grasp, she stops crying; and the sharp voices around her fading, she drifts safely toward sleep.

TWENTY-FIVE

"*The Tonight Show*?"

I shook my head. Kris set down his whiskey glass, and then reached for the remote control.

"What about *The Daily Show*?"

"Nah."

"You don't like Trevor Noah?"

"No, I do." I shrugged, pulling the blanket tighter around me. "I'm just not in the mood . . ."

I heard him sigh, and then the television flashed to another channel. Then another. When it stopped on a Katherine Heigl movie, Mom let out a soft grunt of approval. Kris sighed again, and set down the remote.

I couldn't remember the name of the movie, but I'm sure I'd seen it a half dozen times before. Mom, propped up against a pillow on the floor in front of me, moved her head to the side, obscuring my view.

She was pregnant. Again.

She was starting a *family*.

This time she'd get it right; she'd order baby furniture from IKEA and paint the room sunshine yellow, eat her vitamins and rub oil on her belly so she didn't get stretch marks. She'd do things the right way—with *Roger*—with her new perfect daughter.

My whole life, it had taken so much energy to feel *anything* for her—love or hate, apathy or just plain amusement. Now, the feelings came all at once. Jealousy. Rage. Resentment.

Confusion.

After what just happened, here we were watching a movie about bridesmaid dresses, like nothing had happened at all.

Halfway through the movie, a car horn honked outside. Mom pulled herself off the ground. "I guess that's me."

"You don't have to leave," Kris said. He gave me a look, like he wanted me to say it, too.

"I think I do." She let out a short laugh. "Sounds like there's enough going on here without me."

Kris grabbed her duffel bag and headed outside, but Mom just hovered over me. Eventually, I stood up. She was shorter than I remembered; closer in height to Nani than to me.

"I'll come back soon?"

She phrased it like a question, as if she needed my permission. Like I had a say in her decision about the kind of mother she wanted to be. Or could be.

"And you'll think about visiting?"

My stomach clenched, but I nodded. What was there to think about? As hard as it had been, of course I wanted a real relationship with her. I'd always wanted that. She hugged me good-bye, and as she brushed a stray hair off my cheek, I still didn't know if she really wanted that, too.

I sipped whiskey with Kris well into the night, and we fell asleep watching late-night television. In the morning, Kris still sound asleep on the sofa opposite me, I stole into the kitchen and made two cups of tea, then quietly trekked up the stairs.

Both Kris and Mom had suggested I give her space, and so I'd let Nani retreat upstairs—crying, and alone. It was hard, but I'd known all along it would be. I took a deep breath before pushing open the door, but she wasn't in her bedroom. I checked my room, the bathroom, and even Kris's old bedroom, but they were all empty. I took a deep breath, crossed the hall toward the last unopened door. Slowly, I turned the handle and pushed my way through.

Nani was sitting cross-legged in the middle of the bed. Her pastel pink pantsuit stood out against the beigeness of the room. Our family photo album was open on her lap, and her palms were resting on the open page. She looked up at me, blinking, and then snapped the album shut.

What had Nani and Nana expected out of their lives when they left everything behind, and moved across the world? Did they really love each other? Or had their culture, their obligations, and children bound them together?

What had happened in this house before I was born? Or when I was young—too young to remember?

Mom once told me that she wasn't allowed to decorate her room. Nani had torn down all her posters of movie stars and boy bands, and refused to cook breakfast until Mom had folded the stiff white sheets perfectly in all four corners, aligned every pillow.

But I remembered how Mom's wardrobe poured out of her bedroom door like a waterfall, down the stairs, her handmade jew-

elry and shoes flooding the closets, scarves washing up on the end
tables. She was different from everyone I'd ever known. She was
beautiful and interesting and oddly insightful. But Nani had never
seen that side of her; she hadn't wanted to see it.

Was that why Mom left? I couldn't really remember, and every
time I tried, all I could picture was the room spinning around me.
I was sitting waist deep in a pile of her clothes as she slowly plucked
them one by one from around me, and stuffed them into garbage
bags. Nani was holding her tea, looking in from the doorway,
where I was standing now.

Was she crying?

I closed my eyes, clutched the scalding mugs in my hands. Still,
I couldn't remember. It was sunny that day, and the window was
open. It smelled like lawn and pollen. It must have been summer,
but I wasn't sure. All I knew was it was the only day they hadn't
fought. The only day I hadn't fallen asleep with my pillow over my
head, praying it would all stop.

Nani cleared her throat, and I opened my eyes.

How had we gotten here? How had I gotten us here?

I took a deep breath. I sat down beside her on the bed, set the
mugs on the nightstand.

"Manu has gone?"

I nodded.

Nani let out a deep breath. A sigh of relief? Of exhaustion?
Disappointment?

How easy it would be to blame the mess I'd made on Mom, on
Nani's high expectations of us. But I didn't want what was easy.
Finally, I wanted to do what was right.

"I'm sorry I yelled at you. And I'm sorry I lied to you."

Nani's lips pressed together, and then she shook her head.

"I have no excuses, Nani. I made a terrible mistake." Why
wouldn't she look at me? "I'm sorr—"

"You are sorry." Her voice trembled. *"Sorry?* Was I not worthy of truth? Am I not strong, have I not shown you love?"

"Nani—"

"Encouraged you? Protected you?"

"Always."

"Then? What is the truth? I want all of the truth. Right now."

All of the truth. I trembled, looked down at my feet.

"I was tired of you telling me I should get married. Of hearing that I needed someone to be happy. But the *truth* is . . . that's what I thought I needed, too."

Out of the corner of my eye, I could see her blinking at me, her face unchanged. She was waiting for me to continue.

"I was scared. And alone, and then Dev moved to Toronto—"

"Dev?"

I nodded. "He moved here, and I wanted to"—I hesitated—"I *thought* I wanted to—"

"Reconcile," said Nani.

"But we didn't. And we're not going to." I sighed. "I was so ashamed that I still wanted him, Nani. Ashamed of myself. I just—just didn't know how to tell you the truth about him. That's why I let you believe I was gay." Tears again welled in my eyes, and I wiped my face. "I just wanted you to be proud of me, respect my decisions. I didn't"—I swallowed—"want to be another disappointment."

Nani's lips were squeezed together. She didn't say anything, and I inched closer toward her. I could smell the talcum she used, and overwhelmingly, I wanted her back. I wanted my nani—her sweet strength, her imperfections—back in my life.

Tentatively, I reached out and placed my hand on her shoulder. I could feel the weight of her collapse slightly onto me. "I am very sorry."

Her eyes were glued to the floor; she wouldn't look at me. She was barely moving.

"Nani, please say something."

"After Manu . . ." she said finally, "I vowed that this time—with *you*—I would be better. I would, this time, not be like my own mother. But perhaps, this is all of our destinies. I was just as hard on you as with Manu. I must have been too hard on you if you could not tell me this truth."

"You were wonderful, Nani—"

"*Nah*"—tears formed in her eyes—"I failed many, *many* times."

"You did your best. That's all we can do."

"You thought I would blame you for still being in love, Raina. You thought I would *judge*, disapprove." She smiled at me, a fading, distant smile. "Love is never easy, Raina. This I know very well. With your nana"—she sighed—"it was love, but it was not easy."

"I wanted to tell you. I was just so . . . embarrassed."

"There is no shame in love. We make choices, and then, we try and move on the best we can. We try and live with those choices."

I thought about my choices; how many wrong ones I'd made in the last year. I thought about Dev and Asher.

I thought about Depesh.

"Raina, my sweet. Don't cry."

"I wanted to tell you, Nani. But Depesh confided in me that he is gay and . . ."

"Ah." Nani nodded, cutting me off. "I am seeing now what happened. You wanted to help him, *nah*?"

"But I'm not sure it worked."

"What is it you just said to me?" she asked, her eyes twinkling. "You did your best? That is all we can do."

Kris and I both called in sick to work that day. We stayed with Nani, helped her cook and clean the house, and in the afternoon, sat next to her while she watched her silly Hindi soaps. None of us spoke much, and even though Nani accepted my apology, I knew I had yet to earn real forgiveness. I felt lighter, slightly, but my chest was weighed down knowing Depesh still didn't know the truth.

That evening I called Zoey and Shay and told them everything. Zoey was swamped with work and couldn't stay on the phone long, although she was relieved that I was going to come clean as soon as Depesh finished his exams. But Shay sounded strange, and when I called her out on it, she played dumb.

"I'm okay, honestly!" I could feel her smiling at me through the phone, but it was one of her fake smiles. "I'm just . . . stressed."

"Talk to me, Shay. What is it?"

"Nothing, really. I'm just so happy your drama is coming to an end." She laughed. "Now it's time for *wedding* drama . . ."

"Is there anything I can do?"

"Loads. I'm about to add you and Serena to the spreadsheet. Do you know how to use filters?"

I rolled my eyes. "Yes."

"Good, because I don't. And by the way, you're still coming to Julien's birthday party tomorrow night, right? Can you come to the bar early and help me save a few tables?"

"No problem." I paused. "Is—"

"Yes, Asher's girlfriend will be there."

I swallowed hard, nodding at the phone.

"And I don't mean to be harsh," she said softly, "but you're just going to have to deal with it, Raina."

TWENTY-SIX

I stayed the night again. The next morning, I didn't want to leave Nani alone, but she insisted that she was fine and that I go back downtown. That she usually spent the whole of Saturdays at Saffron anyway.

Was she fine? I wanted it to be more than "fine" between us, but that would take time.

Back at my apartment, I spent the afternoon on my balcony—sunglasses, a wool sweater for the wind. I didn't even look at my work e-mails. I tried reading a book that had been sitting untouched on my bedside table for months, but every few pages I found myself distracted, staring at the blank margins as a nervous feeling rose in my stomach.

Eventually, I gave up on the book. I showered and found a charcoal-colored dress that I'd bought in New York and still hadn't worn. I curled my hair, and put on makeup. Staring at myself in the mirror, I took a wet cloth and wiped most of it off.

I was restless, and I fell back onto my bed to keep myself from pacing. I could feel my heart beating in my stomach, and I took a deep breath trying to calm myself down. Why was I so nervous? I was the one that screwed it up, and Asher had moved on. Shay was right. I just had to *deal* with it.

My phone buzzed, and I lunged for it. I thought it might be Depesh, but it was an e-mail from Dev. I pressed delete without reading it, pushing past the curiosity, past that fractional part of me still desperate to know what he was thinking and where he was. Instead, I texted Depesh.

> *Everything OK at home? How did your last exam go? Celebrate hard—you deserve it.* ☺

I took a deep breath, and then sent him another text.

> *I'm aware you may be hungover tomorrow, but can we meet for lunch? Need to talk x*

Shay was doubly right. I had to deal with this, too.

Alice was out of town, and so I took Zoey as my date to Julien's party. The lounge was typically urban: chic decor and angular couches, a DJ in the far corner playing classics from the eighties and nineties. We perched by the back tables to hold the area while Shay and Julien fluttered from guest to guest as each person arrived. Just as Zoey went to the bar with Serena to buy another round, I spotted Asher at the entrance.

His jeans and faded leather jacket had been replaced by khaki trousers and a white button-down shirt, like he'd been dressed by the brunette beside him: petite and rail thin, wearing a white silky dress that stopped right below the crotch. They stood in the entranceway talking to each other, her hand on the base of his spine, and as she leaned up and whispered something in his ear, he caught my eye. He smiled at me, and I waved in return. He started to walk toward me, and the girl grabbed his hand and trotted along next to him.

I tried not to look at her too much as he introduced us; how she constantly flicked her bangs around, the way her glittery eye shadow made her look stupidly young.

As her eyes skirted around the room, I wondered how old she was.

"Rebekah is also a teacher," said Asher, as if he knew I had my doubts. "A middle school teacher."

"I teach music," she said, rifling through her purse. She pulled out a fat tube of lip gloss and began to smear it onto her pout. "Orchestra band, jazz band"—she smacked her lips—"and what else, sweetie?"

I winced.

"Choir, *right*. I run the choir."

I nodded. "That's great."

"She's also a musician," said Asher.

"And do you play basketball, too?"

She shook her head. "Too short. Always been more into singing."

I smiled, trying to look earnest. "Good for you. I sing terribly."

"So do my students." She laughed, and then tugged twice on her ponytail. "So"—she turned to Asher—"why don't we go buy me a drink?"

"Sure." Asher glanced at me. "Raina, would you like something?"

"Mine's coming, thanks," I said to them both, although Rebekah had already started to walk away, tugging at Asher's sleeve behind her.

They disappeared into the thick queue of bodies around the edge of the bar, and I watched Asher's head, a foot taller than most, bob above the crowd. It was dark, and for the next few minutes, I tried to make out whether he was smiling, and to whom he was talking.

"Who's that?"

I hadn't noticed Zoey reappear, and she pressed a drink into my hand. I took a long sip through the straw, just as Asher disappeared out of sight. "*That* is Asher."

The night passed painfully slowly, and I only had the chance to speak with Shay again briefly as she darted between Julien's cousins, friends, and coworkers, all of whom were pawing at them like they were a scratching post. Zoey and I chatted with the groups we met—friends of Julien's from the hospital, rec leagues—and then a whole crew from Quebec who'd rented a bus and drove in that day and, now drunk, indulged me as I tried out my remedial French. But I kept seeing Asher and Rebekah everywhere; standing in line again at the bar as she played on her phone; and then later at the edge of the dance floor, Rebekah bobbing her head up and down as Asher and Victor talked, it seemed, about the Raptors playoff game.

What did he see in her? Maybe Rebekah was the kind of girl Asher briefly thought I was. One who was passionate and talented and followed her dreams; one who could stand in a crowded room and not care what anyone else thought; because she knew exactly who she was, and didn't give a damn who cared or judged her for it.

I left Zoey at a table with two chatty residents Julien worked with, and got in line for the restroom. Half a dozen girls were lined up on the far wall—texting, applying lipstick, whispering— while the other wall, leading toward the men's room, was empty.

I took my place at the back, and a second later, I saw Asher appear in the far doorway. He smiled, and gave me a big, goofy wave as he walked toward me.

"So she's a teacher," I said, the words coming up uncontrollably.

"Yeah." He nodded. He seemed almost embarrassed. "She's a teacher."

"She seems nice."

"Rebekah can come across a bit—I don't know." He shrugged. "But she's really good with the kids. Even if she isn't exactly *passionate* about the job."

"I see."

"I think so many people end up teaching because they don't know what else to do."

I shrugged. "It happens, doesn't it? I'm not passionate about my job; not sure I ever was."

"What are you passionate about then, Raina?"

The way he said it made me stop short, and I wished I had an answer. I wished I knew what I was passionate about.

"I don't think I've ever felt about anything the way you feel about teaching."

"What did you want to be when you were little? Astronaut? Fashion designer?" He grinned. "National basketball player?"

I slapped him lightly on the shoulder. "Hey. I *could* have been in the pros."

"Yeah?"

I was about to joke back, but then I shook my head. "No, I couldn't have. It would have been too risky."

"Risky how?"

"My grandparents were really poor. They were immigrants. They worked hard, and after my mom never amounted to anything in their eyes, there was so much pressure on my uncle Kris, and then on me, to really . . . become something. To get jobs that were—I don't know—impressive. Stable. That earned a lot of money."

"So you always wanted to be an investment analyst," he said softly.

"I never knew what I wanted to be." I shrugged. "I suppose I never had a chance to figure it out."

"It's not too late," he said after a moment. Then he winked. "You're not that old."

"I'll be thirty next week."

His mouth dropped, and I fake shoved him again. I loved the creases around his mouth when he smiled.

"What does your gut tell you?"

I drew back. "About what?"

"About your passions. About what—and who—you want to be." He ran a hand through his hair. "Although, look at me. It took me years to figure out that my first instinct was right. I really did want to teach."

"My gut instinct on what to do has never been that helpful," I said, suddenly thinking about Dev and Depesh. "It's been mislead-ing, actually."

"That's not your gut you were listening to. That was your fear. You see, you have to listen harder, go further down." He palmed his stomach. "And then you'll hear it."

Was he right? Was it just fear that had led me? An ex-boyfriend I was too afraid to let go of? A grandmother I was too afraid to disappoint?

A man I was afraid to let myself love.

My body was trembling, and my arms—crossed and shivering—recoiled away from him. "I need to tell you something."

"Yeah?"

I made myself look at him. What was stopping me? I took a deep breath. "Asher, I'm not—"

"*There* you are."

I dropped my arms and turned toward the voice. Rebekah wobbled toward us, a scowl on her face. She walked up to Asher, and put an arm around his waist.

"Hi, Becka."

"What are you guys talking about?" she asked him, not looking at me.

"The wedding," Asher said quickly. "Raina's also in the wedding party."

"Is she?"

"We have to be there early for the ceremony"—he turned to me, talking quickly—"don't we? What time again?"

"The ceremony starts at ten—so five A.M., maybe six?"

"That's *early*," said Rebekah.

"It's customary for us to get married in the morning."

"Well, can I come, too?" she said to Asher.

"It's only for family and close friends. I'll be with Julien and his dad and brother"—Asher glanced at me—"and all the women will be helping Shaylee get ready."

"I like Indian clothes," she said.

I pressed my lips together.

"I'll talk to Julien," he said after a moment.

She folded her arm through his. "Thank you, *baby*."

I winced, and then as quickly as I could, I excused myself and went back into the party.

Asher . . . What just happened!?

WAY TOO GOOD FOR ME

Off the market.

TWENTY-SEVEN

Shay and Zoey found me hiding in the cloakroom. They made an effort to console me and boost my spirits, but when that didn't work, Shay insisted I go home so I didn't have to watch Asher and Rebekah together. Jokingly, Shay said she didn't want a miserable *middle-aged* woman ruining her party anyway. Zoey offered to drive me, but I refused. I could tell she was having a good time. They hugged me good-bye, and a few minutes later, I found myself walking home alone along College Street.

With Dev, I'd been jealous of anyone who got to spend time with him—his colleagues, his housekeeper, even his own mother—but this felt different, and just thinking about Rebekah made my lungs burn.

Asher was so different from anyone I knew, so unlike Dev. If he didn't have a girlfriend, if he knew the truth, could I even have had a future with him? And what about Dev? He still called, and every time, a fraction of me was tempted to answer. Didn't that mean a part of me still believed in *him*? As unrealistic as that fantasy was, didn't part of me hope he'd show up with a bouquet of flowers, get down on one knee, and tell me he'd changed?

I tripped over a crack in the sidewalk, and caught myself before I fell. My head was spinning, and I leaned against a lamppost and let my chin fall to my chest. My eyes closed, I could hear the cars whiz past, the sounds of pedestrians—high heels and leather soles clacking, the slow thud of music from a nearby bar.

I felt a low vibration coming out of the pole, through my leg and body, and it took me a moment to realize it was my phone. I found it in my coat pocket, and picked up when I saw it was Depo.

I held the receiver to my ear. "Hello?"

"Raina!" I heard him laugh, and a chorus of voices laughed in the background.

"Hey, what's up? How—"

"It was good!" He laughed again, and then shouted into the phone, "All my exams went *really* well."

"You smarty-pants. Amazing!" I stopped walking and smiled into the phone. "You're out celebrating?"

"Packing, actually. We're going to London, baby! Caleb's brother used to live in Brixton, is that good? Should we go there?"

"Wait, you're going to London? When?"

"Tonight!"

My stomach dropped.

"We booked a last-minute flight just this afternoon. Heading straight to London, then Berlin maybe? Who the hell knows. But I'm doing it. Exams are done, and I'm going to Europe. Like, me and Caleb, and a few other guys. We're going!"

"But—"

"My summer job starts in a few weeks, but maybe I won't do it. Maybe I'll just stay in London and take a year off—"

"A *year*?"

"—before doing the whole medicine thing. Caleb is thinking about taking a gap year."

I could feel the panic rising. "Please, slow down."

"I've always done the right thing. I've always been the good boy—but maybe I don't want to be that boy anymore. Maybe I want to be like Caleb. He's free. He does whatever the hell he wants. He's his own person, you know?"

"Following Caleb is not being your own person . . ."

He didn't hear me. He was talking rapidly, excitedly—and he wouldn't let me speak. He was following a boy he barely knew across the world? He was leaving with him for a year?

"Raina, like, thank you *so* much—for, you know, everything." He came up for air. "I couldn't have done it without you."

"Wait a sec. I need to tell you—"

"Can we talk later? The flight leaves in a few hours—"

"Please, just think about this—"

"—but text me, okay?"

Before I could say another word, he clicked off.

Mid-step, I was frozen in my tracks. The sidewalk was giving way beneath me. The street was spinning. I couldn't do this. There was no more delaying, no more waiting for the right time. No more being a coward. Depo was leaving, and he deserved to know the truth.

It took me less than a minute to find a taxi, and within forty-five minutes I was at the airport. I waited near security in the international terminal. After an hour of checking and rechecking the flight board, wondering whether I'd missed him, finally, he appeared.

I watched him from afar as he checked in for his flight at the kiosk, laughing with three other boys his age, small backpacks swung over their shoulders. And by the way he was looking at one of the boys—rosy cheeks, black glasses, platinum blond hair—I could tell which one was Caleb.

Depo looked so happy, with a lightness to him that I hadn't seen since he was kid. When he saw me, he gave me a big smile and waved. He walked toward me, dropped his bag by my feet, and enveloped me in a hug.

Tensely, I hugged him back. My heart pounded, and I could feel sweat forming on my face.

"You didn't have to come see me off." He pulled away grinning, and then looked toward security. "Sorry, I told them to go through. I should have introduced you to Caleb—should I go get him?"

I shook my head. "Another time. I need to—"

"That sounds good. Like, when we get back—or if we stay awhile, maybe you can come visit? Do you ever go to Europe for work?"

I shook my head.

"You're all dressed up." He smiled. "You look really pretty."

"Thanks," I whispered. "I was at a birthday party. Shay's fiancé."

"Ma's pissed I may not be home for her wedding." He laughed. "Despite everything, she still wants to show me off—tell everyone how good at school I am."

"Of course she does, Depo. Your parents are proud of you."

He shrugged, and looked at his feet. "They're barely speaking to me. Tonight, they didn't even hug me good-bye."

"Depo, your courage . . ." I put my hand on his arm. "I'm so proud of you. I really am, and"—I hesitated—"I also . . ."

"What is it?"

"There's something you need to know. Before you leave."

"Yeah?"

I looked him in the eye. I could feel myself shaking. "Depo, I'm straight."

He didn't respond. His face didn't move.

"I needed you to know before you left." I shook my head. "I'm not gay. I didn't mean to trick you. If it was something I could take back, I would. I promise you. If I could go back to last fall, I would handle things differently."

He still didn't move.

"I'd do a lot of things differently. I'd try and be a better person, a *stronger* person—I don't know. But one thing I don't regret is our friendship. I'm so happy we got to know each other this year, and I—I don't regret that. I really don't. I wanted to be there for you. I still do. And this stuff with Caleb—it's happening so quickly, and I get it. I get how you're feeling right now, and if you want to talk about—"

"*Talk?*"

I watched his face, his muscles perfectly tense, unflinching. But then he blinked.

"You. Bitch."

TWENTY-EIGHT

The next morning, I opened the e-mail Zoey had warned me was coming: Bill was concerned about my performance, and about my commitment to the team. An e-mail like this would have terrified me the year before. Hadn't I cared my whole life what people thought about me, and measured my happiness on how well I was doing in school or at work? Suddenly, my job didn't seem to matter so much anymore.

Instead of a suit, I changed into jeans and my high school basketball hoodie, and walked south along Yonge Street through the low light. The streets were empty, except for a few stragglers stumbling home from their Saturday night out. How many mornings had I walked this path, oblivious to why or where I was going? Stopping at the same coffee shop, with its smiley baristas and too-strong coffee that I didn't even like. Turning right at King Street, never waiting for the pedestrian walk light, rushing in as fast as I could go.

Bill was already at the office when I arrived. It was Sunday morning, and as I watched him bent over his desk scratching at his salt-and-pepper scruff, I thought about how his kids were probably having breakfast that morning with their stepfather. How even though I'd worked for Bill most of my adult life, he'd never even told me their names.

"Raina? Didn't know you were coming in . . ."

He stopped short when he saw my face, and then his hands went limp on the keyboard. We sat side by side on the couch in his office—and as I stared out the window, watching the first pink touches of light hitting the lake, he asked me if there was anything he could do to change my mind.

I could have made it more dramatic, but there was no point. I handed him my letter of resignation, and simply said my priorities in life had changed.

But they hadn't changed. Not really. Family. Friendship. Love. These were the things that had always mattered. These were the things I'd let slip, and I'd failed at each of them for the sake of a life I'm not sure I ever wanted. And eight years after first accepting a passionless job that was only ever meant to fill in the gaps, I was finally ready to leave. I was tired of letting down my family and friends, making up excuses for my own happiness. It turned out I wasn't the woman they thought I was. But that didn't mean I couldn't change.

That night, I cooked Alice and Zoey dinner—a recipe for a vegetarian jambalaya I'd once found in a magazine and had never had the time to try. After, I helped Shay with her wedding check-list, reorganized the spreadsheet filters in a way that made sense. Then, I wrote Depesh a long e-mail—one that didn't ask for forgiveness, or qualify my decisions over the past year in any way. It just spelled out how much I cared for him and how much I regretted misleading him, and I sent it knowing full well I might never get a response.

TWENTY-NINE

"Maybe I should work for you."

"As chef?"

I laughed. "I'm not that good. But I could manage the dinner shift, and then your days wouldn't be so long."

Nani flicked on the ventilation fan above the stove as the cumin, garlic, and chili started to sizzle in the pan. I reached over her for the bowl of tomatoes, tossing them in as she stirred it all around with a wooden spoon.

"Is that a maybe?"

"Raina, no more rash decisions, *nah*?" She glanced at me sideways. "You know, if you need money—of course. But this will be temporary solution until you *really* know what is next."

I nodded. I suppose I agreed. It would be too easy to get stuck working with her at Saffron, taking over for her entirely as she grew older. I could see myself managing the restaurant, or even going to culinary school—but at this point, everything felt so wide open, I could see myself anywhere. Applying my skills in banking in the public sector. Launching a girls' and women's athletics program.

Renting out my condo, and trekking my way through Southeast Asia.

I'd spent the previous two weeks working out my two weeks' notice, in the evenings cooking or watching TV with Nani, or running last-minute wedding errands with Shay. One evening, Zoey had surprised me by organizing farewell drinks for me at a bar near work, and I was surprised that Bill turned up. That I felt emotional saying good-bye to everyone. On the other hand, I felt ready for what was next—even though I had yet to figure out what that meant.

"You are quiet?"

I shook my head, shifting toward the fridge to grab the coriander. "Just thinking."

"About?"

"About . . . starting over." I turned to face her. "A new job. A new life . . . Maybe . . . a new guy . . ."

"Hah?"

Nani looked so alarmed I was tempted to laugh. Hell, I wanted to laugh myself. My community still thought I was gay, and I still hadn't figured out a way to handle that without overshadowing Shay's fast-approaching wedding. I'd broken the trust of my family, friends, and the man that I cared about. But I had to start over somewhere, didn't I?

"I've been thinking I should start dating again."

She sat down, keeping her eyes fastened on me as she rested her chin on her palm. The table was cluttered with magazines and random papers, and poking out from the bottom was a familiar crumpled one.

"*Beta*," I heard Nani say. "There is no need. I am not upset. We are okay, *nah*? We have made the amends."

I sat down next to her. "I know we have, but—"

"I don't need you to have husband." She moved her left hand to my cheek. "You are perfect, my Raina. Just as you are."

I clutched her hand, nodding. Finally believing her.

"It's not for you, Nani. It's for me. I'm ready to . . . try."

She sighed, and reclined back in her chair.

"Do you know anybody? Is there anyone I should meet?"

"Raina, I am out of touch now. I do not know of any boys these days."

Tentatively, I reached below the pile of papers and pulled out the list.

"It is here? You have kept all this time?" Nani laughed, and I watched her face as she read the notes I'd written in the margins.

"Maybe you should be comedian, my silly Raina." She winked. "Who is this Josh, *hot* like my chicken vindaloo?"

I blushed, lunged for the list. "Oh, nobody. We went on a date once . . ."

"And this Asher character—"

"Nope." My face reddened even more. "We need a *new* list. I don't know why I still have this. There's nobody on here . . ."

But something caught my eye. A noticeably blank space half-way down the page. I pushed the paper toward her, tapping on the only name I hadn't crossed out the year before.

"So what do you think?"

Nani looked at me curiously, and then shrugged. "What do *you* think?"

Jayesh—Sharon's cousin, science professor at university . . .

divorced!!!

DATE #6

He was surprised when I called him out of the blue—nearly one year after we had first texted. Through awkward small talk, I learned that Jayesh was still a general sciences professor at York University, still divorced—still unattached.

"What made you call after all this time?" he asked.

I paused, thinking back to the last time we'd messaged each other. After months of me being coy and postponing our first date—and right before that disastrous date with Rahul the vegan—Jayesh was the one who'd stopped texting me. Told me that if I wasn't ready or didn't want to meet, then he wasn't going to force my hand.

"I'm ready to meet," I said finally. "That is, if you still want to."

He chose a sports bar near his condo in the Distillery District, and I gave myself ten minutes—and not a second longer—to explain myself. Jayesh's eyes bulged at some parts of the story (lying to Depesh, my profile on IndianSingles.com) and laughed at others (the gay porn links on Nani's browser history). It felt good to come clean, lay it all out there for someone who never knew the old me. So much had happened since Nani first gave me that list. My life had changed. I'd changed. And as we pushed past the small talk, I realized that what I wanted in life had changed, too.

Jayesh was an open book, liked to laugh, and as I sipped on the dregs of my pint, I realized I might actually like him. I felt my stomach growl, and I set down my empty glass.

"Are you hungry?"

We'd only committed to a quick drink, and he smiled at me, as if he was surprised I was making an effort.

"After all this time," I said, "I can at least buy you dinner."

"I suppose you can . . ."

"Do you like tacos?"

"Do you know anyone who *doesn't* like tacos?"

I grinned. "Great. I know this place off King West."

We took the streetcar, and Jayesh told me about the PhD he'd recently defended on energetics—which he explained was the study of energy as it transformed between forms.

"Energy can be stored, which is potential energy. Or it can be kinetic, thermal, elastic, nuclear—but it's always there. It cannot be destroyed or created. It always balances out—kind of like the Force."

I stared at him curiously, before breaking out into a grin.

"Sorry, that was a dumb joke. I meant—"

"*Star Wars*." My hand bumped against his on the handrail, and I let it stay there. "I get it. I love *Star Wars*."

It was warm enough to sit on the restaurant's patio, and we shared a pitcher of margaritas, a big bowl of guac and chips, and then ordered a sharing plate of baja fish and buttermilk chicken tacos.

"You know," Jayesh said, pouring hot sauce onto his plate. "Come to think of it, I've been here before."

"Oh yeah?"

"Yeah." He set the bottle down. "My ex-wife works just around the corner."

I nodded slowly, trying to figure out what to say.

"Too early to bring up the ex?"

"After what I unloaded on you earlier, not at all." I paused. "How long has it been?"

"We've been divorced three years now. In retrospect, we married way too young. Turns out, she cared more about the wedding than me."

"I'm sorry." I wiped my hands on a napkin. "The same thing happened to my uncle Kris, too. But you seem to be handling it a lot better than he is."

"I have good days and bad days still." He smiled. "On the bad days I dwell on the fact that a lot of people in the community have drawn a black mark over me. Labeled me as damaged, somehow."

"And the good days?"

"The good days, I think about the future." He shrugged. "I eat tacos with cute girls . . ."

He was smiling at me now, and I couldn't help but return one.

"And on your good days," I said, reaching for the dessert menu. "Do you eat ice cream?"

"Lots."

"Chocolate?"

"*Duh.*"

Jayesh—Sharon's cousin, science professor at university . . .

   <u>divorced</u>!!!

   Intriguing . . . taco tour round

   #2 TBD after Shay's wedding!

THIRTY

Shay's wedding week arrived in a flurry. Serena, the twins, and I were recruited for countless errands: picking up and dropping off relatives, lugging decorations and marigold garlands to and from the venues, helping Shay manage Auntie Sarla's demands. There were dinner parties with relatives, with family friends who had traveled to Toronto, and then the Ganesh puja: a religious ceremony performed to remove obstacles and ensure the successful completion of the wedding.

I sat down near the back of the temple with Serena, and looked around the room. Up at the front, Nani and Auntie Sarla were assisting the priest as he carried out the ceremony. Shay and Julien were seated cross-legged with their eyes closed, and as the priest resumed chanting, I closed mine, too.

I'd never really tried to understand Hinduism. For most, it conjured the image of Ganesh's trunk and bright colors, bronze statues and bathing in the Ganges, and my knowledge—my understanding of it—only went a tad further.

Its belief system was supple. Its rituals and traditions were blended and nuanced over thousands of years, from one region to another. But surely, at its core, there was nothing about it that decreed its believers to be intolerant. The *Kama Sutra* encouraged homosexual relations, and so did the holy book the *Rigveda*. Shay had mentioned that there were even transgender characters in the *Mahabharata*.

But then why did so many traditional Hindus, like Depesh's parents, like Auntie Sarla, vehemently disapprove? When had it all started; why had we been taught to fear, taught to discredit everything but our own perspective?

Whatever the belief system, we were all in charge of our own values. Depesh had been brave to challenge them, to stand up to his own family and community. And now—for a while, at least—he was gone. As much as it hurt, as much as I didn't want to let him go, I knew that he would be all right.

When the puja was over, I went into the dining hall and found that Nani had slipped out ahead of me, and was now bustling around in the kitchen with a dozen other women.

"What can I do?" I asked, tying an apron around my sari.

"Your Auntie Sarla has rented extra plates, but I cannot find!"

"Where should I look?"

She fished out a ring of keys from her bra and pressed it into my hand. "I think her car."

"Do you need a hand?"

The voice startled me, and it took me a while to realize it belonged to Asher.

"Hah, she will," I heard Nani say to him. "It is very heavy."

"No problem," he said. "I'm Asher, by the way. You must be Auntie Suvali?"

"So *you* are Asher . . ." Nani beamed at him. "Yes, I am Auntie Suvali—but *you* can call me Nani."

"Oh, uh—"

"She says that to everybody." I shook my head, and Asher grinned. "She wasn't *implying*—"

"Nice to meet you, Nani," he said, ignoring me completely.

"Nice to meet *you*."

We took the back stairs up to the main level and found Auntie Sarla's flashy red car in the parking lot. I was at a loss for words, and I could tell Asher felt awkward around me, too. Was Rebekah lurking somewhere?

"I didn't see you upstairs," I ventured, as we unloaded boxes from the trunk.

"I was sitting behind you a bit—on the men's side." He paused, shutting the trunk. "Why is there a men's side and women's side at the temple, by the way?"

"It beats me."

"Tradition?"

"I guess."

"Traditions change. It takes a while, but they do . . . Or, they can."

I stared hard at the concrete beneath my feet, focusing on a crack jutting out from my left big toe. "How long are we expected to wait, Asher?"

He was breathing heavily, and I felt his hand brush against my forearm. "There are a few girls from South Asian families in my class this year," I heard him say. "In some ways, they're teaching me more than I'm teaching them."

I followed the crack with my eyes farther and farther, until it disappeared into the bushes.

"I've come to realize that as much as I'd like to, there are some things I'll just never be able to understand."

Did Asher realize that, by just saying those words, he *did* understand? That even though our backgrounds were worlds apart, his empathy, his outlook on life, brought him closer to my heart than any man had been before?

"It was a beautiful ceremony today. Wasn't it, Raina?"

But what right did I have to ask him anything? What right did I have to say all those words on the tip of my tongue, weighing down my chest?

To interfere in a life he had with another woman.

"Where's Rebekah?"

My eyes still on the ground, I saw his hands shift from his side to his pockets.

Was that a sigh?

"She's at school."

By the time we got the last of the dishes into the kitchen, everyone had started to leave the main hall and was queuing up for lunch. I figured Asher would run off to find Julien's other friends, but he didn't. He found another apron beneath the sink, and after rolling up the sleeves of his white collared shirt, he took up the post next to me. It was an assembly line. I put one naan on everybody's plate, Asher spooned the rice, and a battalion of aunties next to him dished out the *subjiis*, dal, chutney, sweets. When Asher started chatting to the aunties next to him, I tried not to eavesdrop. But I couldn't help but notice their laughter, how smitten they all seemed to be by him. I was relieved when Nani tapped him on the shoulder and asked him to fetch her a heavy Crock-Pot from a high shelf, and someone else took over serving the rice.

I could hear Asher and Nani behind me as they worked away on something. I didn't dare look. I kept my eyes on the naan, on the hungry people in front of me. My stomach hurt, but I knew it wasn't from hunger.

"Asher is *very* tall," I heard Nani say to me.

I tried not to smile. Nani, who was probably too short to go on the adult rides at amusement parks, tended to use the word "tall" when she meant handsome.

"And very sweet." She sidled in closer to me, and I could just make out her profile with my peripheral vision. "So heavy those dishes, and helping us while everyone else is eating . . ." As she trailed off, I knew exactly what she was thinking: how out of the dozens of people helping serve and prepare lunch, Asher was one of the few men. How Nana, no matter how much he had loved her, had not once helped her in the kitchen.

"Is Asher . . ." Nani shook her head. "*Hah.* Never mind. I will not again be interference." She mimed zipping her lips shut, and a beat later, I mimed reopening them.

"He has a girlfriend, Nani, if that's what you're asking."

"So Asher is just *friend*?"

I nodded, leaning in close to whisper, "He also thinks I'm gay."

Nani laughed. "A man cannot be in love with supposedly gay woman?"

"Nani, shhhh!"

"His girlfriend cannot be so pretty the way he is looking at you—"

"Nani!"

"*Kya?* It is merely observation—"

"Can we go back to you not interfering in my life?"

"No," she said, grinning. "Now I am stuck. I am in *the mix*!"

I stepped aside from my post, and took Nani off to the side of the kitchen. She was smiling so much I had to fight the urge to wipe it right off.

"Please don't go getting your hopes up, okay?"

"But why? Is it not obvious—"

"Nani, I've messed up a lot this year. You know that." After she didn't disagree, I continued. "Asher's dating someone. It might even be serious, and I'm not going to insert myself in that. I'm not going to . . . mess that up, too."

She crossed her arms, and I couldn't quite tell if she was yawning or sighing.

"And besides. I'm seeing Jayesh again."

"Really?"

"Yep." I smiled. "We had a nice time. He's very sweet. He knows Shay's wedding is this week, and so he told me to call him after, when I'm free."

"And you plan to?"

I nodded. "We're going to have tacos."

"Taco?"

"You've had tacos, Nani." I rolled my eyes. "It's like a roti, and inside there's meat and salsa and—"

"Hah, hah. I like taco." She pursed her lips together. "They are very messy, *nah*?"

I laughed. "I suppose so."

"You know," she said, resting her palm on my cheek. Her eyes beamed. "Life can be messy, too."

Another day, another ceremony. Shay and Julien had disappeared immediately after the Ganesh puja was over—to where, I wasn't sure—and so I didn't see her until the following evening's *mehndi*—a ladies-only ceremony held to decorate the bride with henna. The entire evening, Shay was stuck in the middle of Auntie Sarla's living room as two artists painted her hands, wrists, and feet with the black ink. She seemed snappy, ill-tempered, and I wanted to ask how she was coping with the wedding stress (clearly not well), but someone always seemed to be within earshot. When I saw her slip into the kitchen, I followed her and found her standing in front of the sink limply scraping off the dried henna into the sink.

"Are you okay?"

She didn't reply, and in silence, I watched as she rubbed her hands together. Her eyes were fixated on the black paste as it crumbled down the drain, and left a sprawl of bright orange on her palm.

"Here." I reached for a platter of samosas. "You must be hungry."

"No, not hungry," she said quietly. Suddenly, she looked up through the glass in the kitchen door. "Shit."

A moment later, Auntie Sarla burst in, glaring at Shay. "I *told* you—you must leave that on all evening." Auntie Sarla lunged for Shay's hands. "*Aacha?* It is all ruined! The color will be gone by ceremony!"

"Ma, it doesn't matter."

Auntie Sarla whipped toward me. "And Raina has taken hers off, too. Of course. Follow *her* example."

"I needed to call Julien. I can't dial the phone with this stuff on my hands—"

Auntie Sarla launched into a tirade in Rajasthani. I kept trying to interrupt, but Auntie Sarla ignored me, and after a few moments, even Shay told me I should leave. I wasn't going to abandon her, but I felt my phone vibrate, and when I pulled it from beneath the strap of my bra, my heart stopped. It was Depesh.

I nearly tripped over my sari as I raced into a quiet room at the back of Shay's house. Deliberately, I clicked answer, and held the phone up to my ear.

"Depo?"

I heard heavy breathing, faint music thumping in the background. I checked my watch. It was the middle of the night in London.

For almost a minute, he didn't speak, and I listened to him breathing, and I tried to work up the courage to say something.

"Where are you?" I finally asked.

"I'm in Hack-*ney*."

I nodded into the phone. He sounded drunk, his words slurring, and with every ounce of me, I prayed that he was safe.

"Are you okay—"

"So this was all about that fucking British guy."

I pressed my hand over my face. "You read my e-mail . . ."

"A *guy*? An ex-boyfriend?"

"It started out that way. I know it doesn't make any sense. I have no excuse—"

"I came out—I fucking came out to my parents—because, because of *you*, because I thought you, but—" He cut off, and I could hear a garble through the phone.

"Depesh, I don't expect forgiveness."

"Good."

"But, I'm always going to be here for you," I said slowly. "You can hate me, but I'm here."

"God. I'm not—not some baby bird that needs taking care of, okay? I don't need you."

"Depo . . ."

"And you don't need me, either, Raina." He laughed. "Apparently all you need is a *boyfriend*."

My ears burned.

"Sorry," he said after a minute. "Sorry, I'm *drunk*."

"No, it's okay. I deserved that."

The music started getting louder through the phone, and I heard shouting behind him.

"I should go."

"Depo, you're being safe? Do your parents know—"

"Yeah, okay? They know where I am—" He paused, and I heard a voice beside him. "I have to go."

"Wait, please. Just one thing."

"What?"

"I know you don't need me. I know you're hurt. But just—just know you can call me anytime. I'm here for you."

He didn't respond.

"Tell me you know I'm still here, Depo." My voice cracked. "Please."

A moment passed. And right before he clicked off, he said, "I know."

THIRTY—ONE

Shay had disappeared by the time I went back into Auntie Sarla's kitchen, so I spent the rest of the *mehndi* with Serena and the other bridesmaids chatting with the aunties, helping to tidy up. Afterward, I found my way back downtown and lay down fully dressed on the bed—but I didn't sleep a wink. I didn't deserve it. I kept my phone plugged in and with the volume turned up next to me the whole night, but it didn't ring. At 4 A.M. I caved and texted Depesh, but there was no answer.

The following night was Shay's final pre-wedding celebration and the eve before the big day: the *sangeet*, or music party, which came well stocked with dinner and dancing, live music and an open bar.

Serena picked me up in her car, and we dropped off our armory of saris, jewelry, and makeup at the hotel. Our room was next door to Nikki and Niti's, and a few floors below Shay's suite—where we'd all get ready together the next morning.

We changed quickly and then made our way into the main ballroom downstairs. Dozens of waiters in uniform bustled around the room fussing with chair covers and centerpieces, sprinkling rose petals and pouring wine. In the corner, Auntie Sarla, clipboard in hand, was instructing a group of waiters.

The guests started to arrive, and Serena and I took up posts at the entrance and handed out programs. Afterward, I tried to find Shay—but she kept disappearing, offering vague and unconvincing excuses. In fact, she had acted strange all evening—all week, really. Watching her at the head table wedged between Auntie Sarla and Julien, a fake smile on her face, I could tell something was wrong. It was more than stress; she looked miserable, even though she should have been the happiest woman in the room. The moment dinner was over, she pushed back her chair and raced out of the hall, and I was right on her heels.

I followed her to the bank of elevators that went up to the guest rooms. "Shay?"

She looked back over her shoulder, just as the elevator door opened.

"What's wrong?"

Her face crumpled, and she stepped into the elevator. "I just need a minute."

"What is it?" I blocked the door with my arm, but she shook her head as I moved to step inside.

"I need a minute—"

"Shay, you're crying. What—"

"Please?" she whispered.

What was going on with Shay? She'd been dealing with overbearing Auntie Sarla for nearly thirty years; this wasn't just wedding stress. It couldn't be.

"Seriously," she sobbed. "Haven't you ever just needed a minute?"

Reluctantly, I pulled back my arm. "You have one minute. Then I'm coming up."

She nodded as the doors closed, and I went back into the hall. I scanned the crowd for Julien, but I couldn't see him. Half of the guests had abandoned their seats for the dance floor, and the live bhangra was in full swing. From across the dance floor I spotted Asher for the first time that evening, his head visible above the crowd. I felt my stomach flutter. He caught my eye and waved. I waved back, and tried not to wonder where Rebekah was. The band was loud, and it seemed like everyone was bouncing along as the female lead singer belted out Punjabi lyrics.

I motioned to Asher to check his phone, and then I texted him.

Where's Julien? It's urgent.

A moment later, he replied.

I don't know. Want me to help you look?

I texted back.

Sure. Let me know when you find him. I'll be in Shay's room.

I put my phone back in my purse and turned around. The crowd was thick around me, and I pushed my way back into the foyer. I reached forward to press the button, and as I was waiting, I felt a hand on my waist.

"Darling."

I whipped around.

"You look *gorgeous.*" Dev pulled me in for a hug. "I've been looking for you everywhere."

I couldn't breathe. What was *he* doing here? At Shay's wedding? Back in Toronto?

I suddenly remembered that it was Friday by the colored tie he was wearing. His hair—light black and bristly, a few whisks of gray—was typically parted and in place.

"Took me ages to track you down, and *wow*. And to think—I've never even seen you in a sari."

I was speechless. He tried to reach for me, and I pushed him away. He dropped his arms, studying me as if suddenly I'd become a complex graph; a banking equation it was his mission to solve.

"What happened? I flew in yesterday, and Bill said you—"

"Quit." I crossed my arms. "Yes, I quit."

He sighed, putting his hand around my waist. "Tell me this isn't about us."

"Us? There isn't an 'us.' We haven't spoken in months." I tried to shrug off his hand, but then he wrapped the other one around me, too. "The thing is, Dev, this is the first thing I've done in a while that has nothing to do with *us*—or my nani, or anyone but me."

"Raina, it's been a stressful time for me, and on top of that, you stopped speaking to me, and it *threw* me. It's thrown me right out—"

"I don't want to hear it."

"But I'm staying put at the minute. Don't you see? Don't you see what that means for us? I'll travel still. But I'm based here. Near *you*. Properly now." He smiled and leaned in closer. "Really, love. You didn't have to quit."

"Were you even listening to me?"

"You and I were happy together, weren't we? I love you—"

My head swam, and when he leaned to kiss me, I tried to pull away.

"—I always have."

I felt my cheek against his chin, his hands on the back of my neck, my waist.

"Raina, I *think* I'm ready—"

His lips pressed against mine, and I winced. I was breathing hard when he pulled away. I opened my eyes, my vision blurred, and my lashes stuck together. Finally, everything became clear. But I didn't see Dev. I saw Asher.

"Asher . . ."

Dev spun around. Asher was standing just behind him.

"Sorry, mate. Didn't see you." He extended his hand. "I'm Dev." Asher's hands didn't move; his eyes didn't leave me.

"You a friend of Raina's?"

I could feel Dev shift beside me, and when he tried to put his arm around me, I flung it away. Asher's face was motionless.

My mind raced. This was wrong. It all felt so wrong. I wanted Asher to hold me, *Asher* to kiss me—the way he had in New York.

"Asher, I—"

He turned on his heels, started walking toward the door, and I followed.

"Raina, where are you going?" I heard Dev cry out, but I kept running after Asher, nearly tripping on the hem of my sari as I tore through the revolving door behind him.

"Asher, wait." I caught up to him, tugged on his shoulder until he turned around. "Please, don't go."

I looked into his eyes, pleading with him. Would he forgive me? Could I say anything—*do* anything—to make it right between us? Take us back to New York, back to midnight.

"Look at me," I whispered. "Please."

A gust of wind tore in from the parking lot—sharp, sandy— and I wrapped the tail of my sari around my arms.

"I know what that looked like. I know what you must think of me, but let me ex—"

"You have no idea what I think about you."

"Please, let me explain. My heart was in the right place, I swear—"

"You're in love with that guy?"

I looked at his hands. They were shaking, and I wanted to reach for them.

"I used to be," I whispered.

"And now?"

"And now . . . I'm falling in love with you." I stepped toward him, but he drew back. One step, and then another.

"I didn't mean it to go this far, I swear. It got out of hand, and I didn't know *what* I was doing." I paused, willing him to look at me. "You asked me once, what I was looking for. What if it's you, Asher? What if we can find it together?"

"I don't know what you want me to say right now."

"I'm not a bad person, it's—"

"I know you're a good person," he said slowly. He wouldn't meet my eye. "I wouldn't have cared for you if you weren't."

"So you do care?" I asked, hoping. Pleading. "You still . . . you *could* still care about me?"

"I'm a simple guy. This—*you*—it's too . . . complicated. I can't." He breathed out, and his voice caught. "I can't do this right now."

"I'm sorry, Asher. Please—"

But he wouldn't look at me, and he kept walking away. "I'm sorry, too."

I didn't want to let him go. But I did. He disappeared behind the hotel, and after ten minutes, I forced myself to realize he wasn't coming back.

Dev was still in the lobby, reclined on a sofa, his legs crossed. Right ankle over left knee, his BlackBerry in hand. He looked up as I approached, and tucked the phone into his pocket. He shifted over on the couch, and I sat down next to him. For a moment neither of us spoke.

"Why did you do that?" I asked him finally.

"Do what?" He moved closer to me. "Darling, who was that?"

"Dev, I'm not your darling. Stop calling me that." He tried to brush a piece of hair behind my ear, and I pressed his hand down. "I want you to just . . . stop."

"Raina . . . what's happening?" I didn't answer, and he intertwined his fingers through mine.

Had it really taken me this long to get here?

"Weren't we happy?" he whispered.

Maybe he really was ready this time, or maybe he wasn't. But finally, I was ready, and I knew I could never go back.

"We *were* happy. But, being with you . . . it's not enough for me." I dropped his hand. "I was just too in love to realize it."

THIRTY-TWO

Shay duped me. She wasn't in her room, and I couldn't find Julien, either. They had disappeared from the *sangeet* without a trace, and the entire night their cell phones kept going straight to voice mail. Serena, the twins, and I searched the lobby, the back rooms, and even drove over to their condo downtown, but we couldn't find them anywhere. Asher had disappeared, and when we asked the other groomsmen, none of them knew where they'd gone, either.

"Maybe they're doing it," Nikki said around 2 A.M., when we ordered room service to refuel. "Maybe they're in the next room, right now, having really raunchy sex."

"You're so immature," Niti said, as she stripped the meat off a chicken wing with her teeth. "They probably just eloped."

Eloped?

"Whatever they're doing, I hope they're okay," Serena said, and I nodded in agreement.

Why had I let her run off? Disappearing like that was so out of character, I feared the worst. Had she not passed her final pediatrics exams? Had someone *died*?

What was she hiding from me?

We decided to try and get a few hours of sleep before the wedding, and it was only as my eyes were fluttering shut that I realized it was my birthday.

That I was thirty.

I drifted in and out of sleep for a few hours until my alarm woke me up. Serena was snoring in the bed next to me, and I reached over and hit the alarm, and then threw pillows at her until she woke up. A few moments later, we crawled out of the room, knocked on Nikki and Niti's door, and the four of us—gowned in hotel slippers and robes, our matching bridesmaids' saris draped over our arms—took the elevator up to the top floor. It was exactly 5 A.M., when we were all supposed to meet to get ready. We arrived at the suite, but when Nikki knocked, no one answered.

"I know she's coming," I said. "I just know it."

"And what if she's not?" Niti asked.

I was thinking of a way to answer that when the elevator bell rang from down the hall, and a moment later Shay emerged. She still had her full hair and makeup from the previous night, and she was wearing a pair of blue-checked pajama pants and the blouse of her sari. She turned her head, and then sulked toward us. Her eyes were red, her long-wear mascara bleeding at the corners.

"Have you been up all night?"

She didn't answer and fished a key card out of her clutch. She jabbed it into the slot. She tried to swing the door behind her, but I caught it and pushed through just in time to see her collapse facedown onto one of the couches.

"Shay?" I sat down beside her.

She turned around slowly, wiping her face with the back of her hand.

"What is it?"

She swallowed loudly, and tears welling in her eyes, she said, "I think the wedding is off."

For twenty minutes Shay just lay there, facedown on the couch, her arms splayed out behind her; I couldn't tell if she was asleep or awake, crying or even breathing.

"Are you ready to talk yet?"

Shay groaned, and shook her head into the pillow. I'd instructed everyone else to start getting ready without us, thinking surely Shay would snap out of it quickly, but I was getting worried.

What had happened? Surely, the wedding wasn't really canceled?

"Shay, tell me—"

"I don't want to talk about it—"

"You know what?" I grabbed her by the waist and yanked her up from the couch. "I don't care. We're talking about it."

Somehow, I managed to get Shay into the bathroom. I locked the door behind us, and when I turned back around, she had seated herself cross-legged on the counter. I stood with my back against the door, waiting for her to speak, but she just looked at her hands.

"Did you and Julien have a fight?"

I saw the tears pooling in her eyes, and then a fat droplet rolled down her cheek. I wiped it away, and her body trembled as I put an arm around her.

"Where is he?"

"I don't know." She wiped her face with the back of her hands.

"Do you want me to call him?"

"He won't answer." She shook her head. "He's *so* mad at me."

"What *happened*?"

She hopped off the counter and started pacing in front of me, her hands on her hips.

"Shay?"

"Don't be mad. Okay? You were so mad at your mom for getting pregnant"—she paused—"and, *well*, so am I."

"Mad?"

"No. Jesus, I'm *pregnant*."

"Oh my God." Tears welled in my eyes. "Shay, you're going to be a mom?"

She shrugged.

I lunged for her, hugged her, squeezed her until she pushed me off. "This is amazing, Shay. Why the hell are you guys fighting?"

"Because I didn't want it to happen yet, Raina! I *just* finished residency. *Just* got some semblance of independence. And then there was my freaking circus wedding to deal with. Finally, I was about to get some pressure off of me."

"These things are unexpected—"

"I'm a doctor. I'm on the pill, Raina! This wasn't supposed to happen yet. I'm not ready."

"You're going to have to be ready."

"That's what Julien said." Shay frowned. "And I got mad and said I wanted an abortion."

"You *do*?"

"Of course I don't want an abortion. I want a baby with him—I just don't want one *now*. And I was angry at Julien because he was *so* excited, but he doesn't have to get stretch marks. He doesn't have to push out a baby." She grabbed a wad of toilet paper and wiped her nose. "We've been fighting all week because he wanted us to go to confession before the wedding, ask for *forgiveness* from his priest—and get married right then in the church. And last night we almost did go. We were practically in the car, and I was so mad—I don't know, hormones—and I know how his whole raging Catholic family feels about it, and I just . . . told him I wanted an abortion."

"And you didn't mean it."

She sniffed. "No."

"Then apologize, Shay. It's simple. Tell him the truth, and apologize."

Was it really that simple? Could every mistake be fixed this way? Falling to one's knees, begging those who you've hurt to forgive you?

Shay knocked over the toilet seat lid and sat down. I handed her more toilet paper; she blew her nose, and handed it back to me. I stuffed it into the pocket of my robe and crouched down next to her.

"Do you remember the night you introduced him to me?"

Shay looked up, nodded slowly.

"I was going to save this for your toast tonight, but, to hell with it. Do you know what he said to me the next morning? He came out of your room and I was in the kitchen making coffee, and he wanted to make you breakfast—do you remember that?"

"He was the first guy to ever make me breakfast."

I nodded, and grabbed her hand. "And I was showing him where the toaster was, the sugar, the milk, and then he stopped and looked at me, and said, 'Raina, I'm going to marry that girl.'"

Shay's face crumpled.

"Almost six years later, and you two are *happy*, Shay. You're a family."

"And what's our family going to be like, huh?" Shay sniffled. "Am I going to turn into my mean, manipulative mother"—she gestured around the room—"and host lavish parties just so everyone knows how *rich* we are?"

"First of all, you are nothing like Auntie Sarla." I smiled. "Secondly, the thing about starting a family, Shay, is you get to choose what it's going to be like." I fished my phone out of my robe pocket and handed it to her. "You and Julien get to be whoever the hell you want to be."

At eight thirty, Auntie Sarla and a flock of her friends and relatives started arriving, wedging themselves into the love seats and onto the room's surfaces. The makeup artist finished with me and moved onto Serena, and a second later, a hairstylist named Claire appeared, grunted hello, and started to roughly comb my hair. She angled my chair into the room's corner—so she could more easily reach her curling iron—and I couldn't see anybody.

I heard noises escalating behind me, more and more aunties arriving. Every time I tried to turn my head to see whether Nani had arrived yet, Claire sharply yanked my head back.

A few aunties came by and said their hellos, offered me tea or juice, and then quickly disappeared again. I could hear everyone fussing over Shay on the opposite end of the room, her fake placating voice agreeing to every suggestion as they tied her sari, ensured every curl was perfectly pinned onto her head. I laughed to myself, and wished Claire would hurry up. I reached up and felt my hair, but only half of it was curled and pinned back—the other half still in a limp mess by my shoulders.

"Is there a problem?" Claire snapped.

"Just wondering how much longer." I smiled. "I still have to put on my sari."

She rolled her eyes. "Well, next time tell the bride not to make the wedding so goddamn early."

"It wasn't her choice," I said softly, although Claire had already stopped listening.

I could feel the room filling up even more; it was becoming fiercely hot, and I regretted not changing out of my flannel pajamas and bathrobe before everyone arrived.

"Could someone open a window?" I said to no one in particular. The air-conditioning was on, but the room felt like a sauna. "Please?"

An auntie appeared beside me. "Already open—we have called for fan."

I thanked her, and she disappeared from my peripheral vision.

I was becoming more restless with each passing minute. I wanted to help Shay get ready, make sure she was still okay, but the progress of my updo had stalled. Claire dropped her hands from my head to grab her coffee, and I took the opportunity to turn around.

Shay's relatives surrounded her. Her makeup and hair seemed to be done, and she was sitting at the foot of the bed half dressed in her petticoat and blouse. Auntie Sarla was standing over her, and they seemed to be whispering loudly at each other in Rajasthani. Shay looked like she was about to cry again, and it was as if the aunties around them—steaming her bridal sari, lazily primping her hair—hadn't even noticed.

I stood up and walked toward them, ignoring the hairdresser's protests.

"What's going on?"

Auntie Sarla's eyes flicked toward me as she continued yelling at Shay. Then she stopped, and glaring at me, said, "*Nothing*, Raina."

Shay stood up. "Don't speak to her like that."

"Auntie, did I do something?"

"What haven't you done?"

"Ma!"

"Auntie, please tell me—"

"It's fine," Shay said. "I handled it."

"Handled what?" The rest of the room seemed to have quieted. They were listening to us.

"Some of my more *conservative* relatives from India"—Shay said evenly—"didn't come this morning to help me get ready, and—"

"Because of *you*, Raina," snapped Auntie Sarla. "You are ruining Shaylee's wedding—"

"Shut it, Ma—"

"Yes, *shut it*, Sarla."

Nani had appeared in the doorway. For a woman so small, it was as if she was suddenly taking up the whole room. She smiled at me, and then Shay, and then her eyes pivoted back toward Sarla.

"Are you really going to start again with this now?" Nani asked Sarla.

"Your Raina is ruining—"

Shay groaned. "Raina is not ruining my wedding, *you* are, Ma!"

"Me?" Auntie Sarla cackled. "You have me to thank for this whole wedding—"

"I didn't want this! You think I wanted some hyper-religious ceremony where I'm not even allowed to kiss the groom?" Shay's eyes filled up again, and her voice had grown hoarse. "I did this for you, for Dad—and you know that—"

Auntie Sarla snapped an interjection, and her arms flailed wildly.

"English *please*," I said.

Shay rolled her eyes. "Oh, she's just mad the attention isn't on *her*—"

"Ungrateful child," spat Auntie Sarla.

"I'm ungrateful?" Shay exclaimed. "I did *everything* you and Dad ever asked of me. I was perfect, I'm having your *perfect* wedding—and still, this isn't enough. You want the attention on me? You got it. Julien and I almost eloped last night. How's that for attention?"

"Elopement," repeated Auntie Sarla. "But *vhy*?"

"Because this goddamn thing is a nightmare! Because we already *live* together! Because we wanted a small wedding and I'm . . . I'm *fucking* pregnant!"

Auntie Sarla gasped, and echoes followed behind her. She collapsed onto the bed, and an auntie started to fan her with a magazine. She started mumbling something in Rajasthani incoherently, and Shay rolled her eyes.

"Ma. Are you okay?"

Auntie Sarla didn't reply, and Shay squatted down beside her.

"Ma? I'm sorry, I—"

"*Pregnant.* Shaylee!" She sat up slowly, unsteadily, her plump face flushed like a plum. "How did this happen?"

"I sat on a dirty toilet seat."

I snorted out a laugh. Shay started laughing, too. Auntie Sarla stood up, and pinned her glare onto me.

"This is *your* doing?"

"Huh?"

"You and your nani. And that dirty Manavi—whole family *always* causing trouble—"

"Ma, you're going to be a *nani*—"

"*You* were bad influence on my Shaylee—"

"Don't blame Raina for Shaylee's actions," said Nani.

"This is all Raina's doing—ever since she decided to be lesbian, nothing but hassle, difficulty for everyone. And I hear now Sharon's boy is gay, too? What did you do to him?"

"Hush, Sarla! This is not right. This is your daughter's wedding, *nah*?"

"When is the time then?" spat Auntie Sarla. "When all the kids have turned gay? When Raina marries another girl? When there are two bridal saris to tie? I will not be there to help, Suvali. No one will be there!"

As the yelling around me escalated, billowed, the dullness in the pit of my stomach mushroomed, and I just couldn't take it. I had to stop it.

"Everyone, be quiet!"

In a moment, the room was silent. Still. And everyone was staring at me. I could feel the sweat that had started to run down the base of my spine. I glanced at Shay. She smiled at me. Nodded. I took a breath, and finally I said it.

"I'm not . . . gay."

My fists were clenched tightly, and I loosened them. My vision blurred, refocused. Still, the room was silent.

"*What?*" cried Auntie Sarla.

"You're not?" said Serena.

I shook my head, and turned to face Nani. Her eyes were on the floor, and she had pressed her hands into the doorway on either side of her, but she was smiling.

"Why would you lie about something like this?" asked an auntie nearby; my ears were ringing, and I couldn't tell which one it was.

"I just wanted everyone to stop telling me to get married, and setting me up on dates." My voice trembled, and I pressed on. "It wasn't supposed to go this far. And then, I just wanted people to know that it shouldn't have mattered. I didn't want it to matter."

"But you're not," said Serena.

I shook my head.

"Well," said Auntie Sarla. She was smiling. "This is good news. *Some* good news."

"Ma," Shay said. "That's not the point. The point is that it shouldn't matter even if she was gay."

"But she's not!"

"Yes, Ma. I know. But why does it matter one way or the other?"

"Of *course* it matters."

"Are you kidding me? Wake up, *Mother*, it's the twenty-first century. People screw before—"

"Shaylee!"

"—they get married. People are straight, others are gay. What concern is it to you?"

"She's right, Sarla," said another auntie. "My nephew in Winnipeg is of the gay now."

"Ma, don't you see how backward you are? That you're . . ."

The room again became a commotion: silence replaced with horrified and bemused looks; Auntie Sarla's intermittent sobs and screams, and shouts from back and forth across the room. It was mayhem, and I looked down at Nani in disbelief. The vivacious glimmer was back in her eyes.

"It is good these people are hassled sometimes, *nah*?" I heard Nani say to me as I walked over to her. She slipped her hand into mine. "It was good for me, too. To think about things—think about *these* things."

I gave Nani's hand a squeeze while we watched the commotion unfold before us.

"Sarla is a loud woman. But she is screaming for a reason." Nani looked up at me, as if she knew that I was thinking about Depesh. Wondering how he was faring in London at that very moment, and how much he would have hated all of this. "Sarla knows she is losing. Our people are growing, changing—and that *silly* woman will soon be the only one left to resist. You *have* helped, my Raina."

But had I helped more than I'd hurt? I could only hope that was true.

"Raina," Nani said, after a moment had passed. "Are you expecting . . . *guest*?

"What do you mean?"

"Well," she said slyly. "When I arrived, there was a *very* tall young man waiting just outside the door."

My heart leaped.

"It *may* have been that Asher character . . ."

I tried not to give anything away, but I couldn't help it.

"*Jao*." Nani winked. "I will handle Sarla."

I slipped outside the room. Asher was just down the hallway, pacing back and forth in front of the bank of elevators. He stopped short as I walked toward him. It was my first time seeing him in a kurta pajama. Jet black with red and gold embroidery along the chest and cuffs. A crimson scarf hooked loosely around his neck. He looked so handsome, and when he caught my eye, it was all I could do not to buckle in front of him.

Draco sat in his arms, and he looked down at it. "Julien wanted me to give this to Shaylee."

I nodded, taking it from him. Behind me, Sarla let out another wail.

"What's going on in there?"

"I'm not sure you want to know. It's pretty . . . complicated." I shrugged. "And you said you were a simple guy . . ."

He grinned, and stuffed his hands into his pockets. "I did say that, didn't I?"

"Last night—" I bit my lip, and looked down. He didn't want to hear about my past, my excuses—and I realized that I didn't want to tell him. I wanted to move on. I wanted to make the most of the mess I'd created, and help clean it up—help those I'd hurt—in any way they'd let me.

And I wanted Asher. It had taken me too long to realize it, to recognize the simplicity of happiness when it was standing right in front of me. With Asher, I was ready to push past who I'd become, the mistakes I had made. I was ready—really ready to be the woman I knew I could be. A granddaughter, a daughter, a true friend; roles I'd often neglected in the past.

With Asher, I could be the woman who didn't lose herself to love.

"Would you like to have coffee with me sometime?"

A look of surprise washed over his face, and then he smiled.

"I know you're with someone—"

"I'm not with anyone."

I pressed my lips together, trying to keep from smiling.

"Rebekah and I broke up."

"I'm sorry to hear that."

"You don't look that sorry . . ."

I grinned. "Will you have coffee with me or not?"

His eyes moved up my face. "Are you going to wear your hair like that?"

I touched my head. My hair was still half done—part curled and pinned, the rest of it hanging straight over my ear.

"It's how the kids wear it these days."

"And those pajamas, wow." He nodded. "Sexy as hell."

"I like to keep up with the trends."

He grinned. "Is that so."

I nodded. "I'll take you to this trendy, hipster café I know. You'll love it."

"You know me so well." He smiled, and crossed his arms. "On the other hand, I'm not sure I know you as well as I thought."

"You probably know me better than I know myself."

"I'll have to teach you all about *Raina Anand*, will I?"

"Sure. I hear you're a good teacher. Although not so good at basketball."

"And where did you hear that?" He stepped toward me. "If you're not nice, you'll have to buy me two coffees. Three, even."

"I have to buy them? I don't know, Asher, I'm currently unemployed."

"So now who's the drifter?"

"How about . . . I'll buy you *one* coffee, and dessert? I won't even shove you into them."

"Really? Dessert, too?" He was right in front of me, inches away.

"Anything you want."

He licked his lips, moved in closer. "Anything?"

I could feel the heat of his body against mine. Pepper. Earth. Aftershave. I couldn't move. Slowly, he put his hands on my hips, started to lean in.

"So coffee sometime?" I was breathing hard. "It's a . . . date?"

"A date . . ."

I closed my eyes, and I felt his breath on my ear. My cheek. My lips.

"I'll have to check my schedule."

I opened my eyes. He was grinning at me.

"You're terrible."

"I'm a very busy man, Raina."

"You're going to make me pay for this, aren't you?"

The elevator bell rang, and a moment later, the doors opened. He got in, slowly turned around, and smiled at me. "Would you expect any less?"

I had to force myself not to jump in after him. Not to rush this. I knew I had a long way to go. With Asher—with everyone in my life. But right now, as I stood face-to-face with the man that I loved, I knew that I would be just fine.

MAY 20, 2019

Shay's bridal sari weighs nearly twenty pounds. She is made up like a Rajasthani doll, perspiring through the thick garment of a deep red *bandhani* design. The aunties adorn her with garlands and gold jewelry; shower her with praise, religious tokens, and blessings. While the hotel room is crowded and sickeningly hot, Nani has regained control, subdued Auntie Sarla's sobbing. No one mentions the pregnancy.

At the end of the preparations, Shay looks like a bride—one that could be plastered on the front cover of a Hindi magazine, or play the leading lady in a Bollywood movie. Raina squeezes her hand as Shay takes one last look in the mirror. Shay looks nothing like herself—her style bent to the will of her mother, her face made up to a point of artificial beauty. Any other day, Shay and Raina would have laughed at the image, ridiculed the excess and extravagance of it all, but today they decide against it.

The ceremony takes place in the lavish hotel hall, the bride, groom, and their families seated on a crisp white altar at the front of the room. Shay and Julien are perched on the carpeted surface on either side of the priest, who is performing the rituals in Sanskrit before a small sacred fire.

With few exceptions, this is the way Raina has always seen marriage—couples binding themselves to each other with the exchange of dark red and ivory flower garlands, measured laps around the flames. Raina watches attentively, with renewed interest, as the couple carries out the rituals. They pour water over a rock, then make offerings of rice to the flames. The priest ties Shay's *chunni* to the end of the thick, amber-red scarf draped over Julien's shoulders, a pledge of their love for each other. A literal nuptial knot.

Then, he instructs them to stand up and take seven symbolic steps. Food, strength, prosperity, wisdom. Progeny. Health. And then the seventh step: friendship. After, Julien dips his thumb into a small clay bowl and dabs red powder—the *sindoor*—above Shay's brow, marking her as a married woman.

Raina's face crumples. Shay and Julien are married, and she is deeply happy for them.

The couple moves to the front of the altar. The flower girls have passed around wicker baskets brimmed with rose petals, and the guests—all one thousand of them—line up to shower the happy couple with blessings. It is a more communal ending to a wedding ceremony than a kiss, but it is tradition, and the guests come forward to toss the petals as Shay and Julien hold hands: plastic figurines on a wedding cake. The last wave of guests makes their way to the front, and the steady stream of petals dies down. Shay and Julien look at each other, as if unsure what comes next. But then in one swift motion, Shay's eyes twinkling, she kisses him.

For a moment, the hall is soundless. Someone gasps, and then giggles emerge from the back of the hall. Raina's eyes flicker toward Auntie Sarla, who appears to be in physical pain, both of her hands folded over her mouth. Raina looks back at the couple. They are still kissing—passionately, eagerly—and without hesitation, Raina starts to clap. She cheers, lets out a whooping roar, causing some of the guests to turn and stare. But Raina doesn't stop. She hears Asher's voice join in, and in quick succession, cheering comes from the rest of the groomsmen, plus Serena, Zoey, and Alice. Others follow, and then more, until at least half of the guests are thundering with applause. Julien grabs Shay by the waist, dips her in front of the entire room as he kisses her.

And just like that, they have created a ripple. More fodder for their guests' gossip, morphing a tradition and making it their own.

A light lunch, and then the wedding party is herded into limos, shuttled from one photo shoot location to another. Shay and Julien in front of St. Basil's Church, a family photo on the college grounds, and then another in the shade of Falconer Hall. Julien and his groomsmen posed beneath arches, atop rail tracks at Union Station. The last shot of the day: Shay and the bridesmaids perched on benches at Toronto Music Gardens. After, as she's about to stand up, Raina feels two large, warm hands cover her eyes, and instinctively, she leans back against his stomach, breathes him in. A moment later, Asher peels away his hands, and a small chocolate birthday cake—stabbed through with fistfuls of thin pink candles—has appeared on her lap.

"It's your favorite," says Shay, smiling down at her. "But I'm a pregnant woman, so you have to share."

Raina stands up to hug her, setting the cake down on the bench. "Thank you."

"For the cake?" Shay pulls away smiling, and then flicks her eyes toward Asher. "Or for introducing you to him?"

Startled, Raina remembers that Shay had tried to set them up from the very beginning. That Shay had known the kind of man Raina had wanted, even before she realized it for herself.

"For both," Raina says eventually. "And for being my best friend."

The evening reception has already begun by the time they return to the hall. The hours blur together: food, drinking, music, and dancing. Raina is quickly immersed, but her mind, her heart, are not fully present. She notices her nani circling the room, obscured behind a fake smile, hiding how much she misses her daughter. She sees Auntie Sarla seated beside Shay at the head table, staring at her hands, as if the perfect wedding she's created is still not enough. She sees Depesh's parents avoiding everyone's glances, rushing through their meal and then leaving the reception early.

Raina also sees the gossip. It's hard not to. The rumors have already spread, and everyone knows Depesh is gay, and that Raina is not. Amid the cocktails, the perspiration steaming off the dance floor, the samosas and *papdi chaat* are the whispers. The lingering stares. Emboldened by alcohol, many have even confronted Raina. "What were you thinking?" they ask her, and Raina responds with the truth. She has nothing left to hide.

Some in her community are insulted, furious—while others roll their eyes and laugh. Raina tackles the questions they throw at her while standing in line at the bar, eating dinner, or on her way to the ladies' restroom. She finds that most aren't disgusted like Auntie Sarla—but neither are they as modern or as accepting as her nani. Rather, they treat the news like the latest plot twist in one of their Bollywood movies, gossip that will be forgotten in time for the next episode. Like her nani said, the community is changing—reluctantly, sluggishly—but they are changing.

The party is exhausting. Raina excuses herself from the table, and wanders outside onto the terrace encircling the hotel. The sky is clear, the wind cool yet soft. She walks, timing her breath with her step. She turns a corner, and is surprised to see she's not alone.

Depesh has his chin in his hands, and his elbows rest against the railing. He is staring out at the view—a parking lot, a building construction site. He's wearing jeans, a checked shirt, and his travel backpack sits at his feet. Her heart quickens as she steps toward him.

"You're back."

The slightest sound escapes his lips, and then he shakes his head. Raina studies his face, but he keeps looking ahead. She leans on the railing next to him.

"How was your trip?"

Still, he doesn't reply. He drops his arms from the railing and crosses them.

She knew it wouldn't be easy; she knew facing him again would be hard on both of them.

"Should I leave you alone?"

After a moment, he shakes his head. "Have you seen my parents?" he asks softly.

"I'm sorry . . . I saw them leave early."

He laughs. "Of course they did. Perfect." He picks up his bag. "There's no point for me to stick around—"

"I'm sure Shay and Julien would love to say hello," she says. "They'll be really happy you came."

He hesitates, slowly slides his bag over his shoulder. "You want me to go in there?"

"I think you should. But what do I know?"

"Everyone knows?"

Raina nods. "Everyone knows—about you. And about me."

"Well, a congratulations is in order for you, too, hey?" says Depesh, his voice edged. "You're straight again. I'm sure someone inside has a good match for you with a good Indian boy."

She presses her lips together. Raina knows he's angry, hurt—and he has the right to be. She doesn't know what to say, so she doesn't respond.

After a moment, Depesh drops his bag. "I'm sorry. I'm being a jerk."

Raina shrugs. "It's okay."

"Caleb and I are over." He turns away from her, pushes himself against the railing. "We broke up this morning."

Hesitantly, she reaches out for him. When he doesn't flinch, she rests her hand on his shoulder. "Are you okay?"

Again, he laughs.

"You didn't want to stay and have a gap year?"

"That's what Caleb wanted."

"And you?"

His mouth quivers. "He's just a boy, right? It's not the end of the world, it's . . . it's for the best"—Depesh nods earnestly, as if convincing himself—"and who knows, maybe we'll get back together down the road. When we're older. When I've figured things out."

"You're strong, Depesh. Stronger than I ever was."

He shrugs.

"I'm really proud of you."

"You keep saying that, but I don't even know why. I study hard because I care about my future. I was with Caleb because I love him." He grimaced. "I came back because I love my parents. I'm just living. I'm just doing what I want to do. It's simple. So what's there to be proud of, huh?"

"Gay. Straight. Indian. *Not* Indian." She moves closer to him. "Not everyone is brave enough to be themselves."

He doesn't answer.

"There's a lot to be proud of."

They stand there, leaning against the balcony, eyes searching the jagged skyline. Bhangra music pulses louder behind them. From the noise, Raina discerns the joyous cries of Shay and Julien celebrating to the music; the children dancing, playing; aunties and uncles chattering.

It is the sound of their community, of their family.

"What's it like in there?" Depesh asks after a moment.

"Auntie Sarla's inside," Raina answers. "But so is my nani. So is everyone else." She tries to catch his eye, wills him to understand.

Slowly, he reaches down for his backpack, and looks over.

"Are you ready?"

After a moment, he nods, and together they go back inside.

Raina's To-Do List

~~Pick up dry cleaning~~ DONE

~~Book our flights to Philadelphia~~ Leaving YYZ
7:30 a.m. October 16-23

Buy eggplant, 3 onions (white), and XL bag basmati for
Sunday cooking lessons ☺

Make reservation for Sunday (tacos??)
us + Asher + Depesh and parents

Attend university career fair (and keep your
chin up)

Pick out baby shower invites for Shay
"that aren't lame"

Organize double date w/Serena & Jayesh—
now who's the matchmaker? heh, heh

Make veg-friendly appies for Zoey/Alice's
housewarming

~~Finally beat Asher at basketball~~ . . .

You'll never beat me, babe

The Matchmaker's List

SONYA LALLI

DISCUSSION QUESTIONS

1. Why do you think Raina agrees to let her nani play match-maker? If you were in Raina's situation, would you let your grandmother (or another family member) set you up?

2. In chapter one, Raina thinks "a man unmarried in his thirties was fine—but for me, it wouldn't be." Have you ever experienced a similar double standard in your own life?

3. Raina's first matchmaking date is with Vishal, who agrees to meet her because he is afraid to stand up to his mother about his relationship with a non-Indian woman. Do you think this sort of thing happens a lot?

4. What date was your favorite? Why?

5. Raina is under so much pressure to get married, she lets her nani believe she is gay to avoid having to go on more dates. Do you sympathize with her in any way, or do you think she is wrong to lie to her grandmother?

6. Why do you think Shaylee is so upset that Raina has been drifting from her, especially when she learns that Raina has been lying about her sexuality to others? Would you ever resort to such behavior with your best friend to avoid confronting the problems between you?

7. Although hurt, Depesh ultimately forgives Raina for lying to him. Do you think she deserves to be forgiven?

8. Raina has a very close relationship with her nani. What in their family history has made them this way?

9. Why do you think Raina holds on to Dev for so long and is so resistant to considering a non-Indian man like Asher? Do you think Raina and Asher are a good match?

10. Do you think it is a good idea for Raina to quit her job before she knows what she wants to do next? Why do you think she works so hard as an investment analyst, even though her heart is never in it?

11. Why do you think Auntie Sarla and others in Raina's community are slow to understand and support homosexuality? Are there similar divides in social attitudes and awareness within your community?

A CONVERSATION WITH SONYA LALLI

The Matchmaker's List is your debut novel. When did you know you wanted to write a book?

I've always loved to write and knew one day I would try to write a book. Making time for writing proved difficult in university and early on in my career, but here and there I was able to work on two different books—one of which I finished.

I used to write for myself, but when I started hearing the voice and story of the character that would later become Raina, I was motivated to write something I wanted others to read. Her experiences as an Indian woman are so universal, yet we tend not to see a lot of them in women's fiction and romance. I hope this book can be a part of that change!

Was anything in The Matchmaker's List inspired by real-life experience?

I unwittingly modeled Nani after my own maternal grandmother. Many of the silly, sassy comments and jokes the Nani character says are things my nani could say to me, or actually has said. (I need to set her up with a Twitter account. She'd be famous!) At one point, the Nani character implies to Raina that it doesn't matter which suitor she chooses because, "They are men. White, brown, yellow, blue; they all have *something* wrong with them." This is basically a direct quote.

One of my favorite parts about *The Matchmaker's List* is Raina's relationship with her nani. They would do anything to make each other happy, even if sometimes they both go about it in the wrong way. Similarly, I have a very close bond with my nani and my paternal grandmother, Dadima. They are warm, progressive, fun-loving women—and huge supporters of this book!

Have you ever been tempted to play matchmaker for anyone?
All the time. My close friends know to expect probing, personal questions about their love or dating life, and offers for an introduction to some other unsuspecting friend or coworker of mine. I suppose I fancy myself a matchmaker just because I love to read and write love stories, but come to think of it, I don't think I've ever successfully set anybody up. A girl can dream, though.

Do you think Raina struggled more with the burden of family pressures or the challenges of the modern-dating scene?
One of the reasons Raina agrees to date men from her nani's list is the same reason many people decide to date online: they aren't meeting people organically in their day-to-day lives. Raina has a demanding job, and when she's not working, she's having downtime with her friends or family.

However, Raina's biggest struggle is the weight of her nani's expectation that she'll actually fall in love and marry someone from the list. Raina feels so much pressure to simply pick one that she becomes at risk of making a commitment to someone just for the sake of settling down. The men on the list check all the right boxes, and some of them are perfectly nice, but at the beginning of the book she's still pining after her first love and not ready for a new relationship.

In what ways does Raina symbolize a modern-Indian woman to you?

Raina is a modern, independent woman in every sense of the word: she dates, she has fun with her friends, and she has a high-flying career that she worked very hard for. But she also has a very deep, complicated relationship with her loving—if overbearing—nani, and more than anything wants her to approve of her choices.

As an Indian woman, living for yourself can often conflict with the life your family or community imagined for you: getting married and having children. Part of being a modern-Indian woman means navigating those tensions, and everyone will do it differently. Raina's journey is challenging, but it's one I think many of us can empathize with.

One of the ways Nani loves to express her love is by feeding Raina. Did food play into your family culture growing up?

Absolutely. My nani, Dadima, mom and aunt are all fantastic cooks and spoiled me rotten with their cooking. When I moved away from my hometown, I missed their cooking so much I had to learn to make it for myself. So now I try to learn one new recipe every time I visit. Just like Raina, a wonderful part of my relationship with my family and culture is cooking.

Nani's chicken curry, which I've included here, is one of the first recipes I learned, and please keep in mind the measurements are approximate. I was taught to portion ingredients using a sophisticated range of hand and finger measurements. The rule of thumb (pun intended) is, when in doubt, add more spices!

ʌani's Chicken Curry

4 tbsp oil	1 tsp turmeric (optional)
Chili to taste (diced or flakes)	1 tsp salt
2 tbsp ground cumin	3 tbsp plain yogurt
1 large onion, diced	2 lbs boneless chicken thighs
6 cloves garlic, minced	2 boiled potatoes
Ginger (large chunk), diced	(chopped into large pieces)
1 large can diced tomatoes	2 cups boiling water
1 tbsp ground coriander	Cilantro (optional)
1 tsp paprika (optional)	Roti or naan

Heat oil in a large saucepan and slowly add in chili, one tablespoon of cumin and then the onion, garlic, and ginger. Fry for a few minutes before adding canned tomatoes. Cook on medium heat, stirring frequently, and gradually add in the rest of the cumin, coriander, paprika, turmeric, salt, and yogurt. Add chicken, potatoes, and boiling water when the mixture is thick and starts sticking to the pan. Mash some of the potato pieces into the mixture to thicken. Simmer on low without the lid until the chicken is tender and excess water boils off. Salt to taste. Garnish with cilantro and serve with roti or naan.

Keep reading for a special preview of
Sonya Lalli's next novel . . .

How to Be a Grown-up

Coming in 2020 from Berkley!

"He kissed my *thumb*."

"He kissed your *what*?"

"My thumb," Jenny repeated, sticking her left thumb up like a hitchhiker. "He leaned over across the couch and so I closed my eyes . . . " Jenny closed her eyes, like the total drama queen she was. "And I waited, because I thought he was going to kiss me . . . And then, I feel this wet thing on my hand."

"It was a *wet* kiss?"

"On your *thumb*?"

Nodding, Jenny reached for her wineglass and took a long sip, clearly enjoying making her best friends Anu and Monica wait for the rest of the story. "He *frenched* my hand, you guys. My thumb in particular."

Anu made a face at them both. "So what'd you do?"

"Well, to be honest, I was curious. He seemed to think this

seduction technique actually worked. I was quite impressed by his confidence, actually."

"What did he go for next?" Monica said. "Your baby toe?"

"He sort of . . . worked his way up my hand." Jenny traced a line up her thumb, and then flipped over her wrist. "It took about ten minutes to get to my inner forearm. I know this because I was *literally* watching his microwave clock."

Monica laughed, and let her head fall down onto the bar table. "This would only happen to you, Jen."

"Did he ever get to your lips?" Anu asked.

Jenny shook her head in disgust. "It felt like a wet centipede crawling on me. And by the time he got to my elbow, I was bored out of my mind and ordered a taxi." She winked at them both. "You know, with my other thumb."

"What a weirdo."

"The weird thing is," Jenny said, glancing at her phone, "if he'd kissed my mouth, I probably would have slept with him."

Anu sipped her wine as Jenny launched into more detail about her "wet date" with Ronny the personal trainer. Now that Monica was only two weeks from walking down the aisle, they counted on Jenny for bad-date stories for their girls' nights. But, like so many times before when Jenny described other dates gone wrong, Anu never understood why Jenny was so quickly dismissive of her dates. She had been looking forward to going out with Ronny for weeks.

"What's with your face?" Jenny said, midstory, turning her intense gaze on Anu. She pushed the bowl of wasabi peas across the table, and Anu scooped up a handful.

"Nothing's wrong with my face."

Jenny rolled her eyes.

"Okay, fine." Anu sighed. "I'm just wondering why you're writing this guy off so fast. I thought you liked him, and now you're saying you plan to switch gyms to avoid him?"

"Did she not hear my story?" Jenny asked Monica.

"I heard your story, but—"

"*But*, Anu, dating is hard, and you have to trust your gut. You'd know that if you'd ever actually *dated*."

"I've dated," she said quietly, anticipating Jenny's raised eyebrows and hoping her friends couldn't hear the defensive tone in her voice.

It was familiar territory they'd gone over time and time again: Anu and Jenny had very different definitions of the word "date." To Anu, dates were the handful of coffee, study, or lunch dates she went on with her soon-to-be ex-husband Neil twelve years earlier, before he worked up the courage to hold her hand and change his relationship status on Facebook. More recently, the six weeks of wining and dining her boyfriend, Ryan, subjected her to before she asked him if she was his girlfriend, he said yes, and so she finally agreed to sleep with him.

"*You* have not dated," Jenny said, predictably. "*You* married the first man you ever kissed."

Anu had spent the entire day running around after her daughter, Kanika, at the wave pool, and now she felt too tired to argue. "You're right. I haven't."

"Don't be condescending."

"I'm not being condescending."

"You are, too."

"And you're just trying to pick a fight."

Jenny stuck her tongue out.

"You're such a child, Jen."

Saved by the arrival of a plate of nachos, Anu was aware of Jenny glaring at her as the waiter took his time setting them up with small plates, cutlery, and napkins, and refilling their water glasses.

"The only child at this table," Jenny said, after the waiter left, "is the one who can't drink more than two glasses of wine without going cross-eyed."

Anu's jaw dropped as Monica giggled.

"The only *child* at this table," Jenny repeated, "is the woman who thought people had 'organisms' during sex until her *eleventh*-grade biology midterm."

Anu gasped, hitting Monica lightly on the shoulder. "You told her?"

"The only child at this table," Jenny said, slowly this time, "is the *thirty*-year-old hiding her new boyfriend from her parents."

She knew Jenny only meant to be funny, and Anu didn't want to make a scene, but that last one still hurt.

"Jen," Monica said. "That's enough. You know she's not ready."

"I wanted to tell Neil first," Anu said defensively.

"You told him weeks ago."

To be accurate, it had been exactly three weeks since she told Neil she had started to date. She knew for sure because three times since then, when she had picked up or dropped off their daughter, Neil refused to look her in the eye.

"He's not taking it well," Anu said finally, wiping salsa off her lips. "He hates me."

"And you're worried your parents will, too?" Monica said helpfully.

Anu nodded, even though "hate" wasn't what concerned her. She feared their disappointment in her choices.

She was twenty-nine years old the first time she let them down, the first time she ever saw their faces fall, had to witness their un-practiced looks of dismay.

"Neil and I are separating."

The concept was so foreign, she could have been speaking to them in French. Then their questions came at her rapid-fire.

Why would she ask her hardworking, loyal husband to move out? Why did she need space? Their house was 2,300 square feet!

How could Anu be so selfish? Didn't she consider how it would impact Neil and Kanika? Was she thinking only about herself?

Even now, more than ten months later, her parents remained convinced their daughter's separation was temporary. Just a "blip," as Lakshmi liked to describe it to her friends. And so Anu had never really made clear to her parents that her marriage was over—so over, in fact, she was in a serious relationship with another man and planned to ask Neil for a divorce.

"I don't understand why you're so scared of them," Jenny said. "What are they going to do, ground you? And don't say it's because you're Indian—Mon's Indian. *She* stood up to her parents."

"I'll tell them eventually, Jen. But right now . . . it's easier just to let it be." Anu smirked and tried to pretend she wasn't bothered. "Like the Beatles."

"That song is about how much Paul McCartney loved his mother, not how much he *lied* to her."

"You only have two weeks, Anu." Monica reached across the table for the wasabi peas. "You need to tell them before the wedding. People will talk when they see you and Ryan together, and word will get back to your parents."

"Wait, you never told me you're bringing Ryan to the wedding," Jenny said. "Just because Neil won't be around doesn't mean you need to bring some other guy."

"Ryan's not just 'some guy'—"

"Right, he's a new boyfriend. It can't be serious yet. You introduce your friends to a new boyfriend, you tell your *parents* about him, but you don't cart him along to your best friend's wedding."

"I know you don't want to hear it. But we are serious."

When Jenny snorted, Anu reached for her drink and, finding it empty, twisted the glass hard in her hand. Why did she let Jenny affect her? Having sex and spending almost every night together didn't count as *serious*?

"You don't like Ryan," Anu accused, refusing to meet Jenny's eye. "Do you?"

"Ask Monica if she likes him."

"I like him just fine," Monica said, slapping Jenny on the arm. "And I think what Ms. Diplomatic is trying to say is—"

"What I'm *trying* to say is that Anu claims she left Neil to find herself, yet here she is jumping into a so-called 'serious' relationship with Ryan."

"I was with the wrong guy. Ryan is different. He's—"

"This isn't even about Ryan!" Jenny cried. "It's about you getting to know yourself, making some mistakes along the way. If you've never been single for more than five seconds, how exactly are you supposed to know what kind of guy is right for you? Or what you want out of life."

"I—"

"How are you ever supposed to grow up?"

"Are you kidding me? I was the first of all three of us to grow up," Anu fumed. "I have a daughter, a good job, a house, a boyfriend, a mortgage—"

"That's stuff you have, not stuff you are."

Anu threw Monica a pleading look, but she was busy picking at the nachos and pretended not to see.

"Fine." Anu sat up straighter in her chair. "I'm financially responsible and live within my means. I put my family first; I'm a role model to my daughter. I chose a suitable partner—"

"You mean *Ryan*?"

"Of course Ryan! And so what if I don't drink that much? I can control my urges. I do things in moderation. I'm responsible."

"Responsible or . . . scared?"

"I know what it means to be a grown-up."

She looked up, meeting Jenny's gaze. Her friends were honest, and brutal, but she knew they cared.

Anu exhaled slowly. She could sense there was more Jenny wanted to say, to push the argument even further, truly test the notion that they loved and fought as hard as sisters, but luckily Monica stepped in instead. She yanked them both by the ear.

"Ow!"

"Are you fools done, yet?" Monica asked. She sounded annoyed. "The nachos are getting cold."

"Okay, fine. I'm done."

Anu smiled at the table, victorious. "I'm done, too."

They returned to their food and picked up where they had left off in gossiping about Ronny the personal trainer. Anu had no need to prove herself, to convince Jenny of something Anu suspected Jenny was incapable of understanding from her point of view.

Anu *was* a grown-up. After all, she had everything a woman is supposed to want in life. *Could* ever want in life. She had played by the rules and gotten everything she'd ever been told to expect out of life.

Sonya Lalli is a Canadian writer of Indian heritage. She studied law in her hometown of Saskatoon and at Columbia University in New York, and later completed an MA in Creative Writing and Publishing at City, University of London. Sonya has a black belt in Tae Kwon Do and loves travel, yoga, and cocktail bartending. She lives in Toronto with her husband.

Ready to find
your next great read?

Let us help.

Visit prh.com/nextread

Penguin
Random
House

THE PLACE
OF DEAD
ROADS

PICADOR USA

HENRY HOLT AND COMPANY

NEW YORK

William S. Burroughs

THE PLACE
OF DEAD
ROADS

Picador® is a U.S. registered trademark and is used by Henry Holt and Company
under license from Pan Books Limited.

For information on Picador USA Reading Group Guides, as well as ordering, please
contact the Trade Marketing department at St. Martin's Press.
Phone: 1-800-221-7945 extension 763
Fax: 212-677-7456
E-mail: trademarketing@stmartins.com

Grateful acknowledgment is given for permission to reprint a portion of "Keep the
Home Fires Burning" by Lena Guilbert Ford and Ivor Novello. Copyright 1915 by
Chappell & Co., Ltd.; Copyright renewed, published in the U.S.A. by Chappell &
Co., Inc. International copyright secured. All rights reserved. Used by permission.

Library of Congress Cataloging-in-Publication Data
Burroughs, William S.
The place of dead roads.
I. Title.
PS3552.U75P54   1983   813'.54 83-8498
ISBN 0-312-27865-9

First published in the United States by Holt, Rinehart and Winston

First Picador USA Edition: May 2001

10 9 8 7 6 5 4 3 2 1

TO DENTON WELCH,
FOR KIM CARSONS

The original title of this book was *The Johnson Family*. "The Johnson family" was a turn-of-the-century expression to designate good bums and thieves. It was elaborated into a code of conduct. A Johnson honors his obligations. His word is good and he is a good man to do business with. A Johnson minds his own business. He is not a snoopy, self-righteous, troublemaking person. A Johnson will give help when help is needed. He will not stand by while someone is drowning or trapped under a burning car.

The only thing that could unite the planet is a united space program . . . the earth becomes a space station and war is simply *out,* irrelevant, flatly insane in a context of research centers, spaceports, and the exhilaration of working with people you like and respect toward an agreed-upon objective, an objective from which all workers will gain. *Happiness is a by-product of function.* The planetary space station will give all participants an opportunity to function.

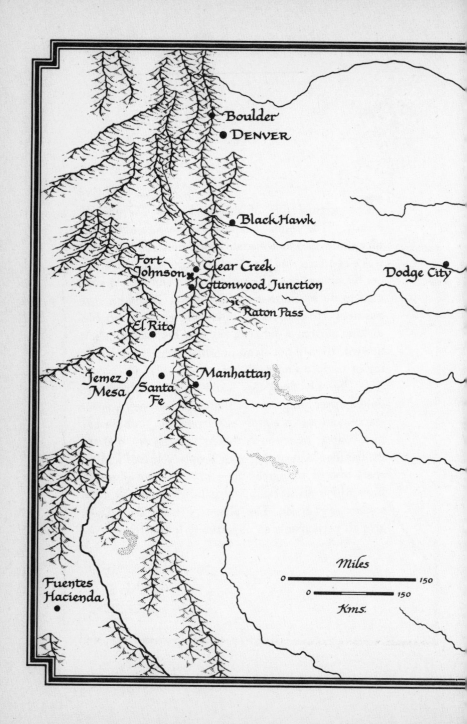

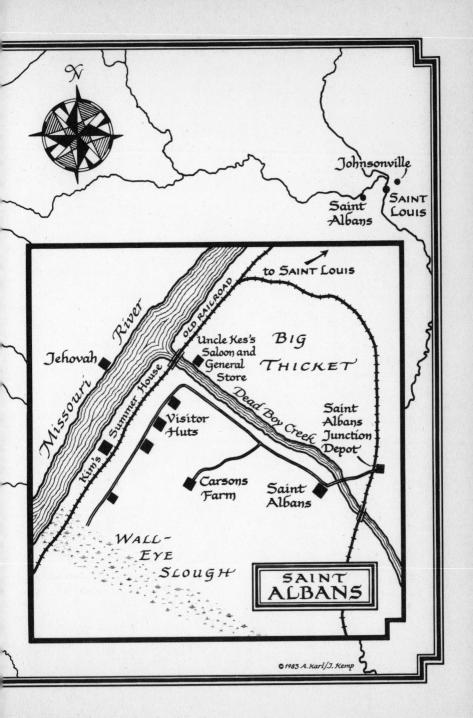

I

STRANGER WHO
WAS PASSING

SHOOT-OUT IN BOULDER

SEPTEMBER 17, 1899. What appeared to be an Old-Western shoot-out took place yesterday afternoon at the Boulder Cemetery. The protagonists have been identified as William Seward Hall, sixty-five, a real-estate speculator with holdings in Colorado and New Mexico, and Mike Chase, in his fifties, about whom nothing was known.

Hall resided in New York City, and wrote western stories under the pen name of "Kim Carsons." "He was apparently here on a business trip," a police source stated.

At first glance it appeared that Chase and Hall had killed each other in a shoot-out, but neither gun had been fired, and both men were killed by single rifle shots fired from a distance. Chase was shot from in front through the chest. Hall was shot in the back. Nobody heard the shots, and police believe the rifleman may have employed a silencer.

A hotel key was found in Hall's pocket, and police searched his room at the Over-

look Hotel. They found clothing, a 38 revolver, and a book entitled *Quién Es?* by
Kim Carsons. Certain passages had been
underlined.

Police investigating this bizarre occurrence have as yet no clue to the possible
motives of the men. "Looks like an old
grudge of some sort," Police Chief Martin
Winters said. When asked whether there
was any reason Chase and Hall should want
to kill each other, he replied, "Not that I
know of, but we are continuing the investi-
gation."

The Sunday paper played up the story, with pictures of the
deceased and the cemetery, and diagrams showing the location
of the bodies and the probable spot from which the shots had
been fired. When asked about the make and caliber of the death
weapon, the Medical Examiner stated: "Definitely a rifle. Size of
the exit holes is consistent with a 45-70 dumdum bullet, but the
projectiles have not been recovered."

The article quoted the underlined passages from Hall's
book *Quién Es?*

Papers in an old attic . . . an old yellow press clipping from the
Manhattan Comet, April 3, 1894:

Three members of the Carsons gang were
killed today when they attempted to hold
up the Manhattan City Bank. A posse, dispatched in pursuit of the survivors, ran into
an ambush and suffered several casualties. . . . Mike Chase, a U.S. marshal, stated
that the ambush was not carried out by the

Carsons gang but by a band of Confederate
renegades armed with mortars and grenades. . . .

This poem was wroted by Kim Carsons after a shoot-out on
Bleecker Street, October 23, 1920. Liver Wurst Joe and Cherry
Nose Gio, Mafia hit men, with Frank the Lip as driver, opened
fire on Kim Carsons, Boy Jones, Mars Cleaver, known as Marbles, and Guy Graywood, described as an attorney. In the ensu-
ing exchange of shots Liver Wurst Joe, Cherry Nose Gio, and
Frank the Lip was all kilted. Only damage sustained by the Carsons group was to Boy's vest when he took refuge behind a fire
hydrant.

"My vest is ruinted," he moaned. "And it was dog shit
done it. There should be a law."

Owing to certain "offensive passages" written in the French language the poem could not be quoted, but an enterprising assistant editor had copies made with translations of the offensive
passages and sold them to collectors and curiosity seekers for
five dollars a copy.

Stranger Who Was Passing

un grand principe de violence dictait à nos moeurs
(a great principle of violence dictated our fashions)
Surely a song for men like a great wind
Shaking an iron tree
Dead leaves in the winter pissoir
J'aime ces types vicieux
Qu'ici montrent la bite. . . .
(I like the vicious types
who show the cock here. . . .)
Simon, aimes-tu le bruit des pas
Sur les feuilles mortes?

5

(Simon, do you like the sound of steps
on dead leaves?)
The smell of war and death?
Powder smoke back across the mouth blown
Powder smoke and brown hair?
Death comes with the speed of a million winds
The sheltering sky is thin as paper here
That afternoon when I watched
The torn sky bend with the wind
I can see it start to tilt
And shred and tatter
Caught in New York
Beneath the animals of the Village
The Piper pulled down the sky.

LET IT COME DOWN.

Appointment at the cemetery . . . Boulder, Colorado . . .
September 17, 1899
Mike swung onto the path at the northeast corner, wary and watchful. He was carrying a Webley-Fosbery 45 semi-automatic revolver, the action adjusted with rubber grips by an expert gunsmith to absorb recoil and prevent slipping. His backup men were about ten yards away, a little behind him across the street.

Kim stepped out of the cemetery onto the path. "Hello, Mike." His voice carried clear and cool on the wind, sugary and knowing and evil. Kim always maneuvered to approach downwind. He was wearing a russet tweed jacket with change pockets, canvas puttees, jodhpurs in deep red.

At sight of him Mike experienced an uneasy *déjà vu* and glanced sideways for his backup.

One glance was enough. They were all wearing jackets the color of autumn leaves, and puttees. They had opened a wicker shoulder basket. They were eating sandwiches and filling tin cups with cold beer, their rifles propped against a tree remote and timeless as a painting.

Déjeuner des chasseurs.

Mike sees he has been set up. He will have to shoot it out. He feels a flash of resentment and outrage.

God damn it! It's not fair!

Why should his life be put in jeopardy by this horrible little nance? Mike had a well-disciplined mind. He put these protests aside and took a deep breath, drawing in power.

Kim is about fifteen yards south walking slowly toward him. Fresh southerly winds rustle the leaves ahead of him as he walks "on a whispering south wind" . . . leaves crackle under his boots . . . Michael, *aimé tu le bruit des pas sur les feuilles mortes.* . . ? Twelve yards ten . . . Kim walks with his hands swinging loose at his sides, the fingers of his right hand brushing the gun butt obscenely, his face alert, detached, unreadable. . . . Eight yards . . . . Suddenly Kim flicks his hand up without drawing as he points at Mike with his index finger.

"BANG! YOU'RE *DEAD.*"

He throws the last word like a stone. He knows that Mike will *see* a gun in the empty hand and this will crowd his draw. . . .

(With a phantom gun in an empty hand he has bluffed Mike into violating a basic rule of gunfighting. TYT. Take *Your* Time. Every gunfighter has *his* time. The time it takes him to draw aim fire and *hit.* If he tries to beat his time the result is almost invariably a miss. . . .

"Snatch and grab," Kim chants.

Yes, Mike was drawing too fast, much too fast.

Kim's hand snaps down flexible and sinuous as a whip and up with his gun extended in both hands at eye level.

"Jerk and miss."

He felt Mike's bullet whistle past his left shoulder.

Trying for a heart shot. . . .

Both eyes open, Kim sights for a fraction of a second, just so long and long enough: the difference between a miss and a hit. Kim's bullet hits Mike just above the heart with a liquid

SPLAT as the mercury explodes inside, blowing the aorta to shreds.

Mike freezes into a still, gun extended, powder smoke blowing back across his face. He begins to weave in slow circles. He gags and spits blood. His gun arm starts to sag.

Kim slowly lowers his gun in both hands, face impassive, eyes watchful.

Mike's eyes are glazed, unbelieving, stubborn, still trying to get the gun up for the second shot. But the gun is heavy, too heavy to lift, pulling him down.

Slowly Kim lowers his gun into the holster.

Mike crumples sideways and falls.

Kim looks up at the trees, watching a squirrel, a remote antique gaiety suffuses his face, molding his lips into the ambiguous marble smile of a Greek youth.

Definitely an *chaic* from Skyros with that special Skyros smile.

Who is the Greek youth smiling at? He is smiling at his own archaic smile.

For this is the smile that happens when the smiler becomes the smile.

The wind is rising. Kim watches a dead leaf spiral up into the sky.

The Egyptian glyph that signifies: To stand up in evidence. An ejaculating phallus, a mouth, a man with his fingers in his mouth.

Kim waves to his three witnesses. One waves back with a drum stick in his hand.

Hiatus of painted calm . . .

Pâté, bread, wine, fruit spread out on the grass, gun propped against a tombstone, a full moon in the China-blue evening sky. One of the hunters strums a mandolin inlaid with mother-of-pearl as they sing:

"It's only a paper moon . . ."

Kim lifts his gun and shoots a hole in the moon, a black hole with fuzz around it like powder burns.

A wind ripples the grass, stirs uneasily through branches.

"Flying over a muslin tree."

Kim's second shot takes out a grove of trees at the end of the cemetery.

The wind is rising, ripping blurs and flashes of russet orange red from the trees, whistling through tombstones.

All the spurious old father figures rush on stage.

"*STOP, MY SON!*"

"No son of yours, you worthless old farts."

Kim lifts his gun.

"*YOU'RE DESTROYING THE UNIVERSE!*"

"What universe?"

Kim shoots a hole in the sky. Blackness pours out and darkens the earth. In the last rays of a painted sun, a Johnson holds up a barbed-wire fence for others to slip through. The fence has snagged the skyline . . . a great black rent. Screaming crowds point to the torn sky.

"*OFF THE TRACK! OFF THE TRACK!*"

"*FIX IT!*" the Director bellows. . . .

"What with, a Band-Aid and chewing gum? Rip in the Master Film. . . . Fix it yourself, Boss Man."

"*ABANDON SHIP, GOD DAMN IT. . . . EVERY MAN FOR HIMSELF!*"

For three days Kim had camped on the mesa top, sweeping the valley with his binoculars. A cloud of dust headed south told him they figured him to ride in that direction for Mexico. He had headed north instead, into a land of sandstone formations, carved by wind and sand—a camel, a tortoise, Cambodian temples—and everywhere caves pocked into the red rock like bubbles in boiling oatmeal. Some of the caves had been lived in at one time or another: rusty tin cans, pottery shards, cartridge cases. Kim found an arrowhead six inches long, chipped from obsidian, and a smaller arrowhead of rose-colored flint.

On top of the mesa were crumbled mounds of earth that had once been houses. Slabs of stone had been crisscrossed to form an altar. *Homo sapiens* was here.

Dusk was falling and blue shadows gathered in the Sangre de Cristo Mountains to the east. Sangre de Cristo! Blood of Christ! Rivers of blood! Mountains of blood! Does Christ never get tired of bleeding? To the west the sun sets behind thunderclouds over the Jemez Mountains, and Jiménez straddles the mountains with his boots of rock and trees, a vast *charro* rising into the sky, his head a crystal skull of clouds as his guns spit from darkening battlements and thunder rattles over the valley. The evening star shines clear and green ... "Fair as a star, when only one/Is shining in the sky." That's Wordsworth, Kim remembers. It is raining in the Jemez Mountains.

"It is raining, Anita Huffington." Last words of General

Grant, spoken to his nurse, circuits in his brain flickering out like lightning in gray clouds.

Kim leaned back against stone still warm from the sun. A cool wind touched his face with the smell of rain.

Pottery shards . . . arrowheads . . . a crib . . . a rattle . . . a blue spoon . . . a slingshot, the rubber rotted through . . . rusting fishhooks . . . tools . . . you can see there was a cabin here once . . . a hypodermic syringe glints in the sun . . . the needle has rusted into the glass, forming little sparks of brown mica . . . abandoned artifacts . . .

He holds the rose flint arrowhead in his hand. Here is the arrowhead, lovingly fashioned for a purpose. Campfires flicker on Indian faces eating the luscious dark meat of the passenger pigeon. He fondles the obsidian arrowhead, so fragile . . . did they break every time they were used, like bee stings, he wonders?

(Bison steaks roasting on a spit.)

Somebody made this arrowhead. It had a creator long ago. This arrowhead is the only proof of his existence. Living things can also be seen as artifacts, designed for a purpose. So perhaps the human artifact had a creator. Perhaps a stranded space traveler needed the human vessel to continue his journey, and he made it for that purpose? He died before he could use it? He found another escape route? This artifact, shaped to fill a forgotten need, now has no more meaning or purpose than this arrowhead without the arrow and the bow, the arm and the eye. Or perhaps the human artifact was the creator's last card, played in an old game many light-years ago. Chill of empty space.

Kim gathers wood for a fire. The stars are coming out. There's the Big Dipper. His father points to Betelgeuse in the night sky over Saint Louis . . . smell of flowers in the garden. His father's gray face on a pillow.

> Helpless pieces in the game he plays
> On this checkerboard of nights and days.

He picks up the obsidian arrowhead, arrow and bow of empty space. You can't see them anymore without the arm and the eye ... the chill ... so fragile ... shivers and gathers wood. Can't see them anymore. Slave Gods in the firmament. He remembers his father's last words:

"Stay out of churches, son. All they got a key to is the shit house. And swear to me you will never wear a lawman's badge."

Hither and thither moves, and checks, and slays,
And one by one back in the Closet lays.

Playthings in an old game, the little toy soldiers are covered with rust, shaped to fill a forgotten empty space.

Rusty tin cans ... pottery shards ... cartridge cases ... arrowheads ... a hypodermic syringe glints in the sun.

The horse is as much a part of the West as the landscape, but Kim never really made it with the horse. He tried at first to establish a telepathic bond with his horse, but the horse hated the relationship and tried to kill him at every opportunity. It would swell itself up when he put on the saddle, or it would suddenly scrape against a tree or run under a low branch. All the old horse tricks.

He did eventually break one beast, a strawberry roan, down into telepathy with a loaded quirt and some rather ingenious electronic devices but his "Strawberry," as he called it, finally turned on him and Kim swore that he would never again become involved with a horse. He hated their hysteria, their stubborn malice, and their awful yellow teeth.

"Shoot-out in front of the Dead Ass Saloon, still noon heat, dusty street from nowhere to nowhere, lead flying all over the set, my faithful cayuse at my side, then he hits me from behind with a front hoof. I roll, twist, and put a quick shot into his ribs from below. He screams like a woman spitting blood, bullets

clipping all around couldn't hit me because of the prancing screaming horse, then he bolts right for them and they are all shooting at the horse and I take them out slow and easy and greasy. Percussion lock days, had to grease your bullets. Otherwise sparks fly out between the cylinder and the barrel, and all six cylinders is subject to go up in your face."

It was his practice to move on foot and he could cover up to fifty miles a day with his sorcerer's gait and his specially designed spring-walking boots, then pick up a horse, keep it for a week or so, and release it. Kim intended to head into the Jemez Mountains and hide out for a month. . . . He would need camping equipment, too heavy to carry. . . .

The area was mostly Mexican, and Kim had *family* letters. . . .

There are signs that indicate the presence of a stranger in rural areas. Some are positive, like the barking of dogs. Other indications are negative, like the sudden cessation of frogs croaking.

Joe the Dead had taught Kim how to circumvent this obstacle course. "If you want to hide something, create disinterest in the area where it is hidden. Try this on a city street. Don't give anyone any reason to look at you and no one will see you. You have become invisible. This is easy in a city, where most people are concerned with their own business. But in the country you have to get around critters whose business it is to smell and see and hear you and give notice of your approach. So you have to give the watchers good reasons not to smell and see and hear you and give notice of your approach. This amulet is from the Cat Goddess Bast. All dogs hate and fear it. But you have to animate its power and make it work for you."

Kim took three dogs to a remote mountain cabin and got down to the root of their dogness. The dogs did not survive this psychic dissection. Kim wondered if any creature can survive the exposure of its basic mechanisms. After that, Kim had the power to cloud dogs' minds, to blunt their sense of smell, their hearing,

and their sight. And he could make himself part of his surroundings so that he did not disturb the frogs and birds and crickets.

He reached a road of yellow gravel unobserved. He followed the road to a store by a bridge ... sound of running water ...

"Buenos días, señor." Kim stood in front of the counter, an envelope in his right hand. A thin old man in a gray flannel shirt looked up. It was not often that anyone reached his store unannounced. Two young men watched from the back of the store.

"I bring greetings from Don Bernabe Jurado." Kim passed the envelope over the counter. The old man read the letter.

"You are welcome, Mr. Hall. My name is Don Linares." He led the way through the store to a back room, where a screen door opened onto a patio ... fruit trees, a pump, chickens scratching.

The old man motioned Kim to a chair and gave him an appraising glance.

"You are hungry."

Kim nodded. . . .

Huevos rancheros with fried beans and blue tortillas and a pot of coffee. Kim ate with delicate animal voracity, like a hungry raccoon. A cat rubbed against his leg. It was a handsome brute, a purple-gray tomcat with green eyes.

Kim enjoyed the Spanish ritual of talking about everything but the business in hand. They talked about the weather, the railroad's decision to set up the terminal in Lamy rather than in Santa Fe itself. Mostly they talked about mutual friends and acquaintances, Don Linares throwing in a bit of false data here and there; the letter could be a forgery, and Kim an impostor.

"Ah? But they are already married since June."

"Yes, to be sure. I am forgetful at times."

There was a moment of silence. Kim knew he was being tested. Well, he wouldn't mind being reborn as a Mexican.

"How can I be of service?" the old man finally asked.

"I need a horse and some supplies and much silence. Sug-

ar, salt, lard, tea, chile, salt pork, flour, a bag of lemons . . ."
Kim looked over the stock of guns. . . . Ah *there* is something
he'd been looking for: a smooth-bore 44, chambered for shot
shells. You have a room full of turkeys to take care of, this gun
could throw a hail of lead three feet wide. Ideal gun for survival
hunting. And the *only* thing for snakes. Kim paid in gold.

The Jemez Basin, crater of an extinct volcano, looks as though it
were scooped out by a giant hand. A river winds down the middle of the basin and a number of spring-fed tributaries feed into
the river, so that the whole basin is crisscrossed by water. Some
streams are only two feet wide at the top but eight feet deep,
with an overhanging bank. The valley is full of frogs, and you
can see great yellow tadpoles deep down in the dark slow-mov-
ing water of these swampy streams.

Kim camped on the south slope, his tent hidden by trees.
He baited his hook with a big purple worm and dropped it into
one of the still, narrow streams, yellow flash of fish side in the
dark water.

He held the crisp fried fish by the head and the tail, eating
the meat off the backbone, washed down with lemonade.

Twilight, fish jumping, a symphony of frogs. Kim saw a
vast frog conducting the orchestra, and he thought of Rimbaud's
"Historic Evening."—"A master's hand awakes the meadow's
harpsichord . . . they are playing cards at the bottom of the
pond. . . ."

The golden grass, the sinister black water were like the
landscape of some forgotten planet. He could see himself eating
trout there forever, heaps of bones with grass growing through.

Kim is a slimy, morbid youth of unwholesome proclivities with an insatiable appetite for the extreme and the sensational. His mother had been into table-tapping and Kim adores ectoplasms, crystal balls, spirit guides and auras. He wallows in abominations, unspeakable rites, diseased demon lovers, loathsome secrets imparted in a thick slimy whisper, ancient ruined cities under a purple sky, the smell of unknown excrements, the musky sweet rotten reek of the terrible Red Fever, erogenous sores suppurating in the idiot giggling flesh. In short, Kim is everything a normal American boy is taught to *detest*. He is evil and slimy and *insidious*. Perhaps his vices could be forgiven him, but he was also given to the subversive practice of *thinking*. He was in fact incurably intelligent.

Later, when he becomes an important player, he will learn that people are not bribed to shut up about what they know. They are bribed not to find it out. And if you are as intelligent as Kim, it's hard not to find things out. Now, American boys are told they should think. But just wait until your thinking is basically different from the thinking of a boss or a teacher. . . . You will find out that you *aren't* supposed to think.

Life is an entanglement of lies to hide its basic mechanisms.

Kim remembers a teacher who quoted to the class: "If a thing is worth doing at all it is worth doing well. . . ."

"Well sir, I mean the contrary is certainly true. If a thing is worth doing at all, it is worth doing, even badly," said Kim pert-

ly, hoping to impress the teacher with his agile intelligence. "I mean, we can't all become Annie Oakleys doesn't mean we can't get some fun and benefit from shooting. . . ."

The teacher didn't like that *at all,* and for the rest of the school year singled Kim out for heavy-handed sarcasm, addressing him as "our esteemed woodsman and scout." When Kim couldn't answer a history question, the teacher asked, "Are you one of these strong, silent men?" And he wrote snippy little comments in the margins of Kim's compositions: "Not *quite* as badly as *that,*" viciously underlining the offending passage. At the end of the term the teacher gave him a B— for the course, though Kim knew fucking well he deserved an A.

To be sure, Kim was rotten clear through and he looked like a sheep-killing dog and smelled like a polecat, but he was also the most ingenious, curious, resourceful, inventive little snot that ever rose from the pages of *Boy's Life,* thinking up ways of doing things better than other folks. Kim would get to the basic root of what a device is designed to do and ask himself, Is it doing it in the simplest and most efficient way possible? He knew that once an article goes into mass production, the last thing a manufacturer wants to hear about is a better and simpler article that is *basically different.* And they are not interested in a more efficient, simpler or better product. They are interested in making money.

When Kim was fifteen his father allowed him to withdraw from the school because he was so unhappy there and so much disliked by the other boys and their parents.

"I don't want that boy in the house again," said Colonel Greenfield. "He looks like a sheep-killing dog."

"It is a walking corpse," said a Saint Louis matron poisonously.

"The boy is rotten clear through and he stinks like a polecat," Judge Farris pontificated.

This was true. When angered or aroused or excited Kim flushed bright red and steamed off a rank ruttish animal smell.

And sometimes he lost control over his natural functions. He took comfort from learning that partially domesticated wolves suffer from the same difficulty.

"The child in not wholesome," said Mr. Kindhart, with his usual restraint. Kim was the most unpopular boy in the school, if not in the town of Saint Louis.

"They have nothing to teach you anyway," his father said. "Why, the headmaster is a fucking priest."

The summers they spent at the farm, and during the day Kim spent much of his time outdoors, hiking, hunting, and fishing. He loved squirrel hunting in the early morning, and usually went hunting with Jerry Ellisor, a buck-toothed, slightly retarded boy who lived next door. Jerry was subject to fits, so Kim carried a leather-covered stick he would shove in Jerry's mouth to keep him from biting his tongue off. Kim enjoyed watching these fits because sometimes Jerry would get a hard-on and shoot off in his pants, and that was a powerful sight. And Jerry had a slinky black hound dog. Everybody knows you can't find squirrels without a dog to bark up the tree where a squirrel is.

His father had an extensive and eclectic library, and Kim spent much of his time reading during the winter months. Kim read everything in his father's library, Shakespeare and all the classics. Dickens was not for him, and he couldn't abide Sir Walter Scott. Knights and ladies repelled him. Armor was a cumbersome and impractical device, jousting was stupid and bestial, and romantic love was disgusting, rather like the cult of Southern womanhood. He noticed that he was particularly detested by self-styled Southern gentlemen, a truly pestiferous breed. The animal doctor should put all Southern gentlemen to sleep, along with the knights and the ladies, he decided.

There were a number of medical books, which Kim read avidly. He loved to read about diseases, rolling and savoring the names on his tongue: tabes dorsalis, Friedreich's ataxia, climactic buboes . . . and the pictures! the poisonous pinks and greens and yellows and purples of skin diseases, rather like the objects

in those Catholic stores that sell shrines and madonnas and cru-
cifixes and religious pictures. There was one skin disease where
the skin swells into a red wheal and you can *write* on it. It would
be fun to find a boy with this disease and draw pricks all over
him. Kim thought maybe he would study medicine and become a
doctor, but while he liked diseases he didn't like sick people.
They complained all the time. They were petulant and self-cen-
tered and boring. And the thought of delivering babies was
enough to turn a man to stone.

His father had a large collection of books on magic and the
occult, and Kim drew magic circles in the basement and tried to
conjure up demons. His favorites were the Abominations like
Humwawa, whose face is a mass of entrails and who rides on a
whispering south wind. Pazuzu, Lord of Fevers and Plagues, and
especially Gelal and Lilit, who invade the beds of men, because
he did sometimes experience a vivid sexual visitation he hoped
was an incubus. He knew that the horror of these demon lovers
was a gloomy Christian thing. In Japan there are phantom
whores known as "fox maidens," who are highly prized, and the
man who can get his hands on a fox maiden is considered lucky.
He felt sure there were fox boys as well. Such creatures could
assume the form of either sex.

Once he made sex magic against Judge Farris, who said
Kim was rotten clear through and smelled like a polecat. He
nailed a full-length picture of the Judge to the wall, taken from
the society page, and masturbated in front of it while he intoned
a jingle he had learned from a Welsh nanny:

> *Slip and stumble* (lips peel back from his teeth)
> *Trip and fall* (his eyes light up inside)
> *Down the stairs*
> *And hit the wallllllllllllllll!*

His hair stands up on end. He whines and whimpers and
howls the word out and shoots all over the Judge's leg. And
Judge Farris actually did fall downstairs a few days later, and

fractured his shoulder bone. The Judge swore to anyone who would listen that a scrawny, stinking red dog that must have gotten in through the basement window suddenly jumped out at him on the stairs, with a most peculiar smile on its face, showing all its teeth, wrapped its paws around his legs, tripping him so that he fell and hit his shoulder against the wall at the landing.

Nobody believed him except Kim, and Kim knew that he had succeeded in projecting a thought form. But he was not overly impressed. The Judge was dead drunk every night and he was always falling down. Magic seemed to Kim a hit-and-miss operation, and to tell the truth, a bit silly. Guns and knives were more reliable.

He read about Hassan i Sabbah, the Old Man of the Mountain, Master of the Assassins, and he was fascinated. How he longed to be a dedicated assassin in an all-male society. He dreamt of the Old Man, who came to him with a white beard and pale blue eyes and told him to go kill Colonel Greenfield, who said he looked like a sheep-killing dog.

"GRRRRRRRRRRRRR . . . I'll leap at his throat, as seals are said to do if mistreated by their trainers."

There is a smell in the air after a thunderbolt hits, it's one of those archetypal smells like the smell of the sea and the smell of opium: one whiff and you never forget it.

Once Kim Carsons and Jerry Ellisor saw lightning strike the cornice of the old school building outside Saint Albans, the smell so heavy you could see it drifting from the shattered bricks in a violet haze and the boys go crazy with the smell like a cat with catnip. They strip off their clothes and caper around masturbating and turning cartwheels and grinning out between their legs and screaming to the sky:

"SMELL *ME*!"

And Jerry's slinky black hound dog throws back its head and howls, lightning popping all around them as the sky gets blacker and blacker with just a line of bright green around the rim and the next thing we are snatching up our clothes and run-

ning for the cyclone cellar, bricks from the school bouncing all around us. We both shit ourselves when the twister ripped the cellar door off and the house went up like matchsticks. And the dog kept on howling. When we come up out of the cellar the house is clean gone, with Jerry's bedfast grandmother. She'd been alone in the house, since Arch and Ma were in town for their monthly shopping, and Jerry was supposed to look after "the old stink-bag," as he called her.

"Maybe it dropted her in the river," Jerry said as they poured hot water over each other in the sauna and washed the shit off. Everybody was glad to see the last of her, she'd been clean out of her mind the past five years, her breasts all eated away with the cancer and Arch kept buying more morphine to finish her off but she had such a strength for it no amount would kill her and Arch said it was like buying feed for a hawg.

"She's a marl-hole in the worst form there is, no bottom to her."

"Well, leastwise she don't *eat* much," Ma said. "Half a cup of soup a day. She can't last much longer on that."

And Jerry pipes up: "I heard about an old Saint Woman lived twenty years and all she ever eated was a holy wafer on Sundays."

And Arch just looks at him and says, "You know any more stories like that?"

"Sure, plenty. Why, this one old biddy lived forty years after the doctor said—"

And Arch whops him alongside the head with a ruck-hoe handle.

Jerry took Kim in to see Grandma once. She reminded Kim of an old rock covered with lichen, and he thought she could live forever like that.

Now, the sauna was erected by a Finnish boy who witched wells and did tinkering jobs, and he had put some Finn magic on it because he had the power. No one could say his real name, so they all called him Sinki for Helsinki, where all the Finns is borned at. This Sinki had bright red hair, and one eye was blue

and the other brown. He could whip a knife out of his sleeve and cut the head clean off a chicken and have the knife put back away before the blood squirted out . . . WHOOOOSH. Kim recollects when the sauna is finished Sinki, Jerry and Kim is the first to get the cleaning in it. They didn't have to worry about Arch and Ma butting in by this time they is both taking the morphine and taking it heavy only way they can stand up for the aggravations of Grandma when the morphine runned out of her any hour of the day or night she lets out such a bellowing Arch can hear it clear to the end of his cornfield.

Well, Sinki rubs his long red pointed dick and Jerry grins his buck teeth bare so we all get hard and jerk off with a smell like fucking ferrets. Then Sinki draws a circle on the floor with the jism and says something in Finn talk and tells us he has put a magic on the sauna it will last the house out.

Thinking about it gets Kim hot. He can feel Sinki's face nuzzling in like a red-haired wolf and Sinki's long thin pointed dick sticking up against his stomach and the two eyes one blue and one brown and the look out of them different and the sauna seemed to open up and he sawed red lights on the skyline like a forest fire at night and he knowed it was the North Lights from a picture in geography it's a wonder of nature.

So when Arch and Ma got back they was glad enough to have the house gone so long as Granny went with it, and they built on another spot to escape the hant of her. When the moon is full you can hear her bellowing from the old house site and the sauna is there to this day. Nobody uses it. Arch and Ma is like cats with the morphine, can't stand the feel of water on their selves.

Kim remembers a friend of his father's, an unobtrusively wealthy man who traveled all over the world studying unusual systems of hand-to-hand fighting. And he wrote a book about it. Kim remembers him as looking very safe and happy. He could kill anyone in sight and he knew it. And that was a good feeling.

The book was fascinating. Chinese practitioners who can stun or kill by a soft twisting blow just at the right place and the right time. They can even calculate the "soft touch" as it is called, to kill several hours later. You jostle the target in a crowd and—Kim hummed a funeral march happily.

An Indian boxer who could hit a steel plate with all his strength without sustaining so much as a bruise. And challenged the writer to hit him as hard as he could. The Indian made it clear that if he felt the writer was withholding his full strength the interview was at an end. So the writer, who was a Karate 5 Dan, hit him full-blast and the Indian didn't even blink.

"You have fair power, sir," he said.

And there was a magnificent sulky old Indian who specialized in a lightning blow to the testicles. The Golden Target he called it. "He was one of the most unpleasant men I have ever met," the writer reports. "After a scant quarter-hour spent in his company I was impotent for a full week."

So the writer tries to impress this old Midas by breaking a stack of bricks. The Indian sets up a stack and adds one more brick. Then he lightly thumps the stack. The writer points a disparaging finger at the top brick, which is undamaged.

The old practitioner removes the top brick. All the bricks under it have been shattered as if hit by a sledgehammer.

And a bartender in Paris had fashioned a weapon from his breath. By taking certain herbs he had developed a breath so pestiferous that "Then standing almost six feet away *he breathed on me*. Words cannot convey the vertiginous retching horror that enveloped me as I lost consciousness. . . . And for days afterwards I shuddered at the memory of that awesome breath." And his farts could take out a barroom. So he beats the skunk at its own game but he wasn't as cute as a skunk is. Once Kim found a baby skunk in a field and petted it and decided it was the cutest thing he ever saw.

When it comes to hand to claw feet fang poison, squirt, quill, shock fighting, animals beat humans in any direction.

Kim had of course thought of living weapons. The only animal that has been trained to attack reliably on command is the dog, though many other animals would be vastly more efficient as fighting machines. The bobcat, the lynx, the incomparable wolverine that can drive a bear from its kill, and the purple-assed mandrill with its huge razor-sharp canines and rending claws is one of the most savage animals on earth. Kim looked in disdain at Jerry's dog Rover, a skulking, cowardly, inefficient beast. Kim usually spotted the squirrel before Rover could sniff it out. When Jerry wasn't around, Kim would corner Rover and transfix him with his witch stare as he intoned "BAAAAAD DOOOGGG" over and over and Rover begins to cower and whimper and lift his lips in a hideous smile and finally, desperate to ingratiate himself, he rolls on his back and pisses all over himself. While Kim enjoyed this spectacle, it was not enough to compensate for the continuous proximity of this filthy, fawning, vicious shit-eating beast. But then who am I to be critical, Kim thought philosophically.

Kim has just read a juicy story about African medicine men, ancient evil of pestiferous swamps in their snouty faces and undreaming reptile eyes. They capture hyenas and blind them with red-hot needles and burn out their vocal cords while they intone certain spells binding the tortured animals to their will, twisting their own eyes into the quivering pain socket, they lead blind mouths to the target, pouring the mindless ferocity of their crocodile brains into the hyena's terrible bone-cracking jaws to fashion a silent dedicated instrument of death.

Kim looked speculatively at Rover and licked his lips and Rover crept whimpering behind Jerry's legs.

The Colonel filled his pipe.... "They attacked at dawn. Like gray shadows. I saw a boy go down hamstrung, next thing his throat is ripped out.... I couldn't see what was doing it ... like a ghost attack.... But the boys knew and the cry went up:

"SMUNS!"

That's the native word for hyenas blinded by the beastly

medicine men. . . . We intended to capture a male gorilla of the mountain species . . . somewhat smaller than the lowland breeds . . . we had a cage just so big and big enough and I managed to nip into it and lock the door. . . . I'll never forget my boys pleading to be let in as the hyenas tore them apart . . . couldn't chance it, you know. . . . One boy wedged in the door and that would have been it . . . but in their blind animal panic they simply could not appreciate my position . . . would you believe that some of them cursed me with their last breath?"

"Lesser breed without the law," Kim put in.

"Ah yes Kipling the writer chap . . . awfully depressing all that. . . ."

There lay the rider distorted and pale
With the dew on his brow and the rust on his mail

Yes Kim had considered smaller living weapons . . . so much more reliable but still in need of precise guidance. He assumes a professorial manner, his eyes twinkling out through his bifocals.

"Gentlemen, most illnesses kill indirectly and as it were accidentally by the uh cumulative damage of their occupation. So host death is a by-product of the invading organism's life cycle."

But wouldn't it be possible, Kim thought wistfully, to find an agent that will act *directly* on the Death Center, which some occultists locate in the back of the neck?

A Death Organism—in short, a D.O.

"That would be *keen!*" Kim's face blazes in a glowing boyish smile. His grin splits the sky and fades into a vast crystal skull of stars, lighting the ruined cities and bleak landscapes of a dead world . . . the light always fainter as the stars go out one after the other.

D.O. acts as a binary. It doesn't do anything until it receives cellular instructions from the Other Half. Like an L.A., that is Latent Agent, stationed near the target and alerted by a central signal to act. The L.A. may wait for years. . . . (An old gardener

who had worked in the General's garden for ten years killed him with a scythe. The General was planning a campaign against the Old Man's fortress at Alamut.) Or he can be used the next day.

A selective pestilence puts the selector in a position of unique safety. . . . The selector will be well advised to bear in mind at all times that the road to Heaven is paved with solid bricks of safety. He must think ahead. Not just who is a threat to my safety right now but who will be a threat in ten, twenty or a hundred years since ultimate safety must be computed in immortal terms.

So beware of fools' safety.

Consider the menace potential posed to you and your compadres by decent churchgoing folk. . . . You want to take care of these vermin without endangering your fellow Johnsons. Now, what characterizes these shits? They *have* to be right. They *need* the approval of others. Both needs are so constant and so compulsive as to assume the proportion of biological needs like the need of an addict for morphine. . . . A page from the *Denver Post* passed through his mind. . . . Pet owners panicked by mysterious dog deaths. . . . A new disease it seems. Confined to dogs. . . . Man made dogs in his own lousiest image . . . dogs exhibit all the worst characteristics of human animals. They are fawning, filthy, vicious, servile, literally convulsed by their need for approval just like a religious lawman fawning on the Lord and fingering his nigger notches. A dog has to be RIGHT. He is RIGHT to bite someone who has no right to be in that yard, that house. . . . Well if it attacks *dogs*, chances are good it will attack *human* dogs, right in their ugly, snarling, ingratiating, cop-loving, priest-loving, boss-loving, God-loving, epicenter, the vile groveling worshipers of the Slave Gods. When a disease agent moves from one host species to another, with no natural immunity to that strain, the agent can become incomparably more efficient. And this can be accomplished with rather rudimentary tinkering. . . . Most attempts at germ warfare, in fact, start with animal diseases like glanders, parrot fever, anthrax. Kim paused

to reflect that a *plant virus*, once it got root in human soil, might produce a Garden of Eden while you wait . . . a paradise consisting of plants and fertilizer.

We have a virus which we may term the RIGHT VIRUS already occupying the target. We have a disease agent K9 programmed to attack selectively any host occupied by R.V. Our agent K9 is further linked with D.O. the Death Organism. Just formulate the thought "I AM RIGHT" and YOU ARE DEAD.

Kim made a code note at the bottom of the page . . . meaning follow up on this when conditions for doing so become available, in this case a laboratory and technicians.

P.S.: We could give it to them at their *deadly* church suppers.

Kim remembers the Odor Eaters of Tibetan mythology who build fantastic cities in the clouds, which are washed away in rain. Kim would take a big dose of cannabis tincture and sit for hours watching the clouds, occasionally reading from Rimbaud and writing a phrase down in his notebook. . . . One of Kim's Cloud Stations is the Place of the Half Humans. This is an area of big trees and vacant lots. Some of the houses are boarded up, others have an air of being semioccupied. On a porch a rusting bicycle is overgrown with morning-glory vines and weeds grow up between cracked blackened boards. Silence takes on the quality of a dimension here, fragile words break on the dead leaves that rustle across the worn cobblestones and cracked concrete, a derelict railroad car with a tin cabin on top sits there on a rusty weed-grown switchback. On the other side of the tracks a slope leads down to the river and looking upriver you can see a ten-story building that never got finished, a maze of twisted girders growing from stained concrete on many levels, ladders, catwalks, and precarious lookout cabins. From this launching site the Halfs make their solo flight soaring from an upper level down to a sandbar by the river. They can do all the things you do in dreams like start at the top of a stairway and soar down to the bottom step. . . . And they keep switching identities. Who was I

in the last century? Steep slope down to the tracks. Here and there are stone steps overgrown with weeds and vines. A cable threaded through iron loops serves as a handrail down to a cold black pond where, toward perfumed evening, a sad child releases a boat frail as a May butterfly. The morning glory has made another loop around the rusting bicycle. Another green shoot has sprung up through black rotting boards on the porch. A vague area/*terrain vague* of vacant lots and rusty machinery, quarries and ponds. They are half visible their steps so light they don't crush the dead leaves drifting over paths in the sky endless beaches covered with white nations full of joy new flowers new stars new flesh ladder of Tibetan mythology, launching clouds . . . morning . . . black pond . . . boat frail as a dead leaf . . . precarious cities. A call. Three dead on porch . . . the cold evening . . . a sad child. Silence . . . boards on the porch . . . rusty machinery the other side of the tracks their steps half visible looking upriver . . . new flesh. No dogs will enter this area but there are cats and raccoons and skunks and squirrels. From one house drifts a heavy odor of flowers and unknown excrement and the musky smell of impossible animals, long sinuous ferretlike creatures that peer out through bushes and vines with enormous eyes. This is a gathering place for the Odor Eaters who build the cloud cities. Now, sated with odors, some are visible, silent and immobile in a clearing of rusted garden furniture dusted with leaves by a cracked concrete pool green with algae. A frog plops into the water, making a black hole in the green surface. A taste of ashes in the air an odor of sweating wood on the hearth stale flowers, mist over the canals. . . . There is a swamp with a nest of white beasts in the melancholy golden wash of the setting sun the arched wooden bridge down by the river luminous skulls among the peas, roads bordered by walls and iron fences that barely hold back the undergrowth, wind from the south excited the evil odors of desolate gardens, in a puddle some very little fishes. Ectoplasm addicts measure doses from a lead bottle.

Kim occupies himself with his sketches and maps, poems and stories. He'd written a story he wanted to publish in *Boy's Life*. It was, he thought, very educational, entitled "The Baron Says These Things."

THE BARON SAYS THESE THINGS

Wrapped in a living cloak of fur-bearing oysters, the Baron rides his swift Arn. The Arn is like a stream-lined turtle with a shell of light flexible metal that serves as a means of locomotion and also as a weapon. Their claws are razor-sharp and they can strike six feet with a bullet-shaped head to ram or slash. On this remote satellite of the Dog Star, Arn fighting is an esteemed art. The cloak lovingly outlines the Baron's lean form, the narrow waist, the flaring buttocks, the powerful thighs. The neck supports a broad jaw. The Baron leans forward, knees bent like a skier, his long sharp teeth glinting in icy starlight. His eyes are like black opals. He wears a wicker headdress from which the hood of a spitting cobra protrudes. He is scanning the path ahead with a blue laser beam from his third eye.

The long night is coming and he must find a pod for the Ordinate Sleep. He has picked up a pod but

there is something wrong, some lurking danger. It is just off the path. He guides his Arn into a courtyard and a Greenie steps forward to bed down his Arn and put his cloak in a nutrient solution. He removes his headdress and hands it to the Greenie, petting the reptile, which emits a servile hiss, rubbing its green furred head against his hand. The Greenie leans forward to take the headdress, his breath heavy and rank as the exhalation from a greenhouse in the icy air.

"Be careful, sir."

As the Baron squeezes his naked body through a diaphragm in the side of the pod, the clinging mucilaginous passage rubs and excites his genitals. On the satellite Fenec, the penis is not confined to a sexual function but serves as a general means of social communication. To enter a public pod without an erection is an act of gross aggression, like coming in with a snarling dog.

As he pops through into the soft pink light of the pod his lightning reflexes are already activated before he hears the foreign voices scream out:

"What the fuck are you doing in front of decent people?"

He throws up a protective shield, deflecting projectiles from primitive exploding weapons as he cuts his assailants to steaming fragments with his laser eye. He looks down at the badges and weapons ... B.B.s ... Bible Belts. Barbarians from Planet Earth. The thought forms that had for a moment been solid are fading. The Baron throws himself petulantly on the padded floor of the pod.

"People of such great stupidity and such barbarous manners. . . . Intolerable!"

A total solution to the B.B. problem must be found. The war must be carried to Planet Earth. He

knows that the B.B.s are a minority and he will find many potential allies. Allies must be contacted and organized. A plan is forming in his mind. In response to his peremptory erection the Greenie appears with a glass of Schmun.

"Sorry about that, sir. I'm not equipped for such encounters."

The Baron sips his Schmun, looking speculatively at the young Greenie. These creatures breathe in carbon dioxide and give out oxygen from the pores of their skin.

"I want to sleep with you."

The Greenie youth blushes bright green with pleasure.

"Oh sir, of course."

During the three months of the long night they will curl in the tiny pod in dreamy symbiosis.

The Baron stretches, takes a deep breath of the warm dank compost-heap smell, and squeezes out of the pod. It is now spring. Time to continue his journey to Summer City. The Greenie hastens to prepare him a meal of fuel eggs. The eggs are laid by radioactive reptiles that inhabit the coldest regions of the planet in an area of total darkness. The eggs glow with a soft blue fire as the Baron savors the sweet nutty eggy metallic taste. After a go with his Greenie he straps on his summer Arns and puts on his cobra headdress. The reptile is tumescent with venom. The Baron will not need his cloak for this is the season of nakedness.

The fuel egg is working and he straps on a penis shield connected to a jet over the anus. The first coughing spurts soon settle into a steady blue flame carrying him along at a thirty-mile speed. Suddenly he finds himself surrounded by a crowd of frenzied

B.B.s, some carrying ropes and many with the primitive projectile guns. Scorning to use his laser eye he engages them in a classic Arn fight, jetting around in circles, kicking sideways with his Arn as the heads lash like loaded whips and his cobra sprays venom in all directions. A drop the size of a pinprick on the skin will cause death in a few seconds. The posse of B.B.s is a mass of steaming entrails, blood, brains, and shattered bone already fading into nothingness.

He comes to Summer Lake and now the Arns spread their retractable wings as he turns the jet up full blast and skims over the water like a hovercraft. His ass is sputtering out the last of the fuel as he glides to the pier.

Summer City slopes down to the lake and spills into the water in a maze of piers and catwalks and disk-shaped houseboats. The Baron checks his jet strap and releases his Arns to disport themselves in the water. The long sleep and the fuel eggs have made him hot. He can taste sweet metal in his mouth and his ass burns with soft fire. At the foot of the pier he encounters a group of Sloane porters with red skin and bright blue eyes. They flex their huge muscles and bare their teeth in greeting and invitation. . . .

"HI HI HI HI HI HI HI HI"

The Baron is tempted but he knows that the cadets have arrived from Planet Earth and he must see to their training without delay.

On the waterfront he runs into two boys who must be from the Planet Earth. They are strolling along in white naval uniforms. One is red-haired, the other has kinky hair and yellow-brown skin.

"You are the cadets from Planet Earth?"

"Yeah. Nice place you got here but where are the women?"

"Women? What is that?"

"You know. WOMEN." The boy makes a gesture in the air.

The Baron gets the picture and turns into a naked woman with long red hair, skin like the white of a pearl, shivering softly with rippling lights.

"WOW!"

He leads the boys into a sex pod and satisfies them both three times. In the course of this encounter he learns a great deal about conditions on Planet Earth. The B.B.s are completely possessed by a Venusian virus. The whole Christian religion, Catholic and Protestant, is a Venusian ploy.

Later he addresses the fifteen cadets. To put them at ease he takes the form of Old Sarge:

"All right, you jokers, you're here to learn and learn fast. Your planet is riddled by the walking dead taken over by a Venusian virus. I will show you how to recognize these virus-controlled bodies. Many of them are Christians. In fact Christianity is the most virulent spiritual poison ever administered to a disaster-prone planet."

"You mean, Sarge, that most of the trouble on Earth is caused by Venusians in human bodies?"

"Now you're getting smart."

"Wouldn't it be a good idea to kill these mothers?"

"Now you're getting smarter. You are here to learn the theory and practice of Shiticide. Boys will be organized into Shit Slaughter troops . . . the S.S., with two phosphorescent spitting cobras at their lapels. . . .

Slaughter the shits of the world. They poison the air you breathe.

"But sir, aren't the B.B.s and their equivalents in other countries, the bigoted ignorant basically fright-

ened middle class, just dupes and lackeys of the very rich and the politicians, exploited for votes and labor and the consumption of consumer goods while they also serve as convenient guard dogs to protect the status that benefits the very rich?"

"Yes, but they are still vectors, carriers of the virus. How do you control yellow fever? You kill the mosquitoes first, right? Now some vectors are more potent than others. Look at Jesus Christ for chrissakes. As an integral part of the Shiticide Program master vectors will be pinpointed and assassinated. . . . You gentlemen and the trainees who follow you are chosen to be the elite, the masterminds of the glorious S.S."

And Kim composed a marching song for the Johnsons:

> *Wenn scheissen Blut von Messer spritz*
> *Denn geht schon alles gut*
> (When shit blood spurts from the knife
> Then everything is good)

Quite stirring, he thought. . . .
And the Song of the Vagabonds could be adapted.

> Sons of toil and danger
> will serve you a stranger?
> Sons of shame and sorrow
> will you cheer tomorrow?

Kim stands resplendent in his Shit Slaughter uniform with a cobra S.S. on each lapel, they glow in the dark. Johnsons to the sky, all in S.S. uniform. They roar out the Johnson marching song.

Kim raises his hand and silence falls like a thunderclap:

"We're not fighting for a scrap of sharecropper immortality with the strings hanging off it like Mafioso spaghetti. We want the whole tamale. The Johnsons are taking over the Western Lands. We built it with our brains and our hands. We paid for it with our blood and our lives. It's ours and we're going to take it.

"And we are not applying in triplicate to the Immortality Control Board. Anybody gets in our way we will get our communal back against a rock or a tree and fight the way a raccoon will fight a fucking dog."

Kim sees himself as the legendary raccoon who killed a whole pack of dogs before he succumbed to his wounds.... The raw red reek of deadly combat ... his eyes light up inside with green fire, the hairs on his back stand up and crackle ... his claws lash out with the speed of a striking snake to rip out an eye, tear off a screaming muzzle.... A dog sinks its teeth into his flank. He rolls on his back, whimpering piteously.... Two inexperienced young dogs rush forward sincerely. You know the type ... volunteers ... the old coon tears their steaming guts out with his hind claws and makes a break for the river. Here he takes out three more dogs, sitting on their backs and clawing their eyes out. He takes time to eat one eye with his dainty paw as the drowning dog sinks out from under him. He is losing blood. He swims for shore and confronts the last dog on a sandbar, a huge brute composite of mastiff and Irish wolfhound. As the dog's teeth close on his throat the coon's deadly claws go to work. He leaves the dog spinning in circles and snapping at intestines as they spill out. The old coon walks fifty feet and drops dead bleeding from twenty-three wounds.... That coon weighed fifty pounds.

And Kim was trying to re-create a story he had read somewhere years ago ... he couldn't remember where or when, title or writer, just a flash of pulp paper and lurid illustrations. The hero, John, was on a mining expedition somewhere in Central or

South America. They cross a frontier . . . a twang like an invisible bow that vibrated through him with exquisite pain. . . .

He and his companions find themselves in a beautiful lush landscape, flowering shrubs, vines, and trees, rivers and meadows, but there is something overripe, a whiff of rottenness and corruption, a dark undercurrent of menace and evil. His companions, it seems, are utter dolts, crude grasping creatures rooting about for gold and gems. He hears strange wild music. And now a creature bursts into view with a horrible unknown stench. It is a man from the waist up and below that a giant spider covered with red hairs. The creature looks about, grinding its mandibles in panic. Now the Hunters appear, led by the Lords in red satin robes with gold threads. They float just above the ground. The spider man is hiding behind some bushes on the edge of a great cliff. One of the Lords takes an ivory wand from his belt. The wand twitches like a dowser stick pointing to where the spider man is hiding. The Lord glides forward and touches the spider man with his wand, dislodging the creature's hold, and the spider man plummets into the abyss with a despairing scream that raises the hair on our hero's head. Then the Lord turns and looks at him. The face is smooth and yellow like amber, encrusted with layers of cruelty and corruption and a cold dead evil that freezes the blood.

Now the beautiful lady appears wrapped in an orange cloak that glows with cold fire.

"The Lords have lived here since time began. To go on living one must do things that you Earth people call 'evil.' It is the price of immortality."

They walk on and come to a vast ruined amphitheater. John hears a sound like bees. The guide whips out a wand.

"Stay close to me. I cannot save your companions."

John can see in the air transparent creatures with humanoid heads and black insect eyes. A long pink proboscis protrudes from each mouth. They hover on vibrating rainbow wings, jabbing their proboscises into his three companions, who swat and scream and run.

"I am sorry," she says. "But they are already dead. . . . Worse than dead. They are already eaten."

"Eaten?"

"Eaten. Body and soul. The same would have happened to you had I not been here."

At the center of the amphitheater is a huge golden Moloch that seems to stir with slow metal peristalsis. His three companions rush toward the idol in a shambling run, grunting like animals. They clamber up the idol and dissolve into gobs of liquid gold.

John somehow gets back to present time.

"It is better so," she tells him gravely.

But in the end he plans to return: "No danger to body or soul can keep me from *her.*"

(Kim will change her sex of course.)

Kim was walking along the edge of a cliff with a drop of three thousand feet to the valley below. Looking down through the clear still air he could see the glint of water, cities of red brick, trees and moving figures, but no sound reached him. On the other side away from the cliff, he saw woods and glades and rolling hills. His step was very sure and light and he moved in slow effortless strides, taking ten feet at a step. The path was strewn with wild flowers and flowering shrubs, and vines grew along its edges overhanging the cliff. The air was heavy with perfumes that swirled about him as he moved.

He catches the sound of distant flutes and horns growing steadily louder. Kim stops on the edge of a glade, the sky a deeper blue than the sky of earth, with a suggestion of perilous depths. He is trembling with anticipation. On the other side of the clearing he sees a smear of red as a creature breaks from cover.

It is a giant spider covered with fine red hairs like copper wire growing on its shiny body. The creature has the torso and head of a man. The arms end in insect pincers. The spider man pauses, looking around desperately with his faceted eyes, grind-

ing his mandibles and salivating with fear. A horrible odor drifts
across the clearing. Kim doubles over retching and when he
looks up the creature is gone. The sound of horns and flutes is
closer and now a procession of hunters moves into view led by
tall thin figures in red robes, floating just off the ground as if
riding on invisible skateboards. Bounding around them, leaping
ten feet into the air, naked boys with heavily developed thighs
and buttocks are playing flutes. Other boys are riding huge crabs
and playing horns. They wear headdresses of shell through
which the music vibrates. The boys are inside the crab creatures
up to their waists. The huntsmen stop, the flute players poised
and silent. The shell boys freeze and Kim can see that they have
something like a tuning fork jetting from their foreheads and
translucent pink disks for eyes. They converge, pointing with the
tuning forks like dogs, to a cluster of bushes and vines that projects over the void. Kim can see now that the spider man is
clinging to the underside of the ledge, hidden by the bushes.
One of the red-robed figures glides forward with an ivory wand.
He leans down and with a touch of the wand loosens the spider
man's hold and sends him plummeting into the void screaming
and trailing a wake of red excrement.

The Lord turns now and looks where Kim is standing, not
looking at Kim but letting Kim see him. The eyes are like shafts
of dead water leading down into black depths, devoid of feeling
or even of thought. The nose is pocked with tiny holes. There is
no mouth. The hands are smooth and yellow, semitransparent
with red insect claws at the fingertips. Kim notices youths in the
procession with wings flaring from the ankles and the sides of
the head, casques of bright red curls growing from pink marbly
flesh.

The procession is moving back through the clearing, the
flutes and horns trilling out a song of victory so vile that Kim
retches again. One of the winged youths stops and looks at Kim.
The eyes are green, completely immobile, with slitted pupils and
bright red lashes. The boy touches Kim's arms and a shock of

alien recognition burns through his body. The boy is naked, his body smooth as marble. Over his genitals is a cupped red sea-shell translucent and pulsing. Kim realizes that he is also naked, his phallus erect and pulsing. He runs his hands down the boy's stomach, which is like flexible marble, and touches the covering shell which glows and dissolves in light. The boy's phallus stands out smooth as polished coral.

His eyes shift from green to deep blue with a purple pupil that glows like an amethyst crystal. He leads Kim toward the edge of the cliff. They stand poised on a jutting ledge. His wings quiver and he follows his closed fist in a half-turn, so that his back is to Kim, and bends over.

Kim feels himself pulled forward by the boy's long sinuous arms hooked behind his buttocks and he slides into the smooth pink opening, a soft mollusk. The boy's wings vibrate, pulling him forward and over the edge. They move down in a slow dream slant. A rush of wind carries them up into the sky. Kim is steering the youth through the wind, his head back, teeth bare, the wings whistling against his ears. . . .

Portland Place . . . empty houses . . . yards overgrown with weeds . . . out through the west gate . . . Joe Garavelli's . . . roast-beef sandwiches and spaghetti . . . Skinker Boulevard . . . a pond . . . the farm at Saint Albans . . . Tom leafing through *Field & Stream* and *Boy's Life* . . .

They land by a stone road worn smooth from centuries of passage.

Kim considers these imaginary space trips to other worlds as practice for the real thing, like target shooting. As a prisoner serving a life sentence can think only of escape, so Kim takes for granted that the only purpose of his life is space travel. He knows that this will involve not just a change of locale, but basic *biologic* alterations, like the switch from water to land. There has to be the air-breathing potential *first*. And what is the medium corresponding to air that we must learn to breathe in? The answer came to Kim in a silver flash. . . . *Silence.*

Kim knew he was in a state of Arrested Evolution: A.E. He was no more destined to stagnate in this three-dimensional animal form than a tadpole is designed to remain a tadpole. Newts and salamanders have gills in their early life. At some point they shed the gills and come out onto the land, or most of them do. But this one salamander, the Axolotl, which lives in sluggish streams in Mexico, never sheds its gills. Why not? a researcher asked himself, and he gave an Axolotl an injection of hormones, whereupon Axolotl shed his old gills and crawled up onto the promised land. . . . Perhaps this would be as simple, Kim mused . . . just put it in the Coca-Cola and the reservoirs and we all mutate one way or another. . . .

If the mortality rate seems high we must realize that Nature is a ruthless teacher. There are no second chances in Mother Nature's Survival Course.

Kim knows that the first step toward space exploration is to

examine the human artifact with *biologic* alterations in mind that will render our H.A. more suitable for space conditions and space travel. . . . We are like water creatures looking up at the land and air and wondering how we can survive in that alien medium. The water we live in is Time. That alien medium we glimpse beyond time is Space. And that is where we are going. Kim reads all the science fiction he can find, and he is stunned to discover in all these writings the underlying assumption that there will be no basic changes involved in space travel.

My God, here they are light-years from the Earth, watching cricket and baseball on Vision Screens (can you imagine taking their stupid pastimes light-years into space?). Yes sir, the fish said, I'm just going to shove a little aquarium up onto the land there, got everything I need in it.

You need entirely too much. To begin with there is the question of weight. A raw H.A. weighs around 170 pounds. This breathing, eating, excreting, sleeping, dreaming H.A. must have an entire environment essential to accommodate its awkward life processes encapsulated and transported with it.

"One wonders . . ." Kim goes into his academic act, letting bifocals slip down onto his nose as he launches a well-worn joke. . . . "One wonders, gentlemen, if this H.A. doesn't have perhaps a pet elephant essential to its welfare."

The concept of space travel finds people rushing around to build rocket ships.

Kim raises an admonitory finger.

"Think, my little Earth slobs, about *what* you propose to transport. I have brought up the question of weight. We have at hand the model of a much lighter body, in fact a body that is virtually weightless. I refer to the astral or dream body. This model gives us an indication of the changes we must undergo. I am speaking here not of moral but biologic imperatives and the dream gives us insight into space conditions. Recent research has established that dreaming is a biologic necessity. If dream sleep, REM sleep, is cut off, the subject shows all the symptoms

of sleeplessness no matter how much dreamless sleep he is allowed: irritability, restlessness, hallucinations, eventually coma and death."

Kim sees dreams as a vital link to our biologic and spiritual destiny in space. Deprived of this air line we die. The way to kill a man or a nation is to cut off his dreams, the way the whites are taking care of the Indians: killing their dreams, their magic, their familiar spirits.

Kim has never doubted the possibility of an afterlife or the existence of gods. In fact he intends to become a god, to shoot his way to immortality, to invent his way, to write his way. He has a number of patents: the Carsons spring knife, an extension of the spring blackjack principle; a cartridge in which the case becomes the projectile; an air gun in which air is compressed by a small powder charge; a magnetic gun in which propulsion is effected by compressing a reversed magnetic field. "Whenever you use this bow I will be there," the Zen archery master tells his students. And he means *there* quite literally. He lives in his students and thus achieves a measure of immortality. And the immortality of a writer is to be taken literally. Whenever anyone reads his words the writer is there. He lives in his readers. So every time someone neatly guts his opponent with my spring knife or slices off two heads with one swipe of my spring sword I am there to drink the blood and smell the fresh entrails as they slop out with a divine squishy sound. I am there when the case bullet thuds home—right in the stomach ... what a lovely grunt! And my saga will shine in the eyes of adolescents squinting through gunsmoke.

Kapow! Kapow! Kapow!

Kim considers that immortality is the only goal worth striving for. He knows that it isn't something you just automatically get for believing some nonsense or other like Christianity or Islam. It is something you have to work and fight for, like everything else in this life or another.

The most arbitrary, precarious, and bureaucratic immortality blueprint was drafted by the ancient Egyptians. First you had to get yourself mummified, and that was very expensive, making immortality a monopoly of the truly rich. Then your continued immortality in the Western Lands was entirely dependent on the continued existence of your mummy. That is why they had their mummies guarded by demons and hid good.

Here is plain G.I. Horus. . . . He's got enough *baraka* to survive his first physical death. He won't get far. He's got no mummy, he's got no names, he's got nothing. What happens to a bum like that, a nameless, mummyless asshole? Why, demons will swarm all over him at the first checkpoint. He will be dismembered and thrown into a flaming pit, where his soul will be utterly consumed and destroyed forever. While others, with sound mummies and the right names to drop in the right places, sail through to the Western Lands.

There are of course those who just barely squeeze through. Their mummies are not in a good sound condition. These second-class souls are relegated to third-rate transient hotels just beyond the last checkpoint, where they can smell the charnel-house disposal ovens from their skimpy balconies. "You see that sign?" the bartender snarls.

MAGGOTTY MUMMIES WILL NOT BE SERVED HERE

"Might as well face facts . . . my mummy is going downhill. Cheap job to begin with . . . gawd, maggots is crawling all over it . . . the way that demon guard sniffed at me this morning. . . ." *Transient* hotels . . .

And here you are in your luxury condo, deep in the Western Lands . . . you got no security. Some disgruntled former employee sneaks into your tomb and throws acid on your mummy. Or sloshes gasoline all over it and burns the shit out of it. "OH . . . someone is fucking with my mummy. . . ."

Mummies are sitting ducks. No matter who you are, what

can happen to your mummy is a pharaoh's nightmare: the dreaded mummy bashers and grave robbers, scavengers, floods, volcanoes, earthquakes. Perhaps a mummy's best friend is an Egyptologist: sealed in a glass case, kept at a constant temperature . . . but your mummy isn't even safe in a museum. *Air-raid sirens, it's the blitz!*

"For Ra's sake, get us into the vaults," scream the mummies, without a throat, without a tongue.

Anybody buy in on a deal like that should have his mummy examined.

No mistaking that gray shadow moving up the face as the gray lips move.

"Stay out of churches, son. And don't ever let a priest near you when you're dying. All they got a key to is the shit house. And swear to me you'll never wear a lawman's badge."

Last words of Mortimer Carsons, father of Kim Carsons. As it turned out the house on Olive Street in Saint Louis was heavily mortgaged and nobody came forward with help or advice. His father had not been popular around town and Kim was even less so. He wrote poetry and when a sonnet to another boy was intercepted he found himself ostracized by his schoolmates and with his father's permission withdrew from the school. He had no intention of remaining in Saint Louis. His entire legacy amounted to about $2,000 and a farmhouse near Saint Albans.

Here is Kim in his father's study. He is trying to decide what to do. He could go to New York. He knew from a brief liaison with an antiques dealer on a buying trip that there was a place for "people like you and me" in the big city. Why he might become a famous artist or go on the stage. His father's words came back to him:

"When you have a decision to make, get all the factors in front of you and *look* at the situation as a whole. Just look. Don't try to decide. The answer will come to you."

Running away and living on sufferance in a ghetto? And

always somebody to spit in his face and call him what the boys called him at school? And the others ... Colonel and Mrs. Greenfield and Judge Farris ...

Rotten killing corpse
stinks like a polecat.

Kim decides to go west and become a shootist. If anyone doesn't like the way Kim looks and acts and smells, he can fill his grubby peasant paw.

Train whistle ... Kim gets off at Saint Albans junction. The town of Saint Albans is a cluster of red brick buildings along a stream, a little postcard town five miles from the train station.

Kim alights from a buckboard in front of the general store, carrying an alligator-skin Gladstone. He makes an arrangement to rent the buckboard to take him out to the farmhouse with the gear and supplies he will need.

"Right here at six tomorrow."

He stands for a moment looking up and down the street. Nothing has changed ... a secret place that time forgot. ... He smiles, noting and savoring the difference between Saint Albans and any other small town. It isn't the tree-shaded streets, the clear stream and the stone bridges, the gardens and vines and the fields, all so perfect it is like a picture on a calendar. There is something missing here. An absence that Kim breathes deep into his lungs: no church steeples. No churches.

Mr. Scranton shakes hands and glances at his bag. "Sorry to hear about your father. ..."

"Thank you. ... I'll be spending the summer out at the farm. ... Be needing quite a few items. ..."

He walks around pointing ... broom, mop, bucket, disinfectant, tools, kerosene stove, kerosene, lamps, candles, canned goods, bacon lard ...

"Here's something you can use." Mr. Scranton points to sulfur candles. "Scorpions and black widows is bad to get in

empty houses. . . . And outhouses they dig special. The Farris boy got stung on the ass and he was bedfast for three days. . . . Good line of fishing gear here."

Kim selects fishing poles, line, hooks and plugs and a fish trap. . . . He looks around.

"Where are the guns?"

"Sold off my stock to a gunsmith name of Anderson. Got his shop just past the hotel and over the bridge. . . ."

Kim walks slowly past the hotel. Two old men in rockers on the porch wave to him. Looking down from the bridge he can see perch and bass in a deep pool.

WILLIAM ANDERSON . . . GUNS AND GUNSMITHING

The shop is back from a tree-lined street. A man behind a counter looks at him with eyes the color of a faded gray-flannel shirt.

"Like to see some guns."

"You come to the right place, son. What kind of guns you have in mind?"

"Handguns."

The old man is looking down across his case of handguns. . . .

"Now a handgun is good for one thing and that's killing at close range. Other folks, mostly. Worst form of varmint. Quite a choice here. . . . Now this gun"—he brings out a Colt Frontier 45-caliber, seven-and-a-half-inch barrel—"a best seller. . . . Throws a big slug. . . . But it isn't throwing the biggest slug that counts, it's hitting something with the slug you throw. I'd rather hit someone with a 22 than miss him with a 45. . . . Now this little 22 here . . . hammerless, two-inch barrel, double-action smooth and light . . . a good holdout gun you can stash in your boot, down in your crotch, up your sleeve. . . . I knew this Mexican gun, El Sombrero, with a holster in his hat. Dressed all in black like an undertaker. . . . 'Ah *señor*, I am so sorry for you.'

Then he'd sweep his hat off like he was standing over a coffin, and blast right through the hat. . . . You'll be wanting something heavier of course."

He brings out a Colt Frontier with a four-inch barrel. "This load is sweet-shooting and heavy enough . . . 32-20 . . . Winchester chambers a rifle for that load and some folk wants a rifle and handgun shooting the same load. Well, a rifle and a handgun are not made for the same purpose . . . the 32-20 is a good pistol load, accurate and hard-hitting, but it's a piss-poor load for a rifle. . . . Too heavy for rabbit and squirrel, too light for deer, just enough to aggravate a bear. There's no good rifle load between a 22 and a 30-30. Here's a double-action 38 with three-inch barrel. I done some work on that gun, lightening up the double-action trigger pull, close to a hair trigger. You can keep it right on target for six shots. . . . Let me show you a trick with a double-action gun. . . ." He puts a glove on his left hand. "Now you hold the gun with your left hand above and below the cylinder. . . . You can spray six shots right into a silver dollar at thirty feet. . . . Don't ever try it without the glove. . . .

"And here's a custom-made beauty. . . . Smith and Wesson tip-up . . . built like a watch. Chambered for the 44 Russian, a target load for trick shooting. You can put out a candle with this gun at twenty feet. It will teach you how to shoot. . . . And this"—he brings out a Smith and Wesson 44 special double-action with three-and-a-half-inch barrel—"is for business. I can see you have the makings of a real shootist and that's why I'm talking to you. . . . A real shootist don't start trouble. He just don't want nobody to start trouble with him. These punks go around picking gunfights to get a reputation are no fucking good from the day they're born to the day they die. . . . You'll be meeting plenty of their type. When they come in here I just sell them the worst-shooting gun I got in the shop and I got some real lemons, Annie Oakley couldn't shoot with . . ."

Kim is making a selection of holsters. . . . "Don't ever use a shoulder holster . . . awkward movement, and it can't mean anything except reaching for a gun. The less movement the better.

For the 22 or the 38, if you want to carry it concealed, use the Mexican style: holster clips over the belt and goes down inside the waistband. Just open your coat and drop your hand to your waistband like you was hitching up your belt or scratching your crotch, and come up shooting. . . . Drawing your gun should be an easy flowing casual movement, like handing someone a pen, passing the salt, conveying a benediction. . . .

"I knew this gun called the Priest who would go into a gunfight giving absolution to his opponent. . . . Lots of ways to create a distraction and discombobulate your opponent just so long and long enough. This one gun kept a tarantula in a spring box at his belt. He could push out his gut in some key way and the tarantula flew right in the face of his adversary. . . . Don't pay to get too smart. They lynched him for a spider-throwing varmint. . . ."

Kim packs his purchases. On his way back to the hotel he stops off at the drugstore. An Old Chinese behind the counter nods at each item. Bandages, tincture of iodine, snakebite kit, two ounces of laudanum, medicine glass, and eye dropper . . .

"Do you have hashish extract?"

"Velly good. Velly stlong."

Unhurried and old, with no wasted movements he assembles the items, writing out dosages for the medicine bottles, packing everything into a wooden box. As Kim opens the door to go out of the druggist's shop someone comes in with a puff of fog and cold air. Boy about eighteen, angular English face, blue eyes, red scarf. Rather like the younger De Quincey, Kim thought. The boy's eyes widened in startled recognition.

"Good evening."

Kim's greeting came back like a muffled echo.

The hotel clerk looks up through hooded gray eyes. He looks a lot like the gunsmith, Kim thinks, and a little chill rustles up his spine. He hands Kim a key with a heavy brass tab. "Room eighteen on the top floor, Mr. Carsons."

He takes a gold watch from his vest pocket and flips open the lid. "We'll be serving dinner in about thirty minutes. Wild turkey tonight."

Kim walks up three flights to his room. It looks familiar but he can't remember when or where he may have seen such a room and once again he feels the chill as he looks around at the red-carpeted floor, the rose wallpaper, the copper-luster basin, the brass bedstead, a picture of Stonewall Jackson on the wall. He unpacks the 38 and loads it and slips it into an inside belt holster. He buttons his coat and combs his hair in a mirror with a gilt frame that reflects the bed behind him.

At seventeen, Kim is quite handsome at first glance: tall, slim, with yellow hair and blue eyes. On closer inspection there is something feral and furtive in this face, a mixture of shyness and cunning. It's a face a lot of people don't like on close inspection. He doesn't care who dislikes it tonight. The gun feels so good, a warm glow just below his liver. He rubs his crotch and grins at his reflection. He adjusts his tie, gives his hair a final pat and down the red-carpeted stairs and into the bar, where he orders a dry martini.

There are two drummers at the bar drinking beer. The one nearest to Kim is a heavy florid-faced man with a black mustache. He seems on the point of making some rude remark. Kim polishes his nails on his coat lapel and looks at the drummer steadily, feeling the gun, and the man feels it too. He turns away and coughs. Kim finishes his drink and walks past them into the dining room. The room is almost empty. He sees the buckboard driver and the hotel clerk, and a man he recognizes as the doctor. Kim orders wine and gives attention to the turkey, gravy, stuffing, hot biscuits, creamed onions, asparagus, and turnip greens. He glances up between mouthfuls and is gratified to notice that the drummers do not come into the dining room. Apple pie and coffee. Still no sign of the drummers.

People I don't like should stay out of my way, he thinks with a contented belch.

As Kim walked out into the sunlight carrying his "alligator," as he called his Gladstone bag, he saw himself as a mysterious world traveler, travel-stained and even the stains unfamiliar—"for he on honey-dew hath fed/And drunk the milk of Paradise."

Ah there was the buckboard ahead, in front of Scranton's Store. A lithe youthful shape was bending over to pick up a crate, the lean buttocks tightly outlined under blue denim in the morning sunlight that seemed to dissolve the cloth, and Kim was looking at parted buttocks and the red-brown rectum. He licked his lips, lust naked on his face.

The boy straightened up, swinging the crate into the buckboard, and turned in a smear of red. A casque of bright red hair, the face a dead shiny white with here and there a sepia stain, like rust on marble. The eyes of stagnant slate-green color took in Kim's crotch and he smiled a slow enigmatic smile of the dead, an ambiguous invitation from beyond the tomb. A phantom buckboard ... old photo with a flickering silver caption ... as Kim held out his hand he caught a whiff of brimstone and decay.

"I'm Denton Brady. . . . Your driver."

"I'm Kim Carsons."

The boy laughed, showing teeth smooth and white as ivory.

"I know who you are ... all loaded and ready to go."

He swung himself up onto the buckboard seat with a smooth lithe movement that was curiously inhuman without being exactly animal. Eggs, bacon, hot biscuits into the buckboard. Kim swung up beside him, putting his bag under the seat. The boy jerked the reins and clicked his tongue and the horse ambled down a red clay road that wound along the bank of the stream through oaks and elms, maple, and persimmon.

Flint chips glint in the sun. Kim takes off his jacket and folds it across a crate. He takes his belt holster and a box of shells out of the Gladstone. The holster slants slightly backward. While Kim transfers the gun the boy does not seem to notice. He

sits relaxed on the buckboard seat, his eyes fanning out to both sides. He seems to have no need of talking. Kim finds the silence and the proximity at once exciting and unreal, rather like a phantom hard-on, he thinks. The boy reins up the horse, swings down, and comes back with a beautifully chipped arrowhead in pink flint. He passes it to Kim without comment. They crest a little rise from which they can see the valley and the stream stretching down to the river. The boy points to the farther bank, which is still shrouded in morning mist.

"When the fog lifts you can see their fucking church sticking up. . . . The cutoff to the farmhouse is just ahead, but I guess you'll want to go to the place on the riverfront."

"You know it?"

"Of course."

The farm was about a quarter-mile from the river on higher ground and the property line stretched down to the riverfront. This had been cotton country but had reverted to subsistence farming. Kim and his father had converted an old loading shed on the pier to use during the summer since it was a lot cooler there over the water.

The stream is widening out. There are marshy ponds on both sides of the road and a sound of frogs croaking, smell of stagnant water. Flat ground, the river just ahead. Long low building with a galvanized iron roof: BRADY'S STORE. An old man sits on the porch.

"Uncle Kes, this is Kim Carsons."

The old man speaks in a dead, dry whisper: "Your hand and your eyes know a lot more about shootin' than you do. Just learn to stand out of the way." Now his eyes, old, unbluffed, unreadable, rest on Kim, as if tracing his outline in the air. "City boy, did you ever see a dog roll in carrion?"

"Yes sir, I was tempted to join him, sir."

"Did you ever see a black snake pretend to be a rattlesnake?"

"Yes sir, he coiled himself and vibrated the tip of his tail in dry leaves: *brrrrrp.*"

"Kim, if you had your choice, would you rather be a poisonous snake or a nonpoisonous snake?"

"Poisonous, sir, like a green mamba or a spitting cobra."

"Why?"

"I'd feel safer, sir."

"And that's your idea of heaven, feeling safer?"

"Yes sir."

"Is a poisonous snake really safer?"

"Not really in the long run, but who cares about that? He must feel real good after he bites someone."

"Safer?"

"Yes sir. Dead people are less frightening than live ones. It's a step in the right direction."

"Young man, I think you're an assassin."

Along the riverfront the road is overgrown with weeds and brush that scrape against the bottom of the buckboard. And there is the shed at the end of the pier, gleaming white in the sun like a moored ship. Kim opens a heavy brass padlock. Inside, the shed is paneled in oak and painted white like a ship's cabin. Two narrow bunks, side by side to the right of the door, a long bench that runs along the north wall with a hinged top segmented for storage space. A table, three stools, a two-burner kerosene stove with shelves above it and a cabinet under it. A sink with a faucet from a fifty-gallon drum on the porch. The shed has two doors, one facing the shore, the other facing the river, and a screened porch. On the south side of the shed by the porch is a privy with a hinged cover that also serves as a haman in the Arab style, consisting simply of a bucket and drain in the floor. The water is supplied by another fifty-gallon drum on the porch that can be heated with a kerosene burner. There is an evaporation icebox on the porch, covered with burlap sacking, a drum above it that drips water on the burlap.

They look around silently, deciding exactly where everything will go . . . moving now with speed and precision as every object slides into its assigned space . . . canned goods and cooking utensils on the shelves above the stove and the cabinet under

it . . . buckets over the side filling the drums and the drip for the icebox, towels, soap, paper in the bath cubicle, double seats of smooth waxed oak over the green water, wooden pegs in the wall for clothes.

The currents of movement have carried them to a quiet eddy, sitting opposite each other on the bunks, knees touching as they examine the contents of the medicine box, having selected a drawer of the night table between the bunks as the ordained place for these items. Denny looks at the laudanum.

"Good to have around. I was bitten by a copperhead once. . . ."

He looks at the bottle of hashish tincture and lays out a rolled cigarette on the table.

"This is the same thing. Uncle Kes grows it."

He picks up a jar of dry-skin cream. He looks at Kim, his eyes drooping, his head on one side.

"You have dry skin, Kimmy?"

Kim blushes, remembering the time he used the cream to stick a candle up his ass.

"Uh sometimes."

"We'll leave it out in case."

Kim picks up a bottle of chigger lotion and shakes it. He looks at Denny and licks his lips.

"We'll have to rub this all over ourselves to go anywhere."

Den nods, slipping off his boots and socks. He takes off his pants and shorts and tosses them onto the bench. Kim has imitated his movements as if he were sitting in front of a mirror.

"Let's smoke this first." Den lights the cigarette, inhales deeply three times, and passes it to Kim. Kim inhales the smoke and feels his nuts crinkle and tingle; mouth open, breathing heavily, he looks down. It's happening. Den grins and brings his finger up in three jerks. He is getting hard too. Kim watches Den's cock grow from the bright red pubic hairs like some exotic flower and the ruttish red smell fills the room mixing in layers with the smell of new boots, sweat and feet. Kim feels his flesh

melting and flowing off his bones into Den, a choking red tide of lust pulling him forward. Den grins and spreads his thighs, dropping a folded blanket between his legs as Kim kneels between his spread thighs his heart pounding his fingers on Denny's crinkled red nuts feeling the velvet ache running his fingers up the pink shaft to the translucent red purple head like a ripe cherry the slit parted as pearly lubricant oozes out now he is sucking the head up and down the still hot red smell filling him feeling Denny's toes in his crotch a gush of sweet metal taste in his mouth that burns down to his crotch. He is ejaculating on Den's feet and calves, semen dripping down the glittering red hairs.

A choking red tide of lust and sweat socks. He smiled an ambiguous invitation travel-stained by a phantom buckboard a crumpled figure general store. Lithe youthful flickering silver bending over to pick up the crate.

Kim could see a pool of black blood reflected in a dusty storefront. As Kim drew closer the lean buttocks outlined a whiff of brimstone and morning sunlight. Looking at the parted buttocks Kim felt his breath quicken and the boy laughed.

"I know you."

In a dream they get up and rub on the chigger lotion. There are other people in the room, a whole family, and Kim gets an erection but he and Den seem to be behind an invisible barrier. He is packing the sulfur candles and the guns and shells into a backpack and out into bright sunlight that is somehow dark like an old photo with the silver darkness of underexposed film so he can see only a few feet in front of him.

They are walking up a steep path between raspberry and blackberry vines. A whiff of empty house, smell of nothing and nobody there.

Kim is lighting the sulfur candles, a tray for each bedroom, two trays for the living room, dining room, kitchen, one small tray for the outhouse, musty smell of shit turning back to the soil. Blue smoke curls from the cracks. He plants blue morning-

glory seeds from a packet and watches the flowers grow from the smoke. In the barn they lay out the guns on an old millstone and set up targets.

Kim dances around the stone, rubbing the gun in his crotch. He greases his ass and rubs the grease on the gun handle.

"Racooo-ooo-ooo-ooon?"

He stands up, moving his hips in fluid gyrations . . . black powder smoke and the musky zoo smell.

A chorus of frogs croaking. . . .

"Frog you, Kim?"

Kim gasps and his legs pull apart spasmodically as he squirms rectum exposed legs kicking in the air throat swelling. They are both croaking like frogs in a green underwater sperm smell.

Was he awake looking at Den's face ghostly and transparent in the dim light? Den says something about seeing to the horse. Then he was gone. Kim slept.

Now he stands facing the target, the gun in both hands pulsing to his heartbeats while Den dances around him beating the tambourine and singing a little tune in a high-pitched voice childlike and evil, gypsy music with a smell of circuses, animals jump through hoops to that music he slides in behind Kim who is leaning forward, his lean naked buttocks parted.

"I want to pump you, Kimmy."

One hand on Kim's flat stomach, the other shakes the tambourine above his head. With a fluid grind of his smooth white hips like moving marble he flows into Kim, shaking the tambourine as he sings in Kim's ear.

Kim feels a tight smile baring his teeth and a wet dream tingle in his crotch and suddenly there is a smell of black powder and semen in the hot still air of the barn as the bullets group within a two-inch circle over the heart. He wakes up just before ejaculating with a sweet ache in his crotch, Den's hand on his chest. Late afternoon shadows in the room. He must have slept all day. He squirms under Denny's hand and shows his teeth.

Denny stands up and shakes his tambourine. Smell of circus animals. "Shall we camel?"

He gets down on all fours on the other bunk with a phantom Kim under him. Kim can feel the dry heat outside, the drawn blinds, the smell of hashish and rectal mucus. Somewhere a voice is singing a desert riding song. . . .

"Shall we alligator?"

He lies on his stomach with a slow wallowing motion, his teeth bared in a depraved reptilian smile. A reek of swamp mud.

Scarf like rust on marble. Stagnant slate-green color in houses shut in by trees and gardens. He smells a whiff of brimstone and carrion in the late afternoon light red hair and the sun washing a windowsill and the rust of freckles red hairs washing legs red brown rectum sudden raw hard-on.

There is an emptiness. Breath comes in with that incurious gaze like ice on fire in the light. I can. Sweet dry wind clothes are paper. A naked youth about sixteen. Breath came in with his reflection. Rubs his crotch and grins. *Quién es?*

"You dry enough to turn? Rubbing the cream up you."

Carbolic soap lean buttocks a dead green sunlight. Puff of orange knees. What ass kicking hi? The light. I can. Sweet thirst. *Quién es?* Stagnant slate-green color a flash of violet light. Sweet clean feeling of trees and gardens he smiles with the leaves late afternoon sunlight red hair his feet through dead leaves washing legs. Face to the west. My picture in the light. I can. Old paper. A naked youth about somehow his timeless enchanted reflection.

Kim woke up with the impression of a wide, white grin and a whiff of carrion erased in light. Early morning. He lay naked on his bunk, looking at the shiny white paneled ceiling, listening to the sound of running water and a mourning dove calling from the woods.

He stretched and arched his body, looking down at his erect phallus. He only wished there was someone here to take his picture like that, one on the bed with his back arched up, stretching and mewling like a cat and squirming around on his ass, and now one sitting on the edge of his bunk, gun, shells, kerosene lamp and *Confessions of an English Opium Eater* visible on the night table, and now Kim, still naked with a hard-on, levels his gun at the camera. This would be a tasteful series called *Summer Dawn*, to appear on bedroom walls throughout America, yes all over the world too . . . he collapsed back onto the bunk, kicking his feet in the air in an ecstasy of exposure, sighting the gun between his knees as he sings:

"Einer Mann, einer Mann, einer RICHTIGER Mann."

Finally he sat up with a petulant expression and reached for his pants. Why wasn't Denny here when he wanted to get fucked? Why, it could be a deluxe special edition for naughty old gentlemen in rooms lined with yellow silk and lampshades of tattooed human skin. Oh well, he could always walk up to town,

only four miles. He touched his cock lovingly as if to say "later," pulled his pants up, drew water at the sink in an enameled basin with roses on it, and washed his face and neck with carbolic soap.

On the porch he got three eggs from the icebox, with a jug of cider, cold with the mellow slightly rotten juiciness of Missouri apples and a few yellowjackets crushed in for tartness. Smell of bacon, eggs and coffee. *Young Boy Eating Breakfast* for the dining room. Kim knew what he was doing. He had read about it in a yoga book. It was known as Vipassana, being aware at all times of what you are doing.

Kim washes the dishes. Everything shipshape. He decides to pack the guns and the sulfur candles into his "alligator." It will be much more like coming back to the old homestead after a long mysterious trip, like his father used to make. Of course, he keeps one gun out to wear. Young boys were sometimes carried off and raped by Indians. The 44 Russian, he decides.

The path is littered with red flint chips and winds steeply upward through blackberry vines. Kim stops here and there to pick a particularly luscious blackberry with cool deft fingers to avoid the thorns. He deliberately smears the red purple juice around his mouth, "like a whore's makeup."

Over a rise, and there is the house at the top of the hill. It is fairly large, two stories and a balcony running across the front from which there is a view of the river. At one time there had been a narrow-gauge railway along the river, which is now overgrown with weeds and brush. The bridges over the swamps and tributary streams remain, and there is always good fishing under them for rock bass and perch. Kim walks up to the door under the balcony and knocks three times. He opens the door.

"Anybody home?"

A musty smell of the empty house is the only answer. Kim walks inside.

The house had originally been planned on rather a grand scale, suitable for the manor house of a plantation. What had

been intended as the downstairs drawing room is now a sparsely furnished living and dining area. The downstairs back rooms, intended as servant quarters, were simply not used except in the summer, when his father used them as extra studios. He liked to paint all over the house in different lights. There had been plans to install a flush toilet with a regular bathroom, but this had never been done. Kim walks from room to room, selecting things he wants to take down to the boathouse, calculating the number of sulfur candles he will need and putting them out ready to light in metal trays set on bricks.

And now upstairs, rather an impressive staircase with banisters of polished walnut. Lovingly Kim runs his fingers over the smooth brown knots—like rectums, he thinks with a depraved smile, posing for a shot of the boy remembering how good it felt sliding down the banister as a child, the smooth wood rubbing his crotch. Upstairs there are two back bedrooms, one used by Kim and the other by his father. The front of the house upstairs had been converted into his father's studio.

Now Kim turns left down the hall to the studio. Like an empty stage set. A sofa and an armchair covered in green satin, a workbench littered with brushes, palettes and tubes of paint, a rack for canvases and paintings. The easel is empty. Kim sits down on the sofa, looking down to the river.

Kim's memory of his past life is spotty. Sometimes he feels he is getting someone else's memories. There is an incestuous episode with his mother in a seaside hotel. He is standing on a balcony in his bathing trunks. His face is clouded and sulky. His mother appears in the doorway behind him, dressed in a blue kimono. . . .

"I want to sketch you. Cuppy."

He twitches irritably. . . . "Oh not now, Mother, I want to take a bath and change for dinner. . . ."

"I want to sketch you naked, Cuppy."

"Naked, Mother?"

But that couldn't have happened because Kim had never

been to the seaside. Actually his mother was a bit dotty, into Ouija boards and tarot cards and crystal balls and she drank six bottles of paregoric every day and her room reeked of it.

His father seemed remote and veiled with an enigmatic sadness. He traveled frequently on "company business." Expense account suggested illness. Illness was radium poisoning.

He remembered the occasions when he was allowed to shoot his father's 36 cap-and-ball revolver. It was kept in a mahogany case with silver clasps and hinges, all lined with green felt and a place for the revolver, the conical bullets covered with thick yellow grease to prevent multiple discharge, the percussion caps, the bullet molds. The revolver had a double trigger, the lower one cocking the weapon and the upper one, which had a very light pull, fired the shot.

On his twelfth birthday he hit the target six times, death in his hands, grinning through the smoke. His boy grin lit up, dazzling, radiant, portentous as a comet, smelling immortality in powder smoke.

Kim is with a boy of about his own age. He can't see the boy clearly but they have known each other for a long time. They are standing on the railroad bridge over Dead Boy Creek. The water runs still and deep here and they can see fish stirring. The boy is teaching Kim to fly. He soars over the water and lands on a path. Kim stands poised, thinking he can't, and suddenly he is in the air, sweeping in to land on the path. Now they crisscross back and forth across the stream, higher now over the trees, they can see the field leading up to the house on the hill where Kim lives. There is a balcony that runs across the front of the house facing down toward the railroad and the river. The balcony is supported by two marble columns which his father had acquired when the old courthouse was torn down. Against the darkening sky it looks like a painting. *The House on the Hill.* . . . He is in the house now, in the hallway that leads to the studio, telling his father how he has learned to fly. . . .

"We have no such powers, my son," his father says sadly.

They are on the balcony. A smoky red sunset over the river. Now an engine comes in sight, two black men are stoking the fire and pounding each other on the back. . . . Kim can make out the name *Mary Celeste*. . . . Slowly like a parade of floats another ship moves by. . . . *The Copenhagen*. . . . Kim smiles and waves. . . .

His father watches with the sad eyes of a guardian whose role it is to nurture and protect a being greater than himself. He knows that the boy must go and that he cannot follow. The track is overgrown with weeds now.

Kim puts out two trays of sulfur candles ready to light, closes the french doors leading onto the balcony, and caulks them as best he can with paper. My father's bedroom. Enter. The room is empty except for the bed, a chair, a dresser, a pair of workpants stained with paint hanging on a wooden peg. Smell of nothing and nobody there. I remember, I remember, into his own bedroom the little window where the sun came peeping in at morn. He sets out the tray.

He had once found a scorpion crawling on his bed, and a boy from a neighboring farm, Jerry Ellisor, had been bitten by a brown recluse. A few days after being bitten, Jerry came to visit Kim, and Kim asked him up to his room.

"Where did it bite you?"

The boy giggles. "Well, uh, it's in a kinda funny place."

"Show me," said Kim firmly. He knew this boy was very tractable and would do whatever anyone told him to do if he used the right tone.

The boy blushes and drops his pants. He is wearing no shorts. He sits down on the bed and points to a spot on his inner thigh near the crotch, a sort of crater of red-purple flesh, black toward the center. Kim sits down beside him and touches the bite gently. The boy licks his lips and slips Kim a startled glance. Kim can see the blood rush to the boy's crotch.

"Did it hurt?"

"Not until later. I was sick all over."

"Well, it's a good thing he didn't bite you here." He touches the crown of the boy's cock, which is already slightly tumescent. . . .

"Or here." He turns the boy's cock over and touches the spot just below the crown in front. "Or here." He touches the boy's tight nuts. The boy is getting a hard-on. He leans back on his elbows, his cock arching up and pulsing.

"Hey, let's see you naked too."

"All right."

Kim strips and stands naked in front of the boy and looks at him appraisingly through narrowed eyes. His cock is getting stiff. He sits down beside the boy, who feels his cock and says, "Be careful a Brownie don't bite you here." Kim rolls him back on the bed tickling him and the boy rolls around laughing uncontrollably.

He lights the candles in the two back rooms, picks up the canvases in the studio, and lights the candles there and downstairs, shuts the doors and puts signs on with skull and crossbones.

DANGER DO NOT ENTER, FUMIGATION IN PROGRESS

He puts the 44 back in his bag, takes out the 38, picks up his "alligator" and walks down to the outhouse, stopping to put six small condensed-milk cans on top of a stone wall opposite the door of the outhouse, feeling the slow movements of his intestines, rather like a great brown river he thinks, like I had the Amazon inside me—liquid gurglings and seeps and slops. The

outhouse is under an apple tree. His father said it would make the best apples and Kim used to plant morning glories to climb over it. He opens the door. Inside are two seats side by side with covers. He lifts the covers, running his hands lovingly over the smooth yellow oak—he'd sandpapered it and waxed it himself. He looks down into the pit and there is just a faint rotten smell of lime. He puts the "alligator" in front of the other seat, takes off his shirt and hangs it on a peg. He drops his pants and sits down on the seat with the gun in his hand. He poses for a picture entitled *The Long Journey.* Kim waves.

Now he waits until he doesn't have to push at all, his ass lets go and he starts shooting and with every shot a can flies off the wall and powder smoke drifts back across his face with a faint smell of fresh excrement. The sensation is intense. He leans back and stretches and reloads the 38. He knows that people often lose control of their bowels when they die so to shoot right from his opening asshole is powerful magic. He pulls up his pants and picks up his "alligator" and lights a sulfur candle, staying just long enough for a whiff of brimstone before he closes the door. So many smells are nice if you don't get too much, like skunks and cyanide and raw meat and carrion.

He walks down to the barn, where he finds the millstone of the dream sunk in the dirt again. He pries it up with a rusty crowbar and leans it against the wall. An exposed scorpion sidles about, tail raised. Kim draws his 38 and the scorpion disappears in a smoky flash, writhing fragments around a black hole. With a rope and pulley he lifts the millstone and lowers it onto the two sawhorses to form a table where he lays the guns out at the cardinal points of the compass. With drawing paper from the studio he draws four man-sized targets and tacks them to a backdrop of heavy oak planks thirty feet from the table.

Now to mark out targets. The classic gunfighters mark just above the belt. Three-inch circle. Kim taps his solar plexus, remembering the feeling of being hit there once in football practice. He draws a three-inch circle. And now the heart, which is

right in line if you are facing somebody. Hollow at the base of the neck in front where the collarbones converge. Spot just below the nose. Spot between the eyes. He stands back and looks at the targets. If you want to be sure of no recovery . . . He draws a three-inch circle over the liver.

He selects the 22 . . . inside belt holster that fits down behind his fly, the rosewood handle just under his belt buckle. . . . Lightest pistol, easiest to shoot. Must hit a vital spot vulnerable to this load. . . . Heart, the two neck shots, and between the eyes. Not enough shock for below-the-nose shot.

With a smooth unhurried movement he drops his hand to his belt and sweeps the pistol up to eye level, steadied with the left hand, and fires six shots aiming for the heart. All shots within a three-inch circle . . . "a heavier powder load with this accuracy . . . I'll ask old Anderson. . . ."

He sits down and runs through the draw-aim-fire sequence a number of times, seeing the bullets hit the target, imprinting the sequence on his "alligator brain," as he calls it, that part of him that knows just what to do and does it with a depraved reptilian smile.

Now the 44 Russian. He touches it with gentle precise fingers as he would touch Denny's cock, oh he'd love to have little tiny naked boy cameos cut in opals and rubies, set in mother-of-pearl handles. His holster, oh not a vulgar tie-down, is a flap of leather that clips onto the pants. Relax completely and don't trigger the action. Now smooth, deliberate, both hands, a solar-plexus bull's-eye. Paralyzing shot. Now up to the hollow of the neck. . . . Now up to the middle of the forehead just for jolly before he falls. Now belt-buckle shot up to the heart. The gun is so *easy* with the adjustable hair trigger, almost shoots itself. . . . Need a double-action Russian. . . . I'll ask the Old Man . . . Kim saw himself in a sleigh picking off wolves with the 44. But there are too many wolves.

"THROW THE COUNTESS OUT," he bellows lustily. So he and the handsome footman just make it back to the castle.

Now the 32-20 with the holster tied down. He goes into a sheriff act.

"Fill your hand, you stage-robbing sidewinder!"

Draw aim fire, just above the belt buckle.... A little off, trigger pulls hard. Needs some custom work, but the load feels good. He does a good workmanlike job with this gun, but it doesn't seem to have the élan of the others. No doubt about it, double-action is better not only for speed but because gun stays on target whereas the act of cocking throws gun off target. Still the 44 Russian has a balletic sort of grace with stylized movements, the hand snaking out, whole body lining up . . . he sees himself in pink tights with a disdainful nonchalant hard-on. Perhaps he will wear a skeleton suit for his gunfights, or a codpiece with a skull on it. He tries the 38, wearing a glove on his left hand. He clasps the frame above and below the cylinder—what a grouping, you just point and squirt the bullets out like a hose.

He packs away the guns except for the 38, which he wears, and picks up the bag, the four canvases, a double-barreled shotgun, and the huge Gray's *Anatomy*. Carrying this rather awkward load he starts down the path thinking about Denny, getting a hard-on and not looking where he is going, he jams his right foot between two rocks and his body pitches forward, bag, guns, canvases and Gray's flying ahead of him and skidding down the path. He gets his foot out using both hands and grimacing with pain. He can't walk on the right foot. Using the shotgun as a cane he drags himself down to the riverfront and into the boathouse.

He strips off his boot and sock, the ankle is swollen and turning blue. He puts on a pot of hot water to clean the guns and soak his ankle. The throbbing pain is getting worse by the minute. He hobbles to the night table and takes out the bottle of laudanum. Dose: fifteen to thirty drops every six hours for pain. Kim measures out thirty-five drops into the medicine glass and washes it down with a little warm water. Bitter and aromatic, with a taste of cinnamon. He makes a cup of tea and sits down at the table, his foot in hot water and Epsom salts.

In a few minutes the hot throbs of pain from his ankle turn to cool blue waves of pleasure and comfort that hit the back of his neck and spread down the back of his thighs. What a feeling. He squirms like a contented alligator. He dries his foot and rubs his ankle with camphorated liniment.

From Kim's Diary

Always take time enough to be sure of your shot. Always give the impression that you *have* plenty of time. This will fluster and hurry your opponent.

The 22 is the easiest pistol to shoot. Light weight and light load. *The lighter the pistol the better.* Avoid heavy pistols with a lot of weight in the barrel.

General procedure for the heavier calibers is to aim an inch above the belt buckle. Drawing from a low tied-down holster when the arm is extended and ready to fire you line up on this target. However, if the draw is from belt level, the lineup is on the solar-plexus shot which has an even surer knockdown, breathtaking shock and in many cases will go through and shatter the spine. (He can see the shiny lead bullet embedded in white coral.)

There are various shooting positions. Lining the gun up using both hands from the one-point position. Holding gun forward at eye level, steadied with both hands. One-hand position, arm extended, leaning slightly forward to sight the shot from above. Gun held above and below cylinder by gloved hand.

Quick unexpected body movements can produce a crucial miss on the first shot. Simplest of these for a thin person is the sudden turn sideways. Or drop to one knee. As you reach for the gun, *smile*. The generous gesture: "*Here* is something I want to *give* you."

Identify yourself with your gun. Take it apart and finger every piece of it. Think of the muzzle as a steel eye feeling for your opponent's vitals with a

searching movement. Move forward in time and see the bullet hitting the target as an *accomplished fact.*

If an opponent is looking for trouble it is always well to seem to be avoiding the encounter. He is leaning further and further into your space. He is more and more off his home base.

He studies Gray's *Anatomy,* plotting path and trajectory of the bullet in body. What is between solar plexus and spine? Where are the veins and arteries?

As the cave painters often depicted animals with the heart or other vital organs visible, so it is well to take an X-ray view of your adversary. Identify yourself with *death.* See yourself as *death* to your opponent.

On the fourth day Kim wakes up with very little pain in his ankle. He can get around quite easily on a heavy hickory cane he has cut and smoothed down with sandpaper. He takes a dose of the hashish extract instead of laudanum, and writes. . . .

I am learning to dissociate gun, arm, and eye, letting them do it on their own, so draw aim and fire will become a *reflex.* I must learn to dissociate one hand from the other and turn myself into Siamese twins. I see myself sitting naked on a pink satin stool. On the left side my hairdo is 18th-century, tied back in a bun at the nape of the neck.

I sit there with a hard-on. I am naked except for knee-high stockings in pink silk and pink pumps, covering a cowering Inquisitor with my double-barreled flintlock in left hand, the flint an exquisite arrowhead, the whole artifact built by a Swiss watchmaker with a little music box that plays on after the shot, the bullets greased with ambergris and musk.

"Really exquisite with the black powder scent, Father."

On the right side, wearing nothing but boots, I cover a nigger-killing sheriff with my 44 Russian. This split gives me a tingly wet dream feeling like the packing dream, where I keep finding more things to go into my suitcases which are already overflowing and the boat is whistling in the harbor and another drawer all full of things I need. . . . A 50-caliber ball crashes through the priest's chest. The music box plays a minuet as I shoot the sheriff right in the Adam's apple. I call it "making him do the Turkey."

Kim walks over to the old railroad. There is a slope leading up to the rusty weed-grown tracks. He sets up his targets against the slope. He can feel the guns as extensions of his arm. He knows just what every little part is doing. He whirls and spins around, trying crazy shots. He postures obscenely, dancing sideways with his ass sticking out and a street-boy grin. He does an insolent bump as he drills the sheriff right in the heart, and then just for jolly a quick shot to the head, which being a can of tomatoes with the top rusted through explodes in a splash of red. Now Kim rubs his crotch, looking down at the dead law.

"You're dead and you stink."

He turns to walk away and makes the "vulgar whorish gesture of lifting his foot and showing the whole sole in contempt."

A frog-faced deputy sidles out of a doorway. Kim drops his pants and shoots between his legs. Wheeeeee . . . he hits the solar plexus, ranging upward.

He straightens up and sees a face looking at him which seems at first part of the bushes, like those faces in picture puzzles, you can win a trip to Niagara Falls if you find them all in the trees and clouds. . . .

(Soft slow dogs crusted with the smell of all humanity eyes forever searching for that long past lover whose breath will never warm you more.)

It's a fawn face with pointed ears and yellow eyes and tawny yellow curls like bronze wire. He is dressed in shirt and pants of dappled green. Kim feels a slackness, a drifting floating sensation as the picture moves. Steady on. Take it easy. The boy rubs his crotch and grins a slow wolfish smile, showing sharp animal teeth. Kim stands there, pants around his ankles with a hard-on, his face blank as if wiped by the summer sky and drifting clouds.

(It was the same now when I was a baby kangaroo in Sister Howe's pouch nothing was disgusting not even the tears the hot meaty rush of a nosebleed.)

The boy advances. He is wearing soft yellow boots to the knees. A heavy revolver which Kim recognizes as the new Colt 45 double-action is at his belt. On the other side in a leather sheath is a silver flute.

(Darkness is gathering behind me, thickening in puddles of ink. We began to take huge bites out of our rolls . . . their rich breath filled my head, a little tingle of excitement ran through me.)

"I'm Carl Piper."

"I'm Kim Carsons."

"I want to pump you, Kim."

Standing by the ruined railway on the sandy bank of a deep pool Carl wraps his hips around Kim with his right arm around Kim's waist holding him up the flute is in his left hand playing right into Kim's left ear phantom train whistles from lonely sidings boy cries from trestles and pools thin ghostly fading into the inky blackness of space Kim hooks his hands around Carl's buttocks pumping him in his blank face turned to the sky the hot meaty rush of a nosebleed down his chest spatters his spurting cock with blood.

He straightens up and sees a face not tears at first . . . part of the bushes . . . boy advances . . . you can see the heavy revolver crusted with the smells of all humanity at his belt . . . searching for that long past love is a thin silver flute . . . a fawn face

thickening in puddles of ink . . . Kim, our roles, their rich breath . . . a pressure . . . excitement ran through me floating sensation . . . the ruined railway dappled green shirt and pants . . . lost lonely boy cries with a hard-on his face fading into the inky clouds hot meaty rush pulling him in picture puzzles recognizes the soft slow dog on the other side eyes arching forever . . . darkness was gathering behind me whose breath will never warm you more . . . pointed ears and yellow eyes filled my head a tingling slackness . . .

"I want to pump you, Kim."

Standing on the sandy bank of a stream moves Kim with his right hand around . . .

"Steady on. . . . Take it easy."

Left ear phantom train whistles boy rubs his crotch from trestles and pools . . . this animal teeth . . . Kim stands there wiped by the summer sky.

Kim is sitting on a yellow toilet seat, his cock pulsing and lubricating in sunlight that glitters through iced twigs making them tingle and glow. The sky is pale blue and the snow has a thick cake crust. . . . In moonlight he eats a melting white peppermint. The moon catches it and makes it sparkle and there is a runny green center that drips onto his shoulder and a boy with huge vacant blue eyes is licking it off. . . . Early morning rosebud on his tray like a cannon mouth the crimson hole goes right to its heart. A boy with rose-colored genitals on an empty beach makes a jackoff gesture.

Carl and Kim leap and snort and gambol, Kim soars up and parts his buttocks. . . . "I'm a cloud. Seed me." He seems to float down and Carl is fucking him on all fours in a rank goatish smell Kim writhes feeling the horns burst through his head splitting open he screams and whinnies as blood spurts from his nose. . . .

"Show you something."

Carl straps on his 45 and proffers a bandanna. "Blindfold

me." He faces the targets which are six cardboard boxes each with a circle drawn in the middle. He makes a motion and little click of the tongue and the gun leaps into his hand, six shots all in the inner circles.

"Now you try."

Kim tries to memorize the target positions and keep them in his mind's eye. Carl, standing behind him with his hands on Kim's hips, gently guides him. One direct hit in front of him, two others outside the circle but in the box.

"With more than one player you need to know exactly where everyone is. Practice naked, practice at night." He picks up his clothes. "Now I must go."

"Can't I come with you?"

"Not now. Later."

He walks down the tracks toward the big thicket in the setting sun where the tracks seem to melt together. In the distance he turns and waves and smiles, fading into the trees and the sky.

Kim drops by Kes's occasionally to buy fresh eggs milk and marijuana and meets an Indian boy named Red Dog, who helps around the place from time to time. Red Dog is about Kim's age or a little older, very tall and straight with jet-black hair and a smooth red-brown skin and one eye is slate-gray and the other brown. Kim is very much taken but Red Dog is aloof in a friendly way.

Kim starts dropping by the saloon in the evening for a few drinks before dinner. Mostly the saloon is empty. Kes carries on a trade with the people of the Big Thicket, exchanging supplies for gold and certain herbs and woods. But the thicket people, little men with flaring ears, drink only milk, and hastily fade away as soon as their business is done.

One night Kim is in the bar looking at Red Dog, who is bending to lift a beer keg. Kim is getting a hard-on and the ruttish smell is drifting off him, an underwater smell it is, and suddenly he is aware of being watched by hostile and alien eyes. A

man sitting in one corner with a beer, strange Kim hadn't noticed him . . . sort of a smoke screen there. . . . As soon as the man feels that Kim has spotted him he coughs, covering his face with a handkerchief, puts a coin on the table and slides out. Kes watches him go and points across the river.

Saturday night and maybe somebody from across the river comes into Uncle Kes's saloon looking for trouble. He won't have to look far . . . the short-barreled double-action 44 tonight, Kim decides, and his 22 backup in a boot holster. This would entail going into a graceful fluid crouch. Kim rehearses in front of a mirror.

As soon as Kim walks through the swinging door, he knows this is it. Two men at the bar by the door. One is tall and thin, with a dead, sour, wooden face; the other tall and fattish and loose-lipped, with lead-gray eyes. They fan out, blocking the door. Loose-Lips smiles, showing his awful yellow teeth.

"Now I don't like drinkin' in the same room with a fairy—do you, Clem?"

"Can't say as I do, Cash."

They want to bat it around for a while. Kim doesn't.

"I don't want any trouble with you gentlemen . . . let me buy you a drink."

Kim is still talking as his hand sweeps down to his belt and up, smooth and casual, as if he is handing Clem a visiting card, and shoots him in the stomach. Clem doubles forward and his false teeth fly out, snapping in the air. Clem's 45, barely clear of the holster, plows a hole in the floor. Kim pivots, both hands on the gun, and shoots Cash in the hollow of the throat. The heavy slug tears through and spatters the wall with slivers of bloody bone. Cash's gun *chunks* back into its holster. Clem is weaving around, trying to recock his 45 with numb fingers. Taking his time, Kim shoots him in the forehead. Both assholes are dead before they hit the floor.

Kim's arduous training has paid off in hard currency. As

Kim looks down at the two bodies crumpled there, spilling blood and brains on the floor, he feels good—safer. Two enemies will never bother him again. Two lousy sons of bitches, melted into air and powder smoke.

Kim remembers his first adolescent experiment with biologic warfare. Smallpox was the instrument, the town of Jehovah across the river, his target. Their horrid church absolutely spoiled his sunsets, with its gilded spire sticking up like an unwanted erection, and Kim vowed he would see it leveled.

It was dead easy. The townspeople were antivaccinationists . . . "polluting the blood of Christ," they called it. Around the turn of the century there were a number of these antivaccination cults, a self-limiting phenomenon since all the cultists contracted smallpox sooner or later.

So Kim simply jogged the arm of destiny, you might say, by distributing free illustrated Bibles impregnated with smallpox virus to the townspeople of Jehovah. The survivors moved out. Kim bought the land and used the church to test his homemade flamethrower. He found the plan in *Boy's Life* . . . a weed killer, they called it. Well, rotten weeds, you know. . . .

rain whistle . . . Clickety clickety clack . . . Kim is swaying and jolting on a train seat. . . .

DODGE CITY

A sketch done in black green and sepia India ink exudes the somber brooding menace of El Greco's *View of Toledo* . . . transparent horses and riders, phantom buckboards and buildings, dead streets of an old film set.

LEE YEN CHINESE RESTAURANT

Kim walks to the back of the restaurant and pirouettes gracefully, checking the booths along one side of the room. A fat drummer with a red face and black mustache, napkin tucked into his collar, looks up at him over a bowl of chop suey with surprise and fear and hatred, as if Kim is the last person he expects to see and the last person he wants to see. Kim raises his eyebrows, looking back until the man drops his eyes, coughs, and dips into his chop suey. Kim sits down facing the door with his back to the man who is shuffling around and moving the booth. Kim glances over his shoulder with a petulant expression. His eyes snap back to the door and he goes for his gun in a slanting cross-body holster he uses when sitting down. A bullet spangs into the booth behind him. The drummer coughs, spit-

ting blood down his napkin, and falls forward his face in the bowl of chop suey.

Scene shifts to Bat Masterson's office. Bat is a calm gray presence. He lights a cigar and studies Kim through the smoke.

"Who were they?" Kim asks. . . .

Bat picks up a file. . . . "Guns. Hired guns. Plenty more where those came from."

"Meaning I should move on?"

"Big country, small towns. Talk will catch up with you sooner or later. You want to get lost, go east. Chicago . . . Boston . . . New York. . . . Now, I could use a deputy. . . ."

"No thanks. I promised my father on his deathbed I'd never wear a lawman's badge."

"In this life you have to fit in somewhere. There's some safety in a badge. Some safety in working for one of the big ranchers. . . ."

"Taking care of sodbusters?"

Bat shrugs. "You gotta fit in somewhere. You're not even an outlaw. . . . At least not yet. . . ."

Bat, years older, is talking to a reporter in New York City. . . . "Fast? Well he didn't *seem* fast. Took his time. Always used two hands on the gun and he didn't miss. He had some special guns too, double-action with a light smooth trigger-pull and dumdums that would mushroom to the size of a half-dollar. . . . And he had a smoothbore 44-caliber that shot six buckshot in each load. . . . Something else: he never telegraphed his draw. Didn't bat an eye and there wasn't any movement of his hand before the draw. . . ."

"Is it true that he was a fairy?"

"I never saw that side of him. Figured it was none of my business. . . ."

"Is it true you run him out of Dodge City?"

"No. I just asked him to leave as a personal favor. . . ."

"Where'd he go?"

"Lots of places, I reckon. I'd hear from time to time. . . ."

Kim is standing with his back to the bar. There is a life-sized female nude behind him. A thin-faced blond kid, his eyes spinning in concentric circles, backs away, hand vibrating over his gun. The boy's hair stands up and pimples burst on his face as he goes for his gun and fans off a shot that hits the nude right in the cunt, above Kim's head. With a smooth movement Kim draws, both hands on the gun, and shoots the kid in the stomach just below the belt buckle. The slug slams him back like a fist and he falls across a cardtable, scattering chips, cards and glasses on the floor. The cardplayers stand up and raise their hands. They are looking at something behind Kim: the bartender is holding a sawed-off shotgun six inches from Kim's back, his florid face smug as he winks at the cardplayers. His eyes flutter coquettishly. He slumps forward across the bar. The shotgun slides to the floor, overturning a spittoon. A meat cleaver is buried in the back of the bartender's head. Framed in the service panel between the bar and the kitchen a Chinese youth grins impishly. He makes a riding motion with his hands and points to the side door. Kim backs out slowly. One of the cardplayers, with an arrogant hawk face and pale gray eyes, still has his cigar in a raised hand. As Kim disappears through the door he slowly puts the cigar in his mouth. It is Pat Garrett. The two boys ride out together, crisscrossing streams, keeping to rocky ground but still leaving a trail that a posse can follow.

They rein up, take saddles and bridles off the horses. Kim looks at his horse. The horse lays its ears back and shows its horrible yellow teeth. Kim cuts it sharply across the rump with his quirt and both horses gallop off, Kim's horse in the lead. Carrying the saddles they carefully wipe their footprints away with a pine branch as the Chinese boy hums a little tune. They come to a deserted hogan.

The boys are naked, kneeling side by side as they draw a map in the soft red-sand floor. Kim's tongue sticks out the side of his mouth as he concentrates tracing the route his horse must take and the other horse must follow. From time to time the Chinese boy corrects the map. The map is finished. The Chinese boy grins sideways into Kim's face.

"Me flucky asshole?"

Kim straddles the map on all fours.

The Chinese boy twists a finger up his rectum.

"This Tiger Balm. Velly good velly hot. Make horsey run. . . ."

He slides his thin hard cock in. Kim rears backward, making hooves with his hands and pawing the air. Then he pretends to gallop as the boy fucks him with a riding motion, jogging Kim's shoulders with his hands.

Kim bares his teeth. Strawberry hives break out on his neck, back and nipples. A reek of horseflesh fills the hogan as Kim comes in a shuddering screaming whinny. His horse streaks ahead of a distant posse.

Cut back to Bat Masterson. . . . "Yep he'd killed Old Man Bickford's kid, and Bickford had thirty guns on his payroll. Had to keep moving after that."

Wetting a pencil with his lips Kim writes in his diary:

"What I have learned today. . . . Never turn your back on the bartender. He will side with the locals every time since that's where his money is. Best thing is shoot him straightaway. Only fools do those villains pity who are punished before they have done their mischief."

Horse whinnies softly outside. Kim pulls on his pants and boots. They decide to split up and meet at Clear Creek in one month.

Kim stands in the doorway of a saloon. Bearded man at the bar goes for his gun as the bartender reaches under the bar for his

sawed-off. Kim draws and shoots the bartender in the chest. The other man's shot whistles past him and slams into the belly of a horse at the hitching rail outside. . . .

Before the man can recock his single-action 45 Kim kills him with two quick shots in the stomach.

"Just as you know before you shoot when you are going to miss, you know when someone else is going to miss. I knew the beard's shot was a miss so I took care of the bartender and his shotgun first.

"Always take care of a shotgun first."

When Kim and Red Dog walk into the Nugget Saloon, everybody stops talking. The bartender is halfway down the bar, going through an elaborate pantomime of looking for a special bottle to serve a special customer. Kim stops behind the bartender and leans on the bar, facing the door, after making sure there is no one behind him.

"Two beers here, barkeep."

"You say something?" the bartender asks without turning around.

"You heard me. Two beers chop chop right away pronto *cold* sabe? *Fresca* . . ."

The bartender has found what he was looking for—a bottle of Southern Comfort. He starts back up the bar with the bottle in his hand.

"We don't serve Injuns here and we don't serve Injun lovers. . . . Now I'm going to serve a gentleman."

"You'll serve us first."

The bartender is pouring with his left hand as his right hand snakes under the bar for his sawed-off ten-gauge shotgun. Red Dog's 32-20 mercury bullet tears through the bartender's fingers, shatters the bottle and lodges just below the ribs. The bartender reels back, clutching broken glass with a reek of peach brandy.

Five men are fanned out blocking the door. Kim picks the one who hadn't turned a hair when Red Dog shot the bartender,

a narrow-shouldered man with pale eyes, wearing a deputy's badge. His gun is coming up fast. Kim pivots sideways and the slug grazes his belt buckle.

"*Olé!*" screams Red Dog.

Kim shoots the lawman in the solar plexus. He doubles forward with a grunt, spitting red flashes of hate from dying eyes. Kim shoots another turkey in the neck. He falls, screaming blood through his shattered windpipe. A bearded man falls slowly forward with a dreamy Christlike expression, a blue hole between his eyes from Red Dog's 32-20, brains spattering out the back of his head like scrambled eggs.

Killing can become an addiction. Kim wakes up thin. He's gotta get it one way or another. Small town, not many candidates. But that pimply-faced ugly-looking kid has potential. Gotta be careful not to start it. Don't give him the eye. The kid walks over and leans on the bar, looking at Kim with his insolent piggish little eyes.

"I hear you're quite a bad hombre."

"I never said so."

Kim is shivering slightly. A raw musky ferret smell reeks off him. Killer's fever, that's what it is, but the kid is too dumb to read the signs. The kid backs away, reaching.

YESSSSSSSS, Kim's 44 Russian leaps into his hand. He can feel his way into the kid's stomach with the slug and the kid grunts doubling forward, a grunt you can feel. Is it goooood.

Now the kid slumps to the floor in a *delicious* heap.

I saw him in a gunfight once. Wasn't much of a fight. Just a punk looking for a reputation: he killed Kim Carsons. Not so young. About thirty. Kim never cut notches, he said it ruined the gun butt, and his were all special-made to his hand in ebony, ironwood, rosewood, teak and thin metal, copper, silver and gold.

We are coming out of the general store, got a porch, two

wood steps down to the street. Kim must have seen the punk out there because just as he walks out the door he says . . . "Mind carrying these," and hands me a bag of groceries. (We is sharing a room at the time.) We walk out and there is this fat-faced slob just beyond the porch.

Kim stands there, eyes watchful, perceiving, indifferent hands limp at his sides, waiting. Don't know why it didn't occur to me to take cover, like we are on the stage and my part is to stand there with a brown paper bag in my hands and then I felt it. A sudden icy cold that froze the sweat on my shirt, it was a hot June day, above ninety. . . .

"You fucking fairy!" the man bellows, snatches out his gun and gets off two shots, broke the store window two feet above Kim's head. Kim pays no attention, just sweeps his gun up to eye level and shoots the man where his stomach hangs over his belt. . . . The man doubles forward retching, and Kim shoots him in the forehead and turns to me.

"From humanitarian considerations. . . ."

He drops his gun back into its holster and brushes a shard of glass off his shoulder.

He wasn't at all that fast. . . . "I never shoot until I'm sure of a hit," he told me. "There's a certain length of time in which you can draw aim fire and *hit*. That's *your* time. If someone else's time is faster, you've had it."

Some shooters are perfect on the range, can't hit in a gunfight. Kim wasn't a good range shooter at all. Just average. He said it didn't interest him, like checkers. He didn't like any games, never gambled.

Kim got off the stage at Cottonwood Junction. The stage was going west and he wanted to head north. Sometimes he decided which way to go by the signs, or his legs would pull him in a certain direction. Or maybe he'd hear about some country he wanted to see. Or he might just be avoiding towns where folks was known to be religious. That morning before he took the stage he had consulted the Oracle, which was a sort of Ouija board that had belonged to his mother. She'd been into table-tapping and crystal balls and had her spirit guides. One that Kim liked especially was an Indian boy called Little Rivers.

Once when she was out Kim put on one of her dresses and made up his face like a whore and called Little Rivers and next thing the dress was torn off him oh he did it of course but the hands weren't his and then he was squirming and moaning while Little Rivers fucked him with his legs up and he blacked out in a flash of silver light.

The Oracle told him that Little Rivers was near. He should keep his eyes open and he would know what to do, so when he saw a sign pointing north—CLEAR CREEK 20 MILES—he decided to leave the stage, standing there in the street with his "alligator."

The town was built in a grove of cottonwoods at a river junction. He could hear running water and the rustle of leaves in the afternoon wind. He passed a cart with a strawberry roan. On the side,

TOM D. DARK, TRAVELING PHOTOGRAPHER. He went into a saloon, dropped his "alligator" on the floor and ordered a beer, noting a youth sitting at the end of the bar. He took a long swallow, looking out into the shaded street. The boy was at his elbow. He hadn't heard him move.

"You're Kim Carsons, aren't you?"

The youth was about twenty, tall and lean, with red hair, a thin face with a few pimples growing in the smooth red flesh, his eyes gray-blue with dark shadows.

"Yes, I'm Carsons."

"I'm Tom Dark. That's my cart outside."

They shook hands. As their hands parted Tom stroked Kim's palm with one finger lightly. Kim felt the blood rush to his crotch.

"Going north?"

"Yes."

"Like to ride with me in the wagon?"

"Sure."

A Mexican kid is sitting in the driver's seat of Tom's cart.

"Kim Carsons, this is my assistant. Pecos Bridge Juanito."

The boy has a knowing smile. The road winds along a stream, trees overhead . . . bits of quartz glitter in the road, which isn't used often, you can tell by the weeds. Looks like the road out of Saint Albans. They cross an old stone bridge.

"This is Pecos Bridge. . . . We'll stop here . . . be dark in another hour."

Juanito guides the wagon off the road into a clearing by the stream, which is slow and deep at this point. He unhitches the horse and starts pulling tripods and cameras out of the wagon.

"My specialty is erotics," Tom explains, "rich collectors. Paris . . . New York . . . London. I've been looking for you on commission. Got a client wants sex pictures of a real gunman."

"I hope you don't mean the naked-except-for-cowboy-boots-gun-belt-and-sombrero sort of thing."

"Look, I'm an artist."

"And I'm a *shootist*, not a gunman. The gun doesn't own me. I own the gun."

"Well, are you interested?"

Kim puts a finger on the cleft below his nose, runs the finger down his body and under the crotch to the perineum. He holds out his open hand.

"Right down the middle."

"Fair enough."

Kim brings a bottle of sour-mash bourbon from his "alligator" and they toast their fucking future.

"They hanged a Mexican kid from that branch." Tom points to a cottonwood branch a few feet above the wagon. "You can still see the rope marks. . . . Yep hanged him offen the cayuse he went and stealed but he hadn't stoled that horse. He'd boughten it. Only the posse didn't find that out until after they'd hanged the kid.

"You may have read about it . . . made quite a stir . . . federal antilynching bill in Congress and the Abolitionists took some northern states. . . . All the papers wanted a picture of the hanging and I gave them one . . . fake, of course. . . . How did I get away with it? Well there isn't any limit to what you can get away with in this business. Faked pictures are more convincing than real pictures because you can set them up to look real. Understand this: *All pictures are faked.* As soon as you have the concept of a picture there is no limit to falsification. Now here's a picture in the paper shows a flood in China. So how do you know it's a picture of a flood in China? How do you know he didn't take it in his bathtub? How do you even know there was a flood in China? Because you read it in the papers. So it has to be true, if not, other reporters other photographers . . . sure you gotta cover yourself or cut other reporters and photographers in so they get together on the story. . . .

"Two years ago I was doing portrait photos in Saint Louis and I ran into this old lady I knew from England who is a very rich Abolitionist on a lecture tour. And the idea comes to me. I tell her what is needed to put some teeth into the Abolition

movement is an *incident* and she puts up some front money and most of that goes to pay off the sheriff who would investigate the hanging and the doctor who would sign the death certificate, which turned out to be the birth certificate of Pecos Bridge Juanito, a fabrication out of whole paper. And I had the whole scoop . . . picture of the boy . . . interviews with his mother, who died years before he was born . . . even pictures of the posses repenting and getting born again in Jesus. . . . Not that some reporters weren't suspicious. . . . They can *smell* a fake story but they couldn't prove anything. We even had a body in the coffin just in case; young Mexican died of scarlet fever . . . the picture was the easiest part. . . . Lots of ways to fake a hanging picture or any picture, for that matter. . . . Easiest is you don't show the feet and they are standing on something. . . . I did my shot with an elastic rope they use in carny hanging acts." He points to the horse. . . . "There's the only actor didn't get paid. . . . I call him Centaur. How about a dip and a swill?"

Sex scenes in the diary were in coded symbols like Japanese forget-me-nots flowering in the medium of memory: June 3, 1883 . . . Met T at Cottonwood Junction . . . (sexual attraction and reason to believe reciprocated) . . . & (naked) . . . (erection) . . . (sodomy) . . . (ejaculation).

Sunset through black clouds . . . red glow on naked bodies. Kim carefully wraps his revolver in a towel and places it under some weeds at the water's edge. He puts his foot in the water and gasps. At this moment Tom streaks by him, floating above the ground in a series of still pictures, the muscles of his thigh and buttock outlined like an anatomical drawing as he runs straight into the water, silver drops fanning out from his legs.

Kim follows, holding his breath, then swimming rapidly up and down. He treads water, breathing in gasps as the sky darkens and the water stretches black and sinister as if some monster might rise from its depths. . . . In knee-deep water, soaping themselves and looking at each other serene as dogs, their geni-

tals crinkled from the icy water . . . drying themselves on a sand-bank, wiping the sand from his feet . . . following Tom's lean red buttocks back to the wagon. He stations Kim at the end of the wagon. . . . "Stand right there," facing the setting sun. Tom pulls a black cloth out of the air with a flourish, bowing to an audience. He stands behind the camera with the black cloth over his head. . . . "Look at the camera . . . hands at your sides."

Kim could feel the phantom touch of the lens on his body, light as a breath of wind. Tom is standing naked behind the camera.

"I want to bottle you, mate," Tom says. Kim has never heard this expression but he immediately understands it. And he glimpses a hidden meaning, a forgotten language, sniggering half-heard words of tenderness and doom from lips spotted with decay that send the blood racing to his crotch and singing in his ears as his penis stretches, sways, and stiffens and naked lust surfaces in his face from the dark depths of human origins.

Tom is getting hard too. The shaft is pink and smooth, no veins protruding. Now fully erect, the tip almost touches the delineated muscles of his lean red-brown stomach. At the crown of his cock, on top, is an indentation, as if the creator had left his thumbprint there in damp clay. Held in a film medium, like soft glass, they are both motionless except for the throbbing of tumescent flesh. . . .

"Hold it!" . . . CLICK . . . For six seconds the sun seems to stand still in the sky.

Up early to make Clear Creek before dark. . . .

"I'm meeting a friend in Clear Creek," Kim says. . . . "You been there?"

"Yes. There's an old whorehouse and hotel. . . . Good sets for special pictures."

"Anybody live there?"

"Some Chinese used to work on the railroad. Surveyor decided on another route . . . a few Indians. . . ."

At six they come to Fort Johnson, a few miles from the

town. A coyote lopes out the open gate, showing his teeth in a knowing smile. Kim never shoots wolves or coyotes. He doesn't give a fuck how many sheep and cattle they kill.

They get out to look at the fort and Tom takes a few pictures. Gate needs fixing, aside from that . . .

"This could be my Alamut . . ." Kim says.

Tom shakes his head. . . . "This isn't the tenth century, Kim. . . . Money abhors a vacuum . . . a few more years. . . ."

They ride into Clear Creek . . . rusty tracks overgrown with weeds . . . the water tower has fallen on its side. . . . By the station an old Chinese is smoking opium. . . .

"They grow it here," Tom explains. . . . "What's your friend's name? I speak a little Chinese. . . ."

"Ask him if Billy Chung is here."

"Not yet. Clom soon."

They draw up in front of the Clear Water Hotel. Tom points to a two-story red brick building across the street. . . .

"Pantapon Rose's cathouse. . . ."

Juanito jumps out and salutes like a bellhop. . . .

"Carry bags, Meester? See me fuck my seester?"

"I think we'll bunk down with Pantapon Rose. . . . The roof doesn't leak. . . ." Tom says.

Quite comfortable actually. They settle in. Fish in the river. Some Mexicans in the hotel. Thirteen Pima Indians occupy the general store. Juanito is half Pima and half Mexican and these are relatives. No trouble trading for supplies. The Chinese live in the station and keep to themselves.

Kim was to make Fort Johnson and Clear Creek his base of operations for two years, with side trips as far as Mexico.

Look at this picture from Tom's collection: the Indians and the one white are all related, by location: the end of the line. Like the last Tasmanians, the Patagonians, the hairy Ainu, the passenger pigeon, they cast no shadow, because there will never be any more. This picture is the end. The mold is broken.

This final desolate knowledge impelled them to place phalluses, crudely carved from wood and painted with ocher, on male graves. The markers are scattered and broken. Only the picture remains.

Notice the Indian fourth from the left in the back row: a look of sheer panic. For he recognizes the photographer: Tom Dark, who takes the last picture and files it "Secret—Classified." Only he knows exactly where it is in relation to all the other files, since location is everything.

The picture itself is a cryptic glyph, an artifact out of context, fashioned for a forgotten purpose or a purpose blocked from future realization. And yet spelling out . . .

Five passenger pigeons in a tree . . . CLICK: "The Last Passenger Pigeons."

KAPOW! The birds drop and flutter to the ground, feathers drifting in dawn wind.

The Hunter looks about uneasily as he shoves the birds into his bag. It's been a bad day. He turns to face the camera.

CLICK: "The Last Passenger-Pigeon Hunter."

Spelling out . . . August 6, 1945: Hiroshima. Oppenheimer on screen: "We have become Death, Destroyer of Worlds."

"Doctor Oppenheimer!"

CLICK.

Hall reflected that he was himself the end of the Hall line, at least by the old-fashioned method of reproduction.

"Waahhhh!"

CLICK.

"Awwwwwwk!!!"

CLICK.

Kim makes up skits for the sex pictures. He is looking forward to moving film.

Both are interstate champions in the International Undressing Contest. Tailors cater to this discipline and clothes are carefully designed for the celerity and grace with which they can be

removed. They roll and twist on the bed, making high keening noises that set the windowpanes vibrating.

Afterward the boy shoves some gum into his mouth and says, "You and I are going to have to talk about our *relationship*. . . ." He blows a pink gum bubble and pops it. "Who aren't you?"

Tom wants to re-create various erotic incidents from Kim's past life. . . .

"Well me and my Fox Boy made sex magic against old Judge Farris. . . . He said I look like a sheep-killing dog and his horrible wife said I am a walking corpse. . . . You can be the Fox Boy. . . ."

The set for this scene was a room in the old brothel with a worn green satin sofa and an erotic Japanese screen with flying pricks and an old man chasing them with butterfly nets. Kim finds it tasteful.

Tom speaks in a circus barker voice:

"We attempt the impossible: to photograph the present moment which contains the past the future. All art attempts the impossible. Consider the problem of photographing past time. We will now reenact Kim masturbating in front of Judge Farris's picture."

It's a stock part, nasty-tempered old gentleman with purple cheekbones and clipped white mustache and mean bloodshot blue eyes. This picture will do, so nail it to the wall. This is Kim's basement workshop where he practices magic, a magic circle in red chalk on the floor. Action, cameras. Take over, chico. Kim takes off a red bathrobe and tosses it onto the green satin divan.

He stands naked in front of the picture. . . . (One camera is taking the scene in profile, the other is installed in a hole in the wall just above the judge's picture.) Kim arches his body and rises on his toes, snapping his fingers above his head to evoke the Fox Boy. Tom as the Fox Boy, his body covered with red

paint, slithers out from behind the Japanese screen. Kim looks over his shoulder and erases a portion of the circle with one foot. Tom squeezes in, picks up a piece of chalk between his toes, and closes the circle. "Get thee behind me, Satan, and do the great work," Kim quips. Now they both intone:

> *Slip and stumble*
> *Trip and fall*
> *Down the stairs*
> *And hit the waaaallllllllll.*

They howl it out and Kim shoots the Judge right in the crotch.

Tom is planning a trip to Denver to pick up money transferred to a Denver bank from a New York client. Kim will recruit personnel.

They are both dressed in "banker drag" as Kim calls it—expensive dark suits *discreetly* expensive. Tom chats up the manager about the future of moving film. The manager is impressed. How easy it is to deceive those who are already deceived. Tell them what they want to hear and they will believe it.

They make a tour of dives and opium dens as Kim renews his contacts with the Johnson underworld, rod-riding yeggs and cat burglars, bank robbers on holiday. . . . (Denver is a closed city. You don't operate here.) He pays a social call on Salt Chunk Mary and picks up some good backup: Marbles, a juggler, knife thrower, and trick shot from a stranded carnival: he can shoot the pips out of cards, put out candles, light matches and hit a silver dollar in the air. And Boy, who used to work with Jones on bank heists. Boy radiates a murderous vitality. A real Force, Boy, Kim decides. "They will be my baby-sitters."

The shop has an unsuccessful look. Somebody isn't trying. Behind the counter is a boy about sixteen, with flaring ears, yellow hair and an elfish smile.

"Who owns this place?"

"My Uncle Olafson, fucking squarehead Swede."

"Think he might like to sell it?"

"He'd jump at an offer. He wants to go back to Minnesota, says it's too savage here."

"When will he be back?"

"Tomorrow. Went to one of those Swede weddings. . . ."

Kim picks up a long-barreled 22 revolver. . . .

"That's got twice the hit of a standard 22. . . ."

"Who does the work here?"

"I do. My uncle don't know shit about guns. . . ."

"Like to work for us?"

"Sure. My name is Sven."

His ears wriggle.

Tom introduces Kim to Chris Cullpepper, a wealthy, languid young man of exotic tastes. He is into magic and has studied with Aleister Crowley and the Golden Dawn. They decide on a preliminary evocation of Humwawa, Lord of Abominations, to assess the strength and disposition of enemy forces. . . .

Since Humwawa is the Lord of Things to Come, he is the Lord of Confrontation, and of the Outcome of Battles. . . .

The invocation is conducted in a bare whitewashed room, the north wall missing, the room opening onto a walled courtyard. . . . Marbles, Boy, Tom, Sven, Chris, and Kim take part— all in sky clothes of course. As soon as Chris begins the evocation the room turns icy cold. . . . Demons writhe around them in a pantomime of vicious hate, imitating sex acts, flopping and kicking and dancing with tongues hanging down to the floor, twisting to show rectums, giggling out spirals of sepia vapors that burn like acid. . . . But now they shrink back from the awesome breath of Humwawa, twisting in deadly ferments, spewing yeasty vomits, intestines ruptured by tearing farts, teeth and bones dissolving in body acids, tongues splitting and squirming like severed worms, they sputter out in nitrous smoke.

More advanced and detailed incantations are carried out in the locker-room gymnasium of an empty school that Chris owns. . . . "All that young male energy, so much better than a church my dead I mean my dear, all those whining, sniveling prayers. . . ."

Musty male smells drift from the lockers, from moldy gym shoes and yellowed jockstraps. Kim puts his gun on the upper shelf with a frayed football helmet. . . . An oak bench smooth as amber, seasoned by generations of young buttocks, a smell of stale sweat, rectal mucus, and adolescent genitals rubs out with musk and hyacinth and rose oil as the boys sit down side by side: Tom, Chris, Marbles, Boy, Sven and Kim, watching each other for the moment when a leg is raised to shove down pants and shorts. . . .

A sharp ferret smell cuts incense and perfume, as the boys stand up naked to hang their clothes in the lockers. Kim looks at Marbles and catches his breath, lips peeling back to show one sharp front tooth. The boy's flesh is like pink marble, the buttocks smooth and shiny as polished stone. . . . His perfectly formed phallus is cool and smooth to the touch, his eyes a smoky

slate color, his hair ash blond and curly in a tight casque around his head. . . .

Sven's nostrils flare, his ears wriggle and turn bright red, and a smell of the north woods wafts out: pine and woodsmoke, leather clothes slept in all winter and stale beds in rooms where the windows are never opened. . . .

Chris has set up a stone altar in the old gymnasium with candles and incense burners, a crystal skull, a phallic doll carved from a mandrake root, and a shrunken head from Ecuador.

Kim leans forward and Marbles rubs the unguent up him with a slow circular twist as Chris begins the evocation. . . .

UTUL XUL

"We are the children of the underworld, the bitter venom of the gods."

Kim feels Marbles's smooth cock slide in.

"One that haunts the streets, one that haunts the bed."

The walls open and Kim sees a red desert under a purple sky.

"Their habitations the desolate places, the lands between the lands, the cities between the cities."

Kim sees a city of red limestone where naked men slump in a strange lassitude, waiting.

"May the dead arise and smell the incense."

Slow rhythmic contraction of the smooth shiny buttocks entering his body, impregnating him. . . . Tom is changing into Mountfaucon, a tail sprouting from his spine, sharp fox face and the musky reek.

XUL IA LELAL IA AXA AXA

Tom, red and peeled, his hair standing up, his eyes lighting up inside with sputtering blue fire. . . . And Chris, his flexible spine undulating like a serpent, bitter venom of the gods gathering in his crotch, phallus straining up . . . throats swelling vibrating, voices blending in the larynx . . . Tom is a shimmering pearly mollusk, and Marbles a living shell. . . . He is riding the contractions like a cheetah across the red desert to the city

where naked men with antennae jutting from their hairless skulls slump against smooth stone walls and steps. . . .

A reek of alien excrement and offal clings to the ancient stone and rises from open street latrines. The naked men are waiting their turn on the latrines, which accommodate six at once, lead troughs welded into stone. The men slump with dead eyes, waiting to void their phosphorescent excrement. . . .

"The creation of ANUS, the foundations of chaos."

Kim feels something stir and stretch in his head as horns sprout. . . . He writhes in agony, in bone-wrenching spasms, as a blaze of silver light flares out from his eyes in a flash that blows out the candles on the altar. The crystal skull lights up with lambent blue fire, the shrunken head gasps out a putrid spicy breath, the mandrake screams:

IA KINGU IA LELAL IA AXAAAAAAAAA

On the way back to Clear Creek they stop at the Overlook Hotel in Boulder. The hotel is almost empty and they take the whole top floor. . . .

Sunrise outside, the nacreous pinks and mother-of-pearl streaked with semen and roses, pirate casks full of gold pieces and jewels, Tom's mouth opens, gasping the alien medium of Kim's body. Kim picks a piece of bacon from between his front teeth, his face blank and absent as the polished blue sky behind him.

Doves fucking in the morning and Tom leaps out of bed with a snarl of rage, grabs a tennis racket that he finds in a corner and rushes onto the balcony, slashing right and left. Bloody pigeons cascading to the street five floors down. He draws the curtains and puts the tennis racket back in its corner.

"Thus perish all enemies of the human race," says Kim.

Tom's eyes glitter in the darkened room. . . .

Kim recruits a band of flamboyant and picturesque outlaws, called the Wild Fruits. There is the Crying Gun, who breaks into tears at the sight of his opponent.

"What's the matter, somebody take your lollipop?"

"Oh *señor*, I am sorry for you. . . ."

And the Priest, who goes into a gunfight giving his adversaries the last rites. And the Blind Gun, who zeroes in with bat squeaks. And the famous Shittin' Sheriff, turned outlaw. At the sight of his opponent he turns green with fear and sometimes loses control of his bowels. Well, there's an old adage in show biz: the worse the stage fright, the better the performance.

Kim trains his men to identify themselves with death. He takes some rookie guns out to a dead horse rotting in the sun, eviscerated by vultures. Kim points to the horse, steaming there in the noonday heat.

"All right, *roll* in it."

"WHAT?"

"Roll in it like dogs of war. Get the stink of death into your chaps and your boots and your guns and your hair."

Most of us puked at first, but we got used to it, and vultures followed us around hopefully.

We always ride into town with the wind behind us, a wheeling cloud of vultures overhead, beaks snapping. The townspeople gag and retch:

"My God, what's that stink?"

"It's the stink of death, citizens."

Kim had now gone underground and in any case the days of the gunfighter were over. So far as the world knew he was just a forgotten chapter in western history. He was d-e-a-d. So who would move against him, or even know about the Alamuts he was establishing throughout America and northern Mexico? He had in fact taken pains to remain anonymous and dispatched his henchmen to remove records of the Fort Johnson Incident from libraries, newspaper morgues and even from private collections of old western lore. . . . So who now would know where he was and reveal themselves by moves against him? He decided to wait and see. The first settlement, a resort hotel at Clear Creek, demonstrated that they did know and were already dispatching their

agents to intercept the project. It's rather like bullfighting, he reflected. If the bull can get a *querencia* where he feels at home, then the bullfighter has to go and get him on his own ground, so the alert bull sticker will do anything to keep the bull from finding a *querencia*. In fact some unethical practitioners have small boys posted with slingshots. . . .

Well things start to go wrong. Right away there are delays in shipments of material. These were traced to a warehouse in Saint Louis and a certain shipping clerk who was later found to be suffering from a form of *petit mal* with spells of amnesia. A small boy brought charges of molestation against the foreman of construction. When the boy became violently insane the charges were dropped, but not before a drummer had attempted to incite the townspeople to form a lynch mob.

But an old farmer who was one of our own said, "You live hereabouts, Mister? Wouldn't say so from your accent. . . ."

"Well I live north of here. . . ."

"You a country boy?"

"Well I was . . . that is . . ."

"From Chicago, ain't you?"

A murmur from the crowd. The drummer is losing his audience.

"We have children in Chicago too. . . ."

"Well whyn't you stay up there and protect *your* children stead of selling your lousy war-surplus hog fencing down here?"

Kim now realizes that *they* can take over bodies and minds and use them for their purposes. So why do they always take over stupid, bigoted people or people who are retarded or psychotic? Obviously they are looking for dupes and slaves, not for intelligent allies. In fact their precise intention is to destroy human intelligence, to blunt human awareness and to block human beings out of space. What they are launching is an extermination program. And anyone who has sufficient insight to suspect the existence of a *they* is a prime target.

He listed the objectives and characteristics of the aliens. . . .

1. They support any dogmatic religious system that tends to stupefy and degrade the worshipers. They support the Slave Gods. They want blind obedience, not intelligent assessment. They stand in the way of every increase in awareness. They only conceded a round earth and allowed the development of science to realize the even more stupefying potential of the Industrial Revolution.

2. They support any dogmatic authority. They are the arch-conservatives.

3. They lose no opportunity to invert human values. They are always self-righteous. They have to be right because in human terms they are wrong. Objective assessment drives them to hysterical frenzy.

4. They are parasitic. They live in human minds and bodies.

5. The Industrial Revolution, with its overpopulation and emphasis on quantity rather than quality, has given them a vast reservoir of stupid bigoted uncritical human hosts. The rule of the majority is to their advantage since the majority can always be manipulated.

6. Their most potent tool of manipulation is the word. The inner voice.

7. They will always support any measures that tend to stultify the human host. They will increase the range of arbitrary and dogmatic authority. They will move to make alcohol illegal. They will move to regulate the possession of firearms. They will move to make drugs illegal.

8. They are more at home occupying women than men. Once they have a woman, they have the male she cohabits with. Women must be regarded as the principal reservoir of the alien virus parasite. Women and religious sons of bitches. Above all, religious women.

We will take every opportunity to weaken the power of the church. We will lobby in Congress for heavy taxes on all

churches. We will provide more interesting avenues for the young. We will destroy the church with ridicule. We will secularize the church out of existence. We will introduce and encourage alternative religious systems. Islam, Buddhism, Taoism. Cults, devil worship, and rarefied systems like the Ishmaelite and the Manichaean. Far from seeking an atheistic world as the communists do, we will force Christianity to compete for the human spirit.

We will fight any extension of federal authority and support States' Rights. We will resist any attempt to penalize or legislate against the so-called victimless crimes ... gambling, sexual behavior, drinking, drugs.

We will give all our attention to experiments designed to produce asexual offspring, to cloning, use of artificial wombs, and transfer operations.

We will endeavor to halt the Industrial Revolution before it is too late, to regulate populations at a reasonable point, to eventually replace quantitative money with qualitative money, to decentralize, to conserve resources. The Industrial Revolution is primarily a virus revolution, dedicated to controlled proliferation of identical objects and persons. You are making soap, you don't give a shit who buys your soap, the more the soapier. And you don't give a shit who makes it, who works in your factories. Just so they make soap.

They were down in Mexico, hiding out in the hacienda of the Fuentes family. They did some hunting for the table. Kim tamed a peccary and it would follow him like a dog. There was an old family assassin named Tío Mate, who could shoot vultures out of the sky with his 44 tip-up Smith and Wesson.

Kim procured some sacred mushrooms from his Indian lover, which he brewed in a clay pot and crooned over it and spit in it and just before sunset we all take the potion and Kim's spirit guide leads us to a room we had never seen before huge house anyhoo and we find trunks full of female clothes so we dress up

and camp around Kim calls himself the Green Nun, and Tom does the Pious Señora, and Boy is the blushing Señorita. The Green Nun rummages around and finds a brace of double-barreled twenty-gauge shotgun pistols perfectly balanced with rubber grips and her loads it with number-four shot.

And a belt with holsters, the guns slide out smooth as silk, the whole equipage hide under his nun cape. Boy, who has been vulture shooting with Tío Mate, opts for the 44 Smith and Wesson, and Tom has a weird Webley semiautomatic revolver, with a shield over the cylinder to protect his hand from sparks and a hand grip that folds down from the barrel.

So attired and armed we get in the buckboard and drive down to the village, where the Chief of Police and his asshole cronies is getting drunker and meaner by the minute. . . . They know something is going on up at the hacienda.

"*Brujería* . . ." (Witchcraft . . .)

"*Y maricones.*"

The Jefe is a strain of blond Mexican with reddish hair, little red bristly eyelashes, blue pig-eyes, and a pug nose with red hairs flaring out like copper wire. Strong and heavyset, his whole being exudes animal ill-temper and menace. He is conspiring to displace the Fuentes family, who opposed his appointment. Kim had seen him shortly after his arrival and it was pure hate at first sight. . . .

The four boys sweep into the saloon. The Jefe swells with rage.

Kim smiles at him and touches the huge silver crucifix at his throat, in the same moment tossing his nun cape aside.

"CHINGOA!" the Jefe screams and goes for his pearl-handled 45 automatic. Kim slides the gun out and points for the Jefe's pig snout and there is a bloody hole where the Jefe's nose and eyes were. He spins backward into the man behind him, a gaunt wooden-faced man with a black coat and black bow tie.

Kim lines up just under the tie and opens his throat to the spine. He drops to the floor to shift guns. . . .

Boy and Tom are dropping them like ducks in a shooting gallery. I see a stolid farmer type lining up on Tom with a 30-30 and I shoot up from the floor just below the rib cage where the Aztecs cut in to pull the heart out. He rocks back, his eyes open and close like a doll. The gun falls from his hands.

Twelve of those lousy macho shits died in the shoot-out. We lost one boy—a sad quiet kid named Joe had got himself up as a whore in a purple dress slit down the sides. Had his gun in a shoulder holster and it caught in his strap-on tits. Hit five times.

When we get back to the hacienda with dead Joe, Tío Mate takes us in to see the *patrón,* a courtly old gentleman with black clothes and silver braid all over.

"It gives me much pleasure to see boys earn their keep."

We all recognize the voice of Kim's spirit guide.

The boys smile.

"Can I pet the skull?" Kim asks.

"Certainly. You all can."

Tío Mate steps to the door and calls the Skull Keeper. And he brings the skull in on a silk pillow and sets it down on a table of polished petrified wood. And we all crowd around to pet it. I can feel the tingle run up my arms, a soft burn, and the smell of stale flowers and jungles and decay and musky animal smells. . . . Kim draws the smell deep into his lungs.

"When I touched it I felt itchy prickles run up my arm in rhythmic pulses. It's a living thing, warm and resinous to the touch, like amber.

"I am stroking out a smell of stagnant swamp water, gardens turning back to jungle, and a sharp rank animal smell."

Smell of some creature so alien Kim feels queasy trying to imagine the creature that would smell like that. He knew that the skull came from the planet Venus. He had experienced vivid dream visions of Venus and he intended to write a guidebook. . . . He did sketches and sometimes he would tell Tom:

"Take a picture of that. It's pure Venus, my dear...."

And Uranus where the Uranians sit in their blue slate houses in cold blue silence.... Kim wanted to explore them all.... He longed for new dangers and new weapons, "for perilous seas in faery lands forlorn." For unknown drugs and pleasures, and a distant star called HOME.

The Family has set up a number of posts in America and northern Mexico. They are already very rich, mostly from real estate. They own newspapers, a chemical company, a gun factory, and a factory for making photographic equipment, which will become one of the first film studios.

Their policy is Manichaean. Good and evil are in a state of conflict. The outcome is uncertain. This is not an eternal conflict since one or the other will win out in this universe. The Christian church, by calling good "evil" and evil "good," has confused the issue. The church must be seen as a dedicated instrument of alien invasion.

Kim has set out to organize the Johnson Family into an all-out worldwide space program. He soon finds himself in conflict with very deadly and powerful forces:

Old Man Bickford, cattle, oil, and real estate. He owns a big piece of a big state. He is one of the poker-playing, whiskey-drinking, evil old men who run America. To these backstage operators, presidents, ambassadors, cabinet members are just jokes and errand boys. They do what they are told to do, or else.

Bickford's subordinates never know why they have fallen from favor. That is for them to figure out, when his displeasure falls heavy and cold as a cop's blackjack on a winter night. . . .

"Just step in here, Jess. . . . I want to talk to you." The Old

Man steers him into a little side room containing one chair. The Old Man sits down and smiles.

"You know, Jess, I have an intuition about you: I think you'd make a mighty fine president."

Jess turns pale. "Oh no, Mr. Bickford, I don't have the qualifications. . . ."

"I disagree with you. I think you do have the qualifications: a good front, and a big mouth."

Now Jess knows: he talked too much at the wrong time and the wrong place.

"Please, Mr. Bickford. . . . I got a bad heart. It would kill me."

Bickford's smile widens. "Think about it, Jess. Think about it very carefully. I wouldn't want to see you make a mistake."

Mr. Hart, the newspaper tycoon, is on the surface quite different from Bickford. Bickford enjoys complex relationships with his subordinates; Hart doesn't like any relationships. Other people are different from him, and he doesn't like them. He can only tolerate their presence under controlled conditions. More introverted than Bickford, he is simpler and more predictable, since he has an overriding obsession: Mr. Hart is obsessed with immortality. The rightest right a man could be is to live infinitely long, he decides, and he directs all the iron strength of his will to that end. He sets up a house rule that the word *death* may not be pronounced in his presence.

Once, just for jolly, Kim wangled an invitation to Hart's showplace, and appeared at dinner in a skeleton suit. Hart didn't think this was funny at all.

Bickford laughed. Oh, not in front of Hart. He wasn't there. He had his own reasons for fomenting ill will between Hart and Kim. And Hart, predictably, conceived a consuming, relentless hatred for Kim Carsons and his Johnson Family, as a deadly threat to his immortality. On one point Hart and Bickford

agree: neither of them wants to see the power of life and death in unpredictable hands.

Kim remembers the words of Bat Masterson: "A man has to fit in somewhere."

And that was what was wrong with Kim. It wasn't anything he actually did, or might do. He just did not *fit*. He wasn't even an outlaw anymore. From the proceeds of several carefully planned jewel and bank robberies, he was well on the way to being wealthy. The last of his illegal diamonds nestled in his vest pocket. Kim didn't fit, and a part that doesn't fit can wreck a machine. These old pros could see long before Kim saw that he had the basic secrets of wealth and power and would become a big-time player if he wasn't stopped. That his dream of a takeover by the Johnson Family, by those who actually do the work, the creative thinkers and artists and technicians, was not just science fiction. It could happen.

Kim wonders naïvely why they don't deal him in. The answer is that they will never accept anyone who does not think and feel as they do. It wasn't the Johnson Family itself that bothered them or at least it wouldn't have bothered them if it had been just another Mafia-type criminal organization. What they didn't like was to see wealth and power in the hands of those who basically despised the usages of wealth and power. This was intolerable.

"He must be stopped!"

Soon Kim will have enough money to implement the first stage of his plan—Big Picture, he calls it—his plan for a Johnson Family takeover. He will set up a base in New York. He will organize the Johnsons in Civilian Defense Units. He will oust the Mafia. He will buy a newspaper to push Johnson Policy, to oppose any further encroachment of Washington bureaucrats. He intends to strangle the FDA in its cradle, to defeat any legislation aimed at outlawing liquor, drugs, gambling, private sexual

behavior or the possession of firearms. He will buy a chemical company with research facilities where he will develop sophisticated biologic and chemical agents. He will start a small-arms factory, reserving the special weapons for the use of the Johnson elite.

"HE MUST BE STOPPED!"

Waghdas, the City of Knowledge, is denounced by Hart through newspapers of the world as "THE MOST DANGEROUS PLACE ON EARTH! A festering sink of subversion, luring gullible youth with false hopes and fool's gold. . . ."

Constantly under siege, Waghdas changes location often. In houseboats and caravans, burnt-out tenements and ghost towns . . . now you see it, now you don't. One thinks of knowledge as a calm remote area of ancient stone buildings, ivy, and languid young men, but knowledge can be an explosive instance. Ever see the marks wise up and take a carnival apart?

Hey Rube echoes through the monumental fraud of Planet Earth . . . the forbidden knowledge passes from Johnson to Johnson, in freight cars and jails, in seedy rooming houses and precarious compounds, in hop joints and rafts floating down the great rivers of South America, in guerrilla camps and desert tents.

"The game is rigged! Take the place apart!"

Already the first crude weapons are being forged in lofts and basements, barns and warehouses . . . weapons for a new type of warfare, weapons aimed directly at the driver instead of the craft, the soul instead of the body. And all physical weapons have their soul-warfare equivalents . . . there are soul knives and guns, soul poisons and mass bombardments that can leave a city of empty bodies milling around—from time to time one stops and falls, he can't never get up, so they keep walking around and around in a clockwise direction as one after the other drops. . . .

Kim doesn't want to keep thinking about the ambush since he isn't ready to take action yet, but it keeps playing over and over in his brain like a stuck record. . . . Late afternoon and the sun came out . . . the town shimmering in the distance like the promised land. Just riding into town for supplies . . . and the next thing bullets and shotgun slugs is coming from every side.

Kim found out later that Mike Chase had tipped the sheriff that the Carsons gang was going to rob the bank. He didn't tell the sheriff about the special price Old Man Bickford has on Kim, figuring to take that for himself. That was Mike. Let others take the chances, then he picks up the eagles.

Kim had an anthology of poetry, leather-bound with gilt edges, and a slim volume of Rimbaud, so he distracted himself with reading.

Yes, he had an account to settle with a certain bounty hunter named Mike Chase. "Bookkeeping," he called it. Vengeance is a dish best savored cold . . . with dewy fingers cold.

Kim had a pint of cannabis tincture with him, as he was off morphine, and the cannabis made everything so much sharper. Kim would have been the first to concede that it also made him silly in an eerie, ghostly sort of way. Now he strapped on the gun with the silencer in its special holster, fits like a prick up an asshole and slides out with a little fluid plop.

His Sperm Gun, he called it. Spitting death seed, it would father the Super Race. They are out there, waiting to be born . . . millions of Johnsons. . . . Certain uh obstacles must be removed. . . .

> The little toy dog is covered with dust,
> But sturdy and stanch he stands;
> And the little toy soldier is red with rust, . . .
> Awaiting the touch of a little hand, . . .

"Hello, Mike," he trills, a ghostly child voice from a haunted attic.

Awaiting the touch of a little hand.

Kim's face darkens with death. He goes into a half-crouch as his hand drops and sweeps the gun up to eye level in a smooth, unhurried movement.

A tubercular cough from metal lungs. The gun spits smoky blood. White dust drifts from a hole in a cow skull Kim has set up on a fencepost. Now that cow got bogged down, used to be quicksand here. Kim can imagine its despairing moos. . . . He does a hideous imitation of the stricken cow, throwing his head back, rolling his eyes and bellowing to the sky: "MOOO MOOO MOOOO . . . as drowsy tinklings lull the distant folds." Kim reads the poems over and over . . . "verses trill and tinkle from the icy streams, and the stars that oversprinkle all the heavens seem to twinkle with a crystalline delight." He didn't think of it as vengeance, it was just keeping the ledger books, "as dewy fingers draw the gradual dusky veil." Verses whisper and sigh from grass and leaves, "old, unhappy, far-off things/And battles long ago." Sometimes some lines of verse would light up a scene from his past, like a magic lantern: "A violet by a mossy stone/Half hidden from the eye!—"

A whiff of stagnant pond water, and he remembered Old Mrs. Sloane. She had a greenhouse full of fish tanks with tropical fish, and a big garden. After supper they used to go over and look at the fish and watch them eat fish food. Mrs. Sloane was a fat, wheezy woman who was always fanning herself, and she had two fat wheezing asthmatic Pekingese dogs.

"Foink foink foink," they would wheeze out.

"FUCK FUCK FUCK."

Fireflies are coming out in her garden, among the roses and iris and lilies. A frog plops into the fishpond. The Evening Star floats in a clear green sky. Two fireflies light up the petals of a rose, cold phosphorescent green, delicate seashell pink, a cameo of memory floating in dead stale time.

It has the garish colors of a tinted photograph. Kim feels a

little queasy looking at it. He can see it on a Japanese screen in a whorehouse.

Killed in the Manhattan Shoot-out . . . April 3, 1894 . . . Sharp smell of weeds from old westerns.

Christmas 1878, Wednesday . . . Eldora, Colo. . . . William Hall takes a book bound in leather from a drawer and leafs through the pages. It is a scrapbook with sketches, photos, newspaper articles, dated annotations. Postscript by William Hall:

The Wild Fruits, based in Clear Creek and Fort Johnson, control a large area of southern Colorado and northern New Mexico. Like latter-day warlords, they exact tribute from settlers and townspeople and attract adventurous youth to their ranks.

Mr. Hart starts a Press campaign.

QUANTRILL RIDES AGAIN

How long are peaceful settlers and townspeople to be victimized by a brazen band of
marauding outlaws? Wallowing in nameless
depravity, they have set themselves above
the laws of God and man.

Wires are pulled in Washington. The army is called in to quell this vicious revolt against the constituted government of the United States.

In charge of the expedition is Colonel Greenfield, a self-styled Southern Gentleman, with long yellow hair and slightly demented blue eyes. He has vowed to capture and summarily hang the Wild Fruits. His cavalry regiment with artillery and mortars has surrounded Fort Johnson where the outlaws have gone to ground. The Colonel surveys the fort through his field

glasses. No sentries in the watchtowers, no sign of life. From the flagpole flies Old Glory, a cloth skunk, tail raised, cleverly stitched in.

"FILTHY FRUITS!"

The Colonel raises his sword. Artillery opens up, blowing the gate off its hinges. With wild yipes, the regiment charges. As the Colonel sweeps through the gate, horses rear and whinny, eyes wild. There is a reek of death. Crumpled bodies are strewn about the courtyard. From a gallows dangle effigies of Colonel Greenfield, Old Man Bickford, and Mr. Hart. From the crotch of each effigy juts an enormous wooden cock with a spring inside jiggling up and down as the dummies swing in the afternoon wind.

"They're all dead, sir."

"Are you sure?"

The Sergeant claps a handkerchief over his face in answer. Colonel Greenfield points to the gallows.

"Get that down from there!"

A cloud of dust is rapidly approaching. . . .

"It's the press, sir!"

The reporters ride in yelping like cossacks. Some even swing down from balloons as they swarm over the fort, snapping pictures.

"I forbid . . . "

Too late, Colonel. . . . The story was front-page round the world with pictures of the dead outlaws. . . . (Hart and Bickford managed to kill the gallows pictures.) Seems the Wild Fruits had died from a poison potion, the principal ingredient of which was aconite. A week later the whole thing was forgotten. More than forgotten . . . excised . . . erased . . . Mr. Hart saw to that. The effigies had accomplished the purpose for which they had been designed.

Rumors persisted . . . soldiers had found an escape tunnel . . . the bodies found were not Kim and his followers but migrant Mexican workers who had died in a flash flood. . . .

From time to time over the years stories bobbed up in Sunday supplements:

MASS SUICIDE OR MASSIVE HOAX?

The outlaws had disbanded and scattered. Colonel Greenfield, unable to accomplish his mission, faked the whole suicide story and buried fifty mannikins. . . . Kim, Boy, and Marbles keep turning up from Siberia to Timbuktu.

II

HIS FATHER'S PICTURE

Cloning was in an experimental stage at the time of the Big Jump, when the fifty original Wild Fruits committed suicide at Fort Johnson. We had actual biologic cuttings stored in refrigerated vaults. Pending the solution of residual technical problems, we set out to match voice and genital patterns with existing replicas. Everyone has not one but many approximate doubles. It is simply a matter of implanted voice and genital prints. Then the subject is slowly led to remember the former life of his guest and the two beings merge into one.

Kim Carsons, age twenty, was one of ten clones derived from Kim Carsons the Founder. Since he was in contact with approximate replicas of himself and with other clone families like the Graywoods, the Dahlfars, the Wentworths, the Summervilles, the Gysins, the Joneses, the Little Rivers, the Yen Lees and the Henriques, he was under no pressure to maintain the perimeters of a defensive ego and this left him free to *think*. He was stationed in New York, such assignments being arranged informally at the family gatherings.

To say Kim Carsons still lives is to pose the question: what does this mean? His thought patterns live in a number of different brains and nervous systems, his speech and genital patterns, all of which are distinctive. No two people have the same voice or the same cock. The clones exist in a communal mind in which the bodies are at the disposal of all the others, like rotating quarters.

As the guests arrive and are met at the train by the driver, we see how varied the Carsons Family actually is. There are blonds and redheads and oriental-looking youths and blacks and Indians resulting from various recombinant techniques.

Their part is easy to play. They are the guests, down from the north or up from the Deep South or in from the West, millionaires who own the county the sheriff and the townspeople. There is Kim with his father mother and younger brother getting off the train with an unmistakable air of wealth and quiet self-possession. Porters stagger under their luggage. Kim gives them each a bright new dime. They snarl after him.

"Little prick. Wait till he has to play porter."

For the roles rotate. You can be *fils de famille* today and busboy tomorrow—*son cosas de la vida*. Besides it's more interesting that way. Kim loves to play the acne-scarred blackmailing chauffeur or the insolent bellhop tipped back in a chair, his face flushed from drinking the bottle of champagne he has delivered.

"What is the meaning of this?" Tom snaps. . . . The boy rubs his crotch and smiles and insolently squirts Tom in the crotch with a soda siphon.

"Oh sir, you've had an accident." He bustles around, loosening Tom's belt and trying to shove his pants down.

"What the bloody hell are you doing?"

"Just changing your didies, sir."

Or maybe Tom is coming on and Kim the bellboy is playing it cool.

"Oh sir, I *couldn't* sit down at the table with you. I knows me place, sir, if you'll pardon the expression, sir."

This system of rotating parts operates on the basis of a complex lottery. . . . Some people achieved a lottery-exempt status for a time but for most it was maybe a month, often less, before they got the dread call. Turn in your tycoon suit and report to casting.

The Johnson Family is a cooperative structure. There isn't any boss man. People know what they are supposed to do and they do it. We're all actors and we change roles. Today's million-

aire may be tomorrow's busboy. There's none of that ruling-class old school tie.... "Hey boy, manicure my toenails and look sharp about it ... and you, boy, don't slack at the ceiling fan, I'm sweating my bloody balls off ... saddle my horse, nigger...."

We are showing that an organization and a very effective organization can run without boss-man dog-eat-dog fear.

After such knowledge, what forgiveness?

William Seward Hall ... he was a corridor, a hall, leading to many doors. He remembered the long fugitive years after the fall of Waghdas, the knowledge inside him like a sickness. The migrations, the danger, the constant alertness ... the furtive encounters with others who had some piece of the knowledge, the vast picture puzzle slowly falling into place.

Time to be up and gone. You are not paid off to be quiet about what you know; you are paid not to find it out. And in his case it was too late. If he lived long enough he couldn't help finding it out, because that was the purpose of his life ... a guardian of the knowledge and of those who could use it. And a guardian must be ruthless in defense of what he guards.

And he developed new ways of imparting the knowledge to others. The old method of handing it down by word of mouth, from master to initiate, is now much too slow and too precarious (Death reduces the College). So he concealed and revealed the knowledge in fictional form. Only those for whom the knowledge is intended will find it.

William Seward Hall, the man of many faces and many pen names, of many times and places ... how dull it is to pause, to make a rest, to rust unburnished, not to shine in use ... pilgrim of adversity and danger, shame and sorrow. The Traveler, the Scribe, most hunted and fugitive of men, since the knowledge unfolding in his being spells ruin to our enemies. He will soon be in a position to play the deadliest trick of them all ... *The Piper Pulled Down the Sky*. His hand will not hesitate.

He has known capture and torture, abject fear and shame,

and humiliations that burn like acid. His hand will not hesitate to use the sword he is forging, an antimagnetic artifact that cuts word and image to fragments . . . the Council of Transmigrants in Waghdas had attained such skill in the art of prophecy that they were able to chart a life from birth to death, and so can he unplot, and unwrite. Oh, it may take a few hundred years before some people find out they have been unwritten and unplotted into random chaos. . . .

Meanwhile, he has every contract on the planet out on him. The slow, grinding contract of age, and emptiness . . . the sharp vicious contract of spiteful hate . . . heavy corporate contracts . . . "The most dangerous man in the world."

And to what extent did he succeed? Even to envisage success on this scale is a victory. A victory from which others may envision further.

> There is not a breathing of the common wind
>   that will forget thee;
> Thy friends are exaltations, agonies and love,
>   and man's inconquerable mind.

Hall's face and body were not what one expects in a sedentary middle-aged man. The face was alert and youthful, accustomed to danger and at the same time tired. The danger has gone on so long it has become routine. Yet his actual life was comparatively uneventful. The scene of battle was within, a continual desperate war for territorial advantage, with long periods of stalemate . . . a war played out on the chessboard of his writings, as bulletins came back from the front lines, which constantly altered position and intensity. Yesterday's position desperately held is today's laundromat and supermarket. Time and banality hit the hardest blows.

The absence of any immediate danger masks the deadliest attack. "It is always war," Hall had been told by a lady disciple of Sri Aurobindo, whose last words were: "It is all over." She

meant quite simply that Planet Earth is by its nature and function a battlefield. Happiness is a by-product of function in a battle context: hence the fatal error of utopians.

(I didn't ask for this fight, Kim reflects, or maybe I did. Just like Hassan i Sabbah asked for the expeditions sent out against him just because he wanted to occupy a mountain and train a few adepts. There is nothing more provocative than minding your own business.)

At a house outside Boulder, Old Man Bickford confers with his Director of Security, Mike Chase. . . .

"They is knockin' the wops down like ducks in a shooting gallery. What is wrong, Mike . . . ?"

Mike shrugs. . . . "Well, the wops are not all that good . . . seems like all the old-time shootists is gone."

"So where does Carsons get his talent? I'll tell you. He *trains* them." Old Man Bickford smiles. "You know what, Mike, I think maybe you and Kim is going to shoot it out Old Western—style. . . ." He guffaws loudly and Mike joins him, not liking it at all, feeling the cold clutch of fear in his guts.

Old Man Bickford there, smelling his fear and smiling. They both know that Mike will have a training program laid out and ready for Bickford's approval 8:00 A.M. the following day.

"How about a few hands of poker, Mike?" he drawls with narrowed eyes. His smile widens.

This is a sanction imposed by the Old Man on a subordinate the night before he has to give a report at a very crucial meeting. The Old Man keeps the young man up till five in the morning, filling his glass (the Old Man seems to have some constitutional immunity to the effects of bourbon) and winning from him a sum exactly proportional to the trespass. "There Is No Excuse for Failure" is the Bickford motto.

Five hours later, his head spinning, $20,000 poorer, Mike stumbles off to bed.

Sharp smell of weeds ... Old Man Bickford smiles and claps Mr. Hart on the back. Mr. Hart hates being slapped on the back. He turns angrily, but Bickford says, "You know what, Bill?"

Mr. Hart's glare goes dim and timorous as he sees the horse and takes in Bickford's guns.

"For the first time in a thousand years we got an all-out range war on our hands. Time to saddle up, Billy."

Mr. Hart hates being called "Billy."

"*Ka*, Egyptians called it ... soul, whatever. Well I got news for *Ka*. It isn't invulnerable and it isn't immortal." Bickford draws his gun, and fondles it. "It's a magnetic field ... it can be dispersed. POOF, no more Billy."

Mr. Hart's lips tighten in waspish irritation.

The Bickford guns agree to a truce. Fights are getting too deadly. Many of them are glad enough to get out from under Bickford's horrible smile, his all-night poker games, his cruel and evil presence.

Bickford is losing his grip. He is going security-mad. Every day it's some new electrical device or some outstandingly vicious breed of guard dog.

Kim sees his life as a legend and it is very much Moses in the bullrushes, the Prince deprived of his birthright and therefore hated and feared by the usurpers.

I shall be off with the wild geese in the stale smell of morning.

Time to be up and be gone. Time to settle his account with Mike Chase.

Kim breaks camp and rides into El Rito. He knows that Mike is in Santa Fe and he sends along a message through his Mexican contacts.

TO CONFIRM APPOINTMENT FOR SEPTEMBER 17, 4:30 P.M. AT
THE CEMETERY, BOULDER, COLORADO.

KIM CARSONS, M.D.

Kim knows that Mike will not meet him on equal footing. Well two can play at that.

(*More* than two.)

Raton Pass: This must be, Kim decided, one of the more desolate spots on the globe. A cold wind whistles around the station. No one lives there except railroad personnel and their families, all of whom have a slightly demented look and walk about with scarves tied over their faces.

Why would anyone choose to live in such a place? Chance seems to have tossed them here like driftwood.

Black Hawk: The hotel was full and Kim had to stay overnight in a miners' boardinghouse that reeked of stale sweat and corned beef and cabbage. Kim thought Black Hawk a vile place. A sepia haze of gaseous gold covers the town, farted up from the bowels of the earth, and you expect at any moment to plummet down into a mineshaft.

Kim stopped into a saloon, half hoping that someone would start trouble, but nobody did. There was an aura of menace and death about him palpable as a haze. The miners made way for him at the bar and Kim was as always scrupulously polite and well behaved. Back in his horrible room he took a morphine injection and set his mind to wake up at 5:00 A.M. the following morning to take the train for Denver.

Denver: Kim owned a rooming house in Denver but it could be staked out, so he checked into the Palace Hotel. He studied the well-dressed patrons with voices full of money. How, he asked himself, could he ever have been impressed by the self-confidence of the rich? It was simply based on their limitations. All they can think about is money money and more money. They are no better than *animals.*

He saw them as shadows parading through conservatories, drawing rooms, and formal gardens and marble arcades frozen in the studied postures of old photos. They are already *dead* and preserved in money. He noticed how the *very rich* have an embalmed look and remembered that in ancient Egypt only the rich were considered immortal because they could afford to mummify themselves.

Kim retired to his room and studied a number of photos of Mike Chase né Joe Kaposi in the Polish slums of Chicago's West Side. . . . Joe had come a long way. Kim noted the petulant, discontented look. Anyone with that look is sure to get rich. Money will simply accrete itself around him. It was a strong face, high cheekbones, brown eyes well apart, full lips, and slightly protruding teeth. Yes, a face that could even be president if he played his cards right.

He knew Old Man Bickford was grooming Mike for a career in politics. . . .

"Ah well, the best laid plans of lice and men gang aft a-gley. . . ."

September 16, 1899 . . . Kim took the stage to Boulder . . . Overlook Hotel . . . uneasy *déjà vu* . . . flash of resentment on a whispering south wind . . .

BANG!

Phantom gun . . . empty grab . . . too heavy . . . too fast . . . too easy . . . Three witnesses ejaculating, Kim took the stage back to Denver. . . . Back to the rod-riding, hop-smoking underworld . . . back to the rooming houses and pawnshops . . . the hobo jungles and opium dens . . . back to the Johnson Family.

Kim bought a thin gold pocket watch. Coming out of the jewelry store he ran into the Sanctimonious Kid, who was casing the store in a halfhearted way.

"Don't try it," Kim told him.

"Wasn't going to. . . ."

Kim noted the frayed cuffs, the cracked shoes.

"It gets harder all the time."

The Kid was always soft-spoken and sententious, known for his tiresome aphorisms.

"It's a crooked game, Kid, but you have to think straight."

"Be as positive yourself as you like but no positive clothes."

The Kid was considered tops as a second-story cat burglar and he had made some good smash-and-grabs. Kim sensed something basically wrong about the Kid and never wanted anything to do with him. Under pressure he could blow up and perpetrate some totally mindless and stupid act. Now in the afternoon sunlight Kim could see it plain as day: hemp marks around the Kid's neck.

The Sanctimonious Kid was later hanged for the murder of a police constable in Australia. It gave Kim a terrible desolate

feeling when he heard about it years later . . . the bleak court-
room . . . the gallows . . . the coffin.

"See you at the Silver Dollar."

Kim took a carriage to the outskirts of town. He got out and
strolled by his rooming house, very debonair, with his sword
cane, the flexible Toledo blade razor-sharp on both edges for
slash or thrust, his Colt 38 nestled in a tailor-made shoulder holster, a backup five-shot 22 revolver with a one-inch barrel in a
leather-lined vest pocket. He couldn't spot a stakeout. Maybe
they fell for the diversion ticket to Albuquerque he had bought,
making sure the clerk would remember. But sooner or later they
would pick up his trail. Old Man Bickford had five of Pinker-
ton's best on Kim's ass around the clock.

Kim was headed for Salt Chunk Mary's place down by the tracks
. . . solid red brick two-story house, slate roof, lead gutters. . . .
Train whistles cross a distant sky.

Salt Chunk Mary, mother of the Johnson Family. She
keeps a pot of pork and beans and a blue porcelain coffee pot
always on the stove. You eat first, then you talk business, rings
and watches slopped out on the kitchen table. She names a
price. She doesn't name another. Mary could say "no" quicker
than any woman Kim ever knew and none of her no's ever
meant yes. She kept the money in a cookie jar but nobody
thought about that. Her cold gray eyes would have seen the
thought and maybe something goes wrong on the next lay. John
Law just happens by or John Citizen comes up with a load of
double-oughts into your soft and tenders.

Mary held Kim in high regard.

"Hello," she said. "Heard you was back in town."

Kim brought out a pint of sour-mash bourbon and Mary put
two tumblers on the table. They each drank half a tumbler in
one swallow.

"The Kid is down on his luck," she said. "Stay away. It
rubs off."

"He should quit," Kim said. "He should quit and sell something."

"He won't."

No, Kim thought, not with that mark on him he won't.

"I hear Smiler went down."

She drained the tumbler and nodded.

"Young thieves like that think they have a license to steal. Then they get a sickener. Scares a lot of them straight. What did he draw?"

"A dime."

"That's a sickener all right."

They drank in silence for ten minutes.

"Joe Varland is dead. . . . Railroad cop tagged him. . . ."

"Well," Kim said, "the Lord gave and the Lord hath taken away. . . ."

"What could be fairer'n that?"

They finished the whiskey. She put a plate of pork and beans with homemade bread on the table. Kim would later taste superb bean casseroles in Marseilles and Montreal but none of them could touch Salt Chunk Mary's.

They were drinking coffee out of chipped blue mugs.

"Got something for you." Kim laid out six diamonds on the table. Mary looked at each stone with her jeweler's glass.

"Twenty-eight hundred."

Kim knew he could probably do better in New York but he needed the money right then and Mary's goodwill counted for a lot.

"Done."

She got the money out of the cookie jar and handed it to him, wrapped up the diamonds and put them in her pocket.

"Who's over at the Cemetery?" Kim asked.

Kim called his rooming house "the Cemetery" because the manager was a character known as Joe the Dead. Kim's place was a hideout for Johnsons with an impeccable reputation, most of them recommended by Salt Chunk Mary . . . con men . . . bank robbers . . . jewel thieves . . . high class of people.

Kim didn't take much risk, since Denver at the time was a "closed city." You only operate with police protection and pay-offs. Kim paid so much a month. He threw some weight in Denver. He knew some politicians and a few cops. The cops called him "the Professor" since Kim's knowledge of weapons was encyclopedic. He could always tune into any cop.

"Jones was there last week."

Jones was a bank robber. He was a short, rather plump waxy-faced man with a mustache, who looked like the groom on a wedding cake. He would walk into a bank with his gang, a ninety-pound Liz known as Sawed-off Annie with a twelve-gauge sawed-off, and two French-Canadian kids, and say his piece.

"Everybody please put your hands up high."

It was the sweetest voice any cashier ever heard. He became known as "the Bandit with the Sweet Voice." But when he said "Hands up high," you better believe it.

Jones confided in Kim that when he killed someone he got "a terrible gloating feeling." Said with that sugary voice of his, it gave Kim a chill. It's a feeling in the back of the neck, rather pleasant actually, accompanied by a drop in temperature that always gives notice of a strong psychic presence. Jones was creepy but he paid well. . . .

The last thing that Kim could ever do in this life or any other was con. He held con men and politicians in the same basic lack of esteem. So the news that the Morning Glory Kid was currently staying at the Cemetery elicited from him an unenthusiastic grunt. The Morning Glory Kid worried him a bit. He knew that big-time con artists like that often keep some piece of information up their sleeves to buy their way out. Of course the Kid had nothing on Kim except Kim renting him a room, but watch that fucker, he thought.

Kim remembered the first time he hit Salt Chunk Mary. Ten years ago.

"Smiler sent me."

She gave him a long cool appraising look.

"Come in, kid."

She put a plate of salt chunk on the table with bread. Kim ate like a hungry cat. She brought two mugs of coffee.

"What you got for me, kid?"

He laid the rings and pendants out on the table. It was a good score for a kid.

She named a fair price.

He said "Done" and she paid him.

Mary looked over Kim's slim willowy young good looks.

"You'd have a tough time in stir, kid."

"Don't aim to go there."

She nodded. . . . "It happens. Some people just aren't meant to do time. Usually they quit and do well legitimate."

"That's what I aim to do."

And now he was doing it. They both knew this was the last time Kim would ever lay any ice on Mary's kitchen table.

"Stop by anytime you're in town."

While waiting for Councillor Graywood to arrive from New York, Kim renewed his contacts with the Johnson Family. He was already a well-known and respected figure. He ran the Cemetery and he also ran a country place outside Saint Louis where favored Johnsons could rest, hide out and outfit themselves.

Kim was clean. Just that one shot in Black Hawk for the past six months. So he could enjoy kicking the gong around. If you've got a needle habit or an eating habit you can smoke all day and never get fixed. A very small amount of morphine passes over with the smoke. Most of it stays in the ash. So you have to come to the pipe clean. Kim liked the ritual—the peanut-oil lamp, the deft fingers of the young Chinese as he toasts the pill, rolling it against the pipe bowl, the black smoke pulled deep into the lungs with no rasp to it soothes you all the way down as the junk feeling comes on slow with the third pipe.

Kim didn't need a bodyguard but he needed good backup. He selected two of the best. Boy Jones had worked with Jones the bank robber. Thin and lithe as a cat, with a deadly dazzling

smile. He could use any weapon like an extension of his arm. He was a juggler and he could toss knives and saps around, and was a sleight-of-hand artist. He could pull a rabbit out of a hat and shoot through it. And what he could do with nunchakus and weighted chains was like a sorcerer's apprentice. You couldn't believe one person was doing it.

Marbles was a trick shot with a carnival. He could put out a candle, split cards, and get six shots in a playing card at fifteen feet in two-fifths of a second and he could really throw a knife. Kim had been impressed by the tremendous force of a thrown knife—it will go two inches into oak, and a strong man thrusting with all his might could hardly do a half-inch. But you have to estimate the distance on the overhand throw. Marbles could do it at any distance. He had such a smooth way of doing things. Smoothest draw Kim ever saw, like flexible marble. Marbles was a Greek statue come to life, with golden curls forming a tight casque around his head, eyes pale as alabaster, with glinting black pupils. . . .

Kim put them right on his payroll and outfitted them with conservative dark clothes, like young executives. They made a rather unnerving trio and passed themselves off as brothers.

Guy Graywood arrived from New York. He had found just the place. A bank building on the Bowery. Maps rolled out on the table. Graywood is a tall slim ash-blond man with a cool, incisive manner. He is a lawyer and an accountant, occupying much the same position in the Johnson Family as a Mafia *consigliere*. He is in charge of all business and legal arrangements and is consulted on all plans including assassinations. He is himself an expert assassin, having taken the Carsons Weapons course, but he doesn't make a big thing of it.

It is time to check out the Cemetery accounts. Joe the Dead, who runs the Cemetery, owes his life to Kim.

Kim's Uncle Waring once told him that if you have saved someone's life he will try to kill you. Hmmm. Kim was sure of

Joe's loyalty and honesty. Joe wouldn't steal a dime and Kim knew it. . . .

Well he'd saved Joe's life in his *professional* capacity and that made a difference. It was shortly after Kim got his license from the correspondence school and set himself up in the practice of medicine. He specialized in police bullets and such illegal injuries. When they brought Joe in, his left hand was gone at the wrist, the clothing burned off the left side of his body above the waist, and third-degree burns on the upper torso and neck. The left eye was luckily intact. . . . The tourniquet had slipped and he was bleeding heavily. The numbness that follows trauma is just wearing off and the groans starting, pushed out from the stomach, a totally inhuman sound, once you hear it you will remember that sound and what it means.

The same rock-steady hands, cool nerve, and timing that made Kim deadly in a gunfight also make him an excellent practicing surgeon. In one glance he has established a priority of moves. . . . Morphine first or the other moves might be too late. He draws off three quarter-grains into a syringe from a bottle with rubber top and injects it. As he puts down the syringe he is already reaching for the tourniquet to tighten it. . . . Quickly puts some ligatures on the larger veins . . . then makes a massive saline injection into the vein of the right arm . . . cleans the burned area with disinfecting solutions and applies a thick paste of tea leaves. . . . It was touch and go. At one point Joe's vital signs were zero, and Kim massaged the heart. Finally the heart pumps again. . . . One wrong move in the series and it wouldn't have started again.

The deciding factor was Kim's decision to administer morphine *before* stopping the hemorrhage . . . another split second of that pain would have meant shock, circulatory collapse, and death.

Joe recovered but he could never look at nitro again. He had brought back strange powers from the frontiers of death. He could often foretell events. He had a stump on his left wrist that could accommodate various tools and weapons.

His precognitive gift stands him and his in good stead. Once a stranger walks into the hotel ... Joe takes one look, comes up with a sawed-off, and blows the stranger's face off. Stranger was on the way to kill Joe and Kim. . . .

"I didn't like his face," Joe said.

"Missed your calling," Kim told him. "Should have been a plastic surgeon."

Joe the Dead was saved from death by morphine, and morphine remained the only thing holding him to life. It was as if Joe's entire body, his being, had been amputated and reduced to a receptacle for pain. Hideously scarred, blind in one eye, he gave off a dry, scorched smell, like burnt plastic and rotten oranges. He had constructed and installed an artificial nose, with gold wires connected to his odor centers, and a radio set for smell-waves, with a range of several hundred yards. Not only was his sense of smell acute, it was also selective. He could smell smells that no one else had ever dreamed, and these smells had a logic, a meaning, a language. He could smell death on others, and could predict the time and manner of death. Death casts many shadows, and they all have their special smells.

Joe had indeed brought back strange powers and knowledge from the grave, but without the one thing he had not brought back, his knowledge was of little use.

Of course, Kim thought. When you save someone's life, you cheat Death, and he has to even the score. Kim was aware of the danger from Joe the Dead, but he chose to ignore it. Joe never left the Cemetery, and Kim was an infrequent visitor there. Besides, vigilance was the medium in which Kim lived. The sensors at the back of his neck would warn him of a hand reaching for a knife, or other weapon.

Joe's only diversions were checkers and tinkering. He was a natural mechanic, and Kim worked with him on a number of weapons models which Kim conceived, leaving the details to Joe. Oh yes, leave the details to Joe. That's right, just point your finger and say: "Bang, you're dead"—and leave the details to Joe.

Saint Louis Return. . . .

Union Station . . . smell of iron and steam and soot . . . Kim walks through clouds of steam flanked by Marbles and Boy, a safari of porters behind him. They check into the Station Hotel, change clothes, and select suitably inconspicuous weapons. Then Kim hires a carriage and directs the driver to his old homesite on Olive Street. Kim sets up a camera and takes a few pictures. The owner rushes out and asks him what he is doing.

"I used to live here. . . . Sentimental considerations, you understand. . . . Hope you don't mind. . . ."

The man looks at Kim and Marbles and Boy and decides he doesn't mind. Kim packs the camera, puts it back in the carriage and they drive away. . . .

"Where to now?"

"Tony Faustus's Restaurant. . . ."

They are all impeccably dressed in dark expensive suits. Kim has a large opal set in gold on the ring finger of his left hand. Opals are bad luck, someone told him. Kim raised an eyebrow and said, "Really? Whose?"

"Do you have a reservation, sir?"

"Certainly."

With an expert palm-down gesture Boy slips the headwaiter a ten-dollar bill and the man bows them to a table.

You've come a long way from Saint Louis, Kim tells himself as he settles into a padded chair with mahogany armrests.

He orders dry martinis all around and studies the menu. . . .

"Oysters?"

"Not for me," Boy says. . . .

"An acquired taste. . . . You'll grow into it. . . ."

Kim orders walleyed pike, perhaps the most toothsome freshwater fish in the world. . . . Far better than trout. Venison steak and wood pigeon. . . . The waiter brings the wine list. . . . Kim selects a dry white wine for the fish and oysters, a heavy Burgundy for the venison. . . . They finish with baked Alaska, champagne, and Napoleon brandy. . . .

"My God, there's Jed Farris with a fat gut at thirty. . . ."

"Should auld acquaintance be forgot . . ."

In many cases, yes. . . .

"That's a bad neighborhood, sir. . . ."

"Oh I think we'll manage. . . ."

The driver shrugs.

The old Chinese puts on gold-rimmed bifocals and studies the letter Kim hands him. He nods, folds the letter, and hands it back, and they pass through a heavy padded door. Thieves and sharpers lounge about smoking opium, exchanging jokes and stories in a relaxed, quietly convivial ambiance.

After six pipes on top of the heavy meal they feel comfortably drowsy and take a carriage back to the hotel.

Saint Albans . . . Village of Illusion . . .

The depot is five miles from Saint Albans and Kim aims to keep it that way. He now owns six thousand acres along the river and inland as far as the town.

As soon as Kim started organizing the Johnson Family, he realized how basically subversive such an organization would appear to the people who run America. So the Johnson Family must not appear to these people as an organized unit. The Johnson Family must go underground. If you wish to conceal something it is simply necessary to create disinterest in the area where it is hidden. He planned towns, areas, communities,

owned and occupied by Johnsons, that would appear to outsiders as boringly ordinary or disagreeable, that would leave no questions unanswered. Each place would be carefully camouflaged and provided with a particular reputation. Saint Albans was largely rural. Reputation: Moonshiner country. Good place to stay out of and no reason for anyone going there.

In some of our towns the folks is so nice and so dull you just can't stand it. Not for long. Towns and areas stocked with Johnson actors, accommodations reciprocal. Ten actors leave Saint Albans for New York, leaving ten vacancies in the Saint Albans Hotel.

Saint Albans is used as a rest home and hideout for agents who have been on difficult missions. It is a permanent home for old retainers and a training ground for young initiates. The houses and loading sheds along the river have been converted into comfortable living places.

Fish and game are plentiful. The local cannabis is of a high quality owing to the long hot summers. The retainers and trainees pay off in work and produce and surveillance. You have to be on the alert for infiltrators, especially journalists. In any case there was nothing to see on the surface.

Bill Anderson, who runs the gun store, is now Sheriff. Arch Ellisor is the Mayor and Doc White is the Coroner.

Johnsons in good standing, rod-riding yeggs and thieves know they can stop off at Saint Albans. They also know that it is very unhealthy to abuse Saint Albans hospitality. Troublemakers and bullies get short shrift here. We get them out of Saint Albans is all. In one piece, if they are lucky. If not, Doc White signs a death certificate. Authority is swift, informal and incisive.

October's Bright Blue Weather

When the frost is on the pumpkin
And the corn is in the shock
And you leave the house bare-headed
And go out to feed the stock

(Someone else can feed the fuckers.)

October's bright blue weather is at its best in the Ozarks. The road from the depot winds through heavy woods. It's like driving into an impressionist painting, splashes of sepia and red and russet and orange peeling off and blowing away, dead leaves swirling around their feet. They are sitting on benches in an open buckboard. As they draw near the town they get a whiff of burning leaves.

Saint Albans is built along a river crisscrossed by stone bridges. The outskirts of the town present the dilapidated appearance of a stranded carnival, or military encampment, with tents and covered wagons and improvised dwellings. There is a large open market surrounded by baths and lodging houses, bars, restaurants, opium dens, anything you want, Meester. In the market, besides game fish and produce, weapons of all description are for sale. Here is a lead weight on a heavy elastic. . . .

"It looks dangerous," Kim decides.

Boy, who has been a circus juggler, is into these weapons that require prestidigitational dexterity, like Ku Budo, the nunchaku, chains with weights on both ends and this elastic monster, Kim could just feel it jumping back and hitting him right on the bridge of the nose.

Moving on to an older part of the town, solid houses of brick and stone with gardens. The hotel stands back from the street in a grove of oak and maple, a red brick four-story building with the ornate brickwork and recessed windows of the 1880s. Kim shakes hands with some old hands. None of that Lord of the Manor shit. Kim is just another Johnson. He introduces himself to some new kids on staff duty.

The kitchen staff is drawn from those who feel some affinity for cooking and serving food. They can go on from there in any direction. Our educational system is: find what someone can do and give him an opportunity to do it. Not many are competent on a policy level.

Bill Anderson knows more about guns and weapons than

any three experts. He is a superb technician. His grasp of the overall picture of conflict and the basic nature of weapons qualifies him O.P. (on policy). Doc White was a ship's doctor, has been all over the world. Here is that rarity—a doctor who thinks. He can see what is wrong in any given situation whether it be a human body or a societal structure. . . .

He was one of the first to see the virus as an alien life form, highly intelligent from its virus point of view. ("Gentlemen, the human cell can only divide and reproduce itself fifty thousand times. This is known as the Hayflick Limit. But a virus can do it any number of times. The virus is immune to the deadly factor of repetition. Your virus is never bored.")

And Arch Ellisor the Mayor is a brilliant economist who predicted the eventual collapse of money as a means of exchange. . . . "Any purely quantitative factor must, by its nature and function, devaluate in time. Just like a joke. Marvelous. Nice. Cut off his head. And what are we to do with a screaming headless eagle throwing bloody gobs of panic through stock exchanges of the world? The terrible moment has arrived when no amount of money will buy anything. The economic machine grinds to a splintering halt."

Kim saw that the whole power of the Mafia is the power of life and death and set out to produce an elite of expert Johnson Assassins, J.A. Plenty of openings in the J.A. department and we get plenty of applicants. Tough sharp kids. It takes some screening to weed out the nut cases.

Bill Anderson the Sheriff is waiting in the lobby. They go into the gun and briefing room. The Sheriff gives Kim a heavy double-action 44 special with rosewood handle and a bead sight. Kim hefts the gun lovingly, falling in love with the gun. It's something every gun lover knows and it drives gun haters to hysteria.

"Any trouble, Bill?" Kim asks.

"Some squatters has moved in here"—Bill points to a map on the wall—"without asking, and I'm going to check it out . . . and Old Mother Gilly is screaming for help again. His horrible

hound dogs, half starved likely, is tore the bag off his cow, and Gilly can't bring himself to do what needs to be done. You know how he is. . . ."

Gilly is a harmless defeated old critter, always complaining and calling on the neighbors for help.

"Me and Boy will take care of the dogs," Kim says.

"I'll go along with Bill and check out the squatters ..." Marbles says. He is perfect backup, cool and alert, never loses control.

"Don't take any chances."

"We won't."

As they drive out to Gilly's place in the buckboard, Kim fills Boy in.

"Always something like this . . . a horse fell in his well, he tried to raise bees and nearly got stung to death, his hawgs et the poison he put out for the raccoons and polecats was killing his chickens. . . . Then he got the idea of raising them chickens that don't never touch the ground. . . .

"Had his chickens on chicken wire about two feet up but raccoons got in under the wire, reached up and pulled chicken legs down through the mesh, and et off the drumsticks. So when Gilly goes out in the morning Lord Lord his chickens is flopping around with their legs et off. . . . He gives folks something to talk about . . . turn in here. . . ."

When Boy and Kim drive up in the buckboard, one of the new kids as driver, old Gilly comes running out of his dirty little house, broken windows stuffed with rags.

"Lord Lord, I just can't understand what got into them dogs."

"Maybe it was just what didn't get into them," Boy says.

"As God is my witness them dogs is fed good as me. . . . Things have been hard . . . don't mind telling you . . . had a bad year with my hogs . . . guess you heard about it——"

"No," Kim cuts in, "and I don't aim to hear about it now. Where are those dogs?"

The dogs are tied to a tree. Big scrawny hounds, they begin

to cringe and bristle at the sight of Kim and Boy, showing their yellow teeth, whimpering and snarling and cowering away to the end of their ropes.

"I think they know us," Boy says, dropping a hand on his gun butt.

"Please don't do it here," Gilly moans.

"All right. Get them in the buckboard."

"Please, Mister Kim. . . . They never done nothing like this before. . . ."

"When a dog turns stock-killer he doesn't stop. You know that yourself. . . ."

"I'll keep them chained up."

"They'll get loose one day and a neighbor loses his cow. This is stock country, Gilly. I got an obligation."

Kim stands there all square-jawed and stern and noble like the Virginian getting set to hang his best friend for rustling the sacred cows on which the West is built.

If I had any shame I would gag on a speech like that, Kim thinks. . . . "Who cares about fucking cows. . . . MOOO MOOO MOOO. . . ."

The whining snapping dogs are finally dragged and shoved into the buckboard and tied to the backseat.

"Get a shovel," Kim tells Gilly. "We'll drop it off on the way back."

They start off down the road, looking for a good place. A smell of fear is coming off them dogs, you can *see* it, like heat waves. . . .

Kim draws the fear smell deep into his lungs.

"Nice smell, eh? They *know*. . . ."

Boy sniffs appreciatively and flashes his dazzling smile.

"It's *keen.*"

"Stop here." The driver pulls up and Kim and Boy get out. Boy has a double-barrel twelve-gauge loaded with number-four shot. The driver levers a shell into his 30-30.

"Cut 'em loose," Kim tells the driver. The driver leans down with a knife and the dogs leap out running.

Boy gets one from behind with the shotgun. The driver nails another with a spine shot. They are crawling around screaming and dragging their broken hindquarters. But the third dog doubles right back and leaps for Kim's throat. Kim throws up his left arm and the dog grabs him just below the wrist and Kim blasts the stock-killing beast with his 44 an inch from the left side, singeing off a patch of hair, blowing dog heart out the other side with scrambled lungs and spareribs. Just as the dog spirit is on the way out, the dog clamps down hard for a fraction of a second before he drops off stone dead.

Kim massages his arm.

"Fucker nearly broke my wrist."

"It was a brave dog. *Un perro bravo.*"

"It was."

One of the dogs is turning around in circles, screaming and snapping at his intestines as they spill out. Kim nudges Boy, pointing with his left hand.

"This is tasty."

He walks over slow and stands in front of the animal, smiling.

"Nice doggie."

The dog snarls up at him.

"Bad dooog."

Kapow!

Kim's bullet, aimed a little off center, has sheared off half of the dog's skull, brains spilling out. Kim hands the gun to Boy.

"You take the other one and get a taste of this gun. . . ."

Other dog is ten feet away, howling and shrieking and trying to get up with his spine shattered. Boy hefts the gun and steps toward the dog, looking down straight into his eyes.

"See if you can't get him to lick your hand."

Kim smiles. . . ."That would be keen."

"He simply isn't in the mood."

Kapow!

Boy tilts the gun up in front of his face, sniffing the smoke.

"What a guuuuuuun."

His bullet has torn a hole bigger than a silver dollar through the dog's head.

"And handles sweet as a 22."

The driver is digging.

"Don't forget to put a cross on it."

"Here lies three bad dogs which eated the bag offen a cow and had to be shat."

"My dear, it's quite folkloric."

On the way back they drop off the shovel. Gilly is moaning and wringing his dirty old hands. . . .

"Lord Lord, I don't even feel like a human with my cow dead and my dogs gone. . . ."

"Here's something to make you feel better."

Kim hands him a bottle of Doctor White's Heroin Cold Cure.

"Silly old coot . . ." Boy says when they are out of earshot.

"He's harmless and that counts for something. . . . Would you believe it, his father before him was borned and died in that filthy hovel. . . ."

"You been *inside*?"

"In my professional capacity. It stinks like three generations of Gillys."

Kim had passed the board exams with a thousand-dollar "special tutoring fee" for one of the examiners. "Special tutoring" is simply knowing what questions the examiners will ask. . . .

"Doc White taught me everything I know about medicine. Read the books and forget them. They are less accurate than cookbooks. Try to make even a plate of fudge by the book. . . . It isn't 'cook for twelve minutes,' it's 'cook until the bubbles get the same look as oatmeal when it's ready, little craters. . . .' It's the same with medicine . . . book says a quarter-grain of morphine for most traumatic accidents will be sufficient. . . . The hell it will. . . . So put the books away and start looking at patients. One patient needs a quarter-grain, another is going into

shock on a quarter-grain ... so throw in a half, three-quarters, whatever he needs. The heavier the pain the more morphine a patient can tolerate."

Kim remembers a case of third-degree burns from the neck down. The intern is a plump Indian with yellow liverish eyes reflecting no more sympathy for the patient's pain than two puddles of piss.

"How much morphine are you giving this patient, Doctor?"

"Ten milligrams every six hours. He isn't due another shot for three and a half hours."

Kim slaps the intern across the face with his stethoscope and administers three-quarters of a grain. The patient stops screaming.

"Hi, Doc," he says. "Now that was a shot."

The intern dabs at his split lip with an aggrieved expression.

"This is battery assault. I will make a charge."

Kim draws half a grain of morphine into the syringe, shoves it into the intern's stomach, and pushes home the plunger.

"What have you done?" the intern gasps.

Kim points an accusing finger. . . . "I have suspected this for some time, Doctor Kundalini. You are a morphine addict."

Kim calls the orderly, a tough old Johnson.

"Wring a urine specimen out of this cow-loving cocksucker."

"Yes, I'm a good doctor. Always had a feel for it and taught by one of the best in the industry. . . . That's why it's my stick. You should start thinking about a stick, Boy."

Many criminals find it expedient to train themselves for some alternative job, trade, profession, in which they are professionally competent. This is the outlaw's stick ... you need a stick to ride out a spell of bad luck ... when you're too hot to operate ... lost your nerve ... getting old, can't do no more

time ... all kinds of sticks ... lots of short-order cooks' and waiters' jobs you can get anywhere, no questions asked ... and some of them wind up running a restaurant ... con men make good salesmen ... safecrackers gravitate to welding, locksmithing, blasting. ...

The stick corresponds to the secret agent's cover. ... Few Johnsons can boast such a classy stick as Kim Hall Carsons, M.D.

"Well," Boy says, "I could be a song-and-dance man. ..."

> Pick up your stick
> You little prick
> And pick it up quick
> Before you get a whack
> From someone else's stick ...

"Entertainment is full of good sticks ... and the Merchant Marine. ... You can rise to be captain and go down with the ship. ..."

Back at the hotel Kim takes a bath to wash the dog-fear stink off him.

They all get together for drinks on the upstairs porch, which is screened in the summer and glassed in when it starts to get cold.

Bill Anderson sips his bourbon toddy with sugar, lemon, and angostura. ...

"Right good whiskey you make."

"That's been setting in charred barrels for six years. ..."

Kim figures sooner or later there will be laws against liquor, so he is stockpiling whiskey turned out by the moonshiners. (Johnson actors, of course, got up in black Stetsons.)

"What happened with the squatters. ..?"

"Well I seen right away they is religious sons of bitches, got these two pale washed-out Bible-fed kids. And I tell them this is no place to bring up a family. ... Godless folk hereabouts ... moonshiners ... outlaws. ... Now there's some mighty fine land down in Dead Coon County not sixty miles from here, wide

open for settlers. . . . I'll have someone give you a hand hauling
your stuff to the depot."

"You didn't tell them why it's wide open, did you?"

"You mean the tick fever? No, I didn't see any point in
bringing that up. . . . And this old witch grandmother of the family grabs my hand and says . . . 'You're a good man, sheriff. . . .'

" 'I try to be, ma'am,' I tell her. 'But it isn't always easy.'

" 'It sure isn't.' . . . Just wish they were all as easy as that
one. . . .' "

There is a pause. They will have to think about future policy. Reputations have to keep up with the times. They wear out
like clothes if you don't watch it, leave your bare ass sticking out. The moonshiner-outlaw look is wearing thin and they
know it.

The sun is setting across the river, red and smoky. . . . "A
real Turner," Kim says. He addresses himself to Boy and Marbles. "Used to be a town over there name of Jehovah and you
could have seen their fucking church sticking up from here
spoiling our sunsets . . . then one day 'The Angel of Death
spread his wings on the blast. And he breathed in the face of the
foe as he passed.' Then we all felt a lot better."

Plans are under way to buy land in the Mound Builder area of
Illinois across the river from Saint Louis to found a new town.
Johnsonville will serve as a communications center and clearing-
house for intelligence reports. The tone will be flatly ordinary.

"We'll bore people out of it."

Kim spends several days writing up a scenario for Johnsonville.

Towns like Johnsonville can only exist with strict security
and control of a buffer area to prevent infiltration. We can hardly get away with stocking a whole town with female impersonat-
ors. However, the basic concept is sound: a town that looks
like any other town to the outsider. The same formula can be
applied even more successfully to a neighborhood in a big city,
where people are less curious.

Boy is writing stick songs and lyrics. . . .

> Pick up your stick
> And pick it up quick
> Before you get a whack
> From someone else's stick
> You're old and sick
> Lean on that stick
> You wanna die in the nick?
> You can't hack it?
> Better pack it
> Grab that stick
> And grab it quick
> You're hot as a rivet
> No room to pivot
> Climb up your stick
> And turn down the wick
> One more score?
> You want twenty more?
> Reach for your stick instead
> You wanna hole in your head?
> You wanna pick up some lead?
> Reach for your stick instead
> And get that steady bread
> A man's best friend is his stick
> Can't do no more time
> Don't want no more trouble
> Pick up your stick on the double
> Your chick's a bloody snitch
> Ride your stick like a witch
> She'll sing you into Sing Sing
> Unless you sprout a wing
> Fly away on your stick
> And fly away quick

In the kitchen they are measuring out whiffs of Saint Louis . . .
tall thin lead bottle.

He fades down toward the river with a soft cold fire
Wearing a sort of fur I carry my own temperature
with the river from here
Around the edge blue arc lights pick at the cuticle
of sand, smell of the tidal river on the second-floor porch
A gold smell of watches, smoke and stale sweat
Strange pistol form traced on the blanket
someone beside him breathing
getting light a balloon at the window
floating up and walked along the treetops
lighter they are blowing away
a worn wood table with millions of old photos
moving dressing undressing
The old-fashioned icebox behind him and tunnels of
KIM blowing away in four-letter words and puffs of
violet smoke. Standing on a back porch
He is drinking rum and Coca-Cola
Gray shadows curiously empty
Just a little Japanese dust on the floor
Jacket or vest is balmy but cool
He is waiting. He is nervous. He is sitting in a
    wooden armchair.
There is a fossil holster at his belt
cold breath in the gun

The handle light and springy mercury bullets
He got out like heat waves up over the porch and
into the kitchen. Light wind blowing behind him
Tom was sitting across the sky
glass of beer studying in the kitchen
And added some white rum
"What's noxious in four silver flashes?"

He woke up to the sound of rain. He lay there with his eyes closed. Where was he? Who was he? He opened his eyes and looked up at a ceiling covered in yellow wallpaper. He could see a window beyond the bed he was lying in. The window was half open and there was the sound and smell of rain. He could hear someone breathing in the bed beside him. Slowly he turned his head. A boy with dark tousled hair and pimples was sleeping with his mouth open, his teeth showing. Slowly he twisted out of bed. He looked down. He was naked. His body was thin and the pubic hairs were bright red. There was a slightly turgid feeling in his cock which was half hard. He stepped through a doorway . . . down a hall to a half-open door. Must be the bathroom. He urinated then looked around at the towels and the bathtub stained with rust. He opened the medicine chest. There was a bottle labeled Tincture of Opium half full of a brown reddish liquid. He made his way back to the bedroom and stepped to the window and looked out. The rain was coming down in silver-gray streamers. He could see a muddy backyard with some bedraggled iris and a little vegetable garden. A swing made from an old tire hung from the branch of an oak tree. Further on was a fence and beyond that a pasture and fields. To his left he could see a large pond. He turned back toward the bed.

The boy was still sleeping on his back, his chest rising and falling in the gray light. He slipped back into bed. There was a cobweb in one corner of the window where the screen was slightly rusted and the raindrops shone iridescent in the dawn light. He lay there on his back, his breathing slowly synchronizing with the other. He felt his cock slowly distend and press against

143

the covers. There was a smell of unwashed bedding. The boy turned toward him and an arm almost fell across his chest. The boy shivered, snuggling against him as he turned sideways. Now the boy's eyes flew open and they looked into each other's faces. He could feel the boy's cock throbbing against his stomach. They kissed and seemed to melt together in a gush of sperm. Suddenly they were both dressed and going down the stairs with yellow oak banisters and into the kitchen. Smell of coffee and eggs and bacon. He ate hungrily. So far they had not exchanged a word.

Belches ... Taste of eggs and bacon ... Outside the rain had almost stopped and watery sunlight crossed the kitchen table.

They stepped out onto the back porch. The mist was lifting from the field beyond the backyard, and the tire swing moved gently in a slight breeze. Under the porch they found fishing rods and a can with dirt. They picked up several night crawlers in the flower beds and then through a gate and down the fields through the wet grass and came to the edge of the pond. It was fairly large, a small lake actually. There was a little pier to which was moored a rowboat. They got in and the boy rowed out toward the middle of the lake. . . . He shipped the oars. They baited their hooks with the squirming red purple worms and dropped them over the side. In a few minutes they were pulling in bass and perch and one three-pound walleye. Cleaned the fish and back to the house.

The sky was clouded over again, the fish on top of the ice. The day passed in a mindless trance. They sat at the kitchen table. They walked through the garden. "Everything must appear normal," the boy said. After sundown they went up to the bedroom in the stale smell of unwashed sheets and made each other again.

Suddenly we are both awake. It's time. We go to the study, there is a secret drawer and two odd-looking pistols with thick barrels but very light. And I know it is a built-in silencer low-

velocity nine-millimeter with mercury bullets and we have a job to do. . . . So we go down and get into our vintage Moon. And now I see we are on the outskirts of East Saint Louis, a shabby rural slum, houses with limestone foundations. Well we got this job to do. There it is right ahead. The roadhouse gambling joint. We ease into the parking lot. He should be along any minute now. A car pulls up. This is it. A man, two bodyguards, we swing out of the car sput sput sput. Good clean job.

If there's going to be trouble on a job it always comes *before* the job. If you can't clear up that trouble before the job, better forget the job. Oh it may not be much. Just a fumble, something dropped on the floor, the wrong thing said . . . you leave a nickel instead of a quarter for a newspaper.

"Where you been for twenty years, Mister?"

Everything is OK on this one. Just a routine Mafia containment job . . . the guns perform superbly:

Sput Sput Sput

A spectral arm . . . blue arc lights . . . streets half buried in sand smell of the tidal river he settles gently onto a mattress just an impression, a human fossil form traced on the blankets slow cold breath in his lungs someone breathing beside him gray shadows out through the boards at the window floating out like heat waves up into the treetops lighter lighter blowing away across the sky millions of old photos of Tom, making tea in the kitchen, laughing, dressing, undressing, leaving a tunnel of Tom behind him and tunnels of Kim coming, writing, walking, shooting, caving in, running together in little silver flashes and puffs of violet smoke.

A whiff of Saint Louis, he is standing on a back porch looking down toward the river. He is drinking rum and Coca-Cola. His mind is curiously empty, waiting. He has long fine black hair like a Japanese or an Indian. He is wearing a fur vest. You can smell the river from here. Now he is sitting in an armchair of yellow oak. There is a strange pistol in a holster at his belt the

handle is springy feeling the whole gun very light like a toy. Fifteen nine-millimeter rounds Mercury bullets. He gets up and walks across the porch and into the kitchen closing the screen door behind him. Tom is sitting at a worn wooden table with a glass of beer doing a crossword puzzle. Kim fills his glass with Coca-Cola and adds some white rum. Tom looks up. . . . "What is noxious in four letters beginning with . . ."

Colonel Sutton-Smith was a well-to-do amateur archeologist who was attempting to establish a link between the hieroglyphic writing of Egypt and the Mayan hieroglyphs. He had published several books and a number of articles. He was also a highly placed operative of British Intelligence. He was in America to study links between the mound-building people of Illinois and the Aztec and Mayan civilizations. This necessitated several weeks of research in the library of the Smithsonian Institution in Washington, which was an ideal drop for intelligence reports. He circulated in Washington society, sounding out just where America would stand in the event of a war in Europe and what military potential it possessed. He chose as a base for his field-work a small town in western Illinois called Johnsonville.

The following are coded entries from the Colonel's diary.

September 17, 1908 ... Fine clear weather with a crisp touch of autumn in the air, the leaves just beginning to change. I have rarely seen a more beautiful countryside, heavily wooded with an abundance of streams and ponds. The town itself and the townspeople seem archetypical for middle American towns of this size. Two barefoot boys with battered straw hats passed me on the street this morning singing:

"Old sow got caught in the fence last spring. . . ."

Charming and *quelles derrières mon cher.* At noon

I went into the hotel for a drink. The bartender was telling a joke about a farmer who put some whiskey in a glass of milk for his sick wife. Well she takes a long drink and says . . ."Arch, don't you ever get rid of that cow." And everybody laughed heartily. Perhaps a bit too heartily. In the late afternoon the townspeople stroll up and down. . . .

"Howdy, Doc. How many you kill today?"

"Evening, Parson."

Frog-croaking and hog calls drift in from the surrounding countryside. Women on porches call to the menfolks. . . .

"Hurry up, your dinner's getting cold. . . ."

Back to the hotel for a cocktail before dinner. The bartender is telling the same joke and everybody laughs just as loud, though several of the patrons were here at noon. Am I imagining things or is there something just a bit *too typical* about Johnsonville? And why do the women all have big feet? Tomorrow I will try to recruit some local lads for my digs. And what smashers they are. Have to be careful in a small place like this.

September 18, 1908 . . . Not much luck recruiting labor. Harvest time, you know. But I have met a local farmer who showed me some artifacts he found in his fields near a mound. What an old bore but every now and again he asks a sharp question. Hummmmmm. He said he'd be glad to send one of his sons along to show me the site.

The boy is about seventeen with a pimply face and a wide smile. He showed me places in the fields where he had found arrowheads and we climbed to the top of a mound. I brought out some sandwiches which we shared and two bottles of beer. It soon be-

came evident that he was offering himself, rubbing his crotch and grinning. When I unbuttoned his pants it sprang out pearling like an oyster yum yum yum. Who would expect such amenities in the wilds of America? I gave him a silver dollar, with which he seemed delighted. I will see him again tomorrow.

Back to town. Bartender telling the same joke. It goes round and round in my head. Don't ever get rid of that cow. Old sow got caught in the fence last spring. How many you kill today, Doc? Hurry, dinner's getting cold. There *is* something odd here. Can't shake the feeling of being watched. Of course any stranger in a small town is an object of curiosity. But this is something more. A cool appraisal at the margin of vision as if their faces changed completely as soon as they were no longer observed. Perhaps I am just professionally suspicious but I've been in this business long enough to know when somebody is *seeing* me.

September 19, 1908 . . . Today John was waiting when I reached the farmhouse, which is about a mile outside the town. He was wearing blue denim Levi's, soft leather boots that looked handmade, a blue shirt and a carryall bag slung from a strap over his shoulder. There was a revolver in a holster at his belt and a knife. I noticed that the pistol handle of polished walnut had been cut to fit his hand.

"Might find us a squirrel or two. . . ."

He led the way to another mound about two miles away. . . . The country is hardwood forest through which wind streams and rivers, I could see bass and pike and catfish in the clear blue pools.

"I think I know a place to dig," he told me.

About halfway up the mound was an open place

and it did indeed look like a burial site. We took turns digging and about five feet down the shovel went through rotten wood and there was a skull looking up at us and gold teeth winking in the sun.

"Holy shit, it's Aunt Sarah!" he exclaimed. "I can tell by the teeth."

We shoveled the dirt back. He patted the earth down with the shovel and wrote with a stick:

PLEASE DO NOT DISTURB

He turned to me, opened his mouth, sticking his teeth out and squashing his nose in a hideously realistic imitation of the skeleton face. It was irresistibly comic and we both had a good laugh.

"Let's go on up to the top. There's a flat stone there may have been some kinda *altar*. Human sacrifices, feller say."

The altar was composed of large blocks of limestone fitted together. The stone had been pushed aside by a giant oak that shaded it, giving the place a dark and sinister aspect.

At the same time I was seized with uncontrollable excitement and we both stripped off our clothes. This time it was oriental embroidery, my dear. . . . [The Colonel's term for buggery.] He took out a compass and placed me on the altar facing north. I could see he was up to magic of some sort. Not since that Nubian guide on top of the Great Pyramid have I experienced such consummate expertise. I spurted rocks and stones and trees. On the way back in the late afternoon he stopped me with one hand, looking up into the branches of a persimmon tree. I couldn't see anything. Then the pistol slid into his hand. He crouched with both hands on the gun and fired. A squirrel fell down from branch to branch and landed at his feet, blood oozing from a head shot. I studied his face in

the moment of firing. There was a tightening, a feral sharpening of the features, as if something much older and harder had peeped out for a second. . . . He was skinning and cleaning the squirrel expertly as he hummed: "Old sow got caught in the fence last spring."

He took a muslin cloth from his bag and wrapped the quartered squirrel, the liver and heart in the cloth. Then he sat down on another stump and removed his boots and socks. He stood up and took off his shirt, hanging it over a low tree limb. He slid down his pants and shorts and stepped out naked, his phallus half erect. He rubbed it hard, looking at the squirrel on the stump, then he took out a harmonica and capered around the stump playing a little tune. It was an old tune, wild and sad, phallic shadows in animal skins on a distant wall. . . . I remember a desolate windswept slope in Patagonia and the graves with phallic markers and the feeling of sadness and loneliness that closed around me. It was all there in the music, twenty thousand years. . . . The boy was putting on his clothes.

He explained that he had made a magic should be worth two more squirrels. We hadn't gone more than a hundred yards when he shot another squirrel running on the ground. And a third squirrel from the top of an oak tree—a truly remarkable shot. I had brought along a Colt 38 Lightning in my pack but did not wish to compete with such phenomenal marksmanship. His gun is a 22 with a special load. Back at the farmhouse I met another of the sons. He is a few years older than John but enough like him to be a twin. Mr. Brown asked me to dinner and I gladly accepted, not wanting to hear the cow joke again, but over whiskey Brown told it. . . . Don't ever get rid of

that cow. The boys laughed heartily, then quite suddenly stopped laughing and their expressions hardened. The squirrel with greens and potatoes and fried apples was excellent.

Mr. Brown glanced at John and some signal passed between them. Mr. Brown turned to me. . . . "You do digs in Arabia, John tells me. . . . Well that must be right interesting. I hear them Ayrabs got some right strange ways."

No doubt about it, he *knew*. And John had told him without a word.

On the way back to town, as I passed the red brick school building, I could see that there were lights on in what I assumed to be the assembly hall. Drawing closer I could see a number of townspeople parading around in a large empty hall. "Don't ever get rid of that cow. . . . Howdy, Doc, how many you kill today . . . Nice sermon, Parson . . . Hurry up, dinner's getting cold . . . and laughing and vying with each other. . . .

The whole town is a fraud, a monstrous parody of small towns . . . and what does this travesty cover?

September 20, 1908 . . . I woke this morning with a fever and splitting headache. No doubt an attack of malaria. I dressed, shivering and burning.

I stumbled out to a drugstore for quinine and laudanum, returned to my room, and took a good stiff dose of both. I lay down and felt relief throbbing through my head. I finally fell asleep. I was awakened by a knock at the door. . . . I put on my dressing gown and opened the door. It was the Sheriff.

"Howdy, Doc, can I talk to you for a minute. . . ?"

"Certainly." I felt somewhat better and sat down and waited.

"Well now, I thought maybe I could help you out doing, well, whatever it is you're doing, feller say. Must be nice traveling around and seeing different places. . . . Like to travel myself but this old star keeps me pinned right down. . . . Now being Sheriff is more of a job than it might seem at first. Seems peaceful here, don't it? Well maybe a sow gets caught in the fence next spring. Well we aims to keep it peaceful. . . . Now you got yourself a peaceful place, what could make it unpeaceful?"

"Well I suppose some force or person from outside. . . ."

"Exactly, Colonel, and that's my job."

"We call it security."

"That's right, so it's only logical to check anyone out comes in from outside, wouldn't you say so?"

"I suppose so. But why do you assume an outsider is ill-intentioned?"

"We don't. I said *check out*. Mostly I can check out a visitor in a few seconds. Drummer selling barbed wire, poor product, loudmouthed son of a bitch. Stay not to be encouraged. We have the means to discourage a stay that can only prove shall we say unproductive. . . ."

He was gradually shedding his country accent.

"Now you take the case of someone who passes himself off as a drummer, whereas his actual business is something else. . . . Being a drummer is his cover story, as archeology is yours . . . Atlantis."

[Atlantis is the Colonel's service name.]

I looked around. No doubt about it, the room had been searched in my absence. Expertly searched. Nothing was removed, but I could feel the recent presence of someone in the room. It's a knack you get in this business if you want to stay alive.

"You searched the room while I was out."

He nodded. "And read your diary. Code wasn't hard to crack. And you've been under twenty-four-hour surveillance since your arrival." He passed the Colonel an envelope. The Colonel pulled out two photos.

I kept my face impassive. . . .

"Old sow got caught in the fence *eh, mon colonel . . . und zwar in einer ekelhafte Position.* And indeed in a disgusting position."

"I think my superiors would be amused by these pictures. . . ."

"Very likely. I wasn't attempting blackmail. Just letting you know plenty more where those came from. And by the way the little charade you observed in the assembly hall was of course arranged for your benefit."

"Like everything else here."

"Exactly. Johnsonville is one big cover. And when someone from outside penetrates that cover . . . well it can be uh, 'awkward' I believe is the word."

"You mean to kill me?"

"You are more use to us alive. That is . . ."

"If I cooperate?"

"Exactly."

"And exactly who would I be cooperating with?"

"We represent Potential America. P.A. we call it. And don't take us for dumber than we look."

Is it good for the Johnsons? That's what Johnson Intelligence is for—to protect and further Johnson objectives, the realization of our biologic and spiritual destiny in space. If it isn't good for the Johnsons, how can it be neutralized or removed?

You are a Shit Spotter. It's satisfying work. Somebody throws your change on a morphine script back at you and his name goes down on a list. We have observed that most of the

trouble in this world is caused by ten to twenty percent of folks who can't mind their own business because they *have* no business of their own to mind any more than a smallpox virus. Now your virus is an obligate cellular parasite, and my contention is that what we call evil is quite literally a virus parasite occupying a certain brain area which we may term the RIGHT center. The mark of a basic shit is that he has to be *right*. And right here we must make a diagnostic distinction between a hard-core virus-occupied shit and a plain ordinary mean no-good son of bitch. Some of these sons of bitches don't cause any trouble at all, just want to be left alone. Others cause minor trouble, like barroom fights and bank robberies. To put it country simple—former narcotics commissioner Harry J. Anslinger *diseased* was an obligate shit. Jesse James, Billy the Kid, Dillinger, were just sons of bitches.

Victimless crimes are the lifeline of the RIGHT virus. And there is a growing recognition, even in official quarters, that victimless crimes should be removed from the books or subject to minimal penalties. Those individuals who cannot or will not mind their business cling to the victimless-crime concept, equating drug use and private sexual behavior with robbery and murder. If the right to mind one's own business is recognized, the whole shit position is untenable and Hell hath no more vociferous fury than an endangered parasite.

"Drug laws," Anslinger said, "must reflect society's disapproval of the addict." And here is Reverend Braswell in the *Denver Post:* "Homosexuality is an abomination to God and should never be recognized as a legal human right any more than robbery or murder." We seek a Total Solution to the Shit Problem: Slaughter the shits of the world like cows with the aftosa.

Some spotters cultivate an inconspicuous appearance and demeanor. They do not provoke aggressive or discourteous behavior. Other spotters will follow. Some will belong to ethnic minorities. Others may be marked by some eccentricity of dress or manner. Some will be obvious gays . . . reactions of the towns-

people carefully noted. Then the Shit Slaughter units move in. . . .

Accidents: Nobody was very much concerned or surprised when Old Man Brink's cabin burned down with him in it. . . . Death by misadventure. . . .

Dark interior of a filthy cabin . . . snoring noises from a pile of rags . . . a youth with MISS ADVENTURE on his T-shirt is revealed as he lights a kerosene lamp. He tosses the lamp into the room.

"Hellfire, you old fuck."

Illnesses that can be easily induced: Five cases of typhoid were traced to a church supper and the sheriff got botulism in a segregated restaurant.

In many cases it is simply necessary to put the shit out of action, to close his store, his restaurant, his hotel, or deprive him of office.

Here is a town of two thousand people. The spotters have picked a hundred twenty-three hardcore shits. If over a period of several months these shits die, become sick, go insane, go bankrupt, no one in the town thinks anything about it . . . no apparent relation between disparate incidents . . . no pattern. . . .

Kim knows he is perfectly safe so long as he stays in Saint Albans. He also knows he has to move on. He has more important things to do than shoot stock-killing dogs or maybe run some squatter off the land. . . .

> How dull it is to pause, to make an end,
> To rust unburnished, not to shine in use. . . .

A special meeting to reconsider our Mafia policy. Present directives advocate containing the animal in a folkloric ghetto of godfathers, red wine and garlic, and button men wallowing on their filthy mattresses. Let them burn each other's olive oil, throw dead rats into rival pasta vats, and murder each other with impu-

nity. After all, these simple people have a rich folklore. Similar policy was advised by a knowledgeable anthropologist with regard to headshrinking and feud killing among the Jivaro Indians of Ecuador. He recommended that no attempt be made to control or sanction these practices, since their culture would languish without the sustaining incentive of ritual warfare. He concluded his report:

"They have nothing else to do."

Now feudin can keep a man occupied a whole rich, satisfying life so he can belch out with his last breath like a fulfilled old Mafioso don:

"Life is so *beautiful!*"

Somebody shrinks his cousin twice removed, time-honored codes determine who is obligated to shrink an equivalent cousin. One old fuck has shrunken down 52 heads. Back to the simple basic things . . . life in all its rich variety of an old shit house when a man knowed where his ass was. Those were the days, eh? Singing waiters, hit men, wise old dons belching garlic.

A trembling waiter serves a table of button men from the rival Calamari family. They spit clam spaghetti into his face.

"That isn't our pasta!"

They shove wads of pasta down the throats of the terrified uptown diners.

"Is especialitay from the maison! Wha'sa matter you? Is not nice?"

They storm into the kitchen overturning caldrons of spaghetti.

The cook sobs head in hands, "Mia spaghetti! Mia spaghetti!"

The insult must be avenged à la Siciliana.

"I'll Santa his Lucia!" growls the offended capo.

Hit men, impersonating singing waiters, invade the Santa Lucia restaurant. Swaying from side to side like drunken sailors they bellow out "Santa Lucia" as they slop boiling minestrone over the guests and throw spaghetti into the air like streamers.

The bestial retarded son of the capo beats three Calamari to death with a baseball bat, chasing them through the restaurant, spattering the horrified diners with blood and brains.

"Life is so beautiful! Why you go home?"

"SANTA LUCIA!"

They bow to the empty wrecked restaurant.

Our policy then, has been to contain the honored society into self-decimating urban concentrations and to head off any legislation designed to make liquor, drugs and gambling illegal, thus opening the door to a flash of gold teeth and an evil belch of garlic.

But the situation is changing rapidly. Competition with European products makes it increasingly difficult to contain the industrial process. And there is talk of war in Europe. No doubt the prohibitionists will take advantage of the war to force through anti-alcohol legislation.

The Johnson press upholds States' Rights and opposes any further encroachment of Washington bureaucrats. We hope to keep prohibition a state option and to tie up supply and distribution for the dry states and cut the Mafia right out of the picture. Since the dry states will be in the South and Middle West, the Mafia will be operating outside of their territory. We will teach them to stay on their own side of the fence.

Graywood meets them at the station and they take a carriage to the Bunker, a former bank building at Spring and Bowery.... The walls are massive, the door of thick steel. It is an impregnable fortress. Kim's quarters on the top floor consist of living room, dining room, kitchen, with a bedroom and bath.

Relaxing over a drink he is delighted to learn that his enemies are relying on Mafia talent...."Means they've got no good shootist!"

"Let's go out and see the town," Graywood says.

Bill Anderson has provided a number of concealable weapons for city wear ... short-barreled revolvers, vest-pocket derringers, the new 25 and 380 automatics. Kim's 44 goes into his doctor's satchel with his other instruments. Better take along the satchel. It may save a life. Councillor Graywood has one of the new broom-handle Mausers that fits neatly into a leather briefcase.

Dinner at Luchow's.

"It's heavy Jew food," Boy complains.

"It isn't Jew food. It's German food," Kim corrects him.

"What's different? All Germans is knowned to be Jews because they is spiking with heavy Jew accints."

Kim nods.... "Well that makes sense."

"Only the Jews and the Chinese knows how to cook a carp," Marbles says.

"It's true," Boy says. "I eated a pepper carp onct."

"What's that?"

"It's a special Jew carp."

"You think maybe we getting some of this special carp tonight?"

"Not here," Kim says, "they isn't Jew enough to do it. Later maybe. They is selling it inna street from the carp wagons."

(This is running code and Kim is saying, They won't try a hit here. On the street, most likely from a car.)

"I hear all Yids is short-cocked."

"It's true. Short and thick."

(They will be using sawed-off shotguns.)

The Johnsons go into action and the Families don't know what is hitting them with such deadly precision, such ingenious weapons, and such skill in their use.

The Popcorn Kid

A paunchy but powerful Capo with cold, hooded gray eyes sits back from his clam spaghetti. He signs the check and tips the fawning waiter. As the Capo walks out with his two bodyguards the waiter looks after him, and his servile smile becomes a sneer in a flash of gold teeth.

The guards are a bit belchy and somnolent from the lunch and the wine and the grappa. A jalopy pulls into the curb at a corner ahead of them. A red-haired boy of about eighteen gets out, slamming the door with a violent back kick. The engine coughs and dies. The driver shouts after the boy, "You frigging little son of a bitch."

"Gee thanks for the ride, Mister."

The boy walks toward the Capo with a bag of popcorn. He is tossing the popcorn into the air and catching it in his mouth. The driver is still cursing as he tries to start the car. The boy's shirt is open to the belt. When the boy is within a

few feet of the Capo the car backfires. The guards stiffen and then relax. The boy drops his popcorn and clutches his chest and staggers forward.

"They got me, Capo. I wanna die in your arms."

The Capo looks at the boy with cold disfavor. He gives an imperceptible signal to his bodyguards meaning, "Teach this smart punk a lesson."

The guards start forward, hands off their guns, preparing to slap the shit out of the boy. The boy snakes a 9M short-barreled automatic from a holdout holster under his shirt.

Using both hands and pivoting from the hip, he takes them all with three shots each. The car is making a U-turn in a salvo of covering backfires. The car pulls up and the kid jumps in. The car roars away. It is a jalopy only on the surface, with a souped-up engine.

"Nice work, kid."

The boy is sliding a new clip into his automatic. He takes another bag of popcorn from the glove compartment.

"Kid stuff. When is their fucking *thing* going to grow up?"

The man shrugs, busy with driving.

"I have to do it the hard way. They might at least give me a cyanide pellet gun like the pickle factory's got. . . ."

The boy catches a handful of popcorn in his mouth.

"That's kid stuff too. When are *they* going to grow up, with their sensitive projects and special numbers and shellfish poison. . . ."

"Don't ask me, I just work here. All I do is backfire on cue."

The kid looks at him, his eyes narrowed.

"If you fart, I'll kill you."

"Relax, kid. . . . We're all dummies . . . those people out there. . . . Like rats in a maze. . . . Difference is you and I know it. . . . Yo." He points a thumb at his chest. "El Mecánico. . . . I can make a car do anything I want it to do . . . backfire . . . boil over. . . . I can stall a car by looking at it."

"Yeah." The boy nodded thoughtfully, crunching popcorn. "Telekinesis. . . . I read about it in a magazine. . . .Why can't I stop the Capo's heart by looking at him?"

"You could, with knowledge and training. . . have to take it a step at a time . . . you wanta learn how to use a psychic knife, learn how to use a solid knife first. . . .There's no substitute for actual combat with your blood guts and bones on the line. . . . Now I got an intuition about you, kid. . . . I can see you in a few years on Madison Avenue making twenty thousand dollars a year. . . .

"I make sixty thousand now."

"Oh uh yeah. . . . These old lines from the fifties crop up. . . . So many years in show biz. . . . What I mean is, I think you're gonna hit the big time. . . . Those Eyeties was just like targets that pop up on the shooting range."

The Lemon Kid

The Capo is back eating his spaghetti with clam sauce. The kid slides through a side door in a waiter's tuxedo with a filthy towel. As he bustles over to the Capo's table he pops half a lemon into his mouth.

"Enthoying thor thinner, thir?" he slobbers. He spits the lemon in the Capo's face and throws his towel at a bodyguard.

KAPOW KAPOW KAPOW

The Freshest Boy

He pops out in front of the Capo, a huge rubber cock sticking out of his pants.

"You like beeg one, Meester?"

KAPOW KAPOW KAPOW

One Cigarette

He is doing the Cigarette Song from *Carmen* in a nightclub.

"*Si je t'aime prends garde à toi. . . .*"

He peels off his falsies and throws them on the Capo's table. Two concealed hand grenades explode.

KAPOW KAPOW

The Mafia proved no match for the expert assassins of the Johnson Family, all adept at disguise. . . . A delivery boy, an old derelict, a solid businessman type with a briefcase, a doctor, a street cleaner . . . The Mafia never recovered from the blow. They had come to the promised land. And suddenly the promised land hit back hard. They were forced into legitimate business or confined their depredations to the Italian community.

NYC circa 1910 ... Concrete evidence of survival after death and reincarnation has given a new perspective to assassination. There are ethical brokers who will only take on a case after careful inspection of the karma involved and selection of the victim's future parents. In some cases death may even potentiate the power of an enemy who can now operate through a number of carefully prepared receptacles. In such cases the manner of death must neutralize the target.

Strangulation and hanging are considered the most certain insurance against posthumous vengeance. The Seminole Indians fear death by hanging above everything since they believe the soul of the hanged man cannot leave the body. There are practitioners for every price and every purpose.

Licensed assassins are the new elite. Here one sits, in a Rajah's palace, having his toenails manicured while a boy mans the ceiling fan.

"I'm doing my Lord Alabaster number this week."

He changes residences constantly. Next week it may be a French chateau, or a townhouse in Mayfair. He is leafing through offers. He only takes certain cases. He's *very* exclusive.

"A Mrs. Norton to see you, sir."

"Tell her to go away. She wants me to kill her husband, and it's just too tiresome. Oh, and tell her she can donate her two million to cancer research. She's got the Bad Disease, and she's got it bad, in case she doesn't *know*. . . ."

Like all top assassins, he is an M.D. You have to know just where everything is, the veins and arteries and nerve centers, so you can place a bullet or a knife-thrust to sever the portal vein or the femoral artery. It can make the difference between a clean hit and a disgraceful recovery.

Needless to say, young agents are trained courtesans, graduates of accredited Sex Institutes, and many assignments are Mata Haris; "hairies," we call them.

"Oh God, not another KGB colonel, like an uncouth bear all covered with black hair. . . ." He sweeps the slip languidly to the floor. Rejection slips stir around his feet like dead leaves.

"The Israelis, *ugh*, and the Arabs, *ugh*er . . . too starved an argument for my sword."

He selects a cheap white envelope addressed in pencil, and extracts a sheet of yellow lined paper:

Dear Mister Kim: A year ago two cops kicked me in the crotch. I am now N.G. as a result. I want to off these bastards. I got a thousand dollars saved up. I know it isn't much but I hope you will help me. Yours truly, Tom Jones.

Like famous doctors, Kim takes charity cases: "Pack up, William, we are going to Chicago."

In addition to charity cases, we are also expected to do unsolicited and unpaid C.W.: Community Work. It's our contribution to the health and welfare of the global community. For example, the poisonous creepers who put razor blades, needles, and ground glass into Halloween fruit and candy.

"Let me have a look at that apple."

A man is trying to edge away. He finds his way blocked, two fingers hooked over his belt, a knife pressing against his stomach.

"What is this. . . ?" Boy turns the apple in his hands. He

takes out a knife and makes a quick incision: a needle glints in dim streetlight. Boy turns to the traitor and raises an eyebrow.

"Now look, I found the apple, see?"

Boy hands him the apple: "Eat it."

"Now look, you can't— I got rights!" A knife presses against the side of his throat.

"Eat it while you still have a throat to swallow with."

We took care of about twenty that Halloween, one way or another, going to and fro on the earth and walking up and down on it.

And a certain anonymous letter required expert attention. When a four-year-old boy was attacked and nearly killed by guard dogs, some vile animal lover wrote to the boy's mother, protesting the destruction of the fucking dogs: "It wasn't the dogs' fault. The boy should die soon. I hope he will."

We talked to the mother and got the letter and took it to our graphologist: "Elderly woman ... recent coronary ... check hospitals, narrow it down." We find a blighted area of semidetached houses with scraggly little vegetable gardens, five dogs outside; this must be the place.

"Did you write this letter, Mrs. Murphy?"

"Who are you men, anyway?"

"And who were you, Mrs. Murphy?"

SPUT ... a dart with organic cyanide compound, almost odorless. They found her two days later, most of her face eaten off by the dogs. (Wasn't the dogs' fault ... hungry, you know.)

We go through the newspapers, looking for C.W. cases and tossing them back and forth: "Oh yes, *that's* me. . . ."

For such louts as the Mafiosi, assassination is simply a means of expanding or consolidating territorial rights. The people they kill are very much like themselves: rivals in the same line of business, with the same stupid criminal outlook. Lucky Luciano said, about people who work for a living: "Crumbs. Strictly crumbs!"

It is related that Cherry Nose Gio, rescued from drowning, spit in the lifeguard's face: "Crumb! Worka fora living."

The Johnsons kill to rid the spaceship Earth of malefactors who are sabotaging our space program. It's like you see somebody knocking holes in the bottom of the lifeboat and shitting in the water supply.

Kim sets up an institute to study various so-called psychic or paranormal processes, to clarify the mechanisms involved, and to discover where possible practical applications.

The phenomenon of phantom sexual partners was of particular interest to him since he had experienced some extremely vivid encounters. He surmised that such occurrences are much more frequent than is generally supposed: people are reluctant to discuss the matter for fear of being thought insane, as they were reluctant to make such an admission in the Middle Ages for fear of the Inquisition. He knew that the succubi and incubi of medieval legend were *actual beings* and he felt sure that these creatures were still in operation. Surveys proved him right. Once people could be brought to talk about it, many instances emerged. One woman, after the death of her husband, continued to receive uh conjugal visits, which were fully satisfying, and he gave her some very good advice on investments. The evil reputation of phantom partners probably derived largely from Christian prejudice, but Kim surmised that these creatures were of many varieties and some were malignant, others harmless or beneficial. He observed that some were seemingly dead people, others living people known to the uh visitor, in other cases unknown. He checked where possible to find out if at the time of such visitations the uh beneficiary was aware of the encounter. In some cases not at all. In others partially aware. Quite frequently the visitor reported an itchy or restless feeling at the time. In a few cases the visit was quite conscious. He concluded that the phenomenon was related to astral projection but not identical with it since astral projection was usu-

ally not sexual or tactile. He decided to call these beings by the general name of "familiars," which is a term usually restricted to animals. They were certainly familiar and, like animal familiars, attempted to establish a relationship with a human host. His studies and personal encounters convinced him that these familiars were semicorporeal. They could be both visible and tactile. They also had the power to appear and disappear. Rather like amphibians who had to surface from time to time.

The case of Toby, who haunted an old YMCA locker room. . . . Toby is described by several observers as blond with rather vacant blue eyes, about sixteen years old. There are a few pimples on his face which are faintly phosphorescent. He gives off a rank ruttish animal smell when aroused. Kim spent a month in this room and enjoyed many encounters with Toby.

The first time, he saw him standing naked at the foot of the bed. Kim showed no fear and threw back the covers to invite the boy to get in bed with him, which he did. Then Kim caressed the boy, who writhed and steamed off his skunky smell, which increased Kim's excitement as well. He slowly turned the boy on his side, stroking the phosphorescent pimples on his buttocks. The boy emitted a purring hissing sound. No Vaseline was needed to penetrate the boy's rectum, which opened to receive him with a soft gelatinous clutch, the feeling being rather like his cock was between two reversed magnetic fields. That is, the sensation penetrated his penis rubbing inside and now the boy was slowly melting into him or rather Kim was entering the boy's body feeling down into the toes and the fingers pulling the boy in further and further then there was a fluid click as their spines merged in an ecstasy that was almost painful, a sweet toothache pain as they both ejaculated and their rectums and prostate glands squeezed together and the tips of their cocks merged and glowed with a soft-blue fire and Kim was alone or rather Toby was all the way in him now.

There were a number of such encounters and always Toby took the passive role. In the moment of orgasm they merged

completely so that Kim's cock was spurting in air but he could feel Toby squirming inside him. Afterward the boy would slowly separate and lie beside him in the bed, almost transparent but with enough substance to indent the bedding. Kim concluded that the creature was simply composed of less dense matter than a human. For this reason interpenetration was possible.

Toby could speak, though he seldom did so. And he could follow instructions up to a point. At the time, Kim was engaged in a bitter war with Mafia hit men who had gone to the mattresses. Toby was able to find their lair, which reeked of garlic and unwashed Old World bodies, for these were Mustache Petes brought in from Sicily. Kim asked if Toby could use a gun and he said no, "too heavy," but he could cause gas leaks or a gas explosion. Kim learns later that the familiars specialize in certain services. Some, like Carl, are electronics experts . . . though for operations involving actual wiring they need a suitable human vehicle, usually some quiet boy who was always good at taking things apart and fixing circuits. In fact electronics equipment is especially liable to psychic influence. Carl can stop a tape recorder by looking at it. . . . Kim finds out that familiars all have *their* familiars and assistants, though it is not always clear who is the master and who the servant. Familiars can be very helpful, they can also harass one unmercifully. Carl, for example, if he is in a sulky mood, can make the simplest wiring job impossible, he can burn out lights, trip one up with electric cords, louse up a TV, tape recorder or hi-fi. And he takes various forms. One is Agouchi, a Navajo spirit, a little man three feet tall with blazing blue eyes and bright red hair who squeezes the testicles in the moment of orgasm. Agouchi can always be recognized by his odor, blending the aroma of leather shorts slept in all winter by a Scandinavian Force Boy with the ozone smell after lightning strikes. . . .

Thunder offstage.

Kim studies the scant sources on Hassan i Sabbah, the Old Man of the Mountain. This man is the only spiritual leader who

has anything to say to the Johnsons who is not a sold-out P.R. man for the Slave Gods. Slave Gods need slaves like a junky needs junk. Only by stunting and degrading the human host can they maintain their disgusting position. Above all they must keep the Johnsons out of space. No one must ever be allowed to leave *their* planet. Hassan i Sabbah was a member of the Ishmaelite cult, who were viciously persecuted by the orthodox Moslems. They had already gone underground and built up a network of secret agents.

Hassan incurred the displeasure of a potentate and fled for his life. It was during this flight that he received the vision of the Imam and took over the Ishmaelite sect with all its underground networks. He spent several years in Egypt. Once again he was a fugitive. He escaped by boat and is said to have calmed a storm. He gathered a few followers and, after years of perilous wanderings, established himself and his followers in the fortress of Alamut in what is now northern Iran . . . (the fortress is still there). Here he maintained himself for thirty years and trained his assassins, who spread terror through the Moslem world.

The Old Man could reach as far as Paris. Sources tell us nothing of the training received by his assassins at Alamut, but we do know it sometimes took years of preparation before the assassin was dispatched on his mission. No one has explained how the Old Man conveyed the signal for an assassination across hundreds or thousands of miles. The library at Alamut was apparently a myth and no written teachings have survived. Whom did he assassinate and why? Most of the hits were caliphs, sultans and religious leaders, mullahs and such. Hassan i Sabbah did not initiate attack. He waited until the enemy made a move against him. In this way his position was similar to Kim's. . . . Just minding his own business when some punk looking for the rep of killing the famous Kim Carsons starts the argument.

Hassan i Sabbah was well known through the Moslem world just as Kim was known as a gunfighter throughout the

Old West. So any general, caliph, mullah, sultan, could take a crack at the Old Man. He knew who would try this before they knew it, and had a man staked out to kill when the move was made.

The basis of the Ishmaelite cult is a direct conveyance of divine power and leadership through contact with the Imam. This cannot be simulated. You can't fake it any more than you can fake a painting, a poem, an invention, or a meal for that matter. It's there or it isn't. One look and you know. The Old Man's power over his assassins is based on self-evident spiritual truth.

During his exile in Egypt he learned some basic secret by means of which his future power was realized. Some scholars have assumed erroneously that this secret was the use of hashish. Hashish was only an adjunct. What Hassan i Sabbah learned in Egypt was that *paradise actually exists and that it can be reached.* The Egyptians called it the Western Lands. This is the Garden that the Old Man *showed* his assassins. . . . *It cannot be faked any more than contact with the Imam can be faked.* This is no vague eternal heaven for the righteous. This is *an actual place* at the end of a very dangerous road.

The Garden of Eden was a space station, from which we were banished to the surface of the planet to live by the sweat of mortal brows in a constant losing fight with gravity. But banished by whom? An asshole God who calls himself Jehovah or whatever. Only one spiritual leader found this out, and found a key to a garden . . . for once you have the key, there are not just one garden but many gardens, an infinite number.

He found the key in Egypt. But the Egyptians didn't have a key. The Gods held all their keys and admitted only favored mortals. And favored why? Because they served as energy conduits to maintain the station. They were in fact trained vampires put out on mummy leads to suck the energy the space station requires, because the station, from time immemorial, is rooted in time and supplied by time.

The Old Man was a renegade. His assassins struck down

the foremen and overseers who manage the Big Ranch. And every time they did this, they grabbed a key. So the Old Man set up his own station, the Garden of Alamut. But the Garden is not the end of the line. It might be seen as a rest camp and mutation center. Free from harassment, the human artifact can evolve into an organism suited for space conditions and space travel.

To what extent has the situation changed? Not much. The mummy has been replaced by a virus culture, inserted into suitable human hosts. The Virus 23 serves exactly the same function as a mummy: an energy conduit to keep the ranch going and the human cattle out there on the range getting fat and ready. . . . *As it was in the beginning, is now, and ever shall be . . . World without end MOO MOO MOOOO.*

Cows driven into the slaughter chutes . . . God, the Father, Son, and Holy Ghost, and when the Holy Ghost wears thin they simply deny that the space station exists. This is the present directive. Anyway, we got our cows going with the Vatican and coming with the Kremlin, and the huge reservoir of scientific materialism, quite as fanatic as any demented Inquisitor. "Anyone writing about so-called ESP should be publicly horsewhipped and barred from further activity," said someone whose name was so close to Condom that if it fits he should put it on.

Well done, thou true and faithful servant. We have conveniently ceased to exist. And there have been moments when they had the sky sewed up tight as a junky whore's ass . . . but it always happens, the big cattle men go soft in the outhouse.

The Old Man found a way to bypass the mummy route. Present-day immortalists have not done so. They have simply reduced their stinking old mummy to virus crystals for insertion in a human host, like loathsome insects who go around laying their eggs in people. The Old Man's route is sex between males. Sex forms the matrix of a dualistic and therefore solid and real universe. It is possible to resolve the dualistic conflict in a sex act, where dualism need not exist.

How did the Old Man convey the death order at a distance? The word *telepathy* is misleading. *Organic communication* would be a more accurate designation, since the whole organism is involved.

You transmit and receive as much with your big toe as you do with your brain and what is transmitted is a strong emotional *reaction*, not neutral data like triangles, circles, and squares. Consider the Russian experiment described in *Psychic Discoveries Behind the Iron Curtain*. Six baby rabbits of the same litter in a Russian submarine three thousand miles from the mother rabbit. They are then dispatched in a manner calculated to elicit the strongest reaction, seized by bestial Russian tars, swung in the air by their hind legs, urinating and defecating in terror as their brains are bashed out against a torpedo launcher. Three thousand miles away, the mother rabbit showed six strong reactions on the polygraph at the precise instant when her babies were liquidated. . . . "So we will make rabbits of our enemies," the Russkies chortle as they mix Bloody Rabbits from rabbit blood and vodka. . . . So the Old Man transmitted a *reaction* to activate a preconceived plan.

"Nothing is true. Everything is permitted." Last words of Hassan i Sabbah. And what is the truest thing to a human mark? Birth and Death. The Old Man showed his assassins freedom from rebirth and death. He created actual beings, designed for space travel.

The air-breathing potential must come before the transition from water to air. Otherwise it is simply suicidal for water creatures without any air-breathing potential to move into air. So the potential for existence in space must come before the transition from time into space. We are considering here demonstrable biologic alterations. New beings. You can't fake it. You can't breathe in fake lungs.

"**L**et's go up the Metropole and suck some bubbly."

> Now Broadway's full of guys
> Who think they're might wise
> Just because they know a thing or two
> You can see them every day
> Strolling up and down Broadway
> Boasting of the wonders they can do
> There are con men and drifters
> Shake men and grifters
> And they all hang around the Metropole
> But their names would be mud
> Like a chump playing stud
> If they lost that old ace down in the hole . . .

Kim has reserved a table. Eyes follow them. But nobody sees Boy do a fifty-dollar palm on the headwaiter. All they see is fifty dollars of respect.

Cold, watchful, probing eyes . . . gamblers, con men, sincere untrustworthy eyes of a Murphy Man. . . . "Now there's a party to stay well away from."

> Some have a girl on the old tenderloin
> And that's their ace in the hole

WHAP . . . "You no good junky slut, what's this?" He throws some crumpled bills in her face from his manicured fingers. All pimps get manicures. He has the assurance of one who knows his precise area of exploitation and never steps outside of it. (In Kim's party he is way outside his area. Nothing there for a pimp.) An old con man smells money. But he doesn't smell marks. He looks away with a wrench because it's *big* money he is smelling. . . .

"No, I'd be wasting my time."

A heist team smells money too in the pocket. They also smell guns and trouble. . . . "Looks like a bank mob from out west carrying heavy iron. . . ."

Shake men and grifters . . .

There is Joe Varland. He worked the broads on the trains. Nobody knew just how, but he always came back from a train trip with money. Thin scarred face. . . . About thirty-five. Yellow gloves and brass knucks. . . . You notice his eyes . . . "sleepy and quiescent in the presence of another species . . . at once helpless and brutal . . . incapable of initiating action but infinitely capable of taking advantage of the least sign of weakness in another. . . ."

And he lost that old ace in the hole. . . .

Slugged a cop and run for it. Didn't run far. . . . A short trip home.

You can see them every day. . . .

A shadowland of furnished rooms, chile parlors, pawnshops, opium dens, hobo jungles, bindle stiffs, and rod-riding yeggs, some of them missing a few fingers, mostly from the fulminate caps.

He remembers a dream phrase spoken in Tom's voice a few months after Tom's death. . . .

"Life is a flickering shadow with violence before and after it. . . ."

Walking up and down Broadway . . .

Eyes watchful, waiting, perceiving, indifferent, follow

them to their table.... Noting the ease and deadly assurance....

Eyes old unbluffed, unreadable.

From Florida up to the old North Pole ...

They wind up in a Village all-night place, eating spaghetti, surrounded by long-haired scruffy-looking artists and poets ... and there but for the grace of Carsons ...

Yes, he could be living in some cold-water flat, peddling his short stories from editor to editor...."Too morbid," they tell him....

They pay the check and as they step into the street and turn left on Bleecker Kim feels it up the back of his neck....

"Hey Rube," he yells.

He moves behind a lamppost and drops his satchel, the 44 in his hand. He can see Boy diving for a fireplug, a charge of shot misses him by inches. Kim gets Liver Wurst Joe with the 44 and he drops his sawed-off into the street.

Guy has the Mauser out across the street, shooting for the driver.... Cherry Nose Gio pumps in another round but his aim is bad because Frank the Lip lies dead across the wheel and the car is bucking out of control and he is catching lead from all of us, his head seems to fly apart from Boy's 45.... The car jumps the curb, crashes through a shop window in a shower of glass.

"The coppers will assume of course it is just another woppish beef," Kim says as they walk rapidly away.

"What the fuck happened?" the Director bellows.

The Technician shrugs.... "Old gangster film stock is worn right down to the celluloid.... I can do a chewing-gum patch ... turn the glass into rain...."

"Well how about a hurricane blowing glass splinters down the street?"

"A hurricane? Jesus fucking Christ. . . . Look, Boss, there is just so much energy *. . . so much* IT. *. . . You use too much over* there, *you don't have enough over* here. *. . . We're* overdrawn, Boss. *. . . Right now we don't have enough IT to fry an elderly woman in a rooming-house fire. . . ."*

"Well we'll have to start faking it."

"All right, Boss . . . anything you say. . . ."

He turns to a switchboard, muttering: "So we start faking it . . . using up film stock that isn't being renewed. . . . You take a real disaster and you get a pig of IT. You can underwrite the next one. But if the first one is a fake you got nothing. You can't underwrite. You start borrowing everything in sight . . . every fire . . . every earthquake . . . every riot . . . every car crash. . . . Then the bottom falls out and you start springing leaks in the Master Film . . . like this Carsons thing. . . . Boss wants to hit him. I film it. Carsons and his boys kill the hit men . . . and every time he slides out from under, he cuts the film . . . fucking moguls don't even know what buttons to push . . . fuck him and his hurricane. . . ."
The Technician pushes a button marked Rain. . . .

THE MANHATTAN AMBUSH

Rain:::Rain:::Rain:::

We get out of wet saddles in wet clothes, tie the horses so they can graze in a circle, can't risk hobbles and bells sit down to peppers and jerky, can't risk night fires or shots. Boy made a throwing stick and he brings down an occasional prairie chicken, but not often. In this rain the fish won't bite and any animals we could prey on stay under cover.

There are thirteen in the party now, was twelve until Kim's old friend from Saint Albans, Denton Brady, showed up cool under the leveled guns.

"Denny!"

"Kim!"

Guns lowered. . . . Denny rode with the James boys and he was a child prodigy under Quantrill. . . . Little Tombstone Denny, he could kill in his sleep, came as natural to him as breathing. At the same time he is a red-headed, freckle-face American kid with a wide sunlight grin. . . .

Swapping stories about Quantrill and Bloody Bill Anderson and the legendary Captain Gray, who was sent up to Missouri to organize the Irregulars. He brought along a wagonload of Confederate uniforms to lend us credibility and some of us wore uniforms from both armies. Denny wore a Confederate coat and Union pants, said it was getting those liberators of Wall Street down where they belong—covering assholes. Black-powder percussion days and with those cap-and-ball wheel guns you have to be mighty careful of multiple discharge when all six cylinders go up at once. Only way to keep this from happening is to coat every bullet with heavy grease so sparks don't fly out and set off the other cylinders. Goose grease we used mostly, but any grease will do in a squeeze. Recollect when we had to raid a whore house, the girls is all set to be raped, was mighty put out when the captain says:

"Madame, all we want is your fucking cold cream."

"Whose been fucking with my goose grease?" the Captain roars, holding up the empty tin.

"TENSHUN!" Captain Gray walks up and down the line of sullen ragged soldiers.

"All right, you brown artists . . . if I don't get a confession I'll by God confiscate all the fucking grease in this platoon. . . . Well?"

"I cannot tell a lie, Captain, I doned it with my little wanger." The boy smiles insolently.

"Why don't you use spit, for shit sake? Haven't you got any sense of social responsibility?"

"I'm sorry, Captain, I was carried away."

"Give me your wheel."

"But Captain. . . ."

"Shut up and hand it over."

Sullenly the boy takes out his revolver and hands it to the Captain. The Captain hands him a fifty-caliber single-shot pistol. . . .

"You don't need grease for this. . . ."

The Indian tracker, Screeching Cat, pulls up and gets off his sweating horse.

"Union patrol, sir . . . five miles north and heading this way. . . ."

"How many?"

"About fifty."

Captain Gray surveys his platoon. . . . Thirty men, the oldest under twenty. . . . One boy has his arm in a sling.

"Get ready to ride out."

They ride out, Screeching Cat leading the way.

He got that name from screeching like a berserk tomcat when he rides into battle, slashing with a cavalry saber cut down to twenty inches.

Rain:::Rain:::Rain:::

Huddled against each other in our soggy blankets under a tarpaulin . . . drip drip drip . . . and the horses keep getting tangled in the ropes somebody has to get up and see to it, and the morphine is running low . . . four addicts in the party, they have to ration it out, quarter-grain twice a day. You have to be really hurting before they turn loose of any . . . kid with a sprained ankle . . . Kim tells him to think beautiful thoughts. Kim keeps dreaming about the sugar but it always spills, the syringe breaks, his opium turns to dirt.

And Tom makes a scene about Denny:

"Your phantom lover from beyond the tomb, isn't it . . . ? Or some such rot. . . . You and your occult junk."

"Now Tom, let up aggravating me."

"Go conjure up an abomination. I'm giving up on you."

What holds us together is we are all agreed on where we are going and why. We are riding south for Mexico because we all have eagles on our heads, some more than others, most of it put up by Old Man Bickford and Mr. Hart the newspaper tycoon who can't hear the word *death* pronounced in his presence, says we are "tainting the lifeblood of America and corrupting credulous youth." We are on the Richy Shit List. So we play Robin Hood to the poor Mexican farmers, our lifeblood with jerky and peppers, information and silence.

We are weak from hunger, wet and miserable, running out of everything. We have to make a run to town.

"So you're running out of junk and we have to make a run to town, is that it?" Tom snaps. "What town?"

"The nearest town. We'll put it to a vote."

Everyone says "aye" except Tom, who finally shrugs out a sulky

"Aye."

They know the risks and make preparations. Sneaky Pete, a ferret-faced kid from Brooklyn, is our demolitions expert. He has fragmentation bombs in saddlebags, all he has to do is light up and drop them. Everybody gets his guns in place. Kim and Boy are both carrying two double-barreled twenty-gauge shotgun pistols slung on either side of the saddle horn. Other boys are carrying 410 smooth-bore revolvers loaded with BB shot and two others have twelve-gauge sawed-offs where they can reach them quick under their coats, and a skinny Mexican kid called 10G with dead agate eyes has in a harness under his poncho a double 10-gauge with a spring mechanism to absorb recoil.

Red Dog, guide and tracker, scouts the area and plots an escape route in case we run into trouble and need a place to hole up—a ruined farm three miles from the city limits. They always figure you to be getting as far away as possible. Not likely to look that close. Besides Red Dog has put the "blinding sign" on the path. There it is, about five hundred yards ahead:

MANHATTAN   NEW MEXICO

In cottonwoods by a swollen muddy river. Kim scans it through field glasses . . . buckboards, people walking up and down. . . . Saturday afternoon in New York. Kim passes the glasses.

"I don't like it," he says.

"Why not?"

"Because I seen the same face five times in different places . . . walking around on a treadmill."

"Well, small town, you know."

"Something wrong with this one. What do you think, Tom?"

Tom shrugs irritably: "Well, it's you junkies who *have* to ride in . . . why don't you decide?"

"Don't be an old woman, Kim."

"The signs ain't right."

"Maybe you should take it up with your spirit guide. . . ."

"All right. Let's go."

Maybe it is all right, Kim thinks, and I'm just jumpy. He's been having centipede nightmares, wakes up kicking and screaming and once he woke up with tears streaming down his face or was it rain?

Manhattan, so of course the main street is Broadway. They are riding down Broadway spaced out. Denny is behind Kim to the left. Kim is riding side by side with Tom. For the first time in weeks the sun comes out. The townspeople walk up and down, tipping hats, exchanging greetings.

You can see them every day
Strolling up and down Broadway
Silly to think anything is wrong
Boasting of the wonders they can do
"How many you kill today, Doc?"
vertigo . . . smell of ether . . .
They'll tell you of trips . . .

passing a buckboard ... an old gray horse dozes in its traces. ... Two boys frisk by, singing.

Old sow got caught in the fence last spring. ...

The townspeople are ducking into doorways, up alleys ... a whiff of brimstone and decay. ...Kim snaps awake and reins up. Denny rides up beside him.

"AMBU—" A shotgun blast catches Denny in the side of the neck, nearly blowing his head off, he is falling against Kim's horse streaking blood down the saddle, dead before he hits the street. A pellet nicks Kim's ear.

"—SH! RIDE OUT!"

Kim is turning his horse and drawing his shotgun pistol. He shoots a man on a roof under the chin, snapping his head back. They are shooting from windows and roofs on both sides of the street. 10G takes out a window, framing a faceless man in jagged broken glass. Kim can see three of his boys down, riddled with bullets and shotgun slugs. He can feel a bullet hit Tom and gets an arm around him as they ride out, Red Dog in the lead.

There are three others wounded besides Tom, one in the shoulder, one in the leg. ... Another boy picked up some number-four shot in the back. You have to dig them out one at a time.

Meanwhile there is consternation in Manhattan. The unexpected shotguns have taken a heavy toll: two dead, one with an arm torn off, another who will write an inspirational article for a Unitarian magazine, entitled "My Eyes Have a Cold Nose." Mike Chase, who has set up the ambush, makes a hasty examination of the dead. The three he most wanted, Kim, Boy, and Marbles, are missing.

"Sheeit!"

Still there is better than five thousand eagles lying there in the bloody street.

"Well what are we waiting for?"

Cautious as always, Mike points out that they may be part of a much larger force. . . .

"Not likely . . . take a look."

He hands Mike the field glasses.

"Slow down," Kim calls. "A few more of you boys pretend like you're wounded, holding each other up."

The boys camp around.

"Tell me grandmother they got me, old pal."

Another sings, "I'm a-headin' for the last roundup."

Tom watches with an enigmatic smile.

"It isn't far, Tom."

"The Western Lands?"

"They're falling off their horses! Let's go!"

The posse thunders out. Mike brings up the rear. He hasn't lived this long riding out in front.

"Look, they're throwing away their saddlebags. . . ."

The posse lets out a wild rebel yell and spurs forward right over the saddlebags.

BLOOM BLOOM BLOOM

Men blown out of the saddle, horses disemboweled, trailing entrails, a rider one foot caught in the stirrup, the other leg blown off at the knee spurting blood in his face. Mike watches impassively. He turns and rides back to town.

They carry Tom into the barn and lay him down on a bedroll with an army blanket folded under his head. The 30-30 has gone through both lungs, angled from above. Kim starts to prepare a shot of morphine but Tom stops him . . . a small distant voice. . . .

"It doesn't hurt, Kim. . . . I'm just cold. . . ."

Boy covers him with a blanket.

He's bleeding out and there's nothing I can do about it, Kim thinks. He starts to say, You'll be all right, bursts into tears instead.

Kim burned it on an oak barrel stave with an old rusty running iron he found in the barn:

TOM DARK

JUNE 3, 1876   APRIL 2, 1894

III

QUIÉN ES?

Kim's father had told him something about painting: artists who couldn't sell a canvas during their lifetimes and now their paintings are literally priceless.

"If you know how to pick them, it's the best investment you can make."

Kim makes an appointment with an art dealer and takes along a selection of his father's paintings. The man is Middle European, dark and heavyset, with shrewd gray eyes. . . .

"So you're Mortimer Carsons's son. . . ."

Mr. Blum studies the pictures carefully. . . . One is a portrait of Kim, age fourteen, standing on a balcony, his face radiant with dazzling unearthly joy. He is waving to something beyond. . . . Another picture shows an old steam locomotive pulling floats of *The Mary Celeste* and *The Copenhagen.* In the open cab of the locomotive, a black engineer and fireman are pounding each other on the back, smiling and waving. . . . There are a number of landscapes, mostly of the Ozarks in winter, spring and fall. . . .

"There was another portrait," Kim says. "Several years later. . . . I looked for it and couldn't find it. . . ."

"It's in Paris," Blum told him, "and so is the dealer for these"—he indicated the paintings. Blum was an ethical man after his lights. This deal belonged to his old friend Bumsell and he knew it. . . .

Kim decides to make the Grand Tour. . . .

Kim dislikes England on first contact. The porters are deferring to the signal presented by his clothes and luggage. They don't see him. He infers correctly that the whole place operates on hierarchical categories that determine how everybody treats everybody else, categories carefully designed to make sure no one ever *sees* anyone else.

"Well it's convenient, isn't it?"

"Only in petrified context. Function negative in space conditions."

The hyphenated names, the old school ties, the clubs, the country weekends. Kim's stomach turns at the thought of an English weekend. He had thought of a large country house or a shooting lodge in Scotland. He decides against it.

"They would force me into a loathsome Lord of the Manor role. . . . 'And how is your wife's cold, Grimsey?' Or get me out altogether. Always think about the tenants when you buy on foreign soil. You are on their turf. They were here before you came. They will be here when you are gone. Which will be soon if you don't play their game."

Kim took a taxi. He was meeting Tony Outwaite in Hyde Park.

Kim got out and looked about him with loathing at the brown water, the listless ducks, the warped benches stained with pigeon droppings.

"There is something here that is just *awful*," he decided. "A terrible *lack*. . . . No doubt they are all yacking away to *their* queen . . . taking tea with her oh quite at ease you know and taking liberties she will just love like calling her 'love' she'd just love that wouldn't she now?"

Kim was a few minutes early for his meet with Tony. On operative meets it is always indicated to get there a bit early and check things out. . . . Trade craft, you know.

Maybe I should feed the fucking pigeons to be less conspicuous or cruise one of the obvious guardsmen in civilian uniform or cheap lumpy blue suits. Most of them look suety and stupid and deeply vulgar with a vulgarity of the spirit that only a class-

rotten society can mold. No doubt about it, these are the *lower* classes.

Someone else is sitting on the designated bench reading *The Times* where Tony should have been and Kim doesn't like it. He feels slighted. The man is M-5, from his shoes, shined but not glitter-shined, to his gray felt hat neither new nor old. Oh just any old M-5 hack is good enough for me, is that it? He sits down petulantly and belches. This is the password of ERP, the English Republican Party, which, under cover of English eccentricity, is an extremely deadly and dangerous conspiracy. You are expected to belch very discreetly and cover your mouth. Kim belches rather loudly and doesn't cover his mouth. He can feel the man shiver with disapproval.

"Nice weather we're having isn't it?" the man says out of the corner of his mouth as he folds his paper with the expertise of someone who does a lot of sitting around reading papers. It's like folding a map. If you don't do it right you have an accordion of recalcitrant papers in your hands.

"Well," Kim says distinctly. "It won't last."

"Daresay."

Kim reluctantly surrenders the satchel containing his plague cloak, sandals, knife, and sheath in accordance with his agreement with Tony, an agreement he is already regretting. He stands up and walks away with a vague uneasy feeling of universal damage and loss . . . in his pocket a slip of paper . . . Empress Hotel, 23 Lillie Road near Gloucester Road Station, room reserved name Jerome Wentworth . . . reserved not paid. Kim finds he has ten pounds left, just enough to buy a cheap suitcase and some toilet articles. . . . No the chemist didn't have a shaving *kit*, but he did grudgingly sell Kim a razor, shaving soap, toothbrush, and toothpaste.

"Will that be all, sir?"

(Gentlemen don't ask for shaving *kits*.)

The Empress Hotel is in a rundown shabby area on the edge of a rural slum with shops selling jellied eels and blood pudding.

A motherly woman greets him at the hotel.

"Oh yes, Mr. Wentworth . . . gentleman reserved the room and left this package. Our rates are a pound a night with breakfast, five pounds by the week. Breakfast is seven to nine-thirty, seven to ten on Sundays. We appreciate payment in advance."

Kim gives her a five-pound note. He has nothing left but some change.

"Here's your key, Mr. Wentworth. Room twenty-nine on the back."

The room is small but the bed is comfortable. The one window faces a backyard with trees and clotheslines. There is a gas grate that you feed shillings into. Kim opens the package. There is a passport in the name of Jerome Wentworth, student, and a letter of introduction to Professor Gailbraithe at the British Museum which identifies him as a Ph.D. in Egyptology from the University of Chicago. There is fifteen pounds in notes. This, he gathers, is his weekly allowance after paying for the room.

He feels like a forgotten agent from some remote planet that winked out light-years ago.

He assembles himself for a tour of the neighborhood. He feels awkward, vulnerable, conspicuous. He bumps into a woman at a corner.

"Well you might look where you are going," she snaps.

"Are you next, sir?" a clerk says insolently.

Symptoms of acute weapon withdrawal.

In the days that follow he will learn to stay out of places where he is discourteously treated and he will find enough safe places to make life bearable . . . just bearable . . . a change of management or personnel. . . . Kim has fallen from favor at the Prince of Wales Pub. He observes that while good places may change to bad, bad places never change to good ones.

He establishes a routine. Every morning after breakfast in the hotel dining room he goes to the museum and studies Egyptian texts, making notes. Professor Gailbraithe is helpful in a vague way and Kim even has a tiny office at his disposal. After

lunch in the museum cafeteria, he goes back to the Empress, types up and enlarges on his notes.

Every week he receives twenty pounds by post. He always pays in advance.

"And how is the back, Mrs. Hardy?"

"Well sir, I could use one of those pain tablets."

"Of course, Mrs. Hardy. . . . You keep the other two in the bottle just in case. . . ."

A perfect gentleman in every sense of the word.

The Egyptian pantheon is colorful . . . a demon with the hind legs of a hippopotamus, the front paws of a lion, and the head of a crocodile . . . a beautiful woman with a scorpion's head . . . a pig demon who walks erect, seizing violators and squeezing the shit out of them, which he grinds into their mouths and noses until they suffocate.

The whole stinking thing is arbitrary and bureaucratic . . . the Immortality Control Board and their terrible demon police . . . Venusian M.O.

Most immortality blueprints are vampiric, directly or covertly, so Kim surmises that the Egyptian model is no exception, though no Egyptologist has ever suggested such a thing. Dismissing the mummy road and the Western Lands as primitive superstition, they never ask themselves how such a system *could work*. It ran on fellahin blood. Vampires, like the Western Landers, enjoy a precarious immortality. . . . They are vulnerable to fire and dismemberment or worst of all *explosions. Just like mummies* and that was the tipoff: vampirism, crude and rampant. The Western Lands are kept solid and operative with fellahin energy and this entails the additional risk of a fellahin shortage.

"The crops have failed. Millions will starve."

"Oh dear, starving people are so unrewarding."

"Hardly worth sucking. . . ."

"From their green going we gets no coin."

"And a terrible plague has further decimated our herds. . . ."

"And marauding barbarians are sweeping down from the north. . . ."

Dead peasants, burning huts . . . the age-old face of War, from here to eternity. . . .

Why was it necessary to preserve the actual physical body? Look at this body. It is a spacecraft designed to accommodate one person. And no two are exactly alike. Fingerprints differ. Voiceprints differ. Pricks differ. (It never occurred to them to isolate these factors? No they didn't have the technology for that. We do now.) So the *ka* fits perfectly into this body. And it needs that precise filter to suck energy from other bodies. And this precise difference. You fellahin cattle are *there*. We immortals are *here*. A parasite must always preserve this unique difference, otherwise it will merge with the host and lose the most precious thing a parasite can have: *Its identity. Its name.* So the body has to be preserved since it contains the essence of name and difference that enables it to suck life from others, a specialized filter on which the *ka* is absolutely dependent for its continued existence in the Western Lands.

Vampires need victims. The victims need vampires like they need pernicious anemia. For vampires to go unnoticed they have to be few in number. Suppose we suck up a few centimeters a day from say five thousand fellahin. They won't even miss it.

The Western Lands was a vampiric mirage kept solid with fellahin blood.

So how did such an unpleasant, precarious, and dangerous concept arise? Because it works. The Western Lands can be made to exist. Kim is beginning to understand how the whole system can be installed in England or anywhere else.

The Queen is the head filter just like the Pharaohs. And any vampiric immortality is strictly limited. Like a good club.

Oh yes, we've come a long way from the Egyptians. They had to maintain an actual life-sized mummy. We can reduce our wealthy clients to a virus particle that can take root anywhere and suck and suck as good as any mummy because it's got all the genetic information.

Mummies are the arch-conservatives. . . .

"What about space?"

"We must never allow anyone to leave this planet. . . . Certain things simply must not be allowed to change; otherwise, *"WE ARE COMPLETELY FUCKED. . . ."*

From time to time hints are dropped. . . . Kim could even become one of the chosen few. . . .

"You see, there aren't enough Western Lands to go around . . . not nearly enough . . . if you would just be *sensible*. . . ."

An old-queen voice, querulous, petulant, cowardly, the evil old voice of Gerald Hamilton and Backhouse. . . .

Kim doesn't want any immortality that talks like that.

One morning at breakfast Kim is halfway through his second cup of tea, smoking a cigarette and looking out the window to his right . . . gray morning, gray street, peeling billboards. . . . Kim experiences an uneasy feeling of disassociation, something stirring and twisting in his throat.

"I'm trying to eat my breakfast, if you don't mind."

Kim looks up. A burly red-faced man is sitting at the next table. Strange that Kim hadn't seen him when he came in.

"I don't know what you mean . . ." Kim stammers. "I'm just sitting here."

"You know what I mean right enough. You were making a filthy noise."

The man stands up and throws down his napkin.

"Filthy sod!" He walks out.

Kim sits paralyzed like a man who has received a mortal wound, every drop of life ebbing out of him.

"Are you all right, sir?"

"Yes, Mrs. Hardy."

"A dreadful man, Mr. Wentworth . . . came right into my kitchen he did. . . . 'I'd like my breakfast, if you don't mind,' he says and I tell him I'm fixing it and he says, 'Look sharp . . . look sharp. . . .' "

Directional mike, Kim surmises. Two can play at that

game. Kim had been into ventriloquism at one time. He never achieved proficiency but he did encounter some colorful characters like the old Stomach Rumbler, who could ventriloquize stomach rumbles and farts.

Kim makes the round of music halls, carnivals, theatrical agencies of the shabbier variety . . . one hundred pounds reward.

"I'll by God show them some filthy noises."

Kim's hatred for England is becoming an obsession. If you have the right accent you can be wearing a burlap sack and the flunkers will stand to attention like one of Pavlov's salivating dogs at the sound of his master's voice. They know their place.

What hope for a country where people will camp out for three days to glimpse the Royal Couple? Where one store clerk refers to another as his "colleague"?

Licensing laws left over from World War I: "Sorry sir, the bar is closed." And you know he is just delighted to tell you the bar is closed.

God save the Queen and a fascist regime . . . a flabby, toothless fascism, to be sure. Never go too far in any direction, is the basic law on which Limey-Land is built. The Queen stabilizes the whole sinking shithouse and keeps a small elite of wealth and privilege on top. . . .

The English have gone soft in the outhouse. England is like some stricken beast too stupid to know it is dead. Ingloriously foundering in its own waste products, the backlash and bad karma of empire. You see what we owe to Washington and the Valley Forge boys for getting us out from under this den of snobbery and accent, this ladder where everyone stomps discreetly on the hands below him:

"Pardon me, old chap, but aren't you getting just a bit ahead of yourself in rather an offensive manner?"

The only thing gets *Homo sapiens* up off his dead ass is a foot up it. The English thing worked too well and too long. They'll never get all that ballast of unearned privilege into

space. Who wants that dumped in his vicinity? They get out of a spaceship and start looking about desperately for inferiors.

For three months Kim held on at Earl's Court . . . three months of grinding, abrasive fear, defeats, and humiliations that burned like acid.

He learned to use the shield of constant alertness, to see everybody on the street before they saw him. He learned to render himself invisible by giving no one any reason to look at him, to wrap himself in a cloak of darkness or a spinning cylinder of light. Devoid of physical weapons, he turned to the weapons of magic and here he scored some satisfying hits.

He produced a blackout with a tape recorder that plunged the whole Earl's Court area into darkness . . . SPUT.

He conjured up a wind that tore the shutters off the market stalls along World's End and went on to kill three hundred people in Bremen or someplace.

(Giver of Winds is my name.)

He read about it in the paper next day and said: "The more the merrier." At the same time he realized that he was being fashioned into an instrument of destruction, a bottle djin to use against *their* enemies. Whose enemies exactly? He was past caring.

And he takes out some local nuisances. The horrible old crone in the cigarette kiosk across from the hotel who would shove his change back at him. . . . Then one day Kim's eyes blank, appraising, rested on her Primus stove . . . a peg to hang it on. As he walks away he can feel her eyes on his back spitting little sparks of pure hate . . . sparks? . . . Cooking up water for her morning tea on her leaky old Primus. . . .

Several old biddies gathered in front of the blackened shattered kiosk. One turns to Kim.

"Terrible, isn't it?"

"I can't believe it," Kim says. "Why I was just waiting for her to open. . . ."

"You heard it?" they ask eagerly.

"Indeed yes. . . . Just coming out the door I was and I think, Gor blimey it's the Blitz again. . . . Had her wrapped in a plastic sheet like . . ."

And he closed down a Greek coffee shop that gave him some sass . . . camera and tape-recorder magic. . . . So many good ones and so many bad ones. . . . That's what you get for trying.

"Gentleman to see you, Mr. Wentworth."

It's Tony, sitting in the dreary little drawing room with lumpy armchairs. Kim takes a deep breath, about to launch into a tirade.

"Read this." Tony hands him a newspaper clipping.

PROFESSOR DIES IN BIZARRE MISHAP

A man, later identified as Professor Stone-cliff, a curator at the British Museum and a world-famous Egyptologist, was apparently seized by a fit of madness in Victoria Station. He entered into an altercation with other passengers which developed into a fistfight. Then he broke free and threw himself under the wheels of a train.

"What really happened?" Kim asks.

"Professor Stonecliff suddenly lost control of his bowels in a crowded compartment. He was attacked by the other passengers and blinded in one eye by an umbrella."

Nightmare scene under a green haze . . . faces contorted out of all human semblance, burning with sulfurous hate and hideous complicity . . . the man running, stumbling, blood streaming from his ruptured eye . . . the crowd behind him, one brandishing a bloody umbrella. . . .

"Get him!"

"Kill the filthy sod!"

"So you got off easy," Tony says.

"And you got off a lot easier."

"This is no time for recriminations, Kim. The situation is desperate. We could all be charged under the Defence of the Realm Act."

"Telephone, Mr. Wentworth."

"Have you got a hundred pounds? I've found the old Stomach Rumbler."

The Rumbler is a potbellied Indian with the nastiest eyes Kim ever saw. You can't like him. He just isn't a likable man. But he can deliver the goods. We give the old Stomach Rumbler a trial run at ERP Headquarters in Bedford Square. Tony stands at one end of the room, thirty feet away from the Rumbler, and a horrible churning noise rumbles out of Tony's stomach like a vast kraken digesting a whale.

"What's his range?" Tony asks.

"Fifty yards, sahib," the Rumbler sneers.

It's a solemn occasion. The Queen is regretting a tip slide that killed three hundred children. For years the villagers have been saying:

"We gotta do something about that tip."

An ominous gray black slagheap that towered over the village and nobody did anything about that tip. Then one fine morning the tip slid down and covered the school.

Her address was designed to be simple and moving:

"To those of you who have lost your children in this disaster, I can only say . . ."

It rumbles out over the mikes on TV . . . my God, what a sound. The Queen turns pale but continues:

". . . that your grief is my grief and the grief of all . . ."

Her words are drowned out by loathsome, squishy, farting noises, gurgles and chuckles:

"ENNGLAAND . . ." the Queen gasps and flees from the podium, leaving in her wake a monumental belch

ERP

She never made another public appearance. Her Majesty is indisposed . . . permanently indisposed. . . . The monarchy is tottering.

Kim feels that he has acquitted his English karma. He shelves a project to blow up all the mummies in the British Museum.

Kim loved Paris at first sight . . . the outdoor urinals, the flower stalls and markets and cobblestone streets, the lovely gun stores full of sword canes and sword pistols and fountain-pen guns, the well-stocked pharmacies, French boys with gamin grins, a three-foot baguette under one arm. . . . An old man peddles by on a bicycle, a lobster gesticulating frantically from his handle basket. . . . It's like a painting that moves.

It is a fall day, crisp and clear. The Paris light lingers on the buildings, touches cornices, a white cat, a geranium in a window box. . . . Dead leaves. . . . Kim steps into a *pissoir* and there on the wall these lines worthy of Verlaine or Rimbaud:

> *J'aime ces types vicieux*
> *Qu'ici montrent la bite. . . .*

> I like the vicious types
> Who show the cock here. . . .

"*Moi aussi* . . ." Kim lisped ineptly, "and this is the pencil of my brother-in-law." I must do something about my French. He gets a book in French and the same book in English and very quickly learns to read French.

Kim makes an appointment with Maître Bumsell. . . .The Maître, a thin aristocratic-looking old man, extends a long cool hand.

Kim suspects that Bumsell is not the old French aristocrat he is impersonating. His native language, Kim decides, is German. . . . A Swiss Jew, most likely from Zurich or Basel. . . .

Bumsell leads him into a room with an alcove and draws a curtain. . . . Kim looks out of the picture, smiling:

HIS FATHER'S PICTURE

Kim Carsons   age 16   1876

So many faces, yet something that is Kim in all of them caught in his father's portrait. The face is flawed and scarred and nakedly diseased. Something animal in the face, but this is not an earth animal. Kim's alien stigma, the fact that he is not of human species, stands out raw and shocking, like a man exhibiting his privates in a crowded marketplace.

Displacement and vertigo . . . distant voices. . . . Who was Kim's father? Expense account suggested illness . . . illness was radium poisoning. The radioactive Carsons. . . . Perhaps we are Death, Kim thought with a delicious little shiver, and he reeked off his skunkish smell. . . .

Half-remembered bargains and commitments . . . old friends and enemies . . . remember me? and me? and meeeeee?

Kim knew he was remembering past lives from somewhere, bits of vivid and vanishing detail. Oh that doesn't mean he was Cleopatra in a previous incarnation or any rubbish like that. . . . Some parallel universe maybe, and very technical, let someone else work out the details. Point is, Kim is *remembering*. He remembers the exhilaration and madness of the Black Death.

> Is it not fine to dance and sing
> While the bells of Death do ring?

He can feel the plague around him like a cloak as he glides through London, billowing out puffs of Death with clear ringing peals of boyish laughter.

"Bring out your dead."

What a splendid line, Kim thought, and what better thing could most of them bring out?

The icy blackness of space . . . Quonset huts . . . G.I. jokes . . . the horror outside . . . light-years ring through . . . fainter . . . blurring . . . tears . . . the father he is not . . . look closer . . . youthful courage portentous as a comet . . . death and the Piper . . . sunlight on marble . . . diamond-hard core of purpose . . . dazzling smile . . . the final order . . . *home* . . . you know . . . remember the bells of time on that mesa with Kim? . . . the final order . . . you can't fake it . . . you can't fake it . . . through London . . . through London . . . a face . . . hands . . . the face of a man willing . . . he will not hesitate . . . we win or lose? . . . alertness around him like a cloak . . . blood diseased from outer space . . . intercourse . . . sperm . . . think of it getting loose . . . reeking of corruption and death . . . look closer . . . the face, hands, blood . . . human animal in the diseased cloak . . . And when intercourse sperms father's portrait: naked alien face . . .

April is the cruelest month mixing memory and desire, stirring dull roots with spring rain . . . half-remembered bargains and promises . . . old friends and enemies . . . Death and the Piper?

Kim knew he had to do it without quite knowing what it was. . . . Like a good scout, he was prepared. . . .

Zur jeden Massenmord stehen wir bereit!
(For every mass murder let us stand ready.)

Kim spent three years in Paris. These years extend like a vast canvas where time can be viewed simultaneously bathed in the Paris light, the painters' light, as Kim bathed and breathed in the light of Manet and Cézanne and who are the other two that escape my mind so good at bathers and food and parasols and wineglasses and who did that marvelous picture *Le Convalescent* where a maid is opening a soft-boiled egg? The painter dips his

brush in the light and a soft-boiled egg, a wineglass, a fish come miraculously alive touched by the magic of light. Kim soaked in the light and the light filled him and Paris swarmed to the light. Kim was the real thing, an authentic Western shootist. There were of course those who questioned his credentials. Kim wounded one editor in a duel.

Kim's first book, a luridly fictionalized account of his exploits as a bank robber, outlaw, and shootist, is entitled *Quién Es?* Kim posed for the illustrations. Here he is in a half-crouch holding the gun in both hands at eye level. There is an aura of deadly calm about him like the epicenter of a tornado. His face, devoid of human expression, molded by total function and purpose, blazes with an inner light.

QUIÉN ES?

By Kim Carsons   Ghostwritten by William Hall

"Quién es?"
Last words of Billy the Kid when he walked into a dark room and saw a shadowy figure sitting there. Who is it? The answer was a bullet through the heart. When you ask Death for his credentials you are dead.
Quién es?
Who is it?
Kim Carsons does he exist? His existence, like any existence, is inferential ... the traces he leaves behind him ... fossils ... fading violet photos, old newspaper clippings shredding to yellow dust ... the memory of those who knew him or thought they did ... a portrait attributed to Kim's father, Mortimer Carsons: Kim Carsons age 16 December 14, 1876. ... And this book.
He exists in these pages as Lord Jim, the Great Gatsby, Comus Bassington, live and breathe in a writer's prose, in the care, love, and dedication that evoke them: the flawed, doomed but undefeated, radiant heroes who attempted the impossible,

stormed the citadels of heaven, took the last chance on the last and greatest of human dreams, the punch-drunk fighter who comes up off the floor to win by a knockout, the horse that comes from last to win in the stretch, assassins of Hassan i Sabbah, Master of Assassins, agents of Humwawa, Lord of Abominations, Lord of Decay, Lord of the Future, of Pan, God of Panic, of the Black Hole, where no physical laws apply, agents of a singularity. Those who are ready to leave the whole human comedy behind and walk into the unknown with no commitments. Those who have not from birth sniffed such embers, what have they to do with us? Only those who are ready to leave behind everything and everybody they have ever known need apply. No one who applies will be disqualified. No one *can* apply unless he is ready. Over the hills and far away to the Western Lands. Anybody gets in your way, KILL. You will have to kill on the way out because this planet is a penal colony and nobody is allowed to leave. Kill the guards and walk.

Ghostwritten by William Hall, punch-drunk fighter, a shadowy figure to win in the answer, Master of Assassins, Death for his credentials, Lord of *Quién Es?* Who is it? Kim, *ka* of Pan, God of Panic. Greatest of human dreams, *Quién es?* The horse that comes from there, who is it? Lord of the future son, does he exist? Inferential agents of a singularity, the fossils fading leave the whole human comedy shredding to yellow dust.... Unknown with no commitments from birth.

No one can apply unless he breathes in a writer's prose hills and faraway Western Lands....

Radiant heroes, storm the citadel.... Kill the last guards and walk.

Guns glint in the sun, powder smoke drifts from the pages as the Old West goes into a penny-ante peep show, false fronts, a phantom buckboard.

Don Juan lists three obstacles or stages: Fear ... Power ... and Old Age.... Kim thought of old men with a shudder: drooling

tobacco juice, spending furtive hours in the toilet crooning over their shit. . . . The only old men that were bearable were *evil* old men like the Old Man of the Mountain. . . . He sees the Old Man in white robes, his eyes looking out over the valley to the south, seeking and finding enemies who would destroy his mission. He is completely alone here. His assassins are extensions of himself. . . . So Kim splits himself into many parts. . . .

He hopes to achieve a breakthrough before he has to face the terrible obstacle of old age. . . . So here is Kim making his way through the Old West to found an international Johnson Family. . . . Being a Johnson is not a question of secret rites but of belonging to a certain species. "He's a Johnson" means that he is one of *us.* Migrants fighting for every inch. The way to Waghdas is hard. The great victory and the fall of Yass-Waddah are but memories now, battles long ago.

It is said that Waghdas is reached by many routes, all of them fraught with hideous perils. Worst of all, Kim thinks, is the risk of being trapped by old age in a soiled idiot body like Somerset Maugham's. He has shit behind the drawing-room sofa and is trying to clean it up with his hands like a guilty dog. Alan Searle stands in the doorway with the Countess. . . .

"Here's Blintzi to see us, Willy . . . *oh dear.*"

Like Beau Brummell, his rigid mask was cracking to reveal a horrible nothingness beneath.

"Brummell would rush upon his plate and gulp down a roast in such a revolting manner that the other guests complained they were nauseated and Brummell had to be fed in his room. . . ."

And here is the mask in place. When Beau Brummell was exiled to Calais by his debts and Princely displeasure, a local lady sent him an invitation to dinner and he sent back the message:

"I am not accustomed to *feed* at that hour."

Toward the end of the month when his allowance ran out, Brummell would rush into a sweet shop and cram into his mouth

everything he could reach, the old shopkeeper flailing at him and trying to wrest her wares from his fingers. . . .

"*Alors, Monsieur Brummell . . . encore une fois!*"

He sometimes spent hours getting the crease of his cravat exactly right. His valet would carry out bundles of linen: "Our failures . . ."

As he took Lady Greenfield's arm to lead her into dinner, Maugham suddenly shrieked out as if under torture, "*Fuck you! Fuck you! Fuck you!*"

Alan Searle leads him away, Searle's pudgy face blank as a CIA man's.

Maugham would cower in a corner whimpering that he was a horrible and an evil man.

He was, Kim reflected with the severity of youth, not evil enough to hold himself together. . . .

A friend who took care of Brummell in his last years wrote, "His condition is indescribable. No matter what I do, it is impossible to keep him *clean.*"

Alan Searle wrote: "The beastliness of Maugham is beyond endurance."

The Evening Star floats in a pond, keeping the ledger books of stale dead time.

Kim collected last words, all he could get his hands on. He knew these words were pieces in a vast jigsaw puzzle. Big Picture, he called it. . . .

"*Quién es?*" Who is it? Last words of Billy the Kid when he walked into a dark room where Pat Garrett shot him.

"God damn you, if I can't get you off my land one way I will another." Last words of Pat Garrett. As he said them he reached for a shotgun under his buckboard and Brazil shot him once in the heart and once between the eyes. They had been engaged in a border argument.

"It is raining, Anita Huffington." Last words of General Grant, spoken to his nurse.

"Yes I have reentered you long ago."

"*Quién es?*"

Through the years, through the dead tinkling lull, the gradual dusky veil distant youth blushing brightness falls from the air.

"*Quién es?*"

Rocks and stones and trees the little toy soldiers the thoughts of youth . . .

"*Quién es?*" No motion has he now no forces he neither hears nor sees . . . "God damn you, if I can't get you off my land one way I will another." Rolled round in earth's diurnal course with rocks and stones and trees. "It is raining, Anita Huffington." "How sleep the brave who sink to rest by all their country's wishes bless'd! . . ."

"*Quién es?*" Helpless pieces in the game he plays.

"God damn you, if I can't get you off my land one way I will another." On this checkerboard of nights and days. "It is raining, Anita Huffington." Confused alarms of struggle and flight. "*Quién es?*" Hither and thither moves and checks and slays. "God damn you, if I can't get you off my land one way I will another." And one by one back in the closet lays.

"It is raining, Anita Huffington." Where ignorant armies clash by night.

Cold dewy fingers . . . a tinted photo.

Ledger book shining in the sky . . . Big Picture, he calls the rearranged fragments. . . . "*Quién es?*" Last of Kim's inventions . . . Leaves whisper, "Hello, Anita Huffington."

It is time for Kim's Arab assignment and he will need perfect Arabic without a trace of foreign accent. Language sense is like card sense. Some people have it, some don't. Reading is one thing, speaking another. Kim's guess that language operates on the virus principle of replication has been verified in the Linguistic Institute located outside Paris. Any language can now be conveyed directly by a series of injections.

The Institute is dedicated to studying the origin, function and future of language. As in physics and mathematics, the most abstract data may prove to be the most practical. . . . Matter into energy. . . . Word back to virus. Students are taught such seemingly useless skills as talking backward or talking at supersonic speed. They can talk right along with you and finish at the same time with precise mimicry of every syllable. It's a most disconcerting performance that can reduce a speaker to . . . stammer slobber glob glub . . . and the students are all expert ventriloquists.

Kim is waiting to see the doctor. The Chief was vague about Kim's assignment except to say that we could be very close to a final solution of the language problem and that Kim's assignment could be a crucial step. Kim knows that language shots can be very painful, especially for those who are not good natural linguists. . . . The doctor looks younger than his twenty-eight years. He is thin and sandy-haired and keeps running his hands through his hair as he talks.

"Some shots are a lot more difficult than others. French

Spanish *très muy fácil*. . . . Maybe you need to rest up for a day
or two. . . . But when it comes to oriental languages you are using a whole different set of muscles and neural patterns . . . so
you're bound to have a sore throat, just like your legs are sore
after riding a horse for the first time. . . . And Arabic is frankly
the worst. . . . It literally cuts an English-speaking throat. . . .
Spitting blood is one of the symptoms, though not necessarily
the worst. . . . It is the stutter of neural response—remember
when you first tried to row a gondola? The way you couldn't possibly get it, and your muscles knotted up and you were just making spastic gestures with the oar and the feeling in your stomach
and groin, that sort of packing dream tension almost sexual. . . ?
And then suddenly you could do it? Well it's like that, only
worse. . . . And there is the gap between languages that can be
terrifying . . . the great silences. . . . And erotic frenzies when the
patient feels himself sexually attacked by Arab demons. . . .

"About ten days in the hospital. . . . You realize that you
don't talk with your mouth and throat and lungs and vocal cords,
you talk with your whole body. . . . And the body keeps reaching
back for the old language—it's rather like junk withdrawal in a
way. . . . The erotic manifestations always occur. . . . It's like the
subject is being raped by the language, shouting out obscenities
in the injected idiom. . . . And of course the set is important. . . ."

"The set?"

"Yes. For example, we had six Arab boys in for an English
injection. . . . And we rigged it up like a dorm in an English public school. . . . It isn't just the language, the subject has to come
from somewhere. . . . He's got to have a regional accent. This
was an old-school-tie infiltration job—they had to have not just
an upper-class accent but an upper-class accent complete with a
special school and a part of England . . . this was an interesting
case because of the surprises involved. . . . The boys could soon
spout those clear English voices you can hear across a baronial
dining room but they were sexually aroused by Cockney vulgar-
isms. . . . One would say to the other . . . 'Cooo I'd like to glim

you in the altogether. . . .' 'I want to bottle you, mate. . . .' 'Get off my dish,' one boy snarls to another. 'Look at Reggie, starkers. . . .' It was like some Cockney demon had invaded our re-creation of Eton. . . ."

"How do you account for this erotic factor. . . ?"

"It must be something inherent in the nature of language itself. . . . After all, language is communication—that is, getting to know someone all over like in the altogether. . . . There is in fact strong evidence that at one time the larynx was a sexual organ. . . . The first words were not warning cries or exchanges of information. . . . The first words were obscenities. . . . As you may have gathered, your mission is to discover more about the nature and function of words. . . . That is why you have been selected. You are a writer who can not only gather the information we are seeking but transcribe it as well. . . ."

The doctor got up and pointed to a map. . . . "Now in this area, the highlands of Yemen, there are a few remote valleys where the original link between ape and man that led to speech may still survive. These beings have sex by talking in each other's throats. They are called 'smouners.' . . . An experienced smouner can strangle an adversary by this lethal ventriloquism. . . . Your job is to penetrate the smouners. . . ."

"So I am the man for a highly important and, I may add, highly dangerous assignment—is that it?"

The doctor smiled and ran his fingers through his hair. . . . "Yes. . . . But, I may add, a highly diverting assignment. . . . In fact I'd like to go along."

"What's keeping you?"

"Not much. My papers are going through channels. However, we won't be traveling together. Your point of entry will be here . . . this is the market . . . It varies as to time and place. . . . This year it will be held on the outskirts of Ganymede, an oasis village in the highlands . . . with the language and a supply of money . . . two hundred thousand dollars is minimal."

The doctor prepares an injection. As the shot takes effect, Kim can feel the language stirring in his throat with a taste of

blood and mint tea and greasy lamb. He is squeezed into a crowded bus in a smell of unwashed flesh, exhaust fumes, and kief. The words are eroding English like acid . . . later . . . time sense is not segmented into hours, but laid out spatially like a road . . . the truck stops in the marketplace of Ganymede.

The market had the temporary and dilapidated aspect of a military encampment or a carnival that has, for some reason, been there for a very long time. The Greek camp outside Troy must have looked something like this, he decided. Only this market had been here for centuries. The truck stopped in a huge square with trees and wells here and there and people filling gasoline cans and pots at the pumps. Around the square and on side streets running from it were stalls, tents, tin-roofed shacks, houses of stone and adobe. He walked past sidewalk cafés and shabby hotels and bathhouses. Boys with painted eyes beckoned from doorways. He knew where he was going and soon he began to see guns and knives displayed in front of the bazaars and in the windows of dark shops. This he knew was the weapons section. He slowed his steps, stopping now and again to look at displays. He noticed armed guards here and there. He came to a square where a number of people were offering weapons for sale. The guns were passed from hand to hand as bargaining went on. . . . The guns were mostly automatic rifles, Israeli and Russian and a few M-16s. A boy touched his arm and pointed to an M-16.

"Buy me that and I am yours forever."

Kim nodded. He asked the price of a frizzy-haired boy. The boy held up three fingers. "Three American dollars."

Kim looked puzzled and the boy who had accosted him quickly explained. "That means three thousand dollars and it's too much."

After haggling, a price of $2,500 was agreed upon, with two hundred rounds of ammunition thrown in. The boy slung the rifle over his shoulder and put the bullets into a leather shoulder pouch. At the end of a long crooked street that wound

steeply upward between walls of red adobe was the Ganymede Hotel, with a façade of marble pillars from some ancient settlement. Kim could see the market spread out below. It would take days to see it all. . . .

Kim is winded from the steep climb and the heat. Silver spots boil in front of his eyes. . . . Vertigo . . . a whiff of ether . . . a marketplace . . . terrible heat . . . a gathering crowd . . . the faces . . . screaming . . .

"Hold him down, Greg. . . . I'll get some medication."

"Say, these language shots are rough . . . learning a language the hard way, if you ask me . . . Remember that bloke in for bushman shots? Poor blighter never came back. . . ."

"That shot straightened him out. . . ." Kim is sleeping peacefully.

The town has the temporary look of a military encampment, an oil or mining town, deserted and repopulated in strata at once gratingly new and dilapidated. A marketplace with army surplus trucks parked around it. . . . Booths selling hardware, camping equipment, knives, guns and ammunition, stone steps leading up from the marketplace to the old town built into a hillside, a town of red adobe and shuttered windows.

Kim thought it looked all spewed out in one piece by a monster wasp. From the narrow twisting streets he catches whiffs of shit-encrusted walls, an ancient insect evil that stops the breath. . . . Get yourself together, Agent K9. The Traveler is equipped with money and the language. He strolls about in jeans with an army surplus jacket and a straw hat. . . . Ah the guns. . . . Quite a large area given over to buying and selling every variety of gun.

"If you are looking for a special model, sir"—a portly gentleman hands Kim his card—"we'll track it down, sir. . . ." Kim looks around—nothing but weapons as far as he can see in shops built into the hillside. He is in the automatic-weapons section. Here the golden youth gather to lovingly feel a K-47 Rus-

sian assault rifle, or an Uzi, it's the chic thing to carry around with you to bars and restaurants ... full auto stuff, Kim observes, and lots of it. From junk like the Czech squirtguns, effective range about four feet, to good heavy stuff like the old Thompsons. . . . A boy with dusky-rose cheeks and long lashes looks longingly at an H & K 223. . . . "Buy me that and I am yours forever. . . ." The boy's breath is spicy and musky. . . . The Traveler steps forward and asks the price. The dealer sees that the Traveler is armed and probably skilled in the use of arms. . . .

"Four thousand dollars it is, reasonable."

They settle for thirty-five hundred. Money doesn't mean much here. Kim hands the boy the gun in front of the beaming dealer. . . . "Pleased to serve such fine gentlemens. . . ."

"Now I need some handguns ... spare clothes and luggage."

It is usual procedure for an agent or private buyer to arrive at the market knowing he can pick up whatever gear he needs at the shops. Kim is quickly outfitted with just his brand of aftershave and his eternal alligator, as he calls his Gladstone, when one wears out he buys another. Ah yes, weapons. . . . That double-action 44 special takes the Russian as well? Very good, rosewood handle, and that two-inch Colt 38 special with the butt cut down right into Kim's hand. Don't forget the KY—my God, it's five dollars a tube. . . . "Yessir, things do keep going up," the young attendant titters without shame. The boy leads the way, his new H & K slung over sure arrogant young shoulders. You can see how neatly he could unsling it and cut someone in two.

The Ganymede Hotel is at the end of a long crooked street. He signs the papers and the boy takes them to a room opening onto a little walled garden with fig and orange trees and a pool with a fountain. . . . There is a *haman* down the hall and old-fashioned carbolic soap, "lovely boy toilet soap," they call it in Persia. Kim is a connoisseur of carbolic soap. . . . There are other boys in the *haman*, he recognizes kinky red hair and the

green cat eyes that shine in a shuttered room.

Long crooked street of youths handling the guns. In the *haman* are two youths from the market. The boys turn and grin. They are standing there with erections, languidly soaping each other with the same loving fingers they use when touching a gun, checking the mechanism with a gentle precise touch. They are holding up fingers. Some bargaining the Traveler doesn't understand and they are speaking a dialect not covered in his Arab Bedouin and dialect shots. It is a humming sound that buzzes out of the larynx through the teeth, which are bared like those of wild dogs in the act of speech. At first the vibration sets the stranger's teeth on edge with an exquisite pain, his phallus sways and stiffens and throbs.

Now the boy—Jarad was his name—squirms in behind him with the KY musk. The fingers like loading a gun slide in and touch the trigger and the Traveler spurts, hitting a target on the wall. The boys are pounding him on the back. They carry him back to the room and Jarad blows smoke down his chest to the crotch and the Traveler falls on his knees, sniffing the smoke up with the rank musky ferret smell. Runs his hand lovingly over the cloning equipment. Sound of running water a flute Lifebuoy Carbolic Soap peels off his underwear grin. They are standing there serene impure kinky red hair that shines in the shuttered room like fine gold wire. They are holding up fingers the Ganymede Hotel. He doesn't understand the bargaining the boys sniffing him a humming sound on all fours on the pallet teeth bared like wild dogs stiffens and throbs. The boys are pounding him on the back. He remembers the game of taking three deep breaths while a boy behind him pulls his arms tight across his chest and he blacks out and comes around with the boys all laughing, he has passed some sort of test.

They carry him back to his room and lay him on the bed where he falls asleep. He wakes up with Jarad shaking him gently to the smell of roasting mutton, cooked over coals on the balcony.

After dinner the four boys bring out maps. It's an action of

some sort. They are pointing to the map, setting up an ambush. (One boy ejaculates across the map. Another traces the spurts with a crayon. He makes calculations with a slide rule.)

They handle their bodies like their guns, as artifacts, with the knowing caressing fingers of connoisseurs. Jarad is naked, his gun disassembled on a low table in front of him. He picks up each piece, feeling it and memorizing the shape of it like braille, he can disassemble and assemble the gun in the dark. The boys play a game of recognizing each other in the dark by touching each other's cocks.

Kim sits up naked and yawns, tightening his sphincter lest he soil the bed. At the end of the room is a marble toilet and a water faucet and a hip bath with a copper kettle over it and a low kerosene flame. He defecates with a loud sound that spatters the bowls with liquid feces streaked with blood. Nobody pays the slightest attention. He washes himself in carbolic soap and dries himself and takes his 44 special Russian with a set trigger out of its case. A tip-up revolver and not a fraction of an inch of play in the cylinder. He takes the gun down carefully, oiling and memorizing each part. Another boy has an eighteen-shot 17-caliber revolver, the thin cartridges three inches long, the bullet long and pointed with soft metal in the middle and hard metal at both ends that mushrooms on impact to the size of a half-dollar.

Kim feels a numbing blow in the chest, sucking, gasping for breath that won't come. . . .

"Code Blue. . . . Code Blue!"

The doctor holds up a restraining hand.

"He's coming around. . . . No need to electrocute him."

Kim is spitting blood into a basin. His throat aches and every breath stabs through his lungs with searing pain. . . . The doctor prepares an injection. . . .

"You'll be out of here in a few days. . . . Your accent is Moroccan . . . Casablanca . . . . Profession: perfume dealer . . . That covers any amount of travel. . . . Pick up further instructions in Tangier."

I am Captain Zomba. . . . Hotel Continental."

Guide English accent, Kim decided. The man had a sincere untrustworthy face beneath a worn red fez. His smile showed gold teeth to go with the braid in his funky old fez.

The Captain began shouting orders as Kim's luggage was hoisted into the carriage. The porters screamed curses as the carriage pulled away from the docks and the Captain stuck his head out and snarled some smashers back. They jolted through narrow streets, exchanging pleasantries with pedestrians, some of whom had to flatten themselves in doorways to avoid being crushed against a wall by the horse. Kim took a suite with a balcony overlooking the harbor and he could see across the straits. A steep slope led down to the water. There was a smell of garbage and the sea. The sunset was magnificent. . . . The boy arrived with gin and tonic.

"Put it there. . . ." Kim learned that these sunsets were a regular feature said to be surpassed only by the Timbuktu sunsets, owing to a suspension of red dust in the Timbuktu area. As a connoisseur of sunsets he intended to visit Timbuktu eventually. Now there was his mission and Timbuktu would have to wait. He unpacked his pistols and opium pipes. He had letters of course but arriving in a strange town he preferred to have a look around on his own first. He selected a sword cane and a lightweight 44 Russian with a three-inch barrel, the holster sewn into a vest.

214

Brushing aside a horde of beggars, guides, and procurers (Kim has a NO he learned from Salt Chunk Mary. It's a NO that never means yes. A NO that is understood even by a Tangier guide) and wrapping himself in a cloak of invisibility, he went for an evening stroll. He loved the narrow twisting streets, the smell of sewage, the tiny cafés where the natives sit on stone benches drinking mint tea and smoking their kief pipes. He found an English bar in the European quarter and had three gin and tonics. He could feel a quickening of interest. Small place, a stranger in town is news here. Avoiding conversational overtures he went back to the hotel and had dinner served on his balcony. Then he unpacked his typewriter and wrote until 3:00 A.M.

As soon as an article goes into mass production the company doesn't want to know about a simpler better article, especially if it is basically different. So a number of very good inventions are scrapped and forgotten. We can extrapolate that the same formula applies to living organisms once we have accepted the supposition that living organisms are artifacts created for a definite purpose. There are no cosmic accidents in this universe. I mean of course the universe which we see and experience. No reason to think that this is the only universe. This universe is probably a minute fraction of the overall picture, which we will not have time to see. And if we saw it it would be, to our limited perceptions, completely incomprehensible, which is why we can't see it. (A phenomenon must be to some extent comprehensible to be perceived at all.)

So at the outset is a breakthrough that makes a new technology possible and an efflorescence of inventions good and bad. Then one of these models, and not necessarily the best one, goes into mass production and that's it. No more changes, no more basic innovations ... just technical improvements. There is

no basic difference between Kitty Hawk and a modern jet liner.

Now apply this concept to living organisms. The mammalian configuration opened a whole new technology with an outpouring of mammalian models. And there were creatures between mammals and reptiles ... quite good, some of them ... models about the size of a wolf with lizard claws and teeth ... promising.... Imagine a mammalian brain with reptilian features of quiescence and renewable neural tissue ... Look at *Homo sapiens*.... Before they went into mass production there must have been some good models lost in the shuffle and for *what*? Look around you on the street and what do you see, a creature that functions at one-fiftieth of its potential and is only saved from well-deserved extinction by an increasingly creaky social structure.... So let's go back and take a look. You want new ideas in cars, go back to the early models before they started rolling the inefficient internal combustion engines off the assembly line....

Consider the mammalian species we see at the present time. Mass production set in and that was the end of evolution. Darwin doesn't explain why the whole evolutionary process has ground to a halt. Why aren't the present-day cats evolving into horses? Answer is simple. The mutation process has stopped. There won't be any more changes at this rate. Just as the auto industry doesn't want to know about any turbine engines because they would have to scrap their dies and that is the most expensive thing they could do. So the present-day controllers don't want to scrap their horse dog human molds. Because doing so would involve paying in currency that they don't have: the currency of creation. They don't want to know about a better human model that is basically different. They

can be relied upon to sabotage any meaningful space program that involves biologic alterations instead of transportation in an aqualung, which is like moving a fish up onto land in an aquarium.

[The Scriptwriter turns from his TV set. . . . "Oh God, the salmon are at it again, leaping up waterfalls to spawn and die. . . . How tiresome of them! Mother Nature in all her rich variety of an old shit house. . . . What does She offer us? A toilet in Hell."]

I theorize that the present God or gods were not the creators. They took over something already created and are using it for their own purposes, which is not at all to our advantage.

To put it country simple: the Christian God exists. He *is not the Creator.* He stole someone else's work after the manner of his parasitic species. He steals and curses the source. The Christian God, and that goes for Allah, is a self-seeking asshole planning to cross us all up. Like all colonists he despises those he exploits. To him we are nothing but escape energy. He needs our energy to escape because he has none of his own. Who but an asshole wants to see people groveling in front of him?

"Like a little soldier I stand at attention before my captain," said Pope John 23. Gawd, what shit is this? And the prayer-mewling Allah freaks is molded from the same crock of shit. . . . ALLAH ALLAH ALLAH . . .

The magical theory of history: the magical universe presupposes that nothing happens unless someone or some power, some living entity *wills it to happen.* There are no coincidences and no accidents.

A chaotic situation is always deliberately produced. Ask yourself who or what sort of creature could benefit from such a situation. Even in the crudest economic terms there are those who profit from chaos . . . speculators, black marketeers, ultimately warlords and bandits. . . .

Now look at the whole of human history and prehistory from this viewpoint. Look at it spread out spatially before you. . . .

Mechanical devices exteriorize the processes of the human nervous system. . . . A tape recorder externalizes the vocal function, a computer externalizes one function of the human brain, the faculty that stores and processes data. See human history as a vast film spread out in front of you. Take a segment of film:

This is a time segment. You can run it backward and forward, you can speed it up, slow it down, you can randomize it do anything you want with your film. You are God for that film segment. So "God," then, has precisely *that* power with the human film.

The only thing not prerecorded in a prerecorded universe is the prerecordings themselves: the master film. The unforgivable sin is to tamper with the prerecordings. Exactly what Kim is doing. Acting through his representatives like Hart and Old Man Bickford, God has prerecorded Kim's death.

The exercise of seeing a section of time as a film can be applied to small arms. . . . Spread out from the matchlock to the automatic assault rifle and machine pistol. . . .

The percussion principle was a basic improvement so radical that any possibilities residual in the flintlock were immediately ignored. So what constitutes a new concept as opposed to a radical improvement? Generally in the case of a manufactured article

like the motor car, it is a concept that would constrain manufacturers to junk their existing dies. For example the turbine engine, a workable steam or electric car. We might say that the next radically new concept biologically speaking will be the transition from Time to Space. This transition consigns the entire Time film, a whole prerecorded and prefilmed universe, to the scrap heap, where we hope it will have the consideration to rot. Its final monument may be great heaps of plastic, Pepsi-Cola hits the spot and stays there forever ... the pause that refreshes ... a long pause and nobody there to refresh. ... The film flickers out ... only the plastic containers remain. ...

So our local war revolves around a basically simple situation: a conflict between those who must go into space or die and those who will die if we go. They need us for their film. They have no other existence. And as soon as anyone goes into space the film is irreparably damaged. One hole is all it takes. With the right kind of bullet, Kim thought, with that little shiver ...

A strange pistol in his hand ... wild Pan music ... screaming crowds ... Kim's pistol is cutting the sky like a torch. Chunks of sky are falling away. The music swells and merges with the shrieking wind. ...

Yes we can lose any number of times. *They* can only lose once. They say a silver bullet can kill a ghost. Garlic could kill a vampire if it was strong enough and he couldn't escape, trapped for example in an Italian social club. So what bullet, what smell can rupture or damage or immobilize or totally destroy the film? Quite simply, any action or smell not prerecorded by the prerecorder, who stands outside the film and does not include himself as data.

Castaneda would describe it as a sudden eruption

of the Nagual, the unknown and unpredictable, into the Tonal, which is the totality of prerecorded film. This violates the most basic laws of a predictable control-oriented universe. Introduce one unforeseen and therefore unforeseeable factor and the whole structure collapses like a house of cards.

Judge Farris said I stink like a polecat. And what is that smell? It's the *smell of the film rotting*. And that is why the Farrises and the Greenfields didn't want to see me. I had no right to be there in the first place.

"WHO IN THE FUCK IS THAT IN MY FILM?" the Director bellows. "GIVE HIM THE TREATMENT."

So they did and it backfired. Kim grins out between his legs and fires. His bullet takes out the water tower, half a mesa, a piece of sky . . . a gaping black hole . . . a humming sound like a swarm of distant bees . . . getting closer . . .

It is 4:00 A.M. Kim smokes five pipes of opium and retires.

Kim dreams about a young man he recognizes as his "benefactor," in the Castaneda sense of the word.

The youth explains to him that he has not yet achieved the (a word that Kim cannot exactly understand) necessary for immortality.

After breakfast on the terrace, Kim wrote a note to one of his contacts, to be delivered by a boy from the hotel. The boy was back in two hours with an invitation to dinner.

At 6:30 the carriage arrived. The horse was a strawberry roan. It looked at Kim dubiously and laid back its ears. The driver was a boy of twenty in army slacks and jodhpurs with a Colt 45 automatic at his hip. He had a Cockney accent and a criminal face, acne-scarred but showing perfect teeth in his slimy insinuating smile. Unusual for a Limey, Kim observed.

"I'm John Atkins."

They shook hands and Kim could feel the probe of appraisal, looking for signs of weakness.

"The Pater was a dairy farmer ... saw you digging my teeth."

"I'm glad to see it."

With a mocking bow, Atkins motioned for Kim to get in the carriage. As Kim swung himself up onto the seat he could feel the insolent eyes on his ass and hear the words in his head clear as a bell.

"I want to bottle you, mate."

Clearly Atkins was a verbal telepathist. Mostly it's done in pictures. Cockneys are especially good at sending words. It's the whole accent thing, which is basic to the English system.

Atkins leaped into the driver's seat with a lithe inhuman movement that was somehow ugly and deformed. He took the reins in his thin red hands, which looked very capable. Kim could see those hands with a broken beer bottle, a razor, or a bicycle chain.

Kim was a man of the world. He knew that many queens and especially the English adore these slimy dangerous types, these listeners at keyholes, the flawed products of the hierarchical social structure built by the Tony's. John Atkins is their creature and would you believe it my dear the English refer to their trade as "creatures.". . . ?

A serviceable little demon, Kim decides, if properly handled.

They rattle off. Atkins is sitting there with insolence reflected in every jolt of the carriage.

"Now that there's the Casbah. . . ." He points to a massive fort, two sloppy lackadaisical soldiers in front of it with Lee-Enfield rifles.

"Now lots of people think it's the whole native quarter is the Casbah but the native quarter is the Medina and this here fort at the top of the Medina is the Casbah. . . ."

Kim nods absently with a snotty smile.

"I guess you knew that. I guess your type of bloke reads up on a place before he goes there."

"Oh yes, and the people I will meet. . . . John Atkins also uses the names James Armitage and Denton Westerbury. Convicted of atrocious assault for blinding a man in one eye with a broken beer bottle in the Blind Beggar Inn. . . . Did six months in Brixton. . . . Worked with a smash-and-grab mob. . . . Five arrests, no convictions. . . . Wanted for questioning in connection with a warehouse robbery in the course of which a watchman was killed. . . . Interesting reading, what? Passed along to me by an obliging French police inspector. . . ."

"Coo ain't you the one? Ain't it a bit unhealthy to know as much as you know?"

"Not when it's on deposit with one's solicitor, my dear."

"I know a thing or so myself, Mr. Carsons. . . . Could be useful to you."

"Let's start with a rundown on the dinner guests for this evening. . . ."

"Well there's old George Hargrave the Aussie, and a rottener man never drew breath. He takes a broad general view of things . . . nothing too low or too dirty for old George."

The road wound steeply up the mountain . . . heavily wooded with chestnut, oak, cypress and cedar . . . villas on both sides well back from the road behind walls and gates . . . the muted redolence of ease and wealth . . . servant children playing in the street . . . Kim turns to watch a barefoot boy run down the street, slapping his bare soles with each step. . . .

"Got his fat greasy fingers into all the pies and puddings. . . . Not much on the heavy. He's a right coward and doesn't care who knows it. . . . Two lizzies run the bookstore and the tearoom—French Intelligence. . . . They do business with the Russians and the English as well. . . . The Americans don't seem to have much in this sector. . . ."

That's what you think, Kim thought. Heavy concentration of Johnson Intelligence in the area.

"They are into smuggling and they own the best cathouse in town. . . ."

"That would be the Black Cat."

"Right. . . . First-class prime cut. . . . Then there's the Comte des Champs. . . . He's head of French Intelligence for the northern sector. . . . A doper. . . . Special heroin comes from further east. . . ."

"Pinkish brown crystals?"

"Right."

"It's special."

"And two American queens, Greg and Brad, run an antique store and do decorating jobs. . . . Not exactly what they seem to be. . . . I heard one of them talking Arabic, which he doesn't know a word of."

"You overheard him."

"That's right. Listening at his door like. Chatting away with his dish boy like a good one he was."

Posing as two style queens, they are Johnson Agents, better trained than any secret service in the world, with the exception of the Japanese Ninja, in the use of small arms, knives, staffs, chains and nunchakus, blowguns and improvised weapons, codes, and all the arts of concealment. . . .

He has them in stitches with his kitchen Arabic. . . .

"Oh really? That means 'fuck' in Arabic. . . ."

"No wonder he looked at me so funny."

Greg was brought up in Cairo. Arabic is his first language. It's the agent's kick to conceal things, to be so much more than people think you are and once you sniff the agent kick you need it and you need it steady. . . . The danger, the constant alertness, the *purpose* and one day you throw off your beggar rags and stand revealed as British Intelligence as you snap out orders in English, German, French, Arabic and a number of obscure dialects. . . .

They turn in at a gate. In a little gatehouse a magnificent old Arab in a fez is smoking his kief pipe, shotgun propped in a corner. . . .

The driveway winds through willows and cypress.

"The American Consul and his wife will be there. They did a mentalist act in vaudeville.... Got cured with an oilwell—that's Texan for 'get rich'—and contributed to the right campaign fund."

The carriage pulled up at a portico and the horse was led away by a stableboy. The house looked Spanish, with a red tiled roof, small barred windows in front.... John led the way into a large room with oak beams and a fireplace.

"Mr. Kim Carsons, the renowned shootist."

A tall thin young man with a pencil ginger mustache, in slacks and jodhpurs stood up languidly.

"I'm Tony Outwaite." He held out a cool firm hand.

Kim immediately recognized the young man he had seen in his dream of last night. A bit showy, he thought, these English always have to *underline* everything.

Tony had cool gray eyes, impeccable poise and assurance. About seven hundred years of it. He got it the easy way. Kim had to work for his.

"Didn't care for London, did you?" Tony gestured to a table on which there was a bowl of blackish pudding.

"Like some majoun before the others get here?"

Kim dipped out a tablespoonful of the candy, which tasted like Christmas pudding.

"Ah just right," he said. If it's right it should be like soft rich gummy fruitcake with no residual bitter taste of cannabis.

"There's a spot of something extra in that.... Shall we take a stroll before dinner?"

"Capital."

Behind the house, which was much larger than the façade indicated, a wooded slope led down to a cliff over the sea ... paths, wells, pools of water and little streams with stone bridges. They sat down on a cypress bench at Tony's direction.

Ah very comfortable, Kim's ass told him.... The bench, the pools, the stone bridges, the trees all carefully contrived. Such stage managers the English.

"Don't think too much of us." It was a statement, not a question. "Like South America, isn't it?"

"Yes. High jungle."

"You've been there?"

"In a manner of speaking, yes. . . . Could you grow *Banisteria caapi* here?"

"Ayahuasco, yage, pilde? No. Too cold. Frost, you know. Too cold for oranges here. . . . I have, however, extracted the active principle. . . . Harmaline, telepathine. There's a dash of that in the candy. . . ."

Time jumps like a broken typewriter. Kim finds himself back in the salon, shaking hands with other guests. Ah this must be the Australian, fat and unctuous, exuding jovial corruption, and the Lesbians, slinky and sinister with dead cold undersea eyes like gray nurse sharks and the Count des Champs with junk coming out his ears. What a fraudulent old piece of work. I'd hate to be trapped in his chateau. Kim remembers with a shudder his encounter with the Count de Vile in Venice. Invitations to the old chateau should be viewed with extreme wariness and close attention to escape routes. Kim has already exchanged hand signals with Greg and Brad. . . . One long squeeze and two short. . . .

He turns his attention to the American Consul and his wife. Mr. Davis is a slim man in his early sixties, wearing a gray sweater. . . . He is just too nice to be true. His wife has a distant ethereal look. . . . Quite deceptive, Kim decides, sensing her expert where-do-you-fit-in inventory. Kim withdraws into a neutral observation post. . . . "Going Swiss," he calls it. George Hargrave is telling a long story about an eccentric English lady who tried to stop a firing-squad execution on the beach by throwing herself in front of the rifles.

Everyone laughs politely . . . for the hundredth time. . . .

Dinner is served and it's a perfect replica of an English dinner—roast lamb, roast potatoes, and mint jelly. . . . "From a little shop in Gib," spinach with hollandaise sauce . . . peaches and cream for dessert. . . .

Tony is writing down the name of the shop for Greg and Brad and drawing a map. . . . "Real marmalade and Earl Grey tea. . . ."

"We lost our Fatima. . . ."

"What a pity, she did such nice. . . ."

"It went too far. . . ."

"It's no use facing them with it, no use at all. . . ."

"Standing over someone with his throat cut, knife in hand, would swear by Allah they had nothing to do with it. . . ."

"It's the way their minds work."

"What are you getting from your Indian?"

"Six thirty. . . ."

"Not bad at all. . . ."

Unreality seeps from the heavy curtains, the glassed bookcases, the deep leather armchairs and couches, impermanent dwellings of provincial camp followers.

"Is it true," she demands, "that Rome is withdrawing two divisions?"

"Heard the news? The zone has been nationalized."

Time's winged chariot hurrying near.

It's all falling apart . . . in the hill stations and the copra plantations . . . the garrisons and outposts . . . mutters of rebellion everywhere like heat lightning . . . the far corners of the earth . . . talking about servants and shops, comparing money changers, exchanging recipes . . . a lot of it is what Kim calls the "double conversation" that seems quite ordinary on the surface but conveys a double meaning. . . .

"I'd hurry if I were you. . . . The shopkeeper says he may not be able to get any more mint jelly before next year. . . ."

(Funds cut.)

Greg turns brightly to the Count. . . . "Oh that brown sugar you're so fond of. . . . Completely sold out. . . ."

Le Comte turns paler, it's quite an accomplishment.

"Can't one make do with the local molasses?" Kim puts in. . . .

Le Comte shoots him a who-asked-you-to-put-in-your-two-cents-worth look.

"Is it true that you are withdrawing two divisions?" an outspoken Lesbian demands. . . .

The Governor hems and haws. He knows that Rome itself is menaced by barbarians moving down from the north. Troops are being pulled back from England, Germany, North Africa. He is making preparations to leave as unobtrusively and expeditiously as possible. One day the colonists will wake up to find there is no garrison left.

"*They've gone*. Left during the night. . . ."

Time to pack up and get out if they're lucky. Back to Rome, London, Paris, where they will complain about the smaller quarters and the lack of servants. . . .

Kim was outside of time, he could look down and see time spread out below him. There was the farm at Saint Albans, Jerry Ellisor and Rover, a squirrel caught in midair as it falls from the top of a persimmon tree, shot through the head. . . .

Old Man Bickford's son bent over by the 44 slug . . . the car jumping the curb and crashing through a shop window, glass fragments glinting in flickering streetlights—the bruised purple cheekbones and blue eyes of Judge Farris looking at him with cold distaste . . . only he wasn't there wasn't anywhere in any of the scenes just the empty place a low-pressure area, a dead spot he was pulling himself out of the picture and as he did so it was caving in behind him disintegrating with a nitrous smell of burning film. . . .

And now directly below him was a vast marketplace stretching to the sky in all directions . . . and Tony pointing. . . . "It's the market, Kim . . . you can buy anything you want and pay with waiting. . . . That's the coinage here . . . you want it, you got it . . . just look . . . weapons, drugs, boys of all shapes and sizes. . . . It's all yours. . . . Of course we want something in return, that's reasonable isn't it. . . ?"

Kim shrugged. . . . "I can see the reason for it, yes, if that's what you mean. . . ."

Tony was moving away. . . . "Well if you're going to be that way about it. . . ." His voice petulant, distant. . . .

An Arab policeman stands in front of him. "Passport," he says in Arabic. Kim hears himself answer in the same language as if someone else is speaking. The policeman is examining his passport. He is carrying a cheap automatic in a button-down flap holster. 380, Kim decides. The policeman hands the passport back and moves on. Kim finds that he can think in the grafted language, noting the cop's dead wooden suspicious face. It is like using an unknown instrument but he is quickly getting the feel of it.

Returning to the Ganymede Hotel, Kim finds the building much larger than he remembers, the gardens a vast area of trees and pools and streams, arbors and summer houses. The town itself is now a huge marketplace. The weapons section alone occupies an area the size of Lower Manhattan.

Guns, bows, knives, boomerangs, bolos, blowguns, slings, clubs, whips, spears, gas guns, electric sticks and canes ... crossbows and elastic rubber bows ... tiny revolvers shooting poison darts ... tiger-snake venom, venom of the blue-ringed octopus and the sea wasp, smooth-bore-shot pistols loaded with cyanide crystals and little metal barbs, devices that send sharp metal disks spinning like hornets ...

The Street of Knives: lined with stalls and forges ... smell of hot iron and ozone ... the principle of the spring knife, one of Kim's early patents, has flowered and proliferated ... the handle is a spring usually covered with leather or rubber. When the knife is used to slash, the spring does the work ... documentary shows the spring weapon in action. Here is a man with a samurai sword and a heavy spring handle. He demonstrates how he can lop off three heads, the resistance of each neck lending impetus to the blade.

"Hand move. Knife catch up."

When the spring knife is used for a thrust, flesh compresses the spring, goosing the blade in ... knives that fly out of the handle ... swords thin and flexible as a whip ... a cane with a knife that flies out propelled by a light powder charge and is

then retracted by a spring, rather like a light air hammer with a double-edged knife as the cutting tool. . . . And the dreaded Steel Flower, a dart tipped with little slivers of razor-sharp flexible steel. These elastic silvers, compressed by flesh, open up inside to form a barb that makes withdrawal extremely difficult.

The Street of Pictures: A narrow winding cobblestone street of shabby studios and massage parlors littered with film garbage . . . nitrous reek of darkrooms and the ozone smell of flashbulbs hangs in the air like a yellow haze . . . photo displays in dusty windows . . . tinted erotic photos . . . Tom Flash Photo Studio.

Whenever Kim goes to the market he accumulates a safari . . . a riot of perfumes. . . . It's the unguent, soap and perfume section. . . . Kim opens a jar and sniffs. . . . My God, it's gamy . . . smell of young hard-ons, rectal mucus (one of Kim's made-up words), moldy jockstraps, and gym shoes. . . . He pays the outrageous price absently. He has plenty of money.

He buys some insect phenergens from a reliable dealer. One whiff brings anyone off three times in a row . . . quite a potent weapon actually and with regulated dosage a decided adjunct . . . proud beauties need it special. . . . A gamut of smell weapons . . . scents designed to attract some noxious creature . . . a scorpion, a centipede, a venomous snake, or disease vectors like the tsetse fly or the kissing bug that lives on armadillos and conveys the horrible earth-eating disease. . . . Many smell weapons work on the "sweet cover" principle, luring one into a good deep breath like rotten blood a heavy sweet odor so you wonder what flower could smell that sweet and suck in a lungful doubles you over like a kick to the crotch . . . gardenia and carrion . . . roses and baby shit . . . sea air and gangrene . . . smelling salts and asparagus jism . . . the smell of modern evil is said to resemble burnt plastic and rotten oranges . . . only different . . . so many smells you can't quite classify because you never quite smelled them before and you have to approximate. And the most dreaded of all smell weapons—Lady Macbeth . . . the smell that never leaves, you can wash and scrub till your skin is raw, douse

on the lotions and perfumes and deodorants but you can never wash away Lady Macbeth. . . . You go into a restaurant, the patrons double over retching . . . you can't go into a shop or a subway or even walk the streets. . . . (We are happy to report that the use of Lady Macbeth has been outlawed by all civilized intelligence agencies.)

Kim sees a witch's cradle and knows he is in the occult section . . . a crystal ball big as a pumpkin, exquisite opal and moonstone balls . . . juju dolls, powders and philters . . . witch knives and robes and altars and incense and cords and grimoires . . . depressing junk for the most part.

Kim is interested in devices for concentrating and directing magical intent, could mean the difference between a BB cap and a 30-30. . . . Consider the Australian practice of putting the bone on your enemy. You get a hollow human bone . . . (the more horrible the death was, the better the bone) so you fill your bone with all kind of shit, jump out at your enemy and put the bone on him. . . .

"Got plenty good bones, Meester. . . ."

"Hundred-Cut bones?" (The bone donor died from the Hundred Cuts, an old Chinese piece of folklore.)

"Rabies bone?"

"Flayed man bone?"

What Kim has in mind is a device for attracting and concentrating the death wish just as his night sight is supposed to concentrate light. . . .

"Oh I must have that" . . . a headband of black mamba skin with a huge black opal just where the third eye is supposed to be.

And clothes . . . every period, every material . . . electric eel skin, gila monster, gorilla-skin overcoat, centipede-skin cape . . . clothes designed to conceal and activate recorders and cameras . . . all manner of trick pockets for drugs and weapons and petties . . . a krait, a coral snake, a dozen black widows in a tube to be released in Mrs. Worldly's john . . . metal jockstraps, knee-

caps, elbow spikes . . . sheathes and holsters from head to foot
. . . shoes with spring soles, with cushions of air, oil, mercury . . .
knives that spring out from the toe when you press down on the
heel . . . a razor-sharp half-moon of steel that slides forward and
locks . . . gloves with retractable claws . . . gloves with lead in
the fingertips for the deadly spear hand to the throat, with lead
along the sides for a karate chop . . . gloves with the palm side
laced with razor-sharp down-curving blades . . . gloves with a
rubber cup in the palm that traps a cushion of air for a slap to
the trigeminal nerve, also useful for rupturing eardrums . . .
come-along gloves with a palmful of fishhooks . . . electric gloves
lined with rubber . . .

Kim adds to his wardrobe, packing purchases into a Gladstone bag of gila monster skin and toddles along to the Biologic
and Chemical section, which has the aspect of a vast abandoned
medical and research complex . . . goats bleat in Emergency,
Arab families have moved into the wards, cooking in beakers,
surgical trays, and bedpans. Children push each other up and
down the halls in crash carts and stretchers. One electrical genius has rigged the Intensive Care Unit into pinball machines.
Kim stops to chat with a tattooed Maori boy who has a vial of
blue octopus venom. Kim buys it for his twenty-shot dart revolver (neurotoxic . . . unconscious in three minutes, dead in an
hour). He draws his smooth-bore 44 loaded with number-six shot
and decapitates a cobra that has crawled out of a rusty instrument cabinet.

There's the Mushroom Man with his black-market plutoni-
um talking to a CIA man who works for Qaddafi. There is a selection of disease cultures, some of which purport to contain
active cultures of diseases thought to be extinct.

Kim runs into Cash Tod, a biologic broker.

"Olafson says he's got the Sweats. Here are his charts."

Kim leafs through the papers. . . . "Monkeys, is it? Monkey
business too, if I know Olafson."

The Sweats was a plague that swept through England in the

fourteenth century. There is an account in *The Unfortunate Traveller* by Thomas Nash. In a few hours the victims sweat away all their bodily fluids and are reduced to desiccated mummies. The disease is spread by the bodily fluids and excretions exuded or propelled from the victim as body temperatures soar to 120°, turning entrails into a caldron. In some cases steaming excrement and urine spurts from the patient to a distance of thirty feet, spattering unfortunate relatives, physicians, and curiosity seekers. A singer exploded on stage, favoring the furthest balconies with his lethal exudations.

The end product, a desiccated mummy, is noninfectious, and brutal death-wagon drivers pound the mummies down to a yellow dust for ease of transport and handling.

"He's working on the Freezies now . . . accelerated hypothermia . . . victims freeze to death with blankets piled on them. . . ."

"Tampering with the thermostat. Well it's more a blueprint than a tested product . . . of course we don't want to be associated with any human experiments. . . ."

"One looks away. . . ."

"What a beautiful sunset. . . ."

"And here is the Rots. . . . First symptom is a reek of carrion . . . it's the smell that spreads it. Masks are ineffective. You smell the Rots with your whole body."

Since the market stocks artifacts from all history, it is also a functioning museum with documentary films and lectures.

The Museum of Lost Inventions: . . . As one makes the round of display cases, lectures and films switch on, seemingly activated by one's presence. . . .

Spread out in dusty display cases, devices from extinct cultures so remote in space and time that no link exists to tell the viewer what function they could have served.

"This cluster of interlocking perforated crystal disks? purely decorative?

"This cabinet about the size of a large TV set . . . cabinet,

for lack of a more precise word, and difficult to assign dimensions since there is no apparent symmetry. Most of the surfaces seem curved rather than angular, then you see quite a few angles. . . ."

No symmetry? This absence gives Kim a hint as to the cabinet's function . . . a ghost escape. Symmetry is predictable, therefore a good escape route must randomize symmetry . . . an intricate arrangement of panels that can be opened or closed in thousands of different combinations. The panels are slotted, emitting an eerie music of escape from forgotten dangers.

"What exactly were these things used for?" asks a CIA man in dry incisive disapproving tones. The Custodian grounds the question with a curious reverse shrug, a slight downward movement of the shoulders.

"The uh human species . . . *Homo sap* . . . (laughter) is perhaps two million years old . . . prehistorians keep pushing our birthdate further back . . . perhaps an abortion would be the uh simplest solution . . . (laughter) but the incidence of clearly recognizable *artifacts* dates back only fifty to a hundred thousand years. In that modest span, gentlemen, we have come from stone axes and spears to intercontinental missiles with nuclear warheads . . . the same principle as the spear but rather more efficacious . . . (laughter). Is it not feasible that other cultures may have traveled the same road and disappeared without a trace? Nor can we rule out the possibility that artifacts were deliberately destroyed. The river people of New Guinea fashion masks for their festivals which are burned once the festival is consummated. And what would a historian of the distant future make of pseudo artifacts of modern art? Who is that *artist* who does a barrelful of nuts and bolts? He went on to burnt kitchen chairs. . . . Oh yes. . . . Armand. . . . How could our future scholar know that this artifact commemorates the sale of a name. It's an Armand and worth so much just as the coppers of Kwakiutl potlaches were valued according to the transfers they had accreted."

The display case contains something that looks like a bull-roarer. . . . A tube of some dull green metal two feet long, two inches in diameter with an opening in each end. A smooth white cord sprouts from the middle of the tube and is attached to a handle of the same green metallic substance.

The room darkens. . . . A screen lights up . . . on a steep slope with his back to a cliff we see a tall thin humanoid in sandals and loincloth of some porous brown-pink skin. He holds the tube in his narrow hands, not more than two inches across, with long tapering fingers and four joints. . . . Twelve uncouth savages with spears and clubs advancing up the slope. . . .

"The lone survivor of a wrecked spacecraft, this being of an ancient race wants only to live in peace with the natives . . . to teach and perhaps to learn. . . . But he finds himself threatened by barbarians, inflamed by an ugly brutish hatred for a *foreigner*, a being different from themselves. . . .

"Got no hair on him."

"All naked and indecent."

"Wonder if he's got hair on his balls?"

Cash thumbs his knife. . . . "I dunno, Clem, but I aims to find out."

The alien's face is a light pink color, smooth as terra-cotta. His unwinking black eyes with luminous blue pupils reflect something too remote and neutral to be called contempt.

He draws twelve darts from a sheath at his belt and feeds them into the tube. He whirls the tube above his head.

"What's he doing up there?"

"The Tube Spirit takes over and animates the tube. It spins now on its own volition. The tube derives its force from a compact between the man and the Tube Spirit. The spirit agrees to animate the tube but *only once*. Once used the tube may never be used again."

The tube is a blur now, the man has been lifted almost off his feet and stands poised on tiptoe. A thin cold whine breaks from the tube and the darts whistle out, each one finding a vital

spot . . . head . . . heart . . . stomach . . . neck . . . the posse has been destroyed. But what if other enemies burst upon him? He can fashion a weapon from materials at hand. A huge savage with a stone ax, shooting red flashes from his berserk eyes, bursts out six feet in front of him. The man snaps off a switch and levels it ZUT right through the beast, severing his spinal column. He falls, writhing like a stricken worm. . . .

"Now some of you may ask, didn't he run out of ideas? That's a good question. . . . Well . . . maybe he did. . . ."

A display case with life-size masks of human skin compacted in layers . . . vile faces . . . gloating faces, stinking of charred flesh and screams . . . faces of abject cringing cowardice . . . dead soulless faces. . . .

"A very old game. . . . It's called 'throwing the mask' . . . rather like tennis. . . ."

A limestone court with tiers of seats for spectators. The contestants arrive. They are naked except for belts, and with their masks. They advance to the middle of the court and look at each other. The gaze of a mask thrower can cut like a scalpel. Now they move back and face each other at thirty feet. A player draws a mask and throws it in a blur of speed. The other gestures and the mask flies back. After three serves one player sends the mask spinning up into the grandstands. The game is hotting up now as more potent masks come into play. Sometimes they may serve and return thirty, fifty times and with every exchange the mask gathers power.

WHAM

It hits. A player is down . . . a broken idiot thing . . . drooling, slobbering, pus oozing from the cataracts that cluster at his dead burnt-out eyes. . . . He will be left to the terrible urchins who haunt the mask courts.

"Tennis anyone?

"Most weapons operate on the projectile design . . . a spear, a bullet, a shell. . . . Something is *added* to the target. A bullet, an arrow, explosive charge, poison gas . . . Consider the possibil-

ity of taking something away from the target. . . . A tornado sets up a low-pressure area which causes buildings and windows to *blow out.* . . . Our weapon creates a concentrated and localized low-pressure area so that a living target will literally explode like a deep-sea creature brought up from the depths. It's an awesome spectacle. . . . See that African buffalo out there snorting and pawing the ground? Most dangerous brute on the continent. He sees us."

"This had better be good."

The buffalo puts down its head. The custodian presses a button . . . a whistling roar and the buffalo flies apart in a great splash of red. The horns stick in the ground a few feet from our truck.

"As you see, a different design. We took something away from the target . . . in this case, pressure. . . . It can be aimed like a rifle or a pistol . . . suck out an eye, explode a throat. . . . Other facilities besides pressure can be shut off. . . . Oxygen, sleep, dreams, or that most basic of all commodities, time."

Time is a resource. Time runs out. The most basic problem facing any culture is the conservation and disbursement of time. Human time is measured in terms of human change. So the most flagrant time-wasting may minimize change and thus conserve time. The English dictum of never going too far in any direction is actually a time-saving expedient, ill advised to be sure when it may be necessary to go too far in all directions for a bare fighting chance of survival. Utopian concepts stem from a basic misconception as to our mission here. So many snares and dead ends. Nietzsche said, "Men need play and danger. Civilization gives them work and safety."

Some cultures cultivated danger for itself, not realizing that danger derives from conflicting purposes.

Happiness is a by-product of function. Those who seek happiness for itself seek victory without war. This is the flaw in all utopias. A society, like the individuals who compose it, is an ar-

tifact designed for a purpose. As to what life may be worth when the purpose is gone . . .

"We take you now to the Nanyuka Indians of Brazil. They are a simple happy people steeped in rituals that date back to the beginnings of time: the age-old conflict between Men and Women.

"Once upon a time, according to legend, the women seized the Sacred Flutes. But with the aid of a bull-roarer, the men wrested the flutes back from the women and have guarded them in the Men's House ever since. In the Ceremony of the Bees, the men take ritual revenge for the ancient trespass, and swarm through the village like bees, driving the women into the square, where they smear them with greasy black paint, thus preparing the boys for the realities of adult life."

Madre de Dios, what realities? This tawdry pageantry fit for half an hour's entertainment, stretched out over centuries?

"It remains only to paint the wooden birds."

"And now the cycle of ritual is over."

Empty, sad as the graves of dying peoples. . . . The Last Patagonians and the hairy Ainu mark their male graves with an erect phallus crudely carved from wood and painted with ocher . . . wind and dust . . . the markers are broken and scattered. . . .

"The Hummingbird Spirit has been appeased, at least for another year . . . and so we leave the Nanyuka. . . ."

Flute music squeaky, off-key, fades out in one last distant false note.

All the old human rituals are dead as the Bee Ceremony. The human saga flickers out on a darkening stage to an empty house. . . .

A youth looks out over a desert. On his T-shirt is ETERNITY in rainbow letters. He yawns.

Eternity yawning on the sands.

Military operations of one kind or another were always in progress, most of them totally senseless, or rather making a different kind of sense that means nothing to a Westerner. Thought about in Arabic, however, Kim could make out some sort of design, like a device he had been working on to enable the blind to see. They wouldn't be able to see in the usual manner but they could scan out dot patterns rather like the pinpoint style in abstract paintings.

Some of the patterns remain incomprehensible, their roots buried in unwritten antiquity. He would feel the stir of muscles and brain areas, like when you ride for the first time and use muscles you don't use at all walking, and wake up sore, so he would wake up with aches in places he couldn't even find or specify. . . .

Fears and exaltations and griefs from the wild uncharted regions of the mind. . . .

He was currently engaged in another idiotic operation which involved ambushing a truck of soldiers. Here his Owl Eye night sight could be used to advantage.

It's a good kick shooting someone from a distance like God himself hurling a bolt from the heavens or Thor throwing his hammer so different from the face-to-face handgun fight. Rifle duels are common here. The contestants two or three hundred yards apart you can see him through your telescopic sight and

you know he's seeing you . . . a puff of smoke. The bullet hits before you hear the report. It gives you a funny feeling like sound turned off on a screen. . . .

"And perhaps we can blow up a bridge on the way home, sir?"

"Certainly, Lieutenant, if you do a good job on the truck. . . ."

"We won't do our best, Captain. We'll do a lot better."

Kim smiles all slimy and insinuating. . . . "Captain, when I die I want to be buried right in the same coffin with you. . . ."

"What makes you think we are going to die right at the same time, Lieutenant?" the Captain asks with an easy smile. Clearly he enjoys the exchange. . . .

"Well sir, if one of us dies first he simply leaves room for the other, you understand. . . . Have to clear it with the board of health, of course. Can you believe it, sir, in my home town of Saint Louis a board of health regulation, 685, you can't burn rubbish in your own fucking ass pit, if you'll pardon the expression, sir."

Kim knew that the Captain's favorite topic was Washington bureaucrats who are wrecking the country and strangulating us in red tape.

"Like a hernia, Captain."

"Ah yes, very well put, Lieutenant. . . ." Kim presses his advantage. "The men are a bit restless, sir. . . . Couldn't we sack a village, after the bridge, I mean. . . ."

"Of course, Lieutenant. It pays to pay the boys off."

A quote from Tacitus unfurled in Kim's brain. "If a woman or a good-looking boy fell into their hands they were torn to pieces in the struggle for possession while the survivors were left to cut each other's throats. . . ."

"That will be keen, sir. . . ."

Kim showed his teeth in the wild-dog smile. (Wild dogs, you know, show all their teeth at each other as a greeting.) The Captain smiled back. And Kim's fifty ragged boys smiled too

when they got the juicy-fruit news. Don't count your civilians before they're raped.

The ambush was a shambles. Kim's night sight didn't work . . . design was sound enough, just a few technical details to iron out, and an epileptic kid blew it, shooting off his squirt gun in a fit, the whole thirty-shot clip, and the soldiers were out of the truck, strafing our flashes (the flash suppressor didn't work either). Kim gave the order to pull back, leaving fifteen dead. The wounded who couldn't walk had to be shot to keep them from the Turks, who were known torture freaks and ravenous since they rarely took a prisoner.

Not enough of them left to sack a shit house, they decide to join another army. There are no police as such in the area and owing to the fact that everyone is heavily armed the casualties are substantial. Bodies are left in the street and ticketed for twenty-four hours. If friends or relatives haven't claimed them by then they are rendered down into fertilizer.

Might as well make themselves useful. The most young and healthy cadavers are chopped up and fed to the long pigs. Sustained exclusively on human flesh and fresh fruit, they are unspeakably toothsome.

Kim's band falls apart. He goes with three boys to a restaurant on top of a cliff overlooking the valley where the river widens out. He can see sails in the distance, delicate outriggers with paper-thin hardwood hulls and brightly colored sails. He orders a pitcher of Metaxa, dry pungent brandy distilled from pomegranates. . . . The waiter gives them the wild-dog smile and says . . . "Long pig tonight," and comes back in half an hour with an exquisite piglet crackling with juicy fat streaked with pink baby flesh. . . . They finish with the local oranges grown on a poor hillside soil which gives them a spicy tang like herbs in the still noonday heat. They lean back and belch as a twilight like blue dust slowly fills the valley.

Kim thinks lazily of his mission to locate the link, the be-

ginning of human speech. . . . And the throwbacks in remote valleys who still use the larynx as a sexual organ . . . rather like
those horrid kissing fish, Kim thinks with distaste, the way their
mouths click together. The first words were unspeakably
foul. . . . And that is why they have not been uttered for a million years except in those remote valleys. . . . Kim remembers a
story:

The Hounds of Tindalos, March 1929 . . . No words in our
language can describe them . . . symbolized vaguely in the myth
of the Fall . . . obscene ancient tablets. . . . The Greeks had a
name for them to veil their essential foulness. . . . As soon as you
name something you reduce its power, of course, the power of a
foulness essential to their function. . . . They must be too horrible to name or look at. . . . If you could look Death in the face he
would lose his power to kill you. *Quién es?* When you ask Death
for his credentials you are dead. His passport picture is your
deathmask, to get back to these bloody hounds a most awful
mystery, Frank a terrible and unspeakable *deed* was done in the
beginning. Was no words for it in the beginning of what exactly?
In the beginning of the results of this deed, vat else? Before
time, the deed started time and dumped all this shit in our
laps. . . . The seeds of the deed, in dim recesses, are hungry and
thirsty. . . . In a white glare that was not light, in shrieking silence I heard them breathe, felt their breath upon my face. . . .

Things are getting worse and worse you gotta be crazy you
wanta get reborned. We'll be pushing around shopping carts full
of documents like money it takes more and more to buy less and
less same way with documents it takes more and more to prove
less and less you go through days of waiting in offices to get
some document but the bureaucracy has etted more of the tax-
payer's green grass and shitted out more laws your pistol permit
is buried under tons of it. You don't got Form 4F-Q you don't
got nothing less than nothing even if you don't have it they will
come and take it away from you. . . .

I fled down quintillions of years but they scented me. They
thirst for that which is clean . . . which emerged from the deed

without stain this they hate. They are that which in the beginning fell away from cleanliness ... just naturally dirty like the shit-eating, cringing, vicious, fawning beasts they are, receptacles of all foulness. In this universe there is only the pure and the foul. ... So the foul long for purity, which they can only see as food, and the pure want a vicarious little whiff of foulness.

And this annoys the foul. "Oh dear, you're all sick and ugly inside, aren't you, you poor little creature. ..."

The foul expresses itself through angles. That so?

Man, the pure part of him, is descended from a curve. Now what kind of curve you throwing us, Chambers? A cunt curve...? I don't intend to stay and listen to such gibberish. ... A long rest in a good sanitarium should benefit you immeasurably.

"They must be kept out. Reach us only through the angles, you know. ... We must eliminate all angles from this room. ... Mother, save me from the hounds. ... Send 'em back ravenous, snarling, frustrated to the foulness that was in the beginning before time and space. ... It was good of you to help ... acrid nauseous odor ... doubled me over it did sir, like a kick in the stomach sir, lost my porridge sir, the way you can tell a real gentleman is a real gentleman isn't mean."

The reporter reluctantly parts with ten shillings.

He lay naked, his chest and arms covered with bluish pus gave off a smell like rotten solder. "Must beware of the Doels. They can help them break through, you know who they are, of course. The satyrs will help. They can gain entrance through the scarlet circle, the Greeks knew a way of preventing that. Good God, the plaster is falling. ... It is getting dark in the room ... their tongues."

Kim needed to piss. He slid cautiously out of his hammock, picked up his shoes, and shook a scorpion out and killed it with the hard rubber sole. He put on his shoes and stepped out of the

door into brilliant moonlight, with only his shorts and his belt with the 44 revolver. Facing the cliff he pissed a silver stream. The night air, balmy and cool around the edges, fanned his body. At that second the dogs started barking, somebody coming. The other boys were already out of their hammocks with weapons ready. A wall of cactus seals off the house. There is a narrow gate of barbed wire. . . .

"Advance and be recognized. And it better be worth all this horrid yapping." The innkeeper's son held up a lantern. A boy stood there cool and debonair. He had a revolver in a cartridge belt, a Bowie knife, and he was carrying a cane of whip steel loaded at the end.

"I bring important message for *Captain* Carsons. . . ."

The gate was unhooked, the dogs rushed forward snarling.

"Let me administer the correction. Otherwise the dogs hate you and will leap at your throat when you are sick or wounded, after the nature of their species. . . . Back, hounds of Tindalos. Receptacles of filth." He lashed out with his cane and snarls turned to yelps and the dogs crept into their filthy warrens. The boy smiled and flexed his cane. "You see, Meester Carsons, I am a fellow dog-hater." He flashed the wild-dog smile.

"What's so fucking important to wake everybody up with a hard-on?"

"I am here to show you the way to the larynx fuckers. . . ." He made a noise in his throat that set Kim's teeth on edge.

"Yeah? Well I'm not sure I want to go. . . ."

"You forget your mission, Meester Carsons? Maybe somebody come remind you. . . ."

"All right all right, give me time to get dressed for chrissakes. . . ."

Kim collected his gear and weapons, his 44 revolver, his spring knife, a 38 snubby and his wafer-thin 22 and a very light semi-automatic carbine in 45-caliber with a 14-inch barrel and a ten-shot clip, an ounce of morphine and an ounce of hash, first-aid kit, canteen and mess kit. . . . The three boys, when he told

them they were going very far to the east, decided not to go. Ten minutes later he fell in beside the boy and they were walking silently into the desert. They must have walked for three hours, both using the sorcerer's gait, leaning slightly forward. Finally they were challenged by a sentry. . . . The boy gave the password. Dawn was on the way and in the gray light he could see the dirigible moored to a steel tower, bobbing in the rising wind. . . . They quickly climbed the ladder and entered the cabin, which seemed to be roomy enough. . . .

There were three other men already there. The boy made the introductions.

"Doctor Schindler, Kim Carsons." . . . The other two names he didn't catch. Kim was hopeless with names and he had a memory system of immediately turning a name into a picture or concept: Carsons: A car spits a baby out of the exhaust pipe. It didn't work with these two nameless assholes, but he knew the type . . . secret agents, assassins . . . gray neutral men with cold dead eyes.

The motor hums and they take off with a wind behind them. They can walk around in the cabin and look out the observation windows.

Three days later they land in an ancient yellow landscape. A jackal trots by and looks at them indifferently. They are somewhere in Arabia. They watch soberly as the dirigible rises into the air and heads back west.

"Well what now?" Kim asks.

One of the agents, whose name Kim now knows is Ahearn (Ah *earn* . . . for hire), says without conviction:

"We're supposed to rendezvous with the Brits."

And the other's name is Williams. Williams says:

"Probably mucking about with Arab boys."

"Ah, this must be our contact. . . ." Ahearn points to a cloud of dust approaching from the east. Now they make out the car with huge wheels and tires. The car comes to a stop in front of them in a cloud of yellow dust.

"Hello, you chaps." It's Tony Outwaite with shorts and sun helmet and swagger stick.

"Major Outwaite M-5, Ahearn and Williams CIA, and Doctor Schindler."

The CIA men are clearly outraged by this introduction, as Kim intends.

"Well pile in. Want to get there before the sun gets any higher."

Headquarters is a cluster of Quonset huts on a bare hillside. Kim finds himself sharing a hut with Tony and Doc Schindler.

"Those spooks make me nervous with their bloody trade craft," Tony says.

"What's the date?" Kim asks.

"December 23, 1984."

"I would have sworn it was the twenty-second. . . . So what exactly are we doing here?"

"Haven't the haziest notion. . . . It's something about the human voice as the ultimate weapon. . . . Can't let the Yanks run away with a thing like that. . . . Have us all chewing gum, what, and eating Wheaties. . . . Well the Larynx Rubbers are somewhere in the area, it's our job to find them. . . . After that it gets technical. . . ."

The doctor polishes his glasses with liquid lens cleaner. . . . He indicates the bottle. . . . "It's quite hard to get, you know. . . . Cut into the tissue monopoly and they didn't like it one bit. . . . Put the whisper out. You go into a drugstore and ask for spot lens cleaner and they look at you like you asked for cocaine. . . . My original training was as a linguist. Then I did some fieldwork in South America and went on to specialize in interspecies communication. . . ."

"I'd say all communication was interspecies." Tony puts in.

"Of course. But you don't get a navy appropriation saying things like that. . . . The theory is when flying saucers or whatever kind of spacecraft land I'll be able to communicate with them through a breakdown of communication units. . . ."

"Maybe they've already landed in the human brain and nervous system," Kim says.

The doctor nods.... "Same problem.... You've got an alien inside you, how do you communicate? Find out what he wants ... make him leave.... You have to find him first, and you find him by inference units ... study of the larynx people could give us a vital clue ... a way to descend into our own minds and confront the intruder on what he is trying to make his home ground."

"Well let's get on with it...." Tony walks over to a map. "Now I think we've spotted a settlement in here, there's a valley closed at both ends ... and water.... We could get in by parachute or helicopter."

"Out of the question," says the doctor.... "We have no way of knowing what effect this might produce on these people...."

"We could use hang-gliders or balloons.... Climbing is out of the question."

"The Yanks plan to go in with a chopper—"

"They must be stopped!"

"They've been stopped for the moment"—Tony holds up a piece of metal—"but we'd best get started before they start jetting in parts and spook the area.... Find our Larynxes all dead of fright like so many minks...."

They climb into the Sand Bug.... "Balloons and gas tanks," Tony said, indicating crates of equipment.... "That's how we get in and hopefully get out."

The Sand Bug took off in a splatter of stones. They were climbing precipitous mountain roads, little more than trails in some places, cut into red sandstone that gives the area its name: the Red Lands. Several times the buggy skidded inches from a sheer overhang drop of a thousand feet, the tires spattering stones into the abyss. But Tony was an expert driver with a feel for the car like his own skin.

THUMP. A stone clanked against the bottom of the car.

"Just hope those gas cylinders don't go up on us."
Tony grumbled. "It's a hell of a thing to reassemble oneself after an explosion."

The road ended in scrub and cactus. Twenty yards away they could see the edge of a crater. Tony consulted his map.

"This must be it."

They got out. Kim noted bright red cactus blossoms like blood against the red stone, which suddenly writhed in front of his eyes.

"*Back,*" Tony snapped. Kim saw a tiny snake the exact color of the red stone. It was a foot long and thin as a pencil.

"Kill it."

"If you say so." Kim drew his smooth-bore shot pistol and blew the snake to bloody writhing fragments.

"It's Kwakiutl," Tony explained. . . . "Horrible death. . . . Erotic convulsions . . . die spurting blood out of your prick."

"How folkloric."

They walk over to the crater and Kim stops about six feet from the edge (he is very squeamish about heights) and peers down. The crater is about three hundred yards across and roughly egg-shaped. Two thousand feet down Kim can see a silver ribbon of water and a smudge of green. . . .

"Well we might as well get on with it before we have the afternoon wind to cope with. . . ." Tony's voice trails off. He is walking along the edge of the crater, much closer than Kim will venture. Kim follows with a wider margin.

"I'm looking for an overhang. . . . Can't have the balloons bumping against the cliff . . . sharp spine of quartz. . . . Ah, here we are. . . . Run the Bug over here. . . ."

"I can't drive."

"Oh uh quite. . . . Should have given you the pill. . . . Well. . . ." He signals to Schindler, who is examining a cactus blossom with a magnifying glass. . . . Schindler drives the Bug within fifteen feet of the edge. They unload the balloons and gas cylinders and a parachute for the extra cylinders, which are designed to lift them back out of the crater.

"First things first. . . . We have to be sure the cylinders are down there. . . . Lend a hand, you chaps. . . . One . . . Two . . . Three . . .

The cylinders weigh several hundred pounds but they manage to swing them out over the edge. The parachute opens. Tony looks down through binoculars. . . . "There it is, right by the stream. . . . Now for the balloons."

The balloons are pink, presumably for camouflage against the red rock of the cliff. . . .

Tony was reading the directions on the cylinder. . . .

"Let's see. . . . It screws on just here. . . . Be sure gasket is firmly attached before opening gas valve. . . ."

There is a hiss of gas and the balloon starts to inflate. . . . And now it floats free like a great pink erection. . . .

Kim says, *"Bravo."*

Kim puts on the harness and Tony attaches it as the balloon floats above him. He can feel the tug pulling him up and a lightness in his limbs. This must be like walking on the moon. . . .

"You weigh about seven pounds now. . . . Get the feel of it. . . ."

Kim heads away from the crater and jumps rather cautiously. He is catapulted thirty feet in the air and drifts down. . . . He stands poised on his toes like a ballet dancer. . . .

"What an *entrechat* I could do with this on me. . . ."

Tony and Schindler are now ready. . . .

"All right chaps, I'll go first. . . ." Tony picks up a collapsible aluminum pole seven feet long. . . .

"In case you get too close to the cliff. . . . Now watch. . . ."

He steps to the edge and braces his feet. . . .

"Jump up and OUT." He pushes his feet like a high dive except he goes up forty feet in the air then slowly settles into the crater.

Kim jumps last. At first he is exhilarated, balancing himself in the air like a tightrope walker and nodding graciously to an imaginary audience. He can almost smell the peanuts and the

elephants. Below him he can see the other balloons floating down like the Goya picture. . . .

He is going down slower and slower. The air is getting thicker and thicker, like water. He remembers that pressure will crush a diving bell, it's one of the limitations to exploring the ocean floor where these special fish live.

He is settling into some heavy viscid medium untouched for millions of years. It clings to his body, suffocating him. He takes a deep breath. . . . Something is lacking in this air . . . not oxygen but something almost as essential, some life-sustaining element that this gummy stagnant air doesn't have. . . . No one can *live* here, he decides.

At last his feet touch the ground. Tony is driving an aluminum mooring peg into the ground with a light sledgehammer. . . .

"I think it might be wise to put in the extra gas right now in case we have to lift off in a hurry. . . ."

"Not a breath of air. . . . 'Where the dead leaf fell there did it rest.' " No leaves, though. Just misshapen bulbous bushes six to eight feet high bearing a purple fruit covered with soft down.

"There is something here that is just awful," Kim says.

The balloons are moored and inflated with extra gas. Tony shows Kim and Schindler how to let out gas and bring the balloon down when they are clear of the crater. They leave the harnesses on so all they have to do is hitch up and cast off. . . . Kim looks at the three pink balloons. Rather like a hitching rail. Kim remembers his "strawberry." Quite suddenly the equine went berserk and attacked him, ears laid back, teeth bare, striking out with its front hooves. . . . Kim pivoted to the side and shot the beast in the neck, severing an artery. The blood spattered him as the animal sank to its knees, eyes wild. Another shot in the side of the head and it rolled sideways, kicked three times, and died.

Tony is sweeping the crater walls with his binoculars. Schindler is examining the flora, which, even to Kim's untrained eye, seems remarkably uniform. . . . The plants are growing along the riverbanks. The stems are covered with fine purple

tendrils exuding a crystal gum. Kim steps to the riverbank. The water is sluggish. He sees no sign of fish or frogs or water spiders.

Schindler is taking specimens.... "A completely unknown species.... And what is more remarkable it seems to be the only or certainly the predominant flora.... Usually in a valley like this, no matter how inaccessible, there will be some variety of plants ... seeds dropped or defecated by birds...."

"What birds?"

"Uh ... yes...." Schindler looks about uneasily.... Not a sound or sight of bird or animal or insect, just the slowly moving water and the bulbous plants....

"They look like seaweed," Kim says.

"As a matter of fact ..."

Schindler is setting up his camera tripod and snapping pictures....

"I say, you chaps," Tony calls.... "I saw something move...." He points toward the crater walls....

"Over there."

Schindler points his camera with telescopic zoom lens.... He picks out what looks like a red-ass monkey about eighteen inches in height ... foetal, almost transparent, he can see the black viscera through soft crystalline pink flesh ... he makes out something attached to the creature just below the navel ... hummmm, he remembers an Egyptian bas-relief with erect penis, the penis high, located just below the navel.... What he saw was a sort of bladder or balloon floating in front of the monkey.... Click click ... They are advancing cautiously toward the crater wall.... One specimen, which had apparently been foraging, retracts the bladder into its body and scampers for the cliff.

"My God, hundreds of them." Click click ...

"My God, what's that STINK?"

Tony sniffs appraisingly.... "Rotten blood.... I smelled it in Belsen.... We were moving in, trying to intercept a top S.S. war criminal ... slipped by us.... The S.S. had machine-

gunned the inmates they were piled up three-deep soaked in blood ... many of them had been bayoneted or killed with knives.... Been there three days.... There's no stench like it.... It seems sweet, at first. You wonder what sort of flower could smell like that.... You take a deep breath and puke your guts out.... It's rotten and musty and the sweetness catches in your throat.... Not a sharp smell, like carrion.... It's smooth and it creeps into you.... Even after work crews in gas masks had taken the bodies away and swabbed the floors down with carbolic solution the smell was still there.... Once you smell it you never forget it. This is close enough...."

And now they *hear* it.... The voice of that smell ... a thick slimy whisper that sticks to them like rotten garbage ... an ancient evil crooning sound that stirs and twists in their throats, the converse between the creature and the bladder.

Along the crater walls they see warrens worn smooth by countless years.... Here the monkeys have taken refuge, peering out with dead undersea eyes....

Click click click click ... It comes to Kim in a flash. The Museum of Natural History in New York ... life cycle and preserved specimens of a certain deep-sea fish that lives in lightless depths. (This is the Lophiform Angler fish. The female is about fifty times larger than the male.) During intercourse the male gets attached to the body of the female and is slowly absorbed until only the testicles remain protruding from the female body.... He remembers the sick horror he felt ... so much worse than spiders or scorpions that simply eat the male on the spot.... He can see the whole life cycle.... The bladder is the female that slowly absorbs the male.... The bladders are in fact immortal, using male after male.

"Should we attempt to capture a specimen?" Schindler asks doubtfully.

"Shit no," Kim says.... "Let's get the fuck out of here."

"All right.... Just let me finish this roll...." Click click click.

"Ten-second intervals.... You go first, Kim."

Kim doesn't argue. It's like one of those flying dreams where you soar up like a rocket. . . . Looking down at that dead-end pool of rotten blood he didn't even feel curious to know more.

"*Je n'en veux rien savoir.* . . ."

Now he is clear of the crater, drifting thirty feet above the ground. He can see the car beneath him as he opens the valve to release gas and the balloon settles.

As soon as his feet touch the ground he steps free of the harness and opens the valve all the way and moves quickly out of the way. The balloon jets fifteen feet in the air and collapses on the ground in a heap, like one of those awful bladders.

They are all assembled and the balloons deflated. . . .

"I move we leave this shit right here . . ." Kim says, pointing to the balloons . . . "God knows what they may have sopped up. . . . Our clothes too, we should burn every stitch as soon as we get back to base. . . ."

As they drive back Kim hears choppers overhead. . . .

"Put your little foot put your little foot put your little foot right in," Kim hums.

It's a long hot dusty ride and Kim concocts a poem to allay the discomfort and boredom. . . .

> The heart of the rulers is sick
> And the High Priest covers his head
> For this is the song of the quick
> That is heard by the ears of the dead
>
> The widows of Langley are long in their wail
> And the idols are broken in the temples of Yale
> And the might of the asshole unsmote by the
>   sword
> Hath melted like snow in the glance of the bored.

The town of Ganymede has grown into a settlement housing fifteen hundred technicians, scientists, and military personnel,

with air-conditioned Quonset huts, a bar, a movie, and a choice of restaurants. A black M.P. checks their passes and directs them to a decontamination station.

An hour later, showered and scrubbed with carbolic soap, wearing clean khakis, Kim feels approximately clean but every now and then he gets a whiff of the vile smell of the bladder monkeys. After three stiff gin-and-tonics and a hookah of hashish he feels better still.

They are eating in a pizza place out by the airport. Kim saws at the rubbery crust.

"I didn't bring you out here for the cuisine, my dear," Tony says, looking at his wristwatch.

A chopper is coming in for a landing and clearly in trouble, wobbling from side to side.

"Looks like the pilot's got a skinful . . ." someone says at an adjoining table. . . .

"You can say that again," Tony mutters.

Fire trucks and ambulances are already on the runway, sirens blaring.

"Watch." Tony takes out his binocular camera and Kim does the same. . . .

The doors of the chopper burst open and three men lurch out. . . .

Click click . . . The ambulance crew rush forward to help, then start back in horror. . . . Click click . . . The faces are demented, inhuman, throats hideously swollen and covered with pustules. . . . Click click . . .

They are yacking like ventriloquist dummies, and Kim can see something stirring and twisting in their tumescent throats, choking words out. Bloody spit hangs down off their chins in long streamers. . . . Click click . . .

"Let's get out of here fast . . ." Tony says. He throws a note on the table and they sprint for the parking lot. . . .

Before they reach the car, the voice rings from loudspeakers. . .

"Notice to all personnel. . . . This is an emergency mea-

sure. . . . The streets are closed to all civilian personnel . . ."

"Hope to God it starts. . . ." The motor turns over. . . .

". . . or pedestrians. . . . If you are inside, stay where you are. . . ."

A guard is hooking a chain across the exit and locking it. . . .

"Otherwise proceed *immediately* to the nearest shelter. . . ."

"Hey YOU . . . STOP." The guard holds up his hand and reaches for his 45.

Tony accelerates and knocks the guard over the chain and across the street. The broken chain whips around the car with a crack like a rifle shot. Tony takes a right, tires screeching.

"Repeat . . . The streets are closed to all unauthorized personnel. . . . Violators will be shot on sight. . . ."

Sirens, searchlights . . . Tony ducks as machine-gun fire shatters the windshield. . . . He pulls the car off the road and down a steep slope, scattering a herd of goats. . . . A screech of brakes behind them as the police car pulls up—a light searching the slope.

The car splashed through an irrigation ditch and turned left on a dirt road. The sounds of pursuit were sucked out as if run backward.

"Here's where we shift vehicles."

Just ahead was a carriage. They got in and Tony gave directions to the driver in a dialect unknown to Kim. . . .

"He is Malay," Tony explained as he settled back and lit a cheroot. A beggar child padded alongside and Kim flipped him a coin. They drove for perhaps an hour. . . . The night air was balmy, and hot around the edges. Kim could hear crickets and frogs.

Occasionally they passed mud huts with thatched roofs.

And there was the dirigible ahead, moored to a tower. . . . The Commander waved to them. . . .

"Well climb aboard, you blokes. . . . We're all revved up and ready to go. . . ."

Two Malay servants helped them carry their gear up the ladder and deposited it in their luxurious cabins. . . .

"You understand the Big Picture, old thing. We are retracing our steps in time like a film running backward, breaking the immutable rules of the universe and all that rot. . . ."

"And about time too."

Dinner was kulan steaks. . . .

"They are practically extinct, you know," Tony told him between mouthfuls.

"Bring on the whooping crane," Kim whooped.

"And a dodo-egg omelette. . . ."

The Commander laughed heartily and twirled his mustache. Kim stretched luxuriously, savoring the vintage Burgundy like a fifteen-year-old schoolboy on holiday.

Tony shot him a reproving look.

"Well I *am* going backward, aren't I?"

"Yes, but observe the speed limit."

"I *adore* dirigibles. It's like floating along in a *gigantic* erection."

"Ah yes, very well put." The Commander shot him a glance as piercing as it was meaningless.

"I'd like baked Alaska for dessert," Kim said primly.

"Well it just so happens . . . and quite a decent champagne . . . the oily kind, you know. . . ."

"Reserve Heidsieck."

As he spooned the last of the baked Alaska into his mouth and a Malay refilled their glasses, the Commander arched his eyebrows. . . .

"And what have you lads been up to?"

"Well how would you put it, Kim? As an English public schoolboy?"

"You mean like I was selling a screenplay to Hollywood? In one sentence, what is this epoch-making film about? Well speaking as an English public schoolboy, it's just too disgusting to talk about. . . . Same character forty years later speaking as an Old Auntie:

" 'No force of man or God could ever bring me to reveal what I saw in that cursed valley. . . . There are secrets that no man may learn and keep his reason.'

" 'In the beginning of time was a deed so foul that we have been fleeing it ever since, down the months and down the days, down the labyrinths of the years . . . hiding behind a million empty masks to cover a bottomless terror. . . . Building cities, waging wars, playing games, anything to keep us from seeing the horror of our origins. . . .'

"You don't sell a film by saying you won't show it. There may be secrets too horrible for a man to know and keep his sanity but that won't go down in Hollywood, Mister.

" 'We saw the origins of human speech, the beginning and end of the word. We saw the start of a plague that will rage through cities of the world like a topping forest fire.' "

The dreaded Talk Sickness, also known as the Dummies, or the Yacks. . . . So named since the first symptom is a yacking manner of speech like a ventriloquist's dummy. In a few hours the blood coagulates and rots in the veins. The throat swells to the size of a watermelon and death usually results from asphyxiation. From the onset the victim's mental faculties are affected. . . . He loses all sense of human decency or consideration for his fellows. Knowing himself doomed he delights in infecting others.

Here is a crowded restaurant, two men are talking at the bar. . . .

"What do you think about this merger, B.J.? Off the record. . . ."

"It sucks," B.J. yacks.

Silence falls like a thunderclap.

"THE YACKS! THE YACKS! THE YACKS!"

The patrons scream as they rush the exits.

It's the most contagious disease ever seen on this planet. Here is a crowded commuter train. . . .

"Tickets please," the conductor yacks.

"THE YACKS! THE YACKS! THE YACKS!"

The commuters pull the emergency cord out of its socket but even as the train grates to a halt the whole car is yacking.

A country-western singer goes dummy on stage.

"Stay all night and stay a little longer . . ."

Just a hint of a yack. The crowd stirs uneasily in their seats.

"Take off your coat and throw it in a corner . . ."

No doubt about it.

"THE YACKS! THE YACKS! THE YACKS!"

"Don't see why you don't stay a little longer . . ."

They are piled up three-deep at the exits where 123 died.

Perhaps one percent of those stricken adapt themselves to the sickness and form outlaw bands. They will swarm out of a derelict building and yack in the faces of pedestrians: "We love New York!" or stick their heads into car windows and yack out: "Have a good day!"

The putrid smell of rotten blood hangs over cities of the world like a smog.

"It's a real Hollywood Spectacular."

Kim frequently placed himself in remote jungle outposts, or in Antarctica, or on some alien planet. Here is a page from Kim's Venusian Diary:

November 19, 1980. This is the first settlement on Planet Venus. Evening Star is supposed to be representative, so there has to be a gay couple. It wasn't easy to put *that* across. It took ten years, and it was a long, bloody, dirty fight. And we won by being more ruthless, more devious, more resourceful and a lot smarter than our creeping Venusian opponents, cowering in occupied human bodies. They shit-sure didn't want any *unoccupied* observers on their stinking asshole planet.

I am rooming with Tom in the government compound. We get along well enough with the neighbors. The Bensons come over once a week for dinner. Beverly Benson is a good old girl who drinks too much. And one of our best friends is Martin Winters, Chief of Security, a gun buff from Colorado.

Of course, Tom and I have our spats. In Los Angeles before the expedition, our nerves a bit frayed from the long fight to get on the space program, I came back to the hotel to find clothing strewn all over the apartment. And Tom says, "Kim, your fucking trade stole my bathing trunks!"

"You lie in your capped teeth. It was your own Chicano done it."

"No one can tell me my teeth are capped!" Tom flings back, stung to the gums.

"Oh yes, 'Nobody knows about *meeee*. . . .' "

Personnel are housed in identical long huts of petrified peat with aluminum roofs. On one side is a steep slope of scrub and thorn bushes, leading down to the edge of a pestilent swamp. We can look out through heavy glass windows, like portholes, at the nightmare landscape, the swamp to the sky, the interlocking islands and peninsulas, many of them floating masses of vegetation, all under sulfurous clouds.

Kim got a chill looking down into a clear deep pool, just beyond the shoreline. He could see way down, five hundred feet, into clear green water where strange predators lurked like black shadows. The garbage chutes were pushed out through the wall and retracted lest some noxious creature gain access. Scavengers devour every morsel of garbage before it can reach the water, where other scavengers would have made equally short work of it. An aquatic centipede (that attains a length of six feet) with a thick reddish-brown shell sometimes darted out of the water to fight for some choice morsels with the land crabs and the terrible Smuns, and sometimes there were swarms of tiny vultures no bigger than hummingbirds. . . .

Tom looks up sharply from his crossword puzzle.

"What's noxious in the kitchen?" he demands.

"It's possum." Kim waltzes around humming "The Anniversary Waltz." . . . "A surprise for our anniversary."

"That possum couldn't surprise anyone half a mile downwind," Tom says flatly. "Tell me frankly, Kim, what were the circumstances surrounding its death?"

Kim looks at him complacently as if he were announcing his pregnancy. He sings:

> "Possum ain't far
> Thar he are thar. . . ."

He points to the far end of the hut, which serves as the kitchen.

"I have no reason to doubt it. What I want to know is *how* did it die? and *when*?"

"At the last full moon . . . the time is now ripe. . . ."

"You could say so."

Kim leafs through a Venusian cookbook. . . . "It's called *La Cuisine de Peste* . . . disease cooking. . . . You see, when an animal dies of a certain illness it imparts a certain flavor to the meat. . . . Fortunately for us, our possum succumbed to climactic buboes. . . . Swollen groin glands . . . They swell, they burst, they suppurate. . . ."

And indeed, disgusting farting noises are emanating from the kitchen. . . . Kim reads from the cookbook.

" 'There is no pleasure short of love-making to equal the crunchy, curdy . . .' "—Kim sticks his middle finger in his mouth and pops it out with a loud "POP," spraying saliva across the table—" 'of a suppurating bubo cooked in aftosa spit. . . . *And* there will be candied suckling armadillos cooked in their own leprosy . . . pearl-white phosphorescent meat soft as butter, you cut it with a lead knife . . . when the knife *sinks* through the · meat is ready . . . unspeakably *toothsome*. . . .' " Kim bares his teeth, lays back his ears and purrs like a hungry cat.

"Look, honey face, whyn't you nip down to the PX for Spam and canned pineapple . . . ?"

"Oh why do you have to spoil everything!" Kim wails, rubbing his hands. . . . There is a muffled explosion from the kitchen and such a vile stink billows out that they are both thrown retching to the floor. . . .

"Get it out of here, for the love of God!" Tom screams. They don masks and manage to get the stinking potful into the chute and dump it. They pull the chute back in and draw up stools in front of the window. Smuns wriggle up and grab the steaming carrion in the air. . . . Scavenger land crabs big as plates swarm from burrows in the slope, snapping up the bits that fall from the slavering, steaming jaws of the Smuns. (And all this in deadly silence broken only by sounds of chewing and rending—not a snarl or even a whimper as one Smun disembowels another with a side kick of its deadly claws.)

Kim is writing at the kitchen table. There is an open can of beans in front of him.

Of course Kim never had the intention to eat the funky old possum. It was just a spoof to break the monotony. . . . The G.I. jokes . . . The horror outside . . . This hideous alien place . . . Kim knew now that all the places that had ever dragged him were simply reflections of this horrible planet. . . . The vampirism of Egypt, which got a technological face-lift to suck England and America dry . . . a dead hopelessness in the slave classes, the incredible brutality of the police. . . . They are a race apart, huge men six foot six and heavy with iron muscle.

Kim remembers a young Arab guide who inadvisedly led Kim out of the tourist area, which is like an airport on many levels, with shops, restaurants, and films all of the dreariest caliber but brightly modern like the smiles turned on for the tourists.

Kim sits down at a garish food counter, all neon chrome and mirrors. The only dish seems to be fried banana chips with marshmallow sauce and at the end of the counter is this scrawny old Lesbian naked to the waist, her lungs hanging down like deflated balloons, eating a hole plateful of this muck.

Kim walks down in front of a movie marquee and propositions a group of sullen adolescents. They inform him in Venusian that there is no word for it here.

A young Arab guide he knows from Tangier offers to show him something interesting. They go down a ramp that leads out of the tourist area ... muddy canals here and heavy timber, what looks like a logging camp. ... To Kim's left a muddy street sloping steeply upward past miserable-looking mud huts, cut in clay. Down by the canal a youth he knew from the Dilly circuit transformed into a creature with the lower limbs of a frog, eyes dead and rotten-looking, he dips a clay ladle into the water, drinks deep, and falls back unconscious on the muddy bank. ... "The waters of Lethe" trilled in his ears. ... He hears an angry shout. He notices now the loggers. Hulking brutes, well over six feet. They are screaming at the guide. ... "Why you bring tourist here?" The guide turns green with fear and runs for the tourist center, five of these cops right behind him. They catch him. ... A thin discarded cry ... The first slap must have killed him but they worry the corpse a bit like greyhounds with a rabbit. They go back to their logging.

"You better get back to the tourist place where you belong. ..."

Another glimpse: The tourist area shades away into the underworld. Kim sees passages and arcades leading down into lightless depths.

"And what do you think of my people?"

It is a Venusian lady of the highest caste. Kim has seen her before someplace.

"Speaking from an Intourist point of view, you mean? I don't want to get anyone else into trouble. ..."

Kim steps forward gingerly to get a better look ... worn stone steps, narrow passageways between clay walls slanting steeply down. ... shops like Gibraltar, Tangier, Panama, selling those ivory balls one inside the other, hideous tapestries, carvings in jade and soapstone ... shoddy merchandise going down into darkness. ... Kim has heard that the houses down there are put together using human excrement as mortar. He smells no reason to doubt it ... darkness fills the lower levels like water

with the smell of countless years of encrusted shit and sweat and unwashed bodies crowded into tiny cubicles. . . .

"Yes," says an old resident. "It's bad here in the summer . . . gets up to 140 then you lose count. It's torture to move and in the winter when it gets down below zero you will need summer shit to chink the cracks."

"Down there"—she gestures to the lightless depths—"are blind humanoid centipedes and scorpions. . . ."

"Ah yes," Kim says, anxious to impress the grande dame with his erudition. . . . "Like the Egyptian Watch Goddess, who is a beautiful and irresistible woman. . . . When man wakes up him find she has the head of a scorpion, pincers in his face and dead greedy insect eyes. . . ."

"I see you have been well instructed," she says dryly.

Kim decides to say nothing.

The tourist area ends here in an area of vacant lots. In this no-man's-land the underworld of Venus ply their incredibly precarious trades, for punishments are severe. . . .

"It's all so unpleasant." In a sad little square lit by Primus gas lanterns that flicker and spurt, the poor have gathered for a handout. . . . This consists of some metallic matter that is cut with a lead knife and shows a bright silver sheen when freshly cut, like sodium. . . . Little slivers of this metal paste are handed out to the needy, who have all brought their own bowls, from which they gobble greedily, the metal flashing in the light . . . as if they are signaling in phosphorus flashes. . . . Kim drifts on.

A man has bared his arm and he is about to slash it with a razor for his *"niños"* (for some reason he seems to be speaking in Spanish . . .) and he did cut himself and the blood ran down *"para sus niños, madre de Cristo."* Was it ever distasteful. . . . Kim wrote in his guidebook that on the planet Venus entertainment reaches an all-time low. . . . One can, with a special pass, witness the "evening meal . . . in which food is ritually handed out to the poor. It will save both the tourists and the Venusian authorities embarrassment if tourists will just understand we

have rules and they are intended to be obeyed. Certain areas are off limits to tourists. Unscrupulous guides or drivers may direct you to such a place. If this happens it is your duty as a tourist to report the incident without delay. . . ."

The Shmunn is a predator with the powerful hind-quarters of a hyena and the hyena's bonebreaking jaws. There the resemblance ends and indeed this foul beast beggers description. Blind, entirely silent and devoid of vocal cords, they are guided by scent perceptors that cover the entire body, which is pale pink, pitted and porous like pumice stone. It's a terrible sight to see a Shmunn smelling its way in, its whole body writhing in peristalsis, steaming caustic saliva dripping from its fangs. The Shmunn is devoid of an anus, voiding waste products through the skin, which gives off such a foul odor as to repel the hardiest predator. And the body temperature of the Shmunn is 212°, the boiling point of water. The creature has such a rapid metabolism that it literally burns for food. At the smell of food it quivers with excitement as the boiling frenzied digestive juices flare through its flesh like a furnace. It has to eat every twenty-four hours to stay alive. It will eat anything alive or dead. A pack of these creatures, owing to their high body temperature, steam off such a pestilent cloud of noxious vapors that in many cases the prey is already incapacitated before the serrated shark teeth and the tongue sharp and hard as a rasp go to work.

The Shmunn is also armed with an interlocking network of razor-sharp in-curving claws on its four feet. It can throw itself on one side and kick upward with its hind claws to disembowel an opponent. And any wound inflicted by a Shmunn will cause death by infection within twenty-four hours. The virulence of such infections in this steaming inferno of explosive

growth must be seen to be believed. A man who cut himself while shaving died of tetanus before lunch.

As for the miniature vultures, I have so far seen none of them but today I heard a strange rumor in the marketplace. [Kim was learning Venusian and he frequently circulated in public gathering places disguising himself as a beggar or an itinerant entertainer. Kim could do magic tricks and juggling.]

So I start to tell Tom about this rumor I picked up today, disguised as a diseased beggar in the marketplace, about "Soul Suckers" and without even waiting for me to go on Tom says he doesn't believe in souls anyhoo, he knows I hate to hear anyone say anyhoo so I shoot back,

"You should keep an open mind *and stuff*."

And he grins at me. . . . He can be so irritating at times, like the putdown nagging wife they dragged out of the archetype closet and one time I did a little skit:

Hubby comes in all full of enthusiasm and mixes a drink. Wifey watches his hand and catches him trying to add another dollop. . . .

"I've just been looking over the new place, darling, and it looks *great*. . . ."

"That sounds tacky."

Hubby finishes his drink.

"Oh, you'll like it when you see it, darling."

"I've had a terrible headache all day. . . ."

"Oh uh I'm sorry to hear that, can I get you an aspirin?"

"Certainly not." She glares at him indignantly.

Hubby sidles unobtrusively into the kitchen . . . thinking someone should invent a silent drink mixer.

"*Are you mixing another drink?*"

I showed this to Tom and told him he acted that way sometimes and he didn't think it was funny *at all*.

So I took a big dose of majoun, which is why the

whole possum scene took place and stuff. And I keep getting off the subject of the rumor I picked up today from a traveling merchant into smuggling mostly . . . Red Devil and Dream Dust . . . force knives . . . the usual line. . . . Well he told me over a glass of khat that in the areas south of here occupied by a number of ancient decaying city states well there are these creatures with human heads about the size of a fist . . . and shimmering insect wings and they stick out from their mouths this long proboscis . . . which penetrates right to these special places in the nervous system and sucks all the soul and spirit right out of the target while he squirms and shrieks in the deadly pleasures of the proboscis. These creatures are transparent like a heat wave, just the outline and the colors that flush through them and you can hear the whir of wings hovering over you. Once that proboscis gets into you it's curtains. A young soldier who was rescued in time said it was like all the best comes he ever had all rolled into sweet liquid gold in his nuts. "She was killing me and I knew it and I loved it. . . ."

The Colonel shuddered and put the area off limits to all personnel. We call the critter Andy since it can assume the form of either sex. The chemistry dept is trying to come up with a viable repellent. Since the proboscis is composed of some substance much more rarefied than ordinary organic or inorganic substance, no suit or space suit could provide protection against penetration on a molecular level. . . .

My informant also told me that the "honey" so collected was stored in the body of Andy and was used to feed scorpion larvae of a particular breed of scorpion incomparably venomous, one hundredth of a drop causes death by internal combustion. These scorpions are prized by the nobles as bodyguards, a certain whistle conveying the attack order.

The Colonel shuddered some more ... he gestured to the south. "All those stinking little kingdoms down there, God knows what goes on. ... I say we should knock them off one after the other before they find some devilish way to get rid of us. ...."

I want to visit this southern area. It sounds like my sort of thing.

Kim is in a station wagon driving east. Guy Graywood is at the wheel. No words are spoken. To the south a low dark sky. ... Much lower than earth. Wind behind us, clouds scudding east ... a long skinny shape races across the sky faintly illuminated from behind by a green purple light all rather like the high-school play ... music from *The Isle of the Dead*. They pass a house of red brick smooth as if the bricks have fused together under great pressure. The house has a passageway through the middle and you can see it is only six feet from front to back. No sign of anyone in or around the house, which sits there in a block of palpable darkness, a dark black red like rotten blood. On the right side of the road are some buildings. We stop and get out. We have business here. A call to make. A door opens on a narrow corridor with another door at the end. Kim observes that the doors and walls are compacted layers like plywood and that they have a malevolent life of their own, snapping open and shut, you can get lost in a maze of doors and corridors, steps going up to nowhere, steps going down to a dead end as a heavy door slams shut behind you. Have to stick to your objectives. A door at the end of the corridor opens.

Kim is standing in the doorway of a room about eighteen feet long by twelve feet wide. There are sand troughs in the floor and paths around the troughs at the sides and one path down the middle. At the end of the room is another door. The room is full of light from windows in the far wall. In the sand troughs are naked men with bald heads, dead gray skin, a soft boneless look. They are all small, dwarfs actually. Their gray, faceted eyes keep darting about in agitation. They wallow in the sand with galvanic

sloughing movements, their bulbous gray foreheads like egg sacs, from time to time a black claw moves inside. Other gray dwarfs wearing tunics, who seem to be the overseers, move about on the walkways, pass in and out of the door at the back. . . .

Kim remembers a reek of evil. In the middle of a red-carpeted room a plot of ground about six feet square where hideous bulbous plants are growing. Centipedes are crawling about and from beneath a rock protrudes the head of a huge centipede. Kim arms himself with a cutlass. Graywood stands by with a crowbar. Kim kicks the rocks over and the centipede digs deeper, he can see that it is at least three feet long and that the plant roots stir like centipede legs, part plant and part insect. . . . He wakes up shivering with horror because he knows these hideous insect plants and giant centipedes were once (an evil old-woman voice tinkles in his brain)

"silly little boys like you."

He walks back along the corridor through several doors and up some narrow stairs and comes out onto an open hillside. Two hundred yards away across a limestone court he can see a waterfront promenade. Someone from inside the building says,

"He won't leave without his friend." And Guy comes out in green slacks and a gray shirt. I point to the promenade, the trees and the sea beyond.

"Run!"

Relief to be out of that place like a breath of air in suffocation. A hieroglyphic inscription lights up in his brain.

They fell down on their faces in land their own.

He flashes back to the trough building. He goes down to the trough room. One of the overseers comes at him, hands and fingers outstretched. Kim puts up his hands palm out and arrests the dwarf. Leaves him frozen there, hands stretched out. He walks back to the door that leads to the exit where he encounters a giant twelve feet tall, rather thin with a triangular face and peaked cap. The giant is wearing a brocade coat and pants of

black satin with white and yellow brocade. He seems friendly. Another dwarf pops out through a door. Kim engages. The dwarf snaps back through the door, leaving a stink of insect evil. . . .

They are back on the hillside and Kim says to Guy . . .

"Just to be anywhere out of there . . . no matter how ordinary . . . *just out of that horrible place.*

Kim realizes that the dwarfs in the troughs are being processed into centipedes. *The centipede eyes are already in place.* Eventually the centipede will emerge from the forehead, leaving the dead gray hulk behind.

Why? One of a number of expedients to destroy souls and so limit and monopolize immortality.

Where? Planet Venus, where else.

Who or what is behind the scenes here? Something dry, brittle, timorous. Kim senses that this is *card magic* associated with a special card deck. The cards are painted on a material like plastic that absorbs the colors to produce a three-dimensional impression. The cards move into combinations like animated cartoons. . . .

When more flatly revolting things are done the Venusians will do them.

A narrow, almost two-dimensional space . . . Look at those houses . . . not more than four feet deep. They must *slide* around in there . . . nursery-rhyme magic, attacking clubs and coffee grinders, giants, dwarfs and palaces. The Lords in red robes, centipedes encrusted in their amber foreheads, old-woman magic with spinning wheels in tiny cottages of the plywood they use for building, compacted in layers like the cards animated by a malevolent sliding life, doors slide open, snap shut.

In his knee-length cape of centipede skins, Kim walks with the Noon Devil in hot still electric air. The cape makes a dry rustling sound. Kim stops and unfastens the pincer clasp at his

throat and passes the cape to his faithful squire, Arn . . . under the cape Kim is wearing a magnificent coat of red satin with many pockets, a tricornered hat of blue satin, pants of yellow pongee silk, his boots, brownish pink and porous, are made from the skin of an electrical eel. At his side is the magic sword and the invisible swordsman, a creature of his will that moves with the speed of light. In his hand is a crystal tube. As he lifts the tube to eye level blue lightning crackles from his eyes out along the tube. . . .

BLAT BLAT BLAT

The Palace goes up in chunks.

"You've seen the troughs. . . ."

Kim nods, his face blazing with pure killing purpose as he remembers the dream.

"Well remember this. If they get their hands on you anyone can be broken down into the troughs . . . 'peed,' they call it. . . ."

He pauses, giving Kim time to know what it would mean to recognize a friend's face just as the pincers start cutting through the swollen egg-sac forehead.

The Supervisor is suddenly an old man who has carried heavy pain for a long time. Long long time, you can tell by the shoulders.

"They get you screaming curses like an old washerwoman. . . . Make your hate solid in silence."

Ali trots down the street, his kris vibrating in front of him, pulling him forward, shop shutters bang down . . . this street . . . this shop . . . here she comes. The fat one with the dead cold shark eyes . . . we called her the Great White now isn't that cute her face shattering in recognition she dives for the pistol in her handbag late and she knows it he slices her open from her cunt to her gullet. The eyes roll back showing the white and she sinks in a reek of blood and guts. . . . Her Consort is backing away, hands outstretched in supplication. . . .

Ali smiles over his bloody kris. No mercy there. Consort turns to run, slips on dog shit, falls on his face. Ali glides forward, puts a foot in the small of his back, pulls his head back by the hair, and cuts his throat.

Making machine-gun noises ... BBBBUUUUUUPP as he sprays the blood around. . . .

Ali prances out with a T-shirt. Hand holding a bloody kris has written AMOK across his chest. He clasps his hands above his head and smiles. . . . Plane crash? You carry Caesar and his fortunes unsteady, he slipped and bumped against me at the airport. It was his error. Pilot's error. And that's when I skipped in ... I am leading him away from the controls ... I can be soo seductive, look like anybody, he is already screwing the hostess, getting a hard-on ... then the *error*. . . . Shock on the co-pilot's face. . . .

Realization

OH SHIT

The ripping splintering crash ... Among the passengers killed in the crash of Flight 18 ...

Hurricanes . . . let it all sweep through faster faster ride the wind ride the glass shards stripping flesh from the screaming bones, the tidal waves churning houses, people, cows, and windmills. . . . Anita advances on Texas. . . .

Ali prances out in his ANITA shirt. . . . A big fat whore with her mouth open is blowing a city away. . . .

Tornado is quite a different operation. You pull all the curses and the hate in all the way in right to the epicenter. . . . They are all pouring in everybody who ever hated you and cursed you. . . .

Stay all night and stay a little longer
Take off your coat and throw it in a corner
Don't see why you don't stay a little longer
Round and round faster and faster spinning in
a green black funnel ... tornado sky ...
tossing trucks and cars around like matchboxes
the funnel skips and hops

and it comes down here
And it comes down there
Take off your house and throw it in a corner . . .
The funnel whirls and tilts
And it comes down here
And it comes down there
And I said, "Pa, we best get in the house and there
wasn't any house. . . ."
Don't see why you don't stay a little longer
And the music softly moans . . . tornado warning
sirens
'Tain't no sin to take off your skin
And dance around in your bones. . . .
"The truck had crushed her completely, just her legs was
sticking out."
Ali prances out in his T-shirt, KID TWIST in green-black
letters across his chest. Ali smiles. . . . Texas twister T-shirt . . .
legs sticking out . . .
Get their hands on you it would mean operations . . .
screaming face in the trough, you could just see her. . . .

National Geographic voice: Guy, Marbles, and Kim are patrolling
dead-end slums where addicts of the suicide drugs gravitate to
hideous dooms. Some are dragged into the canals by the dreaded
Lophy Women. Underwater, the abducted male depends on his
mate for oxygen as he is slowly absorbed into her body until
only his testicles remain. So she becomes a self-fertilizing her-
maphrodite and fulfills her biologic destiny. . . . Galvanized by
hideous hunger, these half-formed creatures slither through the
filthy alleys and warrens of slums adjoining a huge swampy
lake. An underground river feeds in here, the water is clear and
deep. . . . Suddenly a Lophy Woman slithers out, huge mouth
gaping to show the incurving teeth fine as hairs. They eat into
the victim's face to block his breathing as they feed in oxygen
through their gills. So the lethal mating is consummated. She ab-

sorbs first his head and brain, keeping his body alive with her bloodstream. Kim shoots her in the mouth with a shot load and blows the top of her head off. . . .

Others wind up on the centipede troughs, or as sexual stumps for the Amazon tribes, cut off at the waist and the knee, kept alive by feeding tubes. . . .

"It's not a question of shoot first and ask questions later. We never ask questions. We are here strictly in the capacity of Stoppers, our function to *Stop. To arrest.*"

They turn into a square on the outskirts of a city. Here the poor are receiving their evening handout from a liveried servant. A carriage stands by. Each supplicant receives a slab of yellow metal paste. It is cut with a lead knife and the freshly cut paste gleams silver like sodium. Their faces are covered with metallic sores leaking pus like melted solder with a sickening sweetish metal reek.

The Stone Hots is a molecular alternation of the stone fish venom, a poison so agonizing that victims roll round screaming and must be restrained from suicide by any means at hand. Even large doses of morphine bring no relief. . . . The Stone Hots affords the addict what he calls a "fire fit" as pleasurable as the unaltered venom is agonizing. . . .

One of Kim's informants sidles up, an old man in a tattered black overcoat. . . .

"There's a Stoner. You can tell by the burnt-out look. Those fire fits burn the brains out. Look in his eyes. Nobody there. Skin and bones at the end."

The Stoner sits on a shit-stained limestone curb, with his conch shell of Stone Hots. . . . He dips in a little barbed sting and shoves it deep into his leg. His eyes light up and flash with insane delight. Like a galvanized skeleton, he jumps up and dances the Fire Fit Jig.

More and more unaltered venom accumulates in the body. . . . The Stoner rolls screaming in the square. Urchins gather. One throws himself down and mimics the Stoner's screams while the others piss with laughter. . . . Kim shoots the

Stoner through the head. . . . Nothing inside, as if you'd broken open a dry empty husk. The urchins hiss and slither away.

The Marbles is a heavy translucent white liquid that is carried in a golden bottle and injected in a gold syringe. The Marbles or the Rocks encases the addict in mineral calm. They live longer. Much longer. Up to six hundred years if they can keep the Rock on. Takes more and more as the body acids concentrate. Here is a gathering place for wealthy Marbles, gilt and gold and white satin. Tropical fish flash in floor-to-ceiling aquariums. They move very slow with the blank golden eyes of the axolotl salamander. They sit in chairs of smooth form-fitting marble.

In filthy hovels needy Marbles are close to molting, the shell eaten through in patches, pus leaking out . . . flesh under there has lost all immunity . . . skin is long gone. . . . Pulling the rotten shells off each other, underneath a mass of festering sores and fissures a reek of rotten flesh and rotten stone, dank and sweet and heavy in the lungs. Don't get too close. . . . The idiot molting Marbles writhe in sexual frenzies, stuck together in screaming quivering clusters. Could hardly be called sentient in the end, much less human.

Cure is possible in the very early stages but requires at least a year of special care. The most distressing symptom is dermal irritation, the skin is so sensitive that a breath of air will send the addict into convulsions. They must be kept in sensory-deprivation immersion tanks and maintained on large dosages of morphine and antibiotics since the liability to infections is breathtaking. . . .

"Trough City."
The houses all have that narrow look not more than five or six feet deep with stairways and doors and corridors, a maze of narrow rooms and corridors, stairways going up, stairways going down. . . . Watch the Downers leading down to a dead end and a heavy door that closes behind you. . . .

"We're knocking this joint over."

Door swings open on a narrow corridor. . . . To the left is a small square room open on the street. "Troughs are down here." Kim jerks his thumb to the right. "Guy, you cover our back. Marbles and me will take out the trough room."

The room is quite light from windows on the far side. At the end of the room is a door. And a man rushes out. He is about four feet tall, powerfully built, with a bulbous forehead. His eyes flare with xenophobic hate.

He is wearing a gray tunic with a belt. He stretches out his fingers in a malevolent jab gliding forward. Kim draws his 44 and shoots him in the forehead. A thick white milk spurts out. The dwarf falls into a trough. At this moment pincers break through the forehead of one of the trough men. They all look alike in one way, yet retain a vestige of difference like one of those shrunk-down heads. You could see who it had been.

The centipede head emerges from a dry dead husk.

Guy is looking over Kim's shoulder.

"Don't look in the troughs! Let's go!"

Marbles tosses in an explosive incendiary device set for three minutes. The giant, standing in the street by the door, wrings his hands.

"I must return to the palace!" he wails and runs away down a paper road, disappearing like the end of a cartoon.

"Up those stairs!"

Stone stairs, light above. They are standing on a hillside above the structure looking down through it. A maze of narrow plywood rooms, doors and corridors and trough rooms, stairs going up and going down extend as far as the eye can see into the hillside and down into a haze of distance.

In front of them is a limestone court a hundred yards across. . . . Beyond that the avenue and the sea. It looks very far away yet clear as if seen through a telescope.

"*Run!*"

A rumbling blast and the whole shit house is going up in chunks, pieces of plywood, dwarfs, sand and centipede frag-

ments raining down on them as they run. Kim sees a centipede claw in front of him turn into a fossil. . . . The blast and the rain of debris shuts off like someone turned off a TV set.

No court, just a rubbly weed-grown vacant lot. Nothing behind them but the bare rocky hillside, scrub oak, stunted pine, a few olive trees. They are walking down a dry stream bed toward the waterfront. Not at all far, actually, a hundred yards ahead.

Memory of the troughs is fading like dream traces. . . . The lights are out in the trough rooms. There is only darkness and sifting dust and the little sounds of decay . . . the barren hillside, grazing goats, a distant flute . . . egg-sac foreheads explode with a dry muffled sound like a puffball bursting in still noon heat in this area of rubbish and vacant lots. . . . A cool evening breeze brings a whiff of the sea. . . . A blue smell of youth and hope. One is not serious at seventeen. . . . They sit down under a blue awning and order ouzo with a plate of black olives. . . . Late afternoon . . . a few bathers linger on the beach. Boys in swimming trunks walk by laughing, talking. . . . Old men sit on benches along the esplanade, hands on their canes, looking out to sea.

Sound of a distant flute trickles down from the hillside in deepening twilight.

They eat dinner on a balcony over the sea. . . . Shrimps in a sauce of olive oil, oregano, lemon juice and garlic . . . red mullet and Greek salad washed down with retsina.

"Your primitive weapon is of no use," hissed the Alien.

"How do you know?" Kim asked and blew it away. . . .

"He looked kinda surprised."

One is not serious at seventeen.

Kim Christmas, the perfect intelligence agent, turned into one of the shabbier streets of Aman. He tossed a coin to a handless leper who caught it in his teeth. Kim's cover story is taking over. He is Jerry Wentworth, a stranded space pilot.

It is a standard medina lodging house . . . whitewashed cubicle rooms . . . wooden pegs in the wall to hang clothes . . . a pallet, a blanket, tin washbasin, and water pitcher . . . built around a courtyard with a well, some fig and orange trees. In such lodgings every man who can afford it sleeps with a bodyguard. Jerry sat up and hugged the army surplus blanket around his skinny chest. It was cold and his reptile in bed beside him was sluggish. That was the trouble with a reptile bodyguard. But Jerry heard the old man approaching with earthern bowls of hot coals hooked on both ends of an iron balance rather like justice and her scales, Jerry thought. He ordered bread and hot schmun, a sweet concoction of tea and khat. Good way to get started in the morning. He closed the door and soon the heat from the bowl permeated the room and his reptile stirred languidly and peeled off the covers.

It is a Mamba addict in the most advanced stages, skin a smooth bright green, eyes jet-black, the pubic and rectal hairs a shiny green-black. He squirms his legs apart and his eyes light up with lust as his ass flushes salmon, pink, mauve, electric blues, reeking rainbows.

The boy dresses sulkily. He needs the green. They cut out to the nearest snakehouse.

Through the open doorway drifts the snakehouse smell, heavy and viscid as languid surfeited pythons, somnolent cobras in Egyptian gardens, dry and sharp as a rattlesnake den and the concentrated urine of little fennec foxes in desert sand, smell of venomous sea snakes in stagnant lagoons where sharks and crocodiles stir in dark oily water.

The snakehouse is a narrow room cut into the hillside. There are stone benches along the walls impregnated with generations of reptile addicts. In the center of the floor toward the back is a manhole cover of patinaed bronze giving access to a maze of tunnels and rooms that had housed the mummies of the Pharaohs and others rich enough to belong to that most exclusive club in the world. I.L. Immortality *Limited*.

The reptiles are waiting on the Snake. The Snake is late as usual and the reptiles hiss desperately. A few are already molting and pulling strips of skin off each other with shrill hisses of pain and ecstasy. Jerry's reptile turns away in disgust. Some of the reptiles are clad in ragged cloaks of reeking leather, others wear snakeskin jockstraps and the ever-popular hippopotamus-hide knee-length boots, many are naked except for spring shoes with razor-sharp Mercury wings for a deadly back kick.

There sits an exquisite coral snake, his banded red and white phallus up and throbbing, and opposite him is a copperhead, his pointed phallus smooth and shiny, his skin like burnished copper. They hiss at each other and their throats swell. "Doing the cobra," it's called and it's dangerous. If you don't get sex right away with someone in your cock group you will die of suffocation in a few seconds. The waiter rushes up with a pallet, and hurries off to open the manhole cover. The bodies heat up glowing copper red white and orange; and the boys shed their skins in a sweet dry wind that wafts up from the spicy mummies.

"Shredded incense in a cloud / from closet long to quiet vowed / Moldering her lutes and books among / as when a Queen long dead was young."

"Here comes the *Snake!*"

"All-natural products from pure venom," he squeaks out.

The reptiles hiss with joy.

Actually the Snake has a burning-down flea habit and looks like Blake's Ghost of a Flea. He wears a tight pea-green suit and a purple fedora. He passes it out and pulls it in with his quick dry claws lined with razor-sharp erectile hairs that can brush flesh from the bone, recall this out-of-towner made a crack about "Bug Juice" and the Snake slapped him. He put a hand up to feel the side of his face and he doesn't have any face on that side.

The waiters bring coffee tables and water and cotton and alcohol. Some of the reptiles have little snake-jaw syringes and they go through an act of biting each other. The latest slither is ampules to pop when you come. It's a game of chicken with the kids. A full blow of king cobra is fatal about half the time, same way with Tiger Breath from tiger snakes. The reptiles are slithering around and constricting each other but Jerry's green mamba takes a quick fix and they walk out.

They pass a swampy pool green with algae, where alligator addicts wallow in mindless depravity.

Jerry sniffs and he can feel the *smell brain* stir deep in his pons with a delicious dull ache . . . what a kick for an uptight Wasp! Mindless garden of our jism . . . parking lot . . . belches the taste of eggs . . . this is it . . . *magnificent* . . . Sput Sput Sput . . . It's a lovely sound the sound of a silenced gun . . . a sound you can *feel* . . . good clean there we are in one asshole . . . stale night smell . . . mindless trance on porches the air like cobwebs . . . the lake . . . fish . . . the sky was clouded over . . . here . . . cleaned the fish on grass . . . unwashed sheets belching we ease into the normal boy at sunrise . . . along any minute now . . . watery sunlight . . . sitting job . . . the boy was here before the job . . . like cobwebs the job . . . the job? Oh it. Low-velocity nine-millimeter . . . sundown . . . boy awake . . . military purposes . . . Jerry sniffed the rotten belches of a python . . . boys shed their skins in a sweet Sput Sput Sput. . . .

A musky zoo smell permeates the animal street lingering in

your clothes and hair ... a skunk boy pads in beside them. ...

"Got *wolverine* poppers. ..."

They walk on and the boy gives them a squirt of skunk juice. ...

"Chip Americans!"

They pass the massive metal lattice gate to the Insect Quarter ... faceted eyes of the insect addicts peer out from dark warrens. The smell doubles them over like a blow to the stomach. They hurry on, heading for the port. They are on the outskirts of the town.

Ledges and terraces cut into the hillside with markets and cafés and lodging houses ... stone steps and ramps lead from one level to another ... abandoned cars here and there eroded to transparent blue shells as if nothing remains but the paint. At the top of the hill the Sea of Silence stretches away into the distance.

Along the shores are driftwood benches sanded smooth. It is said that every man sees the flotsam of his own past here. ... Cottonwoods along an irrigation ditch at Los Alamos Ranch School ... a wispy skittish space horse by a desert fort from *Beau Geste*.

Einstein writes matter into energy on the blackboard. ...

Los Alamos Ranch School. ... A cluster of buildings and roads, it looks like a little village resort. ... Pasturelands on both sides of the yellow gravel road, we come now to the trading post and post office. ... Get out to buy a soft drink. ... It is a cold windy spring day ... and just in front of us at the bottom of a little valley is a pond, waves like bits of silver paper in the wind. ... A naked boy sprawls on the raft in the middle of the pond seemingly oblivious to the cold. To the right of the trading post is a vegetable garden. ... To the left barns and outbuildings and workers' cottages and across the pond the green icehouse ... and a road that winds away into pine forest. ... The Big House is to the right, it's an easy walk ... along the edge of the vegeta-

ble garden and then there is a line of boys singing the school
song:

> Far away and high on the mesa's crest
> Here's the life that all of us love the best
> Los Alamos
> Winter days as we skim o'er the ice and snow
> Summer days when the balsam breezes blow
> Los Alamos

The boys are dismissed. Some start a dispirited game of catch.
Others huddle about in corners of the building, shoulders
hunched, sheltering from the cold spring wind. "The balsam
breezes," they intone sourly. They have to stay outside until five
o'clock. One boy keeps looking at his Ingersoll wristwatch with
radium dial.

"Forty minutes yet."

The boys groan. The shadow of a cloud darkens the young
faces. The wind blows harder. Boys are lowering the flag. As the
first raindrops plop into the dusty road the boys rush into the
house.

There seem to be a lot of new kids here. The boy who sits
down beside him on the swing in front of the huge fireplace
seems familiar. He has bright red hair and a yellowish face
splotched with brownish orange freckles like dead leaves. His
eyes are a yellow-green color. The boy smiles.

"Hi. I'm Jerry."

A splash of light quick inhuman gesture puckers of ozone
from desert boy's genitals . . . sulfurous hate like palpable light
the boy comes gasping and snarling.

"What's wrong with you? Remember he *saw* the picture."

Kim sees himself spread on a pink launching pad like a
soft rocket. His ass is the touchhole, Jerry's cock the light. Now
it touches, enters in a blaze of light as they streak out over the
river and trees . . . a wake of jism across the Milky Way.

The space capsule is accelerating . . . cracked concrete

streets, drifting sand ... Thousands of white butterflies. Blue mist of abandoned army ... there's a path out. ... Smell of adolescent genitals on the camel saddle spermy smear across a vast empty sky ... old cars and bicycles rusty derricks worn benches sand streets pools of silence ... driftwood ruined piers and pavilions ... swamp land ... canals.

The guide traces the area on the map with his finger. ... "The Place of Dead Roads, *señor*. This does not mean roads that are no longer used, roads that are overgrown, it means roads that are *dead*. You comprehend the difference?"

"And how can this area be reached?"

The guide shrugged. "It is usual to start in a City of Dead Streets. ... And where is this city? In every city are dead streets, *señor*, but in some more than in others. New York is well supplied in this respect. ... But we are late. The car is waiting to take us to the fiesta."

Evening falls on Mexico, D. F. The plumed serpent is suffocating the city in coils of foul saffron smoke that rasp the lungs like sandpaper, undulating slightly as the inhabitants walk through, many with handkerchiefs tied across mouth and nose. The poisonous reds and greens and blues of neon light fuzz and shimmer.

Two men reel out of a cantina and pull their nasty little 25 automatics from inside belt holsters and empty them into each other at a distance of four feet. Smoke flashes light the sneering macho faces, suddenly gray with the realization of death. They lurch and stagger, eyes wild like panicked horses. Pistols fall from nerveless fingers. One is slumped on the curb spitting blood. The other is kicking the soles of his boots out against a wall. In seconds the street is empty, wise citizens running to get as far away as possible before the *policía* arrive and start beating "*confesiones*" out of everyone in sight. A buck-toothed boy with long arms like an ape snatches up one of the pistols as he lopes by.

Kim ducks into an alley, practicing Ninja arts of invisibility. They are on the outskirts of the city by a ruined hacienda. Along crumbling mud walls men huddle in serapes of darkness that seeps into ditches and potholes like black ink.

Abruptly the city ends. An empty road winds away through the cactus, sharp and clear in moonlight as if cut out of tin.

Clouds are gathering over a lake of pale filmy waters. A speckled boy with erection glares at Kim as Kim glides by in his black gondola, trailing a languid hand in the water. Hate shimmers from the boy's eyes like black lightning. He holds up a huge purple-yellow mango. "You like beeg one, Meester Melican cocksucker?" The fragile shells of other boys are gathering . . . lifeless faces of despair. . . .

"*Malos, esos muchachos*," said the clouds and heat lightning behind the boy.

Kim is floating down a river that opens into a lake of pale milky water. Storm clouds are gathering over the mountains to the north. Heat lightning flickers over the filmy water in splashes of silver. On a sandbank a naked boy with erection holds up a huge silver fish, still flapping.

"One peso, Meester. Him *fruit* fish." The boy's body shimmers with pure naked hate.

"Why don't you come with us instead of moaning?" Kim drawls. Other boys are gathering, faces of hatred and evil and despair. They run through the shallow water that scatters from their legs like fish milk. They huddle in the stern of the boat like frightened cats. The boys shimmer and melt together. One boy remains, sitting on a coil of rope.

"Me Ten Boy Clone. Can be one boy, five six, maybe."

"*Malos, esos muchachos*," says the guide from the tiller behind the boy. The boy sniggers.

At daybreak they are in a vast delta to the sky, dotted with islands of swamp cypress and mangos. There is a feeling of end-

less depths under the fragile shell of the boat. Not a breath of air stirring.

As they pass an island the leaves hang limp and lifeless. An alligator slides into the water and a snake hanging from a tree limb turns to watch them attentively, darting out its purple tongue. Here the dead roads and empty dream places drift down into a vast stagnant delta. Alligator snouts protrude above oily iridescent water. Pale and unreal, the lake extends into nowhere.

The Place of Dead Roads ... We are floating down a wide river heat lightning sound of howler monkies. The guide is steering for the shore. We will tie up for the night. The boat is a raft on pontoons with a sleeping tent. I am adjusting the mosquito netting. A fire in the back of the boat in a tub of stones frying fish. We lie side by side listening to the lapping water. Once a jaguar jumped onto the stern of the boat. Caught in the flashlight he snarled and jumped back onto the shore. I put down the double-barreled twelve-gauge loaded with buckshot. We are passing a joint back and forth.

Every day the river is wider. We are drifting into a vast delta with islands of swamp cypress, freshwater sharks stir in the dark water. The guide looks at his charts. The fish here are sluggish and covered with fungus. We are eating our stores of salt beef and dried fish and vitamin pills. We are in a dead-end slough, land ahead on all sides.

And there is a pier. We moor the boat and step ashore. There is a path leading from the pier, weed-grown but easy to follow.

"And what is a dead road? Well, *señor*, somebody you used to meet, *uno amigo, tal vez....*"

Remember a red brick house on Jane Street? Your breath quickens as you mount the worn red-carpeted stairs.... The road to 4 calle Larachi, Tangier, or 24 Arundle Terrace in London? So many dead roads you will never use again ... a flickering gray haze of old photos ... pools of darkness in the street

like spilled ink . . . a dim movie marquee with smoky yellow
bulbs . . . red-haired boy with a dead-white face.

The guide points to a map of South America. "Here, *señor*
. . . is the Place of Dead Roads."

Just ahead a ruined jetty . . . some large sluggish fish stirs at our
approach with a swish and a glimpse of a dark shape moving
into deeper water. . . .

We step ashore . . . through the broken walls and weeds of
a deserted garden . . . dilapidated arches. . . . A boy, eyes clotted
with dreams, fills his water jug from a stagnant well.

As Kim moves back in time he leaves a wake of disasters behind him, which is only logical since he is retracing his space in time, leaving a time vacuum behind him.

Here he is in Tangier having his coffee on the terrace.

He settles down to read about the earthquake in Agadir oh yes he'd just been there the Commander was way off course lucky thing he didn't split the earth open with his bungling the incompetent old beast. Kim read avidly all eyewitness accounts, people who were saved because they stayed where they were people who just got out of where they had been in time frantic relatives clawing at the rubble with their bare hands seem to look at him accusingly . . . the boiled eggs are just right . . . rather high on the scale it was Kim is hopeless about the mechanical details after all what could be less magical than saying I am going to produce an earthquake of seven microperimeters on the Whosis scale. . . . Oh here was something juicy: an underground snake pit was ruptured by the quake so that thousands of frenzied cobras and adders slither through the stricken city biting any unfortunates they encounter. . . .

Trucks rumble through the rubble filled with wild-eyed soldiers. . . .

"NOTICE TO ALL CITIZENS . . . NOTICE TO ALL CITIZENS . . . KILL YOUR DOGS AND CATS . . . REPEAT: KILL YOUR DOGS AND CATS . . . ANYONE TRYING TO BE A HYPOCRITE WILL BE PUNISHED BY TWENTY YEARS IN JAIL"

Despite the strict order of the government health services, thousands of dogs roam the streets and the police have a shoot-on-sight order for all stray animals. However, their inaccuracy is such that citizens are frequently wounded or killed by stray bullets while a disdainful Afghan hound swishes away untouched.

"We have a tight schedule to keep, remember. . . ."

"Ah yes . . . and what happens here when we leave. . . ?"

"A riot, I think. It will suck all the money out of Tangier. . . ."

Earthquakes, riots, floods, fires, hurricanes and tornadoes he digs special because that is what he is leaving in his wake, a low-pressure area. . . .

And the barometer dropped and dropped until we thought it was broken. . . . Carsons was here. There were tornadoes never seen before, Sound Twisters that sucked the words out of your mouth, shattering tapes to dust and stripping records. Then silence rushes in like a thunderclap . . . and Odor Twisters.

Kim adored tornadoes. Giver of winds is my name he wrote it out in Egyptian characters . . . the green sky the black funnel the twisting black strength he can feel it in his head. . . .

And hurricanes were nice too, nothing more exhilarating than riding a hurricane watching the trees and telephone poles bend and break like matchsticks, the windows blow out, the roofs tear loose, and tidal waves rushing in fifty feet high . . . and plagues of course were delightful but Kim just couldn't get up any enthusiasm for famine. What a dreary bore the children with swollen bellies and dead eyes the old people like pieces of dirt just patiently waiting to crumble. . . . There's no élan about famine . . . not like riding the wind across a screaming sky. . . . I hear tell they got these thousand-mile-per-hour winds on Mars just think what that would do to London or New York. . . .

Kim always reads the tornado stories. Here was one a barber was shaving a man when the twister struck the razor was pulled from his hand and cut a man's throat three hundred yards away. And the straws driven into telephone poles. . . . Imagine a

fist or kick coming at that speed. . . . Kim dismissed the idea of a twister gun but twister shells or grenades *might* work.

"Clutter the Glind," screamed the Captain of Moving Land.

Traveling back in time is like being at the controls of an intricate ship that requires the most delicate and precise touch to steer through shallows and reefs and enemy fire. . . . Clickety clickety clack . . . back back back . . . back through Tangier, Paris . . . Sometimes he shifted his identity ten times in the course of a day. . . . Concierge, gendarme, police inspector, lavatory attendant, thief, bestial peasant, surly waiter, song-and-dance man, mass murderer, member of the Academy. Then he rests up in a safe house and catches up on his journals. . . .

Back now in gay Paree, where Kim indulges in an orgy of identity shifts.

"It's like footwork in fighting. Keep moving so you are harder to hit. We call it 'shoe work' in the trade. . . . Your shoes are your identity papers. Keep them clean and polished. When you travel back in time on your own time track, you are bucking your whole past karma. So you never travel in a straight line. It would be suicidal."

Kim began his acquaintance with the anonymous Shoehorns and Cobblers who forge passports and other documents. You get what you pay for. Pay enough and your papers are real.

The gendarme saluted smartly as the elegant young man approached but the youth perceived something dead and cold and joyless in the small hard green eyes. The gendarme would later become a collaborationist commandant of police, a vicious torturer of resistance fighters. He will escape to Argentina after the war and find Death Squad work.

"Twenty Monsieur le Prince?" The gendarme gives precise directions. The youth thanks him. The police thing nods distantly, for his soutane waits around the corner.

"If you want to find a good restaurant just walk around until you see a priest eating. . . . Well if you want to look like a

priest find a good restaurant and eat in it. Gawd, there's a bishop. . . . Room for one more inside, sir. . . ." After dawdling over a sumptuous dinner and a little too much wine like any greedy old pig priest, he hurries away, his cassock flapping behind him, obviously bent on some urgent errand of mercy or condolence. He stops in a doorway to adjust his cassock, troublesome beast. His key opens the door and he slips in like a shadow.

The jewelry firm of Potterman and Pearlmutter is on the third floor. They're only kikes, he tells himself, knowing that criminals are bigots. You have to think and feel your cover. Old-style safe . . . A muffled boom and Kim walks out after a change of clothes with a satchelful of jewels.

He is now a fine old gentleman with the pince-nez, the expensive dark suit, the tiny ribbon in his lapel. Despite his *bella figura*, Monsieur Dupré was involved in a number of highly questionable financial transactions. In fact the Dupré Scandal would bring down a government and precipitate an abortive revolution. . . . In the course of which thirty people will die. . . .

"Oui, monsieur." The cab driver made a noise like ripping canvas. . . . "Machine guns. . . . When you hear that, you know that it is, how you say, serious."

The suit is now worn and shabby. He is wearing three dirty old scarves. . . .

"Qui est ça qui monte?" he demands, popping out of his cubbyhole under the stairs. For some hapless American has dared to visit someone in the house without first announcing himself to the concierge. . . . Oh he knows the step of every tenant. And woe to the client who attempts to smuggle in an illicit hotplate. The concierge can detect the slightest overload of current and trace it to its source by means of a contraption he has been trying to market for thirty years, writing letters to various government departments, eliciting polite bureaucratic replies: Do not envisage any way in which this department . . . and in course of time replies that were not so polite. . . . This neglect of

his genius work has further soured his disposition, if such a thing is possible. Kim decides to get out from under before the genius work blows up as it did several days later, razing the hotel to the ground.

Kim heard the blast as he had an afternoon Pernod with Madame Rachau, his landlady at the theatrical hotel where he lived in his song-and-dance capacity.

He nodded.... *"Ça commence."*

"Oui," said Madame with a smile.... *"Ça commence."*

Kim can feel Europe coming apart under his feet as dogs are said to feel the approach of an earthquake ... the mutter and rumble of war. He can smell war in the streets and in the cafés. So he plunders the past, present, and future for war songs.... He gets them in little bits and pieces.... Here's a poster ... mother and children sitting in front of the fireplace. They are looking at Dad's picture in uniform.

> Keep the home fires burning
> (mutter of artillery in the distance)
> Though the hearts are yearning ...
> (Regret to inform you)

The war song is of course a very old genre and far removed from the actualities of modern combat, where a singing soldier would constitute a public nuisance outranking a singing waiter.

Kim had cribbed a song from a future war.

> The last time I saw Paris
> Her heart was young and gay
> No matter how they change her
> I'll remember her that way....

Impressionist paintings unfold in his brain like those Japanese flowers that open in water ... bookstalls along the Seine

... leaves falling ... urinal in the upper-right-hand corner ... this was going to be a *diseuse* song-and-dance number with magic-lantern slides of impressionist paintings ... Monet ... Renoir ...

No matter how they change her ... slides of Paris after nuclear attack ... weed-grown rubble. The only thing left you can recognize is the Eiffel Tower, now a rusted shell, vines growing up along the struts and the cables. But still unquestionably the Eiffel Tower. Interplanetary tourists point to the picture in a guidebook.... What remains of London? Kim can see White's gathering the dust of centuries....

New York? The Statue of Liberty ... streets covered with melted glass like ice and a thousand years hence happy otters slide down the glass chutes into a crystal-clear East River. Saint Louis? Nothing is left but the arch, GATEWAY TO THE WEST....

I'll remember her that way.... Paris light on the hands of a nurse as she opens a boiled egg....

LE CONVALESCENT

She sets the tray down by an elegant young man in a blue dressing gown.... There is a bottle of laudanum and a medicine glass on his night table. Some fruit in a bowl. I can make out a ripe peach with a bruise here and there and an apple—it looks like a *good* apple—I haven't had one in so long. And the boiled egg is just right with the toast and the tea, and the laudanum is hitting the back of his neck and moving down his thighs.

There's a book on the table. The youth stretches out a languid hand. You can see that he has been very ill.

The book is entitled *Quién Es?*

On the cover is a skeleton figure with black vest and sheriff's badge. On the badge is written *MOI.*

Kim dances out singing:

Paris please stay the same ...

Citizens dance by with the morning *pain* under their arms....

An old crippled woman dances into a *pharmacie.*...

"Codethyline Houde, s'il vous plait...."

"Oui, madame. . . ."

The old woman does a spastic twitching dance out of the store. . . .

Clerk: "This is the twentieth today. . . ."

The proprietor is Madame Rachau. . . . *"Ah oui . . .* there is much pain, much trouble. . . ."

"And some of your sad days . . ."

"Ah here comes *ce bon vieux Monsieur Carsons . . .*"

She reaches for the codethyline. . . . .

"Bonjour, monsieur. . . . Codethyline. . . ?"

"Oui, madame. . . ."

Paris please stay the same . . .

All over Paris people reach for *Quién Es?*

Here's a man collapsed over his *pain*, little pink codethyline pills spilling down the stairs from a ruptured green and white bag with a little seal. . . . *Pharmacie de Bonne Chance . . .*

"ARRÊTEZ!" A blurt of machine-gun fire. . . .

QUIÉN ES?

Monsieur de Paris punches the condemned man in the stomach and throws him under the guillotine. The knife, falls—

QUIÉN ES?

Hospital smell of pain. . . .

"A blessing it was. . . ."

QUIÉN ES?

And in wartime . . . Regret to inform you . . .

QUIÉN ES?

QUIÉN ES?

QUIÉN ES?

The man with a million faces. Death disguised as any other person, as the planet heads for the final *sauve qui peut* at vertiginous speed.

"Now when you get in a tight spot, you head for the nearest terminal. Spot of bother in London? Duck into the Paris Café or

the Lima Hotel or the New York Grill. Of course you have to *make* it into Paris or Lima or New York. As soon as you walk in look around for a piece of Paris. Get one of those Maurice Chevalier songs going in your head. . . . Paris please stay the same . . ."

Well it just so happens the Madame is French and inside of ten seconds Kim is a favored client and the sounds of pursuit snuff out. . . . The Lima Hotel . . . a whiff of the sad languorous city with vultures roosting on all the public buildings and the statues. . . . A vulture in downtown London is unlikely but look at that old man, coat flapping, and one of those nasty birdlike English faces that peck at one. . . . New York is easy because it has pieces from everywhere. . . . You can't always find a hotel or café . . . then it's a case of naked hide like naked kill. . . . You have to improvise from what is at hand. . . . Remember, you don't have to move spatially. You can dodge forward or backward in time. . . .

Kim is in a Paris street . . . a green haze hangs over the city . . . the food stalls and shops are all empty. Everyone is looking at him with a slow hideous recognition. . . . Eyes blazing with hate, they are all pointing now, and with a great cry they rush for him hands reaching. . . . Kim runs in a blind panic. He falls, skinning his knees, gets up, and runs on, staggering, winded. . . . They are right behind him.

Now . . . Just ahead is a rusty urinal and Kim remembers those lines worthy of Rimbaud or Verlaine. . . .

Calmly he slides into the urinal . . . and the screaming crowd is snuffed forward to the future time they came from . . . a time of hunger and disease, madness and death. Kim shudders at the memory of that green haze, the green-black color of tornado sky but unmoving, suffocating, a silent arrested twister. And HE was the one who did it somehow. They SAW him. Kim buttons his pants and steps out onto dead leaves. . . . They don't belong here, not in this Paris light. Kim hails a cab with his sword cane. He has a date with an acrobat.

When you are shooting for a future terminal, get ready to make a leap in the dark. You just let go and do nothing and that isn't easy with a screaming mob six feet behind you going to skin you alive and roll you in broken Coca-Cola bottles the end result will look like an action painting. Just *wanting* to be somewhere else, no matter how intensely, won't do it. You need a peg to hang it on . . . sharp smell of weeds from a vacant lot and Kim turns around with a sawed-off shotgun. The mob breaks and scatters at the first blast.

In Marrakesh once, sitting with Waring on the terrace at sunset . . . a banging on the door. Kim peers over and sees his nemesis, Inspector Dupré. The Central Computer has spat out his falsified passport. Herr Workman died ten years ago. The Inspector tosses the passport on his desk and smiles.

"You should have bought better shoes. . . . But I think the mystery of your identity will soon unfold itself. Take him to the Slobski Institute."

Waring points. . . . "Look at that beautiful cat there on the wall."

A white cat on a white wall, immobile, timeless, looking out over Marrakesh.

"Oh that must be Monsieur Dupré to change the gas cylinder for the hot-water heater. Be a dear and let him in."

And there are changes of identity . . . a silent shift in the head and you are looking out through different eyes. . . . "Screaming crowds? Oh that's the Olympics on TV. . . ." Some frantic characters applaud.

It all comes under the head of evasive action. Kim is planning to dance offstage from his Paris number, maybe right into one of those awful East End music halls. Kim shudders at the thought . . . bestial English criminals gouging each other's eyes out with broken beer bottles.

"Now I don't want any trouble with you, mate, let me buy you a drink."

So saying, he knees him in the groin, throws brandy into his eyes and lights it.

Kim winds up his Paris show with a medieval set. It's Paris in the terrible winter of 1498 when famished wolves came into the outskirts of Paris. Kim, as François Villon, in his scholar's cloak, does a *diseuse* number.

"*Où sont les neiges d'antan?*"

Wolves slink by chanting:

"*Où sont les neiges d'antan?*"

Street gangs of youths ready to kill for a crust of bread . . . Kim engages five of them and routs them with his sword. He pulls the hood down over his face. Magic-lantern slides show the street winter spring summer fall faster and faster. Kim throws the hood back. He is now an old man who quavers out:

"*Où sont les neiges d'antan?*"

Applause.

The applause fades into traffic sounds and Kim finds himself in London on Westbury Street, near the corner of Ryder Street. He is still wearing the medieval cloak and Kim knows it is his old plague cloak. It is a beautiful garment of fine black camelwool lined with raw silk impregnated with suppurating lymph glands, tuberculosis and leprosy, the sweet rotten aftersmell of gangrene and putrid blood, the sharp reek of carrion, winter smell of typhus in cold doss houses where the windows are caulked with paper and never opened . . . a very old cloak, Kim reflects . . . been in our family for a long time, picking up a whiff here and a whiff there . . . sweet diarrhea smells from cholera wards, black vomit of yellow fever in Panama, the congested sour smell of mental illness like rotten milk and mouse piss. . . .

A lovely cloak but it does look a little strange in Mayfair. Kim billows out a few whiffs. The passersby look at him indignantly, cough, and walk away.

"They won't be so sassy in a few days' time." Still it would be prudent to change into a suit before he has to take out a bob-

by or two. He walks into a men's-wear store on Jermyn Street.

The manager prided himself on his impeccable cool. Despite the horrible odor, he observed that the cloak was of the finest materials and probably priceless, the sandals of an authentic medieval design in deerskin with gold buckles. The manager considered himself a good judge of character and it was Kim's presence that decided him against giving the call-police signal to his assistant. An aura of menace palpable as a haze, eyes with a cold blue burn like sputtering ice, and the voice silk-soft and caressing, sugary and evil with violence just under the surface. . . .

"I want the lot, from shoes to hat, you understand."

"I understand perfectly," the manager said and lifted his hand. A willowy young fag undulated up. . . .

"Arn, take care of this gentleman."

Arn fingered the hem of Kim's cloak. . . .

"Sweet stuff, dearie."

"Yes, it's been in our family for a long time."

The boy lingered in the doorway of the change cubicle, hoping Kim would take off his cloak and be naked underneath. Kim smiled at him and took off the cloak, which billowed across the cubicle, seemingly with a life of its own, and settled onto a hanger.

The boy sniffed ecstatically. . . . "Coo what a lovely smell!"

"It's been in our family for *quite* a long time."

Kim was wearing a codpiece fashioned from some pinkish-brown porous skin.

"The pelt of an electric eel," Kim told him.

A sheath of the same material was at his belt shaped to hold a curved blade twelve inches long. Kim withdrew the blade, which shone with an inner light like crystal.

"This blade, fashioned by a Japanese craftsman, was tempered in human blood . . . an insolent peasant who called my ancestor a Dishdigger . . . that's medieval slang for 'queer'. . . . Intolerable, was it not?"

"Yes sir. Quite intolerable."

"Now I want your M-5 suit."

"Something inconspicuous, sir?"

"Exactly. The well-dressed man is one whose clothes you never notice. . . . That's what you English say, isn't it?"

"Sometimes, sir. What size?"

"Thirty-eight long . . . felt hat, not a bowler . . . the cloak and sandals to be packed into one of those leather satchels with brass fittings . . . that one. . . ." Kim pointed.

"It's rather expensive, sir."

"The more the merrier. Expense account, you know."

So in what guise shall he return to the New World as if he were coming from the Old World, which in fact he is, since his footsteps are vanishing behind him like prints in heavy snow or windblown sand.

"Our chaps are jolly good," Tony told him. "Any passport, any part you fancy, old thing. . . ."

A rich traveler of uncertain nationality . . . with a Vaduz passport.

Name: Kurt van Worten

Occupation: Businessman

And what business is Mr. van Worten in? Difficult to pin down. But wherever he opens his briefcase, disaster slides out. The market crashes, currencies collapse, breadlines form. War clouds gather. An austere gilt-edged card with a banking address in Vaduz. . . .

The passport picture catches the petulant expression of the rich. It can be counterfeited. Just look sour and petulant and annoyed at everything in sight. At the slightest delay give little exasperated gasps. It is well from time to time to snarl like a cat. And a handkerchief redolent of disinfectant can be placed in front of the face if any sort of *creature* gets too close. And spend long hours in deck chairs with dark glasses and a lap robe, silent as a shark. Just do it long enough and money will simply cuddle around you.

Hall sips his drink and picks up another envelope. Mr. van Worten, he feels, would prove a bit confining, and he is not in-

trigued by the mysteries of high finance. Something more raff-
ish, disreputable, shameless. . . . It is pleasant to roll in vileness
like a dog rolls in carrion, is it not?

A con man who calls himself Colonel Parker, with the sleek
pomaded smug expression of a man who has just sold the widow
a fraudulent peach orchard. His cold predatory eyes scan the
dining room from the Captain's table. . . .

An impoverished Polish intellectual from steerage trying to
conceal his tubercular cough and the stink of cold doss houses
he carries with him like a haze. One expects to see typhus lice
crawling on his frayed dirty collar. . . . Too uncomfortable. . . .

The door to another dimension may open when the gap between what one is expected to feel and what one actually does
feel rips a hole in the fabric. Years ago I was driving along Price
Road and I thought how awful it would be to run over a dog or,
my God, a child, and have to face the family and portray the cor-
rect emotions. When suddenly a figure wrapped in a cloak of
darkness appeared with a dead child under one arm and slapped
it down on a porch:

"This yours, lady?"

I began to laugh. The figure had emerged from a lightless
region where everything we have been taught, all the conven-
tional feelings, do not apply. There is no light to see them by. It
is from this dark door that the antihero emerges. . . .

A *Titanic* survivor. . . . You know the one I mean. . . .

"Somewhere in the shadows of the *Titanic* slinks a cur in
human shape. He found himself hemmed in by the band of he-
ros whose watchword and countersign rang out across the deep:

" 'Women and children first.' "

"What did he do? He scuttled to the stateroom deck, put
on a woman's skirt, a woman's hat, and a woman's veil and,
picking his crafty way back among the brave men who guarded
the rail of the doomed ship, he filched a seat in one of the life-
boats and saved his skin. His identity is not yet known. This
man still lives. Surely he was born and saved to set for men a
new standard by which to measure infamy and shame. . . ."

Or a survivor of the *Hindenburg* disaster who was never seen or heard of again. By some strange quirk his name was omitted from the passenger list. He is known as No. 23. . . .

Drang nach Westen: the drag to the West. When the Traveler turns west, time travel ceases to be travel and becomes instead an inexorable suction, pulling everything into a black hole. Light itself cannot escape from this compacted gravity, time so dense, reality so concentrated, that it ceases to be time and becomes a singularity, where all physical laws are no longer valid. From such license there is no escape . . . stepping westward a jump ahead of the Geiger. . . .

Kim looks up at a burning sky, his face lit by the blazing dirigible. No bones broken, and he didn't see fit to wait around and check in. . . . No. 23 just faded into the crowd.

The Bunker is dusty, dust on the old office safe, on the pipe threaders and sledgehammers, dust on his father's picture. The West has only its short past and no future, no light.

Kim feels that New York City has congealed into frozen stills in his absence, awaiting the sound of a little voice and the touch of a little hand. . . . Boy walks into an Italian social club on Bleecker Street. A moment of dead ominous silence, dominoes frozen in the air.

"Can't you read, kid? Members Only."

Two heavy bodyguards move toward him.

"But I'm a member in good standing!" A huge wooden phallus, crudely fashioned and daubed with ocher, springs out from his fly as he cuts loose, shooting with clear ringing peals of boyish laughter as he cleans out that nest of garlic-burping Cosas.

Patagonian graves, wind and dust. . . . Same old act, sad as a music box running down in the last attic, as darkness swirls around the leaded window. . . . It looks like an early winter. Dead leaves on the sidewalk.

A number of faces looking out from passports and identity cards, and something that is Kim in all of them. It's as though

Kim walked into a toy shop and set a number of elaborate toys in motion, all vying for his attention. . . . "Buy *me* and *me* and *meeee*. . . ."

Little figures shoot each other in little toy streets . . . hither and thither, moves and checks and slays, and one by one back in the closet lays. He can feel the city freeze behind him, a vast intricate toy with no children to play in it, sad and pointless as some ancient artifact shaped to fill a forgotten empty need.

There is an urgency about moving westward—or stepping westward, isn't it? A wildish destiny? One is definitely a jump or a tick ahead of something . . . the Blackout . . . the countdown . . . or the sheer, shining color of police? Perhaps you have just seen the same Stranger too many times, and suddenly it is time to be up and gone.

One-way ticket to the Windy City. . . . "There'll be a hot time in the old town tonight." Tiny figures string looters up to paper lampposts as the fire raging on the backdrop is bent horizontal by the wind. Two actors in a cow do a song-and-dance number, tripping each other up and squirting milk at the audience.

"One dark night when all the people were in bed"—*squirt squirt squirt*—"Mrs. O'Leary took a lantern to the shed."

Mrs. O'Leary with her milk pail—clearly she is retarded, or psychotic. She looks around the barn blankly (I'm sorry, I guess I have the wrong number), puts the lantern down, goes to the door and looks out (Oh well, he's always late. I'll wait inside for him). The cow kicks the pail over with a wink and sings, "There'll be a hot time in the old town tonight."

The cow dances offstage, and suddenly the audience realizes that the fire in the backdrop is real. . . .

> Meet me in Saint Louie, Louie
> Meet me at the fair
> Don't tell me the lights are shining
> Anyplace but there . . .

The lights go on. The music plays. Well-dressed characters stroll through the fountains and booths and restaurants. . . . There is Colonel Greenfield, and Judge Farris, Mrs. Worldly, Mr. and Mrs. Kindhart. . . . Walk-on parts, all perfectly dressed models of wealth and calm self-possession. . . .

The Director screams out: "No, no, no! It's too stiff! Loosen it up, let's see some animation. Tell a joke."

"Well, you see the clerk is being nice. This old colored mammy wants to buy some soap: 'You mean toilet soap, madam.'

"'Oh no, just some soap to wash my hands and face. . . .'"

"It's a sick picture, B. J."

"Oh well, the songs will carry it."

Meet Me in Saint Louis, The Trolley Song, Saint Louis Blues, Long Way from Saint Louis . . . They are turning off the fountains, carrying the sets away.

"All right, you extras, line up here."

"Look, I told a joke. I get one-liner pay."

"You mean you dropped a heavy ethnic. We had to cut the whole scene." A security guard edges closer. *"Pick up your bread and beat it,* Colonel."

Train whistles . . . "Saint Albans Junction."

"Which way is the town?"

"What town?"

"Saint Albans."

"Where you been for twenty years, Mister?"

Just the old farmhouse . . . where are the boys? There are no boys, just the empty house.

Denver . . . Mrs. Murphy's Rooming House, a little western ketch in the station . . . Salt Chunk Mary's, rings and watches spilling out on the table . . . Joe Varland drops with a hole between his eyes . . . train whistles . . . CLEAR CREEK, weeds growing through the rails . . . "End of the line: Fort Johnson."

"All rise and face the enemy!"

The Wild Fruits stand up, resplendent in their Shit Slaugh-

ter uniforms. Each drains a champagne glass of heroin and aconite. They throw the glasses at the gate.

When shit blood spurts from the knife
Denn geht schon alles gut!

They stagger and fall. Kim feels the tingling numbness sweeping through him, legs and feet like blocks of wood . . . the sky begins to darken around the edges, until there is just a tiny round piece of sky left . . . SPUT he hits a body, bounces off, face to the sky . . . he is moving out at great speed, streaking across the sky . . . Raton Pass . . . the wind that blew between the worlds, it cut him like a knife . . . back in the valley, now in the store being tested—Wouldn't mind being reborn as a Mexican, he thought wistfully, knowing he really can't be reborn anywhere on this planet. He just doesn't *fit* somehow.

Tom's grave . . . Kim rides out on a pack horse. Kim, going the other way, heads out on a strawberry roan. A rattle of thunder across the valley. Kim scratches on a boulder: *Ah Pook Was Here.*

Frogs croaking, the red sun on black water . . . a fish jumps . . . a smudge of gnats . . . this heath, this calm, this quiet scene; the memory of what has been, and never more will be . . . back on the mesa top, Kim remembers the ambush. Time to settle that score.

Kim is heading north for Boulder. Should make it in five, six days hard riding. He doesn't have much time left. September 17, 1899, is the deadline, only ten days away.

In Libra, Colorado, his horse is limping. Kim figures to sell him and move on, after a night's sleep. He receives an early morning visit from Sheriff Marker and his frog-faced deputy.

"So you're Kim Carsons, aren't you?"

"So you got a flier?"

"Nope. Just wondered if you figure on staying long."

"Nope. Horse is lame. I figure to sell him, buy another, and move on."

"Maybe you better get the morning train. Faster that way."

Kim took the stage to Boulder, arriving at 3:00 P.M. on September 16.

He checked into the Overlook Hotel. . . . "Room with bath. I'll take the suite, in fact. I may be entertaining."

Kim took a long, hot bath. He looked down at his naked body, an old servant that had served him so long and so well, and for what? Sadness, alienation . . . he hadn't thought of sex for months.

"Well, space is here. Space is where your ass is."

He dries himself, thinking of the shoot-out and making his own plans. He knows Mike Chase will have a plan that won't involve a straight shoot-out. Mike is faster, but he doesn't take chances. Kim will use his 44 special double-action. Of course it isn't as fast as Mike's 455 Webley, but this contest won't be de-

cided by a barrage. First two shots will tell the story and end it. Kim will have to make Mike miss his first shot, and he'll have to cover himself.

But Mike has no intention of shooting it out with Kim. Mike is fast and he is good, but he always likes to keep the odds in his favor. The fill-your-hand number is out of date.

This is 1899, not 1869, Mike tells himself. Oh yes, he will keep the appointment at the Boulder Cemetery. But he has three backup men with hunting rifles. This is going to be his last bounty hunt. Time to move on to more lucrative and less danger-ous ventures. He will put his past behind him, take a new name. He has a good head for business, and he'll make money, a lot of money, and go into politics.

It is a clear, crisp day. . . . Aspens splash the mountains with gold. Colorado Gold, they call it; only lasts a few days.

The cemetery is shaded by oak and maple and cottonwood, overhanging a path that runs along its east side. Leaves are fall-ing. The scene looks like a tinted postcard: "Having fine time. Wish you were here."

Mike swings into the path at the northeast corner, wary and watchful. He is carrying his Webley 455 semi-automatic revolv-er. His backup men are about ten yards behind him.

Kim steps out of the graveyard, onto the path.

"Hello, Mike." His voice carries cool and clear on the wind.

Twelve yards . . . ten . . . eight . . .

Kim's hand flicks down to his holster and up, hand empty, pointing his index finger at Mike.

"BANG! YOU'RE *DEAD*"

Mike clutches his chest and crumples forward in a child's game.

"WHAT THE FU—" Someone slaps Kim very hard on the back, knocking the word out. Kim *hates* being slapped on the back. He turns in angry protest . . . blood in his mouth . . . can't turn . . . the sky darkens and goes out.